Al
A Bald Knobber Saga

Vonda Wilson Sheets

ISBN-13: 978-1480279414

ISBN-10: 1480279412

Published by:
Yesteryear Hollow LLC
PO Box 252
Kirbyville, MO 65679

www.yesteryearhollow.com

Follow us on Facebook

http://www.facebook.com/absolutionthenovel

Book and cover design, title page
illustration and map by Larry Howe
Cover photograph by Vonda Wilson Sheets
Back cover photograph by Kelly Trimble

Copyright 2012 by Vonda Wilson Sheets
All Rights Reserved

ABOUT THE AUTHOR

Vonda Wilson Sheets is a seventh-generation Taney County, Missouri native, of Celtic, Cherokee, and German descent. Born hearing and vision-impaired, she was a top student in primary and secondary education and in college, mainly because her mother taught her to read by the age of three. Her father was a hard-working history-loving reader himself, and it was his influence that brought her to researching Taney County genealogy. She stayed in from recess in second grade to write short stories, and has continued to write throughout her life in various media, including a two-year stint as a newspaper reporter. The combination of writing and history brought her to close friendships with others who considered the history of the Bald Knobbers to be a continuing influence on Taney County. Years of study and research, and looking for answers, led to a greater understanding of the people of the Bald Knobber era. She continues to make her home in Taney County, as a wife and mother who still enjoys watching people and wondering what makes them tick.

ACKNOWLEDGEMENTS

There is no book such as this written without help.

Since we married, Greg has supported and encouraged local history-related activities, not only for me, but for the kids. Our children have been a large part of the reason we have worked to preserve and teach what makes our corner of the world so special. Our sons, Wayne and Guy, were the perfect tag-team in teaching me about teenagers. Our sons, TJ and Brett, have the family love for history, even if it's not from the same era. And our daughter, Victoria, whose nine-year-old self told me one night, "History is BORING!" and forced me to prove her wrong. (Now it's "Oh, Nat Kinney, I'm never going to get away from you...")

Our parents have always supported our efforts as well. To Joe and Mary Wilson, Dick and Sharlene McKee, and Wayne and Ilene Sheets, thanks are insufficient, but will have to do. Thank you!

Rick Swan and Ingrid Albers have been a huge part of my life since the beginning days of Yesteryear Hollow in 2001. Without them, THIS would not be. The teamwork, the questions, the writing, the productions, the research, the gallivants--all of these things contributed to the journey of wanting to know more.

A special "Thank you!" to Jo Stacey Albers and Leon Combs, as well as other members of the White River Valley Historical Society, who backed and supported our activities and hare-brained ideas with enthusiasm and encouragement.

The number of friends who have been a part of this journey is infinite. Let's just say that if you have been in one of our productions or just listened to me thinking out loud, I owe you more than I know the words to express. In case any of the kids ask, no, I have never regretted banning video games from one of our camping weekends for the play, "The League: Taney County Justice." And yes, I know who kept putting the Frank and Tubal mannequins in hilarious situations.

Marc King insisted I write the book. So I wrote the book, and the journey became so much more intense. A gift I am very grateful to have received.

Last but not least, Larry Howe read the first chapter on January 3, 2012, and demanded more. He had an entire book to design by July 7. Trish Scowden Trimble joined him in reading and encouraging and demanding "More!" all the way to the final chapter. And our journey just continues...

I love you all!

Vonda

INTRODUCTION

It has been a privilege to work with Vonda Wilson Sheets on her book, *Absolution*. It all started with my finding out, through genealogical research that I was related to her through my mother's family. I found my "new" cousin to be charming, witty, unselfish, and incredibly knowledgeable when it came to the history and the people of Taney County and the surrounding area. I grew up there; my father was born in Mincy, Missouri, and was a businessman in Branson. My grandparents carried the mail as Star Route carriers, and the route remains in the family even today. That is a grand total of 60+ years that the Howe family has carried mail to the citizens of the Mincy valley and Kirbyville area.

My grandfather, Roy Howe, was born in 1888, the year of a significant event during the Bald Knobber era. My great grandfather, Thomas J. Howe, was born in 1855 and he died in a mining accident in Webb City, Missouri, in 1916. He and my great-grandmother, Nannie Susan, lived in the Mincy area during the reign of the Bald Knobbers. My grandfather, Roy and his brother Rhody, both carried the mail by horseback in the early 20th century. At that time there was a combination general store, feed store and post office at the crossroads in Mincy. During my time with my grandparents, I never heard any tales about the Bald Knobbers. Not that they weren't there, I was just so young that history wasn't important to me at that time and I neglected to ask any questions. As I have gotten older and become more interested in family history, I have regrets about that. I'm sure that I missed out on a lot of tall tales and family stories.

But enough about that, for now.

Vonda sent me the first chapter of *Absolution* on January 3rd, 2012. I read it. Two days later, chapter 2 came by email, I read it along with chapter 1 again. I was amazed at the descriptive nature of her writing style. The very first sentence of the first chapter piqued my interest. I could touch, feel and smell that sentence. I came to the realization, after the third chapter, that I had been drawn into a chronological vortex that swallowed

[IV]

me and spat me out during my great-grandfathers' time. I could smell the scents, feel the heat, and visually combine the colors and lighting within my mind. These chapters, and the ones to follow, introduced me to the characters. These people seemed uniquely real to me. I met their wives, their children, rode with them, felt seasons change, was with them when they planted, during good times and bad, but the most amazing thing was, I felt like I was a part of it all.

Absolution: A Bald Knobber Saga is an exhilarating journey of trepidation, vengeance, euphoria, devotion, sensitivity, benevolence and anguish.

As Vonda's fingertips caressed the keys of her computer, she drew me down a twisting path of "what if's," "could be's" and "why nots." There were two chapters that were totally unexpected; the first left me holding my breath and the second brought to the edge of my chair. A quick phone call to Vonda and the question, "Where did that come from?" gleaned an answer of "I really don't know, it was just there."

In the subsequent months to come, Vonda would send me chapters as she finished them, asking for comments and wanting me to make sure that there was continuity. I put each and every chapter into "book form" for editing and comprehensive reading. Once she finished the last chapter, I started designing the book and the cover.

I recognized, right away, what a rare talent Vonda has. Words seem to flow out of her like refreshing water from a cool mountain spring. It seemed that it was almost effortless for her to write, although I know that it really wasn't. It took many hours of determination to squeeze out those words; plus a lot of migraine medicine. She battled 2 months of horrendous migraines during the middle to last chapters of the manuscript, but kept right on going. As she was writing, it was difficult for her to pull herself out of the 1880s and place herself back in the 21st century for her normal work day. However, when she was in the 1880s, she would sometimes churn out 2 or 3 chapters a day. In January, she wrote 13 chapters, and 13 more in February. All this while trying to live with a family that I'm sure had no clue what it was going to be like to have an author in their presence.

Nonetheless, I kept asking for more and more. To be honest, I was hooked on it and couldn't wait until the next installment. When she sent me chapter 24, I asked her if 29 was done. I called it "poking the bear" and it started to be a running joke between the two of us. All the while she managed, somehow, to retain her sanity and managed to refrain from strangling me. For that, I will be eternally grateful. I know, at times, she was certain that she would be a prime candidate for the "loony bin", but she prevailed, and the manuscript was completed July 7th, 2012. I then began the layout and design of the book and the cover. It's been a marvelous journey and I look foreward to the next one.

Larry Howe – Ozark, Missouri – November 14th, 2012

When Vonda asked me if I would consider reading the book *Absolution* that she was writing, I was immediately intrigued.

As a sixth-generation Taney County native, I grew up hearing stories about the Bald Knobbers and was terrified; it was like being afraid of the boogeyman. But the day I read my great-great grandfather's name in Vonda's manuscript, and I realized my family had lived through these violent times, that's the day the boogeyman became very real.

The 1880s were rugged times which is evidenced in this riveting story of pioneer life. While reading Absolution, I became a part of this community of people who mourned over death and rejoiced with the birth of a new child. This is a story that has waited a long time to be told.

It has been an extreme honor to be included in this project and I look forward to the next amazing ride.

Trish Trimble – Yesteryear Hollow LLC – November 7th, 2012

DEDICATION

To Daddy and Mom, who gave me history and taught me perseverance.

"Writing a book is an adventure. To begin with, it is a toy and an amusement; then it becomes a mistress, and then it becomes a master, and then a tyrant. The last phase is that just as you are about to be reconciled to your servitude, you kill the monster, and fling him out to the public."

Winston Churchill – November 2nd, 1949

FOREWORD

Taney County, located in southern Missouri on the Arkansas state line was rough country, rolling limestone hills and ridges, covered with trees, underbrush and rife with steep rocky cavernous ravines. Cool clear springs and creeks flowed out of these ravines and valleys and into the White River. During the Civil War and for many years after, outlaws took refuge there. The county government was in disarray, and nearly all crimes committed were totally ignored.

After the Civil War, there was a land rush as the federal government expanded the Homestead Act. Families moved here from other parts of the country and acquired property. The locals, at first, considered them "outsiders" for they had no right, in their eyes, to tell them what they should live their lives. Some of the "newcomers" came from large cities and "civilized society" and they were astounded that this area, called God's Country by the natives, had virtually no judicial system.

Many of the newcomers and, even those who had lived here for many years, were hoping for change. The event that sparked that change was the murder of a businessman, by the name of Jim Everett, and the subsequent trial in which his killer was acquitted.

This unjust event spawned a vigilante band of night riders made up, initially, of notable men; attorneys, merchants, lawmen, and landowners. Stories were published in national newspapers and the group became notorious.

Things, however, did not turn out as expected.

This story takes place between 1883 and 1891. It is eight years of brutality and corruption that, to this day, remains burned into the memories of the people of southern Missouri.

But this is not just about the Bald Knobbers. It is about the people and the land, life and death during hard uncertain times, families and their children, grandfathers and grandmothers, resistance and submission, hate and love, seasons and rural life in southern Missouri during the last part of the 19th century.

After 20 years of research and devotion to the history of Taney County and the surrounding areas, Vonda Wilson Sheets embarked on a challenging journey to give the people of this era a voice and personal recognition. Her descriptions of the characters and incidents will add a new dimension to the story of upheaval and discourse during troubled times in the Ozarks.

Vonda's expertise, intensive research, and intuitive writing style have allowed her to compile a historical novel unlike any other produced on this subject. Her knowledge is vast, she has studied the genealogical records of all of the people involved in this story and, to paraphrase a well-known saying, "she knows where all the bodies are buried."

Larry Howe – Ozark, Missouri, November 2012

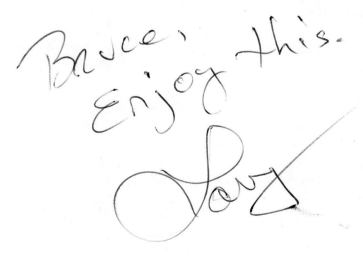

THE PEOPLE

THE BARKERS

Sampson Barker and his wife, Sarah Frazier "Sallie" Barker. Sallie is the sister of Kate Frazier Miles.

Their children are: James, Rufus, Martha Catherine, who married Richard W. Cline, and Edward.

THE BROWNS

John Jasper, "JJ", and his second wife, Caroline Everett Brown. Caroline is the half-sister of Jim and Yell Everett.

THE COGGBURNS

Andrew and Serelda are the orphaned children of James Victor and Frances Serelda Springer Hamblen Coggburn. Robert and Seck are their first cousins, the sons of John Shell and Elizabeth Allen Coggburn.

THE DELONGS

The children of Margaret J. Carriger's first marriage (to William Henry DeLong) are James and Eva.

THE KINNEYS

Nathaniel N. Kinney and Margaret J. Carriger DeLong had two children live to adulthood, Paul C. and Georgia.

THE MILES

William Marion and Kate Frazier Miles had eight children, seven of whom lived to adulthood. Their sons Billy, Emanuel, and Jim are still living at home in the mid-1880s. Kate is the sister of Sallie Barker.

[X]

THE PRATHERS

Alonzo and his wife, Ada Maria, had nine children. Their oldest son, Robert, followed in his father's path of service to the community.

THE SNAPPS

Lafayette, Robert, and Samuel were sons of Harrison "Hack" Snapp and his first wife, Emily Parry.

James Madison "Matt" Snapp was Hack's son from his second marriage to Tennessee Sarah Jane Callen Leathers.

Sam married first to Sarah Sims. Their surviving children were Nannie and Tom. After Sarah's death, Sam married Susie Haggard.

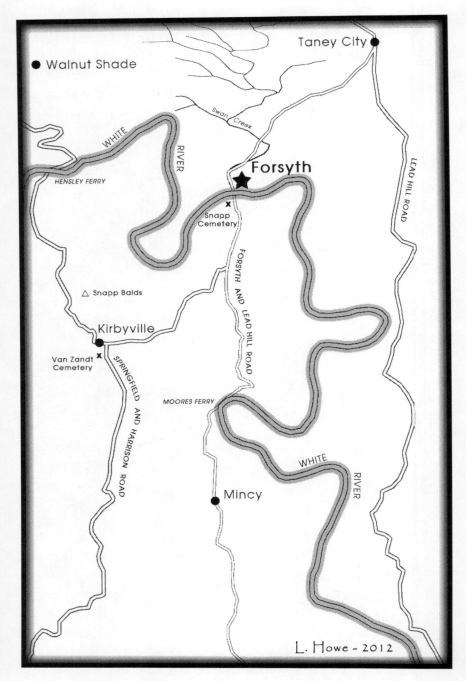

Central Taney County Missouri
1880 - 1890

CHAPTER 1
September 22, 1883

The odors of sweating men's bodies and fresh-cut lumber warred comfortably inside the new mill as Al Layton did a final walk-through, assessing what remained to be done.

He found nothing.

Scowling, he glanced through the window as the final load of debris and sawdust was dumped into the fire outside. It hadn't been a roaring fire--this work crew had cleaned up each day, excited to be working and knowing they were doing an excellent job on the beautiful new building, just downstream from Walnut Shade on Bull Creek. The Everett brothers should be mightily pleased with Al and his crew.

That thought momentarily erased the scowl. Maybe he could get a bonus for finishing the job early?

The air was stifling inside and walking outside proved to be no better. It was early fall, and the only trees that had considered changing were the sycamores. They grew big along the banks of the creek, yellow leaves falling into the clear water at whim, since the air wasn't moving. Hot.

Avoiding the small inferno, Al plodded over to the canopy that served him as an office of sorts, as well as a shelter for Sam Hull, who'd come up from Carroll County, Arkansas to work on this project. Sam had been the key to finishing up the mill quickly. He and Al had worked on other mills in the region together, and Al considered Sam one of the finest sawyers around.

He quite liked Sam, which was good. Al himself wasn't a talker, he reflected as he sat in the only chair and reached for the locked bag which held the men's final pay. Sam didn't appear to notice, however, as he talked enough for two men and then some.

Hull's voice came through loud and clear now, despite the muffling quality of the humidity. He was teasing the other men into something--Al could tell by the tone of Sam's voice. Sam was a prankster, the joker of the bunch, and Al wondered as he opened the job book if he needed to be alert for a trick of some kind.

Concentrating on his notes, he tallied up the men's final pay. While the ink--and the sweat he'd inadvertently dripped on the pages--dried, he quickly pulled out the money, and then divided it into five piles. The scowl returned as he saw his own pay was less than the others', and he glanced again at the book. No, that was right, and he slid the money into his shirt pocket. Damn. Cash was hard to come by in these times, even if it was better than last year.

The thought of last year deepened the scowl even more. Last year, a drought had burned up crops and gardens throughout the White River valley, and jobs such as this had been rare. He'd jumped at the chance to build a mill over in Kansas, and like a fool, had fallen off a rafter and broken several bones. No money coming in, and while he recuperated at home, Jim Everett had extended credit to him, helping his family get through the winter. While the weather had been nearly perfect this year--except for this heat, he grimaced as he wiped his face again--and there was food aplenty to get through this winter, cash was the problem. Everett had been good to him, though. Gave him the chance to work off the debt by building this mill and he was going to have *some* cash.

A nudge on the back of his shoulder turned his head, and a rare smile lit his face. Amanda nickered softly as she pushed him again, her chestnut head almost on top of him under the canopy. She knew it was time for the work day to end, he realized. He rubbed her nose thoughtfully.

If he hadn't bought her--just days before he fell last year--but no, he pushed the thought away. No point in regretting spending cash money on her. Her large eyes flickered at something over his shoulder, and he whipped back around to find his men standing there, silent for a change.

Grins on their faces, too. Concealing his dismay at being taken by surprise by both his horse and his men, Al reached for the pay packets and handed each man what was owed. "Good job, boys," he told them. "Done ahead of time."

Hull whooped, and the others joined in. "We are the best mill-builders in the country!" Sam crowed. The pay packets were stuffed into various pockets and saddlebags. "Let's go swimming!"

This had become a habit of Sam's, inveigling the others to go for a swim in the creek after a sweaty work day. More particular than most, Sam had long ago confided in Al, "I will be damned if I'm going to work with a bunch of smelly men day in and day out."

Sam had a point, Al reflected as his nose picked up the scent of

Absolution | 3

vomit, interspersed with alcohol-reek. Bobby Johnson had visited the bushes frequently that morning; Al hadn't said anything, since there hadn't been much work to do, and Bobby wasn't one to get drunk very often. Al briefly wondered what had caused Bobby to get sodden the night before as he watched the men run and splash fully-clothed into the creek's deep waters.

That thought also melted into the heat as he watched Sam's horse follow him into the water, his neighing like laughter.

God, that was one ugly horse.

Amanda's velvety nose brushed against Al's left ear as he contemplated Hull's horse. An ugly brown that matched cured tobacco, Plug wandered some distance away from the men and kneeled down to roll in the water. His lumbering frame--the colt was tall, Al had to admit--looked like bones piled into a not-so-orderly sack. Plug's legs were sticking up in the air when Amanda again nuzzled Al for attention.

"All right, all right," he told her. Gathering up the job book and unlocked pay bag, he stuffed them in his saddlebag by the tent pole. Amanda looked over toward the other three animals--two mules and the plow horse Johnson rode--as Al picked up his saddle and threw it over her. The mules and horse briefly looked back at Amanda, but their attention was taken by the men in the creek.

While readying Amanda for the ride to Forsyth, Al considered joining the crew for a few minutes. The water did look invitingly cool, but he was not one to tell the boys "See you soon" when a job was over. Especially this time. They knew they'd done a good job, and they knew he'd send for them when he had another one lined up.

Al picked up the reins, climbed on Amanda's back, and again looked at his crew. With a sardonic wave of his right hand in salute when Sam looked his way, he turned Amanda to the widened path to the road, and left at a trot.

The road to Forsyth meandered up from Bull Creek, a wagon trail off the Springfield-Harrison Road that rode the ridges all the way to the Shadow Rock, which overlooked Swan Creek and the town on the banks of the White River. He'd lived in Taney or Christian County all his life, and he was familiar with the old mountains rolling away from view, countless benches and ridgebacks falling down to the river that had carved them. Although Al's senses were alert for the unusual, a hot September afternoon fading into evening wasn't unusual; his eyes noted the clear sky deepening into a dusky blue as the sun dropped toward the horizon, his ears heard the birds and a couple of squirrels chattering, and his skin gleamed as Amanda's coat turned darker with sweat.

Upon reaching Cedar Point, Al turned Amanda right, down the steep hill that led to a backwash of the river. It was time for a drink. She dipped her head after he dismounted and joined her, washing his face with the water that didn't feel much cooler than the air, but was refreshing anyway.

They were about a mile from the city limits when Amanda's ears turned back to listen behind and Al heard hoof beats approaching. His mood was no better, but he had a feeling....

Sure enough.

"Whoa! Layton!"

Hull.

If he'd stayed on the higher road until Swan Creek...well, it couldn't be helped now.

At least no one would ever offer to buy Plug.

"Al! You wanted another race! What do you mean, taking off like that?" Sam yelled while still 50 yards away. That ugly Plug, that bag of bones, was scarcely sweating despite running several miles, and when Hull pulled up, was breathing only a fraction faster than normal. Sam was breathing harder than Plug, Al noted with interest. Plug had done the work.

"You were busy, and I needed to get to Everett's," Al offered by way of apology. He didn't want to risk it.

"Ah," Hull nodded. His shirt and hair were damp with sweat, but he still looked fresher than Al felt. No doubt thanks to his daily swim, the sour thought ran through Al's mind. He glanced at Plug.

"Well, you won't want to race now," he said, tentatively hoping Sam *wouldn't*.

Sam grinned, and slapped Plug on the shoulder. "Eh, he's good for it. What about her?"

Al stiffened. He certainly hadn't ridden hard from Walnut Shade, but Amanda was a quarter horse, and long distance running wasn't what quarter horses were best suited for. She was sweaty, but her breathing was steady.

Absolution | 5

He just didn't want to lose another race.

"She's fine." With a loud "HAH!," Al and Amanda were running the flat road below the southern end of Shadow Rock and next to the river, leaving a startled Hull and Plug behind.

But it wasn't for long.

Plug was a distance runner, which Al had learned to his woe five nights ago. It might take Plug a while to get going, but once he did....

And he and Sam passed Al and Amanda some fifty yards before the Swan Creek ford, splashing into the water joyfully, turning back to laugh with Hull. So it seemed to Al as he and Amanda slowed down, and she gratefully sidestepped down into the water herself, blowing and again dipping her head to drink in the coolness.

Al jumped off to lessen Amanda's discomfort, admonishing her, for whose benefit, his or Hull's? Or was it to keep her from drinking too much at one time? No, he decided. Everyone knew you didn't let a horse drink her fill when she was overheated.

Plug, damn the bastard son of a swamp donkey, was scarcely blowing.

Hull's face, however, was concerned. "Is she all right?" he asked. Al ducked away from Sam's question, feeling along Amanda's sides and crooning to her, telling her what a good girl she was. When he glanced up at Sam, he saw a slight smile on the other's face.

"What?" he asked gruffly.

"I didn't know you were so sentimental, Al," Sam's smile widened as he spoke. He did know what feelings Amanda brought out in Layton--Al was a horse man, through and through.

"Ah, shut up," Al grunted.

Bowing his head in mock obeisance, Sam clucked to Plug, and the two turned toward the buildings of Forsyth. "See you at Everett's," Sam called over his shoulder. "Same bet applies?"

No answer from Al, who was letting Amanda drink again as her breathing calmed and his anxious hands did as well.

Sam rode on, assuming that the same bet, indeed, did apply.

From below his hat brim, Al watched Hull and Plug climb the crest to the city limit sign until they were lost from his sight. He never let his voice change in croon to Amanda, but he hoped like hell no one would find out she'd lost another race to that damned ugly plow horse. He'd gotten lots of offers to sell Amanda, but he

6 | Vonda Wilson Sheets

just knew no one would ever offer to buy Plug.

One of these days, he was going to quit hoping like hell. He hoped.

As he reined in to the tie bar in front of Everett's saloon--Plug acting as if he was asleep, damn him--Al noted Hull was on the sidewalk, talking to the Taylor boys. And Frank Taylor was offering to buy Plug, which Hull was gleefully declining.

Frank Taylor never was a smart person, Al decided. Buy Plug? But then Hilsabeck, the Forsyth Hotel owner, walked up, and offered Hull $300 for the colt.

Three hundred dollars? His eyes closed in disgust. Hilsabeck would use the colt for stud, as he certainly never had time to ride. Footsteps on the wooden sidewalk faded as Hull and Hilsabeck walked off to discuss the offer, leaving Al to contemplate simply riding home. But no, he had to give Everett the job book and let him know the mill was done.

Amanda was quiet, and Al realized she needed some rest before he headed home. Plug looked like he could still haul Sam home tonight, and that was a distance of some 50 miles.

Al dismounted, throwing the reins over the tie bar, and looked up to find Frank Taylor on his own horse, which was standing on the sidewalk above him. He quickly jumped up to the walk, feeling the disadvantage of Taylor looking down on him.

"Lost another race, I hear." Taylor's voice held more than amusement.

Al shook his head in negation, but knew Taylor held the upper hand. He glanced over to his left, where Tubal Taylor sat on a mule, holding the reins to another mule. The Taylors had again captured Oscar Lowell, who was sitting bare-arsed and backwards on a woolen blanket tied to the second mule's back. A momentary sympathetic thought for Lowell, the clerk at the bank, crossed Al's mind--this was the second or third time he knew of that the Taylors roughed Lowell up. The brothers had likely put the blanket in a bed of poison ivy or applied some other substance to it before finding Lowell.

Al's attention returned to Frank. "Eh, she isn't suited to distance races," he said.

"Distance," Frank grinned, and Tubal managed to look interested, "Where'd you start?"

Absolution | 7

"Half-mile marker," muttered Al.

The Taylors laughed, and Al's face went from red with sweat to red with anger. Some people just didn't understand fine horse flesh. In retaliation, he decided to help Lowell escape the brothers. They hadn't bound Lowell, after all, and he didn't think the man a total dunce.

"Amanda can make your horse eat dust!"

Tubal rode his mule forward, leaving Lowell behind him, as Al had intended. "Aw, now, Al, you know Frank's horse has beaten about everyone's," Tubal defended his brother.

Frank nodded in agreement, a nasty grin on his face. His horse touched noses with Tubal's mule, trying to turn in the narrow confines of the sidewalk.

Lowell wasn't a fool. The scrawny little city boy was watching over his shoulder as he slowly inched his way down off the neglected mule. Out of the corner of his eye, Al noted that Lowell's pants had been carelessly left dangling behind Tubal's saddle, which Lowell was now reaching for.

"We can race any time you say," Al told Frank, "Twice on Sunday, if you like."

The Taylors guffawed even louder, if such a thing was possible. Lowell had turned to put his pants on, and Al was treated to a view of Lowell's reddened backside. Yep, poison ivy and wool. Ouch. The man must have been in the company of the Taylors all afternoon.

"Done," said Frank. "I'll catch you up then. You got another horse you're gonna race?"

Oscar Lowell was stepping away quietly, but Al forgot his helpful intention as he understood Frank's insult to Amanda. "Another horse? She's just fine. You'll see on Sunday!"

Tubal chortled again, remembered his "company," and turned to see if Lowell was appreciating the jocularity. He howled as Lowell was disappearing around the corner of the hardware store across the street.

"Frank! He got away!" Tubal dug his heels into the sides of his mule, and went after Lowell.

Frank looked down at Al, who was grinning. Shrugging his shoulders, he turned his horse to grab the reins of the other mule, and then hesitated. After all, he'd had the pleasure of Lowell's company all afternoon, and it was getting on for suppertime. A second glance at Al, who had moved toward the saloon entrance, still grinning, and Frank understood that Al had purposely helped Lowell escape.

"Well, Layton," he drawled, eyes squinting with cunning. "Who knew you were such a softie?"

The grin left Al's face as he entered the saloon while Frank took off, shouting after his brother.

Good cigars, Jim's special beer, and aged whiskey--those scents reached Al easily as he looked through the haze in the saloon to see Jim talking to a table full of men near an open window at the back of the shallow room. Sweat was an undertone, though different, spiced with aftershave and not quite as thick as it was at the mill. Jim's saloon was *the* place for gossip and politics, and the men of the town were in and out all day long and far into the night. With the enlightenment of Sam Hull's finicky sensibilities, an "Aha!" went off at the back of Al's gloomy thoughts. Men who worked and lived in town bathed more often than the men on his work crew.

Snagging a cigar out of the humidor on the end of the bar, he stopped to cut and light it. The job book was still in his saddle bag; he'd retrieve it in a bit. Right now, he just wanted a beer. Nope, he thought, Whiskey. He was going to have to buy Sam a drink anyway, and it *was* a celebration of some sort, finishing the mill for Everett. Damned if he felt like celebrating, though.

Yell Everett, Jim's brother, nodded at Al as he lifted the pass-through and went into the store on the east end of the building. Al returned the greeting while drawing on his cigar, then glanced over at the pool table. Two of the Miles brothers--Billy and Manny, Al thought--were amicably arguing over their game.

"It's slow in here," he said to Jim, who had moved behind the bar.

Jim smiled slightly in agreement. "Busy earlier, though, Beer?"

Letting out a puff of smoke, Al shook his head once, "Whiskey."

Lifting an eyebrow, Jim reached for a glass and bottle, "Something wrong?"

"Nothing you need to worry about." He wasn't ready to tell Jim the mill was finished yet, he realized. Taking a sip of his drink, he rolled it around, and let the smoothness glide down to his empty stomach. Tilting his head in the direction of the pool table, he asked, "Aren't those boys a touch young to be here?"

Absolution | 9

"Eh," Jim shrugged. "Their pa's in town today. They come in ever so often, shoot some pool, and drink a couple of beers. Those two," Jim nodded toward Billy and Manny, "don't cause any trouble. Mind," and a grin broke out, "I'm not saying they back down from it. They don't. But it's got to be brought to them."

Al grunted, and took another sip. Jim looked over at the only other customers in the place. His brother-in-law, JJ Brown, was lifting his glass and turning it upside-down. "I have seen medicine that's able to breathe life into a stone," JJ called to Jim, to the amusement of the men around him. "Alas, I have none before me!"

Smiling at the levity, Jim retorted, "He hath eaten me out of house and home!" Glancing down at Al's face, Jim added, "He hath put all my substance into that fat belly of his!" and waved "in a minute" to JJ and his companions, who were chuckling. JJ was as slender as a broomstick.

"What is it?" Jim asked Al again.

Grabbing the bottle of whiskey, Al snorted and moved away, heading for the table nearest the bar. "I said nothing--"

At that moment, Sam came bouncing into the saloon, laughing and rowdy. "Hah, Al, I'm ready for that drink you owe me!" he called. Jim saw Al's eyes start to roll and his face go dark red, a muscle jumping in his left jaw. The man's shoulders were defensive, Jim noted, and then Hull slapped his hand down on the counter in front of him.

"A glass, since Al's got the bottle," Hull cracked, and laughed some more. Jim handed him a tumbler, and then saw Billy Miles holding up an empty mug. Reaching for the draft, he pulled two more beers while asking Hull, "Who's paying for that bottle?"

"Al is," Hull moved off toward the man he considered a friend. At that, Jim guessed Al had lost another race to Sam. He took the beers over to the Miles boys, who were setting up a second game.

"Alright?" He set the beers on the chair rail shelf, and picked out the coins from the pocketful of change the boys had dumped out earlier. Grabbing the empty mugs, he walked back to the bar to fetch the bottle of rum for JJ. Al was grunting in anger and as Jim passed him and Sam, threw his hat on the table.

Jim paused. "Who's paying for that bottle?" he asked again. He wasn't worried about it, but after years in the saloon business, it was best to make sure one's customers knew who was in charge.

He smelled trouble; he could feel it emanating from Al, whose back was to him. Hull just laughed, Al twitched and exhaled cigar smoke. A muttered "Mine," reached Jim's ears, and he moved back to his friends at the only other occupied table.

"Here." Putting the bottle of dark rum in the center of the table, Jim kept his attention focused on Layton and Hull.

"Is there trouble?" Alonzo Prather's deep voice came through the clatter of the balls on the pool table, and Manny's exclamation of a missed shot.

"Not yet," Jim answered. Alert to the rhythm of the business, Yell came back through the store entry, looked at Layton and Hull, then over at Jim. Jim nodded slightly. It was nearly time to close the store and send the clerk home. His brother would do that and be back behind the bar shortly. Leaving again, Yell glanced up at the cocked rifle above the doorway. It was bad business to shoot a customer, Jim thought with sour humor. He'd much rather not.

His attention half-returned to the discussion at hand.

Prather and Kinney had moved to the Kirbyville area in the past year or so. Prather hung his shingle as a lawyer and newspaper publisher; he was an educated man, dedicated to his family and community. He and JJ became instant friends, and Jim, too, thought of Alonzo as a friend. Prather's soft, white hands moved as he spoke; he was no farmer.

Jim was still a little wary around Nathaniel Kinney, though. Something about Kinney just didn't click. He and his stepson, James DeLong, both appeared educated--Alonzo had hired the younger man to run his newspaper, and hadn't had any complaints thus far.

Kinney was speaking now, complaining about the Taylor brothers. "Those hooligans should be in jail," he said. "There must be plenty of reasons to arrest them."

"There are," JJ replied, "but once in jail, what then? The circuit judge has stepped down, so there are no trials scheduled. One cannot hold men in jail indefinitely; it is against the law. If they make bail," a shoulder shrug indicated JJ's recognition of futility, "they simply keep doing what they have always done."

"Then another route must be taken," Kinney argued, and DeLong nodded.

"What would you suggest?" Jim asked. His attention was solely on Kinney now, but there was still that niggling feeling.

Absolution | 11

"Is there not a posse?" Kinney asked. "Will men not patrol the town to keep order?"

"There is no money in the county budget for a posse, Nat," JJ retorted. "Men have to support their families, and last year was a bad year. They are not going to 'patrol' either the town or the county without being paid."

Nat grunted in acknowledgment, considering. "What about the Masonic lodge? Is there not an oath of community service?"

There it was, Jim thought. Kinney was not a Mason. He, JJ, and Alonzo were lodge fellows, but Kinney was not. Why? He wondered as he left the table, headed back toward Layton and Hull.

Sam was chattering away, excited to be leaving for home the next day. Al had poured himself a second drink, morosely contemplating how much the bottle was going to cost him, and wondering why he'd decided to grab it. The whiskey was settling in his stomach nicely when he felt Jim at his back. He straightened.

"So the mill's done, then?" Jim had heard at least part of Sam's one-sided conversation.

"Finished it up today," Sam raised his glass, finishing his drink.

"Ahead of time? Good job, Al!" Jim wasn't surprised, really. Aside from the debt Al had been forced to take on when injured last year, which was now paid, he and Yell had hired Layton to build the mill because Layton was good at his profession. He picked good work crews, treated them fairly if a bit gruffly, and brought projects in on time, if not earlier. He considered giving Al the bottle of whiskey as a bonus. Well, when Al handed him the job book and bank bag, he'd do so.

Layton had turned in his chair toward Jim when Sam said, "Al hadn't told you yet? Why, he was in here way before I came in!" He reached for the whiskey bottle.

Layton's hand came down over Hull's. "Bet's settled."

"Ah, come on, Al," Sam wheedled. "We ain't racing again for a while."

Al stood, letting go. "That's it. I'll be back to check." He went outside.

Eyes narrowing, Jim watched Layton leave, then turned to Hull. "What's eating him?"

Hull spread his hands wide, shrugging. "He's been pissed all day.

12 | Vonda Wilson Sheets

I thought a race would cheer him up, but I won."

Jim's mouth turned down in amusement. "You couldn't help that?" he asked.

Hull shook his head, seeing the irony. "Not really. I was sawing on the reins as it was." He looked uncomfortable for a moment, then shrugged again. "Al's really going to be mad, though, when I tell him--"

"Tell me what?" Shoving the book and bag into Jim's hands, Layton dropped into his chair, picked up the bottle, eyed it, then poured himself another glass. While Hull paused and Jim waited, he took a drink.

"Ah....Amanda was in heat when we started the job." Hull was speaking slower than usual. He did not want to tell Al whatever it was, and Jim braced for the worst and muttered to himself, "Uh, oh."

"Yeah, what's your point? She was covered by Bilyeu's stud, up on Bull Creek. I built his wife a spring house for the fee," Al said blearily. He put his hands up to his face, rubbing it.

"I know. But Plug got her first." Sam spoke softly.

His hands froze over his face. He stopped breathing. The shock registered, he roared, and went for Hull, but Jim was quicker and slammed him back into his chair with both hands.

"Al! Not in here!"

"You don't know if it's Plug's or not," Sam spoke quickly now, trying to console his friend. His voice continued, placating. "It might not be. Although," he added, "it could have Amanda's beauty and Plug's wind!"

Jim felt Al struggling. A glance at the bottle told him Layton had drunk more than the three glasses he knew about.

"C'mon, Al, we're friends," Sam went on doggedly. "Ain't so bad, is it? You don't like Plug, but others do."

Jim relaxed when Layton spoke. "Amanda's a pure-bred quarter horse, for chrissakes. Hell." Al rubbed his face again, but he had control of himself.

Jim backed off, and suddenly the sounds of the saloon became normal again. He picked up the job book and bag he'd dropped, and went behind the bar to put them in the safe. While he was crouched down, Yell stuck his head in, raising an eyebrow at him.

"It's fine," Jim said. "The worst is over." Yell disappeared again.

Absolution | 13

Footsteps approached the bar, and Nat Kinney was still speaking. Did the man never stop? Jim wondered, and suddenly remembered talking to a fellow saloon owner in Springfield earlier this year. The man's name had been Kinney, too, but he claimed no relationship to Nat.

Jim rose, turned around, and saw JJ and the others were ready to pay up. Thinking furiously, he tallied and made change, and then restrained Nat from leaving with the others. "I would like to talk with you for a moment, Nat," he said. "I have a mare in foal…"

Kinney nodded, his freshly-barbered face and red hair giving off a distinct civilized aroma that didn't match what Jim now realized he knew of the man.

JJ was puzzled. Jim didn't even own a mare, as far as he knew. He started to speak, then realized Jim would tell him whatever he was about the next day. They hadn't been close for twenty years for nothing.

Good-nights were exchanged, while Jim made up his mind what to say.

Kinney claimed to have been a horse breeder in Kansas. However, that had been some years ago. More recent was the story from Abel Kinney, who had hired Nat as a manager of his bar in Springfield. Abel told Jim that Nat killed one of his customers in an ugly fight last December, and it wasn't the first altercation Nat had been in. Nat was a big man--probably six foot three, Jim thought. Abel had said Nat had been in trouble for killings in Topeka, too, although he had not mentioned the circumstances.

Jim was saying, "About your job in Springfield…" when a bellow broke out from Layton again. Dear God, was Sam still talking? He moved off, making the decision to speak with Nat Kinney in the near future. After all, the man was preaching now; maybe he'd realized the error of his ways?

"I just wanted another drink," Sam was telling Al, who was clutching the bottle to his chest.

"You still have some in your glass!" Al bellowed.

Sending Kinney an apologetic look, Jim moved to placate Layton.

Courteously, Nat inclined his head, "Another time, perhaps?"

Jim, speaking quietly in Al's ear, sent a nod Kinney's way, and the man left.

Al was muttering about wasted money or some such. Jim responded, not knowing what he was saying, and jerked his head toward the door, looking at Sam. "Get out!"

Sam made a move as if to leave, and Al yelled again, "Oh, no… double or nothing, you asshole!"

"What is he talking about?" Jim managed to ask.

A wry "He wants to race again" was the response.

"Not tonight, Al. It's late," Jim tried a new tack. "Amanda won't race well in the dark." He glanced out the window. Damn. Not quite…

"Not dark yet, goin' to race," Al grumbled, although he made no move to get up.

William Miles had stepped into the saloon, waiting for Billy and Manny to finish their game. He was watching the drama Jim was managing, his hand stuck inside his vest. A shoulder holster, Jim's mind somehow registered. Jimmy Miles stood outside, watching as well. That one, Jim didn't want inside, and William appeared to have realized it. He made a hand gesture as if he had sensed Jimmy poised to enter.

Al abruptly stood, swayed, and then shrugged Jim off. "Let's play pool," he told the frozen Sam. All thoughts of a horse race were gone, but he wanted to pound Sam's face into a loss somehow.

"Aw, Al, there's a game goin' on!" Sam wasn't totally drunk.

"I'll take care of that!" Al moved over to Manny, who was taking the final shot at the eight ball. Just as he stroked the cue, Al grabbed the stick, causing the shot to go wild, and getting a furious Manny in his face.

"Hey! We're playing!" Layton was taller than Manny Miles, but it made no impression on Manny.

"Game's over." Al growled.

"C'mon, Manny," Billy's soft voice drawled. "Pa's here anyway."

His nose just inches from Layton's, Manny stared Al in the eyes, making mental notes. Only then did he back off, never batting an eye. As he reached the end of the table, he joined his brothers and father. No one spoke until the Miles' were gone, Jim noted with some relief.

Al began setting the rack, and a whoop came from Hull. "Woo, hoo, Al! You sure know who to piss off!" Sam laughed. Jim wondered if the man had a death wish.

Pulling the rack, Al turned to pick up Billy's discarded cue stick. "Those are boys," he told Sam.

"Mean ones, from what I hear," Sam replied. He crossed the room to select his own cue stick.

Jim began picking up glasses to take for washing, alert and ready. He'd already told Hull to get out, and the man had not taken the chance. He could deal with Al--there wasn't anyone else in the saloon. He began walking with his hands full when he heard the crack of the cue breaking the balls.

"Al! You broke your own rack!" Sam yelled and slammed his cue down. "I'm outta here!"

Al cut Sam off at the door, quicker than Jim this time, who'd dropped the glasses and run.

"You're not goin' anywhere!" Al screamed, his hands going for Sam's throat. Jim reached from behind, grabbed Al's hands, and pulled him to the floor. Hull disappeared with a cackle, and Jim wrestled with a sweaty, furious Al.

They ended up in front of the pass-through, where Yell was standing with the rifle, aiming for Al when Jim finished on top. A deadly glint caught Al's attention, and he ceased struggling as the barrel came over Jim's left shoulder, looking Al in the face.

"What's the problem, Jim?" Yell inquired mildly.

"Ah, Al's drunk. Mad, too, though he don't know what about," Jim was panting slightly, but still held Al's arms at the elbows.

"Really? Mmmm. Al, you need to go home. Let him up, Jim."

Relaxing his grip, Jim reached behind his back and pulled his own pistol out. He rocked back on his heels, letting Al see that both he and Yell were armed, but only loosely holding the gun in his right hand. He stood, offering his left hand to Al.

"Come on, Al."

So quickly Yell scarcely saw the movement, Al reached for Jim's gun, twirled it in Jim's hand, and forced Jim to pull the trigger on himself. Jim's hand relaxed its grip as Al pushed him back, red already spraying. Taking possession of the pistol as Yell tried to bring the rifle around, Al continued his lunge toward the door, pushing Jim to the floor and firing twice at Yell. One shot hit Yell in the arm, and he dropped the rifle as Bill Hensley and Charles Groom came running in the door. Hensley and Groom split. Al stood there for a precious second, not able to choose who to fire on next.

Dropping the gun, Al Layton looked down at the dying Jim Everett, who was drowning in his blood. He closed his eyes, turned, and ran right into Sam Hull, who'd returned after hearing the gun shots. Pushing Sam aside, Al fled toward Plug, grabbed the colt's reins, and mounted. The horse reared a bit, but took off, and Al blamed the speed, Jim's blood, and his own sweat for the wetness on his face.

CHAPTER 2
October, 1884

The courtroom had the distinct smell of whiskey when JJ Brown entered. Looking through the audience chamber, he espied his friend Nat's bright hair over to the right, and paused at the row to allow the men to rise and let him enter. He sat down in the space next to Nat, nodding to Nat and Yell as he did so. A deep breath he didn't know he'd been holding filtered out slowly. Sniffing the air cautiously, JJ could still distinguish the whiskey, but it was a subtle scent, enhanced by the dusty courtroom and other men's exhalations.

JJ had aged in the year since Jim's death. He missed Jim with an ache that wouldn't cease. Most of his own family was scattered throughout the middle West, and Jim had been a brother to him in their absence. The close Everett family had taken him up and held him in embrace most of his adult life. Jim's comradeship and support had been returned, even when they stood on opposing sides in argument--which wasn't often.

Today was it. Two weeks of arguments, prosecutor and defense, in the case against Al Layton. Unused to sitting outside the rail, JJ resisted the temptation to rise, turn and look at the defense or the men in the chamber. It would do no good. Frankly, he wasn't sure a "guilty" verdict would do him any good, either. It wasn't going to fix things.

A hand on his left shoulder, and Alonzo's breath in his ear. The big man was sitting a row behind, with James DeLong. "We're waiting on the judge to return from lunch," Alonzo spoke softly. "The jury is ready."

Such was the law in Taney County.

Over to his left, Layton was sitting with his lawyer. Layton glanced over his right shoulder, uneasily aware he could spend his life in jail, JJ thought. Then he saw Al winking at someone between himself and the defense bench, and wondered. Layton didn't really look like a nervous man, JJ realized. With a sinking feeling, he rose with everyone else as the bailiff announced the return of the judge.

The judge looked exhausted and ill. A circuit rider, he had cleared all the other cases on the docket before allowing the Layton case to open. To give him credit, only two or three of the jury members could claim some familial relationship with Layton--the large, extended family had been in the area since at least the 1840s.

A thin voice asked the bailiff if the jury was ready to deliver the verdict.

"Yes," said the bailiff, who was the current sheriff, John Moseley.

The jury was sent for, and filed in from the back of the courtroom. Al Layton was led to the defendant's box.

"He's wearing a gun!" exclaimed Nat in horror. Shushes were made by others, and JJ could hear Yell explaining to Nat that Layton's lawyer had requested a waiver to allow Layton the firearm. Tempers were high over the shooting of Jim Everett, and it was not unrealistic to expect trouble. All this was said in a low voice.

While the formalities were adhered to, every person in the audience chamber shifted to get the best view and prepare for the presumed "guilty" verdict. How could it be anything but? JJ wondered. Then, he remembered the look on Layton's face just minutes ago. He glanced over at Layton again. The angry, drunken man who killed his brother-in-law was nowhere to be seen. Neither was the remorseful man of the past two weeks apparent in Layton's face.

Years of courtroom experience in Taney County had taught JJ lessons in futility, but he had clung to the belief that all evidence damned Al Layton to the state penitentiary. As the jury was seated, there was scuffling, coughing, and averted faces in the jury box-- none in the audience chamber. Everyone seemed to sit as rigid as he did, awaiting the verdict. Again, he looked at Layton without moving his face. Again, Layton looked much too confident.

While the bailiff handed the verdict to the judge, a juror suddenly slumped over, asleep. None of the other jurors appeared to find this unusual. The foreman took the slip of the paper from the bailiff's hand, and again, JJ seemed to feel the weight of past cases.

"We, the jury of State of Missouri versus Albert G. Layton, find the defendant not guilty as charged in the murder of James Everett."

The courtroom erupted, while the judge pounded his gavel and JJ felt James DeLong leaving from behind. Of course, he had a newspaper to print. Everyone else remained in the room, quiet under a contempt-of-court threat from the judge. Not, JJ reflected bitterly, that he had any ability to back it up. However, no one acted as if they

Absolution | 19

knew that--quiet, while the judge released the jury and Layton.

His experienced eyes had roamed over the jurors' faces. The sleeping one was probably dead drunk, JJ knew. He also knew all the men on the jury--there were not that many registered voters in the county to serve jury duty. Which one, which one....there. One of the men had joined the happy group around Layton, shaking his hand and moving off.

JJ, Nat, Yell, and Alonzo had sat quietly, waiting for what? After all, justice was not going to be served here this day. Layton had shown remorse during the trial and it was possible he felt it--Jim had loaned Layton money during the drought a couple years ago, JJ recalled. Well.

He stood. Walking purposefully up the aisle to the front of the court, JJ opened the gate and moved to the right, searching through the jury box for anything that might answer why the men let Layton go. Then he smelled the sot snoring away, and his quest was over. It was rotgut, demon stuff that would make anyone lose his mind. Going to the end of the jury box, he was going to check on the miscreant, and began to reach his hand out to check for a pulse. Would a dead juror mean a mistrial?

"Don't touch him," Nat's voice was soft. For a tall man, Nat moved quietly. One of his stories of his past involved living with Indians on the plains and learning some of their tricks. JJ stiffened, then moved the juror's head, checking for a pulse and ashamed he half-hoped he wouldn't find one. But it was there, and he straightened to look at Nat.

Despite his hollowness, he reached for and found a touch of the humor he and Jim had always shared. "A dead juror would be problematic for Mr. Layton," JJ told his friends. "A hit, a very palpable hit..."

Nat didn't smile. Yell, who had followed the two to the front of the room, did, and responded, "Yes, it would be. We should have thought of poison ourselves."

"How did they find him not guilty?" Nat was shaking his head, looking around the courtroom. "I was on the grand jury. The evidence was overwhelming!"

JJ sighed and sat down. In his own search for answers, his eyes fell on the neck of a flask, poorly tucked into the right pocket of the comatose juror's coat pocket. Pulling it out gently, he took off the cap and sniffed at the contents. He shuddered and hastily replaced the cap, handing the bottle to Yell.

"Poison indeed." Yell was an expert in various whiskeys, moonshine, and bourbons. Although JJ didn't ask, Yell probably knew by the scent of the flask's contents who had brewed it. After a eye-watering, nose-wrinkling shudder of his own, Yell carefully put the flask on the prosecutor's table, whipped out a handkerchief, removed his hat, and wiped his face. He did not offer an answer to JJ's unasked question.

"This is how things are, Nat," Alonzo had joined them. "Trials here are a mockery, if you can get one. No one goes to jail, no one gets convicted. Several of the jurors were related to Layton."

"We all testified for the prosecution! We were there!" Nat continued to protest.

"That fact alone should've precluded you from being on the grand jury," JJ retorted as he stood. "Do you not see, Nat? I make a living--we" his hand waved at Alonzo, "we make a living from business outside the courtroom. I will not say there is no business as a defense lawyer, but it is a damnably small part of my business."

Alonzo was nodding in agreement. "JJ was prosecutor before you moved here, Nat. He has told me of the frustrations in holding office."

JJ's face was a study in frustration, grief, and resignation. "I've held a number of posts. I cannot say it has made a difference here in Taney County."

Nat looked at his friends. "Maybe it is time for a change," he said slowly.

Night was closing in. Paul and Georgia were studying at the kitchen table while Maggie filled a plate for Nat and put it on the back of the stove. Removing the pot of boiling water from the fireplace, she filled her wreck pan and added soap to wash up the supper dishes. The night was peaceful, but Maggie was restless. Nat had stayed in Forsyth last night, waiting for the outcome of the Al Layton trial.

Nearly eighteen years of marriage, and she still missed him when he had business away from home. She hummed softly and smiled, aware that many women married so long would be glad of their husband's absence. Not her.

Absolution | 21

Nathaniel Napoleon Kinney. Mrs. Maggie Kinney. The girlish thoughts ran through the back part of her mind still; her head shook in amusement at herself. A woman in her fifth decade should be a little less silly, she knew. A woman twice-married, who had given birth six times, and buried a child and a husband, should not be so romantic.

Listening to the evening--the windows were open, it had been a beautiful fall day--and zigzagging back and forth in her thoughts, she focused momentarily on the sound of a lone horse traveling on the Springfield-Harrison Road nearby. She knew immediately it wasn't Nat, so returned to her muddled thinking.

Maggie had realized earlier in the day that it had been exactly eighteen years ago when she met Nat on the new railroad from Kansas City to Topeka. She'd been visiting family; he was headed west. Although it was highly improper for a widow to converse with a single man without introduction, they had fallen into conversation at a shared table in the dining car. Traveling on the railroad after the war was still new in Kansas; proper manners were sometimes adjusted as necessary.

And it had been necessary. Although she loved William--indeed, had no thought of marrying again, focusing on raising their three children and living on her father's ranch--she knew when Nat had asked if he could call upon her that he was necessary to her. She wasn't naïve, she wasn't unintelligent, she wasn't dependent, but she was more of a person once she understood the necessity of Nat.

Maggie had been five when her father and uncles had loaded up and left Carriger Landing, Tennessee, under the leadership of her grandfather, Christian Carriger. People had been migrating west to California and Oregon for several years by mid-1845, when her branch of the family left for Westport, Missouri, and wintered near the Missouri River. Early the next spring, her mother was ill, and the rest of the Carrigers left Elliot and Angelina in Missouri. Their wagon train had passed the Donner party, moving fast to avoid winter in the mountains. Still, illness had struck, and her grandfather had died as the train reached the Yuba River. Her uncle Nicholas had rallied everyone, though, moving them on to Sonoma County, California, where they settled, growing grapes and making wine.

Thinking of the wine, Maggie decided to go out to the root cellar and pull a bottle from the last shipment her brother had sent. Wiping her hands dry, she lit another lantern from the fireplace.

"Where are you going, Mother?" It was Paul. A slight frown was on his face--it made him look so much like his father. He was quite protective of her when Nat and James were away.

"Oh, I think I'll go out for a few minutes," she said, smiling. "It's quite nice."

"Will you play tonight?" This came from Georgia, who loved music.

"Now there's a thought," Maggie teased her daughter. She played them to sleep nearly every night. "Is your work finished?"

"Mine is, Mother," Georgia crowed.

Paul's frown deepened. "Mother, those people are probably out there. I do wish you would wait for me to go with you!"

She'd been almost to the dogtrot when she heard Paul's protest. She turned back, setting her lantern on the small table by the doorway, and returned to the big table where the children sat. The oil was low in the big lantern they studied by; she needed to fill it, making a mental note to bring oil in from the cellar as well.

"Those people are your neighbors," she answered Paul's protest calmly. "We live by them, and we want to live in peace. We cannot act as if we are better than they are."

"But, Mother, they have no manners!" Paul hotly declared. "Really, that Andrew Coggburn..."

"is an orphan who has no one to teach him better," Maggie interrupted firmly. What was bothering Paul tonight? Boys were difficult to raise, she thought. James had certainly kept secrets from her, and Paul was approaching that age.

School was going to be opening again next week. Education was spotty here, but Maggie ordered in text books and courses for Paul and Georgia to supplement their learning, and taught them music herself. Paul had taken a load of firewood over to the school building today. What on earth...?

"Andrew was at the school today," burst Paul. "He was saying terrible things about Father, calling him names..."

Maggie took a sharper look at her son. "You weren't fighting, were you?"

His eyes lowered, then raised. "No." His lips, though pressed tightly together, were swollen.

Walking around the table, she reached for Paul's hands. She

brought them up to view in the glow as he protested, but the lantern sputtered and then went out. The sconces on the wall, the fire, and her own lantern across the room shed just enough light that Maggie could tell Paul's hands were swollen at the knuckles. Her fingers brushed over them, so light as to not cause pain.

"Paul." Her voice was disappointed.

"Mother, I hit a tree instead of him. All right?" Defiant. He hadn't eaten much at dinner, and now she saw he was stiff, breathing with some difficulty as if his ribs were bruised.

She sighed. He would not tell her the truth. And she wouldn't make him, because boys had secrets, as did men. She reached for his hair, caressing him as she straightened the red-gold he had inherited from Nat. He was thirteen, and growing up, she thought.

"Paul, I will not be afraid of Andrew or anyone else out there. They come to listen to the music, you know."

"Are you trying to civilize them?" Astute question. He slammed his book shut, and stood, pushing his chair back.

"I don't think--" she began, and stopped. Indeed. Overlooking her own blind spots, instead she held out a hand to him, and asked, "Will you carry the lantern oil in for me?"

Eva and her young man were sitting in the kitchen when Maggie and Paul returned from the cellar. Georgia was sitting on Robert Prather's lap, telling him about her day spent gathering black walnuts, and showing him her stained hands.

Maggie could not keep Georgia out of the woods. She knew Georgia was learning herbals from Granny Haggard. The old Cherokee woman was a skillful healer, and in general, Maggie approved of any educational opportunity. The child was enchanted with the woods; she'd been born on the Kansas prairie, and lived in the city of Springfield before they moved to Taney County. Little wonder--Maggie herself spent a great deal of time outdoors, marveling at the beauty of the old Ozarks Mountains. Georgia had convinced her to plant her vegetable garden last spring in accordance with what Granny Haggard had taught her, and the garden had flourished. However, the amulet with a dried bat in it....

The trip to the root cellar had been without incident, despite some shuffling in the dark. Half of the people were quite wild, Maggie knew, and she did hope that somehow, her music would reach them.

But civilizing them? Maggie didn't know if that was possible. She'd keep that thought to herself.

The lantern re-lit, she shooed Georgia off to bed, and Paul settled with another book--a novel, Maggie noted--in his father's rocking chair, below a sconce. Eva and Robert were holding hands stealthily, dreamy looks on their faces.

Taking a torch from the kitchen fire, Maggie stepped across the enclosed dogtrot and into the parlor, where her prized piano waited for her. She lit the fire in this fireplace, and dusted off her hands. A screen circled the bed in the corner, and the other furniture in the room gleamed with wax. She stretched.

A crock nearby had soft cloths and a small tin of Granny Haggard's beeswax in it. She opened the wax tin, rubbed a cloth across the contents, and then dusted her furniture. The nightly routine settled her, soothed her, and brought the music to her fingers. Lastly, she stroked the piano, running the cloth across the ivory keys from left to right--her prelude to finally sitting in front of the beckoning instrument.

Vaguely, she heard the front door opening, and Robert saying good-night to Eva. That was unusual. As her hands began warming up with scales, she looked up when Eva stuck her head through the door.

"Robert says good-night."

"Oh?" Maggie knew her daughter was surprised.

"He wants to be home when his father arrives," Eva explained. "Apparently, Mr. Prather is at the same trial Father is attending."

"I'm sure he is," she responded.

"Mother…." Eva began.

"Mmm?"

"I don't understand why it's so important."

Maggie wasn't sure she did, either, but she attempted to explain. "A friend of your father and Mr. Prather's was killed last year. This trial was held over the matter, and hopefully, the killer will go to jail." She certainly didn't understand why it was even a question, after Nat told her what happened.

"Why wouldn't the killer go to jail?" Eva asked. She was nineteen, and things were still black-and-white to her. "He should certainly be punished."

"I don't know, dear," Maggie hummed along with her piano.

Then she stopped playing, and turned to her daughter. "Things here are not the same as back home, or even in Springfield. People are different." Her hands longed to play, and she almost raised them back to the piano.

"The law is the same, is it not?" Eva asked.

"Yes, it is," responded Maggie. "But people believe different things, sometimes, and respect lies in differing quantities."

"Oh." Considering this carefully, Eva looked at the back window, which faced Big Bald. Two faces stared back at her and her mother, a woman and a baby. She quickly glanced toward the lighted candle her mother had placed on the table next to the piano, but the vision of the faces did not leave her quickly. The piano was the first in Taney County, and many of the people who lived here had never heard one until Maggie began her nightly concerts. Until it was so cold her mother closed the windows, women, children and the occasional man would sit near the fence surrounding the dooryard and listen to the music for as long as Maggie played. Some of the more bold ones would sit on the porch.

Eva understood the hunger for beauty. Manners dictated she could not discuss this with her mother right now, however. That woman was close enough to overhear, and Eva was well-mannered.

"I think I'll go to bed, Mother. Will you be alright?"

Maggie smiled. "Of course dear, good night." Her daughter kissed her cheek, and went upstairs. Maggie sat for a moment, and then attacked the piano with pent-up emotion.

Her thoughts were not as turbulent as the music was, although nearly so. What was going on in the children's minds? They were suddenly very worried about protecting her, she realized. Well, she would ask them tomorrow.

Her mind drifted back to Nat, and the music changed unconsciously. Softly, she caressed the song from the piano, thinking of the life they had managed to rebuild after the dreadful time in Topeka, and again, in Springfield.

They had lived on her father's ranch, Nat and Elliot breeding and raising horses that had cow sense, and cattle. Being in the midst of her extended family, raising and teaching her own children, she had not paid a great deal of attention to events outside her world. Then one night in 1877, Nat had come home from Topeka, talking about working for the Pinkerton detectives.

She had been asleep, and while warming some dinner for him, he told her how a man had approached him, asking if he had been in the army. Like many in Kansas, he went west after mustering out of the Union Army in 1865 from West Virginia. Marriage to Maggie had anchored him in Auburn, outside of Topeka, but he did sometimes do work for the railroad, as a guard on especially valuable freight. He'd also been to Texas twice, bringing cattle back in the heyday of Dodge City. There was no lack of adventure in his life, he told her.

But he wanted to do this. The kind of work a man hungers for, making a difference in the world around him. Topeka wasn't like the cities back East, where everyone went to the theater, discussed art, and higher education was possible for everyone. Topeka was wild, woolly, and still rough around the edges, and he wanted the chance to tame it.

He took the job, with her support. He was gone a lot, and she didn't always know when he'd be home. But he was alive when he was home, loving her completely and leaving her spent with his energy. The children were happier, the world seemed brighter, and life was good.

The riots of 1878 in Topeka changed it. The newspapers had called Nat and three other men "The Big Four," all good-sized men who'd managed to break the strike of the railroad workers and put some in jail. Until that time, Maggie had thought Nat was doing real detective work--finding out who murdered whom, tracking down bank thieves like the James and Younger gang, that sort of thing. She had no idea he was involved in violent activities.

Despite the heroic efforts Nat had put into his work, after the riots, his bosses seemed to distant themselves from him. The calls for work away from home became fewer and fewer, until he finally decided to leave the company. Maggie knew it was simple jealousy--Nat had told her of snubs, remarks made to belittle him in front of his team, accusations of using his superior strength to promote his own agenda. During his travels, however, he'd been in Springfield, Missouri, and it seemed like a good place to start over.

Her father was against the move back East. Her mother had died before she met Nat, and other family members were close by, but Elliot depended on Maggie for care and love. As the eldest daughter, he told her, she had no right to leave. In her deepest thoughts, she realized she didn't want to go East; the daughter and granddaughter of frontier people, she was bred to always go West.

But her place was beside Nat.

She stopped playing for a rest, taking a sip of water, inhaling the scent of the candle and polish. The fire kept the chill of darkness off her; she rolled her head, stretching her neck muscles, and stopped when she saw Andrew Coggburn's face in the window to her left. The boy was a good three years older than Paul--what was he doing, beating up on a smaller boy? Flexing her hands, she remembered Paul's hands under her own--his hands were bigger than hers. She'd been looking up into his face for some months now. Well, Andrew shouldn't be fighting a younger boy, then. She was going to have to speak to Andrew.

Her water glass was empty, so she rose and went to the kitchen. Paul had retired as well, she saw. Crossing back into the other part of the cabin, she went to the east window, sipped, and saw the moon rising over Big Bald. Silhouettes of a few people who were still waiting for music reminded her of Andy's face, and she glanced over her shoulder as she stepped behind the screen to change into her nightgown. He was no longer in the window, but she had no doubt Andrew was nearby, waiting.

Some people might feel they were being stalked by the watchers, she supposed. Returning to the piano, a lullaby on her mind, she knew she had never felt that way about her audience. She understood what Eva had felt earlier, and couldn't say---a hunger for beauty was one of the first steps to civilizing the wilderness. And it was wild, here. Some people never traveled more than 10 miles from their homes during their lifetimes, living in a log cabin and eating off tin plates.

Glancing up at her walls--you could still see the logs of this house, but it was a house, not a cabin. Nat had told her it was rough, and she'd been prepared for a log cabin. A pleasant surprise to see the walls were finished, inside and out, with siding and whitewash. The upstairs was commodious enough for the children, even James, when he'd joined them here.

A smile lit her face as she heard the distinctive gait of Nat's horse coming down the road. Then she started the lullaby, anticipating pouring him some wine and hearing about his day, and then waking up in his arms tomorrow.

Several minutes passed.

Lost in her music again, Maggie certainly hadn't forgotten Nat was finally home. But her candle spluttered and went out, so she stopped playing again to get a fresh one.

"Don't," he said.

She started, her heart jumping, and then Nat was there, holding her and breathing in the scent of her hair. She clung to him, feeling the chill from outside, laughing softly, and moved to take his coat.

"You're late," she chided. "Robert went home to see Alonzo hours ago."

"Play some more?" Nat asked.

Maggie couldn't see his face well--the fire had burned low--and she turned to go put another log on it. He stopped her, going to add a piece of oak himself.

"Nat?"

He sighed, then turned back to her. "They let him go."

"Oh, Nat…"

"I don't understand. Jim Everett was a good man."

A thought struck Maggie. He smelled as if he'd drank some rum, but not much. "Are you hungry?"

"No. Don't go to any trouble."

"Come. I have food ready."

His coat in her left hand, she reached for his hand and pulled him toward the still-lighted kitchen. He stood still, letting his eyes adjust to the light, while she hung his coat on the peg and closed the kitchen door from the dogtrot. Then she took his hand again, and sat him at the table.

The chicken was no longer warm, but she deftly pulled a potato out of the ashes in the fireplace with some tongs, brushed it off with a potholder, and put it on the plate. Settling the plate in front of Nat, she took butter and bread from her pantry and set them on a cutting board. The gravy was in a crock near the hearth, and she grabbed it before sitting down next to Nat. It was still warm, and her chilled fingers held it a moment. Then she pulled the silverware from crocks on the table, handing the setting to Nat, who was looking at his china as if it were the Holy Grail. She smiled.

"Eat. Then you can tell me."

"Play. Then I'll tell you." His eyes were dark in his ruddy face, and she could see agitation and something else in them.

She nodded, and rose to play at his request. "I want that food

Absolution | 29

gone when I return."

"Two songs. At least."

"Eat."

Nat always wanted to hear Moonlight Sonata. Nights the moon was full, he would watch it rise while she played. Tonight, however, the moon had risen some time ago.

She played it anyway.

Nat's plate was clean and in the wreck pan when Maggie returned to the kitchen. She smiled to herself. He was standing in front of the fireplace, warming himself and gazing down at the flames. He turned slightly to her as she crossed to the pantry, and pulled out the jug of wine she'd put there earlier. The rich red sparkled in the two precious wine glasses she owned.

He quirked an eyebrow at her as he took the glass. "What's the occasion?"

"Talk," she ordered. "Then I might tell you."

Nat searched for the words. Maggie did not know everything he'd done in the past, but she did know a lot. She knew he wanted respect in the community, and it was his own fault they were living in Taney County now. He shrugged. He still would have left Springfield if the man had not died. Springfield was too civilized for a man like himself; he knew it, but she didn't.

But he'd promised to make it up to Maggie, having to move again so soon, and he'd promised to settle down. Horse-raising, preaching, and farming were boring work, though, after spending years as a security guard and riot-breaker. Even militia exercises were boring.

He was running for sheriff next month on the Democratic ticket. Politics mattered little to Nat, the party line even less. There was work to be done here, and he wanted to be the one to do it.

"You know I want the sheriff's job," he told Maggie.

She inclined her head. She didn't like it, but she knew. "What happened today?" she asked, taking a sip of her wine and moving to her rocking chair, wrapping a crocheted shawl around herself.

"Al Layton was found not guilty. Maggie, this place is impossible. No one spends any time in jail, for anything. Scarcely anyone is even arrested. Trials are a joke."

"What about the sheriff?"

"He has two deputies. That's all. One of them is an idiot, the other lazy." He sipped the wine, contemplating. "There's no money for hiring better deputies. They make a pittance. There's no money to deputize a posse. No one wants to join a patrol without being paid, there's no incentive."

"Oh." Puzzled, Maggie rose from her chair and strode to the window facing Big Bald. She took another drink of her wine. "And today?" she encouraged him and turned back to face him.

"Today, it was clear. Everyone here is related to someone else. There's no clear system of complaint, no measure of respect for the office of sheriff or prosecutor, and the men in those offices are simply taking their salaries and putting them in the bank. If someone steals your hog, you take matters into your own hands, or you can ride to Forsyth, file a complaint, and then have the sheriff tell you it's lost."

"Where's the money? Why is there no money in the county?"

Nat shrugged. "There is. Few people pay their taxes, though. The ones who do are supporting the entire county. And with only three officers of the law, people are literally getting away with murder."

Maggie was thinking hard. If Nat found the sheriff's job to be impossible, he would not want to stay. She looked around the room, seeing the effort she and Nat had put into making the cabin hospitable. House, she thought. It's a house. A home. Her hands fluttered, then caught the shawl around her shoulders.

Nat noticed the motion. "What?" he said. "What is it?"

She looked down at the flames, then crossed the room, pacing. She turned back to Nat.

"Why don't you do something?"

"Me? I'm running for sheriff."

"No, I'm not talking about that. If you want to stay here...."

"I do. I've told you before, this is it. I promised you that."

She waved his promise away. "Nat, you are one man. You've said yourself, one man is not enough. Neither is three."

"It's not. The Coggburn boy and his sister are orphans because their father went after horse thieves by himself. His body was never found."

Maggie paused before speaking again. She hadn't known that. Poor Andrew. Still...

"Nat. Are you friends with many good men?"

"You know I am. You've met most of them."

Absolution | 31

"Do these men not want a better community?"

"They do. That's why the trial today was so important. We thought it was the first step."

Maggie shook her head. "Nat. What have you been doing most of your life?"

Nat's eyebrows rose a good inch, then came back down over his eyes as he squinted at her. He looked at her glass, then back at her face. "Living with you. How much wine have you had?"

"You're being silly. Listen to me. What have you been doing most of your life?"

"Besides living with you and raising horses and cattle?" She nodded. As he realized where she was going with this, Nat shook his head. "That won't work here."

"I'd like to know why not."

"Because...." he floundered. "There's no organization like the agency here. There's no money."

"You're missing the point. You have good men for friends, correct? These men are prosperous, are they not?" Nat was nodding slowly as she made each point. "They don't have to make money to feed their families while riding on patrol, do they? They own businesses, and have employees they supposedly trust, correct?"

Nat was agreeing with each item she ticked off in her hastily-assembled list. She moved in closer to him, and jabbed a finger at his chest.

"You do it."

"I'm running for sheriff."

There were times she wanted to hit Nat over the head. Instead, she reached for the wine, refilling her glass and his, and set it back down carefully, so carefully...she didn't want to break the jug in her frustration at not saying the right thing.

"Nat." His eyes were on her face, so she sighed and quickly damped down her feelings. "I know you want that job. Why?"

"So I can help." And get respect from men he liked.

"Alright," Maggie strolled to the window once more, then crossed the room again. She stopped in front of him. Softly, she asked, "You're running on the Democratic ticket in a Republican county. I know politics don't matter to you, but they do to many men. Do you really think you're going to be elected? Really?"

Nat looked floored, she thought, as she took up pacing again.

Surely, he didn't think....

Nat was nonplused. Maggie was very intelligent; she'd figured him out again and again over the years. He had thought he could win the election, however. He'd been talking to every registered voter in the county, securing votes. It was a shock, hearing her say he couldn't win the election. He glanced at her as she paced; too bad women couldn't vote or run for office. He would bet his Grey Ghost on her.

"Oh, dear." She was thinking aloud. She always did that when she was pacing. "You aren't going to want to stay here if you lose the election, are you? Where do you think we should go?" Her face brightened at the thought of her family in California, but she didn't bring that up just yet.

Nat, while admiring his wife somewhere in his mind, was busy putting pieces of the puzzle she'd baldly put in front of him together. "We could do that..." he mused, thinking of getting Alonzo, Yell, and JJ to ride patrol with him.

"Oklahoma Territory should open soon. Or Texas?"

"We'd have to go farther. Need more..." he was muttering. He was at the window, looking at Big Bald. Deer were standing on the bald, eating in the moonlight. He could almost see...

"California? Nat, we could go to the winery, see my family!"

The excitement in Maggie's voice finally got through to him, and what she'd said registered. "California? Who said anything about California?"

"I did. Can we move there? Uncle Nicholas can find work for you, I'm sure."

Shaking his head, Nat saw Maggie's excitement. For a few precious seconds, he felt her urge to leave, to move closer to family. Then his own excitement rose and surpassed hers.

"Maggie, I don't want to move to California. I want to stay here."

Her eyes registered disappointment, but she didn't let it go to her voice. "Why?"

"I told you. I promised you. This was it. It's beautiful country, we have the house, the land, the church. Why leave?"

"You said things were impossible."

"No. They aren't." His tone was emphatic. "I'm going to do it."

"Do what?"

Absolution | 33

"You said to start my own patrol. Set up my own organization. I can do that."

Maggie thought about her family, and let the disappointment go. Her place was by Nat. She moved to the rocking chair, and gently took the shawl from her shoulders, folding it and laying it across the back. Her slender hands tensed on the chair, making it rock.

"Of course you can." She looked up at her love, seeing the excitement in his face, displayed by his body. She kept her worries about the children, about him, to herself. She also didn't tell him why she gotten the wine from the cellar. He came to her, kissed her, then set his chin on her head, as he was wont to do when he was thinking.

"Play for me?" he asked. He felt her move away, and as she went into the other room and began his song, he watched the rocking chair slow.

CHAPTER 3
February, 1885

Snow still lingered in the shadows of the trees and on north faces of the mountains, where the sun couldn't reach just yet on its way to summer. The air was chilly, unless one sat directly in the sun, but Georgia had bounced down the stairs yesterday morning, telling her parents that "Spring is here." She said she'd felt it in her feet when they touched the floor.

Nat grinned in remembrance--he'd looked at Georgia's bare feet, then pointedly outside. Big flakes were drifting down from flat gray clouds. He didn't hold with the superstitious nonsense Georgia came up with--no doubt, through Granny Haggard's herbal lessons. Neither he nor Maggie had any Indian blood, thank God, but there were Scots and Irish grandparents on both sides. Maybe it was the Celtic influence. He'd known Irishmen who had said similar things while working on the railroad.

Georgia had insisted, and instead of admonishing her to put stockings on and hush, he'd swept her up and rubbed her little cold feet with his hands. Maggie had laughed, knowing how hard it was for him to discipline his daughter.

With a loud "Hmpf!" he tightened the girth on Grey Ghost. He didn't interfere with the way Maggie was raising the children, except to insist they attend church. He could fight superstition with the Bible, he knew. Never mind that the snow had moved off a short time later. The abundant sunshine which followed had melted much of it, and the frogs had begun their spring chorus at dusk.

"Well, let's hope she's right," Nat told Ghost as he led the horse outside. "We need an early spring."

Ghost was eager to be off--spring fever, Nat thought with sour amusement--and danced his way up the slope to the road. He glanced over at the house as they passed, seeing Maggie standing on the northern end of the long porch, and nodded back when she waved.

Upon reaching the road, he set the horse toward Forsyth, letting him run to get some of the freshness out of his system. Walkers were even-tempered horses, not given to wildness, but it had been some time since Ghost had been able to go all out. A true gray, even his winter coat had been lighter this year. The horse stood over 17

Absolution | 35

hands, and easily carried Nat as if he was a hundred pounds lighter.

As he reached the road which bypassed Kirbyville, he slowed Ghost to a canter and turned north. His business was in Forsyth, despite Maggie asking him to get the mail today.

The winter was spent making plans. It had been a tactical error to run as a Democrat--Maggie had been right, how did women do that?--and he'd had to invest time in talking to the hard-core Republicans who were suspicious of him as a result.

Down a short slope, pause to drink at a spring. The sun was lower, nearly behind the top of the knob, and Nat heard turkeys calling. Even with his hat on, he had to shield his eyes looking up to the west, but he espied movement in the drabness of a harvested, stalk-silhouetted corn field. There. Two toms were strutting, tail feathers spread, moving among the flock of hens that were ignoring them for the moment. Spring was on its way; Nat noted the blue heads of the gobblers.

Damn. His lips tightened, and he clucked to the horse, which had snorted at the cold water but was now lipping it thirstily. Another snort and final drink, and Ghost jumped the freshet and began moving north again.

At some point after Maggie had given him the idea for the formation of the Citizens' League for Law and Order in October, a change had come over Andrew Coggburn. Before, the boy had obviously worshipped Maggie, his thin face glowing whenever she chanced to speak to him. That worship had not included Nat, although Nat did attempt to reach Andrew. Something had caused Andrew to become more sly and yet, more outspoken, in his contempt of the church and school at Oak Grove.

Nat had stayed up all that night, sipping Maggie's wine and writing his thoughts down. Today was going to be the first test of Maggie's idea, although he would not tell the men he was about to meet that little piece of information. Maggie was his secret weapon. He suspected other men might feel the same about their wives, but no man admitted to it.

The October night had been chilly, but he'd gone outside to smoke a cigar a couple hours before dawn. Used to preaching to the brush and trees out in the woods to practice his Sunday sermons, Nat addressed the bright, clear stars on this night. The moon had already set, and the stars were so close. He tried differing tones of voice, settling at last on majestic, as if the star shine was flowing down into him. It made him powerful, as if no one could question the rightness of what was now his idea. He stood on the edge of the porch, eyes closed, arms outreached.

There had been a brief chuckle. Opening his eyes, he turned in the direction of the noise, but it stopped, and he heard no more. The feeling of power still heated him, but he turned and went back inside to the kitchen, adding oil to the lamp and contemplating its flame as he considered the men of his community and others in the county, who he could trust and who would be best-suited to the task before him.

That feeling of a calling was still with him as the sun rose over Big Bald, and Maggie herself came into the kitchen. She had said nothing, seeming to recognize he wasn't ready for talk, but made coffee and then breakfast.

There was no tiredness in his body as he fed the papers he'd been writing on into the flames of Maggie's fire. No tiredness. Excitement, rightness, hummed through him the entire day. When Maggie had finished playing his song for him that night, he'd lifted her from the piano bench and carried her to the bed in the moonlight, and the power flowed between them, unbroken, unleashed, and forever.

So now he was on his way to Forsyth, about to take a very risky idea to a group of men he needed to make it work, and he was thinking about Andrew Coggburn.

Part of his plan was to preach the necessity of being vigilant, of teaching right from wrong to others. He'd commenced on this course the following Sunday. Andrew had been in church that day, along with his sister, Serelda. Most of the Coggburns couldn't be bothered with church--Andrew and Serelda began attending not long after Nat started preaching. He still occasionally came to church now, but not with any goal of bettering himself.

No, Andrew came to church to bedevil Nat.

Somehow, Andrew Coggburn knew what Nat was planning. He knew, although Nat had been leading his congregation down the path of vigilantism quite stealthily. But Nat could tell Andrew knew, for there had been an abrupt change in the boy's behavior. That first Sunday after Al Layton was acquitted, that Sunday was the first time Andrew burst out laughing in church, and the boy had left the

Absolution | 37

service, gobbling like a turkey.

Now, the whole Coggburn clan, as well as many of their friends, who also did not attend church, called Nat Kinney "The Ol' Blue Gobbler." Their mocking voices, led by Andrew's impudent, grinning face, were beginning to haunt Nat's dreams.

He shook himself, realizing he was less than a mile from the ferry on White River, as Ghost passed the Robert Snapp homestead. The sun had all but gone, and he was expected at the Everett store an hour past sundown. No one's laughter or mockery was going to stop him now.

It was time.

CHAPTER 4
February, 1885 - Agreement

The meeting place had been carefully chosen. The men had been carefully chosen.

Nat rode Ghost to the livery, greeting the hostler and settling his horse in for the evening. He walked west to the Hilsabeck Hotel, reserving and paying for a room he could sleep in tonight. "No, no bath," he told the clerk. "I'll be late." The clerk nodded in acknowledgement, and Nat strode back out, into the chill air between Swan Creek and the White River.

As he passed the hardware store, Nat saw his neighbor, Sam Snapp, and Billy Miles working by lamplight, loading a wagon with seed.

"Good evening," Nat spoke to Sam. The latter finished putting his bag on the wagon, wiped his hands on a handkerchief pulled from his back pocket, and moved to return the greeting with a hand shake.

"Hello, Mr. Kinney." Billy went back into the store for another bag while Sam spoke with Nat.

Indicating the wagon with his head, Nat raised his eyebrows in query. "A little early to be buying seed, is it not?"

Sam chuckled. "No, I don't think so. The frogs were singing last night. By the time we have the ground ready, it'll be time to plant. Early spring this year."

Nat's mouth quirked in response, "Yes, so my daughter says." Another bag thumped into the wagon.

A grin widened on Sam's face. "My wife is kin to Granny Haggard. She says Granny is seldom wrong, so we came to get our seed now."

"You believe in this superstition? You are an educated man," responded Nat. "There could still be a freeze."

Sam pushed his hat back, considering. The wagon loaded, Billy joined the two older men. Sam spoke slowly, as if he was thinking of these things for the first time.

"There could be. I have lived here all of my life, and have witnessed stranger things than frogs singing in February. I have not made a study of it, but weather signs are fairly reliable."

Absolution | 39

The careful response indicated a natural diplomacy on Sam's part. Nat sharpened his gaze at Sam's face, wondering if he should invite Sam to the meeting tonight. But Sam was already moving to put on his coat, the chill having reached through his shirt and dried the warmth he'd gathered while loading the wagon. Billy jumped up on the wagon seat, waiting for his boss to join him.

Shrugging into his coat, Sam reached down for the lantern and handed it to Billy. He then returned his attention to Nat.

"We must be on our way. Good evening to you, Mr. Kinney." Sam climbed onto the wagon, reached for the reins, and clucked to his horses.

Diplomatic, maybe, Nat thought as he nodded in return to Sam. "Good night." But Sam Snapp was damned sure his own man. He watched as the wagon moved south.

As they made their way toward the ferry at the river, Billy did not turn around to look at Nat Kinney. He disliked having his back to the man, however. He had learned from his father to trust his instincts, and his gut was telling him Nat Kinney was a dangerous man. Curious, though. Mr. Snapp had definitely closed the conversation, not wanting to talk to his neighbor any more than politeness indicated. Did Mr. Snapp not realize...?

"He's having a meeting tonight to discuss patrolling the county and put down 'the criminal element,'" Mr. Snapp was reading Billy's mind apparently.

Well, that could be good. Livestock was disappearing off the farms around Taney City, including his father's and Mr. Snapp's other farm. He said as much to Mr. Snapp.

"It could be, Billy. He's not from here, though. It seems to me he is sitting in judgment when he doesn't understand our ways."

"But, Mr. Snapp," Billy protested, "something must be done. Pa has been keeping watch every night, and it's been winter. He can't keep it up once spring does arrive."

Sam nodded. His face was grim. "I don't have the answer, Billy. But I do believe Mr. Kinney is not the man he claims to be." His statement agreed with Billy's instinct. Sam reached up to re-settle his hat as the ferry man indicated he was ready for the wagon to board. "And I do wish you'd stop calling me 'Mr. Snapp.' That was my father."

40 | Vonda Wilson Sheets

The Everett Brothers' Saloon was closed, according to the sign on the door, "Reserved for a private party." Nat smiled to himself, took a breath, and walked in.

When he spoke with Yell Everett in January, Nat considered Yell's suggestion of using the store for his meeting. "No," he'd told Yell. He didn't elaborate, and Yell didn't ask.

The difference in the two rooms housed by the building was immense. The store, at the east end, was light and airy, tended lovingly by Yell's wife, Annie, and his sister, Caroline, who was married to JJ Brown. Merchandise was stacked neatly, placed with an eye to pleasing the customers. The store was painted a light yellow, cheery and warm, much like the Everett family members themselves.

Annie had crinkled her nose when Yell made the suggestion of the store that day. She didn't want any stinking, smoking, tobacco-chewing, drinking men sitting around her store after she'd gone home for the day. Nat had almost laughed at her expression; no doubt Yell would've heard about it when he went home that night.

No, the saloon was much better suited to Nat's purposes. While he and Jim Everett had not been particularly friendly, he had been able to draw closer to Yell and JJ since Jim's death. He wanted the stark reminder of Jim's death, the dark saloon with its nicotine-stained dark walls, the access to the family recipe beer, and the nuances of grimness to aid him in his quest.

He looked around. Yell was probably eating dinner, he decided.

Alone, he walked through the saloon, debating the best place to greet "his" men. If he sat in the corner, with both walls protecting his back, it would look as though he had something to hide, something to be worried about.

No, best be at the bar, friendly with a touch of aloofness. He moved chairs into two lines in front of the bar, as if it was a pulpit. "Guess it is," he said aloud.

He wanted a drink, but it would not do to meet the men with whiskey or beer on his breath. Instead, he reached for a cigar, more to have something to do with his hands rather than a need for nicotine.

There were footsteps on the wooden sidewalk. It was time. He was clipping the cigar as Yell Everett walked in with JJ Brown.

"Good evening," Nat greeted the men. He had expected them first.

James Rice came from the Cedar Creek area. Ben Price, Thomas Phillips, James Van Zandt, and Galba Branson were also from outside Forsyth. Charles Groom lived in Forsyth, on the eastern end of city limits. Polk McHaffie was staying in town--as the newly-elected sheriff, he had prisoners at the jail. Pat Fickle joined Nat at the bar. Alonzo was the last to arrive, with Nat's stepson, James, in tow.

Thirteen men, including himself. Superstitious people would probably be shuddering. None of his picked men were particularly superstitious.

Neither was he.

Captain Van Zandt was the oldest of the men, having turned sixty. Charles Groom was the youngest by two years, under James' twenty six years. Some youth, tempered with experience. A good mix, he thought.

Winter was a time for rest, gathering strength for the upcoming year. They were going to need it.

He'd greeted the men as they came in, shaking hands and indicating seats. Throwing his cigar in the spittoon nearby, Nat realized this....this....was a defining moment in his life.

"I've asked you here to discuss starting a volunteer organization," he began. "Sheriff McHaffie has told me of the difficulties involved in arresting and retaining men who commit crimes. My belief is that prevention of those crimes is necessary to our court system, our communities, and our lives."

Most of the men's heads were nodding in agreement. Encouraged, Nat continued. "I believe the time has come to aid our sheriff and the court system in arresting criminals. We also need to set up an organization which will patrol our county, our lands, to potentially prevent some of these crimes from happening."

The men were listening.

"The circuit court judge only visits Taney County twice a year, on the basis of how many trials we have on the docket. If we can fill the docket more often, it stands to reason the judge must hold court more often, to sentence criminals and send them to jail."

"We don't have a jail," noted McHaffie.

"No, and the Forsyth City Jail will only hold a few men. Maybe the county could add on to the city's jail, since we share it with the city," smoothly responded Nat. "Our state representative should be able to get funding for such a project."

McHaffie nodded--he liked that answer. Traveling back and forth from Ozark and Springfield to transport prisoners was getting tiresome, and took him away from the office several times each month. He could not rely on his deputies.

As if Nat heard Polk's thoughts, he continued. "If we develop an organization which will aid the sheriff in arresting and transporting prisoners by means of patrolling the county, I believe we can cut down on some of the county's expenses."

Nearly all of the men in the room had served in office or by appointment at some point in their lives. The others had large families and were strongly in favor of corralling the stealthy night figures who stole their livestock, maimed their cattle, wreaked havoc upon their lives. Prosperous, upstanding, church people who paid their property taxes and were intelligent; these were the traits Nat looked for in choosing these particular men for this meeting.

The final trait Nat considered was whether or not each man would need to be out in their own fields this spring. These men hired others to work their farms.

"Patrols, like a militia?" Most of the men in the room had served in the Civil War, a few in local militias. Yell had been one of them; he wanted no part of warfare again.

"No," Nat told Yell. "My hope is to deter crime by riding nights in differing parts of the county."

"And if we catch someone in the act of committing a crime?" JJ asked.

"We turn the criminal over to Sheriff McHaffie."

Rice had been largely silent, deep brown eyes watchful, "Big county, Mr. Kinney. This group of men is not enough."

Tricky part here, Nat's confidence never wavered. "We will recruit other men, Mr. Rice."

Eyebrows were raised, heads were nodding slowly. Nat continued.

"We will divide the county into districts. Each of us will recruit men in our districts to aid us in riding patrol. Each district will ride on different nights, in different parts of the county."

Here it came.

"Since schedules need to be coordinated and followed, one person will need to be in charge of assigning nights to each district. I do not have a business to run, and I am easily available. I will volunteer to take on this task." Nat said this in a manner that could be construed as diffident, almost shy. He had had to practice it.

"So one man in charge of each district?" young Groom asked.

"Yes. And that man will come to me to report activities such as arrests, and be assigned nights to patrol."

This was the gamble, that none of the other men would want to be in charge of the entire county for these patrols. So far, none of them appeared to realize that Nat would be in command. He relaxed fractionally. They were busy men, and he was asking them to give up sleep as it was.

"What about retaliation?" this from Alonzo. "Can this be done secretly, for protection of our families?"

"It would happen," Charles Groom said. "If we arrest say, Tubal Taylor, what's to prevent Frank from going to our homes, watching for us to leave, and terrorizing our wives and children?"

James straightened in his chair. "If we wore masks, it would be difficult to distinguish us in the dark. Then how would they know who to act against?"

Nat nodded slowly, thoughtfully.

"If we turned our coats wrong side out, that would be more confusing," added Ben Price.

Captain Van Zandt, practical as always, added, "Horses. We need to ride dark ones. That gray of yours, for instance," he looked at Nat, "would stand out, be easily recognized."

"True," Nat agreed, with a shrug.

"One of us should be taking notes," JJ said suddenly. "We need to have a name for this organization."

"No notes!" Nat shook his head.

"No, no written records," Alonzo agreed. "Do you not see, JJ? Even if nothing goes wrong, we do not need to have a record of it. We are used to memorization."

"We need to stay within the bounds of the law," JJ retorted.

"Which is why Sheriff McHaffie will be in charge of all we arrest," Nat interjected. "We are acting as a posse, not law officers."

McHaffie shook his head. "I can't deputize everyone," he agreed. "And if this plan succeeds, I'll be much too busy to run a posse. Thank you, Mr. Kinney, for offering to take it on."

Nat nodded, hoping no mockery was showing in his gesture.

44 | Vonda Wilson Sheets

Captain Van Zandt was still eyeing Nat. "It'll make you a marked man, Nat."

Gunfire and shouting suddenly erupted to the west of the building, and all the men tensed, watchful in the lantern light. The windows of the saloon were shuttered, and the sound moved toward them. Then past. The whoops were distinguishable as belonging to Frank and Tubal Taylor. Again. Since Oscar Lowell had left Forsyth, the brothers were prone to simply riding through town, shouting and shooting at any time of the day or night.

Nat couldn't have planned it any better.

"Shall we have a drink?" Yell asked, as the group collectively realized that something could now be done with the Taylors. Possibly. McHaffie had arrested them for disturbing the peace twice since taking office, but the brothers made bail and went on to raise even more hell. Alexander Kissee recently filed a complaint against Tubal for cutting the tongues from three cows, which had died. The sheriff made a move as if to leave, but Nat stopped him.

"It will happen. Give us a chance."

With that, the tenseness was broken. Nat understood, but he wasn't finished.

"Yell, if you would wait but a few more minutes," he told the saloon keeper, who had moved behind the bar to serve drinks. Yell nodded, but remained where he was. He'd been sitting for a long time, and he wasn't used to it.

"I think we need an oath, a vow upon us, to clean up this county," Nat continued. "I am not a Freemason, but I understand such a thing exists in the lodge. I nominate JJ Brown to write an oath of membership for the Citizens' League of Law and Order."

Fraternal brotherhood was understood; the oath would make it official.

"I second the nomination," Alonzo's deep voice held a note of amusement. That would certainly keep his friend's mind busy and off his grief.

"What about a future meeting?" asked Galba.

Nat appeared to consider this for a time; Yell took this as a sign he needed a drink, and began pouring from a bottle of whiskey. As his glass was handed to him, Nat answered slowly.

"We'll need a larger place than this for the next meeting, as our recruits will need to join us and take the oath. Big Bald is large enough for such a gathering."

"When will this take place?" Rice was curious.

"Let's say a month from now," Nat responded, "Maybe early April?" Dryly, he added, "My daughter says spring is coming early this year, so the seeding should be largely done, if she's right."

Short-lived amusement rippled through the room as the men moved to get drinks from Yell. None drank, however, until Yell had poured himself one. Ceremoniously, he raised his glass, and the sounds of the Taylors returning for a ride-through filtered into the saloon. In the echoes of the racket, Yell announced, "Here's to the Citizens' League of Law and Order."

As one, the new brotherhood raised its glass, said, "Here, here!" and drank.

He was high, not quite drunk with whiskey, but with power.

Even the cold could not faze him.

Forgetting the room he had paid for, he went to the livery, saddled Ghost, and left for home.

The ferryman grumbled and stumbled and groaned. Nat simply laughed, and offered the man a drink from the flask Yell had filled. Reaching the south bank of the river, he handed over twice the charge, and left.

He rode through the star-studded night; the frogs had gone silent hours ago. His breath and Ghost's were steamy warm, his knees and gloved hands urging the horse on.

Riding into the barn, he quickly unsaddled the horse, fed him, and threw a blanket over him.

Not tired, but he needed home.

Maggie's eyes were shining in the glow of the lantern beside the bed. He shucked his clothes, doused the light.

Not tired.

He was home.

CHAPTER 5
Late March, 1885

It was one of the last of the winter nights. Susie knew it.

She sat in front of the stove, her feet tingling with the warmth. Sam was asleep; his breathing kept time with the flickers of the fire in the stove. The children, whom she was coming to love as her own, were tucked snug in the bed in the loft.

The heat of her indigestion had her sitting up late. The lamp burned steady on the table in the small cabin. The cabin itself was quite warm. It had started snowing yesterday--big, wet, soft flakes, drifting down silently and creating a magic place in the small valley which encompassed her world right now.

Sam and Billy had finished plowing and seeding the fields yesterday. Glancing at the clock, she realized yes, it was not yet midnight, so "yesterday" would suffice.

Billy left to return to the farm on the barrens at Taney City last night. This morning, the clouds of this snowstorm had let them all sleep in for a few precious minutes. She was hoarding the last of these peaceful minutes; soon, it would be full-blown spring, and the days would be long. The service-berry had begun blooming two weeks ago, joined by the dogwood and the redbud. This snow had been a big, wet, deep one. The moisture for the fields would be welcome. Twenty inches had fallen. That wasn't unusual for late spring, and it seldom froze long enough to cause any damage to the garden and crops. She could feel the warmth rising outside. Water was trickling down the roof of the cabin, and she rose to peer out the window by the stove. Yes, the snow was disappearing fast. Her nose crinkled; mud.

Sitting back down and folding back into her shawl, its thickness a comfort on her shoulders and back, Susie sipped at her peppermint tea. Granny had told her to drink several cups a day--it would be a help to the nausea that sent her running at odd moments.

A soft smile brightened her face. A baby. She visited with Granny quite often, but after her first week of battling nausea off and on, she'd asked Granny. "Oh, yes," Granny had grinned. "Two."

She didn't question Granny's wisdom. The native knowledge Granny had passed down to her children, grandchildren, and

Absolution | 47

neighbors, if they were willing to listen, kept them healthy and well-fed. Her own garden would be planted, cared for, and harvested as she'd been taught, careful of moon phases, which plants went where, and more.

In a few minutes, she thought as Sam rolled over in the bed, she'd curl in beside him, enveloped in the feather mattress and wool comforter she'd made while still young. The security of the small cabin, her bed, and Sam's love, was really all she needed. Babies were a bonus.

Contemplating the logs of the back wall in the home, she determined, finally, where she wanted the door to the room Sam planned to add onto the cabin this year. There. Next to the stove, so the heat of it would reach the addition. Sam had promised this room would be their kitchen and living room. It wasn't that the cabin was small--it was, but few people had homes that were bigger. It was too hard to heat a large cabin, and with a summer kitchen and assorted outbuildings, there was no need for a larger place to sleep in. Only in winter did it seem to be cramped.

Nannie murmured in her sleep upstairs. The child was a big help to Susie, eight years old and doing chores without complaint.

A blessing to Sarah Sims Snapp whispered through her mind. Sam's first wife had died of the measles not quite a year ago. Bewildered, grieving, and overwhelmed, Sam had not wanted to marry again so soon. However, the day-in, day-out of caring for young children and trying to run two farms had worn him down to the bone, and Susie made him laugh. They had married in the fall, Susie promising to care for Sarah's children as if they were her own.

They almost were now. Nannie had moments where she disappeared into the woods, seeking solace in a place where water flowed and she could mourn for a little while. She had taken Susie there during one of the warmer winter days, knowing Susie would honor what the little clearing on the creek bank did for her. Susie had murmured a prayer of her own--it had been one of those places Granny would say was filled with the spirit of an Old One.

Indigestion gone, she stood and let the shawl fall from her shoulders. She rinsed her cup, setting it on the shelf, and turned to climb into the bed. Sam's eyes were open, watching her. Susie Haggard Snapp smiled at her husband, and moved to join him.

48 | Vonda Wilson Sheets

She had fallen asleep, almost instantly, on Sam's right arm, lying her neck over it as her head rested on the pillow. Sam had held the comforter open for her, and Susie settled in for a night's rest. The nice shock of her cool flannel night gown had reached him from neck to knees, and she somehow molded herself to him. This was a nightly occurrence, and still new enough to Sam that he wondered at it. A sigh seemed to come from her entire body; she was asleep within seconds of laying her head.

He daren't move. Didn't much want to, anyway, he thought. His left hand was resting on her stomach, as if to add to the protection of the tiny babes inside. He'd known almost immediately when Susie became pregnant; Sarah, too, had suffered from indigestion and nausea when she'd been pregnant with Tom. Twins, though--he almost shook his head. It was very early--Susie's stomach was still flat, although her breasts were filling out, and her skin had started to swell, the texture of a ripe peach. She had laughed, telling Sam that Granny Haggard had said there were twins in there. His hand tingled with the possibility of feeling four feet, four hands, inside their snuggery. He snorted and his left hand twitched.

"Mmmm?" Maybe she wasn't asleep.

"Sleep. I'm here," he whispered in her left ear. He was lying spoon-fashion, almost around her. Another sigh, and she was gone again.

Samuel Harrison Snapp had turned thirty years old in November. As he lay, watching the shadows and light from the small opening in the wood stove, in his warm bed and home, his thoughts were drifting much like the snow had early in the day. It was thick and heavy, purposeful but errant and wandering.

He'd been a little concerned as the snow clouds had moved in while he and Billy were finishing up the seeding on the ridge above the house. It hadn't felt like a blizzard was coming, and when they came down for lunch, Susie was gone, taking the children to visit her grandmother and brother's family. She would not have left if she'd thought the weather was going to be bad, he knew. So he and Billy had made their lunch from the beef haunch roasting in the oven of the stove, demolishing an entire loaf of bread and half a jar of green pepper jelly along with it.

The flakes were starting as they led the horses back up to the ridge. While not entirely flat, the old mountain top held some thirty

Absolution | 49

acres of cleared land. Billy had looked askance at the sky, and then at Sam, his hat covered with big white crystals.

The appearance of the snow--huge flakes, heavy and wet--was reassuring to Sam. What sky was visible was dark, but there was little wind. Late spring snows like this were not uncommon in the hills. It was almost a benediction, Sam felt--one last chance to hibernate like the bears, cold enough to be a little uncomfortable, but not threatening to the seed in the ground.

"It's a good snow," Sam reassured Billy. "Be gone in two days. I would much rather have snows than rain right now. It's better for the wheat."

Billy absorbed this knowledge as he hooked the horses up to the seeder. Thunder rolled from the sky, and both of the men looked up.

"Thunder snow. Guess if it was warmer, it could have been rain," Sam grinned. Perfect.

The sky growled ominously for some time as the two men made a few circuits in the field. The last row wound along the tree line, going west. Two inches of snow covered the crop now; although a mild snowstorm, the sky was certainly unloading. The team curved to the left, and stopped as a big gray horse carrying a large man stepped out from under a tall pine.

Clucking to the horses, Sam continued on when he recognized Nat Kinney. What on earth was the man doing out in this weather? Then remembering Andrew Coggburn's latest stories, he knew, and tightened his mouth. Billy was standing behind him; Sam felt him tensing, and murmured "Easy." It didn't stop Billy from moving closer to the rifles standing just behind the bench seat. Good.

"Why are you seeding in this weather?" Dispensing with the formality of a greeting, Kinney waited until Sam drew up beside him. "Are you not worried about a freeze?"

"Hello, Mr. Kinney," Sam ignored the other's lack of manners. "No, I'm not." Thunder again, as if to mock him, but beyond blinking his eyes, he didn't acknowledge it. "I've seen this type of snow before. It's good for the crops."

"I see Granny Haggard has been influencing you as well," Kinney didn't sneer, but it was a close thing.

Sam raised his chin to get a better look at his neighbor. "I won't say she hasn't, but this..." His left hand indicated the fields he and

Billy had finished. "Thunder snow is not unheard of. I've seen it a few times in my life here."

With that pointed remark, Sam saw Kinney twitch at the implied insult of a native to an outlander who understood nothing. "Much of what Granny 'knows' is native hill wisdom," Sam continued, "Medicinal herbs, times to plant, that sort of thing. It is necessary knowledge to survive in these hills."

"I thought you a man of learning," Kinney returned.

Sam shrugged, smiling slightly. "I read a great deal, Mr. Kinney, but I have not been to college. A farmer has little need for life in the city, even for a degree." In truth, Sam had periodicals sent in the mail, including farming and science journals. It didn't take much wisdom to apply new knowledge to old ways, and he tried to respect both.

The snow was continuing to fall, and all three men were wet. Sam made as if to cluck to his horses again, but Kinney had more to say.

"I am calling a meeting in April, for men of the community to step up and take control of the county," his mid-range voice deepening at the authority in his statement. Sam's reaction was mild, "In what manner?"

"We will establish nightly patrols to catch those who are vandalizing and stealing livestock," Kinney replied. "In time, it will cut down on those crimes."

Sam nodded, appearing to consider the idea. Billy had not moved. Sam could almost hear the timber of his thoughts, though. When Andrew Coggburn had told him what Kinney was planning, Sam had thought it wasn't a bad idea. He had no problems with what Kinney considered 'the criminal element,' largely because he was native, too; but he also didn't go about inviting trouble.

"I have little trouble with those crimes," he spoke his thought aloud.

Kinney's eyes narrowed. "Others do, though, and we are all neighbors. If you do not attend the vigilance, what will happen when you do have a problem? Will you expect us to help you? It is not a matter of if, Mr. Snapp, but when. Do you consider yourself immune?"

"No. My wife will no longer visit Forsyth because of the trouble there." The Taylors and assorted friends had ridden the sidewalks on

Absolution | 51

Susie's last visit with the children; they hadn't been the only ones forced to jump into the mud to avoid being trampled.

"Ah, then you begin to see."

"Mr. Kinney, I have two farms and a family to care for. I will have no time to ride a patrol, come spring."

"But it is spring, according to Granny Haggard, and you are now finished seeding. I believe the patrols will not be necessary, come summer."

More because he was cold and wet--Billy was shivering slightly, whether for the same reason or because of tension--Sam acquiesced. "When do you plan to hold this meeting and where?"

Kinney nodded east, in the direction of Big Bald. "We have not determined an exact date. There will be a bonfire on Big Bald that afternoon and evening, however. One hour after sunset will be the time."

Sam let out a breath, misting in the chilly air. "I'll be there."

A satisfied expression on his face, Kinney took up his reins, and the big gray responded instantly. A few steps, and Kinney pulled back, stopping the horse and turning around. Sam and Billy had not moved, save to watch Kinney leaving.

"The password is 'We ride in the dark,'" Kinney added.

"Password?"

"I want no one at the meeting who is not willing to help," Nat responded smoothly. "If they don't have the password, they will not be allowed on the hill. I would advise you not to share it with anyone who might be a spy." Looking at Billy, he added, "You and your father would be welcome to attend the meeting as well."

"Thank you, Mr. Kinney. I'm sure Pa will be interested in what you are trying to do," Billy spoke politely from behind Sam. The nuance was evident in his voice--William Miles would be interested, but not inclined to join Kinney's group. "If you will excuse us, we need to be going home."

At that, Sam clucked to the stamping horses, Billy shifting a touch to the right as the team rolled onto the trail going down to the warm barn and supper. Feeling Billy directly behind him, Sam clenched his teeth and knew the younger man was acting instinctively to protect.

For the second time in just over a month, Sam Snapp and Billy Miles turned their backs on Nat Kinney, leaving the big red-headed man staring after them.

52 | Vonda Wilson Sheets

His right arm was more than tingling now as Sam thought about Nat Kinney and Billy's reactions to him. Many people liked Kinney, but more than a few of them had only lived in Taney County for a couple of years. Or else they'd fought for the Union during the Civil War, as had Kinney.

When Hack Snapp came to Taney County two years after it organized in 1837, he'd brought a few slaves with him. The Snapps were Southern Democrats; many of the families who made Taney County home were from the mountainous regions of the southern states. The number of families who held slaves before the Civil War could be counted on one hand, Sam thought.

Speaking of hands....he gently pulled his left hand away from Susie, and rolled onto his back. Maybe that would help his right arm--Susie's head was resting just above the elbow, cutting off circulation. Ah, pins and needles were stabbing him, but it was easing slightly.

Water dripping. The temperature was rising; a sure sign the snow would be gone by this time tomorrow night. He briefly wondered if the icicles hanging off the eaves of the cabin would take a little longer to disappear.

Water dripping. Dang, he grinned ruefully. Now he was going to have to move. Carefully, he pulled the comforter up and tucked it in behind Susie's curved back with his left hand. Slowly, he moved to his left, pulling his right arm from under her head. She adjusted in her sleep, burrowing into her pillow and hunching her shoulders in the warmth from his body remaining in the comforter.

Water dripping. More urgently, he rose, his right arm useless for the moment. The chamber pot was on Susie's side of the bed, and he was close to the door. At least he had put on his tailed flannel night shirt, Sam thought, and stoically moved to the door.

Outside, the sense of magic that had come with the snowfall was still enveloping the cabin, but felt different. Stepping to the end of the porch, Sam glanced down to be sure there'd be no tattletale snow--good, a small patch of mud available--and relieved himself, studying the sky while he did so. Cloudy.

Tom would be two this spring. After Sarah had died last June, Sam had little time to be washing diapers. The privy was only a couple dozen yards away from the house, but his heart had quaked at the thought of his very little son going there by himself. Sam himself disliked emptying the chamber pot, so he had taught Tom to urinate off the porch within a few days. They had made a game of it, and he chuckled in remembrance as he listened to the night sounds.

Ordinary ones from the barn. The chickens were in their coop, too. A faint warmth tickled his cheek, and he realized the snow might be gone by sunrise.

Nannie had snorted in a feminine way when she saw what her father was up to with Tom, but Sam put that down to being jealous of the ease men had in this particular instance. However, once Susie had caught Tom "target practicing" while Sam had been otherwise occupied, he learned he had been sadly mistaken.

She had shrieked, grabbed the boy, and brought him to Sam for a father-son chat. Poor Tom had soaked himself and Susie during the trot to the barn, and while he couldn't speak in sentences, had clearly been bewildered. After all, he'd been peeing off the porch for months by that point. Once Sam explained to Susie, he'd been given a much more severe look than Tom had gotten.

"Samuel Snapp. We are a civilized people. We do not pee off the porch around the house. Do we understand?"

Tom's eyes had been watchful, going back and forth from his father's face to Susie's. While his memory of his mother was fading, Susie was still new to him. He didn't cry, but sat tensed as if he might.

He'd spread his hands in surrender. "As long as you are washing the clouts and emptying the chamber pot," he assured her.

"Oh, I will. And you will teach our son to use it properly."

Grinning, Sam cracked open the door and slid back into the cabin, the warmth beckoning him.

It had taken some time to break Tom of his porch habit. There was no going back to wearing clouts, however, and Sam didn't see a need to. Once Susie adjusted to the notion of a little boy wearing nothing under his dress, she'd seen the training for the advantage it was, in terms of laundry. She'd even made Tom a pair of breeches to match his father's for a Christmas present, laughing at the joy on Tom's face when he'd seen them.

Life is good, he thought, sitting in Susie's chair by the fire.

The clock showed well after midnight, its ticking a steady accompaniment to the other sounds inside the cabin. Outside the cabin, something was moving on the porch. Glancing toward the window by the door, Sam saw Andrew Coggburn peering in at him. Motioning silence, he reached for his pants on the end of the bed, and stood to put them on. His socks were on his boot tops; he quickly drew them on, and slid his feet into the boots. As quietly as he could, he grabbed his coat and hat, and again slid outside.

Stepping down from the porch, Sam saw Andy move in the darkness, and followed him to the barn. The door creaked as it opened. The livestock moved, restless, then settled down again once Sam lit the lamp, and he and Andy began talking. The animals were used to this kind of thing.

At about eighteen, Andrew was small and thin. Both of his parents had died when he wasn't much more than ten years old, and his aunt, Minnie Coggburn Webb, and her husband had taken Andy and his sister Serelda in to live with them. Minnie and Albert Webb had been killed a few years ago; Sam didn't know all the particulars, but the couple were shot from ambush while on the Springfield-Harrison road, coming to Kirbyville to get supplies for their farm down by the state line. At that time, Andy had refused to move in with another set of parents, claiming he was bad luck for anyone he lived with. Serelda was living with another uncle and his family.

So Andy had a cave--no one knew where—that he lived in, spending his time roaming the hills, trapping and trading furs to barter for necessities for Serelda and himself. He was a crack shot, but preferred to use traps, snares, and seines to get his meat and hides. He also gathered various herbs and roots for Granny Haggard. Most of the meat made its way to various family members, usually preserved with hickory smoke. Sam himself had found a beautiful haunch of venison in his smokehouse last fall, not long before he'd married Susie.

Sometimes, on bitterly cold nights, Andy would find a friendly barn and bed down in the hay with the occupants. The boy kept to himself, but in return for the shelter, a farmer would find his cows or goats milked, the animals fed, and any small chores done the next morning. This, too, had happened to Sam, but he found it a mixed blessing--having gone to all the trouble of getting out of a toasty bed, putting extra layers of clothes on in the dark chill of a farmer's early morning, and then finding out he could have been drinking coffee and starting bacon to fry instead….well, he was grateful, anyway. Besides, Andy didn't gather eggs. Chickens would give his presence away, especially guinea fowl.

"Saw ya step out. Better not let Susie ketch ya," Andy teased Sam.

No one ever knew when Andy was watching, unless he chose otherwise. Slipping easily into dialect, Sam joked back. "Eh, iffen ya don't tell 'er, she won't know. 'Sides, too much civilization ain't good on a man. Are ya well?"

Rubbing his nose with his coat sleeve, Andy nodded. "Saw Kinney talkin' at ya t'other day."

Sam rolled his eyes, shrugging. "He came here."

"Aye, I saw."

"Do ya foller him all th' time now?" Sam wondered.

" 'Nuff to know this group o' his ain't gonna be good," Andy was chaffing his hands together. Sam supposed that warmth was relative--he had a snug cabin, fire and a woman to keep him warm.

Sam's eyes narrowed as he considered this. "Why do you think that?"

"Bill Hensley's been over to Kinney's house a lot lately. He's wantin' some land downriver, by Arkansas, so's he kin open up another ferry."

"What's that got to do with stopping the Taylors from riding roughshod in Forsyth?" In his curiosity, Sam forgot dialect and spoke naturally.

"Wal. You been going to church up to Oak Grove? Din't see you last Sunday."

"Susie was sick and we decided not to." There was a connection, Sam was sure. He was familiar with the roundabout course of Andy's conversations.

"Ol' Blue Gobbler preached about livin' in sin." Andy dug his fists into his coat pockets, and studied his thick-soled boots. He needed to grease them again before the spring rains came. Thinking aloud, "I cain't say exactly who Hensley is after, but thar's people down on Buck Creek who don't see preachers much."

Sam let that soak in before saying anything else. Taney County was rough country, and rough country didn't civilize quickly--it was much too isolated. And like any mountainous region with plentiful water, high creeks and the White River were often above flood stage. When folks settled in the hills, they learned to be self-sufficient and self-governing. Preachers and lawmen didn't often visit areas that only had two or three large families. Often, a couple would determine to live together, and became handfast, which was traditionally honored for a year and a day. Marriage was a serious business, and the couples usually followed through with vows said by a preacher whenever one came though. Sometimes, the couples would visit Forsyth and make the union official. But it was a long trek, and survival wasn't easy. Why take the time and bother to make a long trip when surely, sooner or later, a preacher was bound to show?

True, some folks who didn't have the isolation of the eastern part of the county took advantage of hand-fasting. But it was still respected by most people. Sam stiffened as he realized that some of Andy's family were likely handfast, and had been for many years. So were a few other people he knew.

"So you think they will go after people whose marriages are not legally recognized?" Sam asked Andy.

"Eh. I don't know thet," Andy mumbled. But his eyes darted to Sam's face. "Be a awful lot of people to go fer."

"True. But if they have good land," Sam continued pondering. "Land that…"

"Land thet would be fittin' to whate'er someone wants."

"Yes." Sam could see it. His first response was horror. His second was caution.

"Andy, are you sure about this?"

"No." Succinct. "I been watchin' Kinney a long time. He's mean, and he's hungry."

Sam himself had no use for Bill Hensley. On the rare occasions he had gone to Springfield, he would not use Hensley's ferry on the White River. Before William Boston had sold out and moved to Washington, Sam had used his ferry and the better road along the ridges between Roark Creek and Bear Creek. Last time, he'd gone to Chadwick and taken the train.

But Kinney had Alonzo Prather and JJ Brown in his bunch--Sam was sure of it. He said as much to Andy.

Andy snorted, and eyed Sam. "Kinney's talked them into it."

"Into taking land?"

"No, not thet. Into the night patrols."

Sam could not believe that Prather and Brown would allow Kinney to bully the county. "I just don't see those men agreeing to break laws, Andy."

"Wal, I'd've sed as much once. But I shore don't like this."

Sam didn't, either.

CHAPTER 6
April 2, 1885

The woman was too tired to listen to music tonight. She sat on her front stoop, gown wadded up past her knees, and let her head droop, making herself appear more hump-backed than usual. Looking at her dirty, bare feet, she resolved to wash them. Soon. Just not this very moment.

Maggie Kinney had started playing the piano with the windows open again, and ordinarily, it being a fine night, she and the children would go listen for a little while. That was surely the most beautiful sound in the world coming from the Kinney home, and she wanted the children to know there was more to life than a run-down farm that grew little in its rocky soil, with a flea-bitten cow and a mean mule.

She got no further in this line of thought when she found herself lying on the ground, her right cheek throbbing and her ears ringing. "Woman!" He shouted. "Where's my supper?"

No matter she'd been back and forth between the wheat field and the barn all day, hauling manure in a basket to coax the promising sprouts along. No matter He'd been down at the creek with his friends, and smelled like rotgut.

Lying on the ground, she eyed Him with caution while she touched her cheek with a dirty hand. Propping herself up on her left elbow, she muttered, "Be on in a minnit."

"You sassin' me? Don't you go sassin' me! I'm hungry!" His nasal voice rose.

She continued the act of rising, cautiously. Her left hip hurt where she'd struck the big rock she used to grind meal sometimes. "Not sassin'. Bin in the field all day."

He grabbed her hair, pulling her face toward Him, and she protested with a squeak as she felt His grip tighten. The squeaks were echoed by the two small girls peering around the corner of the cabin, not ten feet away. Celie and Phebe were four and six years old. They'd seen Him abusing their mother before, but it never stopped them from feeling her pain.

Eight-year-old Randa came out of the woods just as He was howling at her for treating Him like trash. "Hello, Pa," Randa called as His right fist rose. "I'll fix your supper for you!"

He tossed her head as if it wasn't attached to her body, wrenching her neck. This time, she rose faster, and went into the cabin. He sat in the rocking chair to the right of the door.

The windows were open, allowing some light in. She put two pieces of hickory on the fire, and turned as Randa came through the door, trailed by her little sisters. "I've got fresh greens," Randa said, and she sighed. Hopefully, she took down the tin above the fireplace, but she could tell by its weight it was empty. She looked anyway.

"No bacon drippings. No meat," she told her daughter.

"Well, we'll eat without," Randa said. She was still young enough to be hopeful, thought her mother.

Water set to boil, some salt thrown in. She glanced at the daub of butter in its dish, one of the few glass things she owned. Enough there to put on His greens; she and the girls would do without.

Greens surely didn't take long to cook. Within minutes, she was filling the glass bowl for Him--He would not eat off a tin plate--and threw the softened butter on the stringy mass. Greens were good to eat in the spring, she knew--but she never had liked the smell of them, let alone the taste.

Phebe took the plate outside to Him, while she dished up the rest of supper and handed Randa and Celie their tin plates. When a shadow darkened the door, she turned to hand Phebe her plate, and had it knocked out of her hands onto the floor.

"Where's the meat?" He demanded. "Greens without drippin's? D'you think you could fool me with butter?"

"There's nothing else," she told Him. Silently, she handed her own plate to Phebe, who took it and scuttled over to join her sisters sitting on the bed. Although she never took her eyes off of Him, she didn't see it coming, and again found herself on the floor, cringing at his feet.

He walked outside, and she had a few seconds' respite. Then a "whirr!" and the sound of her glass bowl breaking just behind her froze everything.

She did not become aware of anything until much later. Her ribs hurt, and both of her eyes were swelled shut. A silent inventory of her body detailed another broken tooth, and assorted bruises. She could hear Phebe and Celie whispering to each other, but Randa's familiar scent found its way into her senses, and she realized Randa was wiping her face with cool water.

"Ahhhh!" came a soft moan from her mouth; her lips were cut and swollen, too.

"Ma," said Randa. "He's gone. Yer alright."

She didn't feel alright, and couldn't remember the last time she did.

"Where did He go?"

"He didn't say." She could feel Randa shrug.

"Don't matter," she said, taking the wet cloth from Randa, and gingerly wiping her eyes so she could open them. "He'll be back."

Randa took off for Granny Haggard's the next morning. Ma needed a salve for her bruises, and Granny would have some tea that would take the edge off Ma's pain. She hoped Georgia would be there; it had been days since she'd seen her best friend. But she couldn't stay long--Ma would fret, and there was a chance Pa would return. She bit her lip. He was usually gone a couple days after beating Ma.

She called Him "Pa," but He wasn't her father. Her father had left to search for work one day, not long after Celie was born. He had never come home.

"Pa" had seen her mother in Forsyth one day. He'd gotten an introduction, and after several visits, had begged her to marry Him. Ma hadn't wanted to marry again, couldn't marry again, and said as much, finally, to dissuade him. He'd shown up that night in a drunken rage, barging his way through the door. That was the only time she remembered Ma standing up to Him, but it had been enough. He'd backhanded Ma, knocking her down, then dragged her to the bed. Seeing the girls in the bed, He'd demanded they move over. She'd grabbed Celie, who wasn't walking yet, taken Phebe's hand, and nearly fell off the mattress as she tried to get them out of the way. He shoved her, and Ma had come up raging, screeching and clawing at Him for messing with her daughters. The girls, too, started screaming as He pummeled Ma back to the floor, and then threatened to kill her as Randa put Celie down, ready to help Ma. Randa had frozen in place.

Watching Randa, He'd pulled Ma over the edge of the bed, her feet barely touching the floor, and dropped His pants. He did something that made Ma scream once more. "Get away!" Ma had

Absolution | 61

said. Another scream as He plunged into her mother again with His thing. "Randa, go outside!"

Randa had done so, taking her sisters with her. After a time, her mother had shuffled to the door and opened it. She'd made a pallet up on the floor for the girls to sleep on, and that had been life since.

He'd never actually hit Randa. He never even really yelled at the girls, except to demand they call him "Pa." Her mother had pulled her lips in, her face screwed up, but she had nodded. That had been three years ago.

She didn't even know what His Christian name was. Her mother never called him by any name.

Ma seldom spoke at all anymore. When He was home, He demanded her mother's constant attention, and there were times she heard her mother crying in the night after Pa had been humping her. She didn't know exactly what happened in their bed--she couldn't see from her pallet on the floor--but Pa would jerk her mother's gown up over her head, pin her arms, and His scrawny buttocks would bounce up and down maybe a half-dozen times. Protests did no good, and her mother made no attempt to stop Him anymore.

Randa had begun going to Granny Haggard's for salve after the first beating and rape. She had carefully described her mother's injuries, without saying what had happened. Granny had nodded, keeping expression from her face. After the second beating, Granny had handed her a jar of seeds, and told Randa to have her mother swallow a spoonful of them every day, except when she had her monthlies.

"What are they for?" Randa had asked. Ma would want to know.

Granny had shrugged in her slight way. Her brown, wrinkled fingers touched Randa's briefly. "They do not work for every woman," Granny said then. "Your mother will know."

And Ma had. A slight smile had come to her mother's lips, one of the few since Pa had moved in. Since then, Randa knew Ma took the seeds every day, except when she had her monthlies.

The salve that helped Ma the most had to be made fresh every time. Randa handed Granny the tin to be refilled, then turned as Georgia came in. The girls smiled at each other, and listened as Granny explained to Georgia what herbs to grind, and the right amount for the mixture. Randa could make the mixture herself, but she had no goose grease, and that was the best medium for bruises. She was restless, trying to avoid looking at the large old cast iron crock sitting on its hook above the fireplace. The smell coming from it was making her stomach ache. She was starving. There had been nothing save a dry biscuit for breakfast this morning. She had given it to her sisters.

"Sit, sit," Granny spoke as if English wasn't her first language. It wasn't. Granny spoke Cherokee to her family, and to a few others who lived on the big plateau between the northernmost loop of the White River. "The soup is ready," she told the girls.

Georgia wasn't hungry, so Randa ate the contents of both girls' bowls. Granny did not make her feel ashamed to be hungry; she noticed Granny put a lid on a crock of soup and set it gently in her basket. She'd have to be careful going home, but at least Ma and the girls would have something to eat. A loaf of bread joined the soup.

She carefully rinsed out her clay bowls, and set them to air out. She dried her hands on the back of her dress, turning to look at Georgia with an apologetic expression.

"Are you going?" Georgia asked with a small pout.

"Ma needs me back home," Randa answered her friend. She pursed her lips, so Georgia would know she'd much rather stay at Granny's.

She would. For a moment, staying in the safety of Granny's snug little cabin seemed like the best idea in the world. Her eyes brightened as she thought of never seeing Pa again. But Granny's hands gently folded her cloak around her, and handed her the basket of medicine and food.

"It will be better," Granny told her. "Tell your ma."

"Yes, ma'am," Randa replied dutifully. She reluctantly made her way to the door, opened it, and then turned back.

"Thank you, Granny," Randa told the keeper of sanctuary.

"It will be better. Soon. Go on."

୨୦ ୶ଡ଼

Maggie was a little upset. Her prize hen, the one which laid eggs more often than the others, was missing. She had not heard a disturbance in the chicken yard, but maybe a hawk had gotten the brown hen without her knowledge. There was not much one could

Absolution | 63

do about hawks, she supposed.

It was time for dinner, and the family was all home for a change. James usually slept in the little room at the newspaper and print shop, but he was home tonight so he and Nat could discuss the organization.

Setting the butter crock on the table, she smiled as Nat prayed for "the hands that feed us." It was nice to be appreciated.

Everyone was eating--Paul was reaching for a third helping of potatoes and roasted pork. While there was a break in the conversation, Maggie asked her family, "Did anyone notice a hawk getting one of the chickens?"

Everyone thought for a moment, shaking their heads in a variety of rhythms. Maggie noticed an odd expression Georgia's face. Nat claimed her attention, though, by asking, "Are you missing some chickens?"

"Just one. She was my best layer."

Georgia choked. Maggie looked up as her youngest child turned purple with trying to swallow her food. "Are you all right?" she asked. Her complexion returning to normal, Georgia nodded and looked away.

"May I be excused?"

Maggie glanced at the girl's plate. She had hardly touched her food. Georgia had not eaten much for two days. "Are you getting ill?" she asked, reaching across the table to feel for a temperature.

"No, ma'am."

"You're not eating, Georgia."

A pleading look entered the girl's eyes. "Mother, may I be excused?"

Nat put a hand on Maggie's arm. "Yes, Georgia," he answered. Rising from her chair, Georgia took her plate to the garbage pail, but Paul's voice halted her.

"Don't do that. I'll eat it."

Mutely, Georgia handed Paul the plate with its contents, then left the room. Surrounded by her men and oldest daughter, Maggie felt vaguely alarmed as Georgia's footsteps climbed to the attic. The steps receded as Georgia apparently went to her corner of the big open room upstairs.

"Do any of you know what's wrong with her?" Maggie looked around for an answer.

"Maybe she's growing up," Eva answered flippantly.

"She just turned ten," Maggie retorted. "She's not old enough." It was almost, not quite, a wail.

Nat smiled at her. "You've said boys and men can have their secrets. Do girls not have them, then?"

Maggie snorted. "You know better." She nodded her head in Eva's direction. "That one taught us they do."

Nat's smile grew broader. "Then what is the problem?"

"She's my baby!" Seeing what Nat was getting at, she scooted her chair back and started to rise.

Again, he put his hand out to stop her. "Maggie, you can't keep her young forever."

She was tempted to reach for a knife to stab Nat's hand. She was endlessly patient with the children, but he could rouse her to fury faster than Grey Ghost could stomp a rattlesnake. Or a hawk could steal a chicken.

"There is something wrong. She loves roasted pork." She shrugged off his hand, then nearly ran upstairs.

The sun was very low--it was nearly sunset, but not dark. Georgia was already putting on her nightgown, and Maggie hesitated, turning her head to preserve Georgia's modesty. A quick glance from the corner of her left eye assured her that no, her daughter had not started growing into a young woman just yet. But it was close.

"Are you not going to sit outside and listen to music tonight?" she asked.

"I can hear from here." The nightgown was on, and Georgia sat on the bed, no longer attempting to hide her expression. She looked at her mother steadily, guiltily and obviously upset.

"Will Randa not be here tonight?"

"Her mother is ill." But that was not the answer, really--Maggie could tell. She moved to sit beside her baby, who, come to think of it, stood as tall as Maggie's nose.

"Is she seriously ill?" Georgia had become friendly with Miranda when both visited Granny Haggard at the same time one day. Last spring, the friendship had deepened while the children chased fireflies when Maggie played piano. It was only recently Maggie had discovered that Miranda's mother had been one of the women who sat outside in the evenings, listening to Maggie play. The woman never came close to the house, and Maggie didn't see her every

Absolution | 65

night. But she liked knowing her music was appreciated.

"No, I don't think so," Georgia sounded uncertain.

"What is it?"

Taking a deep breath, Georgia blurted, "I took your chicken."

"What?" Shock. What in the world--? Was Granny Haggard--?

"I took it to Granny Haggard." Oh, dear. Oh, no.

Taking a deep breath, Maggie beat back the fear that Georgia was learning some kind of witchcraft. Nothing of that sort had reached Maggie's ears, and Nat would've stopped Georgia going long ago if he'd heard it.

She, too, took a deep breath, pursed her lips, and set a glare on her daughter. "No secrets, young lady," she said severely. "Out with it."

"It's the ointment," Georgia began. In her very-worried world, she didn't hear Nat coming up the stairs. Maggie did. She prompted.

"The ointment."

"Yes, Granny makes a special salve for Randa's mother. Day before yesterday, Randa was there to get it. Granny showed me how to make it, but didn't tell me what it was for."

"Had you seen this ointment being made before?" Maggie asked. Was there a chicken involved?

"Yes, a time or two. But I didn't know what uses all the herbs had then."

"There are just herbs in it?" No chicken?

Georgia fired a look at Maggie that could have scorched her mother. Behind her, Maggie heard an indrawn breath; no doubt, Nat was thinking Georgia had inherited her mother's temper, and was trying not to laugh. She ignored him.

"And goose grease, Mother. Goose grease is the key to making liniment for deep bruises. It goes on lightly, so you don't have to rub the wounds and make them hurt more."

"I see." Was chicken fat acceptable in this case? She wondered crazily. Shaking her head, she doubted it. She used goose grease on her hands in the winter time herself, to keep them supple and soft in the dry air.

"Randa couldn't stay. She ate two bowls of soup like she was starving, and then hurried home."

"Did she?"

"I could hear her stomach, Mother. After she left, Granny seemed

66 | Vonda Wilson Sheets

so tired, I didn't stay very long." True, that. Georgia had been home early for lessons that day. Maggie waited patiently.

"However, I asked her about the ointment before I left. The mix of herbs causes a deep heat, and makes swellings go down. Then I asked why Randa had been so hungry--it was so early, just after breakfast. I couldn't eat any of my soup. Granny said she probably hadn't eaten in a day or two."

A troubled face turned on Maggie, whose heart lurched.

"So I took the chicken and some of our supplies in the root cellar over to Granny yesterday. For Randa and her family. Granny said she'd take the food down in a basket today if Randa didn't come." A sob escaped Georgia's chest. "I didn't know she was your best layer, Mother. I just wanted to help Randa."

Maggie's heart then broke. She reached a hand to Georgia's hair, stroking it, but the young girl hurled herself into her mother's lap. Silence from the stairs; Georgia was tearful enough for her parents, too.

Her arms around this precious girl, Maggie smiled. "It's all right," she told Georgia. "And it will be all right."

The sobbing slowed, and Georgia sat up. Looking at her mother with a small crooked grin, she said, "That's what Granny said."

After he'd finished talking with James about the forthcoming patrol meeting, Nat joined her in their room, sitting on the bed and listening to her finish his song.

She turned to him. "I told you, young girls should not have secrets."

Nat nodded, then held out his arms. She joined him, eyes closed and heart hurting. She was so proud of her children.

"They grow up so fast."

CHAPTER 7
Apr 5, 1885 - Hours before sunrise

Sleep was not going to happen for Nat tonight. He looked across the room at the clock on the mantle, a handsome ebony piece that chimed the hours. Well, it was morning, so to speak.

Maggie had gone to bed. For once, her playing had not soothed him. He was on edge, willing every little thing to work in his favor on this day. He had prepared months....years....all his life for the meeting that was taking place tonight. Yes, tonight--the fifth of April had started nearly 3 hours ago.

Word had gone out to all those who lived too far from Kirbyville to see the bonfire he planned to set in twelve hours' time. Maggie was planning to feed any wives who came in support of their husbands; as far as he knew, Charlie Groom was bringing his wife Ninnie, but his parents were keeping their two small daughters. Ada Marie Prather and Caroline Brown were also going to keep Maggie company while the meeting was going on. Extra bedding was already laid out in pallets for the Grooms; JJ and Caroline would stay at the Prathers' house.

Restless. He wondered about Bill Hensley's proposal to find ways to run off families that had prime land. He shook his head at himself. Yes, he was interested in acquiring land, but he had stalled Bill. The man was ambitious and greedy, he knew. A man like that could and would do almost anything to get what he wanted. And Bill wanted a ferry on the road that was a shorter route from Mountain Home to Forsyth.

Not yet, Mr. Hensley, he thought. Not yet.

First, tonight's meeting.

Nat had borrowed something that would incite the men, get them upset. Well, "borrowed" was a relative term, he considered. He hadn't asked permission, had merely absconded it, and would return it. If he'd asked, the answer would've been an emphatic "No Way In Hell!"

Rehearsing to himself once again, he touched on the finer points of his planned speech. When to get the men roiled, when to calm them.

Briefly, he wondered if Sam Snapp and the men of the Miles

clan, including Samp Barker, would show up tonight. He thought so. There were others he considered on the fence as well--some of the Moores, Snodgrasses, Browns, and the Haworths. Judge Reynolds was a fiery old goat--no telling which way the wind would blow in that quarter.

As he gazed through the window toward Big Bald, he imagined he could see the pile of brush that lay in wait for the moment he would light it. The moon was just past full, and would be late in rising. The impact of the bonfire would be tremendous.

Sam, his brothers, and the others knew the date for the meeting--he'd sent word out yesterday, trusting that James would see to it those men in particular would hear of it.

Restless.

He could not feel sleep waiting for him, so Nat Kinney decided to take a walk up to the top of Big Bald.

A shadow followed him.

ↄ⟋ ⟍ⱺ

It had been two days and three nights since Pa had been home. In that time, her mother's swellings had gone down, helped by Granny's salve and the leeches her sisters had found in the creek. The soreness and discolorations caused by the bruises would take time yet.

Randa lay in the moonlight, listening to the restless night, watching the moon make its trip across the sky through the window. For once, her stomach was full, and she couldn't hear her sisters' stomachs growling as they often did.

She had Georgia to thank for that. Granny Haggard had brought a hamper of food across the ridge and down to their cabin, explaining that Georgia's mother had sent the food. Her own mother had been speechless. She had not been on the receiving end of kindness in a very long time.

Randa followed Granny's advice, insisting on very small portions of the wonderful smelling gift, because their stomachs would be shrunken and could not take in so much at one time. Joy of joys, she and the girls had been gleeful to have the opportunity to eat several small meals yesterday.

Very, very late. Randa thought of the cinnamon buns Mrs. Kinney had sent. Her mouth watered, but she firmly told herself it wasn't fair to sneak a bun and not share with her mother and sisters.

Milk. She dimly remembered her mother giving her warm milk when she was very young and couldn't sleep. She considered briefly rising to warm some milk from the stoneware jug, but a strange lassitude kept her in the moonlight. How much would a true milk cow cost? Or maybe a goat? It would be wonderful to have milk all the time.

She wasn't sleepy, but her body was enjoying the benefits of the day. The moon disappeared from immediate view, and the light was no longer on her face. Hoping the peace of yesterday would last for at least another day, she rolled on her side and began to doze.

Randa had no idea how long she'd been asleep. When her brain first fuzzily acknowledged the vibrations coming from the floorboards beneath her, she thought it was a part of the restless night. Then the door flew open, and Pa was silhouetted in the first rays of the sun.

"Woman! I want breakfast!"

Ma blearily sat up. Randa and the girls, who had all jumped when the door was thrown, feigned sleep.

Pa, meanwhile, stumbled in and plopped on His chair, scraping it across the floor. Randa twitched, but kept her eyes firmly shut. It seemed to be easier on Ma if she didn't have to worry about her and the other two.

Ma stumbled across the floor, tripping on the hamper Granny had left for them. "What do you want to eat?" she asked. Ma had taken medicine to help her sleep without much pain, and was groggy. Randa tensed; she would get up and cook for Pa if she had to.

She heard Him drag the hamper to the table, and begin sorting through what remained. She opened her eyes since He was thus engaged. The packet of flour. The cinnamon buns. A cake, which had caused paroxysms of delight in her sisters. He made a similar noise now, and her eyes squinched shut again.

A menace in His voice. He was asking Ma where the food came from, seeing the remains of their roasted goose on the table. Randa prayed that He wouldn't find the eggs and other things she had hidden in the small creek just yards away. She had wished for a springhouse while building a contraption with branches that would keep the food immersed, cold and away from animals. Now she just hoped there would still be food after this morning.

70 | Vonda Wilson Sheets

The thought that this time was different struck her. After beatings, Pa was generally gone for several days, but always returned in a good mood. He often told Ma that He visited the whores in Forsyth, but Randa had been to Forsyth and hadn't seen any whores. Not that she really knew what one was.

Her mother took a long time answering, it seemed. The medicine had affected her normal instincts for preservation, and she was telling Pa that Granny Haggard had brought it from Mrs. Kinney.

"Kinney?"

Pa was scared of Nat Kinney. The one time He'd attended church at Oak Grove with Ma, Mr. Kinney's sermon had been about men who led idle lives, spending what little money they had on whores and liquor. Taking the sermon personally, Pa had forbidden Ma to attend church any more. The Sundays He wasn't home, Ma sent her daughters to church, but she wouldn't go.

Now Pa was yelling about eating food from the Kinneys. No longer willing to keep her eyes shut, she sat up in time to see the precious cinnamon buns in His hands. However, He'd thrown the bag of flour first, and it had doused the embers in the fireplace. Ma was merely watching Him, not saying anything.

"Don't throw those in the fire!" Randa startled Pa, who turned on her. Then, a thoughtful look came across His face.

"Oh, you like these?" He shook His full hands at Randa.

"Yes, I do, Pa. Please don't throw them in the fire." She did not mention she would simply retrieve them and dust the flour off.

"What'll you do for 'em?"

Not understanding the question, Randa took her eyes off the rolls and looked at Pa's face. "Anything, Pa," she said cautiously.

Pa dropped all but one bun. They rolled about His feet, and He took a step forward, taunting her, waving the bun in her face. Randa's sense of danger was buzzing as she noticed Celie and Phebe crawling for the treats.

He deliberately stepped on the closest roll before Celie could get it. It stuck to His boot, and He tried to shake it off. Ma was coming around the table, suddenly moving faster Randa had ever seen her move.

She found herself on the floor, her face throbbing in time with the knot rising on the back of her skull from the bounce. Celie and Phebe scurried behind her, grabbing the blankets to cover their heads. And

Absolution | 71

then all hell broke loose.

Randa watched as Ma jumped on Pa's back, a knife in her hands-
-where had that come from?--and screaming at Him to leave Randa
alone. In slow motion, Pa bent over, and Ma flew over His head,
landing beside Randa on the floor with a vicious thud. She rose
again, standing between Pa and Randa, the knife still in her right
hand.

Pa laughed. "Ya know whut yer doin'?" He feinted, reaching
for the knife with His left hand, then grabbing Ma with His right.
"I should teach you how to fight," He told her breathlessly as He
took the knife, dropped it, then twisted her right arm, bringing her
hand up behind her back. Still sore, the fresh pain brought a helpless
moan from Ma.

He pulled it further, and Randa heard Ma's arm crack. A shriek
tore from Ma's throat, and Pa thrust her from Him, disgust evident
on His face. She fell to her knees, her useless right arm coming
down to dangle helplessly.

The knife was right there, at Pa's feet. While He was standing
there, deciding what to do, her mother sobbed and cried.

The sun was up. Several rays came through the door, one of them
causing the knife to gleam.

Pa's attention returned to Randa. "Now, 'bout that roll," He
began.

Her eyes went up His body to His face. He was watching her--she
didn't dare reach for the knife.

"I don't want it anymore," she said.

His left foot came up, then down on her stomach. She screamed,
trying to curl up in a ball, but His foot pinned her down. Instant
nausea and vomit came up her throat as she writhed for what seemed
like an eternity; but His footing wasn't solid, and He began to lean
harder on her, cutting off her air.

Motion. Her mother, on the floor, knife in her left hand, driving
it up between Pa's legs.

Blood. Ma pushed Pa away, His body hitting the floor with a
solid thump. The blood was spurting all over the room; she took no
notice as Ma pulled her onto her lap with her left hand, covering her,
shielding her too late, much too late.

A man came through the door, jumping over Ma and Randa and
landing on his knees in front of them. Randa shrieked again, then

realized she knew the man. She just couldn't think of his name.

"It's alright. It's gonna be alright," he spoke slowly, trying to break through the woman's terror. Both of them calmed as he continued to croon, ignoring the moans and dying breaths of the man behind him.

"Where are your other daughters?" He addressed her mother.

Ma shook her head. Standing, he looked about the room, and noticed the covered bundle in the corner. Slender as he was, he blocked the view of the carnage from Celie and Phebe, for which Randa would be forever grateful. "Come, girls," he coaxed the girls, lifting the blanket to see two frightened faces.

"He hit Randa," Phebe told the man.

"Yes, he did," the man replied. "Did he hit you?"

"No, we hided," Phebe answered. "Is Randa dead?"

"Oh, no," the man assured her. "But I think mebbe she needs yer help. Her and yer ma."

Her mother's left arm was shaking. At this, Randa felt Ma pull in a deep breath, painfully, so, so slowly.

"We can help," Phebe assured the man.

"D'ya know how to git to Granny Haggard's house?"

At this, Randa pulled away from her mother, twisted in time to see her little sisters both nod vigorously.

"D'ya think you can fetch Granny Haggard?" the man asked. "Tell her Andy said for her to come, it's all over."

Randa crawled over to the corner where the girls were still shielded by the blood-soaked blanket. Andy Coggburn had been holding it up in his hands, to keep the sight of Pa's body from them. She rose to stand beside him, looking down at her sisters.

Phebe repeated, "Tell her Andy said to come, it's all over.'"

A rare smile lit Andy's face. "Come. We'll walk to the door, then you'll run."

As they walked, Phebe repeated Andy's message. Then, turning to leave, she grasped Celie's hand firmly, and looked at her sister. "Granny's gonna need to make salve fer ya," she said gravely, reaching with her other hand to touch Randa's face gently.

Randa touched Phebe's hand. "It'll be alright," echoing Granny's words. The thought flashed across her mind that maybe, just maybe, it would be. But she put it aside for the moment.

At that reassurance, the girls turned and ran.

Absolution | 73

Even with the pressure of cooking dinner for guests, Maggie was compelled to saddle up and take another hamper to Granny Haggard for Miranda's family. It wasn't long after sunrise; no one would arrive until mid-afternoon, at the earliest. She had plenty of time. The beef was roasting in its own juice, along with potatoes and carrots she had preserved last year, in the big pan she had covered with coals in the fireplace. She'd baked yesterday, inspired by the goodies she'd sent to Miranda's home the day before.

That poor woman. Maggie felt an almost visceral need to help her. How did a woman let a man treat her so badly? Was that what it was like for all the women here?

No, she decided. Certainly not. However, she thought Nat should add the subject to his speech tonight. If she was back in time before he left for the hill--he had not been able to sleep until he knew the sun was going to rise, but was sleeping quite soundly now....if she were back in time, she would tell him that wife-beating needed to be added to the growing list of things gone wrong here.

Some women, like tiny Ada Marie Prather, ruled their households with loving efficiency. Some, like Susie Snapp, appeared to work with their husbands at almost any task about the farm, enjoying the companionship. "I guess you never know," she said to Greta, her mare.

Georgia came out of the house, dressed and ready to climb on back of Maggie's horse, wrapping her arms about her mother's waist and laying her head just below the chignon Maggie wore.

They rode the trail past the school. Greta clopped along steadily, and soon they were on a trail through the woods. Georgia had dropped all hint of secret-keeping once she realized Maggie wasn't upset with her, so the two of them chatted easily. The full saddlebags lay across Maggie's lap, one on each side.

As they reached Granny Haggard's, Maggie noted that her mule was tied to the upright of the porch.

"Something's wrong," Georgia said, and slid off, running toward the low cabin.

Inside, Maggie found Granny putting simples and other supplies into her own saddlebags. Two little girls were being fussed over by Susie Snapp, who was pouring hot water into a tub.

"What is it? What's wrong?" Maggie asked. Georgia was tying knots in the laces of the bags, designed to come loose quickly. "What is it?" Maggie repeated.

Granny turned, tying her own bonnet strings under her chin. Deftly, she grabbed her bags, pausing to look at Maggie for a few precious seconds.

"Randa is in trouble," she said simply. "Will you come?"

"Certainly." She glanced at Georgia, who was ladling porridge from a pot in the fireplace. "Are you coming?" she asked her daughter.

"No place for a girl," Granny put a tentative hand out, then gestured toward Georgia and Susie. "Susie cannot go. You come."

The two women almost ran for their mounts. Granny, who was many years older than Maggie, pulled her mule around and climbed on from the porch. She was riding down the trail before Maggie could collect the reins and go after her.

Catching Granny up, she thought to ask what happened, but realized that talking was impossible at the speed they were traveling. She had no choice but to follow; she had no idea where they were going.

Thinking back to the few seconds she had been in Granny's cabin, impressions of blood--was it the smell? No, she had seen it. The little girls' faces had looked smeared in places. They were both flushed, and breathing heavily. Susie's stepchildren had been nowhere in sight--did Sam actually take care of them? Maggie wondered. Of course he did. He'd done so last year after his first wife died. Susie was expecting a baby, so Maggie had been told by an excited Georgia--Granny had said twins.

So wherever they were going involved something a pregnant woman should not see. Suddenly, Maggie knew who the little girls had been. They were Miranda's sisters--Phebe and Celie. She was pleased she remembered their names, until she'd realized Miranda had not been present.

Granny veered off onto a little-used trail. Down they went, until Maggie realized she was looking down on a roof. As they slid down the leaf-strewn slope, the ground evened out a bit, and then they were at the front of the house.

Miranda and her mother were sitting outside, both covered in blood. Maggie blanched, but jumped off her horse and flew toward them. "Are you alright?" she asked, searching both of them. Neither appeared to answer.

Miranda's mother had a sling for her right arm. Whoever was making the noise inside had done a good job, but Maggie could see the arm was broken, and needed to be set.

Granny went inside the cabin.

"Do you need water?" Maggie called. Granny appeared in the doorway. "No," she answered, somewhat terse. "Andy has set some to boil."

Of course. She'd noticed the smoke, which was a little unusual on a warm spring morning after breakfast. Then she took her bearings. Not having animals to take care of, Miranda's mornings probably ran a little later than her own.

Granny handed her a pot with steaming water and two cloths. She'd carried her bags in, and Maggie could hear her addressing whoever was inside over her shoulder. She didn't even look as Maggie took the pan and cloths, and turned back inside as Maggie knelt to care for Miranda.

"Beggin' yer pardon, ma'am, but would you care for Ma first?" Miranda asked. Her mother was still in a daze, but appeared to be attuned to her daughter's voice. She turned to smile at Miranda and Maggie, the dried blood making the smile somewhat ghastly.

"Certainly," Maggie moved to the left of the open door and stoop, reached a cloth into the boiled water, and began to softly clean the woman's face.

"Miranda, what is your mother's name?" she spoke softly. The woman appeared to be stuck in a nightmare. As the smell from the house wafted out, Maggie realized she probably was.

Shifting uncomfortably, Miranda had whispered. "My father called her Maggie."

Maggie realized Andrew Coggburn was in the cabin only when he came out, his clothes stained and thick with the miasma in the house. Granny had taken a few minutes to set Miranda's mother's arm while Maggie had cleansed the daughter's wounds and dressed them. Miranda appeared to be remarkably unhurt in comparison to her mother's fading and fresh bruising.

Andrew spoke in a low, urgent tone, and Granny had looked at the cabin. Maggie, too, had glanced about. The roof was sagging, and other repairs had been needed for some time. Granny nodded agreement, and Andy started a fire outside to heat some more water.

After removing the belongings which were salvageable, Andy and Granny had calmly poured kerosene about the inside of the cabin. The other Maggie had not noticed until she saw Andy pulling a lighted stick from his outside fire and re-entering the building.

On the other hand, Maggie Kinney had watched the whole thing. It had been a good move, burning the place. As the flames took hold, Miranda simply held her mother; both of them appeared to fear the re-appearance of the man who had traumatized them so severely. Once she saw the flames appear at the opened window, the other Maggie simply turned and began walking up the hill toward the trail.

Andy watched her go. Nodding at Maggie, he helped Grannie onto her mule, and lifted the slight Miranda up behind her. "I'll be by to see you," he told the girl, and Granny headed up the hill behind the other Maggie.

Approaching Maggie, Andy tilted his head back to look up at her. She wore a split riding skirt, and so had climbed on Greta using the stirrup.

Saying nothing, but giving her a slight smile, he reached back and slapped Greta on the rump. And watched Maggie Kinney climb the hill back toward her destiny, her neighborliness nearly at an end.

Andy would go listen to the piano music one last time tonight. Then he figured it would be much too dangerous for him--and the others--to keep lying in wait in the early twilight, hoping to hear beautiful music make up for some of the ugliness in their worlds.

CHAPTER 8
April 5, 1885 - Afternoon

Nat was returning to consciousness slowly.

It wasn't the sound of Maggie entering their room, nor the fact that sunlight was pouring on their bed.

It wasn't the sound of the tub being dragged in front of the fireplace.

It wasn't the sound of the fire being stoked.

It wasn't the sound of Maggie leaving the room.

It wasn't sound at all which brought him to full consciousness and made him sit up rather quickly, although the sounds were odd enough in the middle of the day.

It was the smell of blood and shit.

He looked out the window--not quite noon.

Then he looked as his wife, who was pouring a large pot of hot water into the tub. She left, went back to the kitchen, and Nat heard her pumping at the sink, slinging the refilled pot onto the hook over the fire place in there. Another pot, this one from the stove apparently, and Maggie was gone again, along with the scent that had awakened him.

Maggie smelled like blood and shit. As a farmer's wife, this wasn't necessarily unusual. But today was his day. What the hell? He swung his legs out from under the blanket, his bare feet hitting the floor softly. For some reason, every hair on his body stood at attention when Maggie again entered the room, continuing her cycle of filling the bath tub. Was she using every pot she owned, he wondered?

He knew she was aware of him, but she had not spoken, had not even looked at him. As a matter of fact, she was keeping her face away from him. But he saw determination in the set of her shoulders, which were squared as if she was going into battle. Again, she left the room, closing the door behind her.

To keep in the heat, he realized. He wished for a cup of coffee.

Nat's head turned toward the door as it opened one more time. The tub was fairly full, and steaming. No coffee in Maggie's hand. She poured in the last pot of hot water, dropped the pan.

The humidity in the room made the stench that much stronger, and Nat rubbed a finger under his nose. He started to say something humorous about coffee--she always had a pot on the stove, he drank it all day long when he was home--when Maggie started trying to undo the buttons on the back of her work dress. Nat rose as if to help, but her voice made him wary, freezing him in his tracks.

"Do not touch me."

His hand had stopped just inches from her back. Glancing down the length of her dress, he saw little on her backside that would suggest the stench that swam about his head.

After pulling the dress up to reach the final button that normally rested between her shoulders, Maggie untied her apron, and pulled the two garments over her head. Nat stepped back to give her room, and noticed the odors lightened as her dress and apron were thrown over by the window.

She obviously did not want to talk. Undoing her stays, they, too, hit the floor. Her petticoat and chemise joined the dress and apron by the window.

Still wary of her--he was used to her temper--curiosity made him go over to pick up the dress. The water in the tub hissed as she stepped in it, and he heard the sharp intake of her breath. Why was she submitting herself to a boiling bath in the middle of the day? And a warm day at that?

Again his hand froze mere inches away as Maggie said, "Leave it."

He straightened. Attempting to lighten the heavy atmosphere in the room, he asked, "Is there coffee?"

"Get it yourself."

Uh, oh.

He took his pants from the peg on the wall, and put them on. She had given him leave to get out of the room, and he would take advantage of the opportunity. Glancing over his left shoulder as he walked to the door, he realized she was soaping herself furiously, her eyes not leaving the now-roaring fire. He heard a faint hum, and realized she was growling, much in the way of an African tiger he had once seen in a zoo. Escape was necessary.

Nat crossed the dogtrot and went into the kitchen. This room smelled of roast, fresh bread, and...ugh. Old coffee. The fire in this fireplace was stoked high as well, and he could hear the coffee boiling, getting thicker by the minute. Reaching for a potholder, he nabbed the pot off the back of the stove, and looked for his mug. Given Maggie's current mood, he half-expected to see his mug on the table, with cold coffee in it. But no, she had washed it at some point this morning, and he turned it over on the small counter, wrinkling his nose as the viscous liquid in the pot slurped into it.

Bleah.

He tossed the remainder of the liquid outside in the yard, his eyes roving over his domain. It appeared Galba and Bill were already on Big Bald--he saw the silhouettes of two horses. This reminder of what the night would hold caused him to go back inside, add some milk to his mug, and take a cautious drink.

A shudder and his mouth went into revolt. Alright, then, he thought, and reached for the sugar bowl. Nat didn't mind some milk or cream in his coffee, but sugar?

Hastily, he put fresh water in the pot and added fresh grounds, putting it back on the stove. It was still warm enough from its earlier sojourn to need a potholder. Good, it would be done that much faster.

He forced himself to put aside the urge to join Galba and Bill. A man who could not keep his own household organized....he then realized no one else was about.

Squaring his own shoulders, Nat stopped in the dogtrot to listen upstairs. He recognized James' snore, but didn't detect any of the other children.

Hesitation.

There had been no signs in the kitchen of whatever had caused Maggie's present mood. He made a face, taking another sip of the now-cooled liquid--one could not call it coffee--in his mug, and then opened the door, stepping in and closing it quickly to preserve the warmth for the tigress in her bath.

Other than her skin scrubbed to redness, nothing appeared changed--he sniffed. Christ, she had used lye soap, something she ordinarily only used on the floors and for nasty messes. The stench from her clothes was still in evidence, too. He bore on manfully, pulling his chair back from the fire and into the corner of the room furthest away from their bed. He sat, taking another sip from his mug and realized the stuff had managed to clear any possible cobwebs left in his brain.

Maggie didn't move. Nat had come to think it wasn't anything he had done to make her angry, so was unwilling to leave her alone to brood. He could gentle her like a horse.

The growling ceased after another minute. This was good.

"You don't bully me."

Nat raised his chin, looking at the wraith in the tub through narrowed eyes. That was quite off the path of any thoughts he had been having.

"No, I don't," he agreed thoughtfully.

"You've never hit me, either."

By now, the wariness along his spine had subsided to mere caution.

"No."

Maggie's face was still turned toward the fireplace, but he could almost see her thoughts. Maybe it was time for some levity--whatever she was thinking about was damned dangerous.

"Would you like for me to?" he asked.

A roar from the tub. Maggie stood, turned, and hurled her wash cloth at him, hitting the mug in his instinctively-raised hand and soaking him with both dirty, soapy water and a nasty version of coffee.

High alert. Any incautious smile that may have started on his face promptly disappeared as he sat very still, which was difficult. The coffee he hadn't yet drunk was tickling his ribs, trickling into his pants.

Taking a deep breath, he watched his wife step out of the tub and dry herself off. No more missiles in her immediate reach. Nat spoke softly.

"Maggie. Are you going to tell me what has happened, or do you intend to make me suffer all day? I do have something to do, after all."

No answer. She walked over to the cedar chest at the foot of the bed, rummaging until she found another petticoat and chemise. In the middle of putting them on, she looked at Nat finally. Her attitude had changed completely, he saw. Whatever had gotten to her, she had left in the bathtub.

"Tonight, you will tell your men that any who beat their wives will see retribution from you."

"I've already memorized my speech."

He ducked as the empty china pitcher came at him, crashing into

Absolution | 81

the corner of the wall near the piano. Shards landed on the protective velvet covering the instrument and on his bare shoulders, nicking him.

"Ow!" A roar of his own, and he, too, was on his feet, ignoring the cuts as he advanced on the furious woman, who bent to her left and grabbed the fire poker, holding it steady in his direction.

"Do you really want to, Nat?" Her voice was soft. "Do you want to beat me?"

A new note in her voice, and he stared at her, disbelief on his face. She was not a large woman, but he suddenly realized that a physical disadvantage would not keep her from attempting to kill him if he pushed her any further. Still...

"Maggie. If I do not know what is wrong, I can not help." Speak slow. Words of one syllable. He'd been in any number of dangerous situations in the past, but never with Maggie. What the hell had happened to her this morning?

The poker lowered. "Don't touch me." Menace. "You should know." She, too, spoke in words of one syllable.

Think, Nat, he ordered himself, slightly crouched as his body prepared to leap in any direction called for. Maggie simply looked at him, still as a winter's night.

She had told him to add something to his speech for tonight. Told him. Something about wife-beating...he dimly thought through the past minutes, hours, days...oh.

Preoccupied with tonight's meeting, Nat had forgotten about Georgia's little friend, Miranda. Well, not forgotten, he decided. He had simply pushed it aside to take care of after the meeting tonight. He was going to visit that piece of scum...

Maggie was still watching him. "Miranda?" he asked. "I plan to go there tomorrow. Do you know where she lives?"

Maggie's shoulders suddenly drooped, and she shook her head. Replacing the poker in its stand, she took her Sunday dress down from its peg, and disappeared into its folds, her head emerging.

He had relaxed enough to stand upright, but remained where he was. The tigress was no longer evident, but a new insight prevented him from saying more.

Sitting down to put on stockings and her shoes, Maggie flickered her eyes his direction. Nat suddenly felt the cuts on his feet from the shattered china pitcher, and carefully walked to his side of the bed.

82 | Vonda Wilson Sheets

Sitting, he lifted a foot to examine it, and his eyes fell on the clothes Maggie had tossed under the window. Not tossed, thrown.

She was walking toward the door. Seeing him bend down to pick up the clothes, she said "Don't."

"But…"

"I said don't. I mean it. I want you to burn them when you start your fire this afternoon. I'll put them in a bag for you to carry up there. I don't want you to touch them."

He was totally and completely mystified, had been since he had awakened such a short time ago. Nothing was fitting together, and Maggie saw he still didn't understand. She came toward him, and he straightened.

"Nat, you are not stupid. And you will promise retribution for men who do not treat their women well."

He nodded his head, raising his eyebrows in silent inquiry. Communication was apparently re-established, as Maggie came closer and stood, her face not six inches from his own.

"Miranda's Pa came home last night."

"Oh?"

"Georgia and I took food over to Granny Haggard's for the family."

"I see."

"No, you don't."

Nat didn't respond. He would soon see, he knew. He apparently needed one last cobweb cleared.

"The man decided to beat Miranda."

Suddenly, Nat knew what was coming. Hope the child wasn't dead showed in his eyes, and Maggie answered.

"Miranda is alright," she assured him. Then, the odd tone in her voice returned as she added, "Or she will be."

Well, then, what had gotten Maggie so upset?

"Her mother killed the man."

"Oh?"

She turned as if to leave, then looked back at Nat.

"She drove a knife into his groin."

Shock rippled along his spine. Myriad thoughts came together in Nat's mind, as he understood his wife had helped bury the man, tended the woman. She needed her clothes to burn to pay homage to whatever force stood between herself and her own love.

Absolution | 83

He really, really needed the coffee, which was finished, as his nose ascertained when Maggie opened the door.

Then Nat Kinney discovered he understood much more than he wanted to about this day so far, for his wife's voice, still with that odd note in it, reached him.

"Her name is Maggie."

He was walking to the top of Big Bald, a burlap sack in one hand, a large leather pouch in the other.

One held his wife's nasty clothes.

The other held the things he needed to make this night work as he wanted it to.

The fresh pot of coffee had helped him sort it out.

He had decided, finally, what he was going to say.

CHAPTER 9
April, 1885 - The Power and the Night

Power.

Maggie had made him lunch; whatever the connection between them was called, it had vibrated intensely while he ate and drank the fresh coffee. He did not have to touch her to feel it.

Power.

Nat was not nervous at all. Reaching the top of Big Bald, he saw the faces of Bill Hensley and Galba Branson lighten at his approach. A small cook fire showed the remains of their lunch. He doubted it had been as interesting as his lunch had been. He greeted them, and then did a slow circle, examining the horizon.

A column of smoke rose from a valley some distance away. His wife had told him of the expression on the other Maggie's face when she'd told Andy Coggburn what she wanted him to do with the bloody, defiled cabin.

"Burn it."

The phrase echoed through his mind, in his Maggie's voice.

It was time.

Every motion was deliberate. He lowered the pouch with its contents, and the burlap sack with Maggie's nasty clothes, to the ground, near the pile of wood and brush that reached to his height. The others had made torches, which were soaking in buckets of kerosene.

Without looking at Bill and Gabe, Nat put his hand on one of the torches, pulled it out and let it drip for a few seconds. His breath seemed to catch, and Maggie's voice steadied him.

"Burn it."

This moment would change their lives. They could still back out, still decide to live peacefully, still move.

"Burn it."

Obeisance to power demanded he walk to the cook fire. Lower the torch, watch it catch. Fixedly, he watched the end of the torch move on its own volition from the small cook fire to the huge pile waiting to be lit.

"Burn it."

It took some little time for the brush to catch. They had mixed in green brush and wood, to create the smoke.

It caught. Mesmerized, he watch the flames grow. Eyes fixed, Nat stepped back a little from the bonfire on Big Bald, just crossing the plowed circles around it. The torch in his hand was burning well; he lifted his left foot, crossed his right leg, and knocked the torch's flames into the dirt, where it smoldered for a bit, then died.

A little dizzy, he realized he'd forgotten to breathe. Turning, he smiled at Gabe and Bill, who had been watching him closely, and took a lungful of air. He nodded--the moment needed no words.

Nathaniel Napoleon Kinney turned back to watch the fire grow larger.

Power.

Nat had prepared for his speech the way he did for the sermons on Sunday mornings--writing it, crossing out and correcting, then memorizing and orating while in the barn and the fields, or traveling. Maggie's last-minute demand had derailed him, and he did not have it memorized anymore.

The hours of waiting for the sun to set and the men to appear slipped by, marred only by a small incident that could not deter him.

Captain Van Zandt, the intrepid warrior, who had served in the Florida, Mexican and the Civil Wars, had arrived not long after the smoke from the bonfire began wafting high above their heads. Gabe had made coffee, and handed a cup to Nat, saying "Here you go, Captain."

Nat had taken the cup without thinking, still concentrating. He heard a snort, and looked at Van Zandt, who had been enjoying his own coffee.

"Captain?" Van Zandt asked. Suspicious eyes peered at Nat.

"We thought it would be easier for Captain Kinney to have a title, since he's overseeing the patrols," Gabe explained.

Van Zandt stared at Kinney, squinting. "You were not a captain in the war," he stated.

Nat shrugged--nothing could touch him now. "I did serve," he responded mildly. The errant question of how Van Zandt had known he hadn't made captain didn't register in his mind.

"I'll be damned if you were a captain," retorted Van Zandt, "I'll support the cause, but I refuse to address you with a title that you did not earn, nor deserve." With that, he tossed his coffee onto the cook fire, and rose from the log he'd been sitting on. The fire flickered, and Nat returned his gaze to it. The flames continued to burn.

He scarcely noticed when Van Zandt left the fire and stalked over to his horse. Bill and Gabe made motion as if to go after the captain, and Nat slightly shook his head.

"Let him go." He didn't explain, couldn't explain, but he knew. "We'll be fine."

Power.

About one hundred men stood on the top of Big Bald. Almost as many horses were grazing, waiting patiently for their riders, who were gathered around the west side of the huge fire.

Nat had remained in his trance, automatically noting who was present, who was not. His trusted lieutenants were riding around the borders of the bald, torches in hand; making sure no one came up who had not been specifically invited. Conversation was muted; a buzzing sound encircled Nat's head. Gabe approached him with a whispered message, and Nat nodded.

It was time.

He himself had placed the big chunk of tree on this spot. He had wanted the fire behind him, and the huge full moon to hold him in silhouetted embrace while he spoke.

Power.

The straps of his leather pouch settled lightly on his left shoulder, the bag bumping his left hip. With Maggie's bag in his right hand, he stood, turned his back on the gathering, and tossed it into the fire. It caught instantly, and a faint scent from the contents, of soiled garments, reached him. He bowed his head in acknowledgement of that force, the power that gripped him so fiercely.

He found himself standing on the bench, looking over the men present, silent as the conversations died away.

He shouted, "We meet by the fire!"

The unanimous response was, "We ride in the dark!"

The words that flowed from him, unleashing forces to be reckoned with, had little to do with the speech he had been spending weeks on. He opened his pouch, pulling Jim Everett's bloody shirt from its hiding place, and the men were in his hands. Somehow, the right words flowed into the hearts of the men--his men, he saw--and his own heart left the trance and soared.

By the time he finished, the moonlight showed the faces of the men he knew would lift him up, help him do what appeared to be necessary work. Protect the women and children and show people, by example, the right way to live.

There was excitement on those faces.

As JJ Brown stepped forward to read the oath of membership, and as those present agreed to abide by it, Nat noted who was absent: Sam Snapp and his brothers, William Miles and his boys, the Haworths and some of the Moores. They had been in the group earlier. Obviously, something he had said did not agree with them. No matter.

The intensity, the number of cheers that rose about his head reached him. As the roars died down, he said, "Congratulations, men! You are now members of the Citizens' League for Law and Order!"

And then the roars returned.

Power; He had yearned for it, worked for it, lived for it. Now it had come to him.

Loath to leave the bald, Nat assured the others who had planned staying to watch the bonfire that he would keep an eye on it. It was beginning to die down. So the other men rode away in the early spring chill, the warmth of the fire and meeting symbolized by torches he could see in the distance. The word would spread, much as the news of a man's death by fire this morning had.

Power; He shone, he burned, and he walked. Waiting for something he could not, would not deny. The fire continued to burn, the rake in his hand gathering it into ever-smaller embers.

Then she was there, unrolling a tarp and blankets inside the circle. She reached for a basket, filling two glasses with the contents of a jug from the cellar.

No words were necessary.

She handed him a glass of deep red wine, the color of blood in the fire and moonlight. His clinked against hers, and they both drank, emptying the contents. Then, as one, they threw the glasses into the fire, and fell to the ground, fierce in touch and sound. A final "Burn it!" rang through his mind as he felt himself scald.

Power.

CHAPTER 10
April 5, 1885 - The Women Wait

The house was much too quiet.

Kate Frazier Miles had fed her men lunch, and seen them off to Kirbyville. Well, she liked to think she saw them off, she supposed. They would've gone even if she'd tried to hold them. The smile on her face had faded as she watched them go, not one of them looking back.

She didn't protest when William had allowed Jimmy to go along. He was only twelve, but times were hard, and he was already learning to be a man. Billy and Manny were long past hanging onto her apron strings. Jimmy was her baby; she still thought of him as "Jimmy." Wistfully, she smiled again, thinking of his indignation at her when she'd called him that last week.

Finishing clearing the table and doing the dishes, she wiped her hands on her apron. There were plenty of things to be done. Prepare the boys' lessons for the next week. Go work in the garden. She grimaced--mending clothes. Boys were so hard on clothes; but so were men.

Instead of starting on these things, she took her pipe and the tin of tobacco down from the mantle of the fireplace. A nice cup of tea and a few minutes sitting on the front porch and smoking were just what she needed. A reward.

Pipe lit, tea in hand, Kate walked through the screen door onto her front porch. Her rocking chair was swaying in the breeze. The daffodils had done well this year--they lined her door yard. The lilacs, roses, and her other flowers were almost bursting, racing to bloom first in the early spring.

Feet planted, her back curved slightly to fit her chair. She leaned back, her mind feeling as empty as the house. She rocked, simply trying to enjoy the birds. A hen wandered through the dooryard, five chicks scuttling along behind her. Songs from the trees assured her all was well with her world.

Snorting, Kate's shoulders slumped. Her body curved to try to protect the babies that she no longer carried. William was fifty, she would be so this year. She had to get used to the idea that all of her children would be gone soon. It was a very strange feeling.

Absolution | 89

Trying to shake it, she stood, and stepped lightly down the path. She and her sister, Sally, had always been the small ones in the family, both of them bird-like in their movements. Her walk took her through the gate, toward the corral William and the boys had put around three sides of the barn. She saw Betsy was drooping, too--it wasn't often all the horses were gone, and poor Betsy was lonely.

The mule's head jerked up at her step. As she reached the fence, her hand reached to stroke Betsy's nose.

"Rather quiet around here," Kate told Betsy. "I guess I'll go work in the garden." She considered letting Betsy follow her around for company, but decided against it. Betsy loved to eat flowers.

A stop at the smokehouse to check the fire--this cow had been mutilated, and luckily, William had been able to find her quickly, put her out of her misery. A glance inside showed William had also checked it, and smoored the fire. She needn't check it again today.

As she passed out of Betsy's sight, the mule brayed. And she kept braying, while Kate unlatched the garden gate and checked the bench which held her spade and other tools.

The braying continued. Was something wrong? That didn't sound like a great deal of distress. No, Betsy was lonely. Well....so was she.

Her mind made up, Kate closed the garden gate and went to the barn. Betsy had followed her movements from her side of the fence, and was dancing in eagerness as Kate opened the barn door and walked in.

A saddled Betsy stood just off the front porch a few minutes later, and after securing the bag of mending and her sewing basket, Kate returned for her bonnet and another pocket she tied around her waist. Then she jumped up on the mule from the porch, turned her, and left for her sister's house.

The wait for the men to return would be more bearable if she shared a pipe with Sally, and did her mending. Sally no longer had any children at home; Kate wondered if there was some secret to keeping her own home from feeling so empty.

She rather doubted it, but she and Sally could discuss these things while they waited.

It was Sunday. It wasn't the Presbyterians' turn at the Union Church in Taney City, so there had been no services for Kate, except

90 | Vonda Wilson Sheets

the simple prayer William said over breakfast. Given the nature of the meeting in Kirbyville, she thought as she noticed buzzards flying high looking for food, it was probably just as well.

William was grim about the outcome of this meeting. He was tired, anyway, from trying to get crops planted and protect the livestock at night. It was open range country, but he and the boys were fencing their land, a pasture at a time. Billy had been doing the same for the Snapp place when he was home. Fence-building made for good neighbors, but it was tough, tedious work. Searching for and finding the right trees--William preferred oak--cutting them down, hauling them to wherever the fence was to be set, chopping them into posts, digging the post-holes, setting the posts, filling the holes, then stringing the barbed wire…this was a long process.

Passing the Snapp farm brought Sam to mind. Her tight-knit extended family had moved en masse from Scott County, Virginia, some years ago. They settled close to each other, worked each other's farms as needed. But her brother Henry had itching feet, and sold up to move on. When Sarah Sims was being courted by Sam some ten years ago, Sam bought the Frazier place and moved her onto it. Sam and Sarah had become a part of her clan in the absence of her brother.

Kate mused over this. Although her family had been in America for several generations, her father spoke a mixture of Gaelic and English until his death. It must have been the mountains of Virginia, she thought. Most folks who lived there were Scots, and the old folk kept the clan ways strong, passing it to their children. She herself spoke little of the Gaelic--a lack of practice, she knew, for Sally had refused to learn it, and William just smiled to hear her when they first married.

Betsy turned off the road, down into the protected cove where Samp had built Sally's house. Then a hee-haw from Betsy brought Kate's attention back, and she smiled.

Her sister and niece were on their own mounts, loaded down with Mattie's babies and bags that Kate knew held their mending. Sally's butter cream hair shone in the sun as she smiled at Kate when Betsy drew to a stop, nosing with the other mules.

"Going somewhere?" Kate asked.

"Thought you might need company," Sally replied.

Kate reached a gloved hand up to her own clad head. "You might

Absolution | 91

as well turn around. You forgot your bonnet," she teased. Then Kate's smile faded, and she gestured behind her, toward her empty home.

"You were right."

Kate, Sally, and Mattie spent the afternoon alternately playing with the little girls and mending clothes. None of them were in a frame of mind to cook--despite what William and Samp said, they all knew there was inherent danger in a gathering of men with troubles on their minds. After tending to the animals, they shared a light supper of cornbread and milk. The girls, worn out with so much playing, were down for the night.

Mattie didn't smoke, but her mother and aunt put their shawls about their shoulders and went outside with their pipes. Kate felt skittering along her spine as the night waited for the moon to rise. She and Sally were rocking side by side, as if they were two old women with nothing to do but gossip. Neither spoke for some time. Mattie was singing softly inside, lying down with the children.

When the moon finally made its appearance, Kate rose as if to go.

"Stay," Sally said, calmly. "If they don't bed down at Sam's, it will be hours yet."

Kate shook her head. "They'll be needing to eat, and I may as well try to sleep."

"You won't."

"No," Kate agreed. She shrugged. Her sister said nothing else as she left to fetch Betsy. When she had brought her mule around, Sally was standing at the block used for mounting. They tied the bag of finished mending to the back of the saddle, hands working in harmony. Sally waited until Kate was up, settling her skirts, then tied a second bag on the saddle horn. It was heavy.

"Ham," said Sally by way of explanation. "Let them make sandwiches. You need your rest."

Kate smiled down at her older sister, who never stopped taking care of everyone. Her hand caressed Sally's lined face, and she shook her head in amusement. "I love you," she told Sally.

"I love you. Stop worrying. We have smart men."

With that, Kate was off, riding the trail up to the road by the light of the moon.

They might be smart, she thought. But smart don't stop a bullet, retorted her mocking mind.

❧ ❧

The evening was falling, dishes were done, and the children had all gone over to Ada Marie's house to make candy, under Eva's supervision. Robert and James were on the bald with Alonzo and Nat.

Maggie had only been vaguely aware of Ada Marie Prather, Ninnie Groom, and Caroline Brown through most of the afternoon and early evening. Most of her body and mind were focused on what could be seen or heard from the bald to the east of her house.

For the hundredth time, she strode to the window. The others had settled in chairs in the kitchen, doing what women do best, she supposed. Waiting. Maggie was too antsy to sit without playing the piano. Looking up the bald again, her frustration mounted as she realized only shadows and silhouettes could be seen.

"Do you see anything?" Ninnie asked. Maggie shook her head, then turned back to her guests. Ada Marie and Caroline were discussing some novel the two of them had read.

"Would any of you mind if I played tonight?" Maggie asked.

"Oh, please do." Ada Marie smiled.

One last look outside and then she went into her room to play.

After warming up and playing several songs, Maggie saw that the moon had risen. She settled her hands on the keys, a discordant chime jerking her head away from the window. Then a sound of distant voices, and she found herself standing on the long porch with the others, watching the men's silhouettes and the fire.

None of them appeared to breathe as they formed a phalanx, symbolically protecting home and hearth from whatever waited in the dark, Maggie thought. She pushed the thought aside. She knew who was up there, and not one of those men, including Nat, was a threat to her. After seeing what that other Maggie had gone through this morning, it was a comfort to know.

Some shadows moved to leave, and the women saw men on horses, carrying torches, move to prevent the leaving. A few seconds--obviously a discussion of some sorts, the torches were still--and the horses again began patrolling, the shadows moving out of sight.

Maggie could tell when Nat made a popular statement--the men roared with approval. She smiled, and glanced around the dooryard for her normal nightly audience, feeling a need to reassure the listeners that the music would continue in a few moments.

Gunfire erupted from the bare hill. The four women jerked in reaction to the noise. It continued, but no threat could be heard from the voices drifting down, and all four of them relaxed. Then Maggie noticed--other than the three women beside her, she had no audience tonight.

"Well, that's odd," she said.

Caroline was standing beside her, eyes intent on the bald. "What's that?"

"Oh, I have an audience for the music every night," Maggie responded, her attention no longer on the hill. Where were her music lovers? Did they think she wouldn't play tonight? "They are not here."

Tension eased somewhat, Caroline turned to Maggie.

"Who comes to listen?"

"A few of the neighbors. They are no trouble," Maggie said. "They simply sit and listen on nice evenings. It's a warm night--I don't know why none of them are here."

"Maggie." Ada Marie's voice came from the other end of the line, and Ninnie stepped back, to allow the conversation to continue, but Caroline's voice came first.

"Who are 'they'?" Caroline asked. "Do Ada Marie and Alonzo come?"

Maggie shook her head, laughing a bit. "No, it's some of the neighbors and the children."

Caroline's voice turned acid. "So people who come are not those who attend Nat's church?"

Perplexed, Maggie looked at Caroline. "What are you saying?"

Ada Marie stepped between them, her tiny frame breaching any potential conflict.

"Maggie, do you not understand what the men are doing tonight?" she asked.

"Of course I do. They are setting up patrols to prevent men from beating their wives, stealing cattle, that sort of thing," Maggie replied. "What does that have to do with it?"

"Do you think that's all the men are discussing up there?" Caroline waved a hand at the bald while she asked.

"What else would it be?" Maggie asked.

Caroline glanced back up the hill, and snorted. Ada Marie wasn't going to stop her from stating her mind.

"Do men come to listen?" asked Caroline.

Maggie shook her head. "Only one or two have."

Seeing Maggie still didn't understand, Caroline tapped her toes under her skirts. "Goodness, Maggie, the men of those women you play for are the ones who our husbands will be arresting, after tonight. Do you think the women and children are going to keep coming to hear you play if Nat locks the men up?"

"Nat's not doing this by himself," Maggie defended him. "Your husbands will be out there, too."

"True," Caroline agreed. "But the neighbors don't come to our houses to hear music, thinking we might be a friend."

Thunderstruck, Maggie looked at Ada Marie, who nodded just once. "If the men are in jail, the women won't come," Ada Marie agreed.

Ninnie had been silent throughout the conversation. Now, her attention returned to the bald in time to see some torches coming down this side, taking the path to the main road on the west side of the house. "Look, they're coming," she pointed out. "It must be over."

"Come," said Ada Marie, "they'll be hungry." She shooed Ninnie and Caroline back into the house. Seeing Maggie still staring off into the night, she put her hand on Maggie's sleeve. "Maybe some will come back," she tried to comfort her friend, who had a very strange look on her face.

Maggie turned to Ada Marie, leaving her eyes on the bonfire, which was dying down. Then she shook herself slightly, and looked at her friend.

"Do you think so?" she asked Ada Marie softly. "I think Ninnie may be right." Men rode by the dooryard, the occasional torch lighting their way.

"Those days must be over."

CHAPTER 11
An Oath of Bloodshed

Shock.

That shirt had been carefully hidden away. JJ Brown knew it. He and Yell both stiffened when they realized what Nat was holding above his head, seconds before he told the men around the bonfire.

"How did he get it?" he murmured, sotto voice, to Yell.

"Don't know," Yell's voice was rusty with pain. "The door's been locked since then."

As they listened to Nat, the shock wore to anger.

"He's right," Yell told JJ, "using it to remind us that something must be done."

JJ shook his head. "Did he ask if he could use it?"

"No."

"Well, then."

A few more minutes, and roars of approval began to join the crackling of the high fire. JJ and Yell were silent, watchful. The idea of night patrols was accepted.

Nat then spoke of people who were known throughout the county for various misdeeds, and how those people should be brought to justice. More acceptance.

The plan was going to work.

JJ relaxed, and mentally went over what he would say when Nat signaled him. Although Nat had not used the speech they had agreed upon, the improvisation was powerful. Nat's voice was thundering now; it was almost time, JJ knew.

"Will you stand with me, take an oath of allegiance to fight, to make Taney County safe for our women and our children?"

He felt the fever pitch, the excitement, and waves of it rolled over him as he caught Nat's eye. JJ was drawn to the big man, who still clutched Jim's shirt in his fist. He reached for the shirt, which Nat gave him, and his own hand tingled, feeling Jim's dried blood, which was crumbling into the folds of his palm.

His right hand bringing the shirt to cover his heart, JJ raised his left, palm outward, and stepped up on the bench as Nat stepped down. Nothing of the lawyer's oratory, verbal skills, remained in the pained, raised thunder that rolled from his throat.

"Do you, in the presence of God and these witnesses, solemnly swear that you will never reveal any of the secrets of this order nor communicate any part of it to any person or persons in the known world, unless you are satisfied by a strict test, or in some legal way, that they are lawfully entitled to receive them, that you will conform and abide by the rules and regulations of this order, and obey all orders of your superior officers or any brother officer under whose jurisdiction you may be at the time attached; nor will you propose for membership or sanction the admission of anyone whom you have a reason to believe is not worthy of being a member, nor will you oppose the admission of anyone solely on a personal matter. You shall report all theft that is made known to you and not leave any unreported on account of his being a blood relation of yours; nor will you willfully report anyone through personal enmity. You shall recognize and answer all signs made by lawful brothers and render them such assistance as they may be in need of, so far as you are able or the interest of your family will permit; nor will you willfully wrong or defraud a brother, or permit it if in your power to prevent it. Should you willfully and knowingly violate this oath in any way, you subject yourself to a jury of twelve members of this order, even if it be their decision to hang you by the neck until you are dead, dead, dead. So help me God."

He stepped down, the words of the oath echoing in the yells of the crowd. His head ringing, he walked away from Nat, who had reassumed the bench and was calling his chosen lieutenants to step forward and be acknowledged.

JJ handed the shirt to Yell, who carefully folded it and stuffed it inside his coat. Yell looked up with a weary expression on his face. "Shall we go, Sir?"

JJ responded "What's gone and what's past help should be past grief."

The two men walked away from the near madness they had helped create, for the love of a brother who had died much too young.

Neither ever mimicked Jim's sense of humor again.

CHAPTER 12
Late April 5 - Early April 6, 1885

Jimmy waited until they were nearly to Sam Snapp's before he said something to break the silence of the half-mile moonlit walk from the meeting on Big Bald.

He was tired, impatient, and hungry. Much too excited to eat the meal Mrs. Snapp had fixed when he and his uncle, Pa, and brothers arrived in the late afternoon, all the tenseness of the evening suddenly burst out.

"Pa? I don't under-" he began, half-turning to his father, who was walking behind him.

"I know you don't," William Miles responded, his left hand gesturing in a half-circle. "Soon."

He took a breath, blew out his cheeks to hold it, and let it out, continuing to walk. Sam was in front, leading the group down to his cabin in the bright light of the moon. Hill men bred and born, none of them were breathless or disoriented; all felt the tenseness of the night.

Jimmy's stomach growled, and he heard Manny beside him, softly chuckling. "Me, too," Manny murmured.

A man's shadow came from the right. Jimmy and Manny jumped, hands tensed on the guns they carried. "Hold," their father commanded, and they relaxed--it was Andrew Coggburn who joined them.

Lighted windows in Mr. Snapp's cabin. Maybe there would be food, since Mrs. Snapp was obviously waiting for them. A jump across the creek, and they were soon ranged across the steps and porch, Mrs. Snapp bringing out ham sandwiches and sweet tea.

The others ate in silence, and Jimmy followed suit. The door of the cabin was open, lantern light spilling out to meet the moon. Normal noises of the night--the horses, frogs, water flowing. Jimmy reached for a third sandwich. At the same time, Mr. Snapp rose and left the group, disappearing behind the cabin. When he returned, he carried two large stone jugs, and set them on the porch. Water rolled off the jugs, creating a dark trail in the dimness of the porch floor.

Andrew had produced his own cup for the tea, as did the Miles' and Sampson Barker. Sam started to go in and fetch a mug, but Mrs.

98 | Vonda Wilson Sheets

Snapp handed him one through the door. A murmured "Thank you" and Sam was pouring beer for everyone.

Jimmy occasionally snuck a sip or two of beer from his parents' crocks, but had never sampled beer cooled in a spring before. It was different. Most people brewed beer for home use, he knew. But keeping it cold? His twelve-year-old mind wondered if he could convince his mother to do the same. He liked it much better cold.

A feeling of well-being eased through his body. He should just lay down, he thought. Pa wouldn't mind….he began to stretch out, but a sharp voice halted him.

"James, stay awake." Pa brooked no nonsense, so Jimmy tiredly leaned back against the wall of the cabin, and tried to focus.

"Well?" Andy's nasal voice began the conversation. He was seated on the steps, looking up at Mr. Snapp, whose face was invisible above the light through the cabin door.

"There was an oath," William Miles told Andy. "We left before it was finished.

"Oath?" Andy asked.

"Promise to join a brotherhood based on the night patrols and arresting folks," Mr. Snapp answered, and rubbed his face. Exhaustion roiled through the group, Jim thought.

"So you ain't joinin'?"

"No." William Miles was blunt. "I'll mind my own business."

Nods from Mr. Snapp, Uncle Samp, and Billy. Manny emitted a snore--he had fallen asleep sitting against the post of the porch. William moved as if to poke him awake, and Mr. Snapp stayed his hand.

"William, you and the boys can sleep here tonight."

"I 'preciate that, but we best be getting home," William said. "Kate'll be worried." He then prodded Manny, who jumped. "You and Jim go fetch the horses."

Jim was sorry about that. It was a good three-hour ride home, if they didn't push the horses. Why were they so tired? He and his brothers often hunted through the night. He began to rise to do Pa's bidding, but Uncle Samp spoke.

"They had the Iron-clad Oath, back home," Sampson Barker spoke of Virginia. Jim settled back into his place. Uncle Samp and Pa seldom spoke of the War Between the States, or Virginia. Reaching for his cup, Jim tipped his head back to drain the last of the beer, listening.

"This is nothing to do with that," Mr. Snapp commented.

"Mebbe not," Andy agreed.

"Same thing, though," Pa said. "I don't hold with it."

"Who'd he want to go after?" asked Andy.

"The Taylors, drunkards, wife-beaters, thieves," responded Mr. Snapp.

"Hmm. He din't say nuthin' about folks who wuddint marrit?"

"No," Uncle Samp answered that one.

"I guess I don't understand," Billy began. "The Taylors, and men like them, alright. What's so wrong about them goin' to jail?"

Jim felt Uncle Samp shift; in the darkness, Pa's hat was pointed in Uncle Samp's direction.

Hesitation. Then Pa spoke.

"Your Uncle Samp and me, we seen some awful stuff. None of us had any slaves; that wuddint our reason for joining the Confederates." Jim wondered if he'd ever heard Pa talking like this; he didn't think so.

"One or two men, mebbe a couple more, thet'd be alright, riding patrol. But a big bunch of 'em, when they git to ridin' nights, mebbe drinking some, folks git hurt. Not sayin' some of 'em don't need preachin' and jail, but fer a couple men to make decisions on who needs it, thet's jest wrong. Fer one man to lead a bunch of men, that's trouble."

Uncle Samp was nodding. "We didn't take the oath in Virginia, and that was home. Ain't gonna do it here or now."

Mr. Snapp asked, "What did you do in the War?" Mr. Snapp's Pa had died up in central Missouri during the Battle of Lexington. There was no stone in the family cemetery for him.

Pa snorted again, and his answer was brief. "We was sharpshooters." The silence greeting this statement was tense. Then, "Manny, you and Jim go fetch the horses."

Sharpshooters.

As tired as he was, the phrase circled through Jim's mind as the journey home wound down in the early hours of the morning.

Sharpshooters.

Well, that explained a lot. Jim attended school when it was in session, and to the best of his knowledge, most boys were good shots, hunting for their families and such. The girls usually knew how to handle a gun, but they were kept busy in the family homes and didn't often hunt.

But his mother and Aunt Sally not only knew how to load and shoot a rifle, both of them carried pistols most of the time, away from home. His mother carried hers in a concealed pocket sewn into each of her dresses and skirts. The pouch she wore tied at her waist not only held her pipe and tobacco, but ammunition.

Sharpshooters.

Jim tried to think of when Pa had first handed him a gun, but couldn't remember. He'd always handled guns, far as he knew.

"Target practice." Manny's voice was soft in the darkness. Obviously, his thoughts were swirling around the same track as Jim's.

Target practice. Yep, thought Jim, although he didn't respond to Manny. He didn't think Pa and Uncle Samp would much appreciate the boys talking right now; neither man had said much on the ride.

Murmured words, and Uncle Samp turned off the road, down to his place. Only a couple more miles, and the Miles men would be home.

Sharpshooters. Target practice. Casting bullets, although you could buy them, Jim knew. He tried to think of any other boys his age who had regular target practice, such as the Miles boys did. None came to mind.

Not just target practice. Pa would set them through paces, much as training a horse. Using chunks of wood, straw-filled bags, whatever came to hand, the boys spent hours working their guns, rifles and pistols both. It wasn't unheard of for Pa to ambush them in some way while they were doing chores, and he expected accuracy.

A scene from a couple years ago suddenly came to mind as they rode into the barn, and Jim noted the windows of the house were dark. Had Ma gone to bed? He doubted it, thinking of that day.

He, his mother, and brothers, had been working in the garden one summer day, harvesting some midsummer vegetables for canning. As Ma reached the end of the row, near the border of trees that served as a fence, rattles began vibrating. Ma had not hesitated; in one motion, she had whirled, pulled her pistol and shot the rattlesnake nearby. Jim and his brothers were gape-mouthed as the rattles stopped, and

Pa's laughter came clearly from the woods.

Her eyes narrowed, Ma walked over to the snake, and picked it up, the boys running toward her, "Wait, Ma, it might not be dead!"

"Oh, it's dead alright," Pa said as he came down from the big oak he'd been hiding in. "Your Ma don't miss." He jumped lightly on the ground, and walked toward her, a big smile on his face.

"William Miles!" Ma began shaking the snake at his father, standing her ground. "My stocking!"

Pa laughed, and continued to do so as the boys looked at the "snake," then at their parents. It was, indeed, one of Ma's brown winter stockings, stuffed with leaves. Pa had even gone so far as to add some gray paint in splotches.

"You weren't wearing it," Pa had said, and his mother had jumped him, the both of them falling to the ground and laughing. Then Pa had turned serious, as Ma tried to wrap the stocking around his throat. He held Ma's hands, and looked up at the three sons watching their parents.

"You best not forget--your Ma is the best shot in the family." The grin returned, as he added, "You cain't wear that stocking anymore, anyway, Kate. It has a hole in it."

Examining her pistol, her face averted to her right, Ma's voice was calm. "Oh, I'll fix it," she looked sideways down at her husband, along the barrel of the pistol. "And you." Then she put it back in her pocket, and stood, brushing off her skirts. Then she smiled, and held a hand out to Pa.

The boys slumped toward the back door of the house, exhausted. Ma was sitting at the kitchen table, and Jim smelled the sweet fragrance of her tobacco.

"You boys hungry?"

For once, no one wanted anything to eat. Pa pulled out a chair to sit at the end of the table, taking out his gun and laying it down. His hat came off as well, and he looked at his sons in the glow of the fire from the hearth.

The boys were tired, cold, but their eyes were alert. Pa nodded in satisfaction, while Ma studied each of their faces, no expression on her own.

"You done good. Get some rest--we got fencing to do in the morning."

CHAPTER 13
April 7 - Tuesday - Threats

Kate Miles somehow reminded John Dickenson of some Scotswomen he had seen when he visited Scotland as a lad. She was small, bird-like, red hair fading, her spine straight. Her sister, Sallie Barker, was very much like her. They kept to themselves, these women. John fancied he could hear a bit of the Gaelic when Mrs. Miles spoke; Mrs. Barker, not so much.

He smiled when he looked out the window of his store in Dickens and saw Mrs. Miles alight from her mule. Setting his broom aside, he smiled as she came in.

"Good day, Mrs. Miles," his accent coming through quite well.

"Hello, Mr. Dickenson," Mrs. Miles returned the greeting. She went straight to the counter--no browsing the store for this woman, he thought. She knew what she wanted when she came in, and no fuss about it.

It was a simple order, although his eyebrows rose at the last item on the list. "Two pounds of gunpowder, Mrs. Miles?" That was a little out of the ordinary.

"Two pounds, Mr. Dickenson," Mrs. Miles was quite firm. "And I'll be purchasing at least that much every month for some time to come."

John quickly weighed the bag, then wrapped and tied it. "What else can I get for you today?" he asked.

"Oh, that'll be all," she said, not even looking at the bolts of new calico that had arrived just last week.

Adding up her purchases, he told her the sum, and while waiting for her to count the money out in coin, just for conversation, John said, "A great deal of gunpowder for your boys, Mrs. Miles."

She smiled grimly, handing him the money. "My husband feels they need to practice their shooting more," she responded. "We lost another cow last night. The second one in less than a week."

"Oh," John commiserated. "The people around here..."

"Quite," Mrs. Miles said crisply.

"Will you be filing a report with the sheriff, then?" he asked.

"No," and she looked him in the eye. It made John uncomfortable. "We take care of our own business, Mr. Dickenson."

"Indeed. But surely you have heard of the Law and Order League? I believe I may have seen Mr. Miles there on Sunday night?" He asked the question cautiously; some men didn't talk with their wives the way he did with Mary. He had not only seen William Miles, but also the three young Miles boys, and Sampson Barker.

"Certainly. Mr. Miles and our sons attended the meeting, along with Mr. Barker. But we do not believe that a group of night riders is the answer to the problem of stopping rustlers or other scandalous behaviors."

"And why not?" He was curious. People didn't pay their bills on accounts they held in his store on time unless you asked them for money. He disliked the task.

"My husband saw too many good men go bad during the War, Mr. Dickenson, largely because they rode in mobs which destroyed homes and families. He is not willing to see such action again, let alone be a part of it."

"But Captain Kinney will see to it that men don't go out of control," John protested. "That is why our good-standing citizens put him in command of the organization."

"Well," Mrs. Miles pulled her bonnet back up on her head, and picked up the basket John packed. Keeping her eyes lowered, she said, "It's possible I don't understand the situation. But I have lived through one war, and saw my husband changed; I do not want my sons to live through the same. Is there any mail?" She then raised her eyes, and John saw the reason her sons had the reputation they did. Despite her words, Kate Miles definitely felt she understood the situation all too well.

"Yes, ma'am, there is." He turned to his right, where the post office desk held the letters and journals his patrons received. The slot for Elijah Miles had been empty since he moved north, to the village of Swan. The Miles' oldest son was buying a farm and preparing to marry. John took an envelope from William Miles' slot, and handed it to Kate. She inclined her head in thanks.

"Good day, Mr. Dickenson."

The weight of the basket--and it was heavy--did not pull her spine to the side one inch as she left, and he heard her talking to her mule as she tied it to the back of her saddle.

No, that woman was not going to let her husband join Captain Kinney. Within seconds, she was gone.

"Well, I suppose it's women like that which keep us strong," he said his thoughts aloud.

"Like Mrs. Miles?"

John nearly jumped, but that was unseemly. His wife was standing beside him. He smiled down at his Mary, and nodded. "The Miles family won't be joining with us in the League for Law and Order," he told Mary.

"I wonder why not?" she mused. "One would think--"

"Yes, one would," John wanted to distract her. Mary did not like the idea of him taking turns riding at night, patrolling the area around Dickens and Taney City. She was starting to frown, when he hastily asked, "Did you need something, dear?"

Mary pushed at the reading glasses she wore on the end of her nose with her right hand, and set the accounts book on the counter with her left. He pretended to ignore the marital glare peering at him over the glasses.

"Oh, we did well last month, I see," John was turning pages to the month of March. "Yes, yes…"

"John, you must do something about these outstanding accounts." Her finger pushed one more page forward, and he could see the names of several people who owed the store money. The first name on the list was Frank Taylor. Taylor owed twice as much as the rest of the list combined, he realized.

His store, like nearly all general stores, operated on barter and credit. He earned some pittance for having the Dickens post office in his store. Cash customers, like Mrs. Miles and the Barkers, were few and far between. Most folks paid with hides or some specialty product they were renowned for, such as canned goods. John's mouth watered at the thought of Old Man Johnson's pickles, so tart your lips puckered up for a good hour after eating one. His eyes peeked over at the shelves which held the glass jars of those pickles, while Mary continued.

"Frank Taylor appears to have money. He has not paid one penny on his account since he opened it. His wife is still coming in to purchase. That must cease."

His earlier thought about strong women returned as he reached for his broom. "I had hoped Mr. Taylor would be more responsible once he married last year." Taking the broom out to the far corner of the store, he began sweeping vigorously. It just happened to be near the shelf of Old Man Johnson's pickles. John could feel Mary watching him, but he was hungry…he stopped sweeping, and reached for a jar.

"If you are hungry, I will bring you dinner," Mary smiled as he looked guiltily at her. She closed the account ledger, and went back to the small storage area to put the book on the desk. "It might be a few minutes, John. I need to fry the chips."

He sighed again. Mary reappeared, draping her shawl across her shoulders, and putting her hat on. Her heels tapped on the wooden floors as she approached him near the door, and she lifted her face for a furtive kiss. They did not exchange kisses often outside of their bedroom; he smiled and complied.

Her eyes sparkling, Mary admonished him. "Do not spoil your dinner by eating pickles, Mr. Dickenson!"

"Yes, ma'am," John said in a meek tone, but he, too, was amused. Their house was just across the way, and yet she made sure she always appeared to be a very proper lady.

As the echo of her footsteps faded, John stood near the entrance to the store, distant memories holding him hostage while his broom was neglected.

He and Mary were both English-born. They had immigrated to America some years ago, and settled for a short time in New York. Then, members of their church had decided to move to Taney County and start a self-sufficient community. John and Mary were asked to join the group, managing the store and post office of Eglinton.

It had been a grand experiment, but the man who brought them absconded with all the money one night. Over the next few weeks, members of the commune were horrified to discover no payments had been made on the land or to suppliers. John had been able to keep the store by virtue of Mary's accounting ability, but others of the commune left, starting over once again.

Luck had nothing to do with it, John thought. It was a willingness to work hard that brought success in life. He started sweeping again, thinking of the families he had come to know in recent years.

The rattle of a wagon brought him to the window which opened onto the road between Forsyth and Taney City. Emanuel and Jim Miles were on the seat, Manny handling the reins of the mules. Four mules were hauling the load of wood--that was odd. Hauling wood? Four mules? The wagon slowed, and Jim jumped off, running for the

106 | Vonda Wilson Sheets

front of the store. He stuck his head in the open door, looked around, and found John.

"Hello, Jim. May I help you?"

"Has Ma been in yet, Mr. Dickenson?" young Jim asked.

"She has," answered John. "What are--"

"Good!" With that, Jim wheeled and ran to catch up with the wagon, which Manny had slowed some more, but not brought to a complete stop. John watched the boy jump on the back, and saw Manny twitch the reins, a loud "Giddup" reaching John's ears.

Whatever was the Miles family up to? John wondered. He shook his head, then went to the water barrel in the other corner of the front of the store. Most folks cut their own wood. Maybe someone in Taney City needed a load, he thought as he sipped water from the ladle. The boys might be earning some money.

A horse came through the door, the man on its back ducking to avoid the top. Shocked, John dropped the ladle into the water. The man sat up as the horse halted, and John recognized Frank Taylor.

"Well, howdy, Mr. Dickenson!" Taylor was in a good mood.

Stiffening his shoulders slightly, John decided to pretend having a horse in the middle of his store was nothing unusual.

"Hello, Mr. Taylor," he returned the greeting.

"Good thing I don't want a drink of water," Frank grinned. In dismay, John looked down and to the right, and realized he'd dropped the ladle into the bottom of the water barrel. He closed his eyes, seeking patience.

Returning to his broom meant crossing the doorway behind Taylor and his horse. John went to the back of the store, and appeared to casually lean against the counter near the register. Thinking quickly, he decided to ask Taylor for a payment on his account.

"Just came by to pick up a pair of boots for my brother," Frank said. He took his hat off, and searched the pairs of men's boots hanging from the rafters of the ceiling. John closed his eyes as one boot was yanked down, and Frank pulled his right leg up across the shoulders of the horse to size it against his own foot. The horse didn't like the weight shift, and moved to John's right, almost knocking over a table full of cast-iron skillets and pans. The table rocked, but settled back with a bump.

"Aw, that's too small." Opening his eyes, John watched Frank toss the boot to the floor. The horse didn't like the confines of the display tables in the small room, and was sidestepping nervously. Frank pulled the reins and made the horse go to the other side, where a table full of crockery stood close to the shelves of food preserved in glass jars.

Reaching up again, Frank pulled another boot down and sized it. "That'll do," he nodded in satisfaction, and reached up for the mate. "Jist add 'em to my account."

John cleared his throat. The horse was dangerously close to the crockery table--if he made any sudden movements, it might knock it over. However, since Frank brought up his overdue account--

"I am afraid I cannot do that, Mr. Taylor."

"What?" Frank put his far leg back into the stirrup, and wheeled the horse around to face John. "My brother needs boots. I'm buying them for him. Add 'em to my account."

"Your account is past due. I cannot add your purchase to the account until you have paid your bill." John was slow to anger, but he realized angry was exactly how he felt at this moment.

"Old man, I'll pay you when I'm good and ready. Until then, these boots go on my account."

Seizing inspiration from the Miles boys, John tried placating Frank. "Mr. Taylor, if it is a matter of money, I need some work done. A load of wood, perhaps--"

Frank produced a pistol from his coat pocket, and pointed it straight at John.

"Lemme see if I got this straight. You say I owe you money?"

"You do!" Indignation in John's voice caused Frank's eyes to narrow over the pistol. John didn't think Frank would actually shoot him, so he continued, despite that black hole staring at him.

"Your wife has purchased several items, and neither of you has made a payment since you opened the account. I am forced to close it."

"I'm good fer the money. I'll pay you when I feel like it."

"That, sir, will not do!"

Frank sat back, his tension easing, the pistol resting across his left leg as he regarded John. He was unused to not getting his way; John had never confronted him before. Then Frank's face changed, and he laughed, a short bark.

"Oh, I unnerstan' now. You went to thet Bald Knobber meeting t'other night." Chuckling, he shook his head. "You think thet's gonna amount to sumthin?"

"If you are referring to the Citizen's League for Law and Order, I most certainly do think it will amount to something."

"A bunch of namby-farted outlanders like you, standin' 'round bonfires on top of hills in plain sight and yellin' threats ain't gonna keep me from buyin' my brother a pair of boots! Thet's jist funny." Frank's tone was mocking, "Them Bald Knobbers cain't keep me from doin' whut I want to." The gun returned to his pocket and Frank chortled a little more as he jerked the horse's reins. "Specially if they're like you."

The horse backed up into the table of crockery, then shied as the table went over, knocking jars off the shelves behind it as the crockery smashed. Rearing a little, the animal kept moving as Frank guided it out, ducking again.

Furious, John Dickenson went running for the door, exiting in time to see Mary drop his dinner on the ground as Frank Taylor leaned down and shouted, "Boo!" in her face. She backed up, nearly falling in her haste to get away.

"I will report you to the sheriff!" shouted John, going to help Mary as Frank rode away. The bully sawed on the reins, turned the horse, and came back. John stood in front of Mary, who was shaking.

Frank put the boots in his right hand with his reins, and stuck his left index finger in his ear, rotating it several times. "I cain't believe whut I'm hearin'. Say that again!" he ordered.

"If you leave with those boots, I will have no choice but to report you to the sheriff!" John stood his ground.

"Old man...." Frank leaned down again, his face inches from John's. Horrible breath, mean smile. "Iffen you report me to the sheriff, I'll whip you but good." He backed the horse a few feet, his eyes never leaving John's. "Add these boots to my account."

Frank Taylor rode off, holding the stolen boots where John Dickenson could see. John watched, his mind as empty as his stomach.

He turned toward his wife, who was watching him. "I believe I shall have some of Old Man Johnson's pickles," he told her, then walked back into the store, grabbing a jar of pickles and a handful of soda crackers from the barrel.

Mary followed him in, and groaned at the mess Taylor left behind. Frustrated, she turned to the water barrel, and searched for the ladle.

Settling himself and his meal into a chair by the unlit stove, John propped his feet up on it and saw what Mary was doing. "It is at the bottom," he told her, and bit into a pickle.

Frowning, she said, "I think tea is called for." Without another word, she left again, and he knew she would be gone for a few minutes, bringing a pot of tea when she returned.

John took another bite of pickle, refusing to look at the destruction. He'd earned this pickle, and any others he cared to eat today. After adding the boots, broken crockery, and any other damaged goods to Frank Taylor's account, he would have to ride to Forsyth tomorrow and file a report.

His face brightened. Maybe Mary would let him have another jar of pickles tomorrow night.

Manny and Jim Miles were nearly to their turn-off when a racing horse came from behind. Glancing to see who it was, Jim saw Frank Taylor whip off his hat and hit the gee-side rear mule on the rump as he rode by. The mules all shied to the left, yanking the wagon viciously, and Jim fell out, rolling in the dust. He came up on his feet, shouting at Taylor, who was long gone, wishing he had his rifle in his hand.

Thinking of his rifle, the noise of Manny standing and shouting at the mules, the mules braying and creating a ruckus got through to him, and he ran to the forward mule, grabbing its halter, unmindful of the hooves flying. Mules were damned dangerous when riled, but these animals knew the boys, and began to settle down within a few seconds.

All stood blowing for a few more seconds, then Jim retrieved his hat. Manny was still cooing to the mules while Jim walked around the wagon, picking up the few pieces of wood that had fallen off. He climbed back on the seat, reaching for the canteen and drinking.

"Well, that was a bunch of bullshit," Jim offered the canteen to Manny, who wrapped the reins around his left fist and took a drink himself.

"Better be glad Ma didn't hear you," Manny commented. "You'd be eating vinegar-soaked turnips right now." He took a sip, then eyed the mules. These animals pastured away from the barn, and were half-wild. They appeared to be settled, and he let rein off his fist as he sat down.

"Ma don't have tolerance for cussing," Jim agreed. "But she probably woulda done the same." Looking around, Jim realized Manny had managed to turn the mules into the road home. "Nice work. Didn't even tip off the ground, did you?" He realized he had a few scrapes; his right elbow burned.

"Don't think so. Too much weight."

The boys sat for a minute longer, then Manny started the mules off again, switching the reins to his right hand. "Might see if Pa is done butchering thet cow," Manny said over the rattling of harness and wagon on the dirt road. Jim reached for his rifle under the seat, bringing it to rest on his lap.

Again, a horse came from behind, and Jim whirled, rifle ready to fire as Manny pulled on the reins and grabbed the hand brake with his left hand.

Jim stopped his trigger finger as Uncle Samp shouted, "Whoa!" His horse pranced a little, and he tugged at his own reins, a questioning look on his face.

"Manny drag you behind the wagon?" he asked, noting Jim's appearance.

"No." Adrenaline was coursing through Jim and Manny both, but the boys returned to their seats as Uncle Samp rode up along side the team.

"What happened?" The mules were still excitable, but as Manny clucked, they dug in and began pulling, the slight down slope aiding them. It was a heavy load.

"Frank Taylor spooked 'em," Jim told Uncle Samp.

His uncle nodded in acknowledgement. The boys appeared to have themselves in control so he said, "I'll see you down at the spring," and rode on ahead.

Manny began applying the brake as the wagon rolled down, jouncing in the seat since his hands were busy. He stood as Jim jumped off at the house, yelling at the mules while Jim went in search of Pa.

The second butchering job in a week's time was finished. Pa and Billy were washing up outside the back door, and Ma was wiping the table in the yard down. A large parcel of meat--Jim could tell by the blood seepage--was at the end of the table.

"What happened to you?" Ma had seen Jim first. He must look bad, he thought, for comments on his appearance were becoming common.

"Fell off the wagon when Frank Taylor spooked the mules," he told her. His father and brother turned at the words, Billy tossing his father a towel as both of them looked at Jim.

"Everyone okay?" Pa's eyes narrowed. He still had a splotch of blood on his cheek, which came off when he rubbed it with the towel.

"Yeah, Manny kept the wagon from turning over." Pa nodded in approval, then frowned at the blood on the towel.

"Come eat, Jim," Ma tucked her wash rag into her waistband, and as she entered the house, she told Pa, "I'll send him down after he's cleaned up."

A couple sandwiches of rare beef and a scrubbing from Ma later, Jim rose to leave, feeling a little better. He felt a lot better when he realized Manny would probably forget to tell Ma about the cussing; he certainly wasn't going to tell on himself. Ma's voice halted him as he left the house, and he hesitated, a little concerned, until he realized what she said.

"Take that beef over to Mr. Sims when you deliver the wood," she told her baby. "And watch your mouth."

His mind thought, "Damn!" and his mouth soured, almost puckered, at the thought of vinegar-soaked turnips. Every cuss word uttered on the Miles homestead was met with a whole spoonful of the nasty mess.

"You might not think I know," Ma's voice was amused as Jim had looked back, his face twisted up like he was going to puke. "But I do. In this case, I might have said the same." She laughed.

He relaxed, and picked up the meat parcel. "Thought you might." The mass in his stomach went back down, and Jim set off down the trail to the spring. Along the way, he considered the fact that his mother waited to remind him of turnips until after he was finished eating. That was just mean, he thought.

At the spring, Uncle Samp was firing the smelting log, preparing to melt the lead ore from the vein on his place. The wood which had covered the bottom of the wagon, concealing its load, was tossed all around, and Pa and Billy were setting up to cast bullets. With little breeze coming into the draw, the hot fires had forced the men to shed their shirts.

Manny was exhausted, lying in the shade for a few minutes before he went up to the house. Although his hands were calloused, they appeared swollen from the reins of the mules, which were now unharnessed and grazing quietly.

"Load up that wood," Pa called. "You and your brothers will need to get on over to the Sims place and back before dark."

Grimacing, Jim put the meat parcel on the floorboard, under the seat, and set about throwing the wood back into the wagon. He turned to bend for about the sixth time, muttering under his breath, when his head hit Pa's chest, his eyes landing on Pa's feet.

"Damn."

Pa's voice was as amused as Ma's had been. "You'll load that wood neat, son," he said, not mentioning the cuss word.

"Alright, alright." He jumped up in the back of the wagon, and Pa passed Billy, on his way to help Jim.

"Shit." Very, very quietly, and the taste of turnips screwed his face up again.

Billy handed him two neatly-cut logs, laughing.

"I do that, too," he told his little brother.

"What? Cuss?" Jim had only heard Billy cussing once, some four years ago, when he'd smashed a finger. Ma's retribution had been worse than the throbbing finger; Billy had puked for a long time, between his broken finger and the turnips. It had taken two missed meals before he could eat again.

"Nope, cured of that." Billy smiled ruefully as he handed Jim two more pieces of wood.

"Oh, taste turnips?"

"Yeah." Billy shuddered in friendly misery, then grabbed two more pieces of wood.

"I don't think Pa will tell." Jim wasn't reassured. He noticed two pieces of wood were lying crookedly, and he toed them into place. Then he glanced down at Billy, who was standing with the two logs raised up to him.

"That might help," Billy teased. "He did say 'neat'."

The Miles boys loaded their rifles into the wagon, and left for Mr.

Sims' home, halfway to Swan. Jim had been wondering why Billy was joining them; surely Pa needed him to cast bullets? He asked his brother, who was driving the two mules. Manny was reposing on the back of the wagon, watching the countryside roll past, hat tilted over his face so he could see the road behind without sun glare. His rifle lay casually across his thighs.

"Well, two people would be better," Billy answered, his voice thoughtful. "But Uncle Samp was there. It has more to do with that meeting we went to, I think."

"The Bald Knobbers?" Jim had heard the phrase in the desultory conversation of the afternoon. Uncle Samp's son-in-law had reported that someone in Forsyth had been joking about the meeting.

"Yeah, you heard they wanna arrest the Taylors?" Billy asked.

"What good's thet gonna do?" Jim wondered. "They've bin arrested before, ain't stuck."

"I think thet's the point. It's jist a matter o' time before the Taylors do something Mr. Kinney's men won't like, and they'll go after 'em."

"Oh." Jim considered this. Arresting the Taylors was fairly easy-keeping them in jail long enough to face charges was the problem. They always had bail money, and Jim wondered where their cash came from.

"So....Pa's worried the Bald Knobbers will be out tonight. Ours wasn't the only cow that got carved up."

Two cows in one week hurt a farm family. This last one had been a good milker, too. It would be weeks before one of the other cows would be weaning a calf. He'd been trying to drink coffee in the mornings with his brothers and parents, and adding fresh cream was the only thing that made the bitter brew tolerable.

"Shit." The idea of black coffee, then Ma's cuss concoction, both made his stomach revolt and his face screw up again, as he swallowed bile back down.

"Yeah." Billy didn't like black coffee, either, "Me, too." He clucked to the mules, urging them on.

CHAPTER 14
April 8, 1885 - Wednesday
Frank & Tubal Taylor

Tubal Taylor was asleep when he heard gravel, acorns, and leaves sliding down the hill, announcing the arrival of a visitor. His bed, in the lee of a limestone outcropping which overlooked the creek-fed pool below, wasn't particular comfortable. He'd finished the contents of his flask before he was able to doze off, and now some fool was looking for him. He was cold, but reached through the darkness for his gun....he had no idea who was coming at this time of the night. He pulled his blanket around him and waited.

Flickers from a torch were followed by a gruff oath; Tubal recognized his brother's voice, and relaxed. Then Frank dropped down into the narrow gulch, and looked for Tubal.

"Hey! Stop that!" Tubal howled when Frank's torch found his face. He covered his eyes against the brightness. It had been dark for hours. The walls of the ravine were so steep, light faded early and came late.

"Whyn't you got a fire?" Frank asked.

"Didn't want anyone to see the smoke," Tubal answered from behind his hands.

Frank snorted, then saw the small pile of wood stored nearby. "Well, I'm building one. It's cold, and the torch will be out soon. I forgot my flint," he added, as his actions followed his words. He laid the torch on the wood piled inside the rock circle, and it was soon aflame.

Tubal had simply curled back up in his blankets while Frank started the fire. He was tired--he'd been out the night before, getting tongue meat to make his favorite meal. It took a lot of cow tongues to fill him up, but he still had some of the stewed meat left. Frank was burrowing around, and found the stew pot, which he put next to the fire.

"Hey, thet's mine!" Tubal exclaimed. "It took me all night to get those tongues!"

"Yeah, I heard about it. Dammit, Tubal, you've got everybody all upset. Couldn't you at least have let the Garretts alone?"

"I was hungry for tongue stew. I didn't pay no 'tention to whose cow I cut up." Tubal sat up, rolling his head to crack his neck, and stretched. The fire did feel good. As he blinked in the light, he wondered--

"Why're you here? Jennie kick you out?"

Frank was pissed. No doubt about it, then. "Damn, Frank, you ain't been married six months probly. She said she was gonna kick you out if you didn't fix things."

Tubal wasn't smart. He knew that. Frank watched out for him, but Frank was gone a lot, down to Arkansas, where he kept a still and ran moonshine. It was a small operation, but it kept money in Frank's pocket. And he was considering moving his still here, to this small hollow with a spring that fed Swan Creek. Only problem was, the land didn't belong to the Taylor brothers.

Frank had made the steep descent of well over one hundred feet with his saddlebags over his shoulder, a torch in his left hand, and grabbing saplings with his right when he needed to. It was difficult to do in the daylight--at night, it was perilous. No soft landing.

At the moment, Frank's breathing was calming, and he prodded the pot of tongue stew closer to the fire. Tubal's mule moved closer to the fire, too. He'd brought the mule down the other side of the hill, an easier descent, then walked and swam her through the waters of the creek until they reached the draw.

Nodding at Molly, but pushing her from the fire, he asked Tubal, "Did you find your boot?"

"Huh. Yeah. She'd chewed the top off."

Shaking his head, Frank reached for his saddlebags, and pulled out a pair of boots, price tag still attached. "This is the last pair I'm buying you until next year," he told Tubal. "Iffen you don't keep your boots on when you're sleeping, you'll go barefoot when she gets 'em."

"Aw, Frank, y'know I hate wearin' boots when I'm sleepin'. I like to wiggle my toes." As if to prove it, Tubal stuck a bare foot out toward the fire, long toes waving. That felt so good, he did the same with his other foot.

Frank had pulled his plate and a spoon out of one of his saddlebags as well. In the midst of spooning some stew onto his plate, he looked at Tubal, whose eyes were closed in bliss. Taking a deep breath, he held it in his cheeks, letting the air out slowly.

The brothers were in their mid-twenties. Born in Kentucky,

branches of their family had moved to southern Missouri after the War, continuing to survive on small farms and outside jobs. Although their father had died the year before, their mother was still alive. They took care of their mother's livestock, but neither young man had a taste for farming.

Frank pondered this while he ate. His father had made him promise when he was quite young to always look out for Tubal, who was touched in the head. He wasn't totally simple, Frank knew--but his brother had no moral compass, no sense of when he had gone too far. He could not read, write, or count. Frank could, given enough time. He grunted.

"Good stew," he said, grudgingly.

Somehow, Tubal could cook. Matilda Taylor didn't like to cook, so her food was simple and plain. At a very young age, Tubal had made suggestions which drove their mother mad, and she finally told him, "Look, if you wanna fix it, go right ahead." Since then, every meal Tubal cooked had been so good, no one missed one if they could help it.

This tongue stew was a relatively new dish Tubal had concocted. More than meat and broth, he put some flavoring in that no one could identify, and Tubal wasn't telling. It was addictive, too. Problem was, he wouldn't use meat other than cow tongues for it. There were only so many cows out there.

So when Tubal Taylor got a yen for tongue stew, cows lost their tongue. Not just Taylor cows--any cows Tubal came across.

"Why're you here?" Tubal asked again, now that Frank was carefully scraping the last of the stew from his plate. A well-fed Frank was easier to talk to.

Frank tossed his plate over by his bags, and pursed his mouth. Problems were mounting up.

From a young age, he and Tubal had roamed the hills, helping themselves to whatever they needed. As they grew older, they were gone from home for longer periods, until Tubal was no longer in the habit of sleeping under a roof, except for winter. Tubal had never been particularly civilized, Frank thought; and now, he, too, was more comfortable outside.

But his mother had told him to get married. She was worried. So Frank had made a serious attempt to settle down, marrying Jennie Garrett and building a cabin for her. In the past year or so, he went

Absolution | 117

through all the things a "civilized" man did, putting in crops, getting married, coming home most nights. He only went down to Marion County once or twice a month, staying long enough to make a batch of moonshine when he had to. He smiled. That was one of Tubal's good receets, too.

Elijah ran the still when Frank couldn't be there. Issues arose over money when Elijah made the shine, so Frank was thinking about moving his still here. He didn't mind paying Lige to run the still; what Frank minded was Lige keeping a cut of the profits.

Jennie was alright. He liked her, but she had notions of what a man should and shouldn't do that were higher than even his mother's. He'd been reluctant to open an account at Dickenson's store, but she'd asked, and even just weeks into the marriage, he knew he was not going to be a good husband. So he did it.

As for paying for it, that wasn't an issue, either, really. He'd just forgotten.

In trying to be civilized, yet keep Tubal from getting himself shot, something in Frank had snapped yesterday. Everywhere he turned, someone was telling him what to do. Except Tubal.

When it was just the two of them, Tubal was restful for Frank. But make an attempt to go into town for supplies, or to have a drink at a saloon with Tubal, things went crazy. Somehow, being around more than one person was too much for Tubal. And some people goaded Tubal, not realizing he wasn't just simple--he was insane.

Insane. Frank backed off that thought almost immediately.

Poking at the fire, Frank figured he was thinking too much tonight. Tubal was waiting patiently for an answer to his question.

"Jennie's mad. After I got your boots yesterday, she went to the store and Ol' Dickenson told her she couldn't charge anything else." That had been part of the reason she was mad. Frank conveniently forgot that the other part of why Jennie was mad was that he'd ridden his horse into the store, and broken a few things. "Her dad came by and told me off for you cutting up one of his cows, too."

"Well, thet ain't right." Tubal was very protective of Frank. "You din't do it."

Frank chuckled, although there was no mirth in it. He himself had only a vague notion of "a civilized life," but Tubal had none at all. And folks held him responsible for Tubal's actions.

"Tube....I guess there's a warrant out fer your arrest."

"Why?"

"Someone saw you cuttin' up."

"Well, hell." Tubal threw his blankets off, and stood, stretching and yawning. "Guess I'll go in and let Toney arrest me." He looked down at Frank. "You can come git me out."

Frank nodded as Tubal again rolled himself up in his blankets. "Yeah, that'll work. I have to go back to the house, fix things with Jennie, but I'll be there."

Within seconds, Tubal was snoring softly. Frank listened to the soothing sound and watched the fire.

It was getting a little warm in Taney County, he mused. Instead of moving his still here, maybe he and Tubal should just pack up and go west, out to one of those big ranches, where Tubal could cook and he could work horses. Jennie could come along, and for a few minutes, he envisioned a somewhat normal life. Was that freedom?

He glanced down at Tubal's face, and the dream faded. He felt a tightening in his chest.

Frank Taylor didn't know what to do, but the life he was living now wasn't free.

He woke to the sound of his horse neighing from above the ravine. The fire was out--he noted Tubal had poured water on it, dammit--and Tubal and his mule were gone. The sun was up, but it hadn't been for long.

The horse neighed again. He quickly rolled his blankets up, swished water from the spring on his face, and looked up the hillside while he rubbed his whiskers and eyes with both hands. A helluva climb first thing in the morning.

Grabbing saplings and branches, Frank took some time to get up to the horse, his boots scrabbling for purchase in the leaf mold. Dang, it was rough here....which was why it was a good place for Tubal to stay. No one could find him easily.

The gelding wasn't his favorite horse, and Frank thought about that as he untangled it from the brush and a loose piece of barbed wire. His favorite horse was gonna foal in a few days, and he didn't want to ride her. This horse was about as smart as Tubal, he told himself as he examined the cuts on its knees. Frank had hobbled it, so it could move about, and the critter had fallen somehow.

Well, this day was not starting well.

Absolution | 119

He had to go home for several reasons--to make things right with Jennie, change clothes, pull some money from his hiding place to bail Tubal out of jail, and now to doctor the horse.

Riding was out of the question. He grabbed the reins, and set off to walk. There were some situations where even cussing didn't help.

His father-in-law's wagon was in his front yard. From the time he rounded the bend in the road, he had seen his wife and her dad carrying things from his house to the wagon twice.

The limping horse could not move any faster, and there was a third trip by the time he approached his cabin and dropped the reins.

Dad Garrett turned to halt Frank. "You kin jist stay where you are," he said. "She's coming home with me."

By God, Frank had tried. "Jennie…" he sighed.

"Deserves better than you," Garrett said. "You aren't home, you don't pay your bills, and you'd rather run with that brother of yours."

There was no defense to that. Frank knew it to be the truth. "I forgot about Ol' Dickenson," he told Dad. "I ain't never had an account before."

Dad shook his head, searching Frank's face. He'd let his daughter marry Frank upon several conditions, thinking there was a good man inside Frank Taylor's body somewhere. But damn if he could see it now. Dirty and unkempt were only two of the many problems he had with Frank Taylor.

"You're damned lucky there's no baby. Else it'd git nasty," assured Garrett. "As it is, she'll leave in peace, and you'll leave her alone."

Frank nodded. He had no choice.

Jennie came out with a bag of clothing, and eyed Frank as she said, "That's the last of it, Dad." Frank could not read the expression on her face--he really didn't know her that well--and she added, "I'm only keeping' what I brought, Frank."

He didn't move as she climbed up on the wagon seat, pulling her bonnet over her face. A sound something like a sob may have come from her--it was hard to tell, as Dad Garrett climbed up as well.

She didn't say good-bye, and neither did Dad. He simply drove off, Jennie's mare tied to the gate of the wagon. Neither of them looked back.

The gelding had been smart enough to go into the horse shed on its own, and Frank followed it slowly. He took off the saddle and bridle, rubbed the horse down, and put a salve on its knees. His mare, heavy with foal, had watched the proceedings with interest, and butted Frank playfully as he fed the horses.

The problem of a horse to ride into Forsyth kept him from paying a great deal of attention to the shortness of his breath. He walked into the empty cabin--no, it hadn't been home--and found part of a loaf of bread on the table. Wolfing the bread down, he decided to ride his big mule. It had been a while since Red had been ridden, but the way he felt now, Ol' Red could mess with him all he wanted to.

෨ ෪

John Dickenson was in Forsyth to file a report against Frank Taylor.

He had not eaten the entire jar of pickles yesterday. Mary had pounced on it, taking it from him after Jennie Taylor had come in for supplies, and he had to turn her away. He didn't like doing it; Jennie was a pleasant young woman who was trying to make a man of Frank Taylor. It didn't seem to be working.

"Enough." Mary was firm. He didn't protest, merely returned to cleaning up the mess left behind by Frank. He wasn't even angry anymore. But as the afternoon wore into evening, Mary's list of damaged goods grew, and John resolved to follow Captain Kinney's advice.

Filing a report with the sheriff was the first step.

However, James K. Polk McHaffie was not in the sheriff's office when John Dickenson walked in.

The first thing John saw was his boots, the ones Frank Taylor stole, on Tubal Taylor's feet, which were propped up on the sheriff's desk. Anger returned in full force when John espied the price tag dangling from the boot strap.

"My boots!"

The two deputies were also sitting with their feet propped up. At John's outburst, Toney put his feet on the floor, assumed a professional demeanor, and politely asked, "May I help you, Mr.

Dickenson?"

"Those are my boots! Frank Taylor stole them from my store yesterday! The price tag is still on them!"

Toney raised his eyebrows, and glanced over at Tubal. Casually, Deputy Yeary dropped his feet, leaned over, and jerked the price tag off. Tubal grinned as Yeary dropped the tag on the floor, and resumed his relaxed position.

"I want to see the sheriff!"

"He's transporting a prisoner to Springfield," Toney replied. "Should be back tomorrow morning."

"Then I shall file a report for theft with you, Mr. Toney," John retorted.

Almost wearily, Toney opened the top right drawer of the desk, pulled out a form, and set it squarely on the desktop, in front of John. Then he moved the inkwell and a tin cup holding a selection of pens next to the form.

"You want me to fill it out?" Dickenson was incredulous.

"If you want to file the report, you can fill it out," Toney responded. Some kind of signal sent Yeary's feet back to the floor.

"I need some tobacco," Yeary rose, and stretched. "Come with me, Tubal."

Tubal also rose, his eyes fixed on John Dickenson. Neither young man spoke further as they left the building.

Toney rose, pulled a chair around to the front of the desk, indicating that John should sit and write. Exasperated, John nodded, and sat down with a dogged expression on his face. He watched Toney return to his own seat.

"Why is Tubal Taylor here?" asked John.

"He's under arrest for cattle mutilation," answered Toney. "He's waiting for Frank to bail him out."

John's eyebrows rose. "Should he not be locked up then?" he asked, nodding toward the prisoner cell behind Toney.

Toney's head bent slightly down and sideways as he peered at Mr. Dickenson. "Tubal's a special case."

"What does that mean?"

"It means I don't want to hear him whining while he's waiting for Frank," Toney's answer was smooth. "Frank always shows up and bails him out. I learned a long time ago that Tubal doesn't do well in the cage."

122 | Vonda Wilson Sheets

"But if he deserves--"

"Mr. Dickenson, you have a report in front of you." Irritation and impatience began to come through in Toney's voice as he sat back in his chair, tipping the front up. "Do you want to file it or not?"

"Certainly." John chose a pen from the cup, and dipped it in the inkwell. His eyes still questioning the deputy's actions, he began to fill in the pre-printed form. This was enough of a novelty that his attention diverted for a few minutes, and there was no conversation. But halfway down the page, John raised his head and looked at Toney, who was looking out the door of the office, alert....tense?

"Are you expecting someone?" John asked.

The deputy's smile was grim. "Tubal's slow, but sooner or later, he'll figure out you're filing a theft report against his brother. You don't want to be here when he comes back."

Deputy Yeary had quite understood his peer's silent order to get Tubal outside. Tubal didn't always carry a gun, but he would have a couple knives on his person, Yeary thought.

"I don' like bein' in town today," Tubal was peering around, watching people. The atmosphere was tense. People were walking purposefully, not spending much time getting from one building to another.

On the other hand, Yeary was deliberately slow in pace. He, too, was tense; Tubal could feel it.

"Whut?" Tubal asked.

"The Bald Knobbers visited last night," Yeary answered.

"Them men thet are building signal fires?" Tubal asked. Isolated as he was most of the time, Tubal didn't keep up on gossip, Yeary realized.

"Yeah."

A few more paces; Yeary was thinking back to the days when he and the Taylor brothers ran around together, sleeping in the woods, swimming, hunting. Those had been fairly carefree days and nights, as long as the boys got their home chores done.

Tubal asked, "Whut does the Bald Knobbers hev to do with this?" He waved a hand at their surroundings.

Yeary thought he was used to Tubal's mental processes--or the lack of them--but something had changed. His head nodded as he understood that maybe he had grown up, whereas the Taylors hadn't.

Or couldn't.

The town square was not a big one; they had walked three sides, and Yeary decided he may as well go into Everett's store and get the tobacco he needed, but first things first.

He indicated a bench on the store's wooden sidewalk, and he and Tubal both sat down.

"Tubal, the Bald Knobbers are wantin' to clean up the county," he began. "Do you understand?"

All Yeary got was a blank look of incomprehension.

"Things have gone a little wild," Yeary tried to take a different path. "Folks don't want to come into Forsyth because they don't know if you and Frank are going to be here."

"We're jist havin' fun," Tubal protested.

"Well...." Yeary pondered this. "Mebbe your definition of fun is diff'rent from most folks'."

"We havn't hurt nobody," Tubal was upset, Yeary saw.

"Tube, don't you think takin' a cow tongue is hurtin' someone?" he asked.

"I made stew."

Yeary took a deep breath, exhaled. His uncle JJ had been clear in explaining what the Bald Knobbers planned to do. But the Taylors had been friends of his for a long time.

"Tubal, you and Frank can't keep doing as you've been doing. Or you're gonna end up in jail. Mebbe even the state pen."

Couldn't get any more clear than that, Yeary thought. "I'll be right back."

When he came out with his tobacco, Yeary wasn't surprised to see the panicked expression on Tubal's face. He'd understood.

"Liash, I can't 'bide bein' locked up." He looked ready to bolt. That would not do today, the deputy thought. He took Tubal by the arm, raised him to his feet, and they moved on, back toward the jail.

"I know that," Elias Yeary assured Tubal. "But when a man does something wrong, that's what usually happens."

"Not here." Tubal was stubborn.

Yeary stopped walking, grabbing Tubal by the arm. "Things are going to change, Tubal. People have to change with the times."

Tubal stood quite still, trying to grasp everything. Yeary glanced over toward the jail, his back toward the street. Toney and Dickenson

124 | Vonda Wilson Sheets

were standing in front of the jail, talking. In the noise of the town, Yeary did not hear Frank Taylor ride up behind him.

"There you are. Let's get this taken care of."

Hearing Frank, Yeary dropped Tubal's arm, which proved to be a mistake. A shout from Dickenson, and Deputy Toney and Dickenson were running in their direction. Frank was dismounting when his brother pushed him away, jumping on Ol' Red and lashing the mule, turning him east.

"What the hell? TUBAL!" Frank roared. He ran out in the street, watching Tubal ride away.

"Arrest him!" Dickenson was demanding.

Frank turned to see John Dickenson flanked by deputies Toney and Yeary. Yeary's face bore an expression that Frank could not read; however, he banked on their childhood friendship. Ignoring Toney's voice remonstrating with Dickenson, he asked Yeary, "Mind telling me what the hell's goin' on?"

"Frank." Yeary could hear Dickenson's frustration and anger. An idea came to him that would shut the noise off.

"You're under arrest for aiding and abetting the escape of a prisoner."

Elias Yeary stepped off the sidewalk, to stand face-to-face with Frank, whose features underwent an almost comical change. "Goin' to come peaceably?" his old friend asked. And Frank Taylor was escorted to jail. His bad day had just gotten considerably worse.

John Dickenson was sitting on the bench across from the jail. Frank Taylor was arrested, but not on the basis of the report he had quickly filled out. Deputy Toney had assured him the report would be given to the prosecutor, who would then file charges as he saw fit. John had to trust the process.

After a half-hour of patiently watching the jail, Taylor had not come out, so John rose, assuming Frank would be confined. He walked to his horse, which was still at the jail's post, when footsteps and a low, mean voice reached his ears.

"Old man, I promised you trouble iffen you visited the sheriff's office," Frank Taylor stood close.

John stiffened, but stepped up into his saddle. Seating himself, he replied calmly, "You owe me money."

Frank snorted. "It's not gonna matter. Trust me." And he stalked off.

The deputies were nowhere in sight, John saw. Apparently, Frank made his bail, and the idea of money in Taylor's pocket made peace-loving John Dickenson see red. He backed his horse up, and left for home, wondering if he was going to have to start carrying a gun.

CHAPTER 15
April 8 & 9, 1885 - Wednesday/Thursday
Frank Taylor Goes Crazy

Frank Taylor's rented horse wasn't suited for miles of hard galloping. He was forced to slow down on his way to Tubal's hollow, and the delay was not increasing the likelihood of rational thought.

Images of his day--his life --were passing through his mind in random order. Helpless before devotion and duty to his insane brother, he couldn't fight off the murky chills of bedlam in his own brain. His hands shook on the reins; his eyes did not see the road.

It was well after dark when he rode into his mother's barn. He turned the rented horse loose in the pasture and saddled his brother's horse.

"Why are you taking William's horse?" Matilda entered the barn, carrying a lantern that lighted her son's actions.

"Leaving." He sprang up in the saddle.

"Where you goin'?" Matilda didn't know what had been going on the past couple of days, obviously. She didn't get out much, or else the rest of the family wasn't telling her any gossip.

Frank didn't care. His parents had forced him to take care of Tubal all his life, and look where it got him. "I'm gonna kill Tubal."

"Frank! You can't do that!" His mother was horrified.

"Yeah? Watch me." And he left.

William's horse was smarter than his own gelding, but Frank still tied the reins to a fence post above the hollow.

He scrabbled down the hill, faster than he ever had, fury driving him, making him heedless of scratches and bruises. They didn't matter.

Frank landed loudly on the rock overhang, and then leaped down by the fire below. His senses took no note of the surroundings, all squarely focused on Tubal, who was putting another log on the fire.

Roaring, he leapt for Tubal's throat, his hands instantly putting pressure on the vital spots. Tubal struggled, the wood in his hand hitting Frank on the back, but as he began choking, lying on the ground, he dropped the wood and tried to knock Frank off. His eyes went unfocused quickly, though, and he was fainting when Frank was pulled away by Elijah Sublette.

"What the fuck do you think you're doing, Frank?" Keeping his body between the brothers, Lige had a hard time getting Frank away. He could hear Tubal gasping, but took no time to look. He had never seen Frank's eyes so wild.

"Frank--" Tubal's voice was rough.

Frank continued to struggle against Lige. "Let me at 'im!" he growled. "I'm gonna kill him!"

"You can't do that!" Lige was alarmed. The brothers had fought before, but this was something different.

"I--can--and--I--will!" Frank was grunting, and Lige was forced to keep his attention on his feet, which Frank was stomping on, carrying the both of them back toward Tubal.

Tubal scrambled to his bare feet, crouching to defend himself. "I'm sorry I left you in town, Frank!" he said, panic in his voice. "I cuddint help myself! Liash told me 'bout them Bald Knobbers!"

Frank went still. Lige didn't let go.

"He said they wanted to lock me up, Frank! I can't get locked up!"

Lige didn't trust the rational tone in Frank's voice. "The Bald Knobbers?" Frank's body was still tensed; Lige didn't relax, either.

"You left me to get arrested because of a bunch of outlanders?"

"I said I was sorry!" Pleading.

"I told Ol' Man Dickenson not file a report on me cuz of your boots," Fresh rage tore at Frank's voice. "He did it anyway." He sprung to leap over Lige, which gave Lige the opportunity to grab Frank's ankle and toss him to the ground. Tubal jumped backward over the fire, scorching one of his feet, and he howled.

"Owwwwwww! I said I was sorry!"

Frank watched from his position on the ground; not much choice, as Lige's big foot was planted square on Frank's chest. No sympathy on Frank's face as he watched Tubal leap about in pain.

"Where the fuck are those boots?" The words were as menacing as the tone in Frank's voice.

Tubal sat down on the ground, nursing his injured foot. His left hand gestured toward the bedding close to where Frank and Lige were. "I promised to take care, and I did," Tubal muttered.

Lige let Frank sit up to see the new boots, which had been placed with precise care in the center of the made-up pallet.

A shudder tore through Frank, and he pulled in a breath with great difficulty. His fists clenched and unclenched, and he began to massage his hands. At this, Lige himself relaxed.

"He can't help it," Lige reminded Frank.

His eyes closed, Frank replied, "I know. But I can."

The idea of leaving Taney County was the only bright thread in the knot of Frank's mind.

Lige had brought news that the still had been destroyed, and upon hearing this, Frank gave up.

He would take Tubal and go.

But first, he had to make Dickenson pay for forcing his hand.

CHAPTER 16
April 9, 1885 - Tuesday - Rage

The three of them left Tubal's hollow before dawn. It was raining.

They had no supplies, which bothered Frank very little. He was going to get what they needed at Dickenson's store.

No thoughts. None at all. No regrets at leaving his widowed mother and other siblings. Frank Taylor considered his responsibility to his family stopped with taking care of Tubal. The only way he knew to do that was to go west. William's horse would cover some of the debt he felt his family owed him.

He did not tell Lige or Tubal of his plans. In the rain, there was no conversation at all.

Dickenson was on the porch of his store, watching as the three wet men rode up. The grey light of the rainy morning had not deterred him from drinking his tea and making mental lists of things to accomplish that day. Frank could see the man tense up when he saw who was arriving.

"Howdy, Dickenson." Terse.

He quickly dismounted, walked the few steps necessary, pulled his gun from under his coat, and grabbed John Dickenson by the jaw. "I need some supplies," he said pleasantly, and then brought the gun up, shooting Dickenson through the head. Releasing his victim, he watched in silence as the man fell to the wooden floor. Almost as an afterthought, he fired another bullet into Dickenson's writhing body, and the motion ceased.

Tubal and Lige had watched, dumbfounded.

Frank walked back to his horse, grabbed his empty saddle bags, and turned to walk back into the store. Inside, he began to fill the bags with the supplies they would need. Coffee, flour...

Impatience quickened his movements. Why did Lige at least not understand what he was doing? He forgot that he hadn't told Lige.

Dickenson's wife had come screaming from their house. "Shoot her!" Frank ordered.

Several shots rang out, and he heard nothing else but Mary Dickenson's body falling, too.

Coming out, he noted she had reached her husband before being

130 | Vonda Wilson Sheets

shot. Quickly, he threw the saddle bags on his horse, and mounted. Tubal and Lige were both still, although they had managed to do as he told them.

"C'mon!" he backed, and turned west.

"Are they dead?" Lige asked. He had recovered and was putting his gun back under his coat.

"That's what we came fer, iddint it?" Frank spoke mockingly. "Let's go."

Things went smoothly for about three miles, as Frank led Lige and Tubal on the road south and west toward Forsyth. Tubal was used to blindly following Frank, but Lige was not.

The rain was coming down in buckets, and the three men pulled to a stop under a large, leafy oak. The road to Protem veered off to the left; Lige stared at it, then broke the silence.

"You have a plan?"

"Injun Territoy. Mebbe Texas." A lightning bolt, thunder crashing.

Tubal howled, taking Frank by surprise. "Ma! I dint say goodbye!"

"Did it fer you last night. Don't worry--she knew we wuz goin'." It was imperative to keep Tubal calm. He yelled over the storm.

Elijah Sublett was shaking his head. "Can't leave today."

"Why the hell not? You jist killed a woman!"

Lige obviously wanted to be anywhere but with Frank and Tubal Taylor at this moment. "I dint bring things we'll need," he shouted back at Frank. "Money. My horses."

"I got money," Frank yelled back. The center of the storm was right above them, thunder repeatedly rolling.

Lige kept shaking his head. "You go on. I'll catch you up by Joplin!"

Enraged, Frank nudged his horse close to Lige. "I don't believe you!"

"Then go back to the holler, and I'll meet you there in a few days!"

Tubal had been looking back toward Dickens and Taney City. "Frank!" he reached over and grabbed his brother's reins.

The horse shied, another bolt of lightning, and Frank was hard-

Absolution | 131

pressed to keep control of the situation. When he finally looked at Tubal's face, the panic there was enough to let Lige leave.

"Alright, alright. You got a week. We'll leave without you iffen you don't show," Frank told Lige. Tubal would be stirred up for months if he didn't get to say good-bye to their mother; that was not an option, Frank saw.

Nothing else needed to be said. The Taylor brothers watched Elijah Sublett ride south, back toward Arkansas, and Frank's shoulders slumped. He hoped Lige was coming back.

Tubal led the way down to the creek on his mule, Frank following on William's horse. Both men were soaked, so the swim around the bluff on their mounts didn't do much except make Frank grab the saddlebags and hold them high.

His mind was blessedly empty as he and Tubal reached their shelter, unloading the horses and spreading their coats and clothes out to dry. Tubal started another fire, just inside the wall of water pouring off the overhang. As the flames caught and grew higher, Frank sat motionless, his knees to his chest, arms around his legs. He didn't even notice when Tubal put a wool blanket around his bare shoulders, wrapping and tucking him tight against the chill.

Whistling, Tubal began mixing biscuits, and set them to bake in his lidded pot. He had donned a pair of old buckskin pants, but was otherwise naked. As he knelt to start frying some bacon Lige had brought the night before, Frank noted Tubal's bare feet.

Jerking his head to the left, he saw he was too late. Molly had one of Tubal's boots in her mouth, chewing on the top, the sole flapping with each chomp.

He moved forward, gently, so gently, taking the bacon from Tubal.

"Go get your boots," he said. And began laying the strips of meat in the skillet.

It rained, poured, for three days.

Frank Taylor didn't know what he was waiting for; the emptiness in his mind continued. Tubal didn't say much, either; storms like this made him shut down, protected from anything except the possibility of flooding from the little pool which had risen a great deal.

On the fourth morning, they were awakened by the sound of no rain.

CHAPTER 17
April 13, 1885 - Tuesday
Step it up a notch, Frank

A day of no rain. The brothers watched the spring-fed pool in their ravine rise, nearly to their shelter. They slept and when mood suited, ate. The water began going down as the evening fell.

If Lige was coming back, he should be arriving any time, Frank figured. If the river hadn't flooded all the roads. Too many "ifs," Frank thought. He brooded while he waited. The sense of freedom he'd felt had gone. He was starting to feel trapped, but could not discuss this with his brother.

Tubal handed him a couple of dry biscuits and some sassafras tea as Frank was considering rolling up in his blankets again.

"I gotta go check my snares," Tubal told his brother. "We're outta meat." With that, he sat, pulled his boots on, made sure his knives were in place, and set off for the woods in the dark.

Frank watched the little fire Tubal had built from the last of the dry wood, and let the night into his even darker thoughts. The running water, vague noises of animal movement, the new-leafed trees swaying in the breeze--ordinarily, he didn't really hear these sounds, as they were a part of life. Tonight, they seemed to bore into his skin, beat on his bones.

He had no idea how much time passed. The fire was all but out when Tubal returned, laden with a bundle of wet wood and some rabbits. Neither man spoke, and Frank roused enough to help his brother clean and skin the animals.

The wood was too wet to light; carefully, he arranged it over and around the still-warm embers in the circle. The lid of the Dutch oven clanked discordantly after Tubal put the meat in it to keep.

Tubal was able to fall asleep a short time later. Frank's mind continued its buzzing, but as dawn began, he, too, slept.

Frank and Tubal heard horses. A lot of them. First on one side of their hiding place, then the other. Tubal would want breakfast, Frank knew, but he indicated silence as he unrolled from his blankets and crawled for the mule and his horse. He froze when Molly brayed a short time after the second group left.

Absolution | 133

He was going to shoot that fucking mule, he decided as he grabbed her nostrils, pinching them. He did the same with the horse.

Tense moments. Tubal's eyes were on his face, both of them listening for anyone returning.

Someone was coming around the bluff. They could hear a horse swimming--no, it was two horses. Very brave, thought Frank, considering the roiling waters of the creek, and he reached for his rifle, which he'd managed to dry out over the fire in the past days.

The fire was out now. Unless the mule gave them away--and he didn't think anyone could've heard Molly over the clatter of the group--no one could tell he and Tubal were here.

Aiming his rifle at the spot where the visitors would appear, he let off a shot when he saw movement. It ricocheted off the outcrop.

"Hey, the cave!"

It was Elijah. Astonished, Frank lowered the rifle.

"C'mon up!" Tubal called. A smile was on his face.

Lige Sublett was riding the same horse he'd left on, the horse behind him bearing a tarped burden. Both horses appeared exhausted. Lige himself was mud-covered and wet. He stiffly dismounted, dropping the reins to the ground, and stretched, groaning.

"Managed to avoid your vigilantes," he announced. He rolled his head, neck bones popping. The sound made Frank uncomfortable. He massaged the back of his own neck, standing and stretching as well.

"Vigilantes?"

"Well, they ain't a posse," Lige said. "No one had a badge on."

"Who they lookin' fer?" Tubal asked.

Lige stared at Tubal, then over at Frank. "You." He gave Frank a puzzled look.

Frank shrugged. "We'll leave tonight."

Lige raised his hand in a halting gesture. "Might wanna wait, Frank. Every bald around seems to have a bonfire on it. They'll ride until they find you."

Tubal was ignoring the conversation. He'd gone to the pack horse, pulled off the tarp, and was untying the knots holding the canvas bags on. "Any food in here?" he asked Lige.

"Yep," came the response, and Lige moved to help. "But you might not want a fire," he told Tubal.

They had eaten cold jelly sandwiches, drinking shine. Lige had rescued a few bottles from the wreckage of the still. He didn't know who had found it.

"Don't matter now," Frank said, taking a swig, rolling it in his mouth, feeling the smooth fire go down to his belly, warming him. "We're goin' west."

They were soon drowsy. The sun was making steam rise, and Frank was relaxing in the warmth. Snores emitted from Tubal and Lige both, and he closed his eyes. For just a little while, he would rest. His sleep had been filled with broken fragments of his life, and he was exhausted. Maybe he wouldn't dream…

William Taylor had known for some time where Tubal's hollow was. He was on a duty mission--Matilda had made him leave the farm to search Frank and Tubal out, tell them the news.

As far as he was concerned, it was not his problem, but he understood mothers were different. Tubal had been born slow and crazy, and he felt his parents had indulged his brother in his differences. He had certainly squirmed at school, when the other kids made fun of Tubal, distancing himself from Frank as well. Frank had fought the other kids on Tubal's behalf until their parents kept Tubal home.

He ignored the fact that their father had made Frank responsible for Tubal, or that he himself had eaten many meals Tubal made. It wasn't that he didn't care, he told himself as he looked down the steep hillside. No, he was smart enough not to feel guilty that Frank's life was not his own; that their mother had nearly died giving birth to the blue baby named for her father after being resuscitated; that Tubal had obviously suffered some kind of damage during birth. He did care--just not much.

Plus, he was giving up a horse. Even that was working in his favor, he congratulated himself. He'd gone after Frank's livestock the day of the Dickenson shooting, and hauled or led every single animal on the neglected homestead to Ma's--now his--farm. Frank's prized mare had been slowly, so slowly, walked into his own barn, a stall waiting for her.

She'd given birth to a good-looking colt last night. William was forced to acknowledge Frank did have excellent taste in horses, as he grabbed tree branches and saplings with his calloused hands, working his way down the hill.

He made it to the bottom without hearing anything from his brothers. Landing lightly on the small shelf below the outcrop, his upper lip curled in distaste. He could smell moonshine, and the empty bottle near Frank's hand was the source. Approaching Frank carefully, he picked the bottle up and sniffed--his right brow raised. Tubal's recipe. Looking around, he didn't see any still equipment, but this stuff had been made somewhere.

Elijah Sublett rolled over, talking in his sleep. Tubal was curled up in a ball. What to do?

William debated several ideas.

He could leave. They'd never know he'd been here. But there was his mother to consider.

He could start a fire, but there appeared to be no dry wood under the rock outcrop. The smoke would possibly bring the vigilantes, too, and he certainly didn't want to be around if that happened. He had refused to bring supplies for his brothers, although Ma had wanted him to; it wouldn't do to look as if he was aiding his brothers when they were being hunted.

The third option was the simplest. "Frank!"

No response.

"Frank!" He kneeled to shake Frank. Shaking didn't work.

Grabbing the empty Dutch oven from the fire pit, he climbed down to the pool and filled it with water.

Which one to throw it on? The answer to that was simple.

Tubal yowled as the cold water soaked him, and as William had known would happen, both Frank and Lige jumped to sitting positions, rubbing their faces and looking around for the source of the noise.

"Willie? Why'd you go and do thet fer?" Tubal jumped to his feet, shaking like a big dog. "That's cold!"

"William?" Lige rubbed his eyes, peered at the younger Taylor brother. Sure enough. Then he glanced over at Tubal, who was leaping about, flapping his arms.

It was a funny sight, and William burst out laughing. Lige joined him.

"Shet up!" Frank obviously didn't share their sense of humor. "You've always picked on him."

136 | Vonda Wilson Sheets

"You wouldn't wake up!" William defended himself. Lige had gone quiet immediately, drink-taken as he was. He didn't mess with Tubal or Frank like William did.

Tubal had grabbed one of his blankets and was rubbing himself dry. After ascertaining Tubal was alright, Frank made an effort to get to his feet, moving like an old man. Not even looking at William, he stalked off to take a leak.

When he returned, Frank's mood was no better. Why, he was acting downright surly, William thought indignantly.

"Whut d'you want?" Frank was rubbing his face. Tubal and Lige were moving as if they were drunk; Frank was merely sore.

"Ma wanted me to let you know the Dickensons are alive, no thanks to you."

"What?" That had shocked all three of them. William smiled sardonically.

"They survived getting shot," he repeated.

"Well, well, well…"

Tubal and Lige had looked at Frank, mouths agape. William thought they resembled idiots even more.

"Hmm." Frank was taking the news well, William thought. His eyes narrowed.

"What are you doing?" he asked, curious.

Frank wasn't about to tell William that he was taking Tubal west, along with Lige. Instead, he addressed Tubal. "Go get some wood," he said, looking at the little sky he could see. "Let's have a hot meal."

"You fool!" William was incensed. "Don't you understand? The Dickensons have told the sheriff who shot them!"

"So?" Frank was calmer than he'd felt in days. "They can't file murder charges if folks are alive, now can they?"

Impatiently, William turned as if to go. Tubal had brought one armload of wood, and Lige was preparing to light it. He turned back.

"Them Bald Knobbers have set a price on your head, Frank! Don't it matter to you that they're watching the house, that Ma is embarrassed?"

Frank had been watching Tubal and Lige with the wood. He now turned to William, rubbing his jaw. "How much is the bounty?"

"One thousand dollars."

Gasps from Lige and Tubal. "Well, thet's a sum of money," Frank mused.

"It is." William's response was brief.

Tubal had come to stand beside Frank. "Don't fergit, I need to tell Ma bye before we go," he reminded Frank, who moved as if to shush him.

Frank saw William's eyes gleam, and answered it with a grunt. "Yeah."

"Where?" When Frank didn't reply, William insisted. "Where? Ma'll wanna know!"

"I'd jist as soon not tell you, William," he retorted. "Ain't it enough we're leaving?"

"What's that supposed to mean?" William's question didn't hold curiosity; he knew the answer.

"That means yer embarrassing brothers will be gone, and you won't have to hang yer head in shame," came the quick response.

William made a move forward, but stopped as Lige cocked his gun. None of the brothers had seen Lige pick the rifle up and aim it.

"We appreciate the news, William," Lige said softly. "You'd best get on home."

William eyed Lige, trying to determine just how drunk Lige still was.

"I know you don't care for your brothers like you should," Lige's eyes and hands never wavered. "But I do. You git."

"He means it," Frank added. "You git."

His brothers were standing side by side, protected by a friend. A flicker of shame lit William's stomach like the fire that Tubal kneeled to tend. His mind stamped it out, flooded by relief. Without a word, he turned, walked to the end of the outcropping, and grabbed the first tree branch, hauling himself up. And he left, his brothers and their friend listening as he clambered back up the hill.

Now that a fire was going, Tubal was quick to start preparing supper for the trio. Frank's face was morose as he contemplated William's reaction to the news they were leaving. He figured his livestock, such as he had, was already on the home place. Briefly, he wondered if his mare had given birth yet. It would've been nice to know.

138 | Vonda Wilson Sheets

Lige had set about organizing and packing. He didn't load the big canvas bags on the back of the pack horse just yet; Tubal would have a fit if he couldn't haul his pans along.

Waiting for the meal was proving difficult….it smelled delicious. Lige handed Frank another bottle of shine from his pack, and sat down beside his friend.

"Some brother you've got," he told Frank.

"Eh…" Frank shrugged, took a small sip. He wasn't planning on getting drunk again tonight. It was going to be difficult, leaving the hollow and getting Tubal out of Taney County without visiting their mother. "I'm used to it."

The bottle in his hand might be the key. Could they get Tubal drunk enough to pass out? He could haul Tubal on his horse, and once they reached the top, tie him on Molly.

"Frank?" Tubal had left the fire, came to sit on his other side. "Why'd William come down here?"

"I spose Ma made him," Frank told Tubal.

Frank handed Tubal the bottle of shine, and his brother drank a good swallow.

Tubal considered this information carefully. Then he smiled, appearing almost angelic in the light of the fire. Frank smiled back. "Ma's a good woman," Tubal said. "Too bad Jennie couldn't be like her."

He almost lost his smile, but Frank made a brave face of it. "You're right, Tubal," he answered.

Lige reached across Frank and took the bottle from Tubal. "What happened to Jennie?" he asked, tipping the bottle himself.

"She left." Frank waited for Lige to swallow, then it was his turn again.

Lige's head went back in acknowledgement of the news. Before Frank could hand Tubal the bottle, he'd gotten up to dish up their meal.

"Don't know why anyone wud wanna git marrit in the firs' place," Tubal said, handing Frank his plate. "Though I thought Jennie was alright."

Lige snorted in amusement. Tubal handed him his plate, and Lige began to eat.

"Well, there's advantages in bein' marrit," Frank told his brother, who was again settling next to him. Lige snorted again.

"Like what?" Tubal hadn't asked about marriage before. Frank was speechless, while Lige was trying to stifle his mirth.

"Well, wimmen are nice to have around," Frank began. He knew Tubal had no idea about lying with a woman, and he wasn't going to enlighten his brother. God, problems would multiply.

"Why?" Frank closed his eyes. Lord, Tubal was being persistent.

"Well....they wash yer clothes, and feed yer critters when you ain't there," Frank was searching for reasons to be married. "They smell good, too." He ran out of reasons.

At that, Lige almost lost control, his shoulders shaking and his eyes watering. He choked on the mouthful he had, and hurriedly reached for the bottle of shine, taking a healthy drink to wash the lump of food down. Frank turned a wry face to him, and he thumped his chest, hiccupping. Well, the only cure for that was another bite of food...

"They cook for you, too," Frank was doggedly trying to answer Tubal.

"Well, hell, Frank, I do all that fer you, too," said Tubal. "You oughter jist marry me."

Lige's plate spilled as he lost all control, laughter echoing in the small ravine. Frank was wiping masticated food from his face, trying to not join Lige, who was prostrate, choking and laughing.

Then he looked at his beloved brother, and all humor left him. "Tubal, men don't git marrit to other men," he said, thinking that maybe, just maybe, if he'd loved Jennie as he did Tubal, she wouldn't have left. "Brothers 'specially cain't marry."

Tubal was watching Lige, wondering just what he was finding so funny.

"Well, I don't see no 'vantage to it," Tubal said. "I'll do fer you, jist like I always done."

Lige was recovering, slowly sitting back up, looking at his plate ruefully. He started to rise to get more food, when Tubal snatched the plate and filled it again. "Thet's the last of it."

Lige took the plate a second time, and thanked Tubal. "Some brother you've got there, Frank," he repeated as Tubal returned to his own seat and plate.

Frank's voice was wry. "I know."

The three ate in silence for a few bites.

140 | Vonda Wilson Sheets

Then Tubal asked, "Would it make a difference if I smelled pretty, too?"

This time, Lige bit the inside of his cheeks, shaking with effort to keep from spilling his plate again. Giving up, he simply sat his plate down and walked away from Frank and Tubal, moaning with the pain in his mouth, clamping his teeth even harder on the soft flesh. He didn't think Frank would easily forgive him if he laughed out loud now.

As the night crept on, no one made a move to pack up so they could leave. The fire died down, and the third bottle of the day was making the rounds.

Frank was thinking about William's news. "Y'know, it's possible we don't have to go," he told the other two, who were regarding him with owl-eyes.

"Whaddya mean?" Lige had wholeheartedly accepted the idea of leaving. It was exciting.

"We could turn ourselves in," Frank answered.

Tubal laughed. "I ain't gonna sit in no jail, Frank."

"No," Frank agreed. "We won't have to."

"There's a price on yer heads," Lige reminded him.

"Yeah."

The three of them considered the idea. Neither of the Taylors were happy to leave Taney County. If they had to turn themselves in, maybe face a trial, it would be possible to stay, since the Dickensons were alive.

"I'd have to find a different store," Frank spoke with deliberation. God, he was drunk, but he knew he was right. "Al Layton killed Jim Everett, and he didn't even get jail time."

"Well, I ain't gotta go," Lige told Frank. "They don't know me, couldn't see me. All they saw was a third man."

"True, thet." Frank was beginning to think maybe it was the right thing, turning themselves in. Then what Lige said registered.

"Oh." The third bottle was empty. Lige smiled craftily, then tried to stand. Failing at that, he crawled over to the half-finished packing, and put a fourth bottle inside his shirt. In the meantime, Tubal appeared to have fallen asleep.

Frank was turning the idea over in his mind. Not bad. It was true- -Lige wasn't well-known in these parts. He watched Lige almost fall on the bottle, rolling onto his back to keep it from breaking inside his shirt.

"How'd you like to killeck thet reward?"

His head turned sharply toward Frank. "You're drunk."

"No, well, yeah….No. You cudd colleck."

"It's a lotta money," Lige muttered. His gaze sharpened, and he struggled to sit up. Accomplishing this, he then grew angry. "Are you sayin' whut I think yer sayin'? Whut kin' of fren wudd thet make me?"

"A good one."

"Jesus, Frank, you want me to turn you two in? D'you wanna go to jail?"

"Oh, we ain't gonna."

Lige shook his head, knowing his brains were sloshing inside, but doing it anyway. That didn't help him. He looked over at Tubal, who was rising to take a leak. Well, Tubal stood, anyway. Forgetting what he was standing for, Tubal stumbled slightly toward Frank, then rapidly sat down.

"Frank," Tubal said. "I cain't go to jail."

Patting Tubal on the hand, Frank assured his brother, "We won't spend more than mebbe a night in jail. You could handle a night, cuddint you?"

"Cain't."

"Tubes, we let Lige turn us in, he gets the reward money," Frank explained. "Then he bails us out, and we go off to Texas."

Tubal was stubborn. "Don' wanna go jail. Don' wanna go Texas."

"Tubal, d'you love me?" Frank's voice was thick; it was a low blow, and he didn't like manipulating Tubal. But he'd do it.

Tubal sighed, then lay down, rolling from his side over to his back. He contemplated the overhang above them, what little he could see in the dim light.

"Alright, Frank. But I cain't spen' the night in jail."

"Lige'll git us out," Frank assured his brother.

The three of them were so caught up in the rightness of turning the brothers in and collecting the reward money, they immediately saddled their mounts and headed for Forsyth. The fourth bottle was dry long before they arrived.

CHAPTER 18
April 15, 1885

A knock at the front door of his house brought some consciousness to Polk McHaffie's weary body and mind. Without opening his eyes, he rolled from his right side to his back; he was just about to drift back to sleep again when a variety of sensations registered.

First, Lu was not in bed with him. The down mattress still held the impression of her body, but the flannel sheets were cool to the touch of his questioning right hand.

Second, there was a dim impression of disturbance tickling his brain.

Third, the scents of coffee and bacon were trickling into the small bedroom.

Fourth--he groaned. Elias Yeary's voice was inquisitive in tone in the kitchen.

The sheriff of Taney County opened his bloodshot eyes. Lu had pulled the curtains closed over the window, so the glow of the morning sun didn't batter him as he'd expected.

Fifth--a growl from his stomach brought him fully awake.

Polk's joints and muscles protested as he pushed off the mattress to sit up and bring his feet to the floor. He was stretching when Lu pushed the bedroom door open, his hands high over his head as she regarded him with concern. Handing him the cup of black coffee she'd brought him, she then went to the wardrobe and pulled one of his fresh shirts.

"You're already dressed," Polk sipped from the hot mug as he watched his wife lay his clothes beside him on the rumpled bed.

"Oh, I've been up for some time," Lu reached into the bureau for a pair of fresh socks for him. "You need to wash up and shave."

He raised an eyebrow at her. "What time is it?"

She didn't look at him as she laid his razor and soap next to the bowl on the bureau. "Going on seven," she answered, and then she stepped out to the kitchen. Returning, she carefully poured steaming water into the china bowl, laid a cotton towel over the bowl to retain the heat; she turned to face her exhausted husband with the empty pot in her hands.

"Deputy Yeary is here," Lu said.

"I heard him. What is it?" Something had happened.

"I'll let him tell you."

With that, she went to the window, and opened the curtains. The sunlight poured into the room, and Polk knew whatever news awaited him, it was important. He'd transported a prisoner to Springfield yesterday, and ordinarily, Lu would let him catch up on his sleep when he'd been out half the night.

"I'll get your breakfast dished up." With that, she left the room.

He stood, walked to the beckoning warmth of the water, and held the steamed towel to soften the stubble on his face for a few seconds. Reaching for the cutthroat--Lu kept it sharp--he scraped the itchy growth quickly, wiped himself down, and dressed in record time.

Deputy Yeary was finishing his own breakfast when Polk entered the kitchen. Lu deftly served Polk's warmed plate. He looked appreciatively at it--he'd been too tired to eat when he came in, earlier this morning--and sat down. Greetings over the renewed coffee cup, and he began eating as Yeary filled him in.

"The Taylors are in jail," Elias was talking with his mouth full of the last of his biscuit and gravy.

"That's good. Who found them?"

"They rode in with some stranger."

A mouthful of food went down a little too quickly, and Polk reached for his coffee. "The League didn't find 'em?" he asked after taking a healthy swallow of the hot liquid.

"Nope. Cap'n Kinney was madder than hell yesterday."

Polk took another bite, considering this information. He chewed, and then swallowed again. "Well."

Captain Kinney had set up the Citizens' League for Law and Order to apprehend rogues such as the Taylors, and an unknown man had brought them in.

"The man wants the reward."

"They have to be charged and convicted first."

A small smile hovered on Yeary's lips before he drank the last of his coffee; it did not return as he sat the cup on top of his empty plate, along with his fork and knife.

"I reckoned I'd let you tell him that."

"Why?"

The smile left his deputy's face. At the same time, Lu put two pails of food on the table; part of his job was feeding the prisoners.

144 | Vonda Wilson Sheets

"I know him."

"Who is he?"

Hesitating, he said, "A friend of Frank's."

At that, Polk carefully put his fork down. Chewing, he indicated that Yeary should continue while he sat back in his chair.

Yeary was related to the Everetts by virtue of his uncle's marriage. Some of the extended Everett clan was still down in Arkansas, and Elias had visited them occasionally before taking the job as deputy. On his way back home after one such trip, he'd stopped in a saloon at Lead Hill, and Frank Taylor had been there, sitting at a table in the corner with this man and some others. Frank saw him enter the building, and met him at the bar, never introducing any of his acquaintances to his childhood friend.

Conflicting emotions were on Yeary's face, Polk noted.

"You're sure?" he asked the younger man.

The deputy nodded.

"Does he know you?"

"No," Yeary's answer was grim. "They were all drunk."

Polk pushed his chair back, rising. "You think they want the reward money."

"I know they do."

"Let's go."

Sheriff Polk McHaffie and Deputy Elias Yeary walked to the corner to the square, stopping on the walk outside Parrish's store. Polk could feel the tension rising in Liash.

Keeping his eyes on the two horses and Tubal's mule in front of the jail a block away, Polk's own face tightened. Most businesses wouldn't open for a few minutes yet, but there were usually a few horses in front of the diner; older men often congregated in there before dawn, usually greeting the proprietor with a cup of his own coffee while they swapped gossip and debates.

This morning, horses were all along the rails.

Looking around, Polk saw men sitting on benches outside several buildings, and even in front of the courthouse in the center of the square. A murmur rose as he saw heads turn to look at him. There were probably three dozen armed men watching his jail, he noted.

"How long have they been watching?" Polk asked Yeary.

Yeary shook his head, shrugging slightly, "Frank and Tubal

hurrahed in just after sun-up."

That would be the disturbance he heard in his sleep, Polk realized. This town was ready to explode.

Storekeeper Parrish stepped out with a gun in his hand instead of a broom to sweep his doorway. He nodded to Polk, leaning his right shoulder up against the entry.

"Folks are mad, Sheriff," Parrish said. "Dickenson didn't do anything to deserve getting shot."

Polk appeared to ignore Parrish, and reached for the meal pails Yeary was carrying. "Is Captain Kinney at home?"

Yeary nodded.

"Go tell him." Not even glancing at Parrish, Polk stepped into the street, and walked resolutely toward the jail, uneasily aware of dozens of pairs of eyes watching his every move.

૭ ৫

The bluff on the east side of the Forsyth-Taneyville road blocked the rising sun from view as Frank, Tubal, and Elijah rode south along Swan Creek. They passed Reynolds' Mill, which already had a few customers waiting to get cornmeal and flour. One man ducked into the mill upon seeing the outlaws across the creek, and came out with a rifle. A shot "pinged" off the limestone bluff behind them, and they sped the tired horses up.

Just out of range of the mill, Elijah yelled, "Whoa!"

They were less than a mile from the town as they stopped, Frank's horse sidestepping.

"What?" Frank asked.

"Do we have a plan?" Elijah asked.

Frank considered. No longer quite drunk, he was aware of tightness around his chest, making it difficult for him to breathe again.

"I hear horses," Tubal's hands were tight on Molly's reins.

Frank pulled his wallet out, and tossed it to Elijah. "Colleck the reward, then use my money to bail us out," he told his friend. "We'll meet ya back at the cave when McHaffie lets us go. Be packed, ready to go. We'll leave for Texas."

As the sound of horses came nearer, the three of them sped off again, riding toward Forsyth. Elijah hung back as the brothers rode through the town to the jail, firing their guns and raising hell like they usually did. He caught up just as the Taylors were dismounting in front of the small building that served as the jail.

Deputy Yeary came through the door, gun in his hand. His face held no emotion as Tubal greeted him.

"G'mawnin', Liash," said Tubal.

No response from their old friend, Frank noted. The horsemen who'd followed them from the mill pulled up across the street, in front of the courthouse. Tubal looked over his shoulder, and fright was evident in his eyes.

"It'll be alright," Frank assured his brother. The bands holding his chest hostage tightened.

Elijah was talking to the deputy, inventing a wild tale of how he'd found Frank and Tubal. The brothers walked to join the other two men, and Yeary motioned them inside.

"So I tole thim they was under arrest, and here we are," Elijah's babble came to a stop. Yeary reached for the keys to the jail cell, and then finally looked Frank in the eye.

"You are under arrest for assault on John and Mary Dickenson," Yeary said. His head leaned to the left, indicating Frank and Tubal should enter the cage.

"Frank, I tole you…" Tubal began as they walked in.

A sharp motion of Frank's hand, and Tubal subsided to a whimper as Yeary locked the cell door.

The brothers sat down on the single bed, exhaustion evident despite Tubal's apprehension of being locked up. Yeary turned to face Elijah, hearing Tubal's boots hit the floor. An involuntary smile crossed his lips--Tubal had never been one for shoes--and Elijah misunderstood.

"Alright," the other man was leaning up against the sheriff's desk, half-sitting. The smile left Yeary's face, and Elijah moved, obviously at a loss as to what to do next. Yeary pulled the chair back, preparing to sit down as Elijah walked around to the front of the desk.

"Did you want something?" Yeary asked the other man. The three men stank to high heaven, the deputy noted. Good thing he hadn't eaten breakfast yet.

"I arrested them. I want my reward," Elijah told Yeary.

"You'll have to wait for the sheriff," Yeary responded.

Silence, except for Tubal's whining breathing.

Elijah shifted from foot to foot a couple of times.

"How long will thet be?" he asked.

Yeary shrugged, rubbing his left eye as he did so. "He usually sleeps late after getting back from Springfield," he answered tiredly, "Could be noon."

"Don' knows I wanna wait thet long," Elijah was getting spooked. This wasn't as easy as Frank had made it out to be.

The clock on the wall was just pointing to 6:30 when Deputy Toney came in the door. "Heard the Taylors--" he began, and then clamped his mouth shut as he saw the brothers in the cage. Glancing at Yeary, he nodded. "Breakfast is ready," he said.

Yeary returned the nod, and left. He did not look back at the Taylors.

Tubal's breathing got louder as Toney walked over to the stove, stirred the coals, and opened the lid of the coffee pot. Sniffing the strong liquid within, he reached for a mug, poured himself a cup, then returned, sitting in the chair and putting his feet up on the top of the desk.

Rasping, Tubal asked, "Kin I have a cup of coffee?"

Elijah couldn't take the panicked look in Tubal's eyes. He yanked a mug down from the rack on the wall, poured the thick stuff, and handed it through the bars of the cage. Tubal clasped it with both hands, letting the steam rise into his face for a few seconds before he took a drink.

Frank leaned back against the wall. He had a bad feeling things were no longer in his control. His old friend Elias would not meet his eyes. As Tubal curled into the corner, tucking his bare feet under his legs, he glanced over at his beloved brother.

Best keep quiet, he told himself. And his heart began pounding as he waited.

Sheriff McHaffie entered the office about a half-hour later. He walked straight back to the cage, handing the pails of breakfast over to the prisoners without salutation. Reaching into his shirt pocket, he then handed the brothers each a fork. His movements still abrupt, he turned and poured the coffee Deputy Toney had started a few minutes before. Then he looked at the man sitting in front of his desk.

"You waiting for something?" McHaffie asked the man. His eyes were cold as he looked the sitting man over.

Elijah Sublett rose to his feet, stiff with sitting for so long. "Yes, sir, Sheriff," he answered. "I arrested the Taylor brothers."

"So I see."

Deputy Toney had risen when McHaffie arrived, and now moved back to allow the sheriff to sit. McHaffie did so, sipping his coffee and looking through the papers on his desk. The Taylors were eating their breakfast, watching the other three men.

"I want the reward money," blurted Sublett.

A mild expression was on McHaffie's face as he sat back, took off his hat, and tossed it on the pile of papers. He took another sip of coffee.

"And who are you?"

"My name's Eli--" Sublett broke off. "Thet's not important. I arrested the Taylors. There's a reward for the arrest of 'em."

A cold smile of satisfaction appeared on McHaffie's face. "Did you see the reward poster?"

"No, I heard about it. Found 'em in a draw northeast of town. What difference does it make?" Sublett was getting belligerent. "I brought them in."

"So it appears, Toney, any of those posters in here?"

Toney lifted the sheriff's hat, sticking it on a peg, and began rifling through the papers on McHaffie's desk. Frank had stopped eating, but Tubal took another bite. Sensing his brother's unease, Tubal, too, lowered his fork, still watching.

Finding a copy of the poster, Toney handed it to the sheriff, who didn't even glance at it before passing it on to Sublett. Sublett studied it for a minute while the other four men watched him, reading with his lips moving.

"...con-vick-shun of the Taylor brothers in the mur-der-us ass..."

"I believe the terms are 'for the arrest and conviction of Frank and Tubal Taylor in the murderous assault of the Dickensons,'" McHaffie finished it for him.

"Conviction?" Sublett looked into the faces of his friends behind the bars. Frank was immobile; Tubal was stunned.

"Conviction," McHaffie assured him. He glanced up at the clock. "Toney, go on over to the courthouse. I believe Prosecutor Burns will be in office early this morning." As Toney left, McHaffie told the astounded Sublett, "Mr. Burns will be very glad to hear the Taylors are in jail. He'll be filing charges shortly, I imagine."

Frank snorted. "Charges ain't nothin'," he said. Sublett sank to his chair under the weight of the stare he was getting from Frank-- the message was loud and clear. William had not mentioned anything about conviction or such when he'd told his brothers and their friend of the reward.

Tubal was whimpering again. "Shet it," Frank said. He wished he could see Sublett, but McHaffie was blocking his view. Something was different about the sheriff, Frank knew.

Sublett continued to clutch the poster in his hand. He looked at McHaffie, glad he couldn't see Frank. He could not read well; neither could Frank.

The sheriff's voice continued. "I believe the poster also mentions a reward for the identity of the third man who was with the Taylors."

His face went pale, Sublett knew. Tubal and Frank had both forgotten to finish their meals. Assuming nonchalance, Sublett rose, went to the coffee pot, and poured. His face calm, he turned to McHaffie.

"You want some more?" The sheriff shook his head, again resuming reading the papers on his desk.

Waiting.

Elijah Sublett sat down again.

An hour passed.

The pails of food were sitting on the floor, empty. Frank was still maintaining an air of calm for Tubal's sake, but he was having to focus on his breathing. Noises filtering in from the town were the only sound. Frank didn't try to hear them.

Toney finally re-entered the office. McHaffie looked up, an expectant gaze in his eyes, he watched Sublett while Toney said, "The prosecutor has filed charges on the Taylors."

"I guess you'll have to wait to claim your reward until after the trial, mister," McHaffie told Sublett. Keeping his gaze on Sublett, McHaffie asked Toney, "Bail?"

"None."

There was a sharp intake of breath from Frank.

"Frank? Ain't we getting out?" Tubal asked.

Ignoring the brothers behind him, McHaffie watched Sublett.

The man had broken into a sweat while waiting for Toney's return, and now lifted his hat to run a forearm across his brow. Settling the hat back, he rose from the chair. McHaffie rose as well.

"If you will give me your name and where you can be found, I'm sure the Citizens' League will be glad to reward you for your services," McHaffie told the terrified man.

"I--I--I'll come back for the trial," Sublett wanted out, now. He indicated his friends in the cage. "They won't be able to get out on bail?" he asked McHaffie.

The sheriff was shaking his head. "No, no bail."

Sublett was inching toward the door. "I'll come back for the trial," he said, and bolted.

Toney moved as if to go after him, but McHaffie had whirled to look at the prisoners when Tubal howled. "Don't leave us!"

Frank was at the end of the cell, looking out the window. He could see little of the square, but he was able to see Elijah Sublett riding away, with his horse and Tubal's mule.

"LIGE!" Frank roared, forgetting about staying calm and giving away his friend's name. Shutting his mouth, he realized he had nothing but Elijah Sublett's name left to give. Tubal was pounding his head on the wall, moaning. Despite the racket, Frank saw a number of armed men in the limited view, and his shoulders drooped. Ignoring Tubal, he returned to the cot, sitting and pulling his feet up on the blanket. He didn't want to look at McHaffie, but he did anyway, for a second or two.

"You want to tell me his name?" McHaffie asked.

A chill began creeping up Frank's spine. Tubal's moans were deepening, and his bare feet were shaking with every "clunk" of his head against the wall. "I can't stand bein' locked up," Tubal's voice was a monotone as he rocked back and forth on his hands and knees.

Watching his brother, Frank muttered, "I never caught it." He glanced back up at McHaffie, and realized he could not read McHaffie's face.

Tubal calmed down after a while, which Frank was grateful for. But the spells visited Tubal off and on, all day, until Frank thought he, too, might give in to the same. Tubal was drooling in a semi-comatose state between spells; Frank could do nothing for him.

All he could do was wait.
The waiting was going to kill him.

CHAPTER 19
The Night of April 15, 1885

In the short time since the Citizens' League had formed, Gus Hensley and his night patrols had succeeded in driving one thief and his family out of the South Bee Creek valley, near the state line.

The riders had surrounded the house while carrying torches and wearing flour sacks over their heads. Hensley had shouted to the man, who had been too terrified to respond with gunfire. Giving the family three days to leave Taney County forever, Hensley and his men rode away, went home, and fell into the sleep of the just. The next morning, Hensley had been in his wife's garden across the road from his house, and heard a wagon coming up the draw. It was the family he'd threatened the night before, their belongings tossed under a canvas tarp that one son was trying to tie down as the father whipped the mules to climb. The mother and the rest of the children were hanging on for dear life.

His neighbors reacquired their pregnant sow, Gus discovered later that day when he rode over to make sure the family was really gone. He'd walked through the buildings and yard, discovering a calf and a bee hive which had been left behind.

The bee gum was now ensconced in a new home near his wife's garden, and the calf was in a pasture up on the ridge behind his house. 'Twouldn't do to let the critters go to waste.

Nat Kinney thought about Gus' report as he watched Deputy Yeary leave for the ride back to Forsyth. Gus was still sitting on his own horse--he'd arrived shortly before Yeary came with the news of the capture and arrest of the Taylors.

There was no time to consider the additions to Gus' farm. The idea of seriously scaring the Taylors into leaving Taney County forever and becoming someone else's problem was a good one. How to do that...

He turned toward Gus. "We all ride tonight. Bring two ropes. Make sure they are oiled, not new."

Gus' eyes widened, but he nodded. He clicked his tongue, and left Captain Kinney to turn and look at Big Bald.

Nat had been furious that his night patrol was unable to locate the Taylors. The fury was still running through his veins, and he stalked up Big Bald. He rebuilt the pile of brush and wood for a bonfire, and pulled a flint from his pocket.

He hadn't made a plan when he told Gus to bring prepared ropes, but now he considered the steps to take as he watched the sparks catch and the fire begin to take hold.

It was a bright, clear day. The smoke would be seen for miles, and all would be his tonight.

He definitely planned to scare the Taylors.

Maggie's head showed as she climbed the hill to join him. The smoke was rising in concert with her movements, and she touched his arm briefly when she got to his side, her eyes joining his to watch the smoke spiral ever higher.

Neither spoke for a long time. It wasn't necessary.

In unison, they turned to walk back to the house, Maggie's left hand clasped in Nat's right. When they reached the gate to the dooryard, he spoke softly.

"Play for me?"

"Who is it?"

"The Taylors were arrested this morning."

A small smile came and went on Maggie's mouth. She began to speak again, but he raised a gentle hand, calloused fingers brushing her lips.

"Play for me."

And she did.

ᡍ ᡇ

The Kirbyville and Mincy men who joined the Citizens' League met on Big Bald two hours after sundown. No speech was necessary; all had known of the hunt for the Taylors. The fire was a signal of riding.

"We meet by the fire." Nat Kinney roared.

The men roared back. "We ride in the dark."

Torches.

Riders.

As they rode north, more men joined them. More torches lit the way.

Bonfires signaled throughout the land.

Thundering hooves.

Nat led them down to the river, just south and east of Forsyth.

No waiting for the ferry. Although the river was high, the element of hurry spurred horses and riders alike across the heavy current.

Regroup, rest the horses for a few minutes. Heavy breathing in the dark. Sweaty men, wet horses.

Grey Ghost danced, and the other horses followed.

McHaffie met them just outside the eastern city limits, a small fire signaling the intent men.

Fresh torches.

Some pulled bandanas over their faces. Others pulled out cleaned flour bags with holes cut out for their eyes and mouths. Kinney himself sat still, eyes peering into the darkened village.

"All quiet?" Terse.

McHaffie was equally terse.

"Except Tubal Taylor."

It wasn't a pleasant smile that crossed Nat Kinney's face. "He won't be a problem much longer."

Lieutenants rode up for orders and assignments were issued.

McHaffie fell back. He looked at Nat, shaking his head. "I won't."

It took only seconds and as he saw McHaffie's determination, he nodded and in a commanding voice, shouted "Ride!"

The band surged forward, dozens of men who were tired of the Taylors, tired of people getting hurt, tired of no recourse in a land that could not be easily tamed. The brutal dirt-poor hills, the slumped shoulders of their women, the hunger of their children, all the hard work of their hands and backs in an effort to merely survive--these things rose up in their blood, driven on by Nat Kinney's fury.

They rode west on Jefferson Street, sentries going off the side streets to prevent any one from making an attempt to stop them. The town had eyes, although no one stepped out of their houses and not one window held light. Shouts of warning, yells of fury, kept all who didn't ride in the dark behind the doors of their homes.

Several men dismounted and began to beat on the door of the jail. When Ghost came to a stop in front of the jail, Nat turned and raised his hands. The yelling outside the jail stopped and all could hear Tubal yelling from within the jail.

Absolution | 155

"Lemme out, I cain't be locked up," echoed from inside.

The men began trying to force the jail open once more.

"Oh, we'll get you out alright," Nat yelled back to Tubal Taylor. Seizing an ax from a leather loop on his saddle, he dismounted. The men fell back before him, and he swung the ax at the door, taking only two blows to disintegrate the iron lock. The men on the porch then surged in as the crowd roared approval.

Inside, Tubal was shrieking and Frank was yelling. Neither man was coherent in their terror. They shrank back in the dark, and Tubal fell to the floor, rolling under the cot. Frank turned just in time to keep the metal of the cage door from cutting his face as it flew from under the ax.

Rough hands. Grabbing. Fighting. Yelling. Darkness.

Tubal's voice was hoarse in his relief at being outside, until he looked up from his bare feet and saw a ring of mounted men holding torches in front of him. Frank had doubled over--his captors thought he was trying to escape, and forced him back upright by the hair, not caring that he wasn't able to breathe.

The bright hair of a big man gleamed red as blood in the dark light of the torches. The man's face held grimness in the set of his jaw. Someone thrust a torch in front of him, and the flames made the man's face the stuff of nightmares. He was only two feet from the brothers being held on the porch.

"Frank and Tubal Taylor, you are on trial for the assault and attempted murder of John and Mary Dickenson! How do you plead?"

Frank's legs gave out from underneath him, and his hair was pulled again as he started to go down. His arms were yanked out from his sides, and someone placed a hand over his throat. He screamed.

"I'm not guilty!"

"Really?" the voice was relentless, "You have been identified!"

"It was a misunderstanding!" He struggled.

"So you did shoot the Dickensons?"

"Yes, but--"

At that, the men on horseback roared.

A distinct smell of feces reached Frank's nose as he was hauled down the steps; Tubal had shit himself. He was thrown over a horse, and the force of his stomach slamming into the saddle knocked what little air he had in his lungs out. His last vision before a sack was jammed onto his head was of his brother, struggling hopelessly as he, too, was thrown over the back of a horse.

Frank thought he must have blacked out for a few precious seconds. His tender stomach was trying to come up, or down, since his body was draped over a galloping horse. Occasional bits of gravel were hitting him on the head. "Tubal!" he screamed, and an answering yell came back.

There were sounds of horses all around him, and men were yelling.

Water - they were fording Swan Creek. Frank reared back, trying to raise his head above it. He had no breath. His hands were tied behind him and he could barely move. They had taken the time to tie him to the saddle.

Harsh words and heavy breathing filled the night air, and then there was the vicious abuse that his body was taking.

He felt the horse begin to climb a hill, wondered for a few seconds where he was being taken.

Then he realized....it didn't matter.

A peace began to steal over him as the horses reached the top of the hill. The horse he was on stretched out again and the pace continued furious for a mile or so. Then the thunder quieted, the horses slowing and then halting.

He was untied, pulled to a sitting position, and the hood yanked off his head. He had no idea who was in the group around him; most of the faces were masked. His brother was to his right, he saw. Tubal had gone completely crazy--there was no comprehension in his eyes, which were roaming back and forth. When he saw Frank, there was no recognition and suddenly Frank's vitality surged back into his body.

Frank began to reach for Tubal, ignoring his tied hands, kneeing the horse to move closer, and someone rode between them.

Frank snarled, but whoever was behind the bandana simply laughed.

The big red-headed bastard wasn't done, and he shouted "Frank and Tubal Taylor, you have been tried and found guilty of attempted murder!"

Frank blinked as roughness flew down his face. He felt the scratchiness of a thick rope on his throat, looked up to see Nat Kinney's hands rise into the air. His brother struggled, and Frank knew he, too, had a rope around his neck.

"Have mercy," Frank yelled, "Mercy!"

Kinney had been facing his men, but turned his horse to look Frank Taylor in the eye.

"You shall be shown the same mercy you have shown!"

The mob of men roared again, cries of "Justice!" and more filling the air around the flames of the torches. Kinney's hands rose as he exhorted the crowd, and suddenly, his hands came down.

Frank Taylor rose up into the air.

The horse he'd been on shied, colliding with the horse his brother was on.

Jerking and kicking, his body twirled.

There was the smell of shit and he couldn't breathe.

For a brief second he could see his brother's bare feet, glowing in the light of the torches, and then the rope jerked again.

He came back toward the ground and the rope snapped taut.

There was a crunching noise, a momentary flash of light, and Frank Taylor was dead.

CHAPTER 20
Late Night April 15, 1885 - Shock

"The strongest lye soap won't clean our hands from this night."

Alonzo Prather's voice was raw, strained from purging. His stomach, his mind, rebelled at the thought of the hanged men some two miles back up the night-tossed road. The moon reached cleanly here, at a small spring falling down to meet the river.

JJ Brown's hands were colorless in the moonlight, but gleamed from the water he'd been scrubbing them in. At Alonzo's words, he stilled, and then put his head back, leaving his hands to drip.

Making his way through last year's growth of brush along the small bench between the bluff and the creek, Alonzo went to his horse, dug in his saddlebag, and pulled out a large flask. Silently, he sent a prayer of thanks to his wife, who had not wanted him to ride this night, but prepared him for the worst. He walked to JJ, taking a sip, rinsing his mouth and spitting, then a long pull from the rich, smoky bourbon. After he swallowed, he handed the flask to his friend.

JJ was looking at the clear sky. Shaking his hands one last time, he grasped the flask and let some of its contents swirl down to his stomach. He had been kneeling, but as Alonzo sat down, JJ rocked back onto his heels and closed his eyes.

"I have fought on the side of law all my life," he told Alonzo. He could sense Alonzo's head nodding in agreement. Both men were in shock.

Bringing his head down again for another drink from the flask, JJ looked across the stream, trying to remember where they were, what they were doing here. Ah, yes...

"There is nothing to do, is there?" JJ was speaking rhetorically. He could not look Alonzo in the eye because of the overpowering shame.

Even during the Civil War, neither man had been a part of a mob before. Both men had spent their lives fighting for justice. JJ helped restore the school system in Taney County after the war, and had been elected to office. Alonzo had been a part of the beginnings of the Industrial and Business College at Fayetteville. Education and justice for their chosen people had kept their minds sharp and their hearts keen, as truly good men are when they have found their path.

And in one night, in a few short hours, it was all gone, left in the bloody, odorous mud beneath the feet of the Taylor brothers.

Alonzo was the least emotional of the two men, if such a thing could be said. He was looking back, thinking aloud.

"Our committee rule changed quickly," he told JJ. "I wonder.... when did Nat take control? I did not see this coming."

JJ snorted, a wet sound muffled by wiping his arm across his face, "From the beginning." He pulled to his feet, paced to his horse, then back to Alonzo.

"I see it now. He led us down the wrong path from the start. He took a situation none of us thought we could control, and he controlled us." JJ paused in his steps back to his horse, and then whirled around. "I cannot be a part of this, Alonzo. I cannot do this."

Half-turned to watch JJ's white shirt in the scanty light from the sky, Alonzo began to rise, then fell back to rest on his right foot. "No, and neither can I."

Near hysteria, JJ resumed his pacing. "Jim was my best friend for twenty years, since I came here. I have my business, my land--we have family here. My God, what have we done?"

A passage from one of his philosophy books flitted into Alonzo's mind as he rose to meet whatever decision JJ was coming to in his own mind. "One who is injured ought not to return the injury, for on no account can it be right to do an injustice; and it is not right to return an injury, or to do evil to any man, however much we have suffered from him."

JJ came to a halt. "You quote Socrates to me - to me - now?" He shook his head. "I wrote that goddamned oath, Alonzo. Nat Kinney will come after us. He is bound by oath."

Reaching down for the whiskey flask, Alonzo straightened, and shook his own head in return. "I think not, John. We will not be the only ones who will have no part of things after tonight. And we will not be the only ones who will want the League to meet no more."

"There is the oath!" JJ retorted, and then resumed his pacing.

Alonzo had regained control of his thoughts--the whiskey helped--and now he saw that JJ did not understand what he was thinking.

"I do not think the oath will bind him as it would us, John. Think, man! He has not been a member of the lodge, he does not think as we do. To him, the oath is a tool…to use, to control. He does not feel it, inside."

JJ accepted the flask from Alonzo again. His breathing was calming down, his thoughts were more coherent. "How can he preach again after tonight?" he asked Alonzo.

Eyeing JJ, Alonzo pulled a handkerchief from his pocket, raised his hat, and wiped his face. As he opened his eyes once more, another passage came to his mind. "A tyrant must put on the appearance of uncommon devotion to religion. Subjects are less apprehensive of illegal treatment from a ruler whom they consider is god-fearing and pious."

"On the other hand, they do less easily move against him, believing he had the gods on his side," JJ responded to the Aristotelian quote, and took another sip. "I have to leave. I must move Caroline and the children."

"JJ, we can fight this. I don't believe Nat intended for those men to hang tonight!" Alonzo was emphatic. "I saw his face. He was as shocked as we were!"

"No, he wasn't." Rufe Burns, the prosecutor, and Charles Groom were standing up the stream; how long had they been listening? Alonzo wondered. And where were their horses?

"Were you there?" Alonzo asked.

"No, he posted sentries in front of my house," Groom answered. "Rufe was visiting."

"We rode up after you left," Burns continued. He didn't need to add that he and Groom had followed the older men.

As prosecutor, Rufus Burns had spent the day building a case against the Taylors to keep them in jail and put them on trial in front of a jury. He had been discussing the case with young Groom, who was a newly-made lawyer.

"All the work you put into your case is gone," JJ told Burns. As the previous prosecutor, he knew well the frustration of losing hours spent putting together a fool-proof case, especially in Taney County. "You could not have stopped it."

"Ah, but there's the difference, sir, I wouldn't have," Burns replied. "This case is won."

"They deserved a fair trial!" Alonzo snapped. "They did not kill anyone!"

"They will never hurt anyone else again!" Groom was nettled. "It was only luck that they had not killed anyone!"

JJ jumped back into the fray. "A fair trial does matter. We formed the League to protect life, not take it. What happened tonight was against the law!" He tossed the whiskey flask to Alonzo. "We will regret it." Moving to his horse, he picked up the reins and began to mount. Alonzo followed him, putting a hand on JJ's left arm as he settled into his saddle. The tired horse responded to JJ's touch slowly, allowing Alonzo to ask one final question.

"What will you do?"

"Sell out. Move. I must see my family to safety." Glancing over at Burns and Groom, he looked back down at his friend. "I suggest you do the same."

Incensed, Groom shouted, "It will be safe here, Mr. Brown. It will. Captain Kinney will see to it!"

One more time, JJ snorted, this time in disgust. "That's what I'm afraid of." And he turned his horse back, to take a darker trail up into the night, toward home.

CHAPTER 21
Late April, 1885 - A New Plan for Andy

Everyone settled uneasily into the routine of mid-spring after the Taylors were hung. There were seedlings to be tended, kitchen gardens to be weeded, and buildings to repair after the ravages of winter.

Taney County was open range. Cattle and pigs, especially boars, roamed through the woods, often marked with various cuts through the ear flaps that designated ownership. In the spring, new shoats and calves were cut, the males often gelded. Most farmers generally herded their pregnant livestock into the barnyard to make this task easier after the progeny was born.

One big black sow--Andy thought she must have some razorback in her--had managed to escape her owner this year. During a trek through the woods a week after the Taylors were buried, he heard the grunts of baby porkers coming from the area of Miranda's former home. Investigating, he cautiously soft-footed toward the remains of the house, and then diverted toward the shed that had served the family as a barn.

The sow's small eyes gleamed in the shadows of the opening to the shed. Seven shoats were nursing from her, and she sent a warning squeal as Andy appeared in the door. Smells of afterbirth and blood met him head on, and he stepped back, ducking to the right in case she decided to charge him. Hearing no movement or sound but that of the piglets, he slowly moved his head to the left, his body shielded somewhat by the wall of the building.

Seven, fine, fat little newborn porkers, he thought.

Their mother did not like Andy's presence, and another warning came from her. He backed slowly away, and then turned to go up the hill to the trail that wandered over the ridge to Granny Haggard's house, and points beyond.

Miranda and her family had been much on Andy's mind lately. Maggie was healing, her arm in a sling. They were still at Granny Haggard's home, which was known to be a refuge to all who needed it. What Maggie's future plans were--well, Andy shook his head. It wasn't his decision to make.

Celie, Phebe, and Miranda were in the garden with Granny

Absolution | 163

Haggard, their mother watching from a bench in the shade of the big oak in the corner behind the house. Maggie didn't seem surprised to see Andy; he wondered if she'd been expecting him.

"'Lo, Mr. Coggburn," Maggie's voice was low, still somewhat rusty from disuse.

"I'm Andy," he returned the greeting, sitting on the bench beside her.

"If you'll call me Maggie," the woman replied. Andy smiled faintly at her, and then both turned to watch Granny and the girls, who'd waved when Andy sat down. Granny was showing the girls how to stake tomatoes, and each one was giving her their utmost attention.

Silence was comfortable. Andy couldn't remember the last time he'd felt comfortable in the presence of anyone, save Granny and Sam Snapp. He put that thought aside for the time being, and let his guard down a little farther.

After the tomatoes were staked and tied with bits of rags, Granny told the girls to go wash up. The old woman was spry enough, Andy thought as the girls ran past him toward the house, but there was an air of distraction and she moved slowly through the garden, looking at her plants and checking for things needing attention.

Andy rose to his feet, hefting the bag he'd carried through the morning, and accepted the hug Granny gave him when she joined him and Maggie at the bench. Granny's eyes searched his face--he was used to it--and she smiled. "You're well," she said.

He nodded, and then turned to assist Maggie, who had already stood. Granny looked at Maggie, too, and gestured toward the house. "Come in," she invited Andy.

The trio joined the noisy girls, who had quite soaked themselves in washing up. Such glee was good to see, Andy thought.

Inside the cabin, sassafras tea was creating an aura of warmth, and Miranda began to get down the mugs for a mid-morning break. Andy sat his bag on the table, and Granny's eyes looked questions at him.

"Just some deer meat," he told her.

"Then we'll eat," Granny replied.

The meat was hickory-smoked, lean, and sliced easily. Serving it to the women and girls, Andy noted Maggie was sniffing at it as if she'd never had smoked meat before. Waiting for him to serve himself, the group joined hands while Granny said a short prayer. Then they began to eat.

Maggie cut the meat with her fork, still sniffing at it. She had become adept at using a fork left-handed. Andy took a bite--it didn't smell bad to him, but maybe she sensed something? He relaxed fractionally as she took a bite herself, chewing slowly, letting the flavor fill her senses.

Then she smiled beatifically, the first time Andy had seen such a smile on the woman's face. She swallowed, and then took another bite.

Laying his fork down, Andy sat back in his chair, studying Maggie, knowing Granny was watching the two of them. The girls paid no attention, but were eating and drinking their tea.

Andy was proud of his meat. He took the time to marinate it, then smoked it with hickory, and sometimes some other ingredients. He did not keep a large store of goods in his cave, but he experimented with whatever came to his mind. His family and friends often benefited, for he was generous with the results.

Now, while watching Maggie, he wondered what was going through her mind. He'd never left meat at her home, so this was her first time at sampling his venison.

She was chewing so slowly.

Well, he had time.

She swallowed her third mouthful of meat, and began to shake her head. Seeing Andy's face, she smiled again. He returned the smile cautiously. The smoke shed on Maggie's old home place had collapsed during the rains of a couple weeks ago; smoking meat was the preferred method of preservation, so it wasn't like she hadn't eaten it before.

"What?" Andy finally asked.

"This is good," Maggie answered, "Really good."

Andy nodded. He knew that.

"Really, really, good," and as she took another bite, her eyes closed. After she swallowed again, she opened them to peer.

"You soak the meat, don't you?" Well, that was somewhat startling to Andy. Not many folks he knew would have figured it out. He nodded.

The girls had finished, and Granny excused them to go play outside for a while. Pouring herself another mug of tea, she sat back to listen to the conversation between the teenaged boy she had come to love, and the thirty-year-old Maggie. Her brown eyes lost their sense of distraction as she hummed a slight tune, which neither Andy nor Maggie appeared to hear.

"I can make it better." Maggie was not used to being forthright, and she looked as surprised at herself as Andy did when she spoke.

"I thought you liked it?" he asked. Granny smiled at him; he didn't take offense easily.

"Oh, I do," Maggie's voice was thoughtful, reassuring. "It's the best I've eaten." She took another bite, completely lost in the flavor.

Curiosity had gotten Andy into a few places he didn't like, so he returned to his own plate. He couldn't decide if he was upset or not, so he figured he might as well eat while he waited for whatever was going to happen next.

"It's been years since I've made any," Maggie was thinking to herself out loud. "I don't know…"

She rose, then went to the cupboard near the stove, which held various jars and bottles of herbs and other items Granny prepared. One hand wasn't enough to search through the selection, so she pulled her right arm out of its sling, and winced as she raised it gently to aid the left.

Granny was amused, turning in her chair to watch Maggie, Andy noted. He continued to eat, not registering the hum emanating from the other end of the table.

"There's a spice….no, you wouldn't have it," Maggie turned to Granny. "My grandmother taught me to make a sauce for smoked meat. I haven't thought of it in years."

"What is the name of this spice?" Granny wanted to know.

"It was ground from a certain pepper, one my grandmother grew in her garden," Maggie was still lost in thought, trying to remember. "Ah…she called it paprika when she prepared it."

Paprika. Andy had never heard the word before.

"My grandmother was Spanish, but I don't know the Spanish word for it."

"What kind of pepper is it?" Granny wanted to know. She was always interested in plants, and new ones were sure to gain her attention.

"I don't know that it's been grown here," Maggie said. "We'll have to order it…" She stopped abruptly, faltering.

Granny raised a hand at her. "It can be done," she assured Maggie.

Andy was bewildered for only a moment, then realized what the problem was - money. He didn't have a great deal, but he had enough to order some pepper seeds. He was curious now.

"Iffen you'll write down what it is, I kin order it from Kintrea's," he told the women. "But first, tell me what you do with it."

Maggie came back to the table, her face alight with memories. Granny reached into her pocket for her pipe, filled and lit it, still humming softly.

"We smoked the peppers," Maggie began. "Then we ground them down, and mixed the powder with oil, warming it up to simmer for a time. Grandmother used the oil mixed with tomato sauce and brown sugar….probably some other things, I'll have to try it….and then put it in a bowl next to smoked meat on the table. Oh, it was good."

"Kin you make this sauce without those peppers?" Andy wanted to know.

"Yes, but it's not as good. You can use all kinds of spices," Maggie answered. "Pork was the best meat with the sauce, but we used it on almost anything."

Pork! That reminded him…

"Yu own a pig?" he asked Maggie.

The return to present-day troubles doused the light on Maggie's reflections, and Andy was sorry. "No," she spoke softly.

"Well, you do now," he told her.

Her head jerked back slightly in surprise. "I do?"

"Got a sow nursing her young'uns in your barn," he told her. "Jist came from there."

"Well, I can't take care of her," Maggie said. "I don't want to go back."

Andy considered things for a few moments, enjoying the smell from Granny's pipe. His thoughts were shifting, and a need to help Maggie and her daughters came through them all.

"Tell you what," he began to offer, then shook his head. He was a loner; except for his sister and Granny Haggard, he spent little time with women, and wasn't comfortable around them. He much preferred the company of men.

"Tell me what?" Maggie was curious now.

Absolution | 167

Well, hell. He was in a fix, and it seemed to be of his own doing.

"I'll go pen that sow in," he said hurriedly, before Maggie could protest. "And tear down the rest of the house."

Maggie's brown eyes narrowed. "I don't want to go back there."

"For right now, you don't have to," Andy returned. "But you'll need a place to live soon."

Maggie looked about the small cabin. She had been trying to think of what to do, somewhere in the back of her mind. She did not want to leave, and Granny had been more than hospitable. But it was maybe time to look ahead, after the awful years with Pa. Suddenly, a future was possible. She rose again from her chair, and went to the open door, listening to the sounds of her daughters, who had been joined by Georgia Kinney.

"All right," she murmured. "All's right." Straightening her shoulders, she turned back inside, to see Granny smiling through the smoke wreath, and then looked Andy full in the face.

"You order them peppers, and I'll make you some sauce for your meat," she said. Uncertainty tugged at her lips.

"I'll do thet," he responded with a rare smile of his own. "And we'll go work on your place."

The uncertainty left Maggie's lips, and she put her right hand on Andy's shoulder, wincing as she did so. "Let me write the name down," she said, then went to fetch paper and the ink.

Still humming, Granny made sure her pipe was out, put it in her pocket, then began to clear the table. A small satisfied sigh escaped her, but the two new friends in her home didn't notice. They were busy making plans.

After stacking the dishes in the wreck pan, Granny slipped outside and sat in her rocking chair on the front porch. She could hear the girls' voices from nearby--it sounded as though they had found the green enchantment of the honeysuckle vines which draped down the rocky slope yonder.

The bees' hum as they flew through the yard seeking flowers joined Granny as she swayed with her chair and considered the conversation she'd been privy to. Andy would never marry; and Maggie, although still young enough to bear children, would never want another husband. Both were alone in a way that most people never saw or understood.

Grief had a way of healing, once one got past mourning. As the sun reached its zenith, Granny figured the new friends would soon be able to help each other in that as well.

CHAPTER 22
Early May, 1885 - Aftermath

Three young girls were sitting on the wide front porch of Kintrea's General Store, their bare feet dangling above the ground. Stair-stepped sisters, Nat's first glance told him; then he realized the oldest one was Georgia's friend Miranda.

The child had healed from the wounds she'd received at the hands of her stepfather, he was pleased to see. Miranda's clear skin had the warmth of a peach, and her dark blonde hair was neatly braided. Her sisters looked much like her. Their bonnets hung down their backs, and it was easy to see they were enjoying their horehound candy sticks, chattering excitedly as they waited for their mother.

Nat had never seen "the other" Maggie closely. He paid scant attention to his Maggie's audience when she played her piano in the evening. Still, the woman pushing open the screen door and laughing at her youngest daughter's sticky face bore little resemblance to the scrawny, rabbitty creature he recalled. Still much too thin, this woman was glowing.

Her brown hair was bundled into a braid around her head, highlighted with golden and reddish streaks from the sun. Her skin, too, was sun-kissed, and her soft brown eyes simmered with heat. She obviously had some Spanish or Indian blood in her, Nat thought as he caught the door, bowing and watching her herd her daughters off, favoring her right arm as she pulled her bonnet over her hair. He smiled, and entered the sunlit store.

His good mood abruptly disappeared. Andy Coggburn was paying for a peck of plants and assorted other packages. Nat tensed, expecting to hear Andy's turkey call at any moment. Nat stepped into the corner opposite the counter, and quickly began perusing the merchandise on display. It was fabric, he saw with dismay. He waited, not daring to look in young Coggburn's direction.

Andy left without noticing Nat was watching from the corner. His arms were full of the plants and seeds Maggie had asked for, as well as assorted other items. Juggling his purchases, he called a "thanks" out to John Kintrea, and left the store, walking around and going to the wagon behind the building where Maggie and the girls waited for him.

170 | Vonda Wilson Sheets

Bemused, Nat went to the counter and called for his mail. Kintrea gave him a letter addressed to "Mrs. Maggie Kinney," from her father, and he stuck it in his chest pocket.

"That woman--" he began to ask the storekeeper, who was politely waiting for Nat to purchase something or leave.

"Ah, the Widow Maggie," Kintrea nodded. "Amazing. She looks so well for having so recently gone through such a tragedy."

Nat stared, then nodded. "Tragic, indeed."

"Her arm is almost healed now, you know," Kintrea confided in the man he considered to be a leader in the Kirbyville area. "She tried so hard to save Ol' Hep's life when their home caught fire."

"Indeed."

The storekeeper nodded again, anxious to share the gossip. "Hep was a varmint, that's a fact," he exclaimed virtuously. "But his woman did her best to pull him out of the cabin."

Nat realized the story had changed to protect those who needed protection. He had little problem with it; the people who lived along the ridge bearing the Springfield-Harrison Road and overlooking the White River knew the truth, but saw no reason the whole county needed to know the Widow Maggie had killed her man. It had been a fortuitous thought to burn the cabin to the ground.

And the story of injuries to the family of the man did no harm. Indeed, it made the Widow Maggie appear to be quite brave. She was, Nat thought.

The family had been staying with Granny Haggard, according to Georgia. His daughter was gone from home a great deal, delighting in spending time at Granny's with Miranda. Her school books had been put away for the time being. Abruptly, Nat crossed the store again, looking at the bolts of fabric on the shelves, and pulling one of a yellow sprigged muslin out. He laid it across the nearby cutting table, unrolling it and imagining it as a dress. For the mother of Miranda. He then turned again, and pulled down a bolt of yellow calico, and thought about the fabric against the soft peach coloring of Miranda and her sisters. That, too, would do.

Glancing around, he espied other things that would delight the heart of any female he knew. It was not correct for a man to buy clothing or other items for a woman or girl he wasn't married to or responsible for. Nat didn't much care at the moment.

Kintrea's wife had joined him at the fabric table. "Mr. Kinney,

Absolution | 171

may I be of assistance?" she inquired.

"Miranda and her sisters. The Widow Maggie. What else do they need, besides new summer dresses?" he asked gruffly but quietly. There were others in the store, and he did not want to be heard.

An understanding look came into Mrs. Kintrea's eyes, and she smiled. "A bolt of light linen," she, too, spoke softly. A slight reddening of her cheeks signaled to Nat that she was thinking of smalls, items women wore under their dresses. He nodded, and reached high for the bolt she indicated, setting it on the table as well.

"This will do for Sunday dresses," Mrs. Kintrea was tactfully pointing to the fabric Nat had already set out.

Realizing his mistake, he again looked through the colorful bolts, finally choosing functional brown cotton that would do for everyday dresses for the little family. He looked across the store, thinking of many things a family who had lost everything could use in a new start.

"What else?"

Mrs. Kintrea shook her head, shrugging slightly. "Nearly everyone has sent a gift of some sort to her," she told Nat. "And of course, there's the house-raising tomorrow."

Nat realized that no one had told him of the community's actions on behalf of the widow and her girls. He briefly wondered why, then turned to the woman at his side.

"Can you have this made up for them? Do you have someone--?" he began. This was strictly woman's stuff; now that he saw the piles of fabric in front of him, he wondered at himself.

"Oh, indeed, I do, and she's very good," Mrs. Kintrea spoke assuredly.

"Add the costs to my account. Don't tell anyone I'm paying for them." Forgetting that he was to purchase sugar and coffee, Nat strode off, calling "Good day, Mrs. Kintrea," over his shoulder and slamming out the door.

Her husband joined her in watching Nat Kinney stalk away from the store.

"What was that about?" he asked.

"I'm not sure, but I think Mr. Kinney is quite upset," she said. "It looks as though no one told him or his family about the house-raising for the Widow Maggie."

"His family, or himself?" Mr. Kintrea was appreciative of any man who could cut down trees or raise walls with little effort. "There must have been a mistake."

Mrs. Kintrea shrugged, then began rolling the fabric back onto its bolts for delivery to the home of the woman who did dressmaking in the village.

"My guess would be that Mr. Kinney's neighbors don't much care for him," she told her husband. "I don't understand it myself. Look at the dresses he's having made for the Widow Maggie and her girls."

Her husband sniffed in disapproval. Then he gathered the bolts up to take away. "It's not proper for a gentleman to buy clothing for a lady."

Mrs. Kintrea laughed at his expression, and made a shooing gesture with her hands. "Off with you, John," she said. "Nobody's ever said Nat Kinney is a gentleman. But I'm certain he doesn't want the town to know what he's done for that poor woman."

Kirbyville was bustling with traffic. The Springfield-Harrison Road snaked through the valleys northwest of the White River; it left the Wilderness Road at Spokane, and traveled down along the banks of Bear Creek, crossing it several times. The village of Walnut Shade was tucked along the side of an ancient mountain above the joining with Bull Creek. The heavily-traveled road was hard dirt, except when the rains came. Then it was roiling water.

Bill Hensley did a roaring business at the mouth of Bull Creek, ferrying muleskinners and their teams across the unruly White. It could be a risky business, and he had doubled up in the past two years, acquiring the rights to Boston's Road and the ferrying of drivers who preferred to travel the lonely, dirt-poor rocky ridges that were a chief trait of the Ozark Mountains. Anyone who lived on the narrow ridges between the creeks on the west side of the county sure wasn't making money if they were farming for a living. They were scarcely feeding themselves. But the drivers lost no time due to flooding, a major consideration if one was getting paid by the job.

The broad plateau of the land between the White's northernmost loop into Missouri was by no means flat, but there it was possible to raise decent crops. Kirbyville lay almost in the center of the plateau, a natural place for a commerce center. The Springfield-Harrison

Road ran through the town, and other roads crisscrossed, including a branch connecting Kirbyville to the Leadville-Forsyth Road.

At this hour of the day, the camp for the drivers was largely empty. Depending on how much fodder their teams needed, drivers paid anywhere from a dime to a quarter a night to camp on the outskirts of Kirbyville. Several bunkhouses were available, and enterprising residents ran a harness shop, blacksmith, and other associated businesses nearby. There was even a diner that was open late into the evening, and opened before dawn for breakfast.

Kintrea's Store was one of the largest in the county, by virtue of its location near this resting point on the all-important road. Kintrea, no fool, would put new merchandise out immediately, and was thus able to beat any nearby competition out with selection and cost. Other stores in the county usually had to pay a driver to deliver their goods from Kirbyville, unless the storekeeper himself or a trusted employee was able to handle a full team with a loaded wagon. It wasn't easy.

Nat watched as one such team left the loading area, with "Everett's Store" painted on the side of the wagon. The driver was standing in front of his small seat, calling to his mules.

Restless. Nat would not admit, even to himself, that many of the men he'd considered friends were no longer so. Every time he thought back to that night, the night the Taylors had died, he wondered if there had been any way to change the outcome.

He thought not. There was no regret, except that men he had hoped to form lasting associations with were avoiding him. Strolling to the large clearing the residents called a park, Nat wandered through the picnic tables, finally coming to the band stand. He sat on the steps, and contemplated the view. Reaching down, he pulled up a blade of grass, and began stripping it into small pieces.

It had been a mob. He knew it, and every man there knew it. It was only a matter of time before the Taylors killed someone; luck had been with John and Mary Dickenson that day, or they would have died. He had taken the perfect opportunity to teach a few important lessons, and the outlaws had been on the receiving end.

The message had been received loud and clear, he thought. There had been no more word of anyone seriously breaking any laws of society in Taney County since Frank and Tubal Taylor had died.

The night riders had ridden, though. In much smaller groups, and without the use of a noose, other miscreants had been left messages via bundles of hickory sticks. If a man was known to be thieving from his neighbors, he was generally given three sticks in his bundle, tossed on his front porch or in his door yard--three sticks. Three days to return the stolen goods or livestock, or three days to get out of Taney County.

Reaching down for another piece of grass to strip, Nat noticed the small buggy belonging to Alonzo Prather pulling to a halt next to Kintrea's Store. He started to rise, to speak to Alonzo, then noticed that Robert Prather was assisting his mother down from the seat. Alonzo wasn't in sight.

Hmm. Robert had not been at Nat's dinner table very often lately. And Eva was noticeably solemn these days. Had they quarreled? He hoped not. He liked Robert, and knew Maggie had been quietly making plans for a wedding.

Wash Middleton appeared, climbing the slope from the creek. Nat acknowledged Wash with a glance to his left when the older man sat down. Quietly, both men watched Ada Marie walk back to the buggy, clutching her purchase and a few pieces of mail. Robert again assisted his mother, putting the purchases in the back of the buggy and seating himself once more beneath the fringed canopy. The Prathers were obviously on their way home.

"Howdy, Cap'n," Wash spoke in sly, gravelly tones, menace held back when he was being polite and friendly, as he was now.

"Did you know the Widow Maggie is holding a house-raising tomorrow?" Nat asked Wash, as the latter pulled a knife out of its sheath at his waist, and began whittling a piece of wood from his pocket.

Wash's mouth was permanently twisted from the chaw of tobacco he always had in it. Depending on who was asked, his spitting aim was either the best or the worst in the county. This time, it sailed a good yard from the tips of his boot-clad feet.

"Cain't says I did," Wash answered. "But then, we live over Mildred way. That back road down to Long Beach, it's a good place for keeping to itself."

"I should know about these things." Nat realized he was quite insulted. "Those are my neighbors. My daughter plays with the eldest child."

Rolling his mouth around the chaw some more, Wash considered

Absolution | 175

this in his slow way. It was said the only things he did fast was spit and shoot--he'd been a Union scout, highly-decorated. "Don' know 'bout thet, Cap'n," and another spit punctuated this statement. "There's neighbors, and then there's neighbors."

Exasperated, Nat rose. "My daughter plays with her children, my wife has sent them food....what more could it take?"

Looking up at his leader, Wash eyed the tall, strongly-muscled frame. "They mite could use you to raise the logs."

"I am not a mule!" Nat's voice increased in volume.

Wash made a creaking sound, which caused Nat to look down and left at the slight form on the steps. Incredulously, he realized Wash was laughing.

"What?"

" 'Roun here, folks do whut's got to be done," he told Nat. "En iffen it means they go out and pull the plow they own selves, thin thet's whut they do. Not really used to askin' fer hep. Means others git to knowin' bizness they'd best keep to they own self."

Nat suddenly realized this was why he and some others had not been aware of the beatings the Widow Maggie had endured. And with a shock, he understood that it was because they were outsiders, people who came here from another place, expecting to find similar customs and ways of doing this business called life.

One thing had remained the same however. Tales were often changed to protect someone, and it was usually someone who had been guilty. This time, it didn't matter the accepted tale that was repeated to outsiders or children...it was understood, this time, that the tale was changed to protect the weak.

Most would eventually believe, and remember, the story being told. The Widow Maggie had suffered grievous injuries while trying to pull her man from an untimely fire, and the daughter had been injured while pulling the mother herself to safety. The man had simply been too drunk, a dead weight, the fire too hot and too fast to rescue him.

That was something Nat Kinney could approve of, and he did. His subconscious thought of the colors of the fabric he'd chosen for dresses for Miranda and her family suddenly smacked him upside the brain, and he sat down heavily.

Even here, it was expected to wear black for some time after the death of a family member, at least in public. Black was impractical to wear while doing heavy work.

The Widow Maggie had been wearing faded red calico that showed no evidence of attempts to dye it black. She had, of course, lost what clothing the family owned in the fire, so they were wearing cast-offs, someone else's work dresses. They were not wearing even a black armband, which men often did, in remembrance of their former life.

And Mrs. Kintrea had not chosen to suggest that Nat buy fabric for a black dress for the Widow Maggie.

There were some things Nat Kinney realized he would never understand about these hills.

He'd been halfway home before he remembered he had forgotten to buy coffee beans, sugar, and other things on a list in his pocket.

ço ली

Sometime later, Maggie Kinney heard the sounds of an ax coming from the woods to the south of the house. She was sitting on the porch facing Big Bald, using the sunlight to aid in the mending of a tear Georgia had managed to rend all the way down the back of her dress. Not even her rambunctious son James had been so hard on clothes. While she listened to the rhythm of the axe--it told her Nat was cutting down a tree, and a big one--a faint floral scent invaded her senses. Ah. She lifted the dress to her nose, and realized Georgia had been rolling in honeysuckle at some point in the very recent past.

Sighing, she put down the dress. Nat would be thirsty, and possibly hungry. While questions crossed her mind, she went inside, made some sandwiches, and saw Nat's old Army canteen hanging from a peg near the door. She filled it with water, and then put the sandwiches in a satchel. As an afterthought, she wrapped a piece of chocolate cake in waxed parchment, added it to the bag, and set off to find Nat.

Maggie could even tell that Nat was mad by the tempo of the strokes. There had been a sudden silence as she latched the gate to the dooryard behind her, a slight "whoosh," and then the axe started its chant again.

He'd been different since the Bald Knobbers hung the Taylors.

Shaking her head at herself for using the term--even James was using it to announce meetings in the newspaper--she entered the woods, walking the semi-cleared trail and following the sounds of Nat striking a tree with all of his considerable strength.

The first oak he'd cut down was quite long, big in circumference. He'd taken the time to trim the branches off, and it lay denuded, white wood showing where the limbs had been. The second tree he was working on was almost down, and Maggie stepped back to avoid its fall. However, it caught in another oak, breaking several upper branches before it rested on a long, thick limb that made a distinctly groaning noise.

"Goddamnit!" Nat's voice had always carried well. He didn't know she was there, either.

Nat was considering how to bring the tree the rest of the way down--the oak holding it was too big to suit his purposes--when Maggie's voice reached him.

"Nat, a preacher using that word?" her right eyebrow was raised in disapproval as she leaped lightly onto the first tree, and she waited for him to help her step down. He did so left-handed; he was using his right to wipe the sweat from his face and brow, his hat tossed on the ground nearby.

Grey Ghost was ground-tied some distance away, but Maggie could see the bundle that made up her order from Kintrea's. She handed the satchel to Nat, who still needed to cut a few trees down to work off his temper.

"Thanks," he grunted to her, then tore into a sandwich.

"What is wrong with you?" she asked. "What is it?"

"I don't want to talk about it."

She sat down, "All right."

It only took a couple of minutes for Nat to obliterate the light luncheon; he walked around the felled trees, considering, retrieving and donning the hat, not even noticing chocolate cake. Crumpling up the paper remains, he wiped his mouth on his sleeve and drank thirstily from the canteen. He thumbed his hat back after handing Maggie the wrapper and empty canteen. Then he turned to look at the oak that was still resting in the air.

"Need to get a rope," he muttered.

Wood was a necessity. Cut stove-length for cooking and heating, split or sawn for buildings and fences, everyone had a favorite wood

178 | Vonda Wilson Sheets

they preferred for various uses. Maggie liked the smell of pine on winter evenings, herself. Trees were often cut down and left to dry out, sometimes hauled into shelter to be used as needed. Nat had hauled a great deal of fallen timbers and brush out of these woods for the bonfires on the bald.

She watched him pace. Then he threw his hat.

Raising her chin, Maggie narrowed her eyes against the sun to watch Nat. It was not often he misjudged where a tree was going to fall, but his temper was much more than the tree hanging halfway in the air.

"Would you like me to get a rope for you?" she asked.

"No."

"But you just said--"

"No." Nat stomped over to the second tree, and began to yank on it. It budged some, but not nearly enough to get free of the monstrous half-dead oak it was caught in. Then he walked around, out of Maggie's sight. Next thing she knew, his head and shoulders were slightly visible through the leafed branches of the cut tree-- he'd climbed the bigger one. Then he disappeared from view again, and she watched the tree shudder as he kicked it.

The thing was coming at her, pushed by Nat's feet. It caught on a snagged old limb, and there were more oaths that emanated from the green, shuddering with the impact of Nat's feet. Maggie rose, and moved a bit farther away, going to stand near Ghost and watching as Nat somehow managed to free it from the snag. Progress was made, and then the sounds stopped.

Sun glints off red hair caught her eye, and she was in time to see Nat in the cut tree, as it crashed to the ground with him hanging on to upright branches. As it came to a rest, he jumped lightly through the detritus to the ground, a grim smile on his face.

"Not just anyone can do that," he told her with satisfaction.

"Ride a tree?" she asked, teasing.

"Yank one around," he responded, going to retrieve his axe.

Turkey calls echoed through the small clearing. Nat's shoulders tensed as he grabbed the axe, beginning to sever limbs with a solid crunch which opposed the gobbles riding on the air. Maggie's face was quizzical as she looked at the surrounding treetops and through the woods around her, expecting to see a flock flee from the noise Nat was making. No large ungainly creatures appeared.

Nat was studiously ignoring the turkey calls. Maggie made her way through the green briars and last year's leaves toward him, staying clear of the flying wood chips.

The calls ceased as suddenly as they began. Nat reached the end of the tree, used his right arm to wipe his brow, and then leaned against the axe as he studied the two trees.

"Well, those will do."

"For what?" Maggie asked.

"I'm gonna haul them over to the Widow Maggie's. There's a house-raising tomorrow."

"Oh." Maggie pondered for a few seconds. "Georgia never said anything."

"No, I didn't think so." He carefully avoided looking at his wife's face, pacing over to the big half-dead oak. If he was going to cut it down, he'd need to return to the barn and sharpen his axe, he thought. Resolutely, he turned to face Maggie.

"Georgia should spend more time with Miranda. And you should ask her what they talk about."

This was so unusual, coming from Nat, that Maggie stared at him. "What on earth for?"

Nat took a few precious seconds; his thoughts were turbulent with various emotions, but one landed hard on his tongue and he blurted, "We should not have hung the Taylors."

Maggie stood so still, so pale that at first Nat wasn't sure she'd heard him. Then she blinked. "What does that have to do with Georgia going to Granny Haggard's?"

"I'm worried."

Scoffing, Maggie disputed. "No one would harm her. I do not understand, Nat. The Taylors were dangerous men."

"True. But I didn't set out to kill them."

"You told me yourself it was a mob."

"That is true as well."

Impatient, Maggie's hand spread in the air in front of her. "I cannot read your mind, Nat. Georgia needs friends, but she's going to be educated as well."

"I was the leader that night."

"You are still the leader. The others are still coming to you."

Nat nodded slowly. "They are. But only to tell me of things they are doing on the patrols."

180 | Vonda Wilson Sheets

"Has anyone else been killed?" Her voice was sharp enough.

"No." He ran his hand through his sweaty hair. "Maggie, no one will harm Georgia, true. For fear of me."

Maggie's eyes went round as she looked pointedly at the tree now laying on the ground, then back at Nat. Her chin was pugnacious and her back stiffened as she said, "That's not a bad thing, Nat."

"I've lost them!"

"Who?"

"Alonzo and JJ, the ones who are the influential people in the county."

"Right." Trying to be considerate, Maggie edged slightly closer to Nat. "What have you lost?"

Looking back at her, Nat saw she still didn't understand.

"Respect." She was nodding slowly as he spoke. "Power. No one is telling of things I should know."

"Such as?"

His right arm let the axe fall over as he swept the clearing with his hand, indicating the felled trees.

"We should have been told about the Widow Maggie's house-raising. If Georgia knew, why didn't she say anything? Did someone tell her not to?"

"That's ridiculous, Nat."

"Is it? Tell me, have you taken more food to Granny Haggard's?"

"No."

"Have you spoken to Ada Marie or any of the other women recently?"

"You know I haven't been off the farm."

"And none of them have come to call on you."

Maggie's head was shaking back and forth slightly. "Except for church, I have seen no one, Nat."

"Maggie. If I'm to lead these men, I have to know what's going on in the lives of the people."

"Then tell the men to keep you informed."

"You have to talk to the women!" he bellowed. Taken aback, Maggie was speechless for several seconds.

"Are you saying that because I don't gossip and spend time at Kintrea's store, it's my fault you didn't know about this house-raising?"

Absolution | 181

"Arrrrrrgh." Nat ran his hands through his hair. He stomped several paces, crossing the clearing, stepping over the felled trees.

"The men I need most in the Bald Knobbers are not working with me now. I need to know why. I need to know why Georgia did not tell us of her friend's new house. There's a connection." He came back, looking at Maggie, willing her to see the problem.

Neighbors, people needed others to survive in a community. Nat supposed he should have known there would be a house-raising, but he'd understood from Maggie that Miranda's family was not going to return to the homestead.

The deeper, underlying morass that was bothering Nat most was the loss of his friendships with Alonzo and JJ. He hadn't had a reason to visit Forsyth in recent days--indeed, thought it best to let his lieutenants tell him what he needed to know in regards to the mood of the city since the death of the Taylors. "Peaceful" was what had been reported. Folks weren't worried about the Taylors anymore.

And in peaceful times, folks helped each other with crops, with raising homes; they shopped, they gossiped, they were friends. His daughter had managed to keep her friendship with Miranda; but somehow, he and Maggie had not noticed that the few friends they had were no longer in their everyday lives.

"I do wish you would not use that phrase," Maggie murmured.

"Maggie...." Nat was drawn to her as a moth to the flame of a lantern. "There will not be a League if we do not talk to the people."

"I have no desire to chitchat about the latest fashions with Caroline Brown," she retorted. "It has nothing to do with criminal activities in Forsyth."

"Oh, for God's sake!" Nat's anger rose again. "How is the League going to know who to go after if we don't know what's going on in people's lives?" Deliberately turning his back on Maggie, he picked up the axe, whistled for Ghost, and waited for the horse to approach him. "I'm going to the barn."

Maggie made no gesture to accompany him as the turkey calls started up again. She didn't even look to see Nat's shoulders tense up as he stalked off, Ghost following behind.

Sitting on the tree Nat had ridden to the ground, Maggie didn't even hear the silence around her. She was thinking furiously, and watching various insects as they reacted to this change in their environment.

Would it be her fault if Nat could not retain leadership in the League? She didn't think so. The Taylors were no big loss to any community. Forsyth might be a safe place to visit now, but there was no theater, no musical gatherings, no activities to interest her. Maggie read the newspaper, of course, and ordered in books and periodicals, since there was no library in the region. Her life centered solely on her family and her piano. She had little need for more.

Nat was not gregarious, but he had always needed more than a quiet family life on the farm. She did not begrudge him this. But his desire to become part of the community, to be respected and influential, to provide more for his family, had never impacted her own life a great deal. It certainly had not required her to become social.

Georgia was more like her father in this, Maggie realized. Until now, it was a trait that further endeared the child to her.

But what if it meant losing her? Maggie wondered. What if Georgia's need for friendship expanded past the little damaged family at Granny Haggard's, and she would want to leave, long before Maggie was ready for her to do so?

Maggie's heart began thumping painfully in her chest. She could not stop Nat from his activities, nor James, but she could, and would, certainly do her best to keep Georgia and Paul home. Eva would marry soon; it was evident in the actions of both Robert Prather and her daughter. So that was another loss she was going to have to endure.

The sun was beating down on her now. She had no inkling of time passing.

The sound of mules and chains jerked her head up, and the team came down the stump-studded trail to the clearing, Nat walking behind and jerking the reins. He turned the team, backed them, tied them to a sapling, and began to prepare the log for hauling without saying a word to her.

"Nat?"

Nat hesitated, and then bent again to his task. He yanked the chains back to the log, then stopped and looked at her watching him. Dropping his work, he took a step toward her, then another.

"I want you to understand something. I love this place, this home we've made. I love my church. I want to be a part of the life here."

Maggie acknowledged this statement by dipping her head once. She did not raise her eyes back to him.

"And you may as well know....I'm taking these logs to the widow's place, and I'm going there tomorrow to help with the raising. I want you to fix a basket of food, but I won't ask you to go with me."

The hurt in her heart made her take a deep breath and let it slowly out. Pride made her lift her face to the man she based her life upon.

"There's something else."

Forcing an eyebrow to raise, Maggie waited.

"I bought the necessities for the widow and her daughters to have two new dresses each."

"WHAT?" She was on her feet, and in Nat's face. "You did WHAT?"

Nat wasn't one to lose his temper often, but when he did, it was a maelstrom. "I said, I bought fabric for the Widow Maggie, Miranda, and her sisters."

A sharp slap echoed through the clearing.

As if the sound had been the trigger of a gun at a horse race, Nat grabbed both of Maggie's hands, forcing her backwards. The print of her hand on his left cheek was redder even than his angry face. She tripped, going down backwards, her right buttock hitting the stump of a sapling that had been cut earlier in the spring. It hurt, but she took no time to notice, as Nat had come down on his knees with her fall. Momentum and his own anger continued taking her down; her head thumped against something hard, and Nat's hold on her wrists changed as one of his huge hands took both of hers to the ground beyond her head.

Grunts, and her skirts were thrown over her head. Maggie's corsets prevented deep breathing, and the layers of cotton and linen over her face forced panting as she struggled to fight Nat off. She could hear the tied mules shy away from them.

Domination.

She attempted to knee him in the groin; he shifted. His left hand, holding her wrists, twisted, and his elbow bent. He fell, unable to keep his weight from pushing her harder into the ground and the stumps that were digging into her. He pulled his right knee up against her belly, blocking her left leg. His left leg forced her bent right one wide, and her foot tried to find purchase.

Somehow, her hands came free, and blindly, she scrabbled for his face, and howled when she drew blood. He responded by putting his left hand over her mouth and nostrils, cutting her breath off through the skirt and petticoats covering her face.

As he entered her body, she turned her head from his hand and screamed.

Nat stopped thrusting for a moment, only a moment, and then he laughed a low, rusty sound that terrified Maggie even when she realized that her body apparently wanted him. No matter. Her heart didn't, not like this.

She lay still, no longer fighting, but she refused to join him in pulse, in spirit. A body being a traitorous thing, she knew that she was accepting his domination of her, and her love, which had been the world for her, took the battering with no sound but that of flesh.

It was a blessedly short thing.

He lay on top of her, panting, his anger and passion spent. There was a difference she could feel, and her bruised heart slowed, thumping larger and louder against her ribs. She felt him lift onto his elbows, and she wondered if she would accept his apology.

There wasn't one.

Nat took time to raise himself to his feet, leaving Maggie lying on the ground. He saw blood on the lower half of her white body, and on her smooth legs. Wiping the back of his hand across his stinging face, he noted she'd managed to make him bleed, too. His eyes narrowed as he watched her throw her skirts down, and painfully push to a sitting position.

She did not look at him. He offered her his left hand, and she ignored it.

"I believe I have just proven you have no cause to be jealous," he told her, waving his hand in front of her.

"Was that what that was?" She looked at his hand, but would not touch him. Painfully, she got to her feet, unaided. She would not let him see her pain. Seeing the satchel and empty canteen some distance away, she suppressed a stagger as she retrieved the items, and finally, she looked him in the eyes and smiled faintly.

"It felt like hate to me." Straightening her back--thankful for the aid of her corset--she walked toward home, and a hot bath.

CHAPTER 23
A new home is raised, new ways of thinking

The day of the Widow Maggie's house-raising dawned in soft gray mist, with pearls of color swirling through the slight breezes on the ridges. The fog burned off in response to the sun's ascent, lingering longest in the trees that grew up the northern sides of the mountains.

Andy had not slept last night. The fog curled in with the smoke coming from a newly-built shed up above the razed site on the mountain's bench. Tonight, a new house would shelter Maggie, Miranda, Phebe, and Celie.

In the roughly two weeks since he and Widow Maggie had come to an understanding--he still didn't know what sort of understanding it was, just that it was--the pitiful kitchen garden on her homestead was tended and encouraged, with the results being bright green growing things.

Andy was not a farmer. He had no desire to be one; indeed, he didn't know much about farming for more than subsistence. He had spent most of his life in the woods, gathering and hunting what he needed, bartering for things he had to have otherwise.

Granny Haggard had saddled her mule and ridden off at some point in the afternoon while Maggie and he talked about cooking meat and making sauce. When she returned, she found the two in the garden, discussing tomatoes and spices. The girls had been rowdy in their honeysuckle bower, and the afternoon pleasant.

With assurance, Granny had pushed the two out of the garden and into the front dooryard. "You go there," she told them. Maggie's face had taken on a stubborn look, but she and Andy walked to her old home place, sliding down the hill in concert to the baby pigs squealing in the small barn.

Maggie stood rooted and tentative. She looked around, seeing what was left, waiting to be ambushed, Andy supposed. Then she smiled grimly. "Nothing, there's nothing here."

Andy understood.

In the time since, his sister, the Snapps, and Billy Miles had joined him and the widow in salvaging and clearing for a new cabin. Serelda brought a hatch of chicks with a hen for the new coop from

186 | Vonda Wilson Sheets

their uncle's place. Sam and Susie had helped Andy coax the big black sow and her piglets to their new home, a sty not too far down the slope, the fence reinforced with rocks.

Finding and cutting down the right trees to build a cabin had been the main problem. Yesterday, Andy and Billy were ranging in the cluster of trees which shielded the homestead from the ridge road above. It was growing late, and they needed at least two more logs to roll down the hill and line up for notching. Andy had been silent--he and Billy were not friendly, although there was no enmity between them.

Good oak trees, large enough to use for the walls of a cabin, did not grow often on the limestone-strewn northern exposures of the hills. One could see the White River way down if there weren't more trees below the homesite. Andy had shucked his shirt, tying it about his waist, his eyes wandering through the greenness below them.

Billy had begun to make his way down the hill when both of the young men froze. A team of mules was being driven down the rough trail to the house site.

"Expectin' Sam?" Andy asked in a low voice. Billy shook his head back up at Andy, and shifted the crouch he was in.

The voice reaching the young men's ears was one neither expected to hear. It was Nat Kinney.

"Well, well..." Billy shifted again, slid a little. Andy's right hand shot out, halting Billy's movements.

From the sounds, Kinney had brought a log to the house site. He shouted a questioning "Hello!" but everyone else was gone to dinner at Granny Haggard's. Andy's hackles raised; he briefly considered doing a turkey call. Doing so earlier today had been unpleasant, however, and his throat tightened instead. It had taken every ounce of strength he possessed to sit camouflaged, listening to Nat Kinney rape his wife. The taste of the memory soured his mouth, and he spat.

"Sumbitch," he muttered. Listening, Billy shrugged agreement. Tilting his head toward the left, the two of them began slowly making their way toward the source of the sounds coming from the clearing.

"Put yer shirt on," Billy whispered, although Andy was already doing so. He was browning from the sun, but the pallor of his skin would still be easily seen in the shadows of the hillside, should

Kinney look. Both then clad in homespun shades of brown, they blended in easily with the understory as they made their way to a vantage point behind a deadfall, and looked over it.

There were two long oak logs, pulled in beside the pile waiting for the gathering. Kinney was unhooking the chains, pulling his tackle and bagging it, slapping it over the gee mule on the team. Every few seconds, he would glance off one direction or another, expecting someone to greet him. Even through the dusk wafting up the hillside, Andy saw claw marks on the man's face as he turned the team and leapt onto the haw mule's withers. Both mules fussed a bit, but Kinney yanked the reins and forced them to climb the trail back up to the ridge road.

Andy and Billy waited only a few seconds, then scrabbled down to examine the logs. Exactly what was needed. Billy was nodding to himself. Kinney's logs were longer than the ones he and Andy had cut, but that was easily fixed.

What was not so clear was why Kinney had donated the logs. Billy didn't think it mattered, and said so.

"There's sumthin' behind it," Andy insisted.

Billy shrugged, getting his things together. It wasn't a long walk to dinner, but he was tired, and didn't much care. Brief good-nights, and Billy was gone.

Andy puzzled over this through the night as he tended the cuts of meat hanging from the rafters of the smoke shed. Although there were a few quail, most of the cuts were pork from a fat, corn-fed yearling pig he had traded for. Women would be bringing side dishes, but Andy was supplying the meat.

Widow Maggie and Andy had spent the evening hours of the past week experimenting with the sauce recipe she was trying to recall from her childhood. She'd finally been satisfied with it, and when Andy had dipped a piece of venison in it, he understood what she had been talking about. The thick brownish-red sauce had enhanced the hickory-smoked lean venison to a bone-melting degree. Imagining what it would be like with fat pig had almost brought tears to his eyes.

So today, folks would be eating Andy's carefully-tended pork and Widow Maggie's sauce.

One last time, Andy picked up a bowl of drippings and brushed them on the hanging meat. His stomach growled. Setting the bowl down, he pulled a quail down and stepped back out of the shed, leaning against the shut door. He put pieces of the tender bird in his mouth, chewing slowly and wishing he had some of Maggie's sauce.

As early as it was, echoes of wagons and harness sifted down through the trees. He heard Miranda and her sisters gamboling down the newly-widened trail to the homesite, excitedly chattering about the changes in their lives.

There was still some meat left on the bones of the quail when the sisters espied him, and ran back up and over the stone shelf to the smoke shed. He smiled tiredly as he doled out pieces to them--they couldn't be hungry, coming from breakfast at Granny Haggard's.

Maggie was appraising the site, making sure things were ready, just in time for Sam and Susie Snapp to begin their descent. Cheery greetings resounded, and Andy heard Sam tell Susie that she was not to be dancing around all day long. Susie laughed, and Maggie joined her. It was going to be a good day.

Seeing the women had reminded Andy of Maggie Kinney, and a brief coldness touched his cheek. Brushing away any idea of ghosts, he pushed off from his lean on the shed and came down to join Sam, who was inspecting the trail.

"Reckon it'll be about cleared by tonight," Sam told Andy. "Enough folks come, it'll trample down."

"Yeah." Andy agreed.

There was a fenced enclosure off the barn, and Sam began unloading tools from the horse he'd led down, taking the bridle off and slapping the horse's rump into the barnyard. Tying the gate, he turned to find Susie picking up her basket and smiling at him. She moved away, distracted by the noise of Nannie running to greet Miranda and the others. Sam watched for a moment, then bent to pick up the hatchet and other items.

"I hear you had a visitor last night," he told Andy as they moved toward the stacked logs. "Didn't have to cut any more trees down afterwards, did you?"

"No," Andy replied. "Kinda sticks in my craw, though. Dint want Kinney around."

"Help is help, Andy," Sam had a troubled look on his face. "I know....I know!" he held a hand up as Andy started to speak. "You don't want his kind of help."

"Nope."

More men arrived, and the work of notching, rolling, placing, and setting logs began. Enough hands were available to build the walls three logs high all around before the women came with water. Some of the men began preparing the poles needed to roll the logs higher with the aid of levers and ropes, when another man arrived.

Nat Kinney.

Andy was in the smoke shed, taking down the meat for slicing when he heard Kinney's voice.

Without invitation, Kinney put his horse in the barnyard, calling out greetings to the assorted Snapps, Haggards, Miles, and Coggburns that were building Widow Maggie's new cabin.

Andy could not stay. Trembling, he wondered if Maggie Kinney had come with her husband. But he could not hear her voice.

Rage.

He could not stay.

Slowly, so slowly, he moved to the other side of the shed, where the shadows hid him and he could see Kinney rolling his shirtsleeves above his elbows, pretending not to see the stony faces of the men around him. Greetings had been stilted, abrupt, but Andy knew that Kinney's strength would be needed as the day went on, pulling the logs up and over, settling the notched ends.

He took advantage of the fact that no one was looking toward the shed. Stealthily, he slid out and behind, then he melted into the brush, making no sound that could be heard over the work starting back up below.

One pair of eyes watched for as long as they could. Miranda did not understand why Andy was leaving, but the years of habitually avoiding Pa came back to her, and she didn't go to ask her mother why. And when Georgia Kinney tagged her in their game, she began to run and shout, playing with the other children.

It was cool and dark. He slept.

Ragged, distraught breathing. Shivering.

Came awake, flinging his arms wide, and the rough dirt chafed his face and his bare knees.

Consciousness painful. Darkness confusing.

Awake or asleep, hands pulled at him, and he fought, his eyes wet, his voice hoarse.

Then there was nothing.

Andy was in the cave he called home when his mind rejoined his body at dusk. Without moving from his face-down position on the dirt-packed floor, he listened for any movement, and heard only his own breathing. Cautiously, he turned his head left and opened his eyes. The rocks that circled his fireplace were within a couple of feet; he looked beyond to see the limned opening of the cave, and could see the shadowy deer hide curtain tied back to the right of the entryway.

His hands came up beside his head, and he pushed himself to an awkward sitting position. Slowly, he realized he was sitting bare-assed, his shirt tails dangling in the dirt. He could taste mud, and spat toward the cold fireplace. He leaned back against the cot; no use wondering why he found himself on the floor. It had been some time since the nightmare had been so vivid, so wild. The shivering became a shudder.

Once he got a small blaze lit, Andy grabbed a large piece of cotton and a bar of lye soap, and then made his way to the small pool of the creek that fell down the hill beside his cave. The tin cup sitting on the rock wall aided him in rinsing his mouth, and he again spat dirt. Setting the soap on a rock which had a small bowl carved in its top surface, he soaked the cotton and began to wet his body. After rubbing with the soap, he plunged into the shallow pool, kneeling to bring his head under the water, purging the memory of ghosts.

It was full dark before he returned to the shelter, now warmed by the fire. Grabbing a blanket, Andy crouched down with his arms spread wide, using the blanket to force the heat to his cold body.

He could hear the questions about his disappearance soughing down the hillside over the river; Maggie was wondering where he was. His stomach growled; that was a good sign, it meant he'd managed to beat the devil again.

Quickly dressing, ignoring the scrapes on his face, elbows and knees, he put on moccasins and made sure the fire was banked. Then he set off for the new cabin, traveling deer paths instead of going to the top of the ridge and walking the road.

There was merriment around the big fire filled with scraps and oddments of wood. The cabin was built, layers of oiled canvas

Absolution | 191

tacked down for a roof until shingles could be made at leisure. For now, the house had been blessed, and several children were asleep on the floor, their unlined faces showing contentment in the light of the embers of the fire in the half-finished fireplace.

The rock shelf on the hill behind the house was a good place to watch those below. Andy sat on his heels, his knees against his chest; he was warm now, his hair dry beneath his hat, and he could smell the food now being served by the women. The children had eaten earlier, while the men gathered their tools and sat down to drink for a spell, relaxing in the light of the flames and joking about things that had happened in the day.

He looked for Kinney, but the man appeared to be gone.

Glancing over toward the smoke shed, there was a small figure that drew his attention.

She had been watching for Andy, and once she saw him, she carefully made her way toward him, coming at last to sit on his right. Her sun-browned face was pale in the light of the fire that made its way up the hill; her faded blue dress, paler still. She smelled of smoke and food and light, and she dimpled when she heard Andy's stomach gurgle.

"Hongry?" she asked.

Still unable to speak, he nodded. Still smiling, she put a hand on his arm to stay him, and then slipped down the hill. Andy watched as she went around the front of the cabin, and re-emerged over to the left, where a makeshift table was set up. Maggie laid a hand on her daughter's head, and leaned close to hear the gentle voice.

Never once looking in Andy's direction, Maggie kept her motions smooth and supple as she straightened, then found an empty plate and began to fill it. Andy could almost imagine the smile on Maggie's face--the light wasn't good enough for him to see it. Miranda had gone over to the end of the table, and took down a cork-stoppered bottle, and by the time she returned, her mother handed her a napkin-covered plate.

Back at his side, she handed him the plate and bottle. Maggie had poured some of her sauce on the smoked pork, and it was just as good as Andy had imagined it. He groaned slightly while he savored it. A burst of laughter came from the revelers as the flavor exploded on his tongue.

Miranda was hugging her knees, watching below. She seemed

192 | Vonda Wilson Sheets

to know Andy couldn't talk, and was offering herself as a shield between him and the darkness around them.

He sat the plate down in front of him, empty.

His voice surprised him in its normalcy. "Did it go well?"

Her eyes on the fire, Miranda nodded. "Ma's happy now," she said simply. Then she turned her head so Andy could see her face. "Lotta people."

"Came today?"

She nodded again. "They builded, built, the cabin and did some other chores Ma cuddint do."

Andy nodded with her. It was what neighbors did, helping when they could. In a rough land, a person never knew when they might need help, so they gladly helped others as they could.

"The store owner came." Andy noticed a smile hovering on Miranda's lips.

"Mr. Kintrea? Wal, I kin see why he would. Good food," and he nodded toward his empty plate.

"Yeh. He ate a lot." Her voice was amused. "But he dint help with the cabin."

"I ain't sure Mr. Kintrea is much at that kinda thing," Andy smiled back.

"He went to the smoke shed."

Andy perked up. That was interesting.

"What did he do there?" he asked, curious.

"Wanted to know what Ma did to the meat."

"Ah." For lack of anything to do with his hands, Andy prodded the empty plate in front of him. Miranda's feet shifted, and she looked back down at the fire.

"He wants Ma to make sandwiches for him to sell to the teamsters."

A noncommittal grunt from Andy. Then he heard a note of doubt in Miranda's voice.

"She sed she was too busy to think about it today."

Andy's head bobbed twice in agreement with Maggie's delaying tactic. But her daughter put a little hand on Andy's bare right wrist as it prodded an empty plate, and he stayed himself.

He never touched anyone willingly, nor let anyone touch him. His head shakily bobbed again, and he hesitantly looked down at Miranda's hand, not moving, just resting on his wrist. Then up a short distance to her shy but eager face.

"Wud you teach me how to fix pork?"

Andy's left hand crossed to touch the left hand of Miranda, furtive and quick; his voice was hoarse once more.

"I kin do thet."

And they smiled at each other.

CHAPTER 24
Mid May, 1885 - Blowup

Maggie watched as Nat rode Grey Ghost past the house and up to the Springfield/Harrison Road.

Morning lay soft but heavy on her. The sun had not yet risen above Big Bald, although fingers of pinkish-orange light were grasping for clouds. There had been no dew this morning--it was going to be a hot day. She leaned against the porch post, turning her back on Nat's direction and watching the sky. Once the rim of the sun crested the bald, she went inside, calling for Georgia and Paul to come down; she'd silently fixed breakfast while Nat was tending the animals in the morning dark.

Not talking to Nat for more than three days was taking its toll. She lay beside him at night, stiff as a bundle-board, not once reaching out for him. He had done the same.

Paul and Georgia were not happy to be roused for breakfast and studying again this morning. She knew it was because Nat had snorted in disapproval the day after he helped build the Widow Maggie's house when she'd told them lessons would be starting up again that morning.

At this time, she didn't know if she cared about Nat's approval or not.

Sighing, she poured herself a cup of coffee, liberally adding cream and sugar to weaken the burned taste it often left on her tongue. Listening to the children scratching their math problems on their boards, she walked over to the window, again watching Big Bald.

The sun was more than halfway through the morning before she let Georgia and Paul go from their studies. It was already stifling in the house--they needed to be outside.

Her hands were tapping a tattoo on the open window sill when Georgia's voice cut through the haze in her mind.

"Mother?"

"Yes, dear?" Not quite absent.

"Are you alright?" Maggie turned and looked at Georgia's anxious face.

Maggie smiled faintly. "I am. Why do you ask?" Georgia didn't know about the healing bruises, the hurting heart, she was sure of it.

"You haven't played the piano in a week."

With a jolt, Maggie realized it had been at least three nights since she had played. She hadn't missed it. "Surely not that long, dear," she murmured. "I've merely been tired."

"Oh." Turning to leave, Georgia pulled her bonnet over her head, tying the strings and then again turned back to look at her mother's face.

"Maybe you should sleep today, Mother."

Maggie gestured toward the pans of bread dough she'd moved to the table after the school books had been put away.

"I've Sunday dinner to see to, Georgia," she told her daughter. "Your father will be preaching tomorrow, and he will certainly invite guests for dinner."

Georgia's lips pursed as she sent her mother and the bread dark glances of disapproval. She reached up to untie her bonnet, and began to put it back on the peg by the door.

"I'll stay and help."

Maggie smiled, a real smile this time. "No, you go on to Granny's," she said. "It'll be an hour or two yet; the meat is roasting now."

The dark hair disappeared under the bonnet again, and Georgia left, smiling with her mother's blessing.

Paul was slower to come down the stairs; he had put on work clothes, planning to work in the barn before joining friends for swimming in the river later in the day. However, he, too, stopped in the doorway of the kitchen, watching Maggie's hands restless on the windowsill. Her face was hidden from him, but he knew her thoughts were far away.

He walked into the room, his step nearly as light as Nat's, and put a hand on Maggie's right shoulder.

"Mother." She glanced over the hand on her shoulder, then up into his face. "You and Father have not spoken in days."

His face was so like Nat's, she almost burst with the myriad emotions in her heart. Instead, she turned from him, lightly shrugging his hand off.

"No."

His eyes were intent--she could feel them boring holes into her skull.

She picked irritation out of the morass, and flung it at him. "Paul, do go clean out the barn. I am quite alright!" and turned to face him, shoulders squared. Her right hip sent burning messages along her spine, decrying the sudden movement, but she kept it from her eyes as she looked at Paul.

"Really, Mother," and he indicated the old shirt and breeches of his father, which hung loosely on his fourteen-year-old frame. "Don't be angry."

"Why should I not be?"

"Because he's doing work that must be done," Nat's son told her. He smiled, and her heart began to thaw, just a small drop of blood running down the sides to create a puddle in the shadow of her red pulse. "And he needs you to keep him strong."

He, too, turned to leave her, grabbing his straw work hat and smashing it on his head. She watched through the window as he strode off toward the barn, lean and clumsy still with his height, but the definite markings of a young man with a clear conscience in the set of his shoulders.

ళ ఞ

Forsyth was bustling. It was Saturday, market day.

Alonzo and Ada Marie Prather were in his law office, on the west side of the square, when the door bell jangled. He looked up, and Ada Marie turned to see, a man standing in the open door, his hat brim being twisted by his thin brown hands.

"Mr. Prather?" His face was as thin as his hands, eyes nervous beneath thick brows. A muscle in his left jaw was twitching.

Alonzo searched through his memory....Taber. He stood.

"Mr. Taber!" He came around from behind his desk, and strode to shake the younger man's hand.

The dark eyes searched Alonzo's face. "Kin we talk?"

Nodding, Alonzo stepped back two steps, to allow Mr. Taber enter the room. Ada Marie was settling her hat on her head; she picked up her handbag, and nodded to Mr. Taber.

"I'll be at Everett's, then," she told Alonzo, and smiled at the visitor. "Good day, sir."

Tabor could not smile back, but he did nod at Alonzo's wife as she left the building.

Alonzo's memory supplied him with other information about Taber. He had recently filed a homestead claim down river, along the east bank of Big Creek, and not far from the mouth. It was a good piece of land, and Taber was a good farmer, although illiterate. Alonzo had done the paperwork.

"Your claim has not been returned--" Alonzo began.

Taber's head shook. "Thet's n-not why I'm here," he interrupted, stammering.

Alonzo indicated a chair in front of his desk. "Will you be seated?" he asked, curious. He'd forgotten Taber's speech impediment.

More negative head motion. "N-no, Sary, the young'uns, outside. T-tole them I'd on'y be a m-m-minnit."

Alonzo glanced around Taber's head, seeing a covered wagon outside with more thin faces staring back at him. If he wasn't mistaken, there was fear in the eyes of the children and wife. He looked back at Taber, and saw the same emotion.

Alarmed, Alonzo asked, "What? What is it?"

The strong emotions were keeping Taber from speaking clearly. However, one word had been clear. "B-b-bald N-Knobbers."

Impatiently moving past Taber, Alonzo went outside. Sarah Taber shrank back as he approached her. "What is it?" he asked her, only to find her husband pulling on his arm, keeping him from climbing into the wagon, he supposed.

"Mr. Prather..." Sarah looked down at her husband, and sighed. A tear slid down her cheek. Traces of other tears were clear in the dust-covered face. "John, did you tell 'im?"

Her husband shook his head. Resignedly, he pointed at his throat.

Sighing again, Mrs. Taber leaned forward, speaking low with a parched voice.

"The Bald Knobbers came to our house two nights ago."

"The Bald Knobbers?" Alonzo asked. A certain grimness tightened his mouth. "What did they want?" To the best of Alonzo's knowledge, John Taber was so honest, his own family had disowned him. Until they needed something he had.

"They sed we wuzn't marrit," Sarah told him. "Sed we had to git off the place, leave it."

Confusion was plain on Alonzo's face. He searched Sarah's eyes; she found some grit and stared back. Daring. She wondered if he had anything to do with it, he knew.

"You aren't married?" Alonzo's speech was slow, but his mind was racing.

"We are!" John's voice rang clear and true.

Sarah nodded agreement. "We got marrit nine years ago," she told Alonzo. "There was a big revival, and a preacher marrit us on the last night."

There were five faces peeping through the sides of the canvas, and a sixth, a girl older than ten, poked over her mother's shoulder. Indignant eyes. "Gran told me I was there," the girl said.

"Hush, Lesha..." her mother's hand came up, pushing the daughter back into the wagon's shade. "I won't say we did it afore we lived together," she said, apologizing to Alonzo. "But we was made handfast in front of witnesses afore I moved onto John's pa's place." Both she and John were blushing.

Alonzo stepped back, and John's hand on his arm dropped.

Blushes aside, Alonzo knew it was an accepted practice, to live together until a preacher came through. This was probably only the second or third time John Taber had been in Forsyth since he married Sarah. Some people didn't balk at traveling; others, often the women, never went further than 10 miles from their homes. No wonder the children were staring wide-eyed.

"I have the paper, right here!" Sarah Taber reached through the back, into the wagon, and it was obvious a weight was handed to her. She brought a thick, gold-leaved book out, and set it upon her lap. The Bible opened to a well-marked spot, and a piece of paper was lifted slowly from the thin pages. Alonzo's hand reached for it, and she reverently laid the paper on his palm.

He opened it carefully, aware of the eyes upon him. It was heavily creased, and he winced as the paper gave a little, even with his gentleness.

It was a marriage certificate, handwritten by the cleric who had visited their little village that nestled on the White River near the Arkansas line. Alonzo saw the marks where Sarah and John had "signed" it; witnesses, too, had made marks. The only signature was the preacher's. But the date was more than nine years ago. He folded the paper back up, careful to follow the established creases. Sarah took it from his hand with the reverence of the illiterate for a legal document.

Alonzo turned to John. "Did you ever let the county clerk see that paper?"

No. "We didn't n-know we wuz s-supposed to," Taber said.

Alonzo smiled and nodded reassuringly. "The clerk enters the marriage into the record books," he told the couple. "That is how it is made legal."

"We sed our vows afore God and man," Sarah Taber spoke for her husband. She was plain-spoken, Alonzo noted. She had to be, he supposed. "We ain't broke our promise. Why does the clerk have to see it?"

"So if someone wants to know who is married, they only have to check the records. The government keeps the records, and they'll give you a copy. Nothing is wrong with your marriage, but it does have to be entered." Alonzo hesitated, then asked, "Will you do that, and then stay?"

John reached his hand toward his wife, who slapped a bundle of hickory sticks into it. There were three sticks tied with twine.

"Them Bald N-Knobbers told us to git, and we're gittin'," he assured Alonzo. "This here is the third day."

"But your farm--" protested Alonzo. "You will get the title to it any time!"

John Taber threw the bundle of sticks down, narrowly missing Alonzo's feet. Sarah Taber leaned over, and spat on it.

"That's what we think of yer govermint," she said, her eyes hard. She barely moved as Taber joined her on the seat, having walked around behind the wagon to climb up the left side. "We're goin' to Injun Territory, where it ain't."

"Why, if you've done no wrong?" Alonzo asked as John Taber gathered up the reins, "And why did you come to me?"

John leaned forward to listen as Sarah Taber answered. "You helped us with our land, Mr. Prather," she said grudgingly. "Someone sed you wuz in thet Bald Knobber ruckus, where the Taylors got hung. We figgered you needed to know, so's mebbe someone else won't lose their place. Someone wants our place real bad, we figger."

With that, John Taber clicked his tongue, and the family moved on, leaving a proven claim on their homestead which had been worked by a married couple.

Furious, he bent over, picked up the bundle of hickory sticks, careful to avoid the spittle. Looking around the town, he saw it with new vision--some folks were brisk about their business, even in the

200 | Vonda Wilson Sheets

heat, and others were slow, confident that nothing bad was going to happen to them.

Nat Kinney's voice startled him.

"Where did JJ go?"

Alonzo whirled left. Nat stepped out of the shade of the building housing the printing press and newspaper office, treading lightly on the wooden porch of his law office.

He wasn't sure if he should answer Nat directly, but decided it would serve or sever their friendship.

"He sold up, moved to Ozark."

"Why?" The man was interested, but Alonzo saw no signs of anger. Rather, there was disappointment.

"He thought the Bald Knobbers were out of control the night the Taylors were hung," Alonzo was wary.

Nat shook his head. "No, there was a plan," he insisted.

Alonzo was a big man, tall enough to look Kinney in the eye. "You planned to hang the Taylors, to kill them?"

Nat's face was bland, but there was something in his eyes. "I did not say that."

"Then what do you say?" Alonzo's anger boiled over, and he mimicked John Taber's motion, throwing the hickory bundle at Nat's feet. Nat didn't even glance down, but his face paled.

"I say I know nothing about that family."

"You are contradicting yourself, Sir!"

Nat's eyes narrowed. He stared right back at Alonzo.

"How so?"

"You are either in control, the Taylors were hung by your command, and this family was run out by your command, or else you have no control!"

They were nose-to-nose. "I knew nothing about that family!" Nat shouted. But his eyes darted to Alonzo's left, and Alonzo shook his head impatiently. He began to reach for Nat's collar, when a small fury came between the men, little white hands pushing at Alonzo.

He glanced down to see Ada Marie, her own face red. She half-turned with her right hand on Alonzo's chest and left hand on Nat's.

"Fighting in the street! Shame on you, two grown men, who know better! Alonzo!"

He backed away, taking two more steps and wiping his mouth

with his hand. Nat was standing there, an expression that Alonzo thought could be misconstrued as pleading.

"Sometimes innocent people get hurt, Alonzo."

Alonzo's face was grim as he regarded his right hand, which was shiny from his lips. Had he been foaming at the mouth? He then looked back at Nat, his former friend, and replied, insistent, "No more, Sir. No more."

His left hand pulled Ada Marie behind him, and he raised his right, palm out, toward Kinney. His mouth again full of saliva, he then spit as Sarah Taber had done, on the bundle of sticks at Kinney's feet. "No more."

He had no memory of Ada Marie pulling him back into the stifling air of his office, or giving him some water. She loosened his collar, and was fanning him when he finally came out of the darkness, and he smiled weakly at her--she was scarcely tall enough to see the top of his head while he was seated.

"Better?" she asked.

He nodded, and rubbed his face with both hands. Resignedly, he rolled his head, hearing his neck crack as his shoulder muscles relaxed. With his chin nearly parallel to the floor, and his eyes almost closed, he rolled them toward her.

"Much."

"Have some more water."

He drank.

When he finished the second glass, he sat it down on the desk in front of him. Then he saw the pile of mail--Ada Marie had brought it from the store.

On top was an envelope addressed to John Taber, in care of Alonzo. The return address was Washington, D.C. The Taber family's homestead patent.

Groaning, he put his head in his hands, his elbows on his desk. His fingers ran through his hair, and he finally looked at Ada Marie.

"I need to move you and the children."

She bit her upper lip, and leaned against the desk, next to him. "We'll be fine," and there was a gentle firmness to her voice.

Alonzo nodded. "You will be," he told her. "I cannot have you here. I do not want to worry about you."

She began to remonstrate with him, but he would not budge. He himself would stay in Forsyth, in Taney County, but the family had to leave. He would not have them in danger. He didn't think Nat would come after him, but he would not take that risk with his wife and children. Just in case.

❦ ❧

Deciding to take advantage of the second rising of the bread, Maggie filled the tub in the bedroom, her second bath in nearly 4 days. She added lavender oil to the warm water, and sat with her head lying back, a washcloth under her neck to keep the brim or the tub from cutting into her.

Footsteps in the entry--she'd left the bedroom door ajar, to catch any breeze that came through--and she stiffened. "Who is it?" she called. No one was due home for hours; Paul had left just minutes before she stepped into the tub.

"It's me," Georgia was hesitant.

Maggie's eyes flew open, and she sat up, turning to see her daughter in the doorway. "You're home early," she said.

"Granny said she was going to catch a nap in her hammock," Georgia came all the way into the room. Privacy was not something often found in a small house, even at bath time, it seemed. "I've brought you some tea."

An eyebrow quirked up at Georgia's determined face. "From Granny?"

And then a nod, eyes big and cautious.

Embarrassed, Maggie sighed. Try as she might, she couldn't hide everything. She winced as a twinge shot through her again. "What did you tell her?"

Georgia's face was surprised. "I didn't tell her anything, except you weren't playing the piano because you were tired."

Maggie nodded. "Fix the tea."

They were laughing later as they pulled the last loaf of bread from the oven and covered it. Georgia had helped her mother with the making of Sunday dinner. It had been a fun afternoon, and Maggie had even dusted her piano. She didn't lift the lid covering the keys, though; she didn't know if she was ready for that.

Georgia was in bed asleep; Maggie was in a cotton nightgown, hair down, her body cool in the fabric as she rocked in her chair on the porch, watching fireflies. She was sipping some of the tea Granny sent when the familiar beat of Ghost's hooves grew louder as Nat came home.

Briefly, she considered opening her piano while he was in the barn, so he could hear the music as he put Ghost away for the night. No, he would have to ask. Instead, she went inside and poured him a cup of the same tea. It was the last of the pot.

His face was haggard in the dimness as he approached the house, tiredness evident in the rare heaviness of his step. She held the cup of tea to him, a peace offering. He accepted it, and she sat back in her chair, rocking quietly.

Sitting heavily on the porch in front of her, Nat drank from his cup, and felt peace steal over him as he leaned against the handrail's post. It had been a rough day, and the absence of Maggie's heart had cut him keenly for four days now.

Her white feet were near his left hand. Without moving his head, his hand stole out and gently stroked her ankles, first one, then the other, up and down the tops of her feet. The rocking stopped, and he felt the fire of her coming toward him, sending sparks up his arm and into his body.

"Play for me?" he asked. It was the first time they had touched, had spoken directly to each other since he had taken her in the woods.

Her eyes were inscrutable as she lowered her chin to get a better look at him. Her chair began rocking again, ever so slowly, in rhythm with his hands. Almost against his will, he sat the tea cup down, turned, and watched as both hands began moving up her legs, hesitating behind her knees. The smell of lavender and musk wafted in time with her pulse, at just that spot. He brought his head closer.

Her white hand took off his hat, tossed it to the side, and began to rifle through his matted hair. Maggie could feel her body yearning for him, but she wasn't going to let it go....not just yet.

"Your bath is ready." Soft, voice soft as her heart felt at this moment. She pushed up to her feet, and Nat's hands fell away as he leaned back, stared up into her face. Maggie smiled, a sensuous thing that made Nat's pulse beat harder, and then turned toward the door. She began to offer him a hand to rise, but reconsidered, and went into the bedroom.

204 | Vonda Wilson Sheets

The bathwater and piano both gleamed in the light from the single candle on the nightstand. The screen was folded and put away. Nat was a little slow in coming in, but once he did, she saw him glance around the room as if he'd never seen it before. He walked over to his chair, sat, and began to pull off his boots. The clothes followed.

The tub had been especially made for a big man, and Nat had no trouble sliding into it. His nose crinkled. She had put a scented oil of some sort in it, and had positioned the tub so his back was to the fireplace, which held only banked embers. It was a warm night.

She smiled at his expression, but offered no explanation. She also did not raise the lid on the piano. Not just yet.

He made a quick job of soaping up, then settled back, an expectant look on his face.

"Alright, now I've taken my bath and smell like a riverboat dandy," he said. "Are you through civilizing me?"

That same inscrutable look was in her eyes. "You will never be civilized," she murmured, then stood. She loosened the laces at the neck of her gown, which fell to the floor, and turned. Nat winced, seeing her bruises as she sat down. Slowly lifting the lid, she played a few notes, and then a soft song fell from her fingers.

He was entranced.

Upstairs, Georgia smiled in her sleep.

CHAPTER 25
Mid May, 1885 - Eva and Robert

Eva spent a great deal of time at her friend Rose's home, down in Mincy. Nat raised no fuss about his stepdaughter's absences, as long as she attended church services. She was nearly twenty, an old maid by Taney County standards. Robert Prather's courtship had lasted for almost two years, but he had not proposed.

Late Sunday evening, a day after his father and Nat Kinney had fought in Forsyth, Robert strapped the last of the boxes onto the wagon holding most of his mother's belongings. Alonzo would rent the house to someone, he knew; the buggy held boxes as well, clothes and other essential items Alonzo would need in the little room at the back of his law office in Forsyth.

His heart was heavy in its beat; dread tightened his chest. Going back into the house, he reached for his coat and hat, hanging on his peg near the door. Although his shirt was soaked with sweat, he wanted to be proper when he visited Eva one last time.

Alonzo looked up from a philosophy book, a query raising his brows.

"I have to see Eva," Robert answered the unspoken question. Alonzo took a deep breath, and Robert could see that he wanted to argue.

"She is not Nat's true daughter, you know," Alonzo reminded his son.

"No. But he did raise her," Robert responded.

A pause. "You are a young man, son." Closing his book, he studied Robert with sympathy.

"Are you going to fire James?"

Taken aback, Alonzo took some time to remove his reading glasses, rubbing the bridge of his nose where they left marks. He slowly shook his head.

"No. He is an able editor and writer. Mrs. Kinney has taught her children well."

"Dad...I don't know what to do!" It was anguish on his son's face, and Alonzo could wish things were different.

"Would she leave with you tomorrow?" he asked.

"I don't know. She's been in Mincy, she may not know what has happened."

Ada Marie came in from the kitchen, wiping her hands on her apron. At the interruption, Robert turned and walked out.

"Did I interrupt something?" she asked, as if she hadn't heard the entire conversation.

Alonzo shook his head sadly. "She's got his heart, and he doesn't realize how important that is," he told his wife. "He thinks he is leaving with you tomorrow to get her out of his life. I don't think it will be that simple."

"He could come back after we're settled in."

Alonzo looked out the open door, into the night, and shook his head. "I think he will not." He turned back to the small woman at his side. "He thinks he is being loyal to you, to me." Shaking his head again, he added, "I would rather he was not. Not at this price."

"Can you separate the father from the children like that?" It was a keen question, one Alonzo had struggled with since Saturday afternoon.

"Is there not a passage about the sins of the fathers being passed down to the children?" he asked his wife. "I'm doing my best. I'm not firing the son, because of the stepfather. What Robert does is his choice."

Robert Prather walked the short distance from his parents' home to the Kinney farm. His father's decision to send his mother and brothers and sisters away for a time had brought him to the conclusion that he had to leave as well. Nat Kinney's politics were not the problem; his actions were. He did not want the man for a father-in-law, despite his feelings for Eva.

He had not proposed because he was trying to prepare for married life before he did so. He had come home from college at Christmas time, and realized that with the area in such turmoil, he did not want to go back. As usual, his father was in the thick of things, and as usual, Robert found himself at meetings he didn't really want to be a part of. The confusion this brought on, in addition to his growing feelings for Eva, had made a fine mess of his mind.

So he was going away.

"Go away, see if you can do it, then come back," he told himself. "Maybe."

The thought that this would be the last time he entered the Kinney

Absolution | 207

dooryard brought him to a halt. He saw light shining, and knew Eva would be waiting for him. The music from Maggie's piano reached his ears, and he realized he would miss these evenings.

Eva was waiting for him on the porch. She had seen him, so he went through the gate and turned to latch it carefully. He took a deep breath, squaring his shoulders, and heard her footsteps. She was coming to him. He turned back toward the house.

"Hello," she smiled at him, he knew, and the heart he had hoped was hardened melted again. "I missed you at church this morning." She put a hand on his arm.

Robert tried to smile, but could not bring himself to do so. This was going to be so difficult. His throat tightened.

"Robert?"

"We need to talk." He found that he could not move a step closer to Nat Kinney's home. It would be better to do this in the dark, maybe; then he couldn't see her face well.

But he wanted to.

"So....talk." Her hand had fallen, and he wished for her touch.

"I'm..." His throat was tightening, making his voice croak. He cleared it with difficulty. "I'm leaving tomorrow."

"Oh?" He could hear the hurt. He felt it, too.

"I'm taking Mother and the others up to Appleton City."

"All right." She stepped back, one step. "Are you coming back?"

She knew him better than he had suspected. "No." He felt her flinch, and saw the misty white of her hands go to her left breast, as if to pull on the knife he'd just driven into her with his words. He closed his eyes, but the image remained.

"Are you going to tell me why?" She was tougher than he was.

"No." It was a small answer. But she knew.

"My father. You are leaving because my father and yours had a fight."

"He's not your father!" He felt ridiculous using the argument his own father had given him.

"He is, in every way that counts, Robert. He raised me, provided for me, taught me."

"Yes."

"What our fathers are is not important to us, you know." Stubborn, she was so stubborn. He admired it.

208 | Vonda Wilson Sheets

"It is to me," he told her softly. "It is to me."

"You are wrong!" she cried, and the hands kept pressing into the area of her heart. "You are wrong to leave me!"

"And if I said, 'Come with me!' could you do so, and leave your parents behind?" he asked.

At that, any small movement she was making stilled. "No."

"Well, there you have it," he said sadly. And he turned, opened the gate, walked through it. "I wish you Godspeed, Eva." And he walked away, leaving her to share in his darkness, as alone as he was.

The sun rose on a young woman sitting beside the Springfield/ Harrison Road, near the Kinney homestead. A trunk and a suitcase were her only companions; she was dressed in a traveling suit, smart hat on her head.

Alonzo Prather came over the rise to see Eva DeLong sitting with her back straight, waiting. He had just taken leave of his family; they were headed north, to the Hensley Ferry over the White River, and he was going to Forsyth. He came to a halt, murmuring a gentle "Whoa!" to his horses, but the brake on the buggy squealed as the high wheels bit into the dirt, sliding.

The teamsters had not started coming through yet, so her tweed suit was still fresh. Her eyes were bright with tears as she looked up at Alonzo, then rose to her feet.

"Is he gone?"

Alonzo nodded, as gently as he could. He saw Nat Kinney coming up from the house, watching his stepdaughter as she stepped toward his former friend.

Her face broke.

"I'm sorry, child, so sorry." Alonzo put a hand out to her, as a shout from Maggie came from the direction of the house. Nat was running, Maggie not far behind.

There was no sob, no great tearing of breath, just tears rolling down Eva's face as Alonzo waited until Nat and Maggie arrived to take her back home, then clucked to his horses as they walked away, Eva hanging onto her mother, Nat carrying the trunk and suitcase with little apparent effort.

The sins of the fathers, indeed. He needed to look that passage up.

CHAPTER 26
Summer, 1885

May rolled into June, and June collapsed, sweaty and sticky, into July.

The crops were growing magnificently. Hot as it was, rains came often enough to dust the green back to shiny. The air remained heavy and thick because of it.

The farmers maybe had the best of it. They rose long before sunrise, trying to get heavy work done in the early hours before the sun reached noon. After the midday meal, men and women both did light chores until the need for sleep took them into the early evening. Nighttime chores were the best, done in the minutes painted purple before mists rolled in from the river, bringing cool relief.

The Bald Knobbers met and rode during the nights, their torches lighting the trails to isolated family homes, threatening the men, terrifying the women and children. If the men were foolish enough to try and ignore any warnings, a second visit convinced them of the wrongness of their ways. Whippings, forced removal from their homes....and threatening shouts and shots fired at men who refused to join the group.

Oddly enough, people who lived in the towns and villages of Taney County were not often treated to the sight of men riding through on dark horses, with flour sacks over their heads and torches in their hands. It was the folks whose farms often lay in the steep-walled valleys, with easy access to water and rich dirt for crops, who received the most visits.

And the date and times of the meetings were published in *The Farm and Home*, the newspaper owned by Alonzo Prather, which was edited by Nat Kinney's stepson, James DeLong.

Bonfires burned in late afternoon, their tenders drenched in sweat as they hauled dried brush and wood to remind all--they were watched.

Men began muttering as families were run out of the county, and fear became widespread. Even if a man didn't have a good farm, if his land was host to a Bald Knobber's pregnant sow when she gave birth, and the man put the new shoats in a pen for safekeeping, a visit was usually made. No questions were asked; guilt was the rule.

210 | Vonda Wilson Sheets

Women prayed for an early fall and winter, so their men would stay home, safe against fire and threats, snug against the cold outside. Those women whose men rode at night also prayed for an early winter; on occasion, a man would come home draped across his horse, his friends with bowed heads and dire words against those who fought back.

By day, one could ride from one end of the county to the other, and again across, treated to views of abandoned or burned homes, and gardens with weeds. Those crops began to wither from neglect as the summer melted through August, and the rain stayed away.

It wasn't as bad as it had been during the war. But there were some who were afraid it could be.

ও ও

Andy Coggburn was still whipcord-lean, and still haunted Nat Kinney, by day and by night.

But it was during this fearful summer that Andrew Coggburn was the happiest he could remember being.

There were times no one knew for sure where Andy was. That was nothing new. His family didn't care much, except for his little sister, Serelda, who had been shunted back and forth among uncles and aunts, a half-brother with his own problems, and some cousins. Some didn't have room for a girl-child of eight, even though she did as many chores as she could to earn her keep, and helpful hands were always welcomed. In the summer, it wasn't so much of a problem; in the winter, when large families were crammed into small cabins, there was jealousy.

Andy tried to help out, by giving food and what money he could to whoever kept Serelda.

This summer, he sometimes took her to the Widow Maggie's home for a few days at a time; Serelda was a quiet, shy child. She never complained. But Andy was sure she wasn't getting enough to eat.

The old couple currently boarding Serelda were happy to take the money he provided, and eat the food he left in a cache near their barn. They pretended to be fond of her, complimenting her, but she kept her eyes diverted whenever these things were said in conversation with her brother; she'd heard them mocking him too often.

Absolution | 211

The old woman would not allow Serelda to cook for her and her husband; she prepared a scanty meal twice a day, the door to her small pantry was locked, and Serelda cleaned up after eating soft foods that suited the couple, who'd lost most of their teeth. The milk cow and few chickens on the place took little time to tend, and they didn't allow Serelda in the small kitchen garden, afraid she would eat the few vegetables that it produced. They bought flour and other necessities in town, but being niggardly, they didn't need much.

They didn't touch her, except with their eyes. They complained when she went to church and school, claiming to be worried about her in this troubled summer, but it was more because they had gotten used to having her fetch and do for them. And they shouted as they complained; both were deaf.

Andy watched. When her eyes would not look at his during short visits, he took her down to work and play with Miranda. Serelda was safe in ways that he could not vocalize, but he knew he would have to find another home for her soon. He could not ask Maggie to take Serelda in; her own healing was still a tentative thing, and he would not impose.

Watching Nat Kinney work with his horses one evening, his mind on his sister, Andy wondered if he should move her into his cave this winter. It was damp and cold--he himself wandered in and out as the mood suited, and taking Serelda with him on his treks was out of the question.

He shook his head, forgetting to gobble when the piano music burst from the open windows of the Kinney home. Maybe next time he'd bring Serelda to listen.

No. Georgia Kinney had wandered out to the back porch of the place, disconsolately joining her sister Eva, who was staring moodily up at Big Bald. Neither spoke. Georgia was no longer allowed to play with Miranda, Serelda, and Nannie Snapp. She still visited Granny Haggard, but only for a short time, only when Granny was alone. Granny's eyes had been troubled, telling Andy of it.

He rose, moving silently down the slope to the creek bank, following it till a game trail he was familiar with drew the attention of his feet.

Whatever game Nat Kinney was playing at, more than just his own family members were getting hurt. Andy couldn't see any benefit to bringing Serelda to hear the piano; however, he thought,

212 | Vonda Wilson Sheets

he might start going to church with her. To listen to Nat Kinney preach at Oak Grove.

❦ ❦

The Widow Maggie, Miranda, Phebe and Celie were all kept busy. A temporary summer kitchen had been added to the collection of buildings around their clearing, and as the trail down the hillside to their home cleared back from use, so the breeze coming off the ridge swirled through, tickling drops of sweat from them. Andy and Miranda experimented with methods and ingredients for soaking and smoking meat; Widow Maggie collected her tomatoes and peppers, and finally her sandwich sauce was as perfect as she remembered her grandmother's being. Andy ate a couple of the sandwiches almost every night, and appeared to be gaining some weight, even in summer.

Serelda and Miranda had become good friends, to the point where one was, the other was close by. Serelda, however, kept sneezing in the smoke shed, and none of Granny Haggard's remedies were effective in stopping the attacks. So Serelda worked with the Widow Maggie in the garden and the summer kitchen, while Miranda worked with Andy in the smoke shed. Phebe and Celie ran back and forth, or played with their new rag dolls, ever watchful for rattlesnakes and copperheads. Once or twice a week, the happy little group was joined by Nannie Snapp, and laughter--rusty at first, then as the summer flourished, so did the sound--began to be a common thing at Widow Maggie's.

Andy spent one morning with all five girls, hauling water to the corn field Maggie planted before the cabin burned. It was a small patch, so it didn't take the entire morning, and on the last trip for water, he and the girls had jumped into the creek, splashing and squealing.

Three brown dresses, identical except for size, were laid carefully on the branches of nearby trees, joined by the faded red calico of Serelda's dress, and the light blue cotton of Nannie's. Andy, wearing breeches that had been cut off at the knees, was climbing onto a boulder which bordered the creek. He did a quick glance-over for snakes, then settled into a depression in the rock which had seated many others. His shirt hung near the girls' dresses, and he smiled to

Absolution | 213

see the five shift-clad little ones enjoying themselves.

As alone as he'd been in the past years, he had not been lonely often. But times like this, he reflected, had never come his way, and he treasured them now. His eyes narrowed as little Celie's squeal changed pitch, and he started to rise, but no--it appeared she'd found a crawdad. The other girls clustered around to see, as Andy settled back down. He looked around, espying the forked staff he used in the summer as a walking stick, stuck in the ground behind his rock.

Reflecting on his day, he was in awe of how much life had changed for him. His friendship with Maggie was a strong one, something Andy had never expected to have. She fussed over him, treating him like some combination of brother or son. They talked while the girls napped in the late afternoon hours, lying in hammocks he'd strung up above the cabin, near the shelf rock. They were even comfortable when not talking, Andy thought, and he faintly smiled as he heard her approaching from behind him, settling beside him, wearing her shift and looking at the girls.

"So this is whut yer doin' when you ain't workin'," she teased him, smiling. He smiled back, and both turned to see the girls start overturning small boulders and big rocks along the creek bank.

That wasn't safe, not this time of year. Andy stiffened to call out, tell the girls to stop, and Maggie, sensing his alarm, also half-rose. At the same time, the girls clustered and ran up the bank, screaming. A black sinuous shape followed, and Andy was bouncing through the shallow water, staff in hand, yelling to get the cottonmouth's attention. Maggie was beside him, loud as well.

He missed forking the snake behind its head the first time, and the tell-tale white mouth appeared to yawn in threat as it turned toward Andy. Maggie veered off, giving a wide berth to the snake, headed for the girls. Sensing a threat from Maggie's direction, the head turned slightly, and Andy pinned it, whipping out his knife from its wet sheath. The snake thrashed, but the gravel gave Andy's staff easy purchase, and he cut through the black mottled scales, just behind the pinned head. Quite soon, the severed body and head stilled.

Grinning, he looked up at six scared faces. Maggie had her arms around the smaller girls, and the three older ones were behind her kneeling body. Regaining her composure, Maggie asked, "Do you always swim with a knife?"

"Eh," Andy lifted his staff, using it to toss the remains into the nearby brush. "Only when there's girls around."

Six pairs of eyebrows raised at his statement. What did girls have to do with it?

"Wal, I don't generally wear pants swimming, now do I?" he raised his own brows, his hands indicating the cut-off breeches that clung wetly to him.

"And I don't generally go liftin' rocks along the creek," Andy told the girls. "You get crawly things when you do that."

Celie's face began to crumple; she had been the one who lifted the snake's rock. Andy stepped forward, a grim smile on his face, and swung her damp body up to his hip. His movement made the others relax, and he looked at the little girl clinging to him. "It's a'right this time," he told Celie. "But don't do it lessen I'm 'round, unnerstand?" She nodded. He looked up at the mother, her face pale beneath the tan. "Is it lunchtime yet?"

Maggie nodded, and began shooing her flock back over the creek to the dresses, which were quickly gathered and the group made their way up to the cabin.

The girls' chattering returned to normal by the time they got to the summer kitchen, and their dresses were hung on the clothes line beside it. Andy set Celie on the plank bench at the table, and then turned to see Maggie pull a stack of bowls to the end of the table nearest the fire.

She dished up some beans with loose meat, but this was more than the ham and beans Andy was familiar with. He snagged a spoon from the jar on the table, and took a cautious bite. Beans. Tomatoes. Some paprika. Molasses. Some of his smoked meat. A second bite, and he saw Maggie was watching him.

"This is good," he told her. "What is it?"

"Just a tomato stew."

The girls were cautious as well, but as Maggie filled her own bowl and sat down to join them, appetite took over, and soon they were full and drowsy. Celie was nodding off; Maggie took a final bite of her stew, then got up to carry Celie off to the cabin. The other girls followed, yawning, and Andy rose to rinse out the dishes.

After stacking them neatly, he stretched. It had already been a long day. The sow and her four female progeny had been earmarked and set loose in the woods nearby, but one of the three gelds was nosing through some weeds along the fence. That one, Andy thought, would make some fine bacon--it was already hefty.

Sitting back down at the table, Andy poured some sweet tea into a glass jar, watching Maggie come back down and refill her own jar. Then she joined him.

"What are you thinking 'bout?" she asked, fanning her face. Her shift was still damp, but the air wasn't moving much.

"Pigs."

Both looked down at the pen, Maggie asking, "And?"

"We're gonna need more than whut we got," Andy told her.

She crinkled her nose. "I don't wanna pig farm, Andy."

He chuckled at her. "Wal, you like to cook too much."

Maggie's spine stiffened and she glared at him. "Are you complainin'?"

"No." And he rubbed his full belly, half-hidden by his unbuttoned shirt, grinning. It was getting to where a grin was always tickling his lips anymore.

"But mebbe you should open a diner."

Maggie's eyebrows scrunched as she considered the thought. Then she shook her head. "I don't wanna do thet, either," she told him. "I like takin' sandwiches up to Kintrea's, making some money thet way. It's enuff."

Andy's hand gestured toward the pot of stew, which had been set off the fire.

"Thet's enuff stew to feed us for days."

"I just threw it together, Andy."

"Thet's the point."

She stared at him, then again shook her head. Shyness chilled the warmth in her eyes, and she looked down at the table, then around the neatened clearing. There were no planted flowers this year, but she intended to have them next year. The gate to the garden was no longer hanging off one hinge, and the growing things enclosed behind it were plentiful, for feeding her family and others.

"I like now," she said simply, and the shyness in her eyes increased as she lowered her lashes, glancing at Andy through them. "Got some money comin' in, and we won't starve anymore." A ghost flashed as her eyes widened again, but it was gone quickly, Andy saw. She smiled; the warm brown eyes glowed once more.

"And I have friends." She touched a knuckle to the calloused brown hand on the jar opposite hers briefly, and then took a sip of her own tea. "It's enuff."

§§ ∂

It was nearly the end of July before Kate Miles and Sally Barker were able to go blackberry picking together. Both women had been busy with their gardens, making meals of the fresh produce and preserving the vegetables and tomatoes by drying and canning them. Kate had managed to crock a good deal of meat from the cows Tubal Taylor mutilated, storing the boiled meat in stoneware crocks, soaking it in brine, and pouring fat over the top.

Blackberry jelly was a favorite in the family. Fruit orchards weren't common in Taney County, although nearly everyone had an apple tree or two; there were even a few peach trees around. So gathering fruit off vines, such as grapes and blackberries, was essential if one wanted jelly, and had the money to buy sugar.

William added to Kate's collection of glass jars over the years. She thought she'd had plenty, especially as the children were going off on their own, but she found that she sent canned and preserved foods home with Elijah every time he came to visit; she did the same with her daughters. Sometimes, they remembered to return the jars, but more often, they simply kept and used them for their own growing families. She didn't mind.

What she minded was the sound of rattlesnake, echoing through the blackberry bushes. So Kate and Sally were careful to make a great deal of noise, descending the hillside to the patch, hoping the snakes would hear them coming and leave. Snakes often crawled off upon hearing noise, but Kate checked her pocket for the loaded revolver her father had given her anyway. She knew Sally was doing the same.

Their father, Henry Frazier, had bought a revolver in 1858, a Smith & Wesson Model 1, and even though Kate was married and almost a mother by then, she'd spent time with her father on target practice. He had done the same with Sally; in the troubled years before the war, Henry Sr. prepared carefully.

He'd sent Kate the later Model 3 after his namesake and two daughters moved to Taney County. Sally had received hers in a package the month before.

Absolution | 217

Almost affectionate with the gun, Kate kept it clean and ready to fire, all the time. It was a relaxing thing to do with William in the evenings, melting lead into bullets, making sure the family was well-prepared for anything. Night riders were always a possible threat this summer; William had not made any statements, political or otherwise, but his apparent lack of interest in the Bald Knobbers had been noticed.

So….blackberry patches were notorious for snakes.

This late morning, before it got too hot to be in the breeze-less patches of bushes and vines on the hillside near the Miles' home, Sally and Kate walked down to the patch above the creek. She brought buckets and burlap bags to haul berries home in. Sally would stay to work the jelly and the wine they made, taking a good amount home.

Blackberry wine. She'd better ask William to get some more sugar, next time he visited Dickenson's store. The wild grapes, plentiful everywhere, and the blackberries, made a wine that, if mixed right, would be a definite treat on summer evenings. And winter nights, if she made brandy as well.

It used to be a family thing, going to collect grapes, blackberries, and gooseberries. Now, it was just her and Sally. The boys were working on Sam Snapp's farm, and William was down by the smelter, with Samp, extracting lead from another load of rock; exhausting, hot work.

The sisters chatted comfortably at first, shooing birds away from the enticing fruit and then moving apart as they pulled the dark fruit.

After an hour or so, they stopped to drink water and rest. The two large bags were filled about halfway, and both wanted to fill them if they could.

Then, as Kate headed back toward the side she'd been working, she heard Sally yell.

Keeping a grasp on her empty bucket, Kate ran, ducking and yelling back to Sally as the bushes scratched her and grabbed her; there wasn't a trail. Her ankle rolled against a loose rock, but she didn't slow. Within a minute, she entered the small clearing Sally had found, and saw her sister frozen in place.

Rattlesnake.

Loud.

More than one.

Cautiously, she edged her way around to get a view. Good grief. There were three of them. The snakes' tail rattles pitched even higher as she crept around, moving her hand into the pocket of her skirt, finding her revolver and cocking it. Two of the snakes were intertwined--the third was almost at Sally's feet, mere inches away from striking her.

Pulling her gun slowly out of her dress pocket--sudden movement could make the snakes strike--she debated her next move.

"Do something," Sally's voice could barely be heard.

"Don't move," Kate advised.

Her left hand was holding her bucket. She continued to move slowly, so slowly, so the two snakes a bit farther from Sally were in range of the bucket. From the far right, she could hear William yelling from the creek, but she didn't answer.

The snake closer to Sally struck at her, catching her skirts, and Sally jumped back. At the same time, Kate threw the heavy wooden bucket at the entwined snakes, and brought her revolver up, shooting the one that was caught in Sally's skirts. Then her right hand swung to the left, shooting the other snakes, which were writhing after the bucket's impact.

William burst into view, a shovel in hand, dropping it when he saw--Sally wasn't bitten, the snake's fangs were caught--then grabbed the snake's bloody back above its wound. Stretching it, he pulled the knife he had strapped to his belt, reached down and cut the snake's triangular head off, yanking the body away. Although the head was caught, the adrenaline that had caused the snake to strike was still causing it to wriggle madly in Sally's skirt, and she started trying to shake it loose.

"Stop!" William commanded. He bent to reach for the snake's head as Kate whirled closer to the two, bent to grab the shovel, and aimed it at the two other snakes. One appeared to be dead, but the other, despite a bucket bruising and being shot, was in the process of coiling itself back up, preparing for a strike of its own. It leapt once, and Kate deflected it, left-handed with the shovel. Then William's hand reached around, grabbed the shovel again, and whirled in time to deflect a second strike. The rattles were still sounding as Kate shot it again, bringing her right hand up and taking only a split-second to aim at the head.

Boom. The head disintegrated under the bullet's impact.

Taking a few seconds to breathe again, the three of them stood there, surveying the snakes' bodies and shaking slightly. After decapitating the other two snakes' with the sharp-edged shovel, William dropped it again and reached for the canteen Sally had dropped, shaking it.

"You got enough berries for today?" he asked, uncorking the top and then taking a drink. "Darn, it's water."

Kate nodded, smiling at his grimace as he drank. "Think so." Her forgotten left ankle suddenly throbbed, and she winced. She tried to shift her weight to her right foot, but the slight slope was not accommodating. She turned slightly away from Sally, until her balance was easier.

His eyes questioning, William came to her, offering his hand, "Sit." She did.

He handed Kate the canteen, and she took a drink. Then she passed it up to Sally. William had managed to dislodge the snake's fangs from Sally's skirt and petticoats, and after accepting the canteen, she had bent over to inspect the damage. Two clear holes were just above the hem of the light blue work dress, and her feet and ankles were showing as she lifted it to hold it wide for her sister to see. The fang holes were about the size of small bullet holes.

"You got two out of three," William said, a glint in his eyes as he knelt and lifted the skirt of Kate's dress to her knees, examining her ankle. He unlaced her boot as she reloaded her gun from the supplies in her leather pouch, trying to breathe steadily. Samp joined them, saw that the immediate danger was gone, and bent over to pick up William's knife.

"Want them rattles?" he asked no one in particular.

"Yes," Sally answered him. He quickly severed the rattles from their previous owners, handing one set to Kate, who looked at him questioningly as he gave Sally the other two. William accepted his knife from Samp while considering Kate's quickly swelling ankle, now free of its shoe and stocking.

"I'll make it home," Kate told her husband, and tried to rise. Ouch.

"Nope, don't think so," William rose, extending his hand to Kate. "Don't put weight on it." She came up on her right foot, and gingerly touched her left toes to the ground. Her entire leg seemed to protest, and she held tightly to William's right arm, lifting the foot again.

The men made a chair of their hands, and carried Kate up to the house, embarrassment flaming her cheeks. They settled her in her rocking chair on the porch, and Sally went inside to get rags and make a poultice, putting bread and meat on the table for a quick lunch. The men fixed themselves sandwiches while Sally made Kate comfortable, lifting the ankle onto a pillow stacked on a wooden box. Sally was putting a hot poultice on the violently purple ankle when William appeared in the doorway, Samp behind him.

William had poured Kate some wine, and handed her the glass while she tried to ignore Sally's ministrations. For a few seconds, she seemed to be shocked, then took a sip, closing her eyes, and her face relaxed marginally as Sally stood up. The three of them were staring down at her, concerned, when she opened her eyes again.

"What?" she asked.

"Are you hungry?" Samp questioned.

Considering, her stomach growled in response. Samp, who was half-hidden by the door frame, then brought a sandwich into her sight, and handed it to her. She took a bite almost immediately, and when she swallowed, her attention again returned to the three who were still watching her, now with satisfaction on their faces.

"Ain't broke," Samp said.

"Nope," William agreed.

Sally snorted, sidling between Samp and William to go back inside. "Still plenty hurt," she said. "You'll need some pain powder. You two," she addressed her husband and brother-in-law, "go on down and fetch them berries."

Kate finished her sandwich and wine while the men were gone, and listened as Sally went in and out the back door, preparing to start work on the jelly. At one point, Sally came out the front door, forcing her to drink some water with pain powder mixed in, but rewarding her with another glass of wine.

She was feeling pleasantly wicked, sitting in the middle of the day, the pain of her ankle locked into a distant part of her mind, when she realized she needed to go to the privy. Darn. It took a great deal of effort to rise, finagling herself so the injured foot was kept off the floor of the porch, when she looked up and saw William, who had come in the back door and was now holding a rough crutch.

"I'm glad I'm not a rattlesnake." He moved to help her, setting

Absolution | 221

the crutch against the wall, lifting her left arm and putting it around his neck, encircling her waist with his right arm. "Your dad would be proud."

Kate Frazier Miles made a distinct snort, sounding so much like her father that William smiled. "Take me to the privy," she said, gathering herself for the effort it was going to take.

"In the house," he said. "Chamber pot."

While they were inside, he helped her take her work dress off, and the immediate coolness of air touching her bare arms revived her somewhat. "Would you get the crutch, please?" she asked William.

Shaking his head, he carefully bent and picked her up, carrying her back out to the porch and depositing her in her chair once more. He returned for her pouch, and brought the wine out, filling her glass for the third time. "You need to rest that ankle today," William told his stubborn wife, and he felt better about her when he saw her chin go up as if to argue. She had already lifted the ankle to the foot rest herself. Taking the crutch up, he turned to go back inside with it, and smiled as she squawked. Dropping the smile, he leaned over and said in the same steely voice he used with the children when necessary, "Stay put."

Kate stayed put.

ço ꝛ

The summer peaked and began to wane, and Susie Snapp's belly grew. Her hands, ankles and legs were so swollen, she had difficulty helping Sam around the farm. Nannie helped her at the house, and the two of them grew closer. But as the time for harvesting crops came near, and Susie's discomfort grew, it became obvious more help was needed to prepare for winter.

Sam and Billy Miles would be able to harvest the crops at the Kirbyville farm, storing the corn and grain in the barn and sheds. But preserving the garden produce, picking up nuts this fall, and more, was going to take someone else to help Nannie; Sam could only hope cooler weather would ease Susie's discomfort, if cooler weather ever came.

Tired, dispirited, and hot, Sam was lying on the ground under a big maple late one evening in the front yard of his old home near the Miles' place. He gazed up at the leafy branches, his mind wandering to his childhood, when he would climb maple trees in the fall to sit and marvel at the colors of the leaves.

Susie was home, probably sitting on the creek bank with her feet in the cool water flowing out to the White River. He had asked Andy to fetch Serelda to help Nannie with the household chores and take care of the livestock and Tom. He would go home in the morning; this quick trip to Taney City had only been to try to ascertain the harvest, which was probably a month off.

The rotation of harvesting neighbors had long included his farm here. He groaned, thinking of being away from Susie for at least two weeks while crops were taken in for the winter, so close to her time. He was worried about many things, and simply exhausted.

It was obvious Susie was going to bear more than one child, sometime in November. Although it was now only the end of August, her body had swollen so much that she wore Sam's shirts over cotton shifts cut and sewn to accommodate. Sam had jokingly christened the babies "Pokers," for they prodded him with knees, feet, heads and elbows throughout the nights, their movements through Susie's stretched skin mysteriously sending a thrill through him, intoxicating him with wonder. He could hardly wait.

For now, there were worries.

Granny Snapp was failing, and Susie would want to go visit her tomorrow, when he got home. Another woman to help when the time for birthing had to be found. There were midwives and doctors, to be sure--his own brother-in-law lived in Kirbyville, and was a doctor--but Susie was hesitant to let any other man examine her. Sam snorted at this thought, bringing his hands up to look at them, examining them closely, turning them. Farmer's hands; he could handle helping livestock give birth if he had to. Susie felt he would be enough when her time came, should Granny Haggard be unable. He wasn't so sure.

This was his second year to run both farms, and he briefly touched on the thought of selling the Taney City farm. Both farms had uplands, but in terms of soil, the Taney City farm was the better one. Pondering this, he sat up and looked at the house. It was bigger than the Kirbyville house. He had a well here for water; they drew from the creek at the other house.

There were many advantages to the sudden idea of moving back to Taney City, and briefly, Sam wondered why it had taken him so

Absolution | 223

long to see them.

There was a bigger house, better farm, long friendship with the neighbors, who helped each other and kept their business private. The night riders were active here, true, but the Taney City riders didn't meet as often as the Kirbyville group did on the Kinney farm. Since the Taylors had been hung, Taney City was fairly peaceful. Kirbyville was rowdy with teamsters; they behaved around women, but a person could hear the bells jangling off the harnesses all the time, and traffic was heavy on the Springfield/Harrison Road.

This past winter, down in his little valley, with his children provisioned and Susie's laughter; those memories made him reluctant to think further of the idea. The Kirbyville farm smelled and felt like home; something about it answered to his bones in a way this farm never had.

Well, he didn't have to make the decision now. Time enough, when he and Susie had the winter to talk it over, Tom and Nannie sleeping in the loft, and two babies in the cradle near their parents' bed. The thought of snow blanketing everything was welcome, and he looked forward to getting through harvest, preparing for the cold, and seeing his twin babies for the first time.

Life was hard, but good. He stretched, groaned as he got to his feet, and walked into the house to wash himself in cool water, to dream of happy times to come.

He must have heard the horses riding by, tickling him out of deep slumber. Disoriented, Sam opened his eyes to darkness, dreams of the future still tugging at his fogged mind. Then shouts from the direction of the Miles' place sent him into action, pulling on his pants, grabbing his shirt, and taking up his rifle, which was standing by the door. Nudging a curtain on the open window aside with the end of the rifle, he saw no one outside his own house.

Quietly, he lifted the latch and stepped, barefoot, on the porch, every sense intent on whatever was going on over at Kate and William's. The distance was far enough he couldn't make out words, but Nat Kinney's voice was ringing through the night.

Sam went inside to retrieve his boots, putting them on hurriedly, and hung his leather pouch over his right shoulder. The pouch, laden with cartridges and other things for his rifle, hung down off his left hip.

Slipping into the night, he made his way with caution over to his

224 | Vonda Wilson Sheets

neighbor's home, occasionally stopping to ascertain that no one was watching for him. The path through the woods had never seemed so long; hearing shots fired, he sidled into the shelter of some trees and brush, rifle at the ready, and came on a horrific scene.

At least two dozen men were on horseback, some holding torches, all with faces covered and guns at the ready. The shots he heard had been warning shots, apparently. He crouched, down on one knee, and sighted his rifle on the one unmasked man--Nat Kinney.

The big gray horse was loose-footed as Kinney reined it; neither gun nor torch was in the man's hands, and Sam wondered at the arrogance of his Kirbyville neighbor.

"William Miles!" Kinney called to the house. The windows were dark at this hour, but it was obvious there were five guns trained on the night riders. The torches showed occasional glints from gun metal.

"What do you want, Kinney?" William's voice was steady; Sam still trained his rifle on Kinney, following the horse's movements.

"Why have you not joined your neighbors in riding against thieves and wife-beaters?" Kinney asked.

"I do honest work in the day, and sleep well at night," came the reply.

Kinney laughed, a mirthless thing that sent chills from Sam's spine down along his arms, causing his right index finger to twitch.

"So you say," Kinney growled.

"What are you doing over here, Kinney? Your home is over to Kirbyville," William called out. "I have no quarrels with my neighbors, and don't believe they have such a thing with me. This is not your territory."

Upon hearing this, Sam lowered his rifle enough to take a quick assessment of the riders. He silently congratulated William on this analysis--where were the Taney City riders? There were many, despite the disguises, he recognized, and knew them to be from the Kirbyville area. Seeing one familiar horse, stunned disbelief silenced his mind as his brother-in-law, John Haggard, waved a torch in menace, only a couple dozen yards from Sam's camoflauge.

Still Kinney's horse danced, some twenty feet back from William's front door. Again, Sam trained the rifle on him.

"But your neighbors do have a quarrel with you, Miles! They think you have not taken part in the night patrols because you are

Absolution | 225

afraid."

A shot rang from the house, and despite the movement of Kinney's horse, his hat was knocked off his head. The other riders, who had gone silent, surged forward, yelling, and one slender man--Sam recognized Wash Middleton--dismounted, picked up Kinney's hat, and held his torch to inspect it. Sam knew there must be a hole through the crown.

"Hold your fire!" Kinney barked. The men subsided, only a bit. Middleton handed the hat to his chief, who slammed it back on his head, the horse still sidling about, but the reins tautened. Middleton remained on the ground, and shouted at William, "Jine the band or leave the land!" The torch's flames were pointed at the house, and the guns at the windows were trained on Middleton. Sam watched John ride over to Wash's horse, grabbing the reins with his free hand.

"We do expect honest, good people to join us in protecting our homes, Miles," admonished Kinney.

"Wal, I think I can protect my own," came the wry response from the house.

"Is that so?" Open threat in Kinney's voice. He rode over John Haggard, took his torch, then prodded his horse forward to the house.

"You've heard our case, Miles," Kinney said. "We await your response." He then tossed the torch on Kate's rocking chair, and the action set off a fusillade from the house, Sam holding his fire until he could once again get a clear shot at Kinney. The other torches were also tossed at the house from riders trying to dodge bullets, and a few shots were returned. John had ridden back over to Sam's side of the clearing, moving down to Sam's right, Middleton's horse dancing in agitation as the men and horses in the yard stayed in motion. Sam heard some exclamations and grunts as the Miles found a few targets in the darkness. Incredulously, he watched Wash Middleton running straight at him, and he almost ducked as the man leapt onto his horse and pulled the reins from John Haggard in one fluid motion.

Returning his attention to Kinney with his rifle, his itching right finger squeezed. Kinney's horse shied, and the man had a time with the stallion, finally getting him under control and away. A second shot from Sam missed, but he was fairly certain he'd at least creased the horse with the first shot. Orders to leave were shouted; the riders heard, and obeyed.

There were no bodies in the yard.

When he came out of the woods, Kate was dragging her chair off the porch, and the boys were running for the well in the ground, yanking off the cover and hauling water to throw on to the few hot spots the Bald Knobbers had started. William was standing guard against any returnees, preparing his revolver for attack as his eyes roamed; he relaxed when he saw Sam, who was reloading as he half-ran, looking over his shoulder in the direction the riders had taken.

"Are they all gone?" he asked William, who nodded in assent, grimness in every line of his face.

"They'll be back." William then stuck his own revolver in the back of his waistband, leaving Sam to stand watch.

Once the fires were out, Kate's chair appeared to be the only serious calamity. Sam backed up, still watching, and half-turned as William and Kate surveyed the damage.

"Don't look like they'll be back tonight," Sam commented, and for the first time since he left his house, he felt the freshening air. It was going to rain.

"No, don't 'spect so," William agreed. He gestured toward the house, and the three of them joined the boys at the lighted kitchen table. Kate found her bottle of blackberry wine, handing it to William as she retrieved some of her smaller glass canning jars and set them on the table, limping slightly. William poured the wine, and the room was silent as each person's thoughts rolled around noisily in their heads.

Finally, William spoke to Sam. "I reckon you best watch yourself. He knows those last shots didn't come from the house."

Sam nodded. "I won't sleep anymore tonight, so I'll go on home. He won't know who did the shooting, but if I'm not there when he comes to call, he might figure it out."

The boys nodded along with their father, who gestured toward Kate. "Mighta been better if you'd actually shot the man," he told her, and Sam's face turned toward William's wife. He suddenly realized it had been her shot that knocked Kinney's hat off; wryly, he wondered how he hadn't recognized the sound of Kate's gun at the time. He'd certainly heard it before.

"I was pissed," she told her husband, to the shock of her sons, "I'd have killed the son-of-a-bitch if'n I'd have been usin' the rifle."

Absolution | 227

Exclamations of "Ma!" caused her to grin at the boys, whose mouths were puckered at the thought of her cuss concoction.

"Mebbe he's got a crease on his thick skull," William said with a grin.

"Well, let's hope he learned not to badmouth you around me," Kate answered back.

Sam rode home to Susie, slept for an hour, and was out in the barnyard just after sunrise when the sound of horses brought him running to the front of his house.

"Where's your man?" Nat Kinney was asking Susie as he rounded the corner.

"Right here," Sam answered for Susie, who was standing in the doorway, one of Sam's old pistols in her left hand, concealed from Kinney's view by her skirts. Sam jumped up on the porch, and came to stand next to her, his right hand dangling close to her left side.

Kinney looked a little surprised, despite his evident weariness. There was no bandage apparent under his hat, which had a black-edged hole near the crown. Wash Middleton and Galba Branson also showed signs of fatigue, and Galba had a bandana tied around his right hand.

The big man nodded slowly, eying Sam and Susie, then backed his horse.

"Looking a little tired, Sam," he called out, watchful.

Sam shrugged. "Got a cow in labor." He added, "You look pretty wiped out yourself."

"Been going around, checking on neighbors," Kinney answered. "Thought I'd see how your wife was doing."

"I'm fine," Susie's chin went up.

"That's good, then." Without another word, the three men rode away.

Sam was happy to see a bloodied crease across the rump of Kinney's stallion, but for a moment, he wished Kate Miles had been able to do at least the same to Nat Kinney.

He smiled down at his wife, who'd brought the gun out from the folds of her skirt.

"You and Kate Miles are violent women," he kidded his wife.

She was watching the men as they rode out of sight, and young Tom broke her concentration. "With men like that one around," she

228 | Vonda Wilson Sheets

said as she touched Tom's head, "we have to be."

Sam could only agree. He turned to go back to the barn, halting when he heard a gasp from Susie. Tom had embraced her as best his small arms could, holding her skirt back to her sides, and lying his head on her belly. He was giggling, and as Sam watched, the fabric showed the movement of the twin babies inside her, bouncing against Tom's head. There was a comfort as Susie's eyes met Sam's in amusement.

"Must be girls," she said, her own arms reaching down around her belly to embrace the toddler. "That's the wildest they've kicked yet."

He laughed with her, and en route back to the barn, thought about the babies. He hadn't much considered boys or girls in these months of waiting for them to be born. Now, however, as he put a stool next to the cow and set about milking her, he thought Susie might be right.

৵ ৶

Granny Haggard had suffered with the heat more this year than any she could remember. She spent most of her days inside the cool dimness of her cabin, coming out in the early mornings and evenings to work in her garden. Her needs were few; habit led her to planting and harvesting medicinal herbs and the vegetables in the garden. The family and others, including Andy, kept her supplied with meat.

Late evenings, after the darkness fell, she would rock in her chair on the porch, smoking her pipe and visiting with memories, speaking in Cherokee to those who would answer.

Although she had married twice, she was still called "Granny Haggard" by all who knew her to be a constant in their lives. Her own children were grown, gone to Texas, or even Indian Territory, where their dark coloring was not unusual. Extended family, her clan, lived around her; in this, at least, was some resemblance to life where she was born.

In Taney County, most families had a Cherokee grandmother somewhere, often married to a Scots-Irish grandfather. There were others; the Yoachums over on the James River in Stone County could claim some German and French heritage, if they cared enough. Small family bands of the Cherokee nation back east moved in and

Absolution | 229

out of the Ozarks region, roving around after the Revolutionary War, finally settling in the steep hills that ensured some measure of protection from the white government. This country was wild, often flooded, and difficult to bring wagons through faint trails that meandered through rock-strewn woods. White families with a marked distrust of civilization also moved in, ready to be neighborly but minding their own business. Open discussion of past lives, away from the ancient mountains, was generally avoided. If a person's skin was prone to darkening too much from the sun, he or she wore long sleeves and hats to shield themselves. No one spoke openly, yet everyone knew.

She had been a young woman that dark fall of 1838, carrying one baby and another nestled in her womb when the United States President, Andrew Jackson had seen fit to make the Cherokee leave their homelands. Her husband had died of the bloody flux on the walk toward Indian Territory; she buried him beside the river in northeastern Arkansas, pads tucked between her legs while she bled from miscarriage. She remembered an immense rock bluff soaring high over the group that cold day, forcing her head back to see the stark trees along the top. That night, her brothers and their families slipped off the trail, eventually making their way to established Cherokee communities hidden in southern Missouri and northern Arkansas; she followed, carrying her son on her back.

Her second husband brought her to this ridge in Taney County, and she bore three more children before he left, never to return. She saw his face in the embers of the fire at night sometimes, and knew she had outlived him. She thought it likely some other woman had taken him in; she didn't miss him so much as to go look.

The two sons and two daughters grew, and she took care of other children as well. She was widely known as a healer, and folks would come from miles to seek a cure for their aches and illnesses. Others came to seek love potions and dark draughts; these people had to pay Granny in cash. The idea of eating something from a woman wanting to spell a man made her stomach curdle.

She lived simply and always had. Her cabin provided peace, and she knew her time was coming. The old ways had gone; she had done her best. Granny rather wished she was going to see Susie and Sam's twins born, but she knew this to be her last summer, and it was going to have to be enough.

230 | Vonda Wilson Sheets

Lying in the darkness of a late September night, she was watching the fire when her brother came to her. He held out his hand, and she smiled. Reaching out to grasp it with her own, she felt a great weight leave her, and her brother told her in Tsalagi, "It's time to go home."

It was enough.

CHAPTER 27
Fall, 1885

Hot. No breeze reached the men in the cornfield. Mercifully, the sun was lowering in the sky.

Dusty. Although a violent storm would destroy the crop, a man could wish for some rain, William Miles thought as he reached for yet another husk-covered cob, sticking it in his satchel after plucking a big green corn grub off. It writhed while William finished pulling the ears off the stalk and moved on to the next.

Thirsty. The yellow dust had a way of burrowing into his nose and throat, coating his face and clothes so heavily, he started sneezing some time ago, and only a full drink of scotch every few minutes kept him from having to leave the field. Speaking of which…

William pushed his hat up and pulled down the bandana covering the lower half of his face. Halting his step, he pulled on one of the leather laces crisscrossing his chest, and grasped the flask that had been bouncing off his butt. He hadn't sneezed in a while, but took two full swallows anyway. For medicinal purposes, of course. The smooth clear whiskey had a pleasant taste, and he savored it, closing his eyes and letting it trickle slowly down his throat after his mouth finished taking all the flavor it could handle.

Medicinal purposes were a wonderful thing.

This was the last of Sam's cornfields on the Taney City farm. Unlike his Kirbyville farm, which had much smaller patches waiting to be harvested, it was taking several days for five men to harvest the Taney City farms of the Snapp, Miles, and Barker families. Usually, Kate would be out in the field with them, leaving Sally to fix supper and take care of things. This year, because Kate's ankle was still bothering her, William told her off to stay home.

She ordinarily would have kicked him out of the cornfields days ago, taking his bag from him and telling him to go milk the cows and get out of the way.

But Kate wasn't able to work the fields this year, so William drank scotch. He tipped the flask in her direction at the house, and shook it. What contents were left had far too much room to slosh, in his humble opinion. Supper must be ready.

Billy, on the row to William's left, also halted to drink from his

232 | Vonda Wilson Sheets

own flask. He had not developed a taste for hard liquor; his flask held sweet tea. He liked beer, didn't mind wine, but hard liquor was a creature all its own, and at eighteen, Billy wasn't fond of it. He peered at his father; William's face was restful, but swollen in its dirty ecstasy, a slight frown crossing his face while Billy watched him shake the flask close to his ear. Maybe they'd go in to supper when they reached the end of this row.

Billy knew there wasn't much his parents couldn't do, but Pa was almost useless in the cornfield. He didn't eat cornbread, nor consume much of anything else made from corn. Some liquor was made using corn, and William would drink it once in a while. But that was all.

Pa reacted to corn in a way that Billy never heard anyone else doing. He pondered this as he resumed pulling the ears off the tall plants, bagging them as he stepped up the row. Sam was over to his left, Pa to his right, and Jim was on the other side of Pa. Uncle Samp was on the far side of Jim. Manny was with the wagon, up top at the edge of the field.

Long speculation on the subject of their father's disaffection with corn had dulled the boys' curiosity on the matter the past few years. Kate's absence in the cornfield this season had reopened the discussion, however. Was it because of the corn itself, or something else? After all, some folks sneezed and had phlegm in the spring when pollen was heavy on the air, coating everything with golden haze.

Jim thought it was because of the scotch. The boys had all tried it. A couple of years ago, during the spring planting, Elijah asked Pa if they could take a sip, and Pa had obliged. Billy and Manny didn't much care for it; Elijah, who had learned to make moonshine, preferred the corn whiskey. Only Jim had liked the taste of scotch, which was made from barley. So Jim thought Pa sneezed so Ma would let him drink scotch.

Manny, who hated gathering corn and much preferred to take his turn on the wagon, thought it was because Pa also hated harvesting corn. That was nonsense, in Billy's opinion, but he didn't say so.

The scotch did dull Pa's senses, and he did stop sneezing after consuming a profligate amount of it. The only time Pa drank scotch was when they seeded and worked the cornfields. Other times, Pa didn't drink during the day. As Billy grew older, he came to know

Absolution | 233

there were aspects of farming that were unpleasant, but a man had to do them anyway. He'd learned that by watching Pa, so Manny's opinion didn't count, either.

Elijah was working his own farm now, and therefore was unable to weigh in on this year's discussion.

They reached the end of the row; the burlap bags were so heavy, Billy dropped his to go help Jim lift and dump his bag. The boys panted for a bit, waiting for their father. Uncle Samp and Sam were leaning against the wagon, drinking and resting. Manny jumped down to grab Billy's bag, and helped dump it in the wagon as the older men watched William continue to slowly work his way toward them.

"Don't know as I've known William to be so slow in the field," Sam was commenting as the boys joined their uncle and neighbor. All five were leaning against the side of the wagon. Sam, Manny, and Uncle Samp were wearing sleeveless shirts; Billy and Jim took theirs off, using the sodden cloth to wipe their faces, smearing the dust on them. All of them were various shades of brown- and red-skinned.

Samp Barker turned away, suddenly no longer willing to watch his friend and brother-in-law stubbornly finish his row. As he looked up the fence line, he uttered a sharp exclamation.

"Someone coming."

William was still in the corn, and couldn't see, but something made him look up to see the others turn toward the right. One of the laces crisscrossing his chest had his holster. He dropped his heavy bag of ears, and stole off, tugging on the lace till his revolver reached his hand. A sudden weight came down on his shoulders, and two rows deep into the plants not yet harvested, he went down on one knee. He had to sneeze. The effort to contain it blinded him, and roared through his ears. He put the other knee down, and doubled his body, his hands on his cheeks, covering his nose through the dust-filled bandana. Then he managed to hear someone yell "Sam!" and caught a glimpse of a horse cantering toward his sons at the wagon. Quickly, William turned away and the roaring sneeze he'd been holding in came out as a snort, burning his nose clear up into his head, under his hands.

Eyes watering, hearing no sounds of alarm from the others, he fell back on his rump, put his revolver in its holster, and decided

234 | Vonda Wilson Sheets

he was done for the day. Where was that damned scotch, anyway? William fumbled for a few seconds. Then it was in his hands, and he took a healthy drink. Done for the day sounded good to him. He didn't have anything to lean back on, so he pulled his knees up and leaned forward on them, holding the flask in front of him.

Damn. He hated corn.

Sam had recognized the horse and its rider immediately, and shoved past Samp and Manny. John Haggard was here, on his Taney City farm. Something was wrong.

"Sam!" His brother-in-law rode the same horse he'd been riding as a Bald Knobber on the Miles' place a month ago. He came up, and Sam grabbed the bridle of the horse, waiting.

"John. What is it?"

"Granny died this morning." John's face was filled with grief.

"Where's Susie?" Sam's first thought was for his wife, whose face was so like her brother's.

"Wal, she wuz laying Granny out when I left to fetch you," John said.

"What?" Sam almost shouted. "Shit! Where the hell's your wife?"

John's shoulders shrugged slightly in the face of Sam's anger. He almost whispered, "Ellen's porely. She couldn't get to Granny's."

"Someone's with Susie right now, though, John, right? Someone's helping her? She shouldn't be lifting by herself!" Sam had let go of the horse's bridle, moving closer to John. If John had left Susie by herself…

John nodded quickly as his horse sidestepped. "The Widow Maggie is there, and some of the family."

Sam's shoulders slumped, just a little, in relief. He turned toward Samp and the Miles boys. "I have to go," he said. "I had hoped…" He rolled his neck, letting go of his quick anger with John, then looked at Samp. "I have to go."

Samp returned his nod, eying John cautiously. Sam was tense, but not grief-stricken yet; Samp wondered why for a minute, then looked off toward the cornfield. William had disappeared, but should've returned when there was no alarm raised. Samp took a step to go look for him, but Sam made a slight halting gesture, and Samp waited.

Turning back to John, Sam said, "Go on up to the house, get some supper. We'll leave when I get there."

"No one's at your house."

Impatience tore at Sam, but he held it back. "Go to William's house, John. Supper should be ready."

John's face was stubborn. "I'd rather wait at your house."

"My horse is at William's. Go there. Eat. I'll be right there." Sam's tone was brusque.

"Naw, I'll wait at your house."

Knowing why John was acting in this manner didn't mean Sam would accept it. "You won't get supper."

John's upper lip curled in a sneer. "Don't need it. Don't want any Miles' food." He turned the horse, and rode up the slight slope, then turned right, disappearing behind the highest row of corn.

Sam had already turned back to Samp and the boys before John's horse's hoof beats faded. Samp was watching him, he knew.

Samp's tone was mild when he asked, "What was that about?"

"Granny's been failing. I'd hoped she last until we were done here," Sam half-shrugged, helplessly. There was still half this field to harvest. Then the wheat on all three farms. He sighed. "I'll be back the day after tomorrow."

Samp frowned and shook his head. "Not what I'm askin'," he told Sam.

Tightening his lips, Sam considered what to tell Samp, figured it might as well be the truth. He hesitated, glancing at the three boys, who were alert and ready to move. "Where's William?"

Tilting his head toward the cornfield, Samp shook his head again, "I'll get him in a bit." Suspicious, he prodded the younger man, "Why don't your brother-in-law want to go eat supper?"

"Because he rides with Kinney," Sam answered.

Under any other circumstances, the expressions on the faces in front of him would've caused Sam to smile, they were so alike. Jim ran around the older men, going for Manny's rifle against the dashboard of the wagon. Samp and Manny both put a stop to that however; Haggard was gone.

"I'll kill that sonovabitch," Jim howled. Then his lips puckered up, and Manny and Billy both winced and glanced around, wondering if Kate could hear her youngest child speaking. No sign of Ma or her cuss concoction.

236 | Vonda Wilson Sheets

"No, you won't," Samp told his nephew, the tone in his voice effectively stopping Jim. "He's kin." Samp let go of Jim's arm, and turned his head right, spitting on the ground. A grim smile played across his face. "Pore kin, but kin. You'll leave him be. Not your place."

"But Uncle Samp," Jim began to protest.

"Y'all git this wagon on up and unloaded. Time for supper."

Manny and Jim climbed up to sit on the seat, Manny driving, and Billy clambered over the tailgate to ride with the corn. Samp and Sam watched the boys as they, too, went upslope, Jim holding the rifle propped on his right knee as Manny turned right, taking the load to the crib near Sam's barn.

They began walking along the edge of the field, looking for William. Seeing him lying in the dirt, now shaded by some of the full stalks, Sam picked up the pace, but slowed back down as Samp said with no little concern in his voice, "I hope he's half as smart as William."

"Who? John?" Sensing the older man's nod, Sam didn't turn to look at him. "Why?"

"He'd better stay out o' sight of them boys," Samp responded. They reached William, whose eyes were covered with his right forearm. The other two looked down at him, and the arm came down, eyes rueful as he looked up.

"I hate corn," he told Samp, as he sat up slowly.

Samp put a hand in front of William, who reached up to grasp it.

"I know you do," Samp said, gentle with it. "Ain't no Yankees to watch for in this field, though." He pulled William to his feet, and the three of them slowly made their way out of the row. As they reached the turn left to the Miles' home, Samp added, "Not to say there won't be a Bald Knobber or two afore it's all said and done."

CHAPTER 28
Granny Haggard's Funeral

Kate and Sally made Sam up a quick meal while he saddled his horse, riding up to the front porch of the Miles' cabin to say good-bye. William and Samp were on the porch; at the moment, William was too tired to wash off before he went into the house. His eyes were a touch dull, but Sam knew the men were listening for trouble from his own house.

Brushing past the sitting men, Kate handed Sam a packet of sandwiches as the sound of the wagon returning grew louder. William and Samp relaxed marginally; Samp spat on the ground.

"Reckon one of the boys oughta go with Sam," he murmured to William.

William was considering this when Sam leaned down from atop his horse, protesting. "I don't need protection," he argued.

Samp shook his head. "No, you don't. But you might need a messenger," and as the boys walked tiredly up and joined their father and uncle, Sally could be heard, "My goodness, are we all going to sit outside tonight?"

Kate studied them, then called back, "I think so." She knew Sally was put out, so she hurriedly went back into the house.

"It'll be fine," Sam stated. "It's a funeral. I'll bring Susie and the children back with me, day after tomorrow."

"You don't wanna mess with Haggard," and Samp spat again.

Taken aback, Sam remained stubborn. "We're family. He'll not harm me or mine."

"Was he here with Kinney?" William spoke almost casually.

Sam pulled in and bit his upper lip. He didn't have to say so. The faces of the group on the porch knew.

"I think he would," continuing in the same tone of voice, William raised his head and looked at Samp. "Billy'll go early in the morning." When Sam and Samp both began to protest, William raised his hand to halt them. Billy, who was sitting next to his father, was watching and listening carefully, and William knew he understood. But he said it anyway, mostly for Sam's benefit.

"You'll eat, clean up, get a few hours' sleep," William told his son. "Represent the family at Granny Haggard's funeral." Billy

238 | Vonda Wilson Sheets

nodded; any questions he had would wait, and he glanced up at his mother as her hand handed a plate down in front of him. There was no smile on her face.

Sally was handing plates full of food to Samp and William when Sam Snapp took one last look at his adopted family. Then he turned and rode off.

"Bring Susie here," Kate called after him. Sam didn't acknowledge hearing her, steering his horse through the path in the woods and disappearing from view.

The men and boys ate in silence, too tired to discuss much until the food began settling in their stomachs. Kate was sitting in her new rocking chair; it creaked comfortably as she pulled out her pipe and packed it with tobacco. She scraped one of her wooden matches against the wall of the cabin, and the brief flare showed this to be a long-time habit.

The boys were cleaning up behind the cabin, but William and Samp were still sitting on the floor of the porch, their backs against posts, facing each other. The smell of pipe tobacco wavered on the still air.

The familiar scents and sounds of the night around them soothed William's irritated head. He was reviewing the day, making mental pictures of things left undone and things yet to do, in the absence of Sam.

The boys were coming into the back door of the cabin when Kate asked, "What happened down in the corn?"

Samp shook his head slightly. Sally, who was sitting near him, let her right hand rest on his shoulder, and he reached up and grasped it. "Long day," he responded.

Kate snorted. "I know that." Jim and Manny came through the front door, hair standing wetly on end, shirtless chests pale in the dark.

"You two go on over to Sam's, check the place," William's voice was even in the night, and as his wife began to speak, his sun-darkened hand snaked over and grabbed her foot. Kate stifled her voice, taking a draw on her pipe. "Don't take long."

After getting clean shirts on and grabbing rifles, the two youngest Miles boys loped off the porch, through the yard, and took the path over to Sam's house. Before they were out of sight, Billy came out

Absolution | 239

of the house, leaning on the wall next to his mother's chair. He, too, smelled of soap, and though he often worked without a shirt and had gotten dark in the summer, he was paler than the wall behind him.

"Now will you tell me?" Kate asked.

Samp shifted, seeking an easier position, and waited for William to answer.

There was a shrug, and a sense of uneasiness wafted along with the tobacco smoke. "Haggard came to tell Sam about Granny."

Kate stopped rocking. "William, that's not what I'm asking about. You've been drinking in the corn field again, and you're filthier than the others. And I've already been over to Sam's."

"Wal, I took a nap." Guarded, uncomfortable. He let go of Kate's foot.

Samp snorted in concert with Kate. There was a short yelp of laughter that held no humor. Billy alone did not make a sound. Sally's chair continued to rock, balancing the disturbance and keeping the waves emanating from William from overflowing.

"I hate corn." William muttered, then sneezed.

"I think we all know that," his wife responded.

"Best let it out," Samp advised William.

In surprise, William's head could be made out to raise, and they knew he was staring piercingly at Samp. "Let what out?"

Billy shifted his feet--he was tired, but too interested to move much.

Impatient, Samp snorted again. "Hmpf. Why you hate corn." When William did not reply, Samp began to talk.

"Summer of '63, we was in lower Virginia. Small fight, but he--" and Samp jerked his hand toward William, "he was gone. Took a whole night to find him. Hunkered down over a dead boy at the bottom of a corn field, come sun up."

Stunned silence.

William let out a deep breath, pulled his feet up, and laid his arms across his knees, hands dangling. His head curled down toward his stomach.

Continuing, Samp said, "He was bleeding, shot in the right shoulder. Things was bad. No doctor. Poured some shine on him, made him drink some, and took the bullet out."

William's right shoulder, next to Kate, twitched, and she laid her left hand on it. "You never told me," she said to William. "Not one word." She had seen the scar, of course, but he had several when he came back from the war. They had argued, she remembered, and she'd been hurt by his refusal to talk about it.

William raised his head, looked out over the dooryard. In the watery light from the sky, two shadows emerged from the path to the Snapp home, and the light whine of the gate hinge seemed to jerk William's attention back to the others.

Manny and Jim joined the silent group. "Nothin'," Manny reported.

"Go on to bed," their father replied. "Good job today." The boys said their good-nights, eying their brother, who hadn't moved from his lean on the wall. Then they went into the house, climbing the ladder to the loft and their cool beds.

William rose. "Gotta go oil that hinge," he said, and started to move away.

"William!" Kate, too, rose. William's face was shadowed by her body, and she leaned a bit sideways, so what light came from inside illuminated the haunted eyes.

"Didn't know I was still fighting Yankees," he finally said. He took a step aside, looking hard at Billy. "You best get to sleep." Thinking seemed to be difficult; taking a deep breath, he added. "Wear a coat to the funeral. Don't show your gun."

Sally finally spoke. "Folks don't usually go armed to a funeral," she said, wryness in her voice.

William snorted, his head bobbing with it. He smiled painfully, and looked at Samp, then Kate. "Guess it's looking like war." He moved to fetch his oil can again, then paused.

"I honestly don't remember."

His brother-in-law rose as well, and stretched. "I do. 'Druther not."

◌ ◌

When Sam broke from the path in the woods, he urged his horse to a gallop. John joined him as he entered the road, and neither spoke until they reached the river a half-hour or so later. By that time, Sam had managed to gain control of his temper and his voice, and watched as his horse nosed the water and blew.

The skies were clear, and the temperature had fallen low enough

Absolution | 241

for Sam to be glad he had his coat on. He stretched, then laid his forearms across the saddle of the horse, clasping his hands; the horse's side was heaving a little, and it reminded him of the unborn babies, poking him in the night.

Abruptly, he asked, "Who found her?"

John seemed to be grateful Sam wasn't talking about his normal night-time activities. "Coggburn."

"Andy?"

"Yeah."

"Was it peaceful?"

John nodded; Sam could just make out the motion. "In her sleep."

"Haggard." Sam could no longer keep silent. Speaking as he did, Sam's own head turned toward the river, trying to avoid face-to-face conflict. He looked at the opposite shore as he weighed his words.

"Sam." John seemed to be willing to avoid a fight as well, just yet.

"Why did you come after me? When the family knew I was on the Miles' place?"

"Wal, none of us knew, as such. And you weren't. You was on your own farm."

"What's Kinney got against the Miles? The Barkers?" At that, Sam dropped all pretense of keeping his temper, coming around the back of his horse and facing John.

"What's it to you?" John snapped back.

"They are family," Sam retorted. "Mine."

"No, they ain't. You didn't marry one of theirs."

"Lived next to them for about ten years, Haggard. What's Kinney want with 'em?"

"Cap'n Kinney wants them to join the Knobbers."

"Why?"

John shrugged. Dark as it was, his hat shielded his face. Sam couldn't tell what John was thinking. He half-turned to go around his horse again, then paused. He loomed over John, who was a small man.

"Why?"

From what Sam could tell, John didn't flinch, didn't move. "The Taney City Knobbers needs someone to direct 'em."

"And he wants William or Sampson?" At that, Sam straightened, then walked carefully back around his horse. Again, he sensed John shrugging.

"A man has to jine the band, Sam."

"I've had no visits, no threats."

"You're the husband of my sister." John mounted his horse, Sam a bit slower to follow as he understood what John was saying. "You're my family."

"Did you join to protect all the family?" he asked, temper gone in the wake of cautious curiosity.

John shook his head in response. "I like whut the man says, that's all."

"You like scaring people from their homes, John? Killing people?"

John's horse shifted as his hands moved restlessly with the reins. "I'm making a difference, riding with Cap'n Kinney."

Sam's own horse was more placid under him, bending his head down to drink a bit more water, Sam pulled on the reins, and the horse turned to leave the water. "You're going to his church."

Surprise in his voice, John answered, "Wal, yeah! So do you, when you go."

Sam's head was shaking slowly as he mulled over his words once again. "Not anymore." He rode closer to John, their legs touching briefly as the horses walked down the river bank toward Forsyth and the Kirbyville road. "And the Miles and Barkers are my family. Got it?"

"You're married to mine!"

Sam nodded. "I am." His eyes narrowed at John, who stared back; they were close enough to see each other's faces now. "But they were my family first." At that, Sam clucked his tongue and clicked the reins, and his horse left, moving east toward the ford and south toward home.

Haggard said nothing else to him the rest of the ride. Wearily, the men parted as John turned off to go to his farm, which was just west of the bald Nat Kinney owned. The shorter, smaller bald Sam farmed was a bit farther east.

The horse stumbled down the familiar trail off the road toward his cabin in the valley. Sam was down and running for the house as soon as the creek was crossed, knowing the horse would find its way to the barn and food in a stall.

Absolution | 243

Susie was sitting in a chair at the table, cloaked in her shawl, studying the flames of a five-wick candle. Seeing her safe, and knowing her grief, Sam's own sadness reached hers, and she began to sob as he knelt and put his arms around her.

He was home. Time enough to deal with tomorrow when it came.

※　※

He wasn't surprised to find his horse unsaddled and rubbed down after he slept for a few hours. Andy must've been around when he came home; Sam sent a grateful prayer upwards as he made the rounds of the barn, taking the milk pail back to the house. Andy had done most of the chores again. Nannie had already been out to gather the eggs; the basket wasn't hanging on the chicken-yard gate.

Nannie and Tom were waiting for breakfast; Susie, clad in a new, dark blue calico dress, was reaching for the eggs when Sam told her, "You sit. It'll be a hard day."

Her step was heavy as she clumsily moved the chair back from the fire to give Sam room to cook some eggs. He spooned off the cream into a jar, and then poured milk into mugs. He dropped a kiss onto each head as he gave the children and Susie milk to drink while he fried breakfast.

After a few minutes of somber silence, the scrambled eggs were dished up, bread was toasted, and butter was on the table. Susie joined them at the table after Sam helped her from the rocker.

"I've not been sitting in it much lately," she told her husband.

"If there was arms on it, you couldn't've set in it for the past month," he teased her. She smiled. Then he leaned back a little, chewing his eggs and surveying the new dress. He nodded, indicating the dress. "That take a whole bolt?" he asked, raising his eyebrows in mock alarm at the cost.

"Two," she retorted, taking a bite of her own breakfast. "Thought it would do for curtains after the babies are born."

Nannie had the ghost of a smile on her face as her father joked, "I'm going to have to add windows, then!" and even Tom laughed when Susie threw her napkin at Sam.

The sound of a horse outside brought Sam to his feet, and he strode to the door, finding Billy stiffly dismounting by the end of the

244 | Vonda Wilson Sheets

porch as he opened it. Gratefully, he joined the family after warming up by the fire.

"It's going to rain," he told Sam.

"Hopefully, it won't storm," Sam finished his breakfast, and began the task of washing his plate and fork.

"I'll do that," Nannie rose, gathering her own and Tom's plate. He deftly snagged the last of his jam ladened toast, cramming it into his sticky mouth. Sam tossed Susie a soapy rag, and she reached over to wipe Tom's mouth while he chewed.

He protested, "Me do!" and took the rag from Susie, who smiled at him.

"You do," she agreed. He got down from his chair, and ran over to a small wash table, where her mirror was lying next to the basin. He held the mirror awkwardly with one hand, trying to see his reflection. He missed his mouth, but it was a gallant attempt, Sam thought.

Carefully, Tom replaced the mirror, and then ran to Susie for inspection. "Done!"

She gave him a careful look-over, then took the rag from his hand. "One spot," she told him, and then wiped the jam from around his mouth. "Good job!"

He beamed, then went to the door. "Ready to go!" Tom announced, and his parents smiled at him.

"We'll go soon," Sam promised. He looked at his wife. "I can put a mirror up at his height," he told Susie. She smiled back at him.

Billy was shaking his head in bemusement. Little Tom was a smart boy.

☙ ❧

The solemnity returned as Sam loaded Susie into the wagon, and set the children in the back. It just didn't seem it had been over a year since he'd buried Sarah; life had changed a great deal.

The road from Seven Falls Hill to Kirbyville curved around the first Haggard farm, and the family cemetery was fenced with split rails, set back a little way. The wind was chilly up on the flats between the balds and the river to the east.

Billy hung back from the Snapps as he surveyed the area. He had been through here, of course. His gun tucked safely inside his

Absolution | 245

coat, he hitched his shoulders, glad it wasn't as hot as it had been yesterday. Tiredly, he wondered if Pa was back in the cornfield today; he figured so. He'd thought on the night's revelations as he rode to Kirbyville after trying to sleep, and came to the conclusion that William would win the battle of the cornfield.

Granny had tended a great number of people in the region, but it was a small group at the graveside service. Harvesting season, and the impending rain, kept most mourners working to get the crops in. Granny would have approved, he thought.

It was with some surprise he saw Andy Coggburn with an older woman and three girls, all under the age of ten. The woman's head was covered with black lace; Billy could see dark, sun-streaked hair. She was clad in dark brown, as were her three daughters, whose hair hung down their backs in neat braids. It wasn't until the oldest girl turned to look at Nannie Snapp that Billy recognized who the little family was.

Widow Maggie and her daughters. Wal, that was a shocker. Andy Coggburn and a woman with children.

Andy's sister, Serelda, came running into the cemetery, joining Nannie and Miranda. The old couple she lived with were still footing it, and didn't join the group until the man saying the service had opened his Bible and began his sermon. Billy recognized Wash Middleton, acknowledging the old man with a nod. Standing at the opening into the little cemetery, Billy half-listened as he noted the maples and other early trees--sycamores, hickories--were starting to turn. As little rain as there had been lately, and as early as the spring had been, the colors were vibrant, with strong reds, oranges and yellows. Some of the trees, sugar maples, were still highlighted with green, something which fascinated Billy every fall.

Although a few horses, mules, and wagons were lined up outside the cemetery, his ears caught the sound of one more horse approaching. He half-turned, then finished the turn and planted his feet as Nat Kinney rode up on his grey, with his daughter behind him on the horse's back.

Without a word, Georgia Kinney let go of her father, slid off the horse, and ran to join Miranda and the others at the graveside. Kinney was slower, and Billy noted he was carrying his pistols as the big man dismounted.

The service was brief, and Kinney waited patiently for the girls

246 | Vonda Wilson Sheets

to leave the cemetery. There were tear-stained faces, but death was a part of life and life had to go on. Billy remained on the inside of the fence, nodding at each face when they looked at him.

Wash Middleton did not acknowledge Billy, going through the opening and joining Kinney. They were engaged in a quiet conversation as Andy exited, then he turned to wait on the outside of the fence, not far from Billy. Andy was carrying the youngest daughter of the Widow Maggie, and the middle one was holding his hand. Billy noted that Kinney and Middleton were even more stunned than he had been to see Andy familiar with children.

The gravediggers were almost done covering the pine box when the Widow Maggie stood from kneeling with the four older girls. Sam and Susie were visiting with family, and Maggie apparently had been comforting the girls, murmuring quietly as the family swirled around the grave, some reluctant to leave. As the final shovel of dirt was thrown on the mound, the girls each took a small posy and placed them gently on the grave. Maggie herself followed suit. Then she herded the girls toward Billy, and they walked past, the girls' faces saddened with their loss.

When the girls and Maggie reached Andy, Maggie gently pulled on Georgia's shoulder. The Kinney girl shook her head, but at Maggie's insistence, she reluctantly followed as Maggie turned purposefully toward Kinney and Middleton.

Both Billy and Andy took a step forward as Maggie's intention became apparent. Despite being surrounded by the other girls, including his sister, Andy looked at Billy, biting his lips. Billy felt someone at his side, saw Andy glance to him, and turned to see that Sam and Susie joined him.

The Widow Maggie's voice was clear as it floated through the still air.

"Mr. Kinney, we're havin' a gatherin' at my home in memory of Granny. I come to ask if your daughter, who Granny loved, might join us."

The red-headed man's eyebrows rose as his chin came down and he looked at Georgia. "You know you're leaving today."

Georgia's head shook violently, and she said, "No! I don't want to go to Kansas, Father! I want to go to Miranda's." Tears were rolling down, a drop or two at a time, but she did not cry.

At the sound of her name, Miranda left Andy and ran to the side of her friend and her mother. She turned brimming eyes on Nat Kinney; the man looked from his daughter's face to Miranda's.

"Please, sir, kin she come one more time? Please?"

Tense, Kinney looked up from the faces in front of him, and saw Andy, Billy, and the Snapps at the entry to the cemetery, watchful. Then John Haggard walked past his sister, and came to stand behind the girls in front of him.

"We're going to eat dinner," John spoke quietly. "Widow Maggie has invited the family."

Kinney watched as Billy Miles left the group at the gateway, seeming to glide over to Kinney's left, angling to get a clear view of Haggard's actions. Middleton tensed as he always did when detecting a threat, Kinney guessed. He could not tell if the Miles boy was armed; he himself was the only one wearing visible weapons.

Looking down again at his daughter's face, he let the tension go. There was no harm; trains left Springfield daily, and although Eva was anxious to be gone, another day would not make a difference.

"Go," he said to Georgia, unable to say no for a number of reasons, but mostly because she wanted to do this. "Be home at dark."

"Thank you, sir," Widow Maggie was grateful. He turned away from her warm brown eyes, only to find himself hugged about the waist. Looking down, the mother's eyes were in the daughter, who was embracing him.

"Thank you, sir," Miranda echoed her mother. "She's my best friend."

Awkwardly, Kinney watched as Georgia walked away from her father to join Nannie and Serelda. She didn't look back. He patted Miranda on the arms, and gently pushed the hug away.

"At dark, Georgia," he said loudly.

"I'll make sure of it, Mr. Kinney," Widow Maggie told him as she reached for her daughter's hand.

Nat Kinney realized he was quite jealous as he mounted his horse and rode away, Wash Middleton behind him.

He said nothing until they reached Kintrea's store in Kirbyville, and then it was only one question.

"Is Coggburn living with the widow?" he asked Middleton, who was dismounting.

"Don't know," Middleton replied. "But I kin find out."

Nat nodded, then dismounted and went in to get the mail. He

hoped a letter from his Maggie's father had arrived; he needed something to keep his wife from yelling when he got home.

It had become habit to pick up one of the Widow Maggie's sandwiches to take with him; this time, he eyed the neatly-wrapped wax parchment rolls, and decided he really wasn't hungry.

෨ ෯

Tom had fallen asleep in the back of the wagon, coming home at dusk. Sam carried him into the house and put him to bed, having no little difficulty with the ladder up to the attic in his house. He'd made the steps to suit short legs. He grinned when he stuck his head over the edge, calling for a lantern to see.

"What's so funny?" Nannie asked as she climbed a couple steps to hand her father the light.

"Your cat's up here," he told his daughter.

"She has been for a couple days," Nannie confessed as Serelda Coggburn stood beside her. "Looks like she's about to pop."

The girls climbed up to join Sam, who was eying the loft area with the help of the lantern. He didn't come up here often; he had to stoop in the small space. He knew Susie hadn't been up here in some time, either.

Nannie kept the area tidy, but the big down mattress was beyond her to flip or move. He had laid Tom on it by touch, and now he set the lantern on the small floor space available, sitting down to undress the little boy. There had been quite a few smiles today as Tom followed his father around, aping him in his pants that looked just like Sam's. Susie made him a new pair every couple of months as he grew. Other boys who were still in dresses had followed Tom around, so Sam knew it had been a sight to see him and his herd of boys. He smiled again in remembrance, leaving Tom's shirt on him against the chill of the night.

Nannie and Serelda were yawning. Sam wiped the smile from his lips as he eyed his daughter, who was unbuttoning the back of Serelda's dress.

"We can't leave her up here," Sam said.

Nannie's head bobbed a little. "I wanted to see the kitttens getting borned, Pa," she said.

"I know, honey," he said gently, and allowed the smile to return.

Absolution | 249

"But we're going to Taney City early in the morning." He waggled his hand at the heavy cat, who rose from her nest of straw--did Susie know Nannie had smuggled straw up?--and came to him. "I'll take her out to the barn. She'll be fine." He stroked the cat's head and back, which arched against his hand.

"But Pa--they could come tonight," she protested, turning so Serelda could undo her buttons. "I promise, I'll clean the mess up."

"Well," Sam leaned further down, studying the cat while he stroked her softness. Her sides were not rippling in labor, but he really didn't want to take chances on it. "Honey, she won't like it if we have to move her babies."

"Oh." Nannie knelt down to put her face to the cat's, and received a purring caress in return. "Alright, then. I don't want her upset." She lifted the cat to her shoulder, holding her like a baby, and Sam's brain flooded from the image of Sarah, doing the same with this very child. He smiled again, this time heavily. It had been a day for family memories. He knew there would be more.

He took the step necessary to the ladder, listening for Susie, who had gone to the privy. She wasn't back yet.

"How did you get her up here?" he asked Nannie.

"Carried her in the basket with the straw," and handing Serelda the loud cat, she quickly fetched the basket and stuffed the straw into it. Then she gently put the cat inside. The purring increased at this treatment, surprising Sam.

He stepped down the ladder halfway, and Nannie handed the basket to him. Then as he reached the floor of the cabin, he started for the door, only to halt as Susie came in.

Despite the fact she was pregnant for the first time, Susie's maternal instincts had always been strong. She smiled at the guilty look on Sam's face. "What are you doing?" she asked him conversationally. Her eyes were on the ceiling, as if she could see Nannie and Serelda frozen in place, half-undressed.

"Taking the cat out to the barn," Sam assured his wife.

"Really?" The calico-clad belly came closer, and she sidled over to rub the cat's head. "She seems to travel well."

Sam's eyebrows rose. "What does that mean?"

Susie's smile broadened. "I was looking forward to seeing those kittens being born."

Helpless, Sam gently set the basket near the stove, opening

the grate to stir up the coals. He lit a piece of kindling from them, handing it to Susie who then lit the big candle on the table. She handed the stick back to Sam, who tossed it in the stove and then added some logs.

"Pa! You forgot the lantern!" Nannie's voice came from above.

"Hand it down," he said, and went to the ladder, his back against the wall. To his surprise, Serelda handed it to him, and he smiled at her. "Good night, girls," he said.

They responded, and he joined Susie at the table, sitting across from her as she rested her face on her hands, her elbows on the smooth wood top. She looked at him expectantly.

"What?" he asked, sighing.

"Are we taking the cat or not?" she asked.

"To Taney City? Are you kidding?" he asked back.

"No. When were you going to tell me we were going?" Susie wasn't very good at being angry with Sam, and it showed. She'd overheard Sam trying to ask Andy to watch the farm while they were gone this afternoon, and after thinking it through, she decided it wasn't a bad idea. She didn't like Sam's absences.

"Heard me talking to Andy, eh?" he said. She nodded, the expectant look still in her eyes.

Studying her features, seeing the changes pregnancy had brought to her face, softening it, Sam decided he might as well talk of the things that had been on his mind. Before he said a word though, a murmuring from above stilled them.

"You got a good family," Serelda was telling Nannie. A loud yawn followed, and Sam knew the two girls were in bed, one on each side of Tom, and heard the rustling as the blankets were pulled up to cover the three of them.

"Yeah," came the sleepy response.

"Your parents are nice," Serelda was persistent, even as her voice was fading.

"They're a lotta work," Nannie answered.

At that, both Sam and Susie clapped their hands over their mouths, trying to stifle their laughter. It took a little bit; Sam was snorting as softly as he could, Susie was giggling. When it was safe, when he was sure they were asleep, he looked down at Susie's hands, which were turning and molding the big round candle that lit their faces.

His hands joining hers in the process, they worked the softened wax, and Sam realized his thoughts were being worked in a similar manner.

"Alright." He looked at her face again, but her eyes were on the candle. "We're going to Taney City in the morning. I want you to ride in the bed of the wagon."

"I will not!" she declared, looking up instantly.

"Susie, it's going to be a long ride," and in support, the sound of rain came through the open door. His head tilted that direction, Sam added, "I'll have to put the canvas on anyway. You may as well be comfortable."

"Are you going to put straw down for my nest, too?" she asked, a touch of sarcasm brushing against the cat behind Sam.

"No, figured we'd use the kids' bed," he answered.

"Well, I want to go, and if that's how you're gonna be..." she muttered. Her hands began working on the wax again.

He was more than a little surprised at her acceptance, and decided to wait to ask if she'd move permanently to the Taney City farm.

She looked up again, her eyes misting as her thoughts swirled through the day's events.

"I need something different," Susie said. "For a little while."

Sam nodded, and his warmed, calloused hands, softened by the wax, reached over to stroke hers.

"Let's get some rest," he said. "It's going to be another long day tomorrow. But it'll be a good one."

Smiling through the tears, Susie rose, and he did as well, coming around the table to wrap his arms around her. She stopped him, for just a brief moment. "It always is, with you." She turned, presenting her slender back, curved with the weight of the babies in front. "Unbutton me?"

He did so, quickly. Then he reached up, one hand rubbing her neck and shoulders, and pulled out the wooden pin that held her hair up. It fell with a scented swoosh, enveloping him with lavender and the feel of it against his own skin caused him to wonder if he dared take this any further. She was so big, it might be uncomfortable...

He wondered no more when she let the new dress fall to the floor. Her voice floated, husky in the light, whispering, "Blow out the candle."

"Are you sure?" His hands were pushing the straps of her chemise off her shoulders, even as he whispered against her head, bringing her bare back to his own belly, needing to be touched, completely lost.

"Blow out the candle. You'll be gentle."

He smiled as he leaned over the candle, one breath taking out all five wicks. He hadn't let go of her yet, and his hands roamed around the front of her, finally lifting her clear of the clothing on the floor, and laying her on the bed.

Gentle wasn't something he'd felt in days, but it found him and took him. The smooth hair, soothing and cool between them; her skin, warm and tender against him; purring from the cat, over by the stove; and the musky scent of the candle smoke, settled into him as he wrapped one arm above, one arm below the belly of his wife.

There was no clear memory of falling asleep, but sleep they all did.

The next morning, Sam Snapp took his family, a shy friend, and a loudly purring cat to his home in Taney City by covered wagon, protected against the misty rain from the gentle gray skies. Susie rested comfortably on the big down mattress from the attic; the cat rode in her bed of straw. Tom and the girls took turns riding on the seat with Sam. Despite Sam's anxiety, no kittens or babies were born en route.

Eva DeLong and her half-sister, Georgia Kinney, were also traveling, cloaked in waterproof canvas, escorted by Nat Kinney and Wash Middleton to Springfield. No proof against her daughter's broken heart, Maggie DeLong Kinney sent Eva back home to Auburn, hoping a change of scenery would help. Maggie's intention in sending Georgia was to ensure her sister didn't run off to find Robert Prather. Nat had not wanted Georgia to go, but once men he was beginning to see as enemies saw his feelings for his daughter, he felt she'd be safer at her grandfather's home. He coaxed Georgia a great deal, hoping to get her excited to be riding on a train. In this he failed miserably, as she kept turning her head and looking back as if hoping someone was coming with her.

CHAPTER 29
Late September / Early October, 1885

A day of rain, then the weather turned crisp. The days were warm enough after the sun rose; frost crystals sparkled into oblivion. The wide variety of oak trees followed the seasonal change, dropping acorns onto roofs and unsuspecting heads. Black walnuts fell, too, when the wind picked up and tossed their branches just enough to shake the hard green balls loose.

The men were back in the fields at Taney City. When Sam moved to Kirbyville after Sarah's death, he'd left most of the furnishings in her house, taking only the things a man thought he needed. Of course, Susie had brought her own goods when they married, things carefully made, collected, and stored in a cedar chest or baskets during her youth.

Susie rested after they arrived in Taney City, but two days after Granny's funeral, she began to clean and sort through the house. It was a farm house, not a cabin, with two large rooms on both floors, built for a large family. Its whiteness was offset by the colorful trees around the dooryard this time of the year. While the Miles' boys had tended the fields, the house itself had been empty for over a year; there were spider webs and dust bespeaking loneliness and the heartache of losing Sarah.

Sending the girls and Tom out to collect nuts, Susie stood in the kitchen, assessing her surroundings. It was really *a living* room, Susie thought; the door from the front porch opened into this room, and there was a padded bench and two upholstered chairs in one corner. When he'd been staying here on his trips, Sam had slept on the bench, and the slipcovers were dirty. She eyed them cautiously--a good beating would probably help, and she decided to hang them on the clothesline behind the house to air them out first.

One thing Susie highly approved of in this house was the small addition off the kitchen used as a pantry. Even though a door outside to the back took up most of one wall, the others held shelves. A small table stood next to the door, with a wood rack for towels above it. A dried-out, cracked bar of lye soap was in a small saucer on top of the table; Susie wondered what Sam had used for a wash bowl. Lifting the latch on the door, she stood on the step and espied a tin bowl on a rough set of shelves below her left hand. Taking the second step down to the ground, she wrapped her arms around her belly and bent to look at the rest of the contents of the shelves. There was a bucket, some tools, and some glass jars, one of which was broken. The latched door to the cellar lay within a few feet, secure in its rock-and-mortar walls.

Straightening, she turned around. The cistern was in the corner facing her; the ground cover was askew from the children bringing water in this morning. One of the babies kicked her quite hard as she walked over to toe the heavy cover straight. "Shush," she murmured, stroking the area and humming softly.

The privy was within the fenced yard, in the corner toward the barn and opposite the well. She walked over to the back gate, which had a vine-covered trellis. She turned, leaning against the fence, and surveyed the house from this side.

Although everything could stand a coat of paint--the barn was white, as well--overall, the house was in excellent shape. She could hear the hens clucking in their yard behind her. The ivy from the trellis trailed along the top of the fence toward the coop. When they arrived yesterday, the children had been unable to put straw in the nest boxes when they released the chickens into the yard. Cussing, Sam had attacked the vines with cutters, and the remnants were still scattered about. The shingled and hinged roof opened easily after that. No eggs this morning, but there would be once the hens settled in. The rooster was strutting around the foundation of the house, his feathers still ruffled from having been in a cage for hours.

Nannie's cat, Molly, came from behind the house, freezing as she spotted the rooster. Her sides and belly were heavy, but a rooster... Susie took a step forward as the cat sleuthed toward the rooster, but Molly was slower than usual, and the rooster ran toward Susie, jumping into the air and landing on the fence next to the coop.

"That'll teach you to stay in your own yard," Susie told him. He glared at her, jumped onto the roof of the coop, and crowed angrily. The cat acted as if nothing happened, sitting and licking one of her paws.

Walking along the fence toward the front of the house, Susie admired the way the ivy grew up the exterior of it. The porch posts and roof were decorated with the red leaves.

Movement to her left showed Kate Miles and Sally Barker

coming from the path through the woods. Both women were carrying baskets, wearing faded old dresses. She smiled as Sally opened the gate and spotted her standing under the colorful maple in the corner of the yard.

"Good morning," Susie said.

"We thought you might want some company today," Kate smiled back. "Good morning."

Susie nodded slightly, moving toward the stone steps leading up to the porch. She saw that moss was beginning to grow on them. The Virginia creeper leaves waved as the women went into the house.

Putting their baskets on the bench, the older women accepted Susie's offer of coffee. There was enough left from breakfast for two cups; she quickly dumped the old grounds into the garbage pail and started a new pot. Sally and Kate sat at the table, backs straight and feet on the floor.

While it perked gently, the women began the delicate process of getting to know each other better. The conversation was not stilted, but consisted of impersonal subjects. The tone of the bubbling coffee pot changed in a few minutes, and Susie began to rise; Kate stayed her with a gesture, and performed the task of serving, pouring for Susie and refilling her and Sally's cups. Replacing the pot on the stove, she then checked the fire in it. Over Susie's protests, she tended the smoldering embers in the fireplace, adding two logs and poking them around until the flames began furling along them.

"We're gonna need a lot of hot water today," Kate told Susie. The water bucket was by the pantry door; she took it up, and went through the pantry to the well.

Uncomfortable, Susie sat back in her chair. The babies were active this morning, but she was more ill at ease with the Frazier sisters. When Kate returned, she poured the water into the stock pan, setting it to boil on the stove. She turned to see her sister with an amused smile on her face, and a pink flush on Susie's face.

"I was fixin' to start water boilin'," Susie said. She didn't appreciate the implication of sluggishness.

At once, Kate understood. She didn't smile, but said smoothly, "You ain't had the chance to even go down cellar yet, have you?" she asked.

"No," was the cool response. A pause, "Found it jist before you came." Susie winced at another active kick, unable to hide the discomfort.

"You don't need to be goin' down there," said Sally.

"What? Why not?" Aggravation lay along the edges of Susie's voice.

Kate nodded at Sally, and left for more water. Sally took a breath as Susie looked at her. Sally eyed Susie's belly, tilting her head as she watched another big movement roil while Susie's hands caressed it.

"Sam said it's twins," Sally commented.

A faint smile playing along her mouth, Susie was wistful when she responded. "Granny said it was, long before I was even showing." More movement, and she shifted uncomfortably.

Sally's own body responded to Susie's discomfort, and for the first time, she leaned back in her chair, remembering the heavy days of pregnancy. After pouring a second bucket of water in the stock pot, Kate rejoined them, smiling at her sister, her back remaining straight as she sat.

"Her granny said it's twins," Sally told Kate, whose smile widened. She looked at Susie's flushed face.

"Active today, are they?" Kate asked.

Susie nodded in response. "They were quiet yesterday. Slept most of the way here."

Sally's face was a study in fascination with the movements of the babies. "It'd be hard for you to get down cellar with that," and her left hand made a quick gesture. "Stairs are steep."

Kate's head bobbed in agreement. "I'll go down and get the wash tub," she told her sister.

With effort, Susie straightened her back, starting to protest. "You have been takin' care of Sam and this farm--" she began.

"Sam's family," Kate interrupted. Stealing a glance at Sally, Susie saw the sisters agreed.

"I understand thet--" Susie continued.

Again, Kate smiled. "I'm not sure you do."

At that, Susie's face turned almost defiant. "Then you better tell me."

"He and Sarah were very happy here," Kate began, steady in voice. "The men all worked together, in the fields, butchering…"

"We did the same," Sally put in.

"The same what?" A hurt look was on Susie's face as she asked.

"We did the gardening, housework, children….all together," Kate explained. "Sam and Sarah fit right in when Sam bought this place off our brother."

"Oh."

Sally leaned forward and to her left, touching Susie's right hand, which had braced on the edged of the table against the hurt she felt. "She's gone," Sally said.

"Yes," Kate agreed. "It was a bad time. If it wasn't for the kids, Sam would've been lost."

"We miss her, too," Sally added.

Susie was stiffening her whole body. "But I'm here now. We're happy." A vicious kick caused her to jump, "Ow!" and her hands returned to her belly.

At that, the sisters both grinned, nodding in concert.

"You are," Sally said.

Kate got up again and came around the table to stand at Susie's side. Looking down at the young woman, she asked, a little shyly, "May I?" Still stiff, Susie gave a short jerk of her chin, then leaned back.

Her face lit, Kate gently placed her hands on the fabric over Susie's belly. Gently, she patted and rubbed, feeling the movements of the babies within.

"Sally!" she exclaimed. "You have to feel this."

Her eyes seeking permission from the tentative expression on Susie's face, Sally complied.

Absorbed in the fluid pokes, jabs and prods, the sisters bore rapt looks down at Susie. "Bet your insides feel like mush," Sally said, rubbing what must have been a very small back along the front of Susie's belly.

"They do," Susie admitted, feeling quite strange. She didn't know what to think, but the babies were settling down, and she was reluctant to move.

Nannie and Serelda burst into the kitchen from the front door. Upon seeing Sally and Kate, Nannie dropped her half of the tub they'd been carrying, and flung herself at the sisters. "Grandma!" she yelled, running to Sally and hugged her. Her shining face emerged from Sally's arms within seconds, and she raced around Susie's chair to hug Kate.

Serelda busied herself picking nuts up from the spilled tub, and

258 | Vonda Wilson Sheets

Tom came in, carrying a small pail. Seeing the older women, his face became uncertain as he searched for Susie. Once he saw her, he, too, came running, but to her side.

"Mama!" he said happily, displaying the contents of his bucket. "Nuts!"

"Very good, Tom," Susie said, pushing his hair back off his excited face. She took the offered bucket, looked in it; then, seeing his arms raised to be lifted, she pulled him close to her right side, and hugged him tight.

"The babies are moving today," Susie told him.

He smiled, then shifted his head down to her non-existent waist, and received an obligatory response from inside. The smile grew beatific.

Kate's arms around Nannie, her head nodded at Sally, who then reached down to pat Tom while he clung to Susie. Sally's left hand then rubbed up to Susie's shoulder, and Susie looked at the older woman's face.

Nodding, Sally beamed down. "You'll do." She turned, and saw Serelda still searching for spilled nuts. "Who's this?"

"Mrs. Barker, this is Serelda Coggburn," Susie answered. "Serelda, this is Mrs. Barker."

"Coggburn?" Sally asked, pushing her chair under the table and taking a couple steps to the now-standing Serelda.

"Yes," Susie replied. "Andy's little sister."

"Ah." Then Sally noticed what the girls had been carrying. "Who brought that tub up from the cellar?" she barked.

"I did," Nannie answered. "Yesterday."

Kate suddenly laughed, rueful. Her arms tightened around Nannie, and she continued to chuckle, even as she explained. "Here we came, all ready to help you get things in order," she told Susie. "Seems you're a step ahead of us."

Susie smiled back, accepting and acknowledging. "Nannie's a big help," she told Kate. "Seems she gets it from you."

After a snack of fresh bread and butter for the children, Nannie and Serelda brought in more water, and helped Kate and Sally begin clearing cobwebs and dusting. Windows were opened, and a crib was brought down from upstairs. The bench cushions and the crib mattress were taken outside and beaten with a stout stick, sending

Absolution | 259

out billowing clouds of dust.

Sally left mid-morning to fix lunch for the men, and returned with sandwiches for the women. Susie, who had been sorting through the nuts and sending Tom to dump debris, sat down suddenly with an exclamation.

The aired-out cushions on the bench were comfortable, and after a while, she dozed. Kate and Sally kept the girls quiet as they came in and out of the kitchen, but Tom joined Susie on the couch, and soon, both were sound asleep.

༄ ༅

Sleep.

Phebe and Celie were in the bottom bunk, snuggled down into the mattress against each other. The sweet faces were next to each other, as if they needed the same air to be even more reassured of touch, of love.

The darkness outside fell heavily this night, and the chill crept under the door. Miranda looked out into the clearing, wishing that Serelda and Nannie were visiting. They were in Taney City, with Nannie's parents, and she had been lonely.

Her mother came up behind her, putting her arms around Miranda's shoulders, clasping her first-born to her.

"They'll be back," Widow Maggie said, softly. "Sooner than you think."

Miranda's shoulders rose in protest. "Nannie thought her pa would want to stay over there," she said, quietly.

Maggie nodded, bringing her chin to rest on the top of her daughter's head. "You'll be fine. We got plenty to do, butchering and getting ready for winter."

A slow tear fell onto Maggie's sleeve. Feeling the weight of it, she kissed the fragrant, dark blonde, streaked hair on its straight part.

"Andy will be here to help," she said, and she knew Miranda was smiling, just a little. Then the girl turned and raised her own arms to circle Maggie's neck in a hug.

Miranda drew back from the hug just enough to search her mother's face. Although there were faint lines around the eyes and mouth, she knew her mother to be a beautiful woman. Ma was older than Andy, but...

"Are you gonna marry him?"

In shock, Maggie pulled back a little from her daughter, her hands falling to Miranda's shoulders. She shook her head at the question, and the hard yellow-brown look in her eyes was a new one to her daughter.

"No. I ain't gonna marry again."

"Andy's not like--"

"Randa!" Her mother turned away, and walked around the table to the fireplace. She grabbed a poker, more for something to do with her hands than a need to tend the fire. She prodded at it, anyway, thinking of what to say to Miranda, who still stood by the window. Finally, she looked at the face, now lit by the flames.

"Come here," Maggie said, and set the poker against the stone of the fireplace. Miranda quickly joined her mother, and Maggie's arms again brought her daughter back to embrace.

"I'm sorry, Ma," Miranda began, but her mother's voice cut her off.

"Don't you be sorry," Maggie said fiercely. Her voice became gentler, as terrible memories of the past were pushed firmly into the darkness outside. Her eyes again were warm brown, and Miranda wondered if she'd imagined the yellow just a few moments earlier. Then her attention was grabbed by her mother's voice.

"I won't have no man living with me again," Maggie began. "I want no man. You and your sisters...." at that, she raised a hand to touch the wisps of hair around Miranda's face, no longer daunted by the task of raising her daughters alone, "you are mine to care for, to love. I don't want no man messing with that." She lowered her eyes, aware that Miranda was much too keen for her to hide the latent fierceness for long; but hide it she would, as long as she could.

Mastering it, she again looked at her daughter's face, and even found a smile on her lips. "Andy is a good friend," Maggie explained. "I care about him, too. But he is a friend....that's all. That's all it'll ever be."

Miranda's eyes narrowed. "He's helped us a bunch, Ma," she said. "I know how to do meat like he does now."

"So you do," Maggie replied. "We'll be butchering the pigs tomorrow or the next day. So you got more to learn." She leaned down a little, and kissed her daughter's cheek. "You git on to bed,"

Absolution | 261

she said, and Miranda complied, climbing into the top bunk and pulling the covers up to her chin. Her eyes, so like her mother's, shone in the firelight as she watched Maggie wrap herself in a thick shawl and curl up in her rocking chair, sitting nearly motionless in front of the fireplace.

When Miranda's breath finally slowed into sleep, Maggie felt free to explore her emotions.

No, she wasn't lonely, sitting here alone, her girls safe behind her. She shifted, right foot coming down to gently rock her chair. A thought or two from the past presented a door in her mind, and she went right by it, not even tempted to turn the knob.

There was food, and would be more, enough to get through the winter. She would not have to hear hungry bellies, ever again. She could earn some money, too, and a smile flitted across her face, considering all that had happened since she became "The Widow Maggie."

No, she wouldn't ever have a lot of money, she thought, and that was alright. Some folks cared about it, but she didn't, not now. She had spoken the truth of her heart to Andy, the day that cottonmouth had scared the girls down in the creek. Food, clothing, shelter; these things were hers now, and she and her daughters were safe.

Outside, the wind had picked up; a draft came down the flue, and she realized a storm was brewing. A chill ran through her; it was very late. She stood to bank the fire against the draft, and made her way to her own bed, not far from the girls.

As the sheets and blankets warmed to her body, and she began wafting feather-like into the dark, Andy's face came to her mind. No, he was the brother she never had, the son she would not bear. He was already hers, and even if either of them ever seriously considered the idea, marriage would not do.

The thunderous knocking on her door brought Maggie upright in the bed, throwing the covers in preparation for action. For the briefest instant, "He" was here, and then the world landed back on its feet. She shushed the shrieking coming from the bunks, running to the fireplace and grabbing her knife off the mantel.

The knocking resumed, a dark male voice calling.

Miranda had come down off the top bunk, landing with a soft

262 | Vonda Wilson Sheets

"thump," and bent to shush her sisters with her hands over their mouths. She shook her head furiously at them, Maggie's splintered brain noted, then ran to join her mother, grabbling and finding the poker behind Maggie.

Sidling to the table in an effort to see out the window, Maggie and Miranda saw the flickering silhouette of a man gazing in at them.

Suddenly, voices made sense to the woman and her daughter. "Can't see him!" came from the direction of the window, and the pounding started up again.

"Open up!"

Miranda looked up into her mother's face; calmness drenched her as she realized Ma did have the yellow-eyed rage of a hawk she'd thought she'd seen earlier. Her mother's features were stone cold, and her voice icy as she called back, "What do you want?"

"Open UP!" came over the pounding. The latch on the door held against the knocking, but the door itself seemed to be dancing with each punch.

"No!" Maggie yelled. "What do you want?"

"I want that bastard Coggburn!"

"He's not here!"

"Don't lie to me, woman!"

Miranda whispered, "That sounds like Wash Middleton, Ma."

Maggie glanced down briefly at Miranda's pale face. "Go stand behind the door, close to the bunks. If it comes open, hit the first one in as hard as you can," she whispered back.

Without waiting for Miranda to move, Maggie stepped lightly around the table, going to the wall between the window and the door. A torch's light shone briefly again at the window; Miranda saw Maggie in shadowy profile, the knife in her right hand dark against her nightgown.

Maggie's left hand came to rest just beside the latch. "You're scarin' my daughters!" she said loudly. "Andy Coggburn ain't here. Go away!"

There was no more pounding, but Maggie could hear the men talking outside. Her back to the wall, she silently pulled the rope lace over the latch with her left hand.

"Ain't no back door," a third voice said.

"So he's stuck in there," said the voice belonging to Wash Middleton.

Absolution | 263

"Can't see him," grunted the one from the window.

"Kin you see ever'thing?" Middleton asked.

"Except the corner by the door," was the answer.

Phebe and Celie had covered their heads against the fear, but now Phebe's eyes appeared, huge in the dark. "Ma?" she croaked.

"Stay where you are!" Maggie's whisper was fierce. "Ready, 'Randa?"

Miranda steadied her grip on the poker, raising it over her head with both hands. "Yes," she breathed.

"Middleton!" Maggie called.

She could hear the men's surprise at her voice; then cautious footsteps backed away from the door. Only one man remained, in Maggie's estimation, and she figured it to be Wash Middleton.

"Middleton!" she called again.

"Whut?" came the brusque, nasally voice.

"I tell you this one last time. Yer scaring my daughters. Andy Coggburn ain't here. Go away."

"Prove Coggburn's not there."

At that, Maggie turned against Miranda's whispered, "No!" and lifted the latch on the door. The rope held the door close, but Middleton had a torch, and could just see Maggie's face through the gap.

"I ain't a liar," Maggie said, and Middleton looked bemusedly back at her through the holes in his mask. Her eyes burned steady at him, yellow-red in the glow of the torch. His left hand began to rise, to push against the door, but Maggie shifted, and he knew her foot was blocking any give the latch-string might allow.

The low fierceness in her voice froze him.

"I kilt my man, Middleton," she said, and he knew her words were true. "No man comes in my house now." Her eyes went to his left hand, which was still on her door, preparing to push, and she shifted once again, pointedly passing her knife from her right hand to her left in his sight. He knew she had a better angle on him now, and he lowered his right hand with its torch to protect that side.

The flames seemed to circle Maggie's face as she whispered above the torch's hiss.

"Do you really want to try?"

He stepped back, both hands up, his empty left one unfurling as he took a second step away. Movement behind him reminded him of

264 | Vonda Wilson Sheets

his two companions, and he clenched his fist again.

"I'll take your word for it tonight," he said loudly. Then he whirled, running for his horse. The others were already mounted, and the three men rode off, no further words being exchanged between them and the home of the Widow Maggie and her daughters.

As they left the trail leading up the hillside, going along the ridge overlooking the White River, the men pulled off their masks.

"Shoulda had more men," grumbled one.

Middleton was thinking hard. It did surely appear Widow Maggie was telling the truth, but there had been no denial of a relationship between herself and Andy Coggburn. He smirked to himself. Not many men would walk away from that woman, and here Andy Coggburn appeared to have little interest in her. If he was interested, Andy would've been there tonight, Wash was sure. It was a cold, heavy night.

Then the memory of just why the woman was called "Widow Maggie" returned, and his whole body clenched in revulsion.

"That woman is pizen to any man," Wash told his companions. "Ain't no sinnin' goin' on in that house."

"S' it really matter?" asked one of the others.

"No," Wash admitted. "Cap'n Kinney only wanted to know if Coggburn was livin' there."

At the turn toward Kirbyville, Wash waved the others off. He then backtracked to the road going down to Sam Snapp's cabin, wondering if Coggburn might be there.

There was no light from within the house, and Wash smelled no trace of recent smoke as he halted in front of the door to the empty cabin. He clucked to his horse, and went around to the barn.

John Haggard had said Sam took his family to Taney City, along with Coggburn's sister. Wash dismounted, and opened the barn door, slipping inside to the animal-warm darkness. Satisfying himself the livestock within was being taken care of and Coggburn wasn't there, he winced as thunder rolled, and decided to leave. The rain soaked him before he even got back up on his horse, which only wanted to go home. Wash agreed, giving it free rein to run.

Someone was taking care of Sam's livestock, as Haggard had said. Captain Kinney had only wanted to know if Andy and the widow were living in sin, he recalled. He had the answer to that

Absolution | 265

question. Wash would wait to see what the captain said before he explored further.

༄ ༅

The next morning dawned cold and wet. The sun made little attempt to do more than turn the skies dark gray. In October, folks wise to the hills dressed for nasty weather, taking layers off if and when the day turned nice.

In Taney City, the fields were empty of crops and men. Sam and Billy were in Sam's barn, harnessing the horses to the wagon and putting the canvas on, preparing to leave for Kirbyville.

During their farewell, Susie had handed Sam a long list of items to be brought back here with him. She'd agreed to stay the winter in Taney City without argument, to Sam's surprise. It would take little time, maybe only two days, to clear the fields at the small farm. It would take almost as long, he figured, rueful and wry, to pack what Susie wanted.

Kate wasn't going to accompany them; instead, she'd sent Billy over with saddlebags bulging. Both she and Susie had highly enjoyed the argument of which woman was going to Kirbyville. Neither won when Sam insisted he could deal with the necessary packing. That was before he'd seen the list, of course. He wondered if there had been some conspiracy between the two women after he'd put his foot down; he pulled the list out and studied it again.

Butter churn. Susie wanted her own, when there was a perfectly good one here. Kate knew it, too. Sam's eyes were narrowly focused on the house when Susie came out, holding Serelda's hand and walking toward the barn.

He glanced down at the list again, as Billy joined him. "Canning jars," he muttered to Billy. "I'm supposed to pack canning jars."

Billy peered over at the list. "That's in Ma's writing," he said.

Sam's eyes were still narrowed when he heard Susie and Serelda enter the barn. "Canning jars? Aren't there enough here?" he asked his wife conversationally.

Shaking her head, Susie's face was mild. "Kate says she needs some more. Oh, and add the stone crocks in--we're canning meat, too." Sam was about to remonstrate with Susie, but halted when he saw Serelda's face. She was nervous, and dressed for being outside.

266 | Vonda Wilson Sheets

He tried very hard to be gentle around Serelda, but knew he'd lost ground while attacking the ivy on the chicken coop the other day.

"Serelda has a question, Sam," and Susie's mild expression changed to a cautious one. Her hand released Serelda's, and she gently prodded the girl forward. "I promise, he won't bite," she told the shy girl.

Sam's eyebrows raised in query, and he knelt down to look Serelda in the face.

She stood her ground, and spoke very quietly. "Kin I ride back to Miranda's with you?" she asked.

"May I?" Susie prompted.

"May I ride back to Miranda's with you?" Serelda asked again, unperturbed at Susie's correction.

Sam looked up at his wife, who was nodding.

"Yes, ma'am, you may," he answered gravely, and was rewarded with her rare smile. He stood, pocketed Susie's list, reached for Serelda, and swung her up in the wagon seat.

"Stone crocks," Susie said.

"Got it." Sam was curious about Serelda, but this wasn't the time. He leaned down, kissed Susie on the cheek, and walked around the wagon to climb up the left side, by the brake. "See you soon!" he called, and snapped the reins. As he and his unplanned passenger rode out of the barn, Billy followed on his horse.

It took much longer to cover the distance by wagon. During the trip, Serelda Coggburn managed to lose her shyness with "Mr. Snapp," to the point of calling him "Sam," as he encouraged her conversation.

"I'm larnin' to read and talk proper-like," was one statement. Sam was amused; his curiosity about her lack of reaction to Susie's grammatical correction was answered. Susie herself often spoke in dialect, but she was well aware of the rules.

Another statement led Sam to the conclusion that Serelda was planning to ask the Widow Maggie if she could stay with Miranda this winter. Sam didn't know how to react to this--he'd thought Serelda was going to live with Nannie. He said as much.

"Serelda, you do know you're welcome to stay with us?" he asked.

"Wal, shore, Mr. Sna--Sam," she answered. "But Andy's to home by Kirbyville, and I'll get to see him more at Randa's."

"Ah." His thoughts harkened back to Granny Haggard's funeral. "Does Andy live there?" he asked.

"Oh, no, he still lives in his cave," Serelda was almost bubbling with information, now that the dam had broken. "He and Randa's mother are good friends, though. He's there a bunch."

"Do you know where Andy's cave is?" he asked casually.

"Nope," came the prompt response. "Ain't been there, but I heerd Andy say oncet was near the mouth of a creek."

"Which creek?"

"Don't know," and her voice became solemn. "He ain't telling me thet."

"Hasn't told you the name of the creek?"

"No. Don't think he wants me there," and she put a hand on his right arm. "Thank you kindly for the offer to stay with Nannie, though" and he grinned down at her cold-reddened face. He noted her hands were chafing together.

"Anytime," he replied. Jerking his hatted head back toward the wagon bed, "Would you like to climb back and get warm?" She started to protest, but Sam's offer of a chance to roll up in a blanket out of the wind was too good to refuse. She slept, and Sam missed her conversation.

It was late when they pulled up by the trail to Sam's cabin. "Mr. Snapp? I'll jist get down now," she said in his right ear, her hand grasping his shoulder for balance.

"Sam," he corrected automatically. Then, "Serelda, I'll take you over in the morning."

"Oh, no, sir," she said, and began to climb out on the seat. "I told Mrs. Snapp I'd walk over tonight. I don't want to make no trouble," she added. "Mrs. Snapp saw it my way."

Sam reached down for the brake, stopping the horses with his right hand as he brought the wagon to a halt. He turned to look at Serelda. It wasn't far, and she was Andy's sister; he considered.

"Are you staying on the main road?" he asked.

"No sir, Andy showed me a deer trail some time back. Reckon I'll take thet."

Billy rode back to the wagon, hearing this last in time to understand the situation. "Sam, I kin take her over there. Be back in no time."

Reluctant, Sam took Billy's saddlebags and watched as Serelda

268 | Vonda Wilson Sheets

settled on the back of Billy's horse, clasping him around the waist as the horse danced. It wanted to be home, and suddenly, so did Sam.

"You come to me any time," he told Serelda. "Any time."

She smiled, and with a flick of the wrist, Billy and Serelda were gone.

He drove the horses on down to the barn. By the time Billy returned, Sam was lighting the fire in the cold stove inside. They ate hastily, and bedded down for the night.

๛ ๛

Upon hearing the horse outside, Phebe ran to the fireplace to grab the poker. Maggie stilled her motions, while Miranda ran to the window, then outside, shouting, "Serelda!"

The girls reunited, Billy left quickly, and excited chatter over a piece of cake and some milk soon turned drowsy. Maggie smiled at the sight of two heads in each bunk, heads surrounded by pillows, only noses obvious. Soon all were asleep.

This was the second night after Wash Middleton had shown up. Andy had not been around; Maggie wondered if he somehow knew Wash was looking for him. It didn't matter to her; no one was going to tell her what to do, ever again. Certainly Wash Middleton knew that; the triumph going through her as he retreated the other night had been an intoxicant, filling her with joy. She knew she stood no chance against a bunch of men trying to get into her house--but somehow, she didn't think the Bald Knobbers were going to visit her any time soon.

She slept soundly, waking before dawn and stirring up the fire in the cold morning. The girls slept on, but she slipped outside to the privy, then returned to the house.

Maggie hoped she'd impressed upon the girls the necessity of not telling Andy about Middleton's visit, but Celie was nearly five, still of an age that didn't keep secrets well.

Motion down by the pig pen told her Andy was there, bundled against the chill as the sun tried to shine stronger than it had in a couple days. "He's here!" she called to the girls, who were in various stages of dress in the warm cabin. "We'll butcher today!"

She plated up and took him some biscuits and gravy, along with

Absolution | 269

a rasher of bacon, while he coaxed a fire to roar near the big oak down below the pig pen. He was planning to butcher all three of the young pigs gelded in the spring; it would take a couple days of backbreaking work.

"Good morning!" Her smile was bright as she could make it, handing him his breakfast and looking him over with her usual concern.

"It's no use, Maggie." He knew, goddamnitall, he knew. Seeing her face fall, he glanced up at the cabin, where the girls were erupting, coming to attack him with love. It was no small surprise to see Serelda, but he had no time for questions in the effort of keeping his plate level while trying to hug all four girls. Maggie reached up and snatched his plate, freeing both arms to hug the gaggle of girls clinging to him.

Some hours later, one pig cut down and moved to the smoke shed, where Miranda was busy tending small fires of hickory that was gathered by the other girls, he stopped long enough to take a sandwich with a bloody hand, swallowing it quickly and chasing it down with hot coffee.

"Middleton came here the other night?"

"How did you know?" She was curious. She and the girls had seen no one else.

"He visited Sam's place. I was guessing," and at the look on her face, he quickly added, "It don't take a education to figger out, Maggie."

"Where did you see him?" she wondered.

"On the road between here and Sam's."

"Why are you here today?" she asked, too quietly.

He indicated the gelding still alive, rooting in the pen, oblivious to its fate. "Had to be done."

The distance he was purposefully putting between them hurt her breathing, her heart. He had told her why he lived in a cave, alone; too many people he loved were dead, and he felt he was a curse of some kind, not meant to love or be loved.

He couldn't offer any consolation, either. "Maggie, someone has to stop him. I reckon it's up to me."

"Why you?" she cried. "Why not some of these other men, the ones who won't join, like Sam Snapp?"

"Because Sam has babies coming. A family. I don't."

270 | Vonda Wilson Sheets

"We're your family!"

At that, Andy turned away, began cutting on the pig hanging from the tree. The girls, above at the smoke shed, saw he was working again, and ran down to watch, Miranda most of all. It stopped any further conversation.

As the day wore into night, Andy continued working, letting Miranda cut on the final pig, helping haul the meat to the smoke shed. Maggie worked as well, trying to make sausage for the first time; his directions were terse, and she sternly forbade herself the release of yelling at him.

The girls literally fell into their beds long, long after dark, sleeping in the shifts they wore under their dirty dresses. Maggie herself was exhausted and worn; she resolved to never again butcher three pigs in a day's time, knowing she still had work to do after a nap.

Andy was driven, haggard lines etched into his face, grief held away from him as he had done with the cottonmouth last summer. He looked up at her approach as he was sharpening his knives once again on a whetstone by the fire.

"Are you going to let them do this to us?" she asked as she sank beside him, dully watching the sparks fly.

"I reckon you proved to them the other night they won't stop you from doing what has to be done," he said, his eyes never leaving the motion of his hands, working the knife against the stone.

"How do you know what I did?" she asked, unsure she wanted an answer. Had he been outside the house, hidden in the woods? Did he watch over them?

His answer was not reassuring. "I heard Middleton tell Kinney you threatened him with a knife." He lifted the blade he was working on, testing it, holding it to examine in the firelight. Suddenly, he looked at her and smiled. "Did you?"

"You know I did," she said, "and you know I'll do it again if I have to."

He abruptly nodded, turning back to his work.

"I reckon iffen I see you and the girls at church, you'd best not say anythin' to me anymore," he said. "Iffen you do, I'll be rude."

A chill hit her hard, and she began to shake.

"What are you going to do?" she asked, once more trying to get him to understand how much she counted on his friendship.

"You go on up, get some sleep. This is about done."

Absolution | 271

"What are you going to do?" she repeated, her voice raising only a little, only enough to make him see she meant it.

He finally stopped moving, turning to look at her with a longing in his face that could only have been from his heart.

"I'm gonna stop Kinney, the rest of 'em. It might take a while, but I'm gonna stop 'em." He bent his head, took a deep breath. "I won't be by for a while." She nodded, unable to speak for the chattering of her teeth, despite the fire crackling nearby. "Send Serelda on back with Sam for the winter." At that, he raised his hand to stop Maggie's protest.

"I know Randa needs her," Andy continued. His hand wavered for only a minute. "But if she's here, she'll try to stop me." The hand lowered, reaching over to pull Maggie's shawl closer around her shoulders. "You won't. You know you won't."

He stood, rolling his head and stretching his shoulders and arms, as he prepared to finish up the work Maggie had planned to do. She left him then, understanding that he felt he was meant to be alone, and hoping that he would call after her, saying it was all a joke.

When she reached the cabin, she slowly closed the door behind her, and stumbled to the bed, not bothering with taking off her filthy dress. She rolled up in the top blanket, and took a bleary, sad look around at the home she'd built on the ashes of a miserable life. The sounds of the girls' breathing, the snaps from the fireplace, these sounds of home were a comfort, as was the fact she'd left the latch up on the door, hoping against hope that her friend, the one man she was comfortable with, would come in for some coffee. The pot was burbling contentedly, adding to the sounds of the cold night.

Shadows moved with the flickering of the fire down by the pig sty. And not one of them moved toward the house.

CHAPTER 30
October / Early November, 1885
Andy Bedevils Nat Kinney

Life on a farm rotated around the seasons, around the weather, around the needs of livestock. None of these things were ruled by anything so mechanical as a clock. Fields were seeded, tended, and harvested when the weather and the plants were ready, and no kind of clock ruled over them; even a calendar had little impact. Livestock and game came into heat, mated, and bore young by some kind of internal, instinctive notion of time, which could be measured by the calendar if one was observant.

Life in town was vastly different. Businesses opened and closed by the clock, meetings were scheduled by the clock--a clock being the instrument of humans to organize their lives. Watches were consulted, lunch hours taken, supper on the table--these activities were ruled on the hours ticking though the day.

School sessions not only taught rural children reading, writing, and arithmetic; if a teacher was gifted, students' minds were broadened by learning about different worlds than the one where they lived. Including life ruled by a clock. In Taney County, classes were often held when children were not needed to work alongside their parents in the fields.

Church was a different matter. If there was a preacher to speak, there were church sessions held. In the early days of evolution from instinctive rural life to a society run by the heavy hand of a clock, Sunday school and church were one of the first regular meetings attended by nearly everyone, as long as there was a regular preacher. Some church buildings rotated the different denominations, each taking a turn on Sundays, displaying a spirit of cooperation that was the practical solution to the problem of any one congregation being responsible for a church building's maintenance.

This type of schedule allowed circuit preachers to ride regular routes, preaching in a different building every Sunday, returning at regular times as agreed on by the church boards. These men did not make a great deal of money, and were dependent on their congregation members for room and board as they traveled.

When he moved his family to Taney County, Nat Kinney began

preaching occasionally at the Oak Grove building. As the months were ripped off the calendar, more people came to his services to listen to his messages, and his popularity grew.

Not all agreed with Nat Kinney, though.

This was evident on the Sunday following Wash Middleton's visit to the Widow Maggie.

It was only a short distance from the Kinney home to the Oak Grove building. Dressed in their Sunday clothes, Nat and Maggie, accompanied by their son Paul, walked along the leaf-strewn trail under the tall oaks, and entered the open space surrounding the church and school building to find the congregation clustered outside.

In itself, this was not unusual. Nat halted, though, as he realized the women and men were not off in their separate groups. Men were standing by their families, and tenseness, not voices, circled under the trees. Children were not running and shouting, but kept close by their mothers.

Nat's wife grabbed his arm as she, too, saw. "What is it?" Maggie murmured.

Shaking off Maggie's hand, Nat strode through the people and called, "Good morning!" None responded.

Wash Middleton and Galba Branson were standing in front of the church doors, waiting for him. He glanced over their shoulders to see a small dark object nailed to one of the doors.

"Reckon someone left you a present," Wash said.

"So I see." Piercingly, he eyed the thing. It was a small black coffin, with a piece of paper tucked inside. Impatiently, Nat ripped the whole down from the door, and pulled the paper out, unfolding it.

"To Old Kinney, Pizen and Death is his favorite role," he read aloud, instantly wishing he hadn't. Recovering, he threw the coffin and its paper to the ground, stomping on them, and turned a hurt face to the shocked congregation.

"I cannot believe someone would hurt you by attacking me," he told them. He searched the faces, and halted as he noticed Andy Coggburn, standing with the McClary family. However, Andy's face mirrored the shocked looks of the rest; after pausing, Nat continued.

"Come! Let us gather in worship!" and he threw open the doors. "No one will stop us!"

It was chilly inside; Wash built fires in the stoves, and the people slowly filtered in. Nat instinctively waited to begin services until the atmosphere began to return to normal.

"Mr. Kinney?" Nat glanced down to see Miranda; her mother and sisters stood nearby. "Hev you had a letter from Georgia?"

Looking around for his wife, Nat saw she was in conversation with Galba's wife, Betsy. He allowed a slight smile at the girl, and answered. "She is doing well. Says she is having a wonderful time at her grandfather's home, and is making new friends."

"Oh." Miranda's face fell, but then brightened. "Would you tell her I'm thinking of her?"

"I will." At that, Miranda bobbed a thank-you nod, then rejoined her mother, who shepherded the girls to a seat in the middle.

Striding to the pulpit area, Nat took a few moments to regain his composure and rehearse the main points of his planned sermon. He sat on a bench over to the side, and when it appeared the pews were almost filled, he stood once more.

People quieted as he approached the pulpit, sitting down and arranging themselves. Scanning the faces in front of him--nearly every pew was filled--he again saw Andy Coggburn, seated next to Clarence McClary, not far from the doors.

"Let us pray," Nat opened the service with a certain sense of caution. He placed his treasured ivory-handled pistols on the pulpit, and carried on.

Nothing else untoward happened, nothing out of place occurred. Everyone sang and everyone listened with their usual attention; the final prayer went off without a hitch. Andy didn't speak to the Widow Maggie, which seemed to confirm Wash Middleton's belief that the woman had sent young Coggburn packing.

All in all, Nat felt it had been one of his better mornings at church.

The following Sunday there was no message on the front doors of the church, and again, Andy Coggburn attended services with the McClary family. Again, the Widow Maggie and her daughters sat in the middle of a center pew.

There had been no turkey calls in days. The nights were growing chilly, and no bonfires burned to alert the Bald Knobbers of meetings on Big Bald.

Absolution | 275

Then it was a month since Andrew began to attend church.

Rested and content, Nat devoted a great deal of time to studying and preparing sermons for the Sundays to come. He met with his lieutenants on occasion, making plans for the next year. Maggie, too, appeared to be at peace, and now they had time to spend together. Maggie played the piano more often; Nat would sit listening in wonder, watching her, wanting her.

Maggie's focus began to narrow on Nat since the children were not home. Paul stayed with James in Forsyth, attending school. Sometimes, the half-brothers returned home on the weekends. But through the week, it was only Nat and Maggie for the first time in their married life. While Nat continued to have his meetings and rehearse his sermons, Maggie had only her music, and she grew to be jealous of any time Nat spent away from her, concentrating on people and things other than herself. She had forgotten that Nat was happier when he worked away from home.

Paul was the first to notice Maggie's distraction.

The Spartan quarters he shared with James in Forsyth were chilly. He and James were standing near the freshly-lit stove after the ride back from their parents' home, holding their hands over the open door. The brothers were soaked; it had been a rainy, dreary Sunday. Their heavy coats were hanging on a peg nearby, giving off steam as the stove heated up.

As soon as he could, James began unpacking the food Maggie had sent with them. As Paul thawed out, he watched James dig out a skillet and put it on the stovetop. Roast beef, mashed potatoes, and thick brown gravy were tossed into the skillet, which was soon sizzling and sending up great tufts of mouthwatering scent.

"You want some bread?" James asked.

"No, just a fork," Paul answered. Handing Paul the fork, James fixed his eyes on the contents of the skillet, his own fork stirring the food.

The two began to eat directly from the skillet, not waiting for the food to completely heat.

"I wonder if Mother would be mad if she knew," Paul said, and his brother winked at him.

"We're not going to tell her, are we?" James smiled as he chewed.

276 | Vonda Wilson Sheets

The twelve-year gap in their ages had not made them friends, nor close. James had not lived at home for several years. Paul found his half-brother to be companionable, but rougher than he'd expected. As he chewed another bite, his thoughts were still on their mother.

"Does Mother seem....well....different?" he asked James.

James stopped chewing, turning his head and raising an eyebrow at Paul. A wry grin crossed his lips, and he swallowed.

"I sometimes forget you are fourteen," he told Paul. He took another forkful of food up, and filled his mouth again, seeming to ignore Paul's question.

"What does that have to do with anything?" Paul, his initial hunger momentarily satisfied, stared at his brother.

James shrugged. Continuing to chew his food, he spoke. "Mother has always been 'different'," he said. "I didn't understand that until I left home." He gestured toward the skillet with his fork while he swallowed; Paul began to eat again, listening.

"Most women have close friends," James reached for a rag to use to protect his hand, then removed the skillet to the cluttered table, where he shoved some detritus aside and put it down. Paul, following this movement, pulled his chair out and sat down; James sat opposite. They continued to eat, a bit slower as their stomachs filled.

"Mother doesn't," Paul said.

"No, she doesn't," agreed James. "She doesn't seem to need any friends."

Frowning, Paul considered James' statement. "She has Father."

James nodded. "True. I can remember when he first courted her."

"What was she like before?"

James sat back in his chair, trying to find memories from his early childhood. He wasn't hesitant, but the words were slow as he tried to answer Paul's question.

"I don't remember a great deal." His hand waved, as if dismissing the blurred images of his own father. He'd been five when William DeLong died; while treasuring the few memories he had of William, James considered Nat Kinney his father.

"Mother has never lived in a big city," he continued. "She's always lived on a farm or ranch, except for the time in Springfield."

"Springfield's a big town," Paul protested.

Grinning, James shook his head. "Not really. I lived in Kansas City for a while, and it's not as big as some back east."

Paul snorted. "Mother wasn't happy in Springfield."

"No, but it's not a city. In cities, women have luncheons, socials, visit with each other. There's music, dancing, theater…"

"Who'd want to see some play about the Romans? Or the English?"

Again, James smiled. "You're missing my point. Mother's never known that kind of life."

"She wouldn't like it!" Paul insisted.

Narrowing his eyes at Paul, James pursed his lips as he regarded his brother. "I think she would have liked city life, if our grandfather had let her have the chance."

"Grandfather?" Paul was confused.

"He bought her a piano, Paul, because she insisted. She wanted to study music."

"She has."

James shook his head. "On her own. Not with others who can play as well as she does. Grandfather wouldn't let her leave him. Do you remember his ranch?"

"Of course."

"Out in the middle of nowhere. Mother had no chance to make close friends while she was growing up. She made music instead of friends. And when my father died, she had children to take care of, as well as Grandfather."

Paul was too young to understand. "That's what women do."

Again, James negated Paul's statement. "That's what she's done because there was nothing else. Tell me, Paul….how many boys your age study outside of school?"

Taking a moment to consider, Paul answered, "Maybe two."

"Do you speak like they do? Any of the others?"

"No, because Mother taught us proper grammar."

"Exactly." Satisfied with his explanation, James got up and took the empty skillet to the stove. He poured some stale water in it, and while it was coming to a boil, he turned to look at the gangly boy who was trying to make sense of what he had said.

"But you're not explaining why she's different now," Paul retreated back to his original question.

"She doesn't have us," James said, gently. "None of her children

278 | Vonda Wilson Sheets

are home all the time now."

"But she still has the piano, she still has Father!"

Picking up the skillet with the soiled dishrag again, James hastily went to the door, dumping the hot water and wiping the inside clean. Turning around, he glanced at Paul as he waved the skillet to cool it, and replaced it on the peg next to the stove.

"That's never been enough for her, Paul. And she's never known anything else."

CHAPTER 31
Sam Loses His Heart

The door closed so slowly, Sam waited for his skin to tell him no one else was with him. He watched a drop of water, glinting in the glow of the lamp, travel down the outside of the window. Then his eyes stayed at the bottom, where the rain was freezing into slush that slowly built up on the outer sill.

How long he stood at the window, he never knew. It was a long time.

As the frozen wall grew, he found himself studying the space between it and the window. The room was warm, and condensation caused a wet mist to form, but curiously enough, he could see clearly into that space at the bottom.

He should be making plans, deciding what to do now. He should be comforting Nannie and Tom, making sure Alma and Alvis were being fed, were dry, and were warm.

Right now, it was more important to learn from the slush. How to form into ice. Ice did not feel, he knew. It had no heart.

The condensation prevented the window from reflecting any lighted detail in the room. Amazing, the small things one felt gratitude for. He did not want to feel anything, so he clamped down on that.

He breathed through his mouth. Every now and again, as he stood at the window, small pants of breath flew back at him.

A deep breath caused him to heave, to clutch at the frame of the window, a hand to each side, over his head. Knuckles white, knees buckling, his grip on the thin wood was all that kept him standing.

He dragged himself back up, his eyes never leaving the bottom of the window, focused on that small wet space, warm on one side, cold on the other. The space was growing smaller, pellet and rain drop mixing, filling it in.

Someone was crying in the other room. His ears heard the sobs, the hiccoughing; it was Nannie, but the recognition of her was far away. She was not close enough to the ice for him to feel her. Some latent flicker along his nerve endings heard Tom's howl, but that sound did not spur him to movement. The murmurs of Kate and Sally never registered, either.

280 | Vonda Wilson Sheets

However, the sound of a newly-born baby--not a cry, not a howl, but more like a fierce mewling--jolted him, caused his hands to drop, his eyes to travel up the window, his chin to rise in supplication.

"Please." He did not know what he was asking for, did not know what to seek.

He only knew the door opened by the stir of the air. His eyes were closed; his back was to the door and the bed with his heart lying there, inert. So white. So lifeless. All of the blood was on the floor, the blankets, where it could not help, could not save, could not continue to sustain life.

Then William was there, taking him by the arm, leading him to the chair by the fireplace. It was only a few steps, but the difference between the ice on the window sill and the warmth by the fire was immeasurable. The heat licked at him; he avoided it, avoided looking at the bed, and avoided looking at William. His eyes fell to his hands as he sat, guided by some instinct for preservation.

They were bloody; his whole body flinched, his head jerked.

If he looked up, he would have to say something, do something; worst of all, he would have to think.

His shoulders hunched, warding off the sounds coming through the open door.

"Sam."

He could hear a second mewling, much weaker than the first had been.

William's hand was on his right shoulder.

The second mewling was growing louder. Then Kate was kneeling beside him, thrusting a tiny bundle into his bloody hands, which instinctively clenched around it. William never loosened his grip.

The nerves in Sam's hands flared. He looked down at the face of his child. Jolts were traveling up his arms, into his body; again, he flinched.

Kate spoke. "She's very, very small, Sam."

The effort to take a deep breath, to feel his body do so, was immense. The baby opened her mouth, repeating the weak mewling he'd heard since the door opened. Trying to avoid any sensation when his nerves were jumping throughout him was impossible. Still, without looking at either William or Kate, he began to thrust the baby back toward Kate.

"No." Raw, throaty, the negation in his voice was almost...

absolute.

Quick footsteps, another pair of feet in his peripheral vision, motion sensed; the feet left, and Kate waved a hastily-constructed bottle in his limited view.

"She's hungry."

The smallest finger of one of Susie's good gloves had been cut off and tied tightly around the top of a small bottle. Suddenly, touching that bottle was imperative. His left arm slid under the little bundle, bringing it to his chest, and his heart was suddenly jumping. It hurt, almost enough to make his breathing stop. He watched his chest in motion, the baby next to it, for one....two breaths, then looked at her face again. He sat back in the chair, and as Kate handed him the bottle of warmed cow's milk, the pain in him retreated just a tiny bit, just a little, just enough, that he could feed his baby girl.

William's hand had not left his shoulder.

The baby mouthed the nipple almost accidentally. Small pinholes at the end of the nipple showed white, but the milk did not stay in her mouth; she didn't close her lips around the nipple. He began to croon, under his breath, and her eyes opened in recognition of his voice; she knew him. One of his fingers came up to stroke around her mouth instinctively.

"Come on, little one," he coaxed, and finally, her lips closed hesitantly around the leather. He continued to stroke as she tried to suckle, but milk dripped down her cheeks, into the clout tucked around her neck.

"Oh, no, you can do this." His eyes were shocked as he looked over to Kate, whose face was mirroring his own consternation.

"Try stroking her throat," William said. His hand left Sam's shoulder. Sam moved the baby to allow him access to her throat, and he gently, so gently, stroked it down toward her chest.

Some instinct prompted Sam to rise, to go into the kitchen, clutching the tiny child to his chest, allowing her to feel his heart beat. One-handed, he reached up on a shelf, grabbed a bowl, then went to the table, sitting down. Clumsily, he tried to remove the nipple, but Kate, who'd followed him, understood what he was doing, and did it for him. She poured some of the milk into the bowl, tested it with her finger, then took a spoon from the flatware jar in the center of the table.

"Let me heat the spoon a little," she said, and then whirled to the stove. Opening the grate, she thrust the spoon in for a few seconds, pulled it out, then touched it to her face. "Ouch!" she said, waving the spoon. Testing it again, she handed it to Sam, who then immersed it in the bowl of milk.

He had never stopped his crooning, his humming, and the baby responded as he carefully poured a few drops from the spoon into her mouth. His smallest finger tenderly moved down her throat, and she closed her mouth to swallow.

The room had been unnaturally quiet for a long time when her eyes drowsed shut after several spoons of milk. Smiling, Sam brought her to his shoulder--God, she was so tiny!--and looked over at the group on the bench.

The other baby had taken her first meal and was asleep in Nannie's arms. Tom was also asleep, his head in Sally's lap. Nannie was leaning against Sally, her swollen eyes looking down at her new sister. Serelda Coggburn was in a chair nearby, and looked back at Sam.

Sam's face lost its tender smile as he considered what he had just done. He lifted the twin off his shoulder, and brought her back down to his chest. Her bundling prevented her from moving much, but for a moment, her eyes opened, and the newborn ghost of a smile twitched her cheek. Then she was asleep, listening to her father's heartbeat.

Closing his eyes, Sam took a few moments to let his body recognize the spark in his arms and come to terms with it.

His heart might be in the other room--but his life was here.

It was hard to accept.

"You don't have much choice, friend," William had some idea of what Sam was thinking.

Affirmation of William's statement meant he would go on, he would do whatever he could; get up in the mornings, make life work, for his children.

"No, I don't," said Sam. He felt his eyelids lift, not reluctantly, but hesitantly, just enough to see the tiny face, smaller than his fist, against his chest.

That small spark in his arms would have to be enough.

There was no funeral for Susie; just simple words said over her grave.

Absolution | 283

Nannie and Serelda rode with William and his sons from Taney City to the Snapp family cemetery, which overlooked the White River. The road down to the ferry at Forsyth was nearby; in the downpour of freezing rain, travelers were few. Preacher Haworth spoke simply to the family and the friends of Sam and Susie who did come. Andy Coggburn and John Haggard stood on opposite sides of the grave, studiously avoiding each other.

At first, Sam wouldn't brook the idea of staying home with the twins and Tom. But tiny Alvis, so much smaller than Alma, would only eat from Sam's hand holding the spoon; Kate constructed a sling, and she lay bundled against Sam's heart, under his shirt.

The twins were not born prematurely, but Alvis simply had not developed like Alma. Perfectly formed, Kate marveled at her size every time she got a peek at her.

Alvis would not be able to stand the trip to Forsyth in this weather, Kate felt. She had to be fed by spoon too often, and kept warm, dry, and snug. Finally, reluctantly, to win her argument with Sam, she asked Sam, "What would Susie say?"

Sam did not answer her. Instead, he went into the bedroom, where Susie lay, cleaned and bundled for the coffin. When the door opened once more nearly an hour later, he came into the kitchen, his face closed as he put a bowl on the stove top to warm it up.

Turning, he looked around the room as if searching for Susie once more. His eyes met William's, and his head jerked once.

Torment was feeding Alvis while the coffin was brought into the house. Purgatory was listening to the sounds of Billy and William putting Susie's body in the newly-built box. Hell was the hammer, nailing the lid shut. Two beats per nail. Sam could not help flinching, and the clout he'd tucked in around the baby's neck was soaked with spilled milk.

He kept his head averted as Jimmy and Manny came in and helped William and Billy carry the coffin out. Then Kate came to his rescue, standing between him and the finality of Susie leaving. Nannie and Serelda came running down the stairs, tear-stained faces seeking permission to go with the men. Kate nodded, and the girls grabbed their coats, coming to hug Sam before joining the solemn men outside.

284 | Vonda Wilson Sheets

Once Alvis was fed, cleaned, and again bundled next to his chest, Sam moved the rocking chair over by the fireplace. Fatigue was swirling around him, lapping at him fiercely. Alvis had not had the strength to cry the night before. The custom of sitting with the dead overnight had been interrupted every time he sensed the baby moving, feeding her as often as she opened her mouth.

She was sleeping now, and Sam took the time to lift Alma from the crib that had held Nannie and Tom. Lifting his left foot to his knee, he laid the baby in front of him, his left arm only slightly hampered by Alvis in her sling.

Alma was stirring slightly, but he knew the bigger twin was not hungry--she had eaten just before Alvis, taking a bottle from Kate, who was now cleaning up at the sink. Tom came over with an old rag doll of Nannie's, and settled contently at his father's feet.

Unwrapping the bundling, Sam studied Alma with intensity. He touched her tiny feet, watching her toes spread as he rubbed the soles. His left hand and knee supported her head as he gently examined her, wondering at her perfection. He moved so that he could see her face clearly, and as if she heard the thrum of his mind, her eyes opened, staring back at him.

Not only was Alma bigger in size, she had already begun to fill out--the look of a newborn would be gone in a few days. Her mouth moved as if to suckle, and Sam offered her his knuckle. Within a few moments, her eyelids closed again, and after another couple of minutes, her mouth relaxed as well.

"She's fine," Kate had come over to watch. Sam wrapped the bundling back around Alma, and Kate put her back in the crib. "She's eating well, sleeping through the noise. She'll be alright."

The muscles of his face were strained; his lips, working and trembling, could not form the relief he felt about Alma's health. He rubbed his face, sensed Tom standing up, and his right hand went immediately to fondle the tousled hair of his son.

"Baby is good!" Tom said, and he stood on tiptoe to gaze at Alma in the crib.

"Yes, she is," Kate assured him as well.

Turning his attention to his father, he climbed into Sam's lap, still clutching the rag doll. Carefully, he leaned back against Sam's right side, his head tucking into the bundle of small Alvis, just as he had done when Susie was pregnant.

Absolution | 285

Kate had moved guardedly to prevent Tom from falling, and when she saw Tom's expression, she bit her lip. Her eyes caught a slight movement under Sam's shirt.

"He looks just like--" she began.

"She's trying to kick his head," Sam murmured.

"Is she awake?" Kate asked. Sam eased the cloth of the sling aside; his chin tucked down, and saw that the baby's eyes were indeed open.

Tom had tucked his rag doll in between his body and Sam's. Sam shifted the baby slightly, so that her bottom was resting on top of Tom's head. Kate was forced to smile at the sight.

The movements in the sling were growing a bit stronger, and Kate went at once to prepare another bowl of milk.

"Want to see?" she heard Sam ask Tom. Tom then rose, supported by his father's right arm, and peeked in at Alvis.

"Mama," Tom said.

"No, this is Alvis," and there was the sticky syrup of grief in Sam's response. "Mama went to heaven yesterday."

Kate turned in time to see Tom's head shaking. He pointed at the baby with his right index finger. "Dat Mama."

Struck by a thought, Kate grabbed one of the two bottles and poured the warm milk into it. Securing the nipple, she asked in an offhand manner, "Tom, do you want to feed the baby?"

"Yes."

Although Alvis had not made a sound yet, Kate and Sam's movements to shift Tom on Sam's lap, his arms encircling Tom and Alvis, were quick and careful. Sam watched as his left arm supported Alvis' head and Tom's left arm, and Tom was handed the bottle.

"See if she'll take it," Sam told Tom. With his right hand on Tom's, the two put the nipple to Alvis' lips, and she opened her mouth. Encouraged, Sam helped Tom to move the bottle further in, and suddenly, the baby latched onto the nipple and began to suck.

Tom and Sam were both humming softly--Kate knew it was something Sam did instinctively, and Tom may have been mimicking his father. She was almost afraid to breathe, watching the baby suck for only a few minutes, then fall asleep, her lips slack around the nipple.

Sam looked up at Kate and shook his head after he'd tucked Alvis back into her sling inside his shirt. Breathing again, Kate smiled back at him.

"I think we've found something," she said in amazement.

Taking a deep breath in a sigh, Sam had to agree. Then Tom twisted in his lap, holding up the forgotten rag doll.

"Want dat," Tom said, pointing at the bundle on Sam's chest.

Puzzled, Sam replied, "She's asleep, Tom."

Tom shook his head, then lifted his own shirt, tucking the rag doll inside on his left shoulder. "Want dat!" he repeated.

So Kate fixed a sling for Tom to carry the rag doll as his father was carrying his sister. At her insistence, Sam went to the long bench in the corner of the room, carefully inclining on puffed-up pillows, Alvis at his heart, Tom and his bundled rag doll in his arms. Within moments, all were asleep.

A little less than two hours later, Tom fed Alvis again, with his father's aid. Again, she suckled more milk from the bottle, a critical one more spoonful than she had the first time.

Kate Miles had little hope the baby would survive when she had been pulled from Susie's failing strength, covered in fluid and blood, too frail to wail and too feeble to kick as her sister had done. Now, however, fixing supper and occasionally glancing over at the sleepers, she felt the tiny girl had a chance.

By the time the mourners returned from burying her mother that evening, Alvis Snapp had suckled the bottle in Tom's hand several times, sleeping just a few minutes more between each feeding. Tom stayed tucked up against her, in their father's arms, carrying his own "baby."

CHAPTER 32
December 19, 1885 - Fire

Cold.

His breath was dampening the dark sack masking his head and face. He could feel it, even through his mustache and beard, grown thick and heavy to protect his face and neck in the wintertime. For the time being, he clamped his hat on his head for extra protection.

The residents of Forsyth were certainly not out tonight, this weekend before Christmas. But there were still lights shining in the windows, and the occasional visit outside by a silhouetted figure. He had to wait. He hunkered down in the shadows of the livery, wondering if he could go inside, out of the chill, without disturbing the horses.

Best not.

It was not long after midnight before he could no longer see any sign of wakefulness in the buildings around the square. Even the saloons were dark early, which was not unusual in the winter. Although the buildings around the square were businesses, the owners often lived above or behind their stores and offices. Plus, there were other residences that also had a view of the square.

He waited yet another hour, just to be safe.

The stillness and beauty of the night made no impression on him. His mission was the only thing on his mind.

Finally, he rose, stiff from the cold and enforced inactivity. His knees crackled, and he stood still, letting the achy wakefulness return to his feet. Stretching his gloved hands, the tingling was matched in his fingers, traveling up his arms.

He dropped the hat to the ground. The cold air hit his head, and he inhaled quickly against it.

He picked up the heavy can of kerosene. Carefully, he took a step toward the two-story brick building. He weighed heavily on his foot. Next step, he did the same. He continued in this manner until he was well across the street, and a human would not awake the horses in the livery building. He switched the can to his other hand. Although the unpaved street glowed dimly in the darkness, he cast no shadow. Pleased with his choice of this night, with no moon and a heavy cloud cover, he continued moving slowly toward his goal.

288 | Vonda Wilson Sheets

Although the metal lid was sealed tightly, he could still smell the kerosene through his mask. A brief smile flickered under the black muslin hood as he reached the door and tried the knob. It turned easily, and the door swung inward, disappearing into the deeper darkness of the building.

Familiar as he was with the courthouse, his steps were still measured and quiet when he entered and closed the door behind him.

Setting the can down with a slight "clunk," the contents sloshed inside. For the first time, he was uneasy. He rubbed his eyes through the mask, and was tempted to take it off. Red and white coronas burned through his vision, however, and thus reassured his eyes were still working, he left the mask over his face.

In the entryway of the building, there was only the transom window to admit any light, and it was dark. Still, he picked up the can once more, and crept toward the staircase. He realized he was shaking, but with cold, not nerves, he thought.

His foot hit the bottom step loudly, and he almost toppled forward, the weight of the can balanced against him. When there was no response to the inadvertent noise, he chuckled. The can was set down once more. His fingers too stiff to work well, he pulled off his gloves and put his hands inside his coat, under his armpits.

After a couple of minutes, there was some sense of feeling, and he took a small box of wooden matches from his coat pocket. The match flared, and his eyes reacted sharply, blinded by the small glow. He let it burn almost to his fingertips, then dropped it on the heavily-varnished floor. The smell of burnt wax rose faintly as he lit a second match, and lifted the chimney on the sconce next to the staircase.

Good. The sconce was full of lamp oil, and cast a warm glow. It was the most light he had seen in hours. Taking a candle from his pocket, he lit it from the sconce, and set the chimney back down tidily.

Then he laughed aloud. That was foolish--it would not matter how tidy he was, in just a few more minutes.

Holding the candle in front of him, he lifted his burden and went up the stairs to the second floor. Reaching the top step, he again lifted a chimney for a sconce, but this time, he dropped the fragile glass as he lit the wick. The shards shattered against the can on the floor.

Absolution | 289

His eyes gleamed through the mask. Looking around, he saw that all the doors were closed. No matter. He lifted the mask, blew out the candle, and stuck it back in his pocket.

Each door was opened, and a trail of kerosene poured thriftily on the desks and furniture, leading back out to the hall. He worked methodically--it would not do to run out of kerosene. Papers were tossed down, books knocked off shelves; fuel for the fire.

The can was about half empty when he returned down the stairs, pouring kerosene on each heavily varnished step. His boot had picked up a glass shard from the lamp, and he stopped at the bottom of the staircase again, holding the candle to his raised foot, yanking the glass out.

He repeated his actions on the first floor, paying special attention to the rooms with the land records and treasury books. He did not notice the book on a desk by a window. It was difficult to see through the mask.

Shaking the can, all the trails of kerosene connected at the foot of the staircase, and he stood, breathing heavily through his mask and light-headed from the fumes.

It was time.

The candlewick flared once more, and he climbed the stairs again. The candle was touched to the kerosene, which slowly ignited into a path of flame as it danced and twisted across the floor into the adjoining rooms. Within a minute, fire was in each room, and growing as the paper caught and spread.

Downstairs, he repeated the ritualistic act.

The warmth was reaching him through his coat as he watched to make sure the flames were destroying the records of the county, and could not be easily extinguished. The smoke from the heavily waxed floor became thick and heavy inside, and he judged it was time to go.

Peering through the door, he first made sure no one was outside. Then he threw the door open and ran, back to the safety of the shadows of the livery stable. Once there, he turned to see a glow in every window of the handsome building.

He and his family had profited handsomely in recent years, in land and income. He had capitalized on others' ill fortune, and made his own. Although questions had been raised, the paper trail of his great luck had not been closely examined.

But Taney County officials and citizens had requested an audit by the state of Missouri. The county's finances were in ruins, and there were suspicions of fraud and theft. The accountant had visited once already, requesting land records and more for his review in January.

As the glow became visions of bright flames in the windows, he smiled. There would be nothing for the auditor to see in January, he thought. Everything would be destroyed.

A yell broke through the night, and he knew it was time to leave. Moving cautiously, lest he be seen by citizens rushing to the courthouse, his movements became indistinguishable in the night.

Tom Layton, who was in charge of land records, smashed a window by his desk and managed to snatch a book away from the clutches of the ravenous flames. The fire roared out at him and he hit the ground, smelling of burned hair and smoke, while clutching the one surviving book to his chest. He rolled away from the raging inferno as anxious hands threw a damp blanket over him.

Marriage records. Land deeds. Court files. Tax rolls. All was lost in the courthouse fire of December 1885 in Taney County.

Whoever did it, citizens noted in the days that followed, did a thorough job. Fingers began to point in all directions, from Bald Knobber and Anti-Bald Knobber alike. Neither claimed responsibility nor expressed satisfaction, for to do so would be to paramount to admitting there was something to hide.

After all, who would want to hide the truth?

CHAPTER 33
Open hostilities between Andy and Nat Kinney

In the weeks after the forced break in his friendship with the Widow Maggie and her daughters, Andy Coggburn worked to make his cave a bit more comfortable. He stalked Nat Kinney daily, and checked on Sam and Susie Snapp's cabin in the valley periodically. And he attended church services at Oak Grove, playing the part of a respectful listener to the words coming from the big man who kept his pistols on the pulpit during the sermon.

He saw Galba Branson, Wash Middleton, Bill and Gus Hensley, John Haggard, and others, ride to Kinney's home. Sometimes, at night, the men would meet at the Oak Grove building, their horses stamping and snorting steam in the clear, cold air, huddling close though their reins were tied to the rail. On those nights, with the moon bright white in the skies above the leafless trees, he would huddle between the pile of wood and the building, clutching an old buffalo robe around himself, listening intently.

The daughters of Widow Maggie were obviously perplexed because Andy no longer visited them. Somehow, their mother managed to keep them from running to his side at church services. He missed them, and Widow Maggie, with a fierceness that made him ache if he let it stay on his heart too long.

He also missed Serelda, more than he thought possible. Although he hadn't lived with her in years, the thought of her being "away" from the area wrestled with his heart, even when he knew she was safe with Sam and Susie.

Susie's death from childbirth forced him to reevaluate his plans. Since the Bald Knobbers weren't riding during winter nights, he had refrained from doing anything to antagonize the group. Things were at a standstill until he overheard Kinney talking to the men about himself and Sam in early December.

Andy realized he'd overplayed the part of a worshiper when the men decided Andy was no longer a threat. Such a mistake was easily corrected.

The following Sunday, churchgoers found a hairball, made of skunk fur and beeswax, suspended from narrow black ribbon, nailed to the door of the building. Kinney pulled it off the door and stomped

292 | Vonda Wilson Sheets

on it angrily, appeasing his superstitious congregation by holding his Bible aloft and assuring them he, and they, would remain in perfect health.

The Sunday after that, a trail of soot-blackened salt encircled the building. No one would cross the path until Kinney arrived and promptly crossed it himself. With some inward satisfaction, Andy, again ensconced within the McClary family, noted that some of the more superstitious men and women refused to cross the line, and left, crossing their fingers against bad luck. Members of the congregation who did stay were treated to a sermon on witchcraft, Kinney's irritation evident.

Deciding to visit Serelda and the Snapp family for Christmas, Andy detoured to visit the Haggard family cemetery the afternoon of Christmas Eve. Tying his borrowed mule to the rail fence, he approached Granny Haggard's grave with care, and knelt down beside it. A large rock, encrusted with crystal, marked the grave-- Andy recognized it as one from the rock collection she'd lined in front of her cabin.

The snow-covered ground saturated the knees and lower legs of his pants, but Andy didn't notice as he briefly bowed his head.

"We miss you," he said simply. He brushed snow away from the top of the mound, exposing the dirt still piled higher than the ground around it. His hands dug into the wetness, scraping a shallow hole in the area he judged to be above her heart. Reaching into his coat, he pulled a small muslin bag out of his inside left pocket. He held it to his lips, inhaling the lavender, cedar, and chamomile mix he'd put inside the tribute. Gently laying the bag in the hole, he covered it, and brushed the snow back above the dirt.

Standing, he continued to focus on the rock that served as a headstone. "Bless you," he whispered, and left.

Finding his sister happy at Sam's home in Taney City, Andy elected to stay a few days. He figured his campaign to discredit or drive Nat Kinney away might benefit if nothing happened the Sunday after Christmas. When he returned to Kirbyville, however, he found he was sadly mistaken.

Word had spread of the man's apparent immunity to curses and spells cast against him. Kinney's congregation not only regained its size; even more people showed up for services the Sunday after the

Absolution | 293

new year began. Folks figured Kinney to be a spell-breaker, Andy discovered when he visited Coggburn relations. To his dismay, even some of his own numerous aunts, uncles and cousins attended services on that Sunday, when he again joined the McClary family in their pew. There were extra chairs filling up the entire room of the building, and some men stood outside the half-opened windows, listening to Kinney preach.

After the service was over--Andy wearing the most pious expression he could manage--one of his cousins grabbed him outside and pulled him around behind the building. Along with a couple of horses, there stood several more cousins, which made Andy a little wary, especially when he saw Uncle Seck.

"Boy, what d'ya think yer doin'?" Uncle Seck said.

Puzzled, feigning innocence, Andy responded, "'Bout what?"

Impatiently, Seck jabbed a strong finger at Andy's shoulder. "We cain't talk here. Y'all come down to the house 'bout dark."

Narrowing his eyes, Andy frowned, shook his head. He didn't dislike Seck, but they weren't close. For a short time, Serelda had lived with Uncle Seck after he'd married, but when the babies started coming, Andy had had to find another place for his sister.

Again, Seck jabbed Andy with his finger. "You come. Yer gonna need help."

Somehow, Uncle Seck knew what Andy was doing. "Alright, alright. I'll be there."

Two of his cousins had been posted as lookouts; one drew back. "Outta here."

And the Coggburns melted into the woods around Oak Grove, seconds before Galba Branson walked down the side of the building and turned right, going for the two horses and missing any hint of a Coggburn clan meeting.

Later, Andy visited Granny Haggard's grave. The Christmas snow had melted. Kneeling again before the headstone, his thoughts were calm as he contemplated the possibility that at least some of his family were also interested in the departure of Nat Kinney.

It meant starting a feud, he knew. The message-bearing coffin, the hairball and the soot-blackened salt, these things meant to warn against and ward off evil spirits. Now, mere pranks could get more

294 | Vonda Wilson Sheets

serious, and he wanted to protect his family. A chant Granny had taught him long ago came to mind.

"God the Father is with me. God the Son may be with you. The Holy Ghost is with us all, but I will rise and you will fall."

Just as a precaution, he pulled a small leather pouch from his pocket, and dug out a handful of the cold dirt from the grave to put in it.

Rising resolutely, he turned back north, heading for Seck Coggburn's cabin. It wouldn't hurt to find out just what his uncle had in mind. Andy didn't want anyone hurt; he felt in his pocket for his buckeye, and pulled it out, rubbing it between his fingers and thumb as he walked.

A little luck wouldn't come amiss right now.

Seck walked to his barn about dusk. Andy watched from the trees nearby; seeing Uncle Robert and two cousins join Uncle Seck, he finally entered the barn just after full dark. The men were grouped around a single lit lantern placed on a milk can. The barn was not big; of the four open stalls, two were occupied by a pregnant cow and a horse. The other cows and Seck's team of mules were out in the pasture. Normal barn scents of animals and hay swirled, enhanced with the breath of clear moonshine being passed around in a stone jug. An owl hooted softly and took off through the high, small opening above the wide door.

The meeting was enlightening, to say the least, Andy thought.

After a few comments and statements were made by the others, Seck took charge.

"Wal, I've got nothing to lose by helping y'all go after Kinney. The wife's wantin' to move out to Washington, anyways, and I reckon if things get too hot, we might as well go. I bin working on a way to break up Kinney's church service," he told Andy and the others.

"What's that?" Andy asked.

"Wal, your spells and charms are workin' some, but people hevn't seen Kinney lose his temper," Seck replied. "Need to see him get mad."

"Need to see him crazy," Robert Coggburn said. The lantern-shadowed faces, inscrutable under brimmed hats, nodded in agreement.

"Wal, I figger I kin do sumthin 'long thet line," Seck responded. "Bin studying on thet fer sum time. The man's prouder then a eagle. Gotta make folks skeered of 'im, mebbe make 'em laugh at 'im. Gotta make 'em unnerstan he's not any better then the rest of us."

He looked at Andy, his eyes beady and concentrating. "You bin doin' good work. Got folks talkin'. Iffen we do it now, in winter, mebbe he won't hev so many riders come spring."

Andy nodded slowly in agreement, and somehow, the five men came closer as Seck's voice took up again, lowering in volume but not in intensity. He and Robert laid out plans to discredit Nat Kinney before more families were hurt when the spring came and the Bald Knobbers began riding again. It was nearly midnight before the meeting was over. When each man left, his upcoming role was clearly outlined.

Audacity and tenaciousness were going to ensure that Nat Kinney would not be able to command hundreds of men ever again.

Eliza Boston Coggburn stayed behind to marry Seck when her family left Taney County to move west. In the 1870s, her father and brothers worked for two years to build what was now called Boston Road. An alternative to the Springfield-Harrison Road for its entire length, Boston Road ran along the ridge top from the White River north and west to the Wilderness Road, south of Spokane. It didn't flood, as the Springfield-Harrison road was prone to do, since that teamster-laden road followed the Bear Creek and Bull Creek valleys through much of western Taney County.

Then William Boston put a ferry at the end of his road, not too far upstream from Bill Hensley's ferry at the mouth of Bull Creek. The Boston Ferry was an instant moneymaker, but a feud with Hensley was not part of the Boston family's plan. They sold their homestead to Pat Fickle, a friend of Hensley, and moved to Washington.

So the Coggburns, especially Seck, had family to go to if need be. Traveling in a wagon during the spring and summer, a migrating family would virtually starve the following winter if they had no family or friends nearby. It was not possible to prepare for winter while traveling.

The hill people were a superstitious folk. Healers like Granny Haggard were often called "white witches" or "conjure-women" but Andy knew Granny had not been a witch. The good and bad properties of herbs, roots, and leaves, which ones to use for what illnesses and injuries, was intrinsic knowledge, part of being a healer. Everyone knew enough to be able to treat minor colds and wounds, but healers like Granny were few and far between.

True, some people visited Granny in the darkest night hours for an "ill wish." Granny didn't cast spells, but she did make cash money from preparing a draught to cause stomach cramps for some straying husband, some cheating wife. Or she would make up a posy of herbs to ward off evil, a camphor pendant. Cash was scarce--if a person was going to ask Granny for an ill wish, the time it took to save up the cash Granny demanded most likely allowed that person's mind to change or adapt to whatever made him or her want the ill wish in the first place. Wise in human nature, she still made enough cash to pay her taxes and purchase items she could not barter.

Granny did not share the knowledge openly; Andy had learned how to make ill wishes, what plants and other items to use more by observing Granny than by what she actually taught him.

Cut branches of hemlock were carefully laid on the trail between Kinney's house and the church. Small muslin packets of nasty-smelling herbs were hidden in the rafters of Kinney's barn, and one Saturday night in late January, a packet of grave dust was laid on the top of the inside door frame in the Oak Grove building and in the rafters of Kinney's barn, above Grey Ghost's stall.

But Kinney kept preaching, meeting with his men, and appeared to suffer no ill effect from the charms against him. The congregation and folks who lived in the area came to believe the leader of the Bald Knobbers was impervious to any form of spell-casting, and word continued to spread of this much-admired ability.

Andy didn't plant all the charms with an audience in mind, however; he was forced to search for even more nasty combinations of unlucky items, attempting to spell Kinney enough to at least slow the man down.

Deciding that the dust from Granny's grave held the nature of her good heart, he roamed graveyards for dirt from people who had been notoriously sinful during their lives. Meanwhile. Seck, Robert, some of his cousins, and the McClarys, were making plans for disrupting the second Sunday service in February.

Charles Guiteau assassinated President James A. Garfield in 1881, and was hung for his crime in 1882. A song made the rounds of society in the months after Guiteau's death called "My name is Charles Guiteau." The melody of the Guiteau song was well-known, and would be recognized; the men simply wrote new lyrics for it. They decided that Andy would lead the singing after the service was interrupted. Although he didn't sing often, Andy possessed a clear tenor voice that could be heard for some distance, and the others would join in once they left the building.

Generally, most of the men whose families attended Sunday school or church services stood outside during the service, listening to the preaching through half-opened windows. Galba Branson and Wash Middleton were notable exceptions; Kinney wanted them inside. John Haggard was often outside, keeping an eye on the men and boys who stood around the building, talking quietly in small groups or smoking.

That Sunday dawned with a crispness that belied the coming of spring. If a man stood in the sun's rays, it was warm enough. Andy and his uncles, Robert and Seck, met just north of the Oak Grove building, only minutes before worship services were to begin. In the cold gray shadows of a pine stand, they carefully splattered their clothing with some of the contents from a jug of homemade whiskey. Then Robert filled his flask, and hid the jug in a crouch of juniper nearby.

"Best take a swig," Robert told Andy, handing his nephew the leather-bound flask.

Obligingly, Andy tipped the flask to his mouth, poured some in, and immediately began to choke, sputtering as he spit the drink out. "My God, Uncle Rob, that shit's nasty." He wiped his face with the sleeve of his coat, trying to catch his breath. Hastily, he thrust the flask at Seck.

"Well, I ain't going to waste my own brew, now am I?" Robert grinned.

Seck had also taken a healthy swig from Robert's flask, rolled it around his mouth, and spat it out. As used to various homemade brews as he was, even his eyes were watering. "Damn, Robbie. Where'd you find it? Tastes like turpentine!" He knuckled under his eyes, wiping tears away.

298 | Vonda Wilson Sheets

"Won't say there ain't any," Robert told his brother. Gingerly, he raised the flask to his lips, took a small sip, and let it drool slowly down his chin. "Cain't say age improved it, either."

As Andy and Seck watched in amazement, Robert calmly plugged the flask and put it in his coat pocket. Looking at the others, he asked, "Whut?"

Seck pulled his own flask out and waved it a couple times. "Got my own. Who made that piss?"

Mounting his mule, Robert shrugged and replied, "Don't know. Found the jug huntin' over off Bear Creek a few years ago. It dint taste so bad then. Took me a couple days to get home, though."

Now all were on their mules. The three of them looked toward the direction of the church, set their shoulders; Seck said, "Alright, then. Let's go."

Their timing was perfect. About half the congregation was still outside, talking quietly. Nat Kinney was standing in the doorway, shaking hands with the men who entered, smiling at the women and children.

Robert rode his mule right up to the door, trailed by Seck and Andy. Kinney quickly moved to block the mule from entering the church.

"What do you think you're doing?" Kinney demanded. "This is a place of worship!"

The mule backstepped two paces, and Robert turned it to the right, eying Kinney with a drunken piety. "I am to join in, Kinney. Andy and Seck here tell me you do a mess of fine preachin'!"

Quickly changing from alarm to a mild surprise, Kinney stood his ground.

Andy snickered, "Uncle Rob needs to be saved!"

Taking a deep breath, Kinney caught the scent of old whiskey and his nose wrinkled. However, Robert Coggburn had never attended any church service that he knew about. He realized this would be another chance to impress the Coggburn clan, if Robert joined the congregation. Andy had become a model worshipper, although he had not yet been baptized.

Inclining his head, Kinney half-turned and raised his arms in welcome. The right hand was just inside the door of the building.

"The Lord's house is open to all who would enter. Come, then."

The mules were tied near a cluster of McClary and Coggburn men and boys, most of whom would listen to the service while outside. Moving clumsily, Seck hanging onto Andy as if he would fall, the three of them entered the building, moving to the front pew and trying to sit next to Maggie Kinney. Her expression was frozen as Robert bowed woozily and asked, "Kin we sit here, ma'am?" He blew his whiskey-scented breath out, waiting for her response.

Maggie rose, and imitating Nat's earlier gesture, extended her hand in welcome, gesturing toward the pew. "Certainly, Mr. Coggburn." She then walked across the aisle to sit with Galba and Betsy Branson, trying to not look offended when she realized the entire congregation could see her face.

The disturbance continued as the three "drunken" men argued over who was going to sit closest to Kinney. At one point, Andrew, standing and facing the congregation, appeared to close his eyes in exasperation. Through his lashes, he saw the Widow Maggie and her daughters, halfway back, near the right wall. His right eye twitched--his friend saw it, and quickly covered her smile with her gloved hand. Satisfied that she at least knew he wasn't drunk, he opened his eyes and made a Solomon-worthy decision.

"Uncle Seck, yu hev heard Mr. Kinney's preachin'," Andrew said. "I guess you need to move down 'n let Uncle Rob sit closest."

Seck, who had been first to sit in Maggie's spot next to the center aisle, pushed Robert off his lap. Robert fell to the floor, landing on his bottom, and as Seck stood to argue with his nephew, Robert pushed him away and climbed to the coveted seat.

Nat Kinney took a few strides, put his left hand on Robert's right shoulder, and used his right hand to calm Seck. "Mr. Coggburn, if you'll be seated, we'll begin services."

Grudgingly, Seck plopped down, leaving space for Andy between him and his brother. "I wuz there first," he protested. "Ain't sittin' next to him, no how."

Kinney looked at Andy with disappointment on his face. "I thought better of you," he said.

Andy's eyes tried to focus on Kinney's face, but failed miserably. He pursed his lips, and lowered his head in shame. "They come up with a new receet," he muttered, and tried to sit, landing on Robert's lap. His uncle shoved him over to the empty spot. All three then turned innocent but drunken faces up toward Kinney, who was shaking his head.

Moving toward the podium, Kinney announced, "Let us begin." He put his revolver on the podium, in plain sight of the congregation, and opened his Bible. Then he took off his coat, and laid it on a bench behind him. The stoves had heated the room, and with a packed crowd, it was quite warm, even with the windows halfway open to allow those outside to hear clearly.

Pausing to take a breath, Kinney said, "Good morning!"

The congregation responded, "Good morning!"

"We will start with a hymn asking for God's guidance." Galba then rose from his pew, and began the song "Guide Me, O Thou Great Jehovah."

"Don't know thet one," Robert's voice was clear, about halfway through the first verse.

"Uncle Rob, you don't know any church songs." Andy could also be heard. His tenor rejoined the other singers.

Seck, however, was struggling to keep up with the song. His deep tones were a full beat behind the rest of the congregation, and when the song was finished, he hung on to the last note.

Discomfited, Branson began to announce the second hymn when Kinney made a gesture, halting him. "That will do, Mr. Branson," he said.

Glancing around the room, Kinney's eyes fell upon the three Coggburns on his right. An inscrutable smile on his face, he began to speak.

"Friends, it has become apparent to me that we have a wickedness in our midst." All eyes in the church instantly looked at the front left pew, and whispers were heard. Kinney's smile grew broader.

"Drunkenness."

Pausing for effect, Kinney let the whispers and murmurs die away before continuing.

"Drunkenness is a sin, and it is common among our women...." Kinney paused again, "and our men."

Robert clucked his tongue in rebuke. "Thet's a shame," he agreed with Kinney. Seck and Andy nodded.

"We have some people who come to Sunday school and church with headaches from being drunk the night before," continued Kinney. "Worshipping God in His house after sinning mightily."

Absolution | 301

"Amen!" said Robert.

"God's people, good Christian people, fight sin no matter where they find themselves. It's not enough to go to church. You must fight the sin of drunkenness wherever you see it!"

"Yessir, I believe you should!" Robert said.

Kinney glared down at Robert. "Drinking causes good men to go bad!"

A puzzled look on his face, Robert turned to Andy and Seck. "Now, ain't I here? At church? Is thet bad?"

A titter, some giggles, broke out in the room.

Robert glared back at Kinney. "Is it bad I come to church? I want salvation!"

Kinney appeared to be struggling with a response. "Salvation is available for all who want it, Robert," he finally said. "But you have to follow the word of God in order to gain salvation."

"Wal, I'm here to larn the word of God," Robert replied. "Git to teachin' me."

Although his sermon was memorized, Kinney pulled a piece of paper out of his pocket, unfolded it, and laid it on the Bible in front of him. He studied it for a few seconds, listening to the sounds of the people.

"Drunkenness causes men to beat their wives and children."

"Cain't do thet, don't hev 'em," Robert again spoke.

"Money spent on whiskey and liquor would be better spent on clothing and shoes for men's families," Kinney doggedly continued.

"Eh, thet don't work for me," Robert responded. "Already sed I don't hev a wife or childurn."

"The apostle Paul writes to the Ephesians, in chapter five, verse eighteen, 'Do not get drunk with wine, which leads to debauchery. Instead, be filled with the Spirit."

"I don't drink wine!" Robert stood. "But I am shorely filled with the spirit!"

Branson began to rise, but Kinney motioned him away as he left the podium, moving to loom over Robert.

"Repent of your sins, Robert Coggburn! God loves those of us who seek salvation! Repent, be saved, and join us in heaven!"

"Oh, I am filled with remorse for my sins," Robert yelled back, and reached into his pocket for his flask. Taking a sip of Dutch

302 | Vonda Wilson Sheets

courage, he closed his eyes, and held his hands in the air. "I am shorely sorry for my sins." In spite of Kinney's closeness, he looked down at his nephew and brother, who were watching with interest. "You are, too," he told them.

"No, I ain't," Seck flared back. "Don't know as I'm done sinning." He stood, groping for the flask in Robert's left hand, and put a foot on Andy's own booted foot.

"Ow!" Andy howled, and then he tackled Seck, taking him down neatly at Kinney's feet.

Kinney reached down, knocking their hats off, and grabbed each one by their shirt collars. "Enough!" he roared, picking them up and throwing the two of them in the pew. Both began to dust themselves off, stubbornly refusing to look at the other.

Robert bent over and picked up the hats, handing the wrong ones to Andy and Seck. Andy threw Seck's hat at his face, causing Seck to go for Andy again. This time, Robert put a stop to the nonsense, telling his brother and his nephew, "Y'all told me I needed to come to church to hear some preachin'. Now stop, so's Mr. Kinney can preach!"

Seck and Andy subsided. Turning back to Kinney, Robert looked up. "I'm ready to hear some more, Mr. Kinney," he said politely.

Kinney held out his right hand.

"Give me the flask, Robert. That's the first step."

Mystified, Robert looked down at the flask, still in his left hand. He looked back at Kinney.

"I have to give you my flask?" he asked.

"You must cease getting drunk in order to go to heaven," Kinney assured him.

Most of the congregation could not see Robert's face, and those who could, only saw him in profile. Taking a step, he stumbled against Kinney, dropping the flask, and counting on Kinney to catch him, which Kinney did. In recovery, he picked the flask up with his right hand and turned to the right, enough that all except Seck and Andy could see his face, at least in profile. His right hand, holding the flask, appeared to have a will of its own, refusing to release the flask to Kinney's outstretched hand.

Appearing to force the flask toward Kinney, Robert looked aghast. "I cain't seem to do it," he said mournfully.

Patiently, encouragingly, Kinney said softly, "You can hand me the flask, Robert. Give up the devil drink!"

Shakily, the hand inched toward Kinney again. Finally, Robert's left hand pulled the flask out of his right, and dropped it into Kinney's left hand. "I did it!" he crowed, and the entire congregation shouted, "Hallejuah!" and "Amen, brother!" as Kinney pocketed the flask and then shook Robert's hand in congratulations.

"See? Giving up the devil drink will make you feel so much better, and happier," Kinney said.

Seck and Andy were dumfounded. Muttering back and forth to each other, the two glared at Robert as he sat down and Kinney returned to the podium.

"Drunkenness had become an obsession with Robert, brothers and sisters in Christ," Kinney told the congregation, which was settling back down after witnessing the miracle. "Paul said to us, 'Do not offer the parts of your body to sin, but rather offer yourselves to God, as instruments of righteousness!'" Again referring to his notes, Kinney failed to notice the three Coggburns in conference on the front pew at first. When he looked up, Robert stood, protesting.

"Whoa, whoa, whoa," he said, his hands gesturing a halt. "Whut's thet mean?" he asked Kinney.

Still triumphant, Kinney fell right into the Coggburns' hands.

"Well, Robert, no part of your body should sin," he answered.

"Wudd thet include visiting Becky the whore?" Robert asked.

Gasps and shock rustled through the room. Two women whose names were Rebecca were in the building. Both looked indignant; one was a young single woman, the other was married to a man who was glaring at his wife. Others in the congregation didn't know whether to watch the women or the Coggburns or Kinney, so noise grew as eyes darted around.

Kinney answered, a little impatiently, "Becky, the whore? She's in Forsyth. But yes, Robert, that would include visiting whores. A good man, a God-fearing man, does not seek relations with a whore." Nat studiously avoided the furious expression on his wife's face; the two Rebecca's in the room relaxed, marginally.

"Hmpf." Considering this, Robert reached into his right coat pocket. Taking out a different flask, he unplugged it and took a long drink. "Thet puts a diff'rent light on things." He turned to Andy and Seck. "Y'all dint tell me 'bout thet."

In shock, Kinney stood immobile at the podium.

304 | Vonda Wilson Sheets

"Wal, I don't think I'm gonna seek 'salvation' after all," Robert told his brother and nephew. "Y'all dint tell me ever'thing. Let's go."

The other two stood, shrugging, and followed Robert out of the building, leaving the door wide open. The shocked congregation and its preacher, Nat Kinney, were treated to the song which was written expressly for this moment. Andy's voice soared, joined by the other men who had waited for Nat Kinney to choose drinking as the topic of a Sunday lesson.

"Adieu to old Kirbyville,
I can no longer stay,
Hard times and Bald Knobbers
Has driven me away.
Hard times and Bald Knobbers
Has caused for me to roam,
My name is Andrew Coggburn,
Near Kirbyville's my home.
My friends and relations,
It's much against my will
To leave my dear old mother
And go from Kirbyville.
But for the sake of dear ones,
Who wants for me to go,
I'll arm myself with weapons,
And I'm off to Mexico.

There's one big Bald Knobber
Who is a noted rogue.
He stole from Joseph Bookout,
Some sixteen head of hogs.
Walked boldly in the courthouse,
And swore they was his own.
He stole them by the drove, boys,
And horsed 'em over home.

There's one big black rascal
Whose name I will expose
His name is Nat N. Kinney,

And he wears his Federal clothes.
He tries to boss the people,
And make them do his will.
There's some that does not fear him,
But others mind him still.

To raise Bald Knobber excitement,
I made a splendid hand.
I don't fear judge nor jury,
I don't fear any man.
If the Knobbers want to try me,
They've nothing else to do,
I'll take my old Colt's patent
And I'll make an opening through.

These Knobbers run the country,
But they can't keep it up.
They'll stick their tail between their legs,
Like any other pup.
And there's a day a-coming, boys,
When they will hunt their dens
And if I'm not mistaken
There's some will find their ends.

There was no further preaching that day. Some of the families left the building, never to return. When he met with his men later that afternoon, Kinney was still in shock, wondering how he'd lost control of the service. His mind simply could not analyze just what had gone wrong.

"Well, it was planned, Cap'n," said Bill Hensley.

"Planned?" Kinney asked. Robert Coggburn's flask was still in his pocket. Thoughtfully, considering Hensley's words, Kinney pulled the flask out and took a large drink. For one second, the nasty old moonshine stayed in his mouth; then he spewed it out, gagging and coughing, dropping the flask. The other men wiped their faces, distaste and queasiness evident as Kinney ran to a nearby bush, and threw up. Finally, Kinney returned and bent down to pick the flask up.

"Planned," he growled. "Indeed." Wiping his mouth with the

back of one hand, he looked at the flask, then at his men. "Well, then. I guess we will make our own plans."

CHAPTER 34
Mid to Late February, 1886

At some point during the winter, Sam Snapp realized he wanted to move back to Kirbyville.

No one traveled much during the cold weather, but a warm spell in mid-January brought Sam's stepmother, Jane, to visit for a few days. Susie's daughters were seven weeks old; little Alma was smiling, while Alvis--now called Allie--was finally taking a bottle from someone besides young Tom and Sam. She was still carried about in a sling next to Sam's heart much of the time. Allie was growing, but she was smaller, more delicate than her twin.

Emotions suspended, Sam had not been looking ahead, living from day to day with the five children under his roof. He rose in the mornings. He tended the livestock. He usually fixed breakfast, while Nannie and Serelda took turns with the other meals. He and the girls did baking, laundry, and other chores necessary for survival. Kate visited nearly every day, and for once in her life, refrained from making plans or prodding about the future.

For all that Sam loved and cared for his children, it was evident to Kate that he was merely going through the motions of living. Sam's vitality, his personality, his grit--these things were changed so much, Kate feared for his sanity.

She and Jane discussed the situation over their pipes one evening.

Tennessee Sarah Jane Callen Leathers Snapp Moore was widowed twice before she was forty years old. Her first husband left her with three young children; she'd married Hack Snapp not long after his first wife died. Sam had barely been walking, Hack's oldest daughter had just been married herself, making Jane an instant grandmother. Jane bore two sons to Hack. Times had been hard during the War Between the States, but somehow, she and the children had managed to survive. Sam was in his fourteenth year when Jane married Zach Moore; she'd had the love and responsibility of mothering thirteen children by then, and Zach had eight of his own. Some of the children died young, others died in early adulthood.

Jane Moore knew as much about love, responsibility, and grief as anyone, thought Kate Miles. And the resultant conversation between the two brought Kate to a bit of grief herself.

The next day, Jane fed tiny Allie while Kate was teaching Nannie and Serelda how to make gingerbread. Sam took advantage of the opportunity to escape the house, walking in the snowy woods for a long while. Tom was playing with Alma on the floor near Jane's feet when Sam stomped the snow off his feet on the porch outside the front door.

He walked in, his expression more cheerful than it had been since Susie's death. Hanging his coat on a peg near the stove, he rubbed his cold hands over the heat, dipping a finger in the gingerbread batter and teasing the girls by making a dreadful face. Then he joined Tom on the floor, watching Alma fisting a rattle.

Kate slid the bread pans into the oven, using her apron to shield her hands. "Alright, we've an hour before it's ready," she told the girls. "Y'all go on over to the house, fix William and the boys some lunch." As if in afterthought, she added, "Tell 'em to bring my milk jug over here, and we'll have some hot gingerbread."

Nannie and Serelda bundled up and left. Jane laid Allie in her crib, swaddling her as she fell into sleep. Alma fussed, and Sam brought her to his shoulder, leaning back against the bench where Jane was sitting, Tom snuggled against his side. Kate walked to the rocking chair purposefully, sitting down with a sigh. She fixed her eyes on Sam, who was studiously avoiding her face.

Jane laid a hand on Sam's head, tousling his thick hair, as Kate rocked and watched Tom fall asleep as well. The house was as quiet as it ever was.

"So what are you going to do?" Kate finally asked.

Finally looking back at Kate, Sam didn't try to dodge the issue. His head shook back and forth a couple times. "I really don't know," he admitted.

"You'll go on," Jane said softly.

"I'm doing my best," Sam responded.

"Spring's comin'," said Jane.

Hampered as he was with Tom half on his lap, he turned his head enough to flash a dark look at his stepmother. "I'm well aware of it," Sam said dryly. "Usually does."

"There's a widow down---" Jane began.

"I'm not marrying again!" Sam's voice was low, but fierce.

The two older women expected this. People married for the

Absolution | 309

convenience of extra hands on a farm, to keep house, to bear children, because of necessity. There was usually at least an attraction between the man and the woman, if not a great love. Sam's first wife had been that for him; a helpmeet, someone to care for, to raise a family with, build a life with. Love rather grew with life, if one was lucky.

Susie had sparked a passion in Sam that few people ever experienced in their lives.

Alright. So remarriage wasn't an option.

"What are you going to do, then?" Kate asked. "You can't plant with Allie in a sling on your chest."

"No," Sam admitted. He shook his head again, and Alma stirred.

Jane leaned forward. "Here, let me take her," she said, and Sam lifted her to Jane, who laid the baby on the bench beside her, tucking an old quilt around her. Tom didn't stir.

"You can't run two farms," Kate said. "Not this year, maybe not next year, unless you're going to remarry."

Sam was stubbornly shaking his head. "Not doing it."

"So then what are you going to do?" Kate asked.

His shoulders shrugged. "Serelda wants to go back to Kirbyville."

Kate's left eyebrow raised. "She's not your daughter. Let her." Trying to be impartial in this matter was proving difficult for Kate. She knew what she wanted Sam to do, and she knew the old Sam would've taken her opinion into consideration. This Sam might not.

A small smile tugged on his lips. "She's mine as I'm yours, Kate," he told her. "Or even as I'm Ma's," he added, his head tilting back toward Jane. "I can at least give her a place to call home."

Kate took a deep breath, her cheeks blowing out in a sigh. "So you're going back to Kirbyville," she said, barely succeeding at keeping her voice even.

"Not just because of Serelda," Sam's voice was raw with grief and tenderness both. "The house is smaller, the farm is smaller...I think I can just about manage the farm, with Nannie and Serelda in the house."

"By yourself?" Jane asked.

Sam's head again shook back and forth. "No, I'm hoping to hire Serelda's brother to work with me." His eyes again rested on Kate's face. "If you and William want to work this place, it's yours."

Kate shook her head. "We have enough."

"The boys could do it."

Kate thought for a few moments. "With the Bald Knobbers comin' round, I don't know that William would even think of it."

"Yes, there's that." The three sat in silence. Then Sam continued, slowly. "I don't like the idea of living close to Kinney. But it's 'home,' there."

"You won't find her there," Jane touched Sam's hair again.

Stiffening, Sam replied, "I know. But it's home."

"Will you sell this farm?" Kate asked, her eyes shining with tears.

"If someone makes an offer, I guess." He looked around the room, warm and comfortable without being cramped. Then he shook his head. "I don't know."

Kate and Jane's eyes met again, both of them satisfied that at least one decision had been made. The other decisions would just have to be made in their own time.

The Monday night after the Coggburns dared Nat Kinney and the Bald Knobbers to open up a full-scale war, Sam Snapp and the five children he called his own stepped onto the porch of the cabin in the little valley north of Kirbyville, and Sam built a fire in the cold stove. There was none of Susie's laughter to make the small cabin warm any faster, either. The large bed was quickly made up. After feeding the twins, Sam put them next to each other on top of quilts in the chest at the foot of the bed, making sure the lid would not fall shut. Then he joined the three older children in the bed, pulling Tom onto his chest, and stared at the ceiling until sunrise.

Sam had written Andy Coggburn the week before returning to Kirbyville. He'd been surprised that Andy was not at the cabin, waiting for his sister's arrival.

Aside from the team pulling the wagon, Sam only brought the two milk cows back to Kirbyville with him. The Miles boys were due to arrive sometime late Tuesday, bringing the rest of the stock and another wagonload, including the chickens. Tuesday morning, breakfast was made using goods from a basket Kate had packed.

Absolution | 311

With Allie in her sling on his chest and Alma tucked in his right arm, Sam walked the farm, assessing and weighing the importance of various necessary jobs. Tom, Nannie, and Serelda were with him, walking along the edge of the field on the ridge when Andy found them.

The reunion between Andy and Serelda convinced Sam he'd made the right decision.

He said nothing to Andy about working on the farm with him then. He knew Andy wasn't a farmer; it would be difficult to convince Andy to join him.

Over the next few days, Sam set about making the cabin and farm habitable once again. He saw Susie everywhere, and if not for the pleasure of seeing Andy's joy in Serelda's company, he might have reconsidered his decision to move back. Watching the Miles boys leave on Wednesday had been a bleak moment, and the immensity of what was before him rested irritably on his mind.

Saturday morning, Sam rode into Kirbyville. The sky was clear, and he needed to buy coffee, sugar, and a few other things, as well as check for mail. The news he heard while visiting at Kintrea's store alarmed him to such a degree, his temper rose steadily as he galloped back home.

Forgetting that Serelda and Nannie were near, Sam began yelling as soon as he saw Andy on the porch, showing Tom his hunting knife.

"What the HELL do you think you're doing?" He jumped off the horse, leapt onto the cabin, and pulled Andy up by the collar. Tom backed off at Sam's fury, and went running inside, only to meet his sister and Serelda as they came running to the door. Nannie picked Tom up, plopping him on her left hip, as she watched her father shaking the bejesus out of Serelda's brother.

"Wh-wh-whut are you-you t-t-t-talk--" Andy teeth's rattled as his head bopped up and down. He put his hands on Sam's wrists, and finally forced Sam to let go. Andy landed on his feet, and turned to face the bigger man, ready to defend himself. "Whut are you talkin' 'bout?" he managed to ask.

"You and your family! Your uncles! What game are you playing with Kinney?" Sam's voice didn't let up.

"It's no game," Andy had never seen Sam so furious. "We aim to make him leave."

312 | Vonda Wilson Sheets

"He's not going to leave here," Sam bellowed. "except in a pine box. He's been heard to say he wants to live here the rest of his life."

Grimly, Andy replied "Wal, if thet's what it takes--"

"You are crazy!"

Andy shook his head. "Nope. We aim for him to be gone, one way or t'other."

Jumping off the porch, Sam paced back and forth. He threw his hat on the ground, running his hands through his hair. "Goddammit! Goddammit!" The horse shied a little, and then walked quickly toward the barn, supplies still tied behind the saddle. Sam continued to pace and curse for another minute; then he grabbed up his hat, slammed it on his head, and almost ran off, in the direction of the creek.

Stunned, Andy and the children watched Sam disappear. Then Allie began crying in the sling around Serelda's small chest, and she turned back inside to prepare a bottle of milk.

Allie had eaten, and Andy was feeding Alma a bottle on the porch before Sam returned, much calmer than he had been. Seeing Andy with the baby, his voice was quiet as he told Andy, "I want no part of this."

"Ain't no call fer you to be in it," Andy answered.

Exasperated, Sam shook his head. Nannie and Serelda had reappeared at the door, and Nannie handed her father a sandwich of cold meat. He took it, bit into it, chewed and swallowed as he considered the situation.

"He's gonna come after you," Sam finally said. "They all will."

"Let 'em come. I got no one to worry 'bout."

Seeing Serelda's face at Andy's assertion, Sam jerked his head and asked, "What about her?"

"She's good here with you." Andy was resolute.

"What about your uncles? The rest of them?"

"Aunt Liza's got kin out west. Things get hot, they're goin'."

Sam had to look away. He bit his upper lip, scratched his head. No, he could tell Andy would not listen to him now. Persuasion was the love Andy had for Serelda, and maybe only a few more days in her company would make Andy see reason. He swallowed, and looked back at all of them. Both lips between his teeth, he nodded at Andy.

Absolution | 313

"Who wrote the song?" Sam finally asked.

Andy smiled. "We all did."

There was no smile on Sam's face. "It's a fine piece of work," Sam commented, then walked a few steps off. He turned back, and told Nannie, "Best start heating water. We're all gonna take baths."

Sam was not complimenting the song, and Andy knew it. He also knew the conversation was not finished.

Puzzled, the girls turned to do as Sam bid them. Puzzlement was also on Andy's face.

"I'm taking them to Kinney's church in the morning," Sam told him, then went to fetch the bathtub from its place in the barn.

When he returned, Sam shouldered into the cabin with the bulky metal tub, and set it beside the stove. He put the supplies he'd bought in Kirbyville on the table. "Wash the babies first, then Tom. When that's done, I'll empty it for you." The girls nodded, and set about the task.

Walking back outside, Sam closed the cabin door. After he'd finished feeding Alma, Andy had returned to the chair on the porch, waiting.

Even with the door closed, Sam kept his voice low. "I came back to Kirbyville wanting peace. You should have told me." His words were clipped, his anger still evident.

"Why're you goin' to church tomorrow?" Andy asked.

"Because I want the Bald Knobbers to know I'm not a part of this," Sam replied curtly.

"You weren't here."

"No, but I am now." Sam indicated the cabin door. "My life is in there."

Andy eyed Sam from below his hat brim. "Mebbe so, but mine's not."

"Serelda's not important to you?" Sam asked, eyes deliberately assaulting the younger man. It was Andy's turn to look away. "You're all she's got."

Sighing, Andy looked back up at Sam, and shook his head. "No. There's you now." He rose, and stepped off the porch. "Someone's got to stop him." He walked off, calling over his shoulder, "Tell her I'll be back in a couple days."

Sam stood alone, wondering what to do next. If half of what John Kintrea told him was true--and Sam had no cause to doubt the

314 | Vonda Wilson Sheets

storekeeper--all hell was going to break loose. Hearing the voices of the children inside, he went in to get the bucket, and began hauling more creek water for baths.

৯ ৶

Maggie Kinney had never walked home so quickly as she did after the Coggburns' disruption of church services. Unable to remain by Nat's side in the chaos, her fury and other emotions drove her to the sanctuary of her home. There were no coherent thoughts or ideas in her mind as she nearly ran, her steps only slowing when her corset did not allow her breathing to sustain the pace. Even then, she was home, shedding her cloak, hat and gloves, tossing them on the bed, before she realized she had abandoned Nat.

She bent over, hands on her knees, trying to compose herself without a great deal of success. Only the thought that Nat might bring the other Bald Knobbers home for a meeting caused her to run to the kitchen, checking the dinner roasting in the oven. She stirred the coals in the stove, and the flames came back to life as thoughts roared through her veins.

That stupid song! Even now, the lyrics ran through her like ice, and she automatically went to her chair by the fireplace, putting a shawl about her shoulders. She sat down, reached for the poker, and stoked the flame, throwing in another log. As the fire grew and began to reach her with its warmth, she still remained on the edge of her chair, unable to relax. Her hands clenched and unclenched in the folds of the knitted shawl.

She wished the children were here.

Rising, she walked over to the window facing Big Bald; there was a half-hope Nat and the men were in the barn, taking care of the horses. But no, she would have heard them. Shaking her head, she paced for a few minutes.

Maggie had known the instant Robert Coggburn entered the church building that worship services would be disruptive. Although she was not a social person, she was instinctively astute about people. Her ferocious intelligence absorbed knowledge as easily as her body took in air.

She was so cold. Pausing in front of the fireplace, her back to the stove, the two fires could not warm her. Glancing around the cozy

Absolution | 315

room, she saw Nat's work coat hanging on its peg by the closed door. Dropping the shawl, she was drawn to the coat, and pulled it around her shoulders, snuggling into its flannel-lined depths. It smelled liked Nat, she thought, as she pulled the collar up to her cheeks and returned to the fireplace and her chair.

Enveloped as she was in his coat, Maggie finally allowed her mind to review the morning's events. She tucked her feet up, curled in the chair, and stared into the heart of the fire, Nat's familiar scent wafting around her face.

Trying to be objective, she replayed the Coggburns' masterful drama, her eyes seeing Robert confessing his sins, then recanting. He had played Nat like a violin, she thought, and the fury began to rise in her again. This time, she let it color her thoughts in red and orange tones for a few seconds, until it dangerously began to look as though she was furious with Nat.

She couldn't possibly be furious with Nat. How could that be? The very idea of being angry at Nat caused a white-hot surge through her, finally warming her, until she forced it back into the shadow of thought, again trying to be objective.

Somehow, Nat had not seen what was coming, had not been prepared. She had never seen Nat lose control of any service, any meeting he was leading, like what had happened this morning.

Small black darts flitted in and attacked the white fury as she tentatively touched upon past incidents she had not witnessed, but had been told of. Involuntarily, she glanced up toward the ceiling, at the logs still visible above the plastered walls.

If she considered the past, the events that had brought them here, to Taney County, with the light of her current fury at Nat, doubt would replace the sustenance of her life. She gave Nat Kinney her heart and her life, more than nineteen years ago. "No!" she said aloud to the logs, and stood.

Studiously ignoring the logs, she replaced his coat on the peg, and checked the oven's contents. Then Maggie put more wood in the fireplace, and curled up in her chair, once more tucked up in her shawl.

Time beat with each tap of her foot, rocking her chair in its sonorous rhythm. She closed her eyes, and resolutely tried to be objective again.

That song.

316 | Vonda Wilson Sheets

"He did not do those things," she protested once more to the logs, opening her eyes and looking at them. "We are not rich."

Nat had opened accounts wherever Maggie cared to shop. He gave her money for her books and music, but she never asked where it came from. Nat took care of the bills each month. The black darts began to return, and again, her mind protested.

There were no unexplained additions to the livestock on the farm, Nat was not taking care of another farm somewhere else-- he was almost always home--and he didn't have a business or an office that he was running. Their income had not increased in some insidious manner. So those accusations were baseless, she decided. Nat made judicious investments, and with those and the farm, they were comfortable.

So there, she told herself.

Maggie closed her eyes once more. Finally warm, in the security of the home Nat provided for her, the chair slowed even more as she slipped into a light doze, the smell of the roasting dinner tickling her hunger. She would wait to eat until Nat came home...

James DeLong had been quite accurate in his analysis of his mother, unaware that his people-reading skills had been finely honed by her acuity.

While Maggie slumbered fitfully that cold, bright Sunday afternoon, images and feelings collided painfully, causing darts of doubt to chill her warmth as the fire in front of her began to die down. Unconsciously, her love for Nat, her need for him to be her everything right and wonderful, stomped on the doubts, splattering them against her intelligence. Common sense told her Nat wasn't perfect--no one was--but she had a life with him that she treasured. No matter she was ill-suited to being a farm wife; her mind insisted that any doubts of Nat were wrong.

When she awoke, she was shivering. The sun was fairly low in the west, and the smell of burned dinner was strong. With an oath, she quickly rose and tended the fires, throwing the meal out to the dogs.

Insisting to herself she was warm and relaxed, Maggie decided she would make pancakes for supper. While she was mixing up the batter, she thought about her children.

Naturally, she thought. The children must be home next Sunday, for church services. By presenting a united front to the community, Nat's family would support him in any manner possible.

Putting the bowl of batter aside, she fetched her stationery from the bedroom, lit a lamp against the growing darkness, and sat at the kitchen table. "Dear Eva," she began to write.

The familiar sound of Ghost's pace ran down the side of the house, going to the barn. Maggie nibbled on her pen for a brief moment, then continued to write.

When Nat Kinney came into the kitchen, he was finally hungry after the sickening day. His heart leapt as Maggie looked up from her letter to her daughter, her eyes bright and focused on him.

"Hello, darling," and she raised her face for his kiss.

He sniffed. There was a faint odor of burned food, but no scent of anything cooking now. "Is there coffee?" he asked hopefully. He shrugged his Sunday coat off, turning to hang it on the peg.

"In just a few minutes." Maggie rose, dumped out the old coffee, and began a new pot. After this, she turned to see him staring at her.

"What?" she asked, a little crossly.

Nat shook his head, uncertainty on his face. "What have you been doing today?" he asked.

Maggie smiled, the picture of reassurance. "Oh, I fell asleep after church. The dinner burned. Will pancakes be all right for supper?" she asked, reaching for a skillet and setting it on the stove top.

She was pouring bacon grease into it when Nat crossed the room and grabbed her wrist. "Maggie!" he exclaimed, turning her to face him. She looked up innocently.

"What?" she repeated, her eyes meeting his challenge.

He searched her face for any doubt, any confusion. There was none.

She blinked. "If you're worried about that silly song this morning, don't be," she said. He had not let go of her wrist; she reached up with her other hand, fussing with Nat's hat-flattened hair. She patted his cheek. "No one will believe it."

"Enough of them will," he growled down at her, grim and unhappy.

"Nat," she spoke softly, her gaze suddenly sensuous and melting him on the spot. He felt the frustrations and anger of the day fading, replaced by uncertainty.

318 | Vonda Wilson Sheets

"You're not angry?" he asked.

She smiled. "You must be hungry." She pulled her wrist out of his grasp, and turned back to the skillet, pouring in enough batter to fill the bottom. The coffee was beginning to boil as Nat still stood there, hovering over her. She flicked a hand at him.

"Go," she said, and he retreated to the table, where he glanced down at the letter she had been writing to Eva.

Maggie had written, "I do think it is time for you and Georgia to come home. I will be expecting a telegram alerting your father and me as to the date of your arrival in Springfield."

Confusion flirting with his mind, he looked over his shoulder at his wife, who was humming as she deftly flipped his pancake, and cracked eggs into another heated skillet. It was wintertime, and she wanted the girls to come home.

He sat down heavily, wiping his face with his hands, trying to sort the pieces of the day into a coherent pattern. There wasn't one. The Coggburns had fooled him, through and through. He had been like putty in their hands, in front of his wife, his men, and his congregation. This afternoon, Gabe Branson suggested that Nat file charges of disturbing the peace against the Coggburn men. Nat wanted to serve the warrant for arrest himself; he was going to have to do some negotiating with Sheriff McHaffie, he knew.

Nat knew Maggie for the talented intellectual person that she was; it was one of his major attractions to her, the way her mind worked. He had come home prepared to apologize to her and outline his plan of action for the Coggburns, his retribution on them. Instead, he found her acting as if nothing had happened. Something was very wrong, for if she wasn't angry with him, why was she asking Eva to bring Georgia home from Kansas in February, when a blizzard could come down on travelers at any time? Even trains couldn't move in a real blizzard.

A plate was plunked down in front of him, two pancakes covered with fried eggs. He automatically reached for the syrup, then over at Maggie as she returned to the stove and began preparing her own meal. He realized he still had no coffee, and rose to pour himself a cup.

The coffee and the burned dinner were other puzzle pieces. Maggie generally had coffee going all the time, and as for burned meals, those usually happened if she had been playing the piano and

Absolution | 319

was lost in her music. He knew she hadn't touched the piano today--
he had seen the closed piano when he entered the house, through the
open bedroom door.

Again, he hovered over her, sipping from his mug as he watched
her fix her plate. She walked to the table, and he followed. She
moved the letter to the side, and sat in her accustomed place, then
looked up at him once more.

"Do eat, Nat," she said.

Silently, he sat and began to eat. There was no conversation.
Covertly, he watched Maggie's white hands as she ate, occasionally
glancing at the letter on the other end of the table.

When the meal was over, he helped clean the dishes and the skillets,
drinking coffee and wishing Maggie would say something. Anything.
The silence was so uncomfortable, his skin was crawling.

She sat back down at the table, and continued her letter. When
she finished, she let the ink dry as she addressed the envelope in care
of her father's address. Finally, she sealed the letter.

He had been sitting in his own chair near the fireplace, his back
to her, his shoulders hunched. She rose, and there was a hitch in his
posture as she scooted her chair under the table in reaction to the
sound.

Maggie came to stand behind him, and her arms fell into place
around his neck, reaching in front to grasp his shirt.

"I'll post your letter when I go into Forsyth tomorrow," he told
her, reaching up to run a finger along the back of her right hand.
He was almost afraid to touch her--his need for reassurance was so
strong, it was crazing him, making him dizzy with fear that he had
somehow lost her. Since the children had been gone, Maggie had
been available to him any time, any place. Tonight had been the first
time she had put him off in months.

Her head came to rest on top of his. "Thank you," she replied,
still matter-of-fact in tone. Her breasts were against the back of his
head and his neck, and he could feel her vibrating.

Still, his finger stroked her hand, and he kept himself in check as
the both of them looked at the fire. Finally, he grasped her wrist, his
fingers seeking her pulse. He counted the beats. Somehow, he could
feel her heart pounding in time, through her clothing, and the pulse
in her wrist throbbed faster and faster. His own heart began to match
the rhythm. She had not moved, was not giving him permission to

320 | Vonda Wilson Sheets

do what he wanted to.

Enough.

He stood, knocking his chair out of the way as he reached for her. She was stiff, resistant, holding her body back, even as she met his eyes. In her eyes, he saw faint disappointment, but no anger.

"I'm sorry." Nat's voice was rough. "I was a fool." He cleared his throat, waiting.

No reply.

"When did you know?" he asked, acknowledging her disappointment in him. Maybe that would do it. He didn't know how much longer he could control himself, with her up against his body. He watched her lips.

"When he walked in," she whispered.

That brought him up short. Surprised, he asked, "How?"

"I never smelled liquor on Andrew Coggburn before." Her gaze dropped to his neck, which showed his own pulse.

"Ah."

While the surprise still had him in its grasp, Maggie put her hands on his shoulders and pushed her body away from him, ever so slightly. Her head leaned slowly in the direction of the envelope, exposing her throat to him.

His eyes traveled from her lips down to the blue vein just under her left jaw. If he touched his mouth to it...

Maggie smiled just a little, just enough. "I love you," she said, and then he was free. The first thing he did was to lick that blue vein in her neck.

ভ ৵

Eva's reply to her mother's summons came via telegraph on Thursday. "Cannot come home right now. Letter to follow."

Maggie anxiously opened Eva's letter on Saturday, after Nat returned home from Kirbyville with the mail and news of Sam Snapp's return to the neighborhood.

Scanning it quickly, Maggie slowed down to re-read it aloud to Nat. "Nothing's wrong," she told him, disappointment evident. "One of her friends is getting married next month, and asked her to be the maid of honor." Georgia was fine, Eva had written. The snow was deep in Kansas right now, but the train tracks were clear. They would be home after the first of April, more than a month away.

Straightening her shoulders, Maggie carefully folded the letter and put it in the cedar box where she kept personal mementoes. When she returned to the kitchen, Nat was standing at the window, looking at Big Bald and sipping one of his eternal cups of coffee.

"The boys should be here in a little while," he noted. Maggie came to stand beside him, and his arm went around her, his right hand settling on her hip, possessively turning her into his side. Her left arm went around him, and her right hand went down to grasp him where it would do her the most good.

This was something she seldom did, and his eyebrows rose as he grinned down at her. But a shout came from outside; James and Paul rode alongside the house and into the barn, having raced most of the way from Forsyth.

Maggie's grip did not loosen. "You'll be fine tomorrow," she told Nat. "There will be no trouble." Her gaze was steadfast and hot, but her smile was rueful.

Nat nodded, and slowly backed away from her, finally turning to get another cup of coffee. By the time the boys came into the house, having rubbed down their horses, their mother was playing the piano, and their father was leaning against the bedroom door, watching her.

Maggie had been right, as usual, Nat thought as he watched James and Paul preparing to return to Forsyth after worship services on Sunday.

Except for Sam Snapp's attendance, there was no further trouble. Sam himself sat in church with the children, one baby tucked against his chest, little Nannie holding the other. Sam was at the far end of the pew, and the Widow Maggie at the other, the girls and young Tom in between. The girls had been ecstatic at their reunion, and it was with some difficulty that Nat finally stepped up to preach. He missed his Georgia.

James was mounted and Paul was kissing his mother good-by when Nat made his decision. "Wait a few minutes," he told the boys. He turned to Maggie.

"I'm going into Forsyth," he said abruptly. She didn't respond, and he continued. "I'm going to talk McHaffie into deputizing me."

322 | Vonda Wilson Sheets

"If you must." Maggie's head inclined slightly.

"I want to be the one to arrest Andrew," Nat said. "Today was proof that I should."

Attendance had been half of what it previously had been.

"McHaffie's going to listen to me this time," Nat told Maggie.

"I'll pack for you." And she went inside, promising herself a hot bath and a long night at the piano while he was gone.

CHAPTER 35
February 28, 1886 - Grave Dust

Andrew Coggburn had not visited his sister in over a week when she espied him through the window at Oak Grove church on Sunday morning.

Sam Snapp, who was helping Serelda and Nannie get settled in the pew to wait for services to begin, caught the mixed emotions crossing the Coggburn girl's face. Joy and anger were immediately followed by tense alarm, and Sam whirled to look out the same window, nearly upending small Allie in the action.

"What is it?" he asked the little girl, glancing down at the baby, then back out the window. To say it was a nasty day was being very polite, he thought. A mix of snow and freezing rain were pelting the glass panes as Serelda moved around him to get a better look. He had almost decided to skip bringing the children to Sunday school, but his desire for peace had driven him to harness the horses and put the canvas tarp over the wagon box. Each child was carefully bundled, and he'd put fresh-baked potatoes in the pockets of the three older children to keep their fingers warm. A flat stone that heated in the fire overnight was wrapped in a quilt and strategically placed in the wagon box. It was a short distance from his home to the church, but he wanted no frostbitten fingers and toes. Or noses, come to that.

Serelda, who had grown noticeably more quiet through the long week, sent a hollow glance at Sam, then resumed her search, wiping the glass with her bare hands.

The only thing Sam could think of that would elicit such a reaction in the girl was her brother being outside.

Oh, surely not.

Hastily, Sam pulled Allie out of her sling. Three months old, Allie had just begun to smile, and she sent a toothless grin to her father, who instinctively smiled back as he handed the smallest baby to Tom.

"Here, watch your sister," he told Tom, who was no longer clumsy with Allie, but held her head and body close to his chest. Nannie was still unwrapping Alma while Sam grabbed his coat and hat, nearly running out the door. He brushed past Galba Branson, not even noticing the deputy, and plunged into the weather.

324 | Vonda Wilson Sheets

The team was under a big pine; he'd blanketed them against the wet. Other horses were similarly clad, but there were not many present. It was a raw day to be getting out for Sunday school. He cursed as he turned right around the building, trying to stay under the eaves, raising his arm to keep the rain off his face. Serelda was still watching out the window when he reached it, and he turned to look in the same direction. There.

"Dammit, Andy!" Sam muttered under his breath. He looked to his left, to his right, but there was no one about. Then he dashed out into the freezing rain, cursing himself for being fool enough to come to church this morning.

He reached the semi-shelter of the woods surrounding the building, and something made him pause to look again. He turned right, and saw someone crouched down behind a tree, under a dirty old canvas that nearly blended in with the surroundings.

A few short steps and he had Andy by the scruff on the neck, shaking the canvas down and lifting the younger man half off his feet.

"Where the hell have you been?" Sam demanded.

"Shhh." The boy shrugged inside his oversized coat, and Sam let him go. Landing, Andy pulled Sam away from the church, soaking them both as he made his way through the cedar brake, moisture instantly drawn to their absorbent woolen clothes.

Neither of them had noticed Galba Branson standing outside the building, watching.

When they were several feet into the brake, Andy came to a halt in a deer rest, largely sheltered by big pines overhead. He turned to Sam, an appalled look on his face.

"I dint think you'd bring the young'uns today," he said.

Sam was breathing heavily, stomping his feet and blowing on his cold hands. He pulled his gloves out of his coat pocket, and jammed them on.

"I told you the children and I would be attending Kinney's church," he reminded Andy.

"It's turrible nasty out," Andy said.

"Yes, it is." Sam peered at Andy's face. The young man had been out all night, and it showed. He sniffed, but detected no odor of whiskey. "What are you doing here?"

Andy smiled secretively. "I got a present for Kinney," he said.

He reached into his upper left coat pocket, and pulled a piece of paper, folded into a small square, out. There was writing on it that Sam couldn't read in the quick glimpse, as Andy quickly tucked it back away.

"What is it--no, never mind," as Sam saw Andy begin to shake his head, still wearing that secretive smile. "Why are you here? Why didn't you come see Serelda?"

Defensively, Andy continued to shake his head, adding a shrug. "She's happier with you," he replied, hunching down in his coat.

"You are still welcome at my house," Sam told him. "You're what she's got."

"No, she's got you now." Andy looked away. "Yer doin' the right things for her, things I cain't do. It's best I leave soon."

"Leave? Leave?" Sam was shaking with cold, but puzzled nonetheless.

"Uncle Robert and Uncle Seck are goin' west," Andy answered. "I aim to go, too."

"West? West where?"

"Aint 'Liza's got kin out in Washin'ton." He returned Sam's gaze.

Stupefied, Sam stared at Andy, who again hunched down defensively. "I see."

And Sam did see. He walked a few paces away, putting what he knew of the Coggburns' actions against Kinney into place against the news he'd heard at the store in Kirbyville yesterday. Stomping back, once more he glared down at Andy.

"When are you leaving?"

Andy again looked away, muttering.

"What?" Sam asked.

"This week."

"Just like that. You're just up and leaving," Sam's hands flew wide in questioning gesture.

"Naw. It's been planned, fer a long time," Andy replied.

"Really?" Sam's head was shaking in disbelief. "You've been planning to go to Washington for a long time? How long?"

Muttering again. "Coupla months."

"A couple of months." Sam began stomping again, pacing in agitation as he considered the little girl he had been providing for, Andy's little sister, and what Andy's leaving would do to her. He

326 | Vonda Wilson Sheets

didn't notice that the freezing rain had turned to sleet, pellets making racket on the trees and the fallen leaves, the dead grass that would be green again within a month or so. He stopped to stare at Andy once again. What was there to say? He would try anyway.

Biting his upper lip against saying the wrong thing, Sam tried anyway.

"Are you planning to take Serelda with you? You're all her family," he commented in a much calmer voice.

If Sam had one trump card to play, it was Andy's love for Serelda. He intended to use it.

"No, she's happy here," Andy closed his eyes, his face going even paler than it was from the cold.

"You think so? Do you know, she's cried herself to sleep the past couple of nights, worried about you?"

"Well, she'll have to grow up," Andy rejoined. "Times come hard, we'd be separated anyway."

"She's just turned nine," Sam responded. "Her parents are dead, and the only family member who gives a shit about her is taking off. Were you even going to tell her?"

Andy's eyes shifted away. He had no answer for Sam.

The silence between them was punctuated with the pellets of ice slamming down.

Breaking it, Sam spoke dryly. "I have an idea I'd like you to listen to."

Andy nodded, his cold hands curled in his pockets, his shoulders around his ears. All Sam could see of his head was the hat, agreeing to listen.

"I need help," and as Andy began to break away, Sam grabbed his left arm, holding him, making him listen.

"I have those babies. The children. I came back here because Serelda believed you would come work for me, help me with the farm."

"I ain't a farmer," Andy responded angrily.

"Just for this year," Sam's voice was persuasive. Andy continued away, with Sam following, encouraging. "I need someone on the farm all the time. Billy can't do it. You can."

"I don't know how!"

"Andy, you know animals, and you can do this. Everyone does it."

"I don't!"

Absolution | 327

"No, you'd rather tromp out west, leaving your little sister to deal with loneliness that she doesn't deserve!" Sam stormed.

"There's Maggie's girls, and you, and your girl," Andy countered, turning back to face Sam down. "She's happy taking care of those babies."

"She's a child who needs a home of her own!" shouted Sam.

"You're giving it to her! I CAIN'T!" Andy yelled back.

"Why the hell not?" Sam demanded. "If we build you a cabin on the place, you can give Serelda what she's never had."

At that, Andy's stubbornness began to fall away. Sam knew it. He lowered his voice, continuing.

"It'll be a small one, but it'll be all you need. I need help, getting the crops out, taking care of the place. Those babies need me home sometimes, all babies need their parents." Sam's voice broke, just barely, but Andy heard it, and knew that Sam had given a great deal of thought to his plan.

Andy's hands rose to rub his face, and his arm brushed against the paper packet in his chest pocket. He heard it crackle.

"If you'll stop this game with Kinney, stop harassing the man, settle down, things will be all right." Sam spoke in his normal tone of voice, but there was a great deal of effort to do so.

"Lemme think."

Was it true? Andy wondered. After Wash Middleton had visited the Widow Maggie, just to be sure Andy wasn't spending nights with her and her family, it had been clear to Andy that someone had to stop Kinney from riding roughshod over people. The crackling of the paper inside his coat pocket had reminded him of his goal--to make people see just what Kinney was capable of. His uncles' plans to move west had little to do with anything except timing. Ramping up the mischief with Kinney over the winter, before the Bald Knobbers started riding again, joining Andy in his pranks and tomfoolery, the uncles were having fun. They knew it was serious, but they were leaving and would not be here to face the consequences.

If Andy stayed, and did as Sam asked, could he stop harassing Kinney? He'd been hounding Kinney now for more than two years. Would Kinney simply think Andy was pulling another fast one? His hand crept inside his coat, and clutched the paper packet.

"You'll come to church with us, and you'll see." Sam was coaxing him.

328 | Vonda Wilson Sheets

He loved Serelda, and truly thought his leaving was best for her. Now...

In the noise of the falling ice, and with their arguing, neither Sam nor Andy heard anyone approach them. They were just off the trail leading from the church to Kinney's home, having taken a circular path through the cedar brake.

Andy's right hand gripped the packet tighter, and he began pulling it out once more, but it snagged on something. He heard a ripping sound at the same time as a loud male voice yelled, "Andrew Coggburn! Throw up your hands!"

Stunned, he turned toward Sam, searching for the voice in the cedar around them. Sam, too, was surprised, but he recognized Nat Kinney's voice.

"Throw up your hands!" Kinney ordered again. "I have a warrant for your arrest!"

Sam's hands were up. Andy's left hand was up, but he was trying to get the packet out of his pocket, and gave a mighty jerk. "All right, all right," Andy called, and simultaneously pulled the torn packet out, spraying himself and Sam with its contents as his right hand started to rise.

Andy jerked just as Sam heard the shot.

At his feet. Andy was lying at his feet, bright red beginning to come through his coat. A neat black hole was directly above his heart; the fabric had singed.

"Andy!" Sam knelt, grabbing the young man as Kinney came out of the cedar into the clearing. Clutching Andy's head, checking for vital signs, a pulse, anything...He stuck his hand inside Andy's coat, and it came out red, with dust from the packet. There was no gun. Sam's left hand traveled down Andy's right arm; he felt the paper packet in Andy's hand, and took it.

"Step back away, Snapp." It was Wash Middleton's voice.

The clearing was full of men within moments. Sam stood, his hat dripping water, wiping his face with his gloved right hand, smearing blood and dust on it.

"He was reaching for a gun," Sam heard Kinney telling the others. "I ordered him to throw up his hands, and he was reaching for a gun."

That made no sense to Sam. He knew Andy hadn't been reaching for a gun; the torn packet was in his own left palm, his fingers clutching it. Unfolding his hand, he looked down at the paper, saw the words "Taler Grave" scrawled along a fold, and stuffed it in his pocket hastily, as he met Kinney's eyes.

"He was unarmed!" Sam exclaimed. His skin pulled tight across his face in shock, he saw that Kinney would deny him. Sounds from the church, including women's voices, came to him. He looked down again at Andy's face, eyes open still.

"No, he wasn't," Kinney's voice was soft, his eyes steely blue. "He has a gun."

"No, he didn't--" Sam began to move, to show Kinney the empty right hand of Andrew Coggburn, only to see Wash Middleton kneeling down beside Andy, and as Wash shifted, it was clear there was now a gun in Andy's right hand.

"What are you doing?" Sam demanded, beginning to reach for Middleton, who ducked.

"What are you doing?" Kinney echoed. At that, Sam halted. He looked back over his shoulder at Kinney, whose gun was now trained on him.

"I'm unarmed," and Sam raised his hands once more.

Kinney nodded slightly, eyeing Sam with disfavor. "Yes, you would be," he said.

Serelda burst into the clearing with Nannie behind her, unmindful of the sleet still pelting down. Screaming, she fell at Andy's side, disregarding the gun, Nat Kinney, and everyone else, begging Andy to move.

Some women had also entered the clearing, just a few feet off the trail. As orders began to be barked for the coroner to be brought, Sam started to move toward Serelda, whose back was being sheltered by Nannie. Nannie was looking at her father wildly, checking him over for injury. As Sam moved, however, a rifle was placed between him and his daughter.

"Don't think I'd do thet, jist now," menaced Wash Middleton.

On the other side, John Haggard was talking to Kinney, who nodded. Haggard came around, toward Sam, and bent down to pull Nannie to her feet. "Go to your pa," Haggard told the little girl.

Alone, Serelda continued to wail, and Tempa Middleton stepped forward to pull her up. "Whyn't you jist have a fit?" the woman said as Serelda came to her feet, and she turned, her eyes blazing. Tempa Middleton backed up one step from the child, who began to look for

Sam, her mouth open without sound.

Haggard turned, jerking Serelda toward Sam and Nannie, who was clutching her father. "Best take your children on home," he told his brother-in-law. "It's not safe for you here, now."

Taking one last look at the body on the ground, he turned away, both arms around the girls. In the pelting sleet, Sam walked away from Andrew Coggburn's body. He found his son standing guard over the sleeping babies inside the church building, a grim Maggie Kinney and Betsy Branson not far away.

"Come, let's go home," he told the children, and woodenly began to bundle them back up for the short wagon ride. Mrs. Kinney moved as if to help, but he met her eyes, stopping her from approaching him.

Serelda was hiccoughing, and Nannie's face bore tearstains as she lifted small Alma to her shoulder. Tom, who didn't understand what had happened, looked bewildered, and Sam said, "There won't be any Sunday school today, Tom."

Fitting the sleeping Allie carefully into her sling on his chest under his coat, he took hold of Serelda's hand, and she looked up at him. "You'll be fine," Sam told her. Sobbing quietly now, she nodded, and reached for little Tom's hand.

Surrounded by his children once more, Sam went out into the darkening day, and the impact of the words on Andy's packet struck him full force as he drove home.

In his final act before Nat Kinney murdered him, Andrew Coggburn had burst a packet of dust into the air, covering himself and Sam Snapp with dirt from the graves of Frank and Tubal Taylor.

ço~ ~ço

It was unintentional. Sam knew it. True, he was somewhat educated, and knew he shouldn't believe in superstitions.

That afternoon, after getting the children home, he'd left Nannie to fix them a meal while he took the team to the barn and scrubbed them down with hay. The roughness warmed the horses faster than a warm gruel alone could, and Sam needed to be alone. To think.

If he moved back to Taney City, he would be no safer than he was on this farm. If anything, he would be bringing danger with him, for surely Kinney would see Sam's removal from this neighborhood as guilt by association.

His only hope, as he saw it, was to stay home, and if he went into town for supplies, make it a quick trip and go unarmed. His children, and now Serelda, needed him, and it would be an ample excuse if anyone wondered why he no longer sat and listened to the old timers gossip, visited with his sister and brother-in-law, or went to Forsyth.

He wasn't without friends or family nearby, he realized as he went in to the house to heat water for the horses. His sister, Addie, had raised their orphaned nieces, and her husband, Dr. Anderson, kept office in the parlor of their two-story home in Kirbyville. Taking the water back out, he mixed their gruel and tended the rest of the animals.

By not attending the coroner's inquest--surely being held by now, Sam thought as he realized the storm had passed, and a weak light heralded the sunset--Sam hoped that Nat Kinney would understand he had no intention of telling anyone Andrew Coggburn was unarmed when he died.

Except for grave dust. He'd scrubbed and scrubbed his face, and tossed his good gloves into the fire before donning his work gloves to go to the barn. He couldn't afford to burn his good coat, but it would wash. It might be superstition, but Sam had seen enough during his lifetime to know that if there was belief, it was superstition no more.

Robert Coggburn rode up and knocked on the door after dark. Sam had expected someone from the family to arrive, but remained cautious in admitting Robert inside.

"Rilda, get your coat," Robert told his little niece soberly. "We're gonna bury Andy tonight."

The girl had not spoken, merely stared at the window most of the day. Nannie had made her a plate, but she didn't eat. Busy with the babies and Tom, Nannie had been unable to spend much time comforting her friend, but would pat her arm or hug her when she could. Now, with Robert's arrival, Nannie was afraid for Serelda. Would she come back?

Seeing the questions in Nannie's eyes, Sam knelt down beside

332 | Vonda Wilson Sheets

Serelda. "Serelda, you must go to your brother's burial," he said gently. She turned to him, grief etching the small face, tightening the hands into fists. "We'll be here when you get back home."

Serelda nodded. Sam fetched her coat, and put it on the unresisting little girl, then pulled her to her feet. He knelt once more. "You can do this," he told her. "Andy would want you there."

"No, he wouldn't," she replied, just as softly as Sam had spoken. "He didn't want me at all."

"Well, now, there you're wrong," Sam smiled just a little. "He was going to come here to live, I know it."

"Do you think so?" Her eyes pleaded with Sam for some small hope, some consolation.

"I do. Now you go on," and he stood, turning her toward Robert.

Robert had eyed the scene with some guilt. He wasn't married, and had no children. He had seldom given thought to Serelda, her comfort or how she lived. Children had no great part in his life, but he figured they would in the future, just like everyone else.

Nodding at Sam, there was nothing to say at this moment. He opened the door, and went out, his niece following slowly.

ॐ ॐ

In the dark of night, the Coggburn family buried Andrew at Van Zandt Cemetery, on the south edge of Kirbyville. Lantern light was not warmth as the frozen ground was tossed back on top of the pine box, no words spoken except for a brief prayer; the sobs of Serelda Coggburn did nothing to assuage the guilt and anger of her uncles and aunts.

From the dark window of his warm house, Captain Van Zandt watched the group as they said their good-byes and left, as quietly as they came. The killing of the Coggburn boy was a sorry business, he'd told his wife earlier. Somberly, he shrugged, wondering what would happen next as he got into his warm bed.

No one saw the woman in the shadows of Van Zandt's barn, nor heard her as she approached the unmarked grave, kneeling in silence even though her heart was pounding "Your fault, your fault, your fault" through her stricken mind. For the Widow Maggie was sure that Andrew Coggburn had gone after Nat Kinney, protecting her and her children, for her sake. And now her valiant friend was gone.

CHAPTER 36
Early March, 1886 - Anti-Bald Knobbers

Although his family was in Appleton City, Alonzo Prather was still working out of his office in Forsyth three weeks a month. He spent at least a week per month with Ada Marie and the children, although, he reflected the night of Andrew Coggburn's death, trying to glean his law books for information while with the family was wasted effort.

In the small room he lived in, behind his law office and next door to the entry to James DeLong's room at the back of the newspaper office, the walls were lined with legal books and studies. There was no window; there was no room for one. Only the back door to the building, and the door leading into the front office interrupted the flow of leather-bound tomes containing the legal language he loved.

There was no real reason for the Coggburn boy to be killed, he thought as he rubbed his tired eyes. His reading glasses were on top his balding forehead, and he had the knack of crinkling his face to drop them back to his nose.

"Bah!" Fingerprints. Rather, forehead prints, he sarcastically pointed out to himself. He pulled a soiled linen handkerchief out and took the glasses off, squinting at the page in front of him while rubbing the lenses. Then he used the cloth to wipe the reddened spots on each side of his nose, where the glasses rested while he was reading.

The unconscious routine of studying and cleaning his glasses was interrupted when a piece of paper sailed to the floor after Alonzo tossed the handkerchief to the corner of the small table. A flash of white pierced his peripheral vision and he glanced at it, realizing his weekly letter to Ada Marie had just fallen onto the chamber pot.

"Shit!" he uttered irritably, then he chuckled at himself. Appropriate oath or not, irritability was settling into a knot of muscle at the base of his neck, traveling down his spine to rest between his shoulders. Raising his arms, he stretched, yawning and wishing he could fall into the bed just behind him. But a rueful look at the letter reminded him--if Ada Marie did not receive a letter from him in a timely manner, she would be back here in a heartbeat. A mental

Absolution | 335

image of his tiny wife going after Nat Kinney with a horsewhip, or, God forbid, a gun, galloped through his mind, and he stood, the chair scooting with a loud scrape across the planked floor till it hit an uneven board and tilted back over the bed.

There had to be a way to stop Nat Kinney and the Bald Knobbers. Alonzo had fought in the Civil War as a lieutenant in the Indiana infantry; he had helped organize the Industrial and Business College in Fayetteville, Arkansas, in the years of Reconstruction. He had been a prosecutor in Madison County, Arkansas. He was a Mason, a teacher, a lawyer--he was even thinking of running for the elected office of state representative for Taney County. Why could he not think, find, a way to stop the bloodshed that was coming?

It was so obvious. Men were taking their families to safer locations, like he had done. Movement along the roads, even in winter, was almost continuous. And now Kinney appeared to have committed murder. Alonzo yawned and stretched a bit more, then took off his glasses and threw them on top of the law book. The thought came to his mind that maybe he was being presumptuous in assuming Nat had killed the Coggburn boy in cold blood--but he didn't think so. The county coroner would not be in his office until tomorrow, he was sure.

A letter to his wife. Damn. Banging into the table with his first step, Alonzo walked around it and opened the door leading to the front office. The cold air hit him with a refreshing slap, and he shook himself like a bear in the dark, as he walked deliberately to the desk, retrieving another tablet of paper to write Ada Marie and make more notes to himself.

After stoking the fire and pouring himself a glass of water, he sat once more at the cluttered table. Sighing, he regarded the tablet of paper in front of him, and began massaging and flexing his hands, preparing to write again. As dry as his hands were in the winter, he realized that if he put salve on them, the paper would absorb the grease. Another sigh. He slid his wedding band off, setting it on the open law book to the right of the lamp, and rubbed his third finger on his left hand. Ah....that felt so good. He repeated the motion with his right hand, taking off his Masonic ring, rubbing the third finger on his right hand, his eyes randomly focused on the gleam of the two rings from the lamp.

Alonzo wasn't a vain man. Although it was uncommon for men

336 | Vonda Wilson Sheets

to wear jewelry of any kind, the connection to his wife through their gold wedding rings had helped him get through periods like this, when they were parted for one reason or another. The Masonic ring had been a gift from her; its silver contrasted nicely with the gold in the glow of the light.

Still massaging his hands, he reflected on the satisfaction of his Masonic membership. When he transferred his membership to the Taney County lodge, Alonzo had made instant friends with JJ Brown and Jim Everett, along with other men in the fraternal organization. He desperately missed discussing philosophy and law with JJ. Perhaps he should write JJ as well, he thought. This last bit of violence by Kinney would certainly interest his friend, who was practicing law in Ozark, and searching for a way to stop the Christian County Bald Knobbers from following the lead of the Taney County membership.

Membership.

Alonzo glanced back at his silver ring.

Membership.

He picked it up, studying the symbol on it.

When he came to Taney County, he'd brought papers from his Masonic lodge in Arkansas, a letter of introduction to the Forsyth lodge.

Membership.

Although his formal swearing into the Forsyth lodge had had to wait until paperwork came back from the Missouri Master Lodge, Alonzo had been allowed to attend meetings and rituals in Forsyth.

Membership.

The codes of conduct and the purposes of Masonry were ethical and served the community. But a lodge could not be started without permission from an older, established lodge. Alonzo and JJ had often debated whether states should be governed as strictly as Masons were. If a Mason wanted to establish a new lodge, a charter had to be filed with the upper echelons of the society.

Membership. A charter.

A charter stated the intents and purposes of the group, where it would meet, who its founding members were. Charter members.

Unconsciously, the hand holding his Mason ring lowered as his mind sorted through the myriad details, following a path that landed upon the original meeting of the thirteen men who founded the Bald

Knobbers.

Charter members. He was one, although his mind flinched at the thought.

A charter.

There was no head organization for the group to report to. The rules, the membership, were established at that meeting, a little over a year ago. The purpose was stated as "aiding the sheriff in finding and arresting criminals." The sheriff was a county official. Would that not make the Bald Knobbers a part of the government? And if the Bald Knobbers were a part of county government, were they not ultimately answerable to the governor of the state?

And, most importantly, would they not need to be a part of the county's charter with the state? Or at the very least, regulated by the state's laws? So, in order to form, the Citizens League for Law and Order should be registered with the state?

Alonzo Prather knew no such registration existed.

Nat Kinney, who was not a Mason and did not know of the rules for establishing a new lodge, did not understand that if he remained true to the purpose of the group--to aid the sheriff--that his Bald Knobbers would have to be acknowledged as a rightful part of law enforcement, by the state of Missouri. And Alonzo was damned certain no such acknowledgement existed.

He had found it. There was a way to stop the Bald Knobbers before the entire region went up in flames. Hastily, he set the Masonic ring back down, and took up his pen.

"My dear wife…" He had to write Ada Marie first, so the letter would go out in the morning's post. But his next letters would be to JJ Brown, then the governor of the state of Missouri, John S. Marmaduke.

ം ∾

Exiting through his back door the next morning, Alonzo came to an abrupt stop. Pastor Jurd Haworth was just raising his fist to knock. As the pastor was a smaller man than Alonzo, two less serious people would have burst out laughing. Alonzo, however, stopped the reverend's fist with his own hand.

"Sir!"

The founder of the Christian church at Pleasant View, Jordan M.

338 | Vonda Wilson Sheets

Haworth was related a good third of the families between Forsyth and Kirbyville, all the way south to the Arkansas line, and then some. He was kin to Sam Snapp by a series of marriages, including that of Sam's stepmother to Z.P. Moore. If one looked far enough back, Alonzo guessed, there would likely even be a blood tie to the Miles and Barkers. He shook his head, as if to clear it, then gazed down into Jurd Haworth's worried face.

"Mr. Prather. We must do something, quickly." Jurd's alarm was contagious, and the nerves in Alonzo's tired body seemed to fire, rousing him.

"Is there news?" Alonzo did not pretend to misunderstand the subject of the conversation.

The pastor nodded. The fire in his eyes was not dimmed, despite the silver of his beard and hair. "The inquest was over last night. There will be no charges pressed against Nat Kinney!"

"Damn." The oath slipped out of Alonzo's mouth, but there was no condemnation from Jurd.

"Agreed."

Rubbing his nose where the glasses had rested all night, Alonzo stepped back into his room. "Come in, Jordan." Alonzo and Pastor Haworth had long ago become acquainted on a first-name basis. Now he attempted to calm the pastor by using his Christian name, purposely skipping a more-formal address.

"There is no time, Alonzo!" Jordan didn't even notice the difference.

"Why not?"

"My kinsman--John Haworth--has called a meeting of those who will rise up against the Bald Knobbers."

Taking a deep breath, Alonzo rolled his head on his neck, then looked skyward. The cold morning was clear. "When?"

"This afternoon, on his place." Stepping back a pace, rocking on his feet--an unconscious habit the older man had--Jurd Haworth stood as straight as he could, eying the lawyer as he did so. When Alonzo looked at him once more, he once more stepped forward, desperate to get his point across to the lawyer.

"They're calling for a militia, sir!"

"Militia?"

"Yes. Messages are being sent now to family in Christian and Douglas counties."

Alonzo's brows drew together in consternation. "To what purpose?"

"Some of the men are calling in their brothers, cousins, uncles."

Alonzo's eyes grew wide as the implication of the old preacher became clear. Still, once more, he hesitated.

"How many men are we talking about, Jordan?"

The pastor looked down, shaking his head as he thought for a moment. Then he once again met Alonzo's eyes, and said softly, "There could be over 100 men riding against Nat Kinney by tomorrow night."

Stepping out, Alonzo closed the door behind him. He and Jordan Haworth walked quickly down the side of the building, and as the square came into view, turned in the direction of the home of Henry Everett, who was the current postmaster. Henry was Yell Everett's father-in-law, and a Bald Knobber sympathizer. Jordan Haworth stood waiting outside while Alonzo posted his letters, inhaling the crisp air and worrying, again rocking back and forth.

Having considered the situation, Alonzo only posted the letter to his wife. It appeared he would need to add a postscript to the letters for JJ Brown and Governor Marmaduke. Before he rejoined Jordan, however, he turned back to Henry, whose eyes were clear and fiery under his bristling brows.

"Have you any news, Mr. Everett?" Alonzo asked courteously.

The postmaster reached over and flicked the window curtain, spying Jordan Haworth standing outside, rocking impatiently. "Imagine you've heard it already, Mr. Prather," the man said.

"I would like to hear it from you," Alonzo responded.

"The Coggburn boy tried to pull a gun on Captain Kinney," Henry Everett said. "Clear case of self-defense."

Nodding his thanks, Alonzo was curt in his movement as he opened the door and walked out. He turned and closed it carefully. This time with measured anger in his step, he and Jordan Haworth walked back to his office. There, Haworth's small horse stood patiently. Jurd was reaching for the reins when Alonzo stopped him.

"Hold, Jordan. I have questions."

"Can't you ask them on the way?"

"What happened exactly?" Seeing Alonzo as immovable, Jordan bit his upper lip.

"From what I heard, Snapp and Coggburn were talking in the

340 | Vonda Wilson Sheets

woods out behind the church, and Kinney was going to arrest Andy," Jordan finally answered.

"For what?"

"Disturbing the peace. Don't know as how Kinney got the deputy badge, but he had one on his coat at the inquest."

"Was the warrant valid?" Alonzo wanted to know.

"Far as I know. I guess you heard what the Coggburns did at Kinney's church a couple weeks ago."

"I did. Why Andrew?"

"Heard tell Andy's been stalking Kinney for a long time. Pranking and calling Kinney names."

Some men came down the sidewalk, obviously headed for the diner in the next street and gossip over coffee and breakfast. Jordan clamped his lips shut until the men were out of earshot.

Alonzo himself had been witness to some of the Coggburn boy's catcalls and pranks. Nothing had been so bad as the worship service that Robert Coggburn had attended, however, and Andy had merely been a part of that, not the instigator, Alonzo was certain. It had taken several people to come up with that elaborate scheme. Still…

"Did you attend the inquest?"

"John did. I was too late." The pastor stamped his feet, interrupting his rocking. "It was over by the time I got there." Jurd took a small pouch of tobacco from his pocket, and inserted a large pinch into his mouth. His left cheek bulged as he pocketed the pouch and looked back at Alonzo.

"No charges against Mr. Kinney?"

"No. Self-defense, they said."

"Was there a panel, or just the coroner?"

"Coroner led the inquest. Bunch of Bald Knobbers inside the building." Jurd spat carefully away from Alonzo.

"Who saw Andrew trying to shoot Mr. Kinney?" Alonzo asked.

Jurd began to speak, then snapped his jaw shut, still working the tobacco.

"I have to know, Jordan."

"Sam Snapp was the only eyewitness."

"What did he say at the inquest?"

Jordan turned back to Alonzo, eying the lawyer. "He wasn't there."

"What?"

Absolution | 341

"They said he couldn't be found."

"Who is 'they'?" Alonzo wanted to know.

"The coroner, the Bald Knobbers."

"Why was he not at the inquest?"

"His brother-in-law escorted him home, along with his children."

"After the shooting, of course." Alonzo turned this information over in his mind, matching it against what he knew. "Who escorted Sam?" It could have been any one of half a dozen men, Alonzo knew. The only other man besides himself who had been publicly successful in walking the middle ground between the Bald Knobbers and Anti-Bald Knobbers was Samuel Snapp. He had friends and, more importantly, relatives, on both sides.

"John Haggard," came the retort.

"Shit!" Alonzo's response was swift, and he glanced at the pastor, who was impatiently waiting to leave.

The preacher's eyes were as demanding as his voice. "Now do you understand why we have to go?"

Without another word, Alonzo began trotting toward the livery, patting his pockets to make sure he had his glasses. He heard Jurd calling, "I'll be at the ferry!" as he broke into a run.

Waiting for his horse to be saddled, Alonzo's orderly mind began to sort through what Jordan Haworth had told him.

If Sam Snapp was the only eyewitness to the shooting of Andrew Coggburn, and had been escorted from the church by his own brother-in-law, it was possible that Nat Kinney would not target Sam.

If those who were infuriated by the Bald Knobbers--and Alonzo found himself one of that group, as he mounted his horse and took off at a gallop for the ferry--began a militia in response to the Coggburn killing, and called in family members from all over southern Missouri and northern Arkansas, the number of Anti-Bald Knobbers riding for blood in a matter of days would far outstrip the number of Bald Knobbers who were ready to defend themselves.

It was quite possible hell had already broken loose, and Alonzo Prather was just now realizing it. He wondered, as he saw the little pastor at the ferry being joined by the Miles and Barker men, how many others were seeing eternal flames dancing at their feet as well.

There was no conversation as the Parrish ferry worked across the cold waters of the White River. Although the sun was up, the snow and ice from yesterday's storm wasn't melting yet, and the air was cold.

The mounted men disembarked, and began climbing the road leading south past the Snapp Cemetery and Robert Snapp's home. The silence continued as each man noted a number of horses stamping in the cold outside the Snapp house. Someone was riding toward the group, and Alonzo himself joined the alertness as the rider galloped past, face muffled against the air.

"Fayette Snapp," muttered Jurd Haworth.

"Got here fast," said Samp Barker.

"Must've got a fresh horse in Kirbyville," Jurd commented. There were nods of assent. Lafayette Snapp owned several businesses down in Woodruff County, Arkansas, and traveled frequently.

"Couldn't hev been home," William Miles said in his soft, steely voice. "Thet's two hunderd miles, at least."

More murmurs and nods of assent. By road, the trip would have been impossible to make inside of four days. Even cross-country, it was at least two days' journey, and that was if a horse could be changed out at various posts and towns.

"Might've been in Harrison," Samp Barker was making small talk. It was uncharacteristic, and Alonzo wondered why.

"Could jist about make it from there, since last night," William Miles agreed. It was only mid-morning, not even close to lunch time yet. The group fell silent once more.

A "friend of Sam's" had ridden to the Miles home under cover of darkness late the night before. Something had set the dogs off to barking, after midnight, and William had gone to the window, trying to see what might be causing the disturbance. A silhouette, barely visible, had let a glow show from his pipe, and quietly, William donned his pants and grabbed his coat, going stocking-footed out onto the front porch of his home. He shushed the dogs guarding the figure, commanding them to sit and be still.

He wasn't familiar with many folks over toward the western side of Taney County, but William had been fairly certain it was a

Coggburn family member or relation who had swiftly spoken the news in a nasal voice with a very quiet edge. The pipe glow was not brought to the face, which was muffled against the cold anyway. William's alarm grew as he heard that Sam had been the only witness to the actual killing of Andrew Coggburn, although others had been nearby.

"Meeting at John Haworth's, mid-afternoon Monday." The final sentence, and no good-bye as the informant slipped back off the porch, footsteps crunching in the snow. The dogs did not bark again, waiting for William to release them from silence. He didn't do so until he went back inside, and then he called out "Stay!" as they began to run for the woods. The dogs returned to their nests on the porch, still barking and growling.

Kate had been adamant. "You have to go," she said after he told her the news. "We can't ride this out. We have to know what's going to be done."

William dropped his pants and climbed back into bed. It was damned cold, and Kate pulled him against her, letting her body heat warm him. They lay quietly, both thinking of what had been done; Kate's thoughts were on Serelda Coggburn, mostly. She felt sorry for the girl. As the importance of Sam's role in the mess began to rumble through her mind however, her alarm grew.

"I don't want to join no group," William's voice was soft against her ear. "Hed enough of thet."

"I know." Kate's mind began to see the implications all around. "Is there a chance for Sam?"

She felt William's head began to shake "No," and tears came to her eyes. "Are you sure?" she asked.

"No. I'm not sure about anything, except the killing's not done," came William's reply. He nuzzled her neck, wrapped his arms tighter. "We'll go."

"We?" she asked.

"I'm taking the boys." Grim. She moved as if to protest, but his lips found hers in the dark, and William stopped her with a kiss. She felt his breath on her mouth when he continued. "They have to be ready for war."

His mind on war, William Miles glanced around the group of men--and boys, his own thoughts said--he was riding south with. He

344 | Vonda Wilson Sheets

had known Samp Barker nearly all his life, knew his brother-in-law's mind as well as his own. There was an excited air around Jimmy, his youngest son. That would bear watching. Manny and Billy were both in their own minds, obviously watching and willing to think about what had been told them, what they were going to do.

Pastor Haworth was Sam's kin of a sort. One carryover from the old Virginia days was the establishment of familial networks throughout the Ozark Mountains, much like the mountainous western side of the Shenadoah valley in Virginia. It was a comfort to know you had help in such rough country. You helped your neighbors, in the sure sense that if you needed to call upon them, they would help you. Familial obligations were even deeper. Although he had been born in Virginia, William felt a strong sense of his Scots in-laws when he considered family connections. His father-in-law had known some of the older Scots who emigrated to America as very small children after the Stuart Rising in 1745. Freed from the English laws forbidding and discouraging clan ways, even before the Revolutionary War, small Scottish settlements in the mountains of Virginia had continued their familiar patterns of life.

As children were born and land was eventually passed down the generations, as the population grew, some would venture west. Letters from the absent family members would convince others to join them, so entire branches of some families would move *en masse*. The Civil War had also increased the likelihood of emigration, as men marched through the sparsely-populated hills in the Ozarks while serving in either army, seeing opportunities for their families.

It was a rare family that moved to Taney County without some prior connection, some family link, some sense of what to expect. Alonzo Prather had lived in northern Arkansas after the Civil War, and had his valuable Masonic membership. Nat Kinney had not.

Thinking of war once more, William Miles watched Alonzo Prather, who was in the front of the group. What role would the big man play in the forthcoming days? He had been an original Bald Knobber. He'd been known to take Nat Kinney on in heated debates on the streets of Forsyth after breaking from the Bald Knobbers. He'd sent his family away to safety. He'd been a Union officer, and was highly educated for the times, both formally and informally. Why was he with this group, now?

The pastor and lawyer turned off towards Haworth's house as the

Absolution | 345

road led on to Kirbyville. The Miles and Samp Barker rode on a few hundred yards, then broke off west, cutting across the barren hills beginning to be called Snapp Balds, after the popular family.

They did not ride down to Sam's house. Instead, William and Samp left the boys building a small fire near the river, just inside Sam's property line. The two older men walked swiftly, quietly, up the narrow creek valley, coming to a stop at the edge of a sharp limestone bluff. Stealth was familiar, almost a comfort between the two, as William knelt and Samp hunched over him. As one, the two took off their hats and carefully looked around the bluff edge.

Smoke was spiraling from the chimney of Sam's house. No one appeared to be outside, and there was no alarm detectable in the livestock. William noted that the dogs weren't even aware of him and Samp; either the dogs were lazy, or he and Samp had not made enough racket to alert them. He was more inclined to think "lazy dogs" when a sharp "crack" stiffened both him and Samp. The dogs began to bark, and jumped off the porch, but Sam came out and called them back, while Samp and William slowly turned around to see Billy, standing right behind them.

He had a rueful look on his face. "Sorry, Pa," he mouthed. He knelt down, took off his own hat, then lay on his belly, as Samp and William returned to their watch, Billy slowly moved to be a third pair of eyes watching Sam walk around outside with the bright sun glinting off his rifle, even at this distance. Once Sam returned inside his home, the three backed slowly away from the bluff, and walked a few yards back toward the river.

Samp was the first to break the silence. Both he and William looked at Billy, a measuring approval in their eyes as Samp said, "Well done."

Billy began to smile, then shrugged it away. "Been practicin' a long time." He continued on toward his brothers, who were holding their hands over a small fire some distance away, still stealthy.

He didn't know what to think about that, William discovered. He was nonplussed when Samp said, "We fooled the dogs, but Billy fooled us."

Bemused, he looked at Samp. "He didn't fool the dogs, though."

"No," Samp agreed. "So that leaves us..." his voice trailed off. They watched Billy remain stealthy and quiet until he emerged from the woods near his brothers, his step purposely loud enough for them

346 | Vonda Wilson Sheets

to hear him coming.

William shook his head. "Getting' old." He took a step, then half-turned to Samp. "C'mon, ol' man," William said, offering his arm to Samp in jest. "He was even smart enough not to spook Jim."

William watched his namesake carefully as the group remounted and rode back toward the John Haworth place on Silver Creek, northeast of Kirbyville. As if he didn't have enough to think about, William discovered that a part of his mind was still considering Billy's abilities at stealth, wondering just what he didn't know about his own son. It made him aggravated with himself--if he hadn't seen Billy going through the woods back to Jim and Manny, he wondered if it would have even occurred to him--did Billy purposely crack a twig so he wouldn't startle Samp and William into drawing their guns? Had Billy been sneaking up on him for some time, and if so, how long?

He certainly wasn't going to ask Billy. That would not do.

A faint smile hovered over William's mouth for most of the ride as he pondered these questions, even in the face of the great danger inherent in the meeting. And it was dangerous, he thought, the prideful twinkle caused by Billy carousing through his mind. Enough. There was work to be done.

୬ ୭

Over a dozen men were in the Haworth barn when Samp Barker and the Miles men dismounted in the pasture nearby. Jimmy, excited to be included in this meeting, let the reins of his mare fall to the ground, while the others tied their horses to the fence posts, down and away from the barn. William eyed the mare as he joined his sons and Samp.

He's just thirteen, William thought. So he spoke. "Jimmy, best tie Star's reins."

Jimmy deplored having to ride the elderly mare, and waved his father's advice off. "Pa, she won't go anywhere."

William sent a hard-edged glance at Jimmy, who was too keyed up to notice. He'd spoken once.

Sam's brothers Robert, Lafayette, and Matt were among the group. There were Moores and Haworths, Monroe Snodgrass, Judge

Absolution | 347

John Reynolds, and others, including the McClarys. Alonzo Prather was not evident; William briefly wondered where the lawyer was. The meeting was called to order before he had the chance to ask Jurd Haworth.

John Haworth climbed to sit on the top rail of a pen holding a pregnant cow. "All right, I think we're all here that's gonna be," he said to claim everyone's attention. He looked around the small barn, lit by the open door and two lanterns standing on upended kegs. Catching the eye of each man in the center area of the barn, he hesitated after seeing Jimmy and Manny Miles. Glancing briefly at William, he shrugged and continued.

"I think we all know why we're here. Nat Kinney cold-bloodedly killed Andrew Coggburn yesterday morning near the Oak Grove church building. We must decide on a way to stop Kinney and his friends from killing anyone else."

"I say we go after them. Kill them all!" demanded one of the McClarys.

"Yeah, until they're all dead!" Some men voiced agreement; others were shaking their heads.

"Gentlemen!" Jurd Haworth stepped on the second rail of the pen, trying to be heard. He yelled, "Gentlemen!"

The voices quieted, and faces turned back toward the Haworths.

"Of course, presuming we are gentlemen!" The sarcasm in John's voice was evident.

Anger coursed through the room in response, and Jurd raised a hand acknowledging it. "We're all angry! A boy is dead, through no fault of his own."

"No, it's my fault!" Seck Coggburn came forward, where the others could see him.

"And mine." Robert Coggburn's voice rang out, but he remained at the back of the room.

"I suppose thet boy hed nothing to do with it," another Moore returned in sarcasm.

Again, the room broke out in noisy tirades, each man seeming to want to speak. Billy and his father stood back against a wall, watching. Billy swooped down and picked up a long piece of straw, broke it in half, and handed one half to his father. Both of them put the straw in the right side of their mouths, more for something to do while the fussing was going on.

"Gentlemen!" Again, Jurd Haworth commanded attention from the group. "We ARE gentlemen, and I presume we are Christians. Are we not?"

"I'm more Christian than Kinney, and I say we kill him!" Snodgrass stomped his foot. "Are we going to let him get away with this?"

"Monroe, if we start killing Bald Knobbers, just because we can, we're no better than they are," asserted John Haworth.

Seck Coggburn joined the Haworths on the rails. He held up a hand, and all fell silent.

Grief was etched into the set of his shoulders. He searched the room for his brother, who shouldered his way through to stand beside him. Seck's eyes fell to the floor, the glint of a gun, the lantern, anywhere but on the faces of the men standing before him. William Miles dropped his foot to the floor, came off the wall, and removed his hat. Billy was a second behind him in those motions. Jimmy, Manny, and Samp also removed their hats, and as the other men noticed, their hats, too, were taken off in recognition of the Coggburns' loss.

Seck swallowed hard, nodded, and the hats went back on. His eyes met William's, and the older man nodded. Finally able to speak, Seck's voice was slow and meaningful.

"Reckon y'all might as well know, we're leaving. Going to Washington, where the wife's family is. Thet wuz our plan, to begin with. Just thot we'd slow Kinney down some, and now we're payin' for it. Didn't know he'd kill one of ours. Thet wuzn't the plan."

Robert spoke. "We started this trouble, and we're leavin'. Mebbe ain't fair to you, and mebbe you'll hate us for it. But we got womenfolk to think about, and Seck's got babies. Don't know whut Kinney'll do next, but we ain't gonna be here to find out."

"You're right to go," Samp Barker called out. "No call for anyone to hate on you fer it."

Seck finally looked at the men in front of him. "My thanks to you. We're leavin' in the mornin'." At that, he and Robert left, the silence about them heavy on their shoulders.

No one spoke until the Coggburns rode off. Then William, who had resumed his lean against the wall, called out, "I'd like to know whut happened yesterday."

"With the weather like it was, no one came to services at church

Absolution | 349

yesterday." John and Jurd Haworth both preached on occasion at the Pleasant View church building, near the road coming up from Silver Creek. John continued.

"My horse was fresh, and the rain wasn't sleet yet, so I rode over to Oak Grove to hear Kinney preach. Don't get to hear others much. Got there in time to see John Haggard leading Sam Snapp's wagon away, toward home. Sam was sitting on the seat, and started to call out when Haggard stopped him."

"Why'd Haggard stop him?" Will Moore asked.

John Haworth shook his head, shrugged, and went on. "By that time, Galba Branson had already left for Forsyth, to get the coroner. No one let me near the place. When the McClary boys showed up, no one let them back of the church, either."

"Who was there?" Robert Snapp asked.

"Bill Hensley, Wash Middleton, Kinney and some of the others. Your brother-in-law came later, but they didn't let the doctor even look at Andy."

"Doc Anderson's a good man," said Snodgrass. "Tweren't no call not to let him look."

"Except for his relation to Sam," retorted Matt Snapp. Murmurs of agreement whirled, and the men turned their attention back to John.

"It was cold out. Not many women around to start with, and once Kinney's wife left, the other women did, too. They finally let us in the building, waitin' for the coroner. Once he got there, with Gabe Branson, he went 'round the building and stood back there for only a couple minutes. Then he came inside and began asking questions."

"Was it official?" Will Moore asked. He was married to Jurd's sister, and the Snapp men were his stepbrothers after Jane Snapp married Zack Moore.

John again raised his shoulders, a shrug of acknowledgement. "Claimed to be."

Fayette Snapp burst out, "But he didn't call Sam to the inquest?"

"Said Sam couldn't be found. I didn't see anyone go look for him, either," John replied.

Agitation. Restless movement. "This is our government now? These are our officials?" Monroe Snodgrass called out once more. "This means war!" Voices rose.

350 | Vonda Wilson Sheets

Again, John Haworth quieted the group, and again, he resumed explanation of what he had seen.

"Kinney had a warrant for arresting Andy on disturbing the peace. He showed the piece of paper to everyone. His son and a couple others said they saw a gun in Andy's hand, right after the shooting. Coroner said it was a clear case of self-defense. I left after that, went down to Sam's. By that time, the family had come to get Andy's body for burying, and the storm had broken."

"What did Sam say?" William Miles' voice was steel against the chilly room.

"Said Andy didn't have a gun." John Haworth closed his eyes and bowed his head against yet another outburst.

All three of the Miles boys watched their father as he digested this information, while the room was circled and surrounded with the voices of the other men. William's face whitened and his head nodded slowly as his eyes searched the straw-covered floor. He pushed off the wall with his foot, and quietly said, "Thet'll be enough of thet." He looked around the room, then at Samp, who was nodding in agreement.

None of the other men heard him.

Jurd Haworth once more took command of the room. "Gentlemen! Please! We must unite in order to decide on action!"

"We kill him!" came the cry.

"Kill who?" Jurd wanted to know. "Are we going to kill all of them? How, and what about their families?"

Judge John Reynolds yelled above the din, "We'll raise a militia! We can do it!"

"And who will take care of our families while we're out fighting?" John Haworth wanted to know.

"No killing!" called Fayette Snapp. "No more!" At the sound of his voice, others began to quiet, and he walked to the front, standing with John and Jurd.

"I got a brother with a houseful of children and no wife," Fayette said. "If we start killing Bald Knobbers, they'll go after Sam, sure as shit!"

The Haworths and some of the other men were nodding in agreement. Others moved as if to speak, but Fayette stopped them. "I see it this way," Fayette went on. "By sending Sam away with his own brother-in-law, Kinney thinks Sam won't talk, thinks Haggard will stop him from talking."

As the room quieted to listen to Fayette, however, another noise began growing louder. Hoofbeats.

"Get down!" William pushed Jimmy and Manny to the floor, and all the others realized who it was.

"Bald Knobbers!" someone yelled.

Billy jumped to the wall, climbing the boards that made a ladder to the hayloft. Matt Snapp was right behind him, and the two crawled over to the shuttered doors. There were shouts from inside and outside, voices hoarse as the hoof beats began circling the barn. A couple of other men made their way into the loft, crawling over last year's hay to get to the other side of the barn. As he looked through the gap between the floor of the loft and the bottom of the big door, Billy realized he was hearing gunfire. He pulled his gun out from his coat pocket, Matt Snapp next to him, also ready to fire.

"Get a clear target!" yelled someone.

Darkness had already fallen, and the torches brandished by the riders outside shed no clear light on them. Movement was constant, and while a few inside the barn popped off some shots, Billy did not hear his father's gun, nor his uncle's. He would not fire before they did. He knew they couldn't see any better than he could. As seconds seemed to slow and keep pace with the circling torches, it became apparent the Bald Knobbers were merely threatening, letting the Snapps, their families, and friends, know that this meeting wasn't as secret as they had hoped.

A little over a minute after beginning their snake dance, the Bald Knobbers rode off.

"Anyone hurt?" Billy heard William call out.

"I got a splinter in my ass!" yelled someone from the far side of the hayloft.

Shaky laughter greeted this complaint, as breathing evened out and guns were re-holstered and re-pocketed.

"Better wood than lead," William responded.

A few moments later, all were back on the ground floor of the barn, and it became apparent that Monroe Snodgrass indeed had a splinter in his ass.

"Bring me thet lantern!" Samp Barker took charge, much as he had in the past.

The lantern brought, Samp made Snodgrass drop his pants just

352 | Vonda Wilson Sheets

enough to yank the two inch-long splinter out of his right buttock. When Snodgrass began to pull his pants back up, Samp stopped him. "You git Doc Anderson to look at that, make sure it's out," he advised Monroe. He held the splinter in front of Monroe's face. "Anyone got some whiskey?"

"Yeah, I could use a drink!" Snodgrass said, rubbing his behind and still trying to yank his pants back up. Samp put a hand on Monroe's back, keeping him bent over. Of several flasks offered, Samp took one from Robert Snapp and splashed some of the contents over Monroe's back side, smiling grimly at William as Monroe yelled again.

"Why'd you do thet for?" Finally allowed to pull his now-damp pants back up, Monroe turned around, grabbed the flask from Samp, and took a healthy drink.

"Gets rid of infection, sometimes," William told Monroe. "At least till you git to the doc's."

Things settled down a bit, until Judge Reynolds started on about the militia again.

"That's just proof we'll have to form a militia," Reynolds began.

"Nah, they wuz jist letting us know they were around," William replied. "Organize a militia, it'll give 'em more reason to get rough."

Matt Snapp was looking at Billy Miles with a new respect in his eyes. Matt had fired his revolver when he'd first gotten a glimpse outside. When he realized no one else was pumping lead into their guns repeatedly, he'd pulled back, and copied Billy's patience.

Reynolds fired back verbally. "How else would we stop them?" he asked. "It was fortunate no one was hurt just now!"

William started to shake his head, but Jurd stepped in between them. "Gentlemen, I believe someone has a way." At that, John Haworth walked over to the small tack room and opened the door. Out stepped the lawyer, Alonzo Prather.

"What's he doin' here?" Monroe Snodgrass straightened up, forgetting about his injured butt.

"He's on their side!" Will Moore jumped as if a snake had threatened him.

Jurd Haworth walked over to join Alonzo and John.

"Mr. Prather has found a way to get the governor involved," Jurd

Absolution | 353

announced.

"The governor?" Excited murmurs were mingled with suspicious glances.

"Gentlemen," Alonzo bowed his head in greeting. "You all know me. You know I was with the Bald Knobbers the night the Taylors were hung. You also know I have sent my family away. I think....no, I know, there's a way to get the governor involved, without having to raise a militia."

Interested, alert, all listened to the wise lawyer speak. He told them of searching for a legal means to end the Bald Knobbers' night rides, and how he came to find a way.

Despite some of the more fiery-tempered and suspicious remarks, it became apparent that somebody was going to personally deliver a letter to the governor in Jefferson City. It would be in the form of a petition, and all present would sign it.

Alonzo also advised the men to send letters to the newspapers in the three largest cities in the state, and for printing in newspapers where the men might have family members. These letters were to describe the actions of the Bald Knobbers in moderate language, and ask for help from the state of Missouri.

For a beginning, it was a good one, William Miles thought. His mind was busy, watching the men around him, ticking off characteristics and what he knew of each man. He knew Samp was doing the same thing, and a certain prideful twinkle shot through him when he realized Billy was also assessing and thinking.

Prather's plan wasn't a bad one. It just didn't go far enough.

After signing the petition, it was decided that Jurd Haworth, Dr. Burdette of Forsyth, and Judge John Reynolds would ride to Jefferson City Wednesday morning. William Miles, Billy Miles, Samp Barker, Monroe Snodgrass, and Robert and Matt Snapp would accompany the men as a guard detail, getting them through Christian County and on their way north. On the way back, the Miles group would stop at JJ Brown's home in Ozark, delivering Alonzo's letter to his friend.

It was quite late when the men dispersed. Alonzo's horse had been sheltered in Jurd Haworth's barn, and the two men had ridden in an old horse-drawn buggy down to John's house. Alonzo accepted

354 | Vonda Wilson Sheets

Jurd's invitation to eat dinner and stay the night.

William and Samp were quiet on the way out to the pasture where they had left their horses. Quite alike in their thoughts, both men knew the night wasn't over, nor was the planning. As the men and boys approached the horses, Jimmy was looking for his mare.

"Hup! Star!" he called.

The others were untying their horses, mounting them.

"Pa! Star's not here!" Jim was tired and confused. His voice carried, and his brothers shushed him.

"Serves you right," Manny told Jimmy.

William turned his horse to look at Manny, then down at Jim. His lips pursed as he considered leaving Jim to walk home. But no, Kate would have a fit, especially if she discovered the Bald Knobbers were out this night.

A more discerning eye would have seen the glint in William's glance as he turned to ride. "He rides with you."

"Pa!" Manny protested.

William and Samp rode off, with Billy only a heartbeat behind. Manny saw Billy turn and look at his brothers before they got far.

"C'mon, get on," Manny held his left hand down to Jimmy, who climbed on.

"Hell!" Jimmy clutched Manny's waist as the gelding took off, and both boys tasted Kate's cuss concoction.

"Shoulda listened to Pa," Manny told his brother over the hoof beats.

"Well, then, why am I riding with you?" Jimmy wanted to know.

"Shoulda kept my mouth shut," Manny replied.

It was quite late and all were cold as Samp pulled the bell rope for the ferry. Even though the river was fairly low, Samp was willing to pay the ferryman an extra night toll to haul them back across, rather than ford it themselves. It would have been a shorter, but much colder and wetter, way home.

As they heard the night ferryman come out of his house, hoof beats thrummed and grew louder. Instantly alert, Samp and William relaxed when they realized it was only one horse, and a familiar gait at that. Billy took a few seconds to ascertain the horse was

Absolution | 355

riderless.

Manny shrugged his shoulders as the ferryman came up, stomping his feet and greeting them. "Hey, Jim, there's Star!" Manny told his dozing brother. He pushed his body backwards, and Jimmy nearly fell to the ground, but managed to land on his feet.

"Yeah, she showed up a couple hours ago," the ferryman yawned. "Tried to corral her, but then the Bald Knobbers came through, and she took off."

Star nuzzled Jim's face, and Manny shivered when he realized he'd lost protection from the cold. Jimmy reached for the reins, but his father's hand was quicker. William grabbed the reins away from Jimmy, who stood dumbfounded.

"Did they go in to Forsyth?" William asked the ferryman as he clicked to the horses, leading Star up the ramp.

"What?" Yawning again, the ferryman shook himself. "Oh, yeah, shot the town up, from the sounds of it."

Jimmy scampered aboard behind everyone else, and helped the ferryman lift the gate. Slowly, the ferry creaked and groaned north across the cold river.

Samp paid the toll, and five tired male bodies took off once more for home.

CHAPTER 37
Wednesday, March 3, 1886

The air was charged with change the day after the meeting in the Haworth barn. The weather suddenly turned, melting the snow and ice, freshening the hills with the idea of spring and promise, hope bursting up along with the two-inch high daffodil spikes and other new greens.

The Anti-Bald Knobbers continued with the plans they had put together, messages and conversations leading men to pull out their old Confederate Army uniforms and soberly considering the necessity of once more standing and fighting for their land and their way of life. The women anxiously watched, keeping the children close to home and quiet. Precious sheets of paper were inked with letters of indignation, outcries of injustice, and the intensity grew as word spread of new atrocities.

In Forsyth, men known to be compatriots of the Bald Knobbers rode up and down the streets, occasionally firing their guns in threat as others sought supplies and news. As the temperature rose through the day, so did tempers, and Sheriff McHaffie and his deputies were kept busy as complaints of bullying and assault were filed.

Just after sunset Tuesday, the night riders stalked the Haworth, Moore, and other family members' homes. Children's eyes grew big as the sound of horses and gunfire peppered the dark. Curiously enough, although Sam Snapp watched through another restless night with his rifle never out of reach, not one Bald Knobber set foot on his land.

Sam had begun to wonder if the threat he felt from Kinney in the minutes after Andy's death had only been in his imagination. But when his sister Addie had come Tuesday morning with news of the Anti-Bald Knobbers' plans, Sam realized that the danger was indeed real, and not just for him.

He was pondering all this in the dark of midnight, and rolled over into Wednesday with an impatient sigh. Like most men, Sam preferred to keep busy, and he was determined to start preparing the fields for planting this year's crops in the morning. He dozed off and on, lying in the bed Susie had shared with him. Occasionally, a sob would fall down the ladder and curl through the air between him and

Absolution | 357

the loft where Nannie and Serelda were ensconced. As the hours fell heavily, he and Serelda both managed to finally sleep, weariness and grief forcing them into the escape of unconsciousness.

Birdsong woke him just before sunrise.

Stoking the fire in the stove, Sam shrugged into his clothes, putting on his coat and going out to the barn. After milking the cows and doing the necessary chores for the other livestock, he returned to the house to find Serelda frying bacon and checking the oven anxiously. When the biscuits were almost perfectly golden-brown, she pulled them out and was turning to put the hot baking sheet on the table when footsteps sounded on the porch.

"Who on earth--?" Sam had known instantly it wasn't men-- the sound of their steps were harder, louder. Plus, the dogs hadn't barked. A soft knock barely registered as Sam opened the door to find the Widow Maggie and her three daughters standing in the chilly morning sunlight.

Nannie rushed down the loft ladder, and the girls were all greeting and hugging each other as Tom's feet dangled over the loft. Reaching up to pull his son down, Sam grinned as the babies gurgled along with the excited girls. The small cabin echoed with the cheer of Maggie's daughters, and Sam thought he even spied a small smile on Serelda's face.

Maggie had gone over to flip Serelda's forgotten eggs frying in the skillet, and deftly spooned melted butter over the tops of the steaming biscuits. With an exclamation, Serelda put little Celie down and picked up Alma, carefully moving around the other children and the table to join Maggie at the stove. There was no way Sam could get through; small Allie was passed to him by Nannie, who'd continued to chatter with Miranda as she'd changed the small twin's diaper.

"How do you want your eggs?" Maggie asked Sam. She'd taken off her cloak and put it on the back of the rocking chair by the stove, and for an instant, Sam saw Susie's shawl. He shook his head, then determinedly faced Maggie.

"Over, with the yolk hard," Sam told her. "You don't--"

"I know I don't, but I do, and you do, too." She turned back to the stove, grabbing a plate from the rack nearby.

Considering her curious statement, Sam's left eye squinted almost shut, and he glanced down at the girls, who were making

358 | Vonda Wilson Sheets

some order out of the chaos by setting Tom, Phebe and Celie at the table. Serelda handed Alma to Nannie, who put the baby in the high chair with padding to prop her, and began to make bottles for the twins. Glancing down at Allie, Sam saw her smile. He shifted the baby to his shoulder, and told her, "Your bottle's coming," when she began to fuss.

He realized as Serelda handed the baby bottle to him with another smile that he completely understood what Maggie had said. Pursing his lips, he settled Allie in the crook of his left arm with the bottle, and began to look for a place to sit. There wasn't one, so he walked the few steps over to his bed, yanked the comforter into a tidiness of sorts. Then he laid Allie down with pillows tucked around her, the bottle propped.

Serelda ladled some oatmeal into a bowl, and Miranda was feeding little Alma very small spoonsful as instructed by Nannie. The oatmeal was also shared by the other children. Maggie passed Sam's plate to him via the older girls, and Nannie's grin was shared with him when she handed him the plate.

Sam ate with bemusement evident on his face and in the set of his shoulders. Maggie stood at the stove, watching the children crowded around the table, and when the time came for Alma's bottle, she deftly picked up the baby and held her.

Rising, Sam told her, "Here, I can do that." He reached down and adjusted Allie's bottle, then tried to find a way to take his own empty plate to the dish pan. Maggie reached over the top of the children's heads, shaking her head and taking his plate while holding Alma's bottle with her chin.

Allie had sucked down several ounces of milk. Sam decided it was time to burp her, so he threw a diaper over his shoulder and returned to his seat on the bed. He picked the baby up, shouldering her and patting her back.

The warm brown of Maggie's eyes held a hint of wonder along with a good dose of amusement.

"What?" Sam asked.

"Jist not something I've seen much of," she answered. As Sam started to speak, she shook her head again. She knew why, and she knew the necessities of parenting alone. Man or woman, a parent did what must be done.

Sam spoke anyway. "I think I understood what you said a few

Absolution | 359

minutes ago."

The glow left Maggie's face momentarily. She looked down at Alma, who was studying her face.

"Mebbe you did." Maggie's reply was very soft, but the children were still finishing their breakfasts, so Sam was able to hear her. Then she sent a glance toward Alma's father. "So you'll go work in the fields today."

Sam nodded. "I'm not planting much this year. Just enough."

A burp came from Allie, and Sam felt her small body relax. She and Alma still slept almost immediately after eating. Her scent however, made Sam reach for a diaper and he changed her, while she smiled a toothless milky grin at her father, her eyes nearly closed. Maggie edged her way around the group at the table, and changed Alma. Both babies were sound asleep before being put back in the big crib.

Straightening, Sam and Maggie realized the room was eerily quiet. All five girls and Tom were watching the adults. Both of them began to shake their heads. Sam abruptly turned, opened the door, and walked outside, closing it gently behind him.

He stood on the porch, looking at the dreary hill rising in front of him, watching the sun's rays light it up as if spring was really, really coming. He could hear the Widow Maggie's voice as she rounded up the children still at the table, starting them on chores.

No, neither of them was interested in being married again. For the sake of Serelda, he and Maggie had not brought up why the widow and her children were in his house this morning.

Sam had known of the friendship between Andy and Maggie. As he stepped down off the porch to go hitch the team to the plow, grief struck him anew at the loss of Susie. It had been just over three months, and he momentarily faltered, then shouldered his way through it.

It hadn't been necessity that brought the Widow Maggie and her children to the Snapp home this morning. The good Lord knew she had plenty of work to do at her own place, and she hadn't been married to Andy. But Sam discovered as he took down the mended harness from the hooks on the barn's wall that grief shared was just a little easier than being alone.

༄ ༄

360 | Vonda Wilson Sheets

It would be painful to leave this place.

With a last pat on the lead mule's rump, he turned to look over the covered wagon with a critical eye as the sun's first full rays lit the barnyard up. His wife and children were settled under the canvas; assorted other relations were in their own wagons, waiting for him.

It wasn't possible to take every treasured possession. They had given some items to family members and friends who were staying. He glanced at the house, and noticed the front door was open. Frowning, he crossed to the gate of the dooryard, entered, and quickly walked to the house.

He couldn't resist looking around before closing the door one last time. There was a memory. Suddenly, all of them were there-- the faces of loved ones who had been long gone, or who had died recently. Some, like his brother, had never even seen this house before he died. Feeling a bit strange, he nodded stiffly, and felt the benediction of their approval wash over him. His eyes were moist, and he bowed his hat-covered head as he left, closing the door of his home one last time.

Finally, he crossed the dooryard, and without looking at any of the others who were carefully not watching him, he closed the gate. It was silly of him, he knew--it was only a matter of hours before someone would be going through the gate. There had been no time to sell out, and most everything was in decent shape.

He resolved to live in a finer place once they were settled out west.

The chilly air was full of burdens and the weight of love. Still standing at the gate, an idea came to him. He pulled a bandana out of his pocket, and laid it carefully on the ground. Then he gathered up a handful of the damp dirt from below the gate. Two more fistfuls, and he knotted the bandana. Carefully, he folded the improvised bag, and stuffed it into the inside left pocket of his coat.

Although no one was watching him closely, he felt somewhat foolish as he walked back to his wagon and began to climb up on the seat. He wished he'd thought of taking some Taney County dirt with him yesterday, when he had visited the cemeteries for the last time. He could have filled a Mason jar with memories of treasured places.

No need to shout to the team. He simply clicked the reins, and they were off. The other wagons fell in behind him.

Absolution | 361

Spring was near, he thought as they descended the hill down to Hensley Ferry. His wife was sobbing quietly in the back.

Down at the river, he paid the toll for the party to cross. Bill Hensley wasn't working the ferry today, and he was glad of it. Hensley wasn't particular as to who he insulted or made fun of, and that was one man he would never miss. A brief smile crossed his face as he realized it would no longer matter who knew he was taking his family away from here--he would not know, unless someone wrote a letter to him. And it would not matter then, either.

The wagons followed his lead up the Springfield-Harrison road. They would likely stop tonight at Kentling's, up in Christian County.

The jingle of the harness, the creaks of the wagon, the hooves stepping along the wet road, these things were in his ears. He filled his eyes with the sights of the hills, the sun's continued rise, and noticing the signs of the earth beginning to awaken from winter. His gloved hands were warm, but every now and then, a drop of moisture would appear, darkening the place it landed as the woolen threads slowly absorbed it.

It was a fine place they were going to, with rich soils and a sparse population. Mountains and plenty of rain. Family members who were already there. Letters had been sent, notifying them that his group was going to arrive sometime in the summer. It was a very long distance from here. He knew the time would come, probably on this journey, when he would begin to look forward. But for now, while he was in the valley of Bull Creek, driving northwest toward Spokane, he let his senses fill with Taney County.

This was home.

He would never see it again.

৯ ৶

The town of Forsyth had been full of Bald Knobbers on Tuesday. Crowing about their knowledge of the Anti-Bald Knobber meeting, one Bald Knobber went so far as to confront the McClary men, telling them, "Y'all think you're jist so slick, greased pigs slippin' 'round, hevin' meetings. Some slicker you are!" he shouted. By the end of the day, the Anti-Bald Knobbers were being derisively called "Slickers," which amused the Bald Knobbers to no end. Fights broke

362 | Vonda Wilson Sheets

out, but no one was seriously injured, nor even arrested.

Talk of a local militia being raised to fight the Bald Knobbers swirled through the day, and on through the night in the two saloons of the town.

In the hours after midnight, even the most argumentative men were sleeping it off when William Miles shook the shoulder of his son Billy, and shushed him awake. "C'mon," William barely whispered, not wanting to wake Manny and Jim.

Carefully, father and son crept down the stairs of the house, entering the kitchen. Billy quickly dressed as William explained.

"We're escortin' Judge Reynolds up past Ozark, so he kin take the letter and petition to the governor," William said. "One of Doc Burdette's patients threatened him if he went to Jeff City. And Jurd Haworth's house was shot up a little while ago."

Hearing noises outside, Billy grabbed William's arm.

"It's Uncle Samp," William told him. "He's getting the horses."

"Anyone hurt?" Billy asked, rubbing his face after he finally got his boots on. "At Haworth's?"

"Naw, but there'll be hell to pay. One of the boys found a slug in his bed."

"William!" He turned to see Kate, holding up loaves of bread cut in half and filled with meat and horseradish sauce, wrapped in paper and tied with twine. He took the food, setting it on the table while Kate turned to fill two canteens with hot coffee.

"Tell Samp to bring his canteen in," Kate said softly. About that time, Samp came through the back door, carrying the canteen. She smiled at him, and filled his canteen with the remnants of a second pot of coffee.

Within five minutes, the three men were on their way to a crossroads north of Forsyth. Billy's pockets were weighed down with hot potatoes, and when they came to a halt, an owl called out.

"Thet's a sorry owl," Samp said quietly.

"It's a sorry night to be out," Judge Reynolds replied, riding out in response to the password.

"Thet it is. Snapps coming?" William asked.

"They should be here any time." The four of them rode down a short path through the bare trees, and waited for the sound of horse hooves.

Billy took a drink from his canteen, nearly burning his mouth with the coffee. After replacing the stopper, he dropped the strap over his saddle horn. With his reins still in his right hand, he stuck both hands into his coat pockets, wrapping his cold fingers around the hot potatoes.

He could sit and wonder why his father had chosen to bring him and not his brothers, but he was nineteen and assumed that would be the reason. Emanuel would be seventeen in a couple weeks, and Billy knew Kate would not have let William bring Jimmy.

"Riders coming." Samp and William had dismounted, and could feel the vibrations of sound in the air and ground.

"Too many," growled the judge, who was also on the ground.

Quickly dismounting, Billy could feel the same vibrations, and agreed with the judge. They could see the crossroad from where they were standing, in the lee of an old shed. His horse nudged him in the back, but he planted his feet, reaching to hold the gelding's nose. This horse liked to greet company; the thought crossed his mind that Uncle Samp knew that. His uncle was testing him, and a quick glance sideways told him Samp had noted his actions.

The horsemen were Bald Knobbers, masked and carrying torches. Only Nat Kinney held no torch and wore no mask. He was easily recognizable on his favorite horse, Grey Ghost. They came to a stop at Kinney's raised gesture, and the four men back in the woods stood motionless. If the moon had been shining, it would not have been difficult to see them, Billy realized. Luck was with them.

"You said they would be here," Kinney turned to the man on his right. If he looked past his companion, he'd see the four men in the woods.

The voice was muffled through the mask. "I heard Haworth telling Snodgrass," said John Haggard, and his shoulders raised in a shrug.

"Well, mebbe we convinced Haworth not to go," came Wash Middleton's voice. Short barks of coyote laughter rippled through the group.

Kinney did not reply to this. He rode his horse boldly into the center of the crossroad, circling, searching. Billy's horse sidestepped, trying to shake his hold on its nostrils, but he clung, softly whistling through his teeth, "Sssssssshaish."

He froze as Kinney appeared to look straight at them, but the big man continued to rotate. It was if he sensed something, someone,

364 | Vonda Wilson Sheets

watching. Taking a deep, slow breath of cold air, Billy watched as Kinney said, "Let's go back to Forsyth. Someone may have found something out." The other horses parted and turned, letting Kinney guide his horse to the front once more.

"Damn, they're gonna ride straight into our bunch," Judge Reynolds said softly.

Tense. Waiting for gunfire to start was one of the hardest things to do, some small pocket in Billy's mind noted. The four continued to stand, horses still kept quiet, as the sound of horses fell away again. Only when the silence continued long enough for it to become obvious that the oppositional groups on this road tonight had not met up did Billy sense the older men relaxing.

"Why'd you bring Socks?" William muttered to Samp. Releasing his clamp on the gelding's nose, Billy flexed his fingers as the horse butted him in retaliation. He rocked on his feet, and pulled the horse's head down again, this time holding the bridle. Turning his head toward his father, he was surprised to see his uncle shrugging.

"Fergot about his place on the welcoming committee," Samp replied. "Jist remembered when Billy grabbed him."

Discovering a smile on his face, Billy quickly turned back to his horse so Samp and William wouldn't sense his amusement. Then he thought about Uncle Samp choosing the horses to saddle in the dark barn while William and Billy were getting ready to leave. Since Socks didn't greet humans the way he did horses, it was obvious his uncle was thinking in terms of speed and dark color--Socks was so named for his black leg markings on his otherwise brown body. And he was a tough horse, if a tad friendly. Even now, Socks was trying to nudge the judge's horse, which was making friendly sounds of its own.

It was some time before three men on horseback appeared. Billy grasped Socks' nostrils again. When the men reached the crossroads, Judge Reynolds once more hooted, and Snodgrass' voice was clear.

"Thet's a sorry owl."

Billy and the others mounted as Judge Reynolds replied, "It's a sorry night to be out."

Joining up, the seven riders took the road going north, into the hills dividing Bull Creek from Swan Creek. The cloudy night was cold, with a tang that bespoke of the interest of spring. Up on the ridge tops, the wind forced Billy to take turns with his gloved hands, one holding the reins of his horse and the other wrapped around the still-warm potatoes in his pockets.

Descending into Bull Creek Valley, there was a mist that chilled the face, made the night heavy, especially in the hour before sunrise.

Skirting the town of Ozark, the men continued on until Judge Reynolds called a halt near the Finley River. The men dismounted, stiff and cold while the horses rested and drank.

"This is far enough," the judge told the others. "You go on back to JJ Brown's office, deliver Alonzo's letter."

There wasn't much else to be said. All knew that a large party of men would attract attention, and they still held hope the Bald Knobbers did not know exactly what the contents of their letter and petition to the governor were. All the Bald Knobbers knew was there was going to be organized opposition of some kind.

Riding back to Ozark, a good-sized grove of trees less than a mile from the town, still above the Finley river valley but on rocky ground, promised some measure of camouflage. Here, all of them dismounted once more.

Here, Samp took charge.

"Billy, you'll ride into town, deliver the letter to Mr. Brown." Monroe Snodgrass and Matt Snapp began to protest, but Samp waved them down. "If they come riding through, they'll see one of y'all. One young tired man going into a lawyer's office won't be noticed." Then he looked at Billy, measuring his nephew visually. He reached into his pocket, pulled out a bandana, and dropped it on the ground. He bent over, rubbed the cloth into the dirt with a few swipes, then shook it out as he once more stood. "Tie thet 'round yer neck."

Billy did as instructed, then took Alonzo Prather's sealed letter from Robert Snapp. Even though his face was partially hidden by his hat and coat collar, the handkerchief, knotted in the back, rode along Billy's jaw and made it more difficult to see his features. He mounted Socks, but William stayed him for a moment.

"Set a meeting with Mr. Brown later today," William told his son, voice low as the others began to pull canvas-wrapped bedrolls off their horses. "As a lawyer."

Nodding, Billy left for Ozark.

The little town was the seat of Christian County, and the brick courthouse stood majestically in its square, surround by the businesses which paid suit to the courthouse like so many lovers in a contest of law. Tired as he was, Billy remained alert to anything that might seem unusual, but even as he dismounted in front of JJ's office, nothing out of the ordinary for a busy morning in a bustling town appeared.

Tying Socks to the rail of the covered porch, Billy took the two steps up and then halted, surveying the square once more. There. There was a horse he recognized, then he realized he knew the rider. Bill Hensley. Others appeared, seemingly from behind the courthouse as they circled around the square. They were coming in his direction. Haste would draw attention, so Billy hitched his shoulders slightly, ducking his head and forcing his chin into the folds of his uncle's handkerchief. He turned to walk the few steps across the porch to the door of JJ Brown's office.

There was no entryway to shelter behind, and his heart began to beat loudly as he realized the door was locked. Again without haste, he raised his gloved fist to knock just as he heard the door knob click.

"I beg your pardon," said JJ Brown. "I'm leaving for court." The older man thwarted Billy's entrance by stepping out and pulling the door closed.

"Mr. Brown," Billy said, allowing a note of urgency in his voice. He imagined he could hear the horses of the Taney County Bald Knobbers getting closer, despite the din.

"Young man, I must leave. Whatever it is will have to wait." It was obvious JJ did not recognize Billy as he started to move away.

"Mr. Brown, I have a letter for you," Billy said, low, keeping his hat brim tilted toward the street slightly, but allowing JJ to see him.

"Oh, well, hand it over. I have business," JJ stopped. Looking past Billy, he recognized Bill Hensley and others, his eyes going wide. Keeping his body still, he raised his chin to acknowledge Hensley's recognition, and then glared as the Bald Knobbers kept on riding past.

Only after most of them had continued by did JJ look back at Billy, whose head had slowly, carefully, tilted in response to the closeness of the Bald Knobbers. JJ saw the envelope with Alonzo's handwriting being held out to him, and he took it, calmly acting as this happened all the time.

Glancing from the letter up to Billy's face, the older man realized who Billy was. Still without excess movement, he asked Billy, "Are they out of sight yet?"

Turning as if to check the reins of his horse, Billy watched as the last of them left the square. "Now they are."

"You had best wait inside," JJ returned to the door and opened it. "I must go over to the courthouse, but it shouldn't take long."

Billy nodded, went inside, and then turned to look out the window as JJ closed the door. He watched the attorney cross the street to the courthouse, displaying no fear from Nat Kinney's henchmen as he walked into the two-story brick building, and disappeared.

As tired as he was, Billy could not relax in the quiet of Brown's office. He pulled a chair over the corner near the window, placing it at an angle and adjusting the curtain so he could see the entrance to the square where the Bald Knobbers had exited.

It was a scant half-hour later when JJ Brown returned. Billy jumped to his feet as the door opened. Hurriedly, JJ walked to his desk chair and sat down, removing Alonzo's letter from his pocket and laying it on the bare wood in front of him. He gestured Billy to return to his chair as he stared thoughtfully at the envelope.

"There is coffee, if you would like some," JJ murmured, and then broke the seal and began to read. Billy rose and went to the small wood stove at the back of the room, pouring coffee so thick and black that the aroma alone was enough to revive him. Carrying the cup with him, he returned to the windows and watched the activity in the town square, trying to give the attorney a sense of privacy.

"Hell is empty, and all the devils are here." JJ had thrown the letter on his desk and was resting his forehead on his hands when Billy turned, startled.

"Beg pardon?" Billy asked.

Sitting back in his chair, JJ was shaking his head, and gestured toward the letter. "Shakespeare. No matter. Will you take a letter back to Mr. Prather?"

Biting his upper lip, Billy nodded.

Noticing the gesture, JJ asked, "Is there more?"

Nodding again, Billy continued to stand in front of JJ's desk. "My father would like to meet with you."

"Is he here?" JJ was surprised.

Billy tilted his head toward the north, where he'd left William and the others. "Close," he answered.

368 | Vonda Wilson Sheets

Looking at the clock, JJ thought for a moment. "In what manner?"

Shrugging, Billy told him, "He said 'as a lawyer,' Mr. Brown."

"Ah." JJ stood, came around the desk, and the two men stared out the window, side by side, for the space of a few thoughts. Then JJ turned to look at the young man before him, his eyes full of speculation as he rubbed a finger below his nose. Billy met the attorney's gaze without guile.

"Do you know why?" queried JJ. Billy's face changed instantly, closing down as his jaw twitched and hardened. Raising a hand before Billy could speak, JJ told him, "It's enough that you know. I can guess." A pitiful sympathy welled through JJ as he considered, then gave Billy the directions to his home.

After repeating the directions in his mind twice, Billy had it and put a hand on the door knob. "Good day to you, sir," he told JJ.

JJ Brown nodded, closing the door behind Billy and parting the curtains on the door window so he could watch the young man mount his horse and leave.

Even before JJ moved his family to Ozark from the Forsyth area, the Miles boys had reputations as tough young men. But so had Andy Coggburn, whose death had been detailed in Alonzo's letter. After Billy rode out of JJ's sight, JJ murmured another of Shakespeare's lines, this one from Hamlet. "There is special providence in the fall of a sparrow," and returned to his desk to write a response to his friend.

Alonzo's plan to pursue the Taney County Bald Knobbers and force them to disband for lack of a charter was a good one. JJ suspected a deeper, more insidious plan was afoot, and knew that somehow, Billy Miles would be involved. As he wrote a salutation to Alonzo, another line from Shakespeare crossed JJ's mind.

"So wise, so young, they say never do live long."

CHAPTER 38
Wednesday - Thursday March 3 & 4, 1886

After riding into North Springfield, John Reynolds stopped off at the livery near Commercial Street to board his horse. It was Wednesday afternoon, and business was lively in the railroad town. Trains were arriving and departing regularly; the rail yards, with the stock barn and other railroad-dependent businesses were noisy and interesting to watch. But Reynolds, his mind on his task, paid no attention as he hurried to the depot.

The ticket and his leather pouch were the only things in his hands as he boarded the train. The pouch contained the precious letters and petition to the governor from "Concerned Citizens of Taney County." Once seated, Reynolds relaxed for the first time in days. He had seen no one he knew, and was thankful. So far, it appeared the Anti-Bald Knobbers were living up to the nickname of "Slickers."

Amid much huffing and puffing, the train built up a head of steam and began to move. Reynolds pulled out his watch, clicked it open, and noted the time. It was a practiced movement, and he glanced out the window as he placed the watch back in his pocket.

His railway coach was passing the big livery barn where he'd stabled his horse. The porter was speaking with the passenger in the seat ahead of him when Reynolds caught a glimpse of a group of familiar horses and men riding between the barn and himself. Some of the faces were turned in the direction of the train departing North Springfield on time.

Reynolds quickly sank down in his seat, although he knew no one could possibly have seen him. Then he smiled. The smile broadened when the porter asked, "Ticket, sir?" and punched a hole in the precious bit of thick paper.

Judge John Reynolds was still ahead of the Bald Knobbers. Chalk another point up for the Slickers.

༖ ༕

Word spread quickly through Taney County. Men were meeting in small groups, assigning roles to various individuals, and planning out the strategies for local militia. Messages were sent from one group of men to another through women and older children.

Although the Bald Knobbers were riding in broad daylight, there were too many isolated areas for their opponents to meet for them to be able to threaten and harass all of the small groups.

Jimmy Miles was one of the message carriers. Emanuel was working with a group south of Kissee Mill that included his Barker cousins.

At home, Kate Miles worked in her garden, attacking the cold ground with her shovel and pick. Her confidence in William and her sons was absolute. The only thing greater, in her mind, was the tenseness between her shoulders, sending out warning prickles that occasionally made her shudder.

The three children she had left at home had not been born until after the War Between the States. Kate Miles was appalled to realize that, somehow, she and William had raised warriors who had never seen war, yet were ready when it came.

In the mid-afternoon, Kate decided to ride to Dickens and then over to Sally's. As usual, she felt an inordinate need to be close to her sister when the men were warmongering.

Riding out of the barn, she was headed up the road when she saw Sally riding toward her. Pulling on the reins, she waited for Sally to join her.

"If you were going after gunpowder, Dickenson is out," Sally greeted her sister. Kate's head bobbed in acknowledgement and they turned their mounts back toward the Miles barn.

Sitting on the porch after trying to eat some stew, the women were smoking their pipes when the hair on Kate's head began to vibrate and rise. She recognized the symptoms of panic, and more for something to do, she quit rocking and stood. "I'm going to fix a big dinner," Kate told her sister.

Sally's eyebrows rose. "Do you think they'll be back in time to eat it hot?"

Looking at the shadows cast by the lowering sun, Kate raised her chin. "I don't care. I can't just sit here, and they'll be hungry."

Jimmy came in for a sandwich when his mother's hands were full of kneaded bread dough. While he was eating at the kitchen table, another bolt of panic shot through Kate. This time, Sally felt it, too, and the sisters looked closely at each other. Nodding, Kate touched a flour-coated hand to Jimmy's face.

"Tell Richard and the others to be here three hours after dark," Kate told Jimmy.

Confused, Jimmy asked, "Did you get a message from Pa?" and stuffed the last of his sandwich in his mouth, rising to put his coat and hat back on.

Too worried to smile, Kate's face was rueful. "You could say that." She glanced over at Sally, who was peeling potatoes at a slow pace. Sally's own face had a half-grin on it.

"You might as well tell them there'll be a hot meal," Kate told her youngest son. "Your aunt has peeled enough potatoes for an army."

Billy was able to sleep for about two hours after returning to the clearing where his father and the others were waiting. It was a scant half hour's ride to JJ's home, and the group once more skirted the town of Ozark.

The Brown's house was on a well-traveled road between Ozark and Sparta, some miles from the Chadwick-Springfield railroad trail. The tired men tied their horses behind the house, and walked around to the front door.

Caroline Everett Brown wasn't an easy hostess, but she had made coffee and set out some pastries for the guests. She shooed the children into the front room while JJ sat at the kitchen table with William Miles, Billy Miles, Sampson Barker, Robert Snapp, Monroe Snodgrass, and Matt Snapp.

The Snapp brothers took the lead in the conversation after the coffee was poured. Sending a questioning glance toward his father, Billy waited until William and Samp took a pastry before reaching for his own.

He stopped chewing at the first question.

"What constitutes murder in the state of Missouri?" Robert Snapp asked.

After a lengthy answer from the attorney, Matt Snapp was next. "Would you define self-defense?" Again, the answer was long-winded. Billy sensed JJ was trying to throw up obstacles in the conversation, and he knew there was no time for loquacity.

Matt held up his hand to forestall any further comments from JJ. None of the men were ignorant, but the lawyer's tergiversations were purposely confusing. Then William reached for an unshelled walnut from a bowl on the table, and picked up the nutcracker.

Carefully placing the walnut in the vise, William looked up to see all eyes were on his hands. He squeezed, and the pieces of shell and nut fell on his plate, which still held half of his pastry.

"Mr. Brown, we know you for a good and honest man," William began to pick out the meat of the nut, brushing the shell to the side. "Break it down, if you please."

JJ rubbed his face tiredly, and ran a finger under his nose, rubbing his upper lip.

"Self-defense, in the eyes of the law, is protecting your home and your property, or your life, against a threat," the attorney said. "Murder is killing someone who is unarmed. There are varying degrees, depending on whether it is done in cold blood or under stress." He looked at William's plate, not wanting to see the answer to his forthcoming question. "Are any of you charged with this?"

All replied, "No."

William continued. "But, if one of us were so-charged, would you be willing to defend him?"

Looking back up at the faces around his table, JJ replied, "I know why the Snapps are here, Mr. Miles. Alonzo wrote that Sam is in trouble. What I don't understand is why you, your son, and Mr. Barker are here."

Billy spoke then. "My brother and I work for Mr. Snapp on one of his farms. All Mr. Snapp was doing was asking Andrew Coggburn to work for him on his Kirbyville farm, like we do on his Taney City one."

Sending a hard glance at Billy, William added, "Sam is a good neighbor, Mr. Brown. I don't want his land taken over by some Knobber."

JJ nodded, thinking hard. Reaching a decision, he spoke abruptly. "My retainer is $500. I'm warning you now--stay within the boundaries of the law."

William, Samp, Robert and Matt reached inside their coats, pulling out wallets and counting money. When the pile on the table reached the desired amount, Robert picked it up, and began to straighten it. He spoke once more.

"Some of them at home are drawing names and wanting to hunt men down. Some of the hunted are good men, if misguided. A home guard is being formed. We have a different route."

JJ held up one hand, causing Robert to cease talking, and the other hand was held out for the cash. "I don't want to know more at this time, Robert. You are retaining my services, should you need them."

The six men rose, and JJ stood with them. He shook hands with all of them, including Billy. "There are Bald Knobbers in Christian County now. I'm certain Kinney had a hand in their start. They've killed no one yet, but if they aren't stopped, it will happen. I pray God this ceases soon."

"We hope so, too," Samp Barker finally spoke.

The old attorney wished the men Godspeed, and saw them through the front room and out the door. He stood at the window, watching, as his wife joined him.

"I don't know what they're planning, but I hope it works," JJ told Caroline, who tucked her hand inside the crook of his elbow. He pulled his shoulders back, and once again quoted Hamlet.

"Now whether it be bestial oblivion, or some craven scruple, of thinking too precisely on th' event--A thought which, quarter'd, hath but one part wisdom and ever three parts coward--I do not know why yet I live to say this thing's to do, still I have cause, and will, and strength, and means, to do't."

She smiled slightly in response, then both watched the riders leave. "You will," Caroline assured her husband. "You will find a way."

"I think the way has been found," JJ patted her hand. "God may grant me absolution yet for the role I had in starting it, by allowing me to help end it."

୨଼ ଼ର

The men were tired and ready to eat the hot meal Kate and Sally readied for them. The lack of conversation was punctuated by forks scraping the fried potatoes and onions, along with biscuits and sausage gravy.

Kate did not count heads as the men trickled in, ate, then made their way out to the barn to bed down until William and the others arrived. Under no illusions about the appearance of a meeting here, the various horses and mules were sent to a clearing down the hill

374 | Vonda Wilson Sheets

toward the creek.

Only Sally's son-in-law, Richard Cline, remained in the house. Kate and Sally had cleared the last of the dishes, and were just beginning to sit at the table with Richard when he halted their footsteps with an open palm. Although the mud softened the sounds of the horses, he heard his kinsmen and the Snapps riding in, and went out to greet them, averting any alarm that might be raised in the barn.

Grabbing the reins of Snodgrass' and the Snapps' mounts, Richard relied on the weariness and habits of the other horses to follow him into the barn. A couple of men rose to help remove harnesses and saddles, while William, Billy, Samp, Monroe, Matt, and Robert walked tiredly into the house.

Kate and Sally had their plates filled and on the table. Sally was pouring coffee while the men sat. Again, there was no conversation. Jimmy and Emanuel came in from the barn as William finally leaned back, finishing a third cup of coffee.

Upon asking Emanuel who was in the barn, William and Samp seemed satisfied with the twenty or so men present. After thanking the women for the meal, William rose, nodding at the three sons present in the kitchen.

"You'll come, and you'll listen," he said. Jimmy, delighted to be included, was at the door when his mother murmured a soft protest.

"He has to know," William told Kate. "He must know who to trust, who to turn to. He needs to make those decisions for himself."

"But what are you going to do?" Kate asked. The other men were quiet, waiting for an answer.

Tired, William made an attempt to smile and failed. He looked his wife in the eyes, and shrugged. "Not sure we know now. But we will, soon."

Then the men, and Jimmy, put on their hats, and left the house. Not one of them glanced in Kate's direction as she watched them walk out the door. She turned to her sister.

"He's thirteen," and Kate's voice was a moan. Throughout the day, she'd been remembering the waiting, the worrying, from the war. But until this moment, not once had she remembered the enthusiastic youth of many members of the Confederate Army.

Sally made no response, except to begin pouring water into the dishpan to wash up once more.

There really wasn't anything to say.

The small barn was full of men's bodies and their associated odors. Sweat, exhaustion, fumes of whiskey and moonshine, tobacco, hay, straw, leather and milk from the nursing cow in the corner stall; these odors were sharpened with the dew of fear rising along spines, causing scalps to tingle underneath the winter hats the men wore, despite increasing evidence spring was coming.

Richard and Emanuel were lighting lanterns and placing them on nails along the sides of the central area when William entered the building last, softly closing the door behind him. It was of long habit, as well as the gift of command, that Samp Barker took the lead in calling the meeting. He tossed a goods box on its side and stood on it, scanning the group. He didn't have to clear his throat to get the men's attention.

"Think you all know why we're here," Samp began.

"Cain't say as I do," Will Moore spoke from the center of the room. William and Billy had taken positions by the big door, shoulders against the wall, each with his left foot brought up and tucked under their legs. Billy listened as he reached over to the cow's stall, found a straw, broke it in half, and handed one half to his father, Both then used the straw to pick their teeth and waited.

"Judge Reynolds is on his way to Jefferson City," Samp continued. "He carries our letters of petition for help in stopping the Bald Knobbers."

"We can stop them ourselves," came another voice. Murmurs of agreement rose up and swirled with the smoke from the lanterns.

Allowing tired men to continue in this vein would bring a fight, Samp thought. He glanced over at William, who shrugged.

"If y'all want to keep on doing militia drills, you kin leave now," Samp told them. "Ain't likely to do much good to declare war on the Bald Knobbers."

"How's that?" Moore wanted to know.

"If the governor agrees to help, he'll be sending the state militia in," Samp answered. "If y'all are practicing military maneuvers, they'll be gunning for you and the Bald Knobbers."

Samp's assertion brought the room to silence.

"Well, it could take a long time for them to get here. Someone else is going to get hurt, with the waiting," another voice spoke.

When Billy looked to see who it was, he was surprised to see the old preacher, Jurd Haworth.

Samp nodded. "Y'all kin go on and do it then. I thank you fer comin," he told them.

"But we wanted you to organize our home guard," Jurd protested. "You have the experience--"

"I do, but I won't," Samp cut in.

Haworth turned toward William, who shook his head. "Nope, won't do it."

The doughty preacher took a deep breath and straightened his shoulders. "So you've decided to do something else."

Monroe Snodgrass spoke. "Whatever it is, I'm in." Some of the others nodded as well. Billy had been assessing and watching Snodgrass since the night before. Monroe had been uncharacteristically silent most of the trip; his position had been largely that of an extra gun, if one was needed. He was a friend of the Snapp brothers.

Jurd Haworth shook his head. "I trust you, but I'm already in danger. I cannot wait for the governor to respond. Not now."

Samp nodded, then tilted his head toward the door. "You do as you see fit, Preacher. Thank you for comin'."

Haworth and the others understood the dismissal. They chose to leave, and while blankets were being rolled and the members of the newly-formed home guard left, Billy and William stepped to the side of the door, nodding to each man as he left.

When William grimly closed the door once more, he paused for a moment before turning to look at each man--and boy--left. For Jimmy Miles was still in the barn.

Richard Cline, his nephew by marriage.

Jim Berry, who'd recently moved to Forsyth and bought the building that had housed the Everett brothers' store and saloon.

Robert and Matt Snapp, Sam's brothers.

Sampson, Billy, and Emanuel.

William took the straw from his mouth, and eyed the others once more. He didn't know Jim Berry, and said so, brusque in his weariness. "Mr. Berry, we don't know you that well. Why are you here?"

Berry looked steadily back at William. "Had a visit from thet bunch a few nights ago. Said if I didn't join up and ride with them,

Absolution | 377

they'd run me out of town."

William raised an eyebrow, but nodded.

Before he could say anything, Robert Snapp joined in. "Mr. Berry, we understand you don't want to be a part of that. But we mean serious business here."

"I want to help. Don't like being told what to do," Berry replied.

There were several moments of silence. William replaced the straw in his mouth, and there was no motion to continue conversation.

Hesitantly, Berry said, "I know I'm from Stone County, and I'm not known to you." The others in the barn were watching him closely without appearing to do so. Billy had returned to his lean against the wall, one foot raised, head lowered. The silence lengthened, and Manny joined Billy.

Finally, Berry said, "Alright, I'll go." He walked over and picked up his saddle bag and bedroll, then headed for the door. "But I'm on your side," he added quietly, then slipped out and was gone.

When they were sure Berry was gone, Matt Snapp said, "I've had a few drinks with him. He seems to be alright."

Samp replied, "Well, he ain't dumb."

William nodded. "Thet he ain't."

Samp returned to leading the conversation. "Alright. Let's get this done. We know why we're here. Mr. Brown was clear in stating what constitutes murder, and what is self-defense."

"So we need to provoke him into it being self-defense," Robert Snapp commented.

"Easier sed than done," Monroe added.

The men were nodding slowly, each one weighing and discarding thoughts. Jimmy Miles was watching closely, but kept quiet.

"Someone sed today that Kinney hasn't left his farm since the shooting," Emanuel said.

"We saw him last night," said Matt Snapp.

Some more thought, then William said, "We kin assume he's gonna hev someone with him when he does come into town."

"So someone needs to get close to him," said Robert.

William shook his head. "Thet'll take time."

Samp walked over to one of the stall feedboxes, and picked up a handful of hay. He sorted through it, pulling out six pieces. Breaking one off shorter than the others, he fisted the straw, then put it behind his back.

378 | Vonda Wilson Sheets

William asked, amusement in his voice, "We're gonna draw straws?"

"Name me a better way," Samp retorted. Holding the fist in front of himself, he nodded to Robert and Monroe, who each took a straw. Their choices were long.

Then Samp indicated William, who also pulled a long straw.

Manny stepped up and pulled a long one.

Billy yanked the straw in his mouth out, coming to stand on both feet. He touched his uncle's gloved hand while pulling his choice of straw.

It was short.

Samp let the remaining two straws--one for himself, one for Matt--fall to the floor as he stared hard at his nephew. Matt cursed, and Jimmy asked, "Now what?"

Billy stared back at his uncle, then realized his father had tensed. He faced William and said, "I guess I better get a job in town."

"I should be the one to do it!" Matt was incensed.

"You're a Snapp, and he'll know right away what you want to do," Billy replied. "And you got a wife. I don't."

"Goddammit, it's my brother!" Matt was nearly yelling.

"And my friend." Billy's voice grew quieter. "I'm going to bed." With that, Billy went to the door, opened it, walked out, and gently shut it once more.

Inside the barn, the men realized that whatever they had started was now moving ahead, with Billy's hand firmly in control. William sighed, and looked at Samp questioningly.

"William, we'll bed down on your kitchen floor," Robert said.

Matt shook his head. "Not me, I'm going home."

A grim smile on his face, Robert said, "Alright, then. We'll go home."

They saddled their horses, Matt muttering under his breath, still protesting the straw vote. Emanuel opened the door for the brothers to lead their horses out, and looked over at Jimmy after the Snapps left.

"C'mon, Jimmy," Manny said.

"Monroe, you stayin?" William asked.

"Yeah," was the tired answer. "I'll bed down on the kitchen floor."

Jimmy and Manny each grabbed a lantern and waited till the

older man joined them, then shut the door behind them.

Samp moved to take down the two remaining lanterns. He had a minute or two until Sally joined him, and the two would ride home. He was joined by William in saddling up and waiting.

Neither spoke a word through the action, but while waiting for Sally, William finally asked.

"Did he break the straw?"

Samp's shoulders shrugged. "Hard to tell with my gloves on. Makes sense, though." He led the horses to the door, which William opened, and then closed after the horses came through. Sally came out the back door at that point.

Looking wryly at his brother-in-law, William's hand rubbed at his face and jaw, pushing his hat back slightly. Then he glanced over at the house.

"You got you a smart one," Samp commented, just before handing Sally's reins to her. She led her horse over to the block used to mount horses, stepped up on it, then seated herself comfortably. Samp also mounted.

William snorted, still thinking things through and wondering at his son. He scarcely heard Samp and Sally's "good night" as he barely saw them leaving.

It was another chilly night, and he knew Kate was waiting. He plodded toward the house, his bones and muscles aching from so many hours in the saddle.

Well, it was done. A job in town, Billy had said.

William Miles would sleep tonight, but tomorrow, he and his smart son were going to have a long, long talk.

CHAPTER 39
Wednesday through Friday, March 4 - 6, 1886

The kitchen floor was covered with muddy footprints.

Contemplating the floor with her hands on her hips, Maggie Kinney stood in the doorway with her chin lowered. Damn. There was even mud on the legs of the table and chairs. Lips compressed in a tight line, she dropped her hands and walked over to the counter with the wreck pan and opened the door under it. Her ragbag was hanging on a nail inside, and she knelt down to retrieve it and a bar of lye soap. She looked over her shoulder at the floor again, and picked up a second bar of soap. Standing, she laid the soap and bag on the counter, then crossed the room again, taking one of Paul's old coats off the peg on the wall, and donned it.

Stepping outside, she walked to the well and began drawing water.

The process of drawing water, carrying it inside, heating it to almost boiling and then pouring it on the floor to scrub the dirt away with the more coarse rags from her bag and the strong soap began to have an almost soporific effect on her. She had been alone since Paul left for Forsyth after the inquest for Nat's shooting of Andy on Sunday. When Nat had been home, he was working in the fields, meeting with his men, or sleeping during the day, leaving her unable to play the piano except during the night hours he was gone.

For three days--now four since the shooting--Maggie had been numb.

She washed the legs of the chairs and table first, wanting them to dry so she could wax them when the floor was done.

Moving the chairs away from the table, she knelt down and began to scrub

The lye made her hands sore and reddened, but she didn't notice as the tangle of emotions and thoughts began to unravel, much like the rags were shredding, leaving small pieces of the fibers in places where the knots in the boards were not sanded smooth enough.

She worked slowly, moving away from the corner where the counter and stove were, toward the door, following the muddy path the men left. Working with the pungent cleanser, even with the kitchen door and outside door open, brought tears to her eyes as the

Absolution | 381

sun rose higher in the morning sky. The tears had nothing to do with the train wreck inside her head, she told herself firmly.

Maggie's conscious decision to support Nat after the Coggburns made a debacle of worship services a few weeks ago had tamped down any number of emotions. She saw no connection between her need to play the piano since Andrew's death and her current numbness, despite the words that fell out of her subconscious along with the shreds of cloth. She was having to stop scrubbing and wipe her nose and cheeks on the upper sleeves of her work dress.

Clean.

She tiredly threw the last bucket of muddy water off the big rear porch--any plant there would have a difficult time growing this year, she thought. She stumbled barefooted back into the kitchen, and found the furniture wax.

A little chilled with the open doors, despite her warmth from scrubbing and the fire in the open hearth, she set the wax tin down next to the flames and added more wood. She poured the last of the coffee on the stove in her cup, and started a new pot. No telling when Nat would awaken.

The noise covered the sound of a horseman outside.

Cross-legged on the floor between the fireplace and the kitchen table, Maggie began applying the softened wax to the table legs, working her way up from the floor. She was taking a sip of coffee and eyeing the first leg with satisfaction when footsteps rumbled up the porch and into the entryway of the house. Startled, her view was limited to a pair of muddy boots and legs entering the kitchen.

"Get out!" Maggie yelled, and scrambled to her feet, carefully not spilling her coffee. "GET OUT!"

Pat Fickle stopped three paces after the doorway, his fresh footprints gleaming on the still-wet floor.

"Where's the captain?" he asked,

"Sleeping," Maggie told him tersely. "Get out of my kitchen!"

Pat rubbed a dirty hand under his nose, eying the wrath in front of him. "Need to talk to him." He took a step toward the perking coffee pot on the stove. "Need some of that, too."

His next step resulted in being hit with Maggie's coffee cup, right in the center of his chest. There wasn't enough coffee to soak him, Maggie noted as she reached behind her for the fire poker. "Woman!" Fickle yelled. "Nobody does that to me!"

382 | Vonda Wilson Sheets

Maggie advanced toward him with the poker. Fickle was too stunned to realize his immediate danger, and was briefly immobile when Nat burst into the room.

"Fickle! What do you want?"

His muddy boots continued to leave a trail as Fickle turned toward Nat. Maggie howled again, "GET OUT OF MY KITCHEN!"

Nat looked over Fickle's shoulder at his wife, who held the poker high in preparation to throw it. Hastily, he grabbed Fickle and pulled him out of the kitchen, shoving him through the door to the porch. The poker followed them, hitting the door frame, and Nat realized that Maggie had run after them. He ran down the porch and leapt off it, expecting Fickle to follow. His bare feet squelched in the mud, and drops landed on his ankles. The strong scent of lye attacked his still-drowsy senses.

Fickle must have no sense of self-preservation, Nat thought. He looked back, turning to watch.

"No woman tells me what to do!" Fickle yelled.

Maggie had retrieved the poker, holding it aloft with both hands. Nat saw that her beautiful hands were raw and red, and with the scent of lye jerking him unpleasantly alert, he understood that she had been cleaning something. Oh. The kitchen floor.

She swung the poker, hitting Fickle on the left arm, and he howled, ducking as she took aim for another swing.

"Maggie!" Nat yelled. He started to climb back up on the porch when she looked at him, hell in her eyes with no place for him. She swung once more, hitting Fickle's right arm, and he turned, ducking and running in Nat's direction.

Nat stepped aside to allow Fickle room to land, then took two more paces away from the porch to get out of Maggie's reach. The poker was swinging for a third strike, this one on Fickle's head, and Nat jumped between the man and Maggie, his arms up to stop her.

He didn't. The poker was coming down as he grasped her wrists, spreading her arms wide. The shock of the poker hitting the porch support caused her to drop it.

Simply holding her wrists, he looked up at her face once more. "Maggie!" he said sternly.

Fickle, the idiot, was yelling from behind Nat about what he did to women who crossed him. "Shut up, you ass!" Nat told him over his shoulder. The poker lay on the ground beside him, and he had no

Absolution | 383

doubt that Maggie would be after it if he let go.

She stopped writhing to free herself. Looking at Nat squarely in the face, she paid no attention to Fickle. Eyes still burning, there were tears when she finally felt Nat's hands gripping her wrists so hard, she would have bruises. The odor did nothing to help.

There were a few seconds of silence as the two of them contemplated each other. Nat was clothed in nothing but his union suit, and his body was responding to Maggie's nearness in a familiar fashion.

She felt nothing. Glancing down with what would have been contempt, if she could feel, she swallowed. Then, Nat's iron grip still keeping her from moving far, she leaned over to see his muddy feet.

Fickle then spoke. "Beat her, Captain. She deserves it!" He was rubbing his arms--Maggie had hit him hard, but his coat had prevented her from breaking any bones.

Maggie did not respond to Fickle's suggestion, although Nat was grimly sure she heard it. She tensed, and he did as well, not sure what her next move would be. If she'd had a gun, he was certain Fickle would have been shot. He wasn't sure that she wouldn't shoot him.

Then he sensed hell had frozen over. Scorn, condemnation, and disgust.

Maggie's eyes were still burning, but her voice was coldly polite. "Let go of me, please."

Nat shook his head. "Are you finished beating Fickle?"

She didn't move. "Do not bring him into the house. Ever again."

"What I'd do?" Fickle demanded.

"I said shut up!" Nat growled. Then, "He will not come back in today."

Maggie's chin barely nodded. "Let go of me."

He did, and her wrists flexed in relief. They were still regarding each other as Nat reached down and picked up the poker. He attempted a smile as he handed it to her, and sensed that Fickle was finally wary.

The poker was muddy, but Maggie didn't notice as she took it, and turned to walk away without another word. It was not until she went back into the house that Nat turned to Fickle.

"Did no one ever tell you not to walk on a freshly-scrubbed

384 | Vonda Wilson Sheets

floor?" Nat asked mildly.

"Hell, I don't care about no scrubbed floors," Fickle answered, still rubbing his arms. "I think my arm's broken."

Standing in the mud outside his house, wearing nothing but a union suit, Nat sought some dignity and found it. He raised an eyebrow as Fickle repeated, "I'd beat her."

Nat smiled, supercilious and cool. "Your arm's not broken. What do you want?"

"The doc."

"No," Nat answered patiently. "Why are you here?"

"Oh," Fickle finally quit rubbing his arms and shook them out. "The Coggburns are gone."

News. Ah. "Both of them?"

"Yep. Left yesterday morning."

Nat turned to walk around the corner of the porch, back to the steps, Fickle following slowly. What was left of last year's grass was sharp against Nat's feet, but he would not wince with Fickle present. Reaching the steps, he dared not put a muddy foot on them. Instead, he sat down, and dampness immediately soaked the backside of his union suit. Yes, she had washed the steps, too.

He rubbed his eyes, and when his hands came away, there was a cup of coffee just over his left shoulder. He reached up and took it. "Thank you, Maggie," he said, and her footsteps returned inside.

"Where's mine?" Fickle wanted to know.

Maggie's voice answered, dripping with ice, "Mr. Fickle. I am so sorry, I did not know you were here. Most people knock on the door when they arrive for a visit."

Nat eyed Fickle with surprise. "You didn't knock on the door?"

"Hell, it was open."

Shaking his head, Nat raised his eyebrows. "Mr. Fickle is leaving, dear." He tossed the words over his shoulder, not taking his eyes off Fickle. He took a long drink of coffee.

"I shan't bother bringing him fresh coffee then," his wife responded, still hidden from view.

Fickle was outraged. "I'm not done talking," he said.

Nat rose. "But I am finished listening for now. We will talk later."

"I want the Coggburn place!"

Nat took the steps to the porch, and turned to prevent Fickle from following him.

"I said, we'll talk later. For now, you have caused me to lose sleep and pissed off my wife."

"I don't care about your wife!"

Nat placed a hand on Fickle's shoulder, and leaned over, causing Fickle to back down a step. "But I do, Pat, and that is your misfortune. Thank you for the news."

The threat emanating from Nat reached Patterson Fickle much quicker than any threat from Maggie. He turned to leave, and tossed off, "I'd beat her."

Nat shrugged and chuckled as he watched Fickle walking back toward the mule standing outside the gate. "Next time you come to visit, knock before you enter my house. Oh, and Pat?"

The man turned, once more rubbing his arms, surly and angry. "Yes, sir?"

"I don't have to beat my wife." Nat saluted Fickle with his coffee cup, then turned. As he expected, there was a bucket of warm water by the door, and he reached for a nearby stool to sit on.

Pat Fickle rode away in disbelief, noting Captain Kinney was washing the mud off his feet before he went back inside his own house.

Maggie was waiting for the bucket of water when Nat returned to the kitchen. She took it from him without a word, then added some more hot water to it. Gingerly, Nat walked to the stove, avoiding the tracked-in mud and poured himself another cup of coffee. His chair was shoved to the side of the fireplace. Rather than move it back in front, he sat in it with his coffee, once more feeling the wet union suit making his posterior uncomfortable.

The feeling grew as he watched Maggie hike the skirt of her work dress up and tuck the hem into the waistband. Her lower legs freed, she knelt and cleaned Fickle's prints. Discomfort grew entangled with arousal at the sight of Maggie's cold bare feet and calves, the long line of her shin bones white against the wet floor. As she sat back and wiped her eyes and forehead against her upper right arm, she dropped the rag into the bucket. He saw the bruises on her wrist from his hands, and for a moment, stopped to consider a woman's strength. His eyes went to her left wrist, the darkening blue circling her bones like a bracelet. She appeared not to notice as she uncrossed

386 | Vonda Wilson Sheets

her legs and brought her knees up to inspect. They were red with bearing her weight on the floor, and the dress fell back to expose her upper legs.

Maggie's hands rubbed over her knees and down her legs to her feet. She wasn't quite facing Nat, and didn't even watch him through her lashes, but her motion was not sensual. She didn't want him in any manner at this moment, not even to talk to.

They had scarcely spoken since the shooting. She made meals for the men who invaded her home, kept away from Nat the few hours he was in the house, and had risen in the mornings when he had finally come back from his rides to sleep. Her schedule had not changed, although her work load had significantly increased.

Men had pissed off her porch, used her cups for spittoons, and eaten her food without anyone even pausing to say, "Thank you." But for the tobacco, that had included Nat.

"You have not played for me in days." His voice was quiet.

"No."

"Would you like to now?"

"No."

She wasn't speaking to him, she decided. Unconsciously, she wrapped her arms around her knees like a young girl, her hands massaging her wrists one at a time.

Maggie was used to quiet, to silence. She used it as a defense now. He would not come close to her until she could come to terms with Sunday's events. In the past, when someone had died as a result of injuries inflicted by Nat, he had moved his family. She was trying to prepare herself for another upheaval, and could not bring herself to wonder, once more, if Nat's actions were justified. She had already decided the means used to quell the Coggburn family were probably necessary. The lye soap had caused her eyes to tear.

He rose to fill his cup again, then slowly walked toward her, sipping coffee. Towering over her, he looked down at the silver in her hair, the slender hands still massaging her wrists. A great weariness fell on his shoulders, and he could bear her silence no more. He put a hand out to help her up. She moved away, shifted herself away from him.

"Maggie." A caress was in his voice.

"Don't touch me." She could smell horse, leather, sweat, and worse, on him. She was not some poor woman who had to deal

Absolution | 387

with her man no matter his offense. She was not some whore, paid to suffer in silence whatever her customer chose to inflict upon her body. Her wrists began throbbing.

He knelt down to her, awkwardly landing on his rump, keeping his coffee cup aloft and balanced. When he stretched his legs out, one on each side of her, leaving his manhood vulnerable to her, she turned her head. The bucket of water kept her from shifting her body further away. She heard him taking another sip of coffee, then set the cup on the floor.

"Let me see your wrists."

"They're fine."

The silence returned with her adamant statement.

"I don't believe you," Nat finally said. "I'm sorry." He put a hand on top of hers.

There were tears in her eyes again, although the odor was not as strong. A sudden vision of the Widow Maggie, beaten and defeated, fell into her mind, and she thought of Andrew Coggburn doctoring the woman's wounds with a gentle, deft touch.

Maggie Kinney raised her reddened eyes to her husband, and found she could face him with no fear. "Why did you kill him?"

"He was reaching for his gun, Maggie." Searching Nat's eyes, his face, Maggie saw no reason to doubt he was telling the truth.

"He wasn't a bad boy," she said softly.

"No." Nat pulled her hands toward him, and began inspecting her wrists, his head lowered to avoid her eyes. He caressed the bruises, wincing as they appeared to darken before his eyes. He stroked her arms, pushing her sleeves up above her elbows to touch the fragile skin hidden there.

She let him.

The voice that told Maggie she was a fool to trust him prodded her to speak once more.

"Why don't you beat me like Mr. Fickle does his wife?"

His sudden movement startled her. He lunged at her, picking her up and bringing her to his chest as he rose, knocking over his coffee cup and staining the floor again. She began to protest when his mouth came down on hers, carrying her through the entryway, kicking the door shut, and on into the bedroom. He laid her down on the bed, gently, not letting the kiss end, and his hands grabbed her sore wrists and pulled them over her head. She bit him.

Retaliating, he kept her wrists captive and weighed her down while leaning on an elbow and yanking her skirt and petticoats higher. His knee held her legs down while he unbuttoned the opening in his damp union suit. His body shifted, and just before he pinned her writhing body to the mattress, Nat answered her question.

"Because I don't have to."

It was the same thing he had said to Pat Fickle, she realized as her body responded to him, despite the pain in her wrists. Even though the smell of lye soap wasn't immediately apparent, tears trickled down the sides of Maggie Kinney's face as her husband showed her who controlled whom. Nat didn't notice, as her hands came down to bring him closer, that she let him.

John Reynolds read the headlines of each newspaper as it was delivered to the stand near the capitol building in Jefferson City early on Friday morning. Some were several days old, and didn't have the headlines he was seeking. Others, printed in the days since news of Andrew Coggburn's murder at the hands of Nat Kinney spread, were quite satisfying. There was sure to be an uproar. That would only help his case with the governor. He bought copies of the papers to add to his arsenal.

The appointment was not so satisfying. Governor Marmaduke listened intently to his argument for the state to intervene in Taney County. A sharp knock at the door interrupted, and Marmaduke excused himself briefly. When he returned, he was carrying an open folder that he appeared to be studying. He sat at his desk once more, and when Reynolds attempted to resume the conversation, Marmaduke held up a hand to halt him.

"I understand the other side is now requesting an appointment, Mr. Reynolds," Marmaduke said. "The Bald Knobbers."

Pursing his lips, Reynolds squinted and nodded twice. "So now you see the urgency of my request," he told Marmaduke.

"I'll make no decisions until after Mr. Hensley's appointment," retorted Marmaduke. "I certainly do not wish the situation to deteriorate in Taney County by sending in militia unless it is called for."

"But, sir--"

Absolution | 389

"Mr. Reynolds, you have been a judge, correct?"

Trapped, Reynolds nodded.

"Then you know one must hear both sides of the argument. Your time is up."

"But the petitions, the letters--"

"Leave them. I will read them." The governor stood, and held his hand out to Reynolds. As they shook, the governor seemed to realize he had been abrupt. "You will hear from me no later than tomorrow night." His glance at the papers on his desk was rueful. "Good day, sir."

Bill Hensley and assorted other Taney County residents were in the anteroom. An aide--presumably the one who had knocked on the governor's door--was speaking with the group as John Reynolds exited the governor's office.

It did not help that John Reynolds was the only "Slicker" in appearance. He straightened his tie, took out his watch for a glance, and then walked out at a pace to indicate he was needed elsewhere.

Once outside the building, Reynolds looked about to get his bearings. His hotel was that way. What to do now? He headed back toward the news stand, wondering if any more newspapers had been delivered.

His stomach growled as Reynolds perused the headlines. Deciding he needed to eat breakfast, he began to walk back toward the hotel when he was addressed by a man not far away.

It was a newspaper reporter who had been tipped off by the owner of the news stand about Reynolds' purchases. At first reluctant to talk to the man, John Reynolds found himself sitting in a diner eating bacon and eggs when it occurred to him he was talking to someone who could help.

A story appearing with this afternoon or evening's headlines could tilt the governor's hand in favor of the Slickers. John Reynolds began to discuss the home guard forming in Taney County because Nat Kinney had cold-bloodedly killed an innocent boy.

After paying for his meal, he watched the reporter stride off, nearly running in his haste to make a deadline. Reynolds went back to the hotel to sleep for a few hours; he was exhausted.

The messenger came Saturday. Reynolds accompanied the boy

back to the governor's office.

Governor Marmaduke's greeting was terse; he quickly got to the point.

"Your opponents had me convinced that the situation in Taney County is not at all as severe as you claimed," the governor told Reynolds. "Since my aide has spoken with them, however, I have read your petition and the letters you brought. Mr. Prather's, in particular, shows him to be an educated man, not given to overstatement nor exaggeration."

John Reynolds felt hope rising from the soles of his feet, coursing through his body, until his heart was pounding so fiercely, he could scarcely hear the governor's next words.

"Presuming you have not given copies of those letters to the newspapers," Marmaduke's voice was wry, "I shall send a man down to investigate the situation. I see no reason to call upon the state militia at this time."

Reynolds leapt to protest, "But, sir, I assure you--"

"Mr. Jamison will be in Forsyth quite soon, Mr. Reynolds. And if your compatriots start a war before then, may God have mercy on them. Because Jamison won't."

Reynolds stared in disbelief. "They are beginning to organize, sir. Why, a full-scale war could be going before I get back to tell them."

Marmaduke nodded. "Mr. Hensley assured my aide the men you call 'Bald Knobbers' will not be starting it."

"You believe this? After the evidence I brought you?"

"Mr. Reynolds." The look on the governor's face was distant. "I was in the Confederate Army, a fact I'm sure you are acquainted with. I am familiar with hotheads instigating trouble."

"We are defending ourselves!"

"Mmm. So, claim the Bald Knobbers, are they, according to my aide. They are also adamant I need send no one to Taney County to investigate any activity."

Reynolds clamped down on his jaw. The Governor indicated the newspaper in front of him.

"I want no more reports of trouble in Taney County, Mr. Reynolds." He looked down at the newspaper and picked it up, holding it to show the interview Reynolds had given the day before. "I'm sending Jamison, Mr. Reynolds. Consider that enough." He

Absolution | 391

tossed the newspaper back onto his desk, and picked up a bell, ringing it. An attendant opened the door with a murmured, "Sir?"

"I'd advise you, Mr. Reynolds, to send a telegraph home, telling your Slickers to halt any attempts to form a militia or start a war." The governor then sat in his chair, rolling to the desk and avoiding Reynolds' face. "I will give Mr. Hensley the same advice." He paused. "Good day, and good luck. Mr. Jones, please give Mr. Reynolds direction to the telegraph office as you show him out."

The young man spoke in a low voice. "This way, sir."

John Reynolds was slow to follow, but a look at the governor's bowed head and the pile of papers on his desk caused Reynolds to realize that he was probably lucky to have gotten the man to send someone to investigate. He put his hat on his head, and followed the aide from the office.

While going down the stairs, Reynolds stopped the aide. "Mr. Jones?"

The young man halted on the landing. "Yes, sir?"

"Has the governor actually spoken to Mr. Hensley?"

Jones hesitated, then frowned. "I do not believe so. The governor was quite unable to see him yesterday. I have not seen Mr. Hensley today."

"Has he made an appointment?" Reynolds asked.

"Certainly. For next week."

"Can you tell me when?"

The younger man thought for a moment, then shook his head. "It is later in the week. The governor is so busy, you understand."

"How did I manage to get in so quickly then?" Reynolds asked.

Jones was surprised at the question. "You are a Democrat, aren't you, sir?"

"Yes. But..."

Jones began descending the stairs once more. "It is my understanding that Mr. Hensley is a Republican. He also claimed he had to wait for a delivery of important paperwork before he was ready to see the governor."

Slowly following the governor's aide, John Reynolds gave thanks for two things. One, that the current governor was the first Democrat elected to the position since the war. And two, whatever evidence Bill Hensley was going to give to the governor had been left behind in Taney County. The Bald Knobbers weren't prepared to defend

392 | Vonda Wilson Sheets

their actions just yet.

He thanked the aide and set off for the telegraph office, to alert Alonzo Prather of the governor's decision.

ϡ ᷔ

Billy Miles left for Kirbyville before sunrise Saturday morning. He had his mind set on a job or a farm--he was old enough to be working his own land. It was time he left the home of his parents.

His first choice was to buy Sam Snapp's Taney City farm and work it this summer. If that failed, then his second choice was a job in Forsyth. He was too independent to work as a farmhand anymore.

He stopped at Kintrea's store in Kirbyville to buy some candy for the kids. While waiting to attract John Kintrea's attention, however, Billy realized that the noise in the store had died down. Billy turned to see Sam standing in the entryway, holding the door half open and scanning the late Saturday morning shoppers.

It must have been the first time Sam had been seen in public since last Sunday, Billy thought. John Kintrea had looked in Sam's direction, then began bagging the purchase of the customer in front of him. Murmurs arose as Sam continued into the store, and Billy was aware of people moving away from Sam while he strode to the end of the line Billy was standing in.

The quick glance Billy had of Sam's face had shown the normally-mobile features appearing to be carved from stone. He quickly assessed the situation as Kintrea inquired as to what he wanted to buy.

Transaction completed, Billy moved to the left and turned, leaning against the counter in a casual manner. He caught Sam's eye, and smiled.

Sam smiled back, but there were three or four people between him and Billy. Conversation was impossible.

The store quieted again as the door opened once more to reveal Nat Kinney's tall form. The Bald Knobber captain appeared not to notice Sam's presence as he walked to the far front corner of the store, appearing to be interested in fabric. Mrs. Kintrea had an anxious look on her face as she went to wait on Kinney.

She had begun to cut a length of rich red silk that Kinney pulled out of the shelves of fabric bolts when Sam's turn at the counter

Absolution | 393

came. Some people left the store, others came in. There was space around both Sam and Nat, Billy noted, as if they were tainted. He moved closer to Sam.

After giving Kintrea his list, Sam acknowledged the younger man. "Well, hello, Billy." He smiled slightly.

"Howdy, Sam."

"What brings you this way?" Sam asked. Kintrea muttered something about going to the back room, walking away momentarily.

"Came to see if you was gonna farm in Taney City this year," Billy answered.

Sam looked perplexed. "No, I told your parents I wouldn't." He gazed questioningly at Billy.

"Well, then." Billy's face brightened, which was not the reaction Sam expected. "I'd like to buy it."

That was unexpected as well. Sam's smile disappeared.

"It's not for sale, Billy."

"But, Sam, if you ain't gonna work it--wait, you're moving back, ain't you? Ma'll be so--"

"No, Billy, I'm not moving back. Not now, maybe not ever," Sam replied.

It was Billy's turn to be confused. Some small part of him realized nearly everyone in the store was listening to their conversation. He continued: "Why not? Are you just gonna let that house fall in?"

Sam's face grew hard. "If it does, it does. If you want to work the land, go ahead. We can do it in shares, just like we done last year."

Billy's head shook as he said, "Nope, I want my own place. I want to buy that place from you."

Kintrea had returned, and gave Sam his total. Pulling his wallet out, Sam appeared to consider what Billy was asking, but he really was not prepared to give up the Taney City farm. Neither was he interested in working both farms this year. He wasn't even planting the entirety of the Kirbyville farm, and it was not a large acreage.

He paid his bill, pocketed his change, and picked up the brown paper bundle. He tucked it under his right arm and turned to the left, thanking Kintrea. Then he grabbed Billy by the shoulder to take him closer to the door. Billy let himself be dragged, then straightened after Sam let go.

"Now, you look here," Sam's tone was menacing. "Work the

damned farm. Live in the house. Come here once in a while. I don't have any work for you this year, but I'm not going to sell that farm. Not yet."

Billy continued to argue. "Let me buy the farm from you. I want my own place."

"Are you thinking about getting married?" Sam asked. He had not noticed that Kinney was listening, as were most of the other people in the store.

"Mebbe," Billy answered, jerking his coat straight. "But thet ain't your business."

Sam's head jerked in reaction. "What? We're friends, you and I."

"If you're not gonna sell me that farm, then we ain't."

Hurt, Sam asked, "Really? You want it that bad?" He lowered his voice. "That house is bad luck for women, Billy."

"I'll make my own luck, Mr. Snapp. One last time. Will you sell me that farm?"

"Mr. Snapp?" Sam's head began to shake negatively. "I can't do it, Billy."

Billy looked down at the small brown paper package he held in his hand. It had the candy he had come to buy, peppermint sticks for Sam's children. He lifted his head, brought the package up, and tucked it into Sam's right coat pocket.

"That's for your kids, Mr. Snapp. Sorry to hev bothered you." Billy then turned, opened the door, and walked out, closing the door gently behind him.

Sam Snapp was totally bewildered. He had known Billy Miles for at least ten years, and looked upon him as yet another younger brother. He gazed at the door, which opened to admit a woman and her children, then shook his head at the added noise.

Somehow, his eyes landed on Nat Kinney, who was watching closely. Kinney had no emotion on his face as Mrs. Kintrea folded the fabric and added the necessities for a finished dress. Sam's eyes fell to the rich red silk, the color of love, passion....and blood. Involuntarily, he looked once more into Kinney's eyes.

The eye contact didn't cease, even as Kinney asked for a catalog to order shoes to match the dress. While Mrs. Kintrea looked for the catalog, Kinney nodded just once at Sam.

It was too much. Clutching his package, Sam opened the door and left Kintrea's store. Hopefully, he had enough coffee in the package to keep from having to come back to Kirbyville for a while.

CHAPTER 40
April 7 through 10, 1886

Spring was well on its way. The dogwood and redbud, along with the serviceberry trees, floated their blossoms through the woods, appearing otherworldly and divine in their understory growth. Both wild and planted flowers were members of a blooming riot of color. Even the rose bushes were developing buds, preparing for their share of glory come June.

The Everett Saloon was no more. Jim Berry bought the place and christened it "Berry Brothers," although there was no evidence of a brother in sight. Jim had been born and raised in Stone County, and traveled frequently, selling goods from Taney County and returning with goods for the store attached to the saloon. His wife ran the hotel across Benton Street. Berry had tidily snapped up the corners as they became available for sale, and rumor had it he was looking for someone to run the diner on west, down Jefferson Street. The Bald Knobbers, who did not know of Jim's long-ago familial relation to the Miles and Barker families, harassed Berry about joining the group, but treated it as a joke. Jim did not take it as such; Knobbers still met in his saloon and the profits were quite high. He held them off, saying he traveled too much to want to spend more nights away from his wife. This, said with an elbow in the side and a sly wink, kept the Knobbers from getting too rowdy in his businesses.

When the Everetts owned the saloon, a certain level of society and intelligence had been the mien of a majority of the customers. Now that Jim Berry owned the place, the joke was he let just anyone in, as long as they paid cash. Even Bald Knobbers who had to steal their drinking money.

The entire county was tense. The Haworths and Moores, along with their associates, continued to meet and practice military maneuvers. Fistfights broke out in town, and no one could lay a finger on who started them. Guns were fired, but there was no gossip of anyone's death. Just the riders of the night, making their presence known by patrolling the county roads. Alonzo Prather's newspaper only reported meeting times for the Bald Knobbers; James DeLong was still the editor.

Billy Miles moved into Forsyth in late March, taking a job with room and board at the hotel run by the Berry couple. He was a quick study, learning to run the desk efficiently and competently. It was not advertised fact that he had broken with his family--such tragedy was a disgrace only hinted at in whispered conversations at church and in the town. It was well-known that Kate Miles was a formidably wonderful mother; other mothers dubiously looked at their nearly-grown sons, wondering what horrible event had occurred to cause Billy to leave his family home before he married. They certainly never asked their husbands; thus, the men of the area were slow to learn Billy was living at the hotel.

His quarters were in the basement, a damp place fortified with rock walls and obstructionist in nature. His shins were bruised from running into boxes and furniture tossed down the stairs by earlier management; it seemed as if they were moved around nightly while he worked. The nights were long, but he usually read between guest calls. He slept during the day despite the racket of life in town. No one saw him, save the guests. He seldom left the building, never appeared in the town's saloons, and was in and out of the Berry store as soon as his shift ended in the mornings.

On April 7, an early Wednesday evening, Wash Middleton was sitting outside the Berry Brothers Saloon, keeping an eye on people as they went about their business. He was carving a toy for one of his sons, and Jim Berry had told him to keep the shavings outside. Jim Berry had few rules, but his patrons followed them, for fear of more restrictions. One rule was no wood shavings inside; Jim hated sweeping the mess up.

Three horses in martial step meant something to a former soldier, and Wash's ears picked them up immediately. He watched as a small, trim man with erect posture dismounted in front of the Berry Hotel. The two men with him were in soldier's uniforms.

Wash stood to watch the men enter the hotel, absently brushing the shavings off with his free hand. He was not a slow man, but he operated mostly on instinct. He walked into the building, searching out Nat Kinney, who was sitting at his customary table in the far corner, his back to the wall so he could see the door. Galba Branson and Bill Hensley were with him.

"Hey, Wash, you get you a broom and sweep that up," Berry called from the counter where he was washing glasses, stacking them carefully to dry.

Middleton ignored the command, carefully avoiding the pool players as he made his way through to Kinney. He stood, almost at attention, while waiting for Nat to acknowledge him.

Nat had seen Wash walk in. Careful and deliberate in his actions, he waited until Wash was about ten feet from him before raising his glass to sip at the beer, keeping his eyes averted. It was a power trick he had learned from Maggie in the early years of their marriage, and now almost instinctive in him.

He counted to five after setting his mug down, then looked at Wash. Wash did not squirm, but there were those who did.

"Wash?"

"Soldiers outside, Capt'n." Galba and Bill turned their attention to Wash.

Nat's head bobbed slightly while he considered. "How many?"

"Three. Two in uniform."

"Really. Hmmm." Thinking through the information, the corners of Nat's lips turned up in a small smile. He turned to Gabe and Bill.

"It must be the governor's investigator. What do you think, Bill?"

Bill shrugged. "He sed the man's name was Jamison." Hensley thought about it for a few more seconds, then added, "Don't know as I'd want him to investigate too far."

Nat's eyes narrowed at Bill. "The governor obviously doesn't believe all of the stories, Bill."

"Then why send anyone?" Gabe asked.

"Judge Reynolds and most of the others in the so-called home guard are Democrats, Gabe." Nat pushed his chair back, and stood. "They are voters, so the governor has to do something." He paused. "It is really rather insulting to them, to send only one person with a two-man detail." Nat chuckled, and the others joined in. "Shall we welcome him?"

The four, led by Wash, made their way through the saloon to the counter, where Nat, in good humor, paid the bill. He started to leave, then paused to look at Jim Berry.

"Jim, a bottle of brandy, if you will," Nat said. "Not the stuff you serve in here."

Jim Berry raised an eyebrow. "I don't serve horsepiss in any form, Mr. Kinney." He walked through the pass-through, carrying a broom and handing it to Wash. "Shavings, Mr. Middleton."

Nat put a hand out. "I'll buy what you keep in the back, and add a quarter if you won't detain Mr. Middleton, Jim."

Berry's other eyebrow raised, then he turned and made his way back behind the counter. "All right, Mr. Kinney." He disappeared into the store, and within a few moments, returned with a small bottle. "This is what my wife likes," he told Kinney. "Expensive stuff."

"I'm sure you have more tucked away somewhere, Jim," Nat returned smoothly. "Would you bag it, please?"

The transaction completed, with a quarter added so Jim Berry would sweep his own saloon floor, the four men left. Wash once more led the way, across Benton and onto the porch of the hotel.

Turning to halt Nat, Bill, and Gabe, Wash said, "Jist a minnit. Lemme look first." He opened the door, stuck his head in, and quickly withdrew, shutting the door behind him.

"Capt'n, Billy Miles is in there," Wash told his companions.

Bill frowned. "Wonder why? Is he a guest, do you think?"

Nat's interest was piqued. After witnessing the conversation between Sam Snapp and Billy Miles in Kintrea's store the previous month, he'd wondered what Billy planned to do.

"Naw, he's in a suit," Wash answered. "Must be working."

"Interesting," Nat said. "I wonder how long he's been in town."

Gabe's face was rueful. "I guess I knew. Betsy said something about him leaving home a couple weeks ago." The other three looked at him, and he shrugged. "Women's gossip. I don't pay a lot of attention to it."

Nat pushed his hat back off his forehead, rubbing it in irritation. "Gabe, that's information I would like to have known." He pulled his hat back down, aggravated at Gabe. "This is what we've been talking about, keeping an idea of where the opposition is at all times." His face brightened. "Well, it'll be easier to keep an eye on young Mr. Miles if he's working here." Moving past Wash, Nat opened the door and went into the hotel's lobby. Wash scurried to get back in front of him.

The bell over the door had tinkled, and Billy was waiting for them with a small, tight smile on his face. He was dressed in a suit, and his hair and face were carefully barbered.

"Good day, sirs. May I help you?" he said politely.

"Well, this is a surprise," Nat smiled good-naturedly at Billy. "I thought you were a farmer."

The smile left Billy's face. "I am."

Nat raised his eyebrows, gestured widely with his hands, looking around the small room. "This doesn't look like a farm to me." The other three laughed, but Billy and Nat stared at each other. Billy was the first to break the stare, a slight flush on his face. "I'm waiting," Nat added.

A trace of bitterness, then Billy raised his chin in a manner that, had Nat but known it, was an exact duplicate of Kate Miles' motion when she was determined to get her way.

"Well, Mr. Kinney, I don't know that it's any business of yours," Billy said.

The three men with Kinney all stiffened, but Nat merely stood motionless. His eyes pierced the younger man. "Come now," Nat said. "I'm merely interested."

Reluctant, Billy's chin went down a fraction of an inch. His eyelids lowered, breaking the stare between himself and Nat. "I want to buy a farm."

"Ah," Nat nodded encouragingly. "But I understood you work for Sam Snapp, on both of his places. Am I wrong?"

"No, sir," Billy's voice and head lowered. He looked up at Kinney's face from beneath his brow. "I did until this spring."

"What happened?" Nat's voice was creamy with encouragement.

"Mr. Snapp ain't gonna to run the farm out by Pa's this year," Billy finally answered. He raised his head, hair slick with Makassar and parted neatly. "He wanted me to help him some in Kirbyville, but I don't want no part in the trouble he's having."

"I see," said Nat. "Are you going to buy his place?"

"Don't know as I can talk him into it," Billy replied. "I'm gonna try."

Nat continued to nod while the others looked on. He glanced at his men, and remembered his reason for coming to the hotel. Time to change the subject.

"You had guests arrive in the past few minutes."

Billy nodded. "Yes, sir."

"Who is it?"

Absolution | 401

A slight shrug. "Men from Jefferson City." Billy indicated the guest register.

Gabe took two steps forward, and read the name aloud. "Adjutant General James C. Jamison."

"Thet's him," Bill Hensley said.

Nat lifted the bottle in his hand. "We would like to welcome Mr. Jamison to our fair city," he told Billy.

Billy nodded. "I'll see if he's available to you." He walked around the counter and went up the stairs, disappearing from view. The men in the lobby heard a knock, and a door opening. Billy's voice was indistinct in its query; the answer was inaudible. The door shut, then Billy returned down the stairs. On the bottom step, he stopped and looked at Nat.

"Mr. Jamison sed he's not ready to receive visitors at this time."

Nat was insulted. Being snubbed in front of his men wasn't something he liked. "Did you tell him who I am, Billy?" he asked.

"Yes, sir. He knows you, or at least of you."

"He recognized my name."

"Yes, sir. Said he would send a message tomorrow to set up a time and place for a meeting."

"Is that so?" Nat rubbed his chin. "Well, I hope I'm available for this Jamison's meeting. I am a busy man."

"Yes, sir." Billy walked around the group, returning to his place behind the counter.

Thoughtful, Nat looked at Gabe. "You'll stay here in the lobby until he sends out the message. Then bring it to me at home."

Gabe nodded, "Yes, Captain," and walked over to the velvet chairs by the windows, choosing one that gave him a view of the stairs.

Nat turned to Wash and Bill. "Let's go." Then, remembering the bottle in his hand, he turned back to Billy. "Take this to Mr. Jamison with my regard."

Billy took the bottle, and once more walked upstairs. Another knock, the door opened, and again, Billy's voice was indistinct. After the door closed, he returned to the lobby, walking past the others and returning to his position.

"Well?" Nat asked.

Billy shrugged. "He said to thank you, and took it."

Smiling, Nat turned to Wash and Bill. "Now, we can go."

The sun was merely hinting at rising when Billy Miles approached Galba Branson in the lobby of the hotel.

"Mr. Branson?"

Galba had been asleep for several hours, snoring loudly on occasion, restless in the confines of the parlor chair. His neck and back were so stiff that it took him several moments after opening his eyes to focus on Billy.

"Yes?" He wiped the sleep from his eyes. "Any word?"

Billy handed Gabe a folded and sealed piece of paper, along with the unopened bottle of brandy. "Mr. Jamison has told me the meeting is scheduled for ten this morning in the room over the Berry Brothers store."

Gabe sat straight up, looking at the missive and bottle in his hands.

"And Mr. Branson?"

Not quite awake, Gabe gazed up at Billy, who appeared tired but otherwise unchanged from the previous evening. "Yeah, Billy?"

"Mr. Jamison has requested that I pass on the information that the Slickers will be present as well."

Billy backed up a step or two as Gabe urgently rose from the chair. He watched Gabe gather his thoughts, tuck the paper in the chest pocket of his coat, set the bottle of brandy on the table, and put his hat on. Gabe made as to leave, but Billy halted him.

"Sir? The brandy?"

Gabe turned to look at Nat's welcoming gift to the governor's investigator. The bottle gleamed in the light from sconces by the door. He shook his head.

"Reckon Mr. Kinney might want that back," Billy said, obviously attempting to be helpful.

Gabe's mouth quirked under his mustache; he reluctantly picked up the bottle.

"No, I don't reckon he will," Gabe replied. "But I'll take it to him." He sighed.

"Sir..." Billy began.

"I know. I have to--"

"Yes, sir."

As soon as the morning desk clerk appeared, Billy tiredly went downstairs to his room. The sun was coming up, and he was hungry, too.

On his bed was a basket of food from his mother. He took his suit off, hanging it neatly on the pegs in the wall, and removed his tie, shirt collar, and cuffs. These, too, were put neatly away. Last was his shirt, and he stood in his underwear, absently scratching himself while he perused the basket.

Emanuel had left the basket on his bed last night, waiting for the message from Jamison that would need delivering to the Anti-Bald Knobbers. He left shortly after midnight.

Billy unwrapped one of Kate's sandwiches, and put the basket on the floor. He pulled the crumpled blanket down--Manny must have taken a nap--and tossed the pillow up against the wall for comfort. Making himself comfortable while he chewed, he reached for the copy of a Charles Dickens novel he had been reading.

Damn. Billy's mouth curdled at the unspoken word, but Manny had lost his bookmarker. He took another bite of his sandwich, and began searching for the last page he remembered reading.

While searching, the image of Gabe Branson's face came to him. The man had not wanted to return the bottle of brandy to Kinney.

Luckily for Billy Miles, a jar of Emanuel's moonshine had been in a basket of food Kate sent last week. Mr. Jamison must be a bit Scottish, Billy thought, but he had not been sure, when he offered the man a choice between Kinney's brandy and the jar of moonshine in his room.

Ah. There. He popped the last of the sandwich in his mouth, and settled further down in his bed, reading.

It was a few minutes past ten when Nat Kinney, Bill Hensley, Galba Branson, Wash Middleton, John Haggard, and assorted other Bald Knobbers rode into the square at Forsyth. They tied their horses on rails in front of the courthouse, since it was evident the Anti-Bald Knobbers had taken possession of the rails near the Berry Store and the hardware store.

Cursing, Kinney dismounted and strode across Jefferson, trailed by Hensley, Branson, Haggard and Middleton. The rest remained in

404 | Vonda Wilson Sheets

the square, obviously armed but strangely quiet.

Taking the stairs two at a time, Nat slowed as the door opened at the hands of a young man in uniform. He took a deep breath, then walked in.

His men flanked him as he walked toward a short, trim man with erect posture. Pointedly ignoring the Slickers seated on the right side of the long table, Nat proffered his hand to shake with Jamison.

Jamison had turned when Kinney and his men entered the room, his hands clasped behind his back. Now he glanced down at Nat's hand, and said, "Yes. You are Nathaniel N. Kinney, are you not?"

Nonplussed, Nat pulled his hand back. "Yes, I'm Nathaniel Kinney."

"You are late," Jamison snapped.

"Yes--"

"Be seated, please." Jamison indicated the empty left side of the table, away from the door. Nat waited until his lieutenants walked around and pulled the chairs out, then joined them in sitting down.

One folder lay on the long table, at the head where Jamison stood. He reached down and touched it with a finger, aligning it with the edge of the table.

"I am sure you know why you have been called to this meeting," he began. He watched the men seated in front of him, meeting each pair of eyes with a steely gaze of his own.

To his right sat William E. Moore, Jurd Haworth, John Haworth, and Judge John Reynolds of the Slicker faction. To his left were Kinney's men. He met Nat Kinney's eyes last before continuing.

"Governor Marmaduke has sent me to investigate the continuing claims of warfare on the citizens of Taney County."

"Warfare? Isn't that a bit extreme?" Nat asked. He was looking for a way to grab control of the conversation.

"I said they were claims, Mr. Kinney. I've not said they were true." He paused briefly. "As Judge Reynolds has pointed out, there is a militia, a home guard, if you will, that has been formed in reaction to land-grabbing, house fires, and other acts of violence perpetuated by men who are yet unknown."

Nat interrupted with, "Which is why the Citizens League for Law and Order has taken action."

Jamison eyed Kinney again. "Yes." He tapped the folder in front of him. "Mr. Kinney, these claims state you and your men are the

Absolution | 405

perpetrators. You are named, sir! As is your 'Citizens League'!"

"MY men?" Kinney appeared surprised. "We work together," he gestured in the direction of the men seated to his left, "to help the sheriff and his deputies enforce the law. I am no leader of men."

There were snorts of derision from the Slickers. Jamison turned a gimlet eye toward them, and the noises subsided.

"So far as I see it, and the governor will agree, there are two unlawful organizations represented in this room. Unless either of you can produce a charter and registration with the state?"

None of the men in front of Jamison moved.

"No? Hmm. I didn't think so." He remained standing, but shifted his stance to better focus on the Slickers, his back to Nat Kinney.

"Sirs, you will disband your home guard. No more drills, no more patrols." He waited as if expecting an outburst, but there was none. Alonzo Prather had warned them what to expect.

Continuing, Jamison then pivoted to face Nat.

"And you, sir. You will disband your 'Citizens League,' also known as the Bald Knobbers. No more public meetings, no more notices in the local paper, no more bonfires, no more night patrols by any man in any district of this county. You both have twenty-four hours to disband. You are dismissed."

The outcry came from the Bald Knobber side as the Slickers rose to leave. Nat spread his left arm wide, halting and quieting his men until the Slickers were gone. Then he rose, feeling that being seated left him at a disadvantage to the shorter man in front of him.

Jamison appeared to be expecting this. He merely raised his chin, peering at Kinney over his glasses. "You, sir, are wasting your time."

Nat beamed down at Jamison, then said, "But I have no organization to disband, Mr. Jamison."

Jamison's neck stiffened, and his spine straightened in a manner that made him appear quite a bit taller than he really was. He stood his ground, retaining the dignity inherent to his nature that Nat Kinney had struggled all his life to achieve.

"Oh?" Jamison's voice was mild, but the men present saw through it. "The league was organized, but cannot be un-organized? Mr. Kinney, find someone else to play your fool. Please. I know better." He turned to pick up the manila folder, but halted as he felt Nat's anger rising.

406 | Vonda Wilson Sheets

"All right, but mark my words. The sheriff will continue to need our help."

Jamison allowed faint amusement to show with a small smile. "Really, Mr. Kinney? I believe it was a William Hensley," and Bill was startled to hear his name, "who told the governor your sheriff is a capable officer of the law. An elected sheriff, voted into office by the people." As if in afterthought, he added, "You, sir, are not."

"No! I'm not!" Nat's temper was lost, and he kicked the chair behind him. Then he turned and pointed at his men. "You! Get out!"

Wash had been seated by Nat. He stopped to pick the broken chair up, and the others followed him out. Nat refused to speak more until the door was closed by one of Jamison's escorts. Once alone with Jamison, Nat slumped and sat on the edge of the table.

"I have run for office, Mr. Jamison. The people did not elect me. However, they do appear to believe I am having some effect on the lawlessness in this county. Something had to be done."

Jamison cleared his throat. "Mr. Kinney, your organization seems to have begun with the honorable intentions of a few good men. Many of those men are no longer living in this county, is that correct?"

Nat rubbed his face, a combination of emotions conflicting with the anger he still felt. Then he eyed Jamison, whose face was now at a level with his own, and his hands fell in shock. "You know that. You've been in town less than twenty-four hours, and you know. How is that?"

"I have ways of finding correct information when I need it. It is not the point at this time. Governor Marmaduke wants you to put a stop to Bald Knobber activity immediately. You will cease and desist."

Nat stood and paced a few steps. He was just beginning to fully enjoy his power, and to have it stripped from him by this man was galling. He stopped at the second-floor window, looking east.

"And if I don't?" He did not face Jamison. He wasn't sure he wanted to hear the answer.

"A state militia will be here within two days to lock down the county. Any unrest while they are here will be punished. You, sir, will be charged with obstruction of justice, arrested and incarcerated to await trial in Jefferson City. You will also be charged with any

Absolution | 407

other crime committed after this meeting, and a full investigation into the death of Andrew Coggburn will commence. A full audit of the county's records will also take place, complete with interviews of any and all parties involved in any land transactions."

Jamison paused to let his words sink in, and began walking toward Nat. "The state penitentiary is not a pleasant place, Mr. Kinney. I understand you have a nice farm, a home with a lovely wife. Quite a difference."

Again, Jamison paused. Nat still did not turn to face him.

"Do I have your word, Nathaniel Kinney? You will cease and desist from all activities related to the Bald Knobbers?"

Nat finally turned. Jamison's hand was out. Nat slowly reached for it, and shook it twice. He attempted to let go, but Jamison held him.

"Your goals have been accomplished, Mr. Kinney. I suggest you return to your farm, your wife, and your preaching. Your word, sir?"

Nat nodded, and Jamison's grip loosened. He turned, but Nat's voice stopped him.

"Twenty-four hours is not enough time. Will you give me forty-eight?"

Jamison considered the reasonable request. "I will do that. But I expect full disbandment."

Nat was nodding thoughtfully. "Yes."

Jamison walked over, picked up his folder, and proceeded to the door. As it was opened by one of his detail, he turned and told Nat, "I will await your message of disbandment at the hotel. Good day, sir."

Nat was left alone. He marched to the table, picked up another chair, and hurled it at the door, where the hateful Jamison had so recently been standing. It broke as the door opened once more, showing Wash and Bill entering the room. John and Galba stood anxiously on the landing outside.

All of them appeared unnerved. Nat, impatient, said, "Put the word out. A meeting on Big Bald tonight. I want all districts to report." He smiled at Gabe as he walked to the door. "Gabe, you come with me. We have a bonfire to build."

Stopping at the landing before descending the exterior stairs, Nat watched Jamison and his escort enter the hotel where Billy Miles worked. He remembered the bottle of brandy Jamison had rejected, and felt anger surging through him again. "I wonder if you'll like my message, Mr. Jamison."

გა ლე

James Carson Jamison was in the fifty-fifth year of a very adventurous life. Beginning with the California Gold Rush in 1849, then fighting in Nicaragua, he built a reputation on going into chaos and subduing it into some semblance of order. He had been a Confederate soldier, and spent part of the war in a Union prison. It was this that caused Governor Marmaduke to send him to Taney County. His ability to gather information and use that information to create order was second to none.

About mid-morning on Friday, there was a knock on the door to his room. The day clerk told him that William Moore and John Haworth were waiting in the lobby to speak with him. Jamison asked if he could use the side parlor to meet with Moore and Haworth, and the clerk agreed.

The Slicker faction was outraged, Moore and Haworth reported. Nathaniel Kinney had held a meeting, complete with a bonfire. Jamison was not surprised.

"He has one more day to disband the Bald Knobbers," he told Moore and Haworth. "He asked for that, and I saw no harm in it."

"Sir, we have done as you asked us. We've told our men there will be no more meetings. We gave them our word that you have the situation in hand." Will Moore was furious. "If Kinney is allowed to continue, we'll have no choice but to carry on!"

"Mr. Moore, if you and your relatives continue to practice drills and patrol, I will have no choice but to declare martial law," said Jamison sternly. "Nat Kinney gave me his word that there will be no more threats of harm to the citizens of this county."

"You believed him," John Haworth's temper also was high.

"Gentlemen, as I told Mr. Kinney, if there is any reason for me to suspect he has broken his word, there will be repercussions."

Moore and Haworth looked at each other. Biting his upper lip, Will Moore turned back toward Jamison. "What would those repercussions be?"

"There are several, but one would be a full investigation into the death of Andrew Coggburn."

Moore and Haworth nodded slightly, absorbing this information. Then Moore asked, "What else?"

"I will bring a team of investigators to trace all land records and question all parties involved in any transactions over the past five years. If they must, they will visit every home in Taney County to ask questions."

"What about the people who have already gone?" Haworth wanted to know, thinking about the families who had gone west, including the Coggburns.

"We'll track them down as well," Jamison's reply was smooth. "Since your courthouse has burned once more, it will take years. The county will remain under the control of the state militia during that time. There would be no elections for public office, a curfew, and even more restrictions."

Both men's eyebrows raised.

"That's going too far," Haworth said.

"Yes, well," Jamison paused to let them think for a few seconds. "Governor Marmaduke wants the citizens to feel safe in their homes, which is a Constitutional right. He will take any action he must in order to make Taney County a safe place to live." Turning and walking toward the closed door, Jamison halted before opening it. His back to Haworth and Moore, he added, "Gentlemen, thank you for following orders. Mr. Kinney has twenty-four more hours to do so. Good day." And he left.

CHAPTER 41
Saturday, April 10, 1886 - Disbandment

The evening held an almost festive air, quite different from the day's dawning. Alonzo Prather had just returned from walking around the courthouse square in Forsyth, enjoying the almost-balmy spring evening and a few drinks at the Berry Brothers Saloon before settling in his bachelor quarters for the night.

He left the door open while lighting a candle lamp and setting it on the table. He wished Ada Marie and the children were here to share in his exuberant mood. The next best thing would be writing them, he supposed, taking off his rings and flexing his fingers.

Although he and Ada Marie would discuss today's events face-to-face, he felt an urgent need to write her now. The candle flickered in the slight movement of the air through the door. He sat at the table, watching the flame and feeling as he was a part of it.

Taking his pen up, he dipped it in the open inkwell, and began to write.

"My Dearest Wife…"

He wanted to remember everything.

Alonzo had not been present at Jamison's meetings with the Bald Knobbers and Anti-Bald Knobbers. While he knew of Jamison by reputation, and had corresponded with him since Judge Reynolds delivered his letter to Governor Marmaduke, Alonzo had not actually met the man. And now Jamison was gone, his mission for the governor accomplished.

Slight noises last night, long before the sun came up, had awakened Alonzo. Getting out of bed, he'd stubbed his toe against the table in the darkness, and limped through the passage into his office. His eyes could not make out any one person in front of the burned remains of the courthouse, but it was evident there were several men out there. No one disturbed them.

He had some idea of who they were, however. And now, as he wrote Ada Marie, he once again felt the thrill of the past two days.

"Nat Kinney came to my office on Friday, to seek my advice…"

Forsyth being a small town, Nat had been forced to acknowledge Alonzo's presence on more than one occasion since their argument last year. On his part, Alonzo remained polite, but had no wish to resume his friendship with Nat.

"He wanted my professional help in writing a speech to his men..."

Alonzo had accepted Nat's request, and the two men spent an hour or so writing it. Being in a foul mood when he arrived, Nat's temper was touchy as Alonzo tried to diplomatically write a speech. The trick was to make it appear Nat had chosen to disband the organization because it was no longer needed, not because of any wrongdoing on anyone's part.

"I believe I accomplished this task..." Nat's mood had lightened considerably as Alonzo ruminated and made notes. He had even laughed once or twice as Alonzo finally wrote the speech and read it aloud.

"Yes, yes, I knew you could do it," Nat Kinney told his former friend. His eyes twinkled as he waved the sheet of paper about, letting the ink dry before folding it and putting it in his shirt pocket. "What do I owe you for this?"

Alonzo put him off. "Not a thing." He lifted his chin, and scrutinized Nat's face before continuing. "It will be enough to bring my family home."

Nat appeared wounded. "Alonzo, your family was never in any danger. Surely you didn't think--"

"I didn't know what to think, Nat. You changed what had been agreed upon by thirteen gentlemen, and it was not a change for the better," Alonzo's voice was sharp.

"Did I hunt you down? Did I make you afraid?"

"If you were not going to follow the rules we had set forth in the agreement in regards to aiding the sheriff, how was I to know what other rules or laws you were going to break?"

Nat was nodding, his eyes thoughtful. "Yes....yes, I can see why you would feel that way." He lifted his shoulders in a sigh. "But it's all over now."

Alonzo indicated the paper in Nat's pocket. "If you follow that, it will be."

"I intend to. The Bald Knobbers will not meet again." Nat put his hat on, and turned to leave. "I believe you should bring your family home, Alonzo," he said, his hand on the doorknob. "I promise that your family--nor you yourself--are in no danger from my hands." He turned back to look Alonzo in the eye. "I would like to call you 'friend' again."

Alonzo made a small snort, but gave Nat a small, brief smile. "We shall see, Nat."

Nat nodded once more. "Good day," and left.

Staring at the flame once more, Alonzo straightened his back and stretched. He had until tomorrow night to finish the letter, since the mail would not be posted until Monday. He set the first page of it aside to dry, and laid a fresh piece of paper down.

"The noises I heard during the last night proved to be Bald Knobbers…"

It had been a misty sunrise, fog rolling off the creek and the river, wandering purple, pink and orange around the treetops. The birds were singing and playing hide-and-seek as they flew about, seeking nesting materials and food.

There was no hiding the large pile of wood and brush laying in what had been the lawn of the courthouse, directly across from the hotel Jamison was supposedly sleeping in.

Alonzo regarded it soberly as he took a cup of coffee through the office and went to sit on the bench in front of the building. James DeLong and Paul Kinney were standing in front of the newspaper office next door, also looking at the preparations for a bonfire. None of the businesses were yet open, and there were only a few men about. No one went close to the wood.

While he sipped his coffee, he wondered if James would approach him. It had been difficult to refrain from firing James over the past year, but Alonzo had not done so, nor had he seriously considered shutting the newspaper down. Men were entering the diner for breakfast when he stood, going to fill his coffee cup once more.

James DeLong, Nat Kinney's stepson and a Bald Knobber, was waiting for him when he returned to his bench.

"Good morning, Mr. Prather," James was hesitant.

"Good morning, Mr. DeLong," Alonzo returned the greeting. Paul joined them, handing his half-brother a mug of coffee. "Paul."

"Sir," Paul returned the acknowledgement.

Alonzo returned James' gaze, waiting for whatever was coming next. James wasn't hesitant by nature, so it wasn't long before he spoke.

"I would like to tender my resignation as the editor of your newspaper," James had the look of a man whose mind was made up.

Affecting mild surprise with raised eyebrows, Alonzo merely asked, "Why?"

"I do not have to answer that."

It was times like these that Alonzo wished he smoked or chewed tobacco. Instead, he sighed and scratched the back of his head. "True." He took a deep breath, and said, "Very well. I refuse to accept your resignation."

"What?" Both of the young men were incredulous, Paul looking at James, who was staring down at the seated Alonzo. "Why not?"

Alonzo shrugged. "I do not have to answer that."

"But sir--" Paul took a step forward, only to run into James' hand, halting him.

"Mr. Prather, I do not understand," James told his boss, once Paul was still.

Alonzo smiled, his manner mild. He quite liked James DeLong and Paul Kinney, but he would remain professional for the moment.

"James. If you are resigning because of that--" and Alonzo tilted his head and gazed over at the wood pile across the street, "it's rather late, don't you think?"

"I do not understand."

"Let me ask you this--did I try to stay your hand when you published meeting notices about the Bald Knobbers?"

"No, sir."

"Did I say, 'James, you must publish all letters to the editor you receive?' or 'James, you're fired!' once in the past year?"

James eyed Alonzo, his head tilted and his eyes filled with trepidation. He had shown an obvious bias in favor of the Bald Knobbers in the paper. "No, sir. Not once." His head tilted the other way, still eying Alonzo. "Why didn't you?"

Alonzo shrugged. "Did you ride with your stepfather often this past year?"

James shook his head. "No, we only visited the farm to see Mother a few times."

"So you can say you did not participate in the activities of the Bald Knobbers, correct?"

Silence.

"Alright, you can say that you may have participated in some of the activities, correct?"

414 | Vonda Wilson Sheets

Silence. Paul was watching both of them, his face puzzled.

"James, do you have another job offer?"

"No, sir." James finally spoke.

"Do you wish to farm?"

His face wry, James answered Alonzo with an almost forceful "No, sir."

Alonzo took a drink of his coffee, and smiled up at the young man. "Let us be clear. You do not have another job and you have no wish to farm. You took sides with your stepfather in the past year, appearing to approve of actions you know to be wrong. And you censored my newspaper, correct?"

Chagrined, James nodded. "I did. Which is why--"

Interrupting, Alonzo spoke tersely. "Young man, you made a mistake many newspaper reporters and editors make. You chose sides. It happened to be the wrong one. Own up to it, and don't censor my newspaper in the future."

James appeared to have been slapped and relieved at the same time. "But sir--"

Drinking the rest of his coffee, Alonzo rose from his seat and moved to the door of his office. "James, you're a smart young man. Too smart to waste my time and your intelligence. I don't have time to run the paper, nor find someone else to do it. I would prefer that you do your job, thus allowing me to do mine." He raised an eyebrow at the brothers. "Am I clear?"

James nodded, swallowed. "Yes, sir."

Alonzo nodded back. "You will be fair in the future, or I will fire you. Understood?"

"Yes, sir. Thank you, sir."

Finally, Alonzo smiled. "No thanks necessary. Just don't take sides in the future. That's not your job as a reporter, nor editor. Now…" he nodded toward the pile of wood across the way. "I believe you may have a story to write shortly."

James nodded, and took a deep breath. "So it appears." He reached a hand out, to shake Alonzo's hand. While doing so, he added, "Now I know why my sister speaks so highly of you and your son."

"Eva? How is she?"

"She'll be home in a couple of weeks, I think."

"…so I will not have to find someone to run the newspaper."

Alonzo yawned, and stretched. He pushed his glasses up on his forehead, and rubbed the bridge of his nose. Despite his outward assurance on the matter, he was uncertain James DeLong would be able to refrain from censoring the paper. Sitting back in his chair and easing his tired back and shoulders, he kicked off his shoes and flexed his feet and leg muscles. There was a hole in his sock, he saw. He shook his head, anticipating Ada Marie's reaction when she saw the state of his room and wardrobe. His smile grew broader. Ah, it would be good to have her and the children home.

The flame in the candle flickered in warning, and Alonzo hastily rose to find another before this one went out. The candle box on the shelf over the door into the office was nearly empty. He turned to light the new candle, setting it in a second holder, then bent to blow the first one out. Sitting down, Alonzo waited a few seconds for the wax of the spent candle to cool, then began peeling it and working it into a small ball. It was good exercise for his hands.

Engaged in this homely business physically, his thoughts returned to the pile of wood in front of the remains of the courthouse. Once the wax hardened, he tossed it in the direction of the unlit wood stove, dropped his glasses back down on his nose, and began writing again.

Saturdays were the days many farmers came to town, often bringing their wives and children. Alonzo was drinking from his second pot of coffee by the time wagons began rolling through the square, avoiding the area around the pile of wood. It was nearly 7:30, and he noticed there were few families present. The lack of women's voices and children's excited squeals made it seem ominously quiet in Forsyth, for a Saturday morning.

The adjutant general had given Nat Kinney exactly forty-eight hours to disband his group, and Alonzo knew Nat's sense of theatrics was orchestrating the disbandment down to the last possible minute. He went inside to retrieve his coat and hat. Breakfast at the diner seemed to be a good idea.

Even the diner was less busy than usual. The regular Saturday morning crowd was conspicuously absent, and the woman who took his order of ham and eggs didn't pause for chitchat. Alonzo watched as Billy Miles came in to pick up orders for the guests in the hotel, and wondered if Jamison's breakfast was included in the box of covered plates.

"Working late this morning?" the waitress asked as she handed the box to Billy.

"Couldn't get to sleep," Billy answered. "Too much going on."

"Huh. Yeah," the woman replied. "Whatever Kinney's planning to do, it's shore puttin' a damper on business."

Alonzo saw Billy shrug as he settled the box on his hip and signed for the bill. "It might pick up later," the young man said.

"Hope so," the woman replied. "Them old men don't leave tips worth a shit in the mornings. Want their coffee on the double, though."

Billy smiled, commiserating. Then he left, taking hot breakfast to guests in the hotel.

Although he dawdled as long as he could, Alonzo still managed to finish his breakfast too soon. He found that he was caught up in the town's sense of dread and anticipation, even though he knew what was going to happen.

Back at his office, he tried to work on an upcoming case. After losing his place on one page of a law book the third time, he slammed the book shut. "Damn."

It was a little after nine.

Again donning his coat and hat, Alonzo left the office and walked around the town square. No one remained outside for long, except a few men, who, like himself, were too restless to stay inside. He saw William Miles standing in front of the hardware store, his wife next to him.

"Good morning, Mr. Miles," Alonzo greeted William, and tipped his hat to Kate, "Ma'am."

"Good morning, Mr. Prather," Kate responded. William merely grunted a greeting, nodding back at Alonzo, and tilting his head toward the wood pile.

"Gonna be a show, I hear," William said.

Alonzo nodded. "Let us hope it isn't a farce," he told William and Kate. "I see your son is working at the Berry hotel."

Snorting, William said, "Boy's born to be a farmer." Her face sad, Kate laid a hand on her husband's arm, a motion that made Alonzo ache for his own wife.

"We have to let him make his way," Kate Miles told her husband. "If he thinks this is the way--"

Absolution | 417

Another snort, then William straightened, glancing around Alonzo at the hotel's balcony over the veranda. "Reckon it's about to begin," he said in a low voice.

Alonzo turned to see Jamison standing on the balcony, accompanied by his detail, standing at attention. He pulled his watch from his pocket and checked the time. It was 9:45. He moved to the right of William and Kate.

William stepped off the porch casually, then turned to step back up. "Horses," he said briefly, as he returned to stand between Alonzo and Kate.

Within seconds, the sound of many sets of hooves was rolling down Jefferson Street, and people began coming out of businesses and their homes to watch Nat Kinney ride in from the east, accompanied by hundreds of men. Many in the first rows were carrying torches, although the sun was climbing and the skies were clear. All except for Nat Kinney were masked or hooded. If Nat Kinney had not stood out from the crowd behind him by reason of his horse, the glint of red hair from his hatless head would have marked him as easily as a deer.

Some of the citizens cheered as the men rode by. Others stood silent, then followed the men to the square.

As if it had been rehearsed so often it was routine, Nat rode to the front of the hotel, pulling Grey Ghost to a halt beneath the balcony from which Jamison was watching. His riders formed in patterns of half-circles, leaving immediately bare the area around the wood pile in the courthouse lawn.

Nat waited for silence to creep in among his men before he spoke. When he was assured of having the attention of every person in the square, he began.

"Only a few short months ago, the citizens of this county came together for a noble purpose. Since then, we have dealt quickly and effectively with border ruffians and roving gangs of thieves and outlaws. We have helped the courts obtain convictions. Above all, we have responded every time a law officer needed help. We have brought law and order to our community. Peace and quiet reign supreme!"

Nat then rode through his men to the woodpile. Pulling a bottle from his saddlebag, he proceeded to dump most of the contents on the wood, then nodded at those carrying torches. The dozen or so men approached the wood, and tossed their torches onto it. Within seconds, the wood began burning. Nat waited until it was well and truly caught afire, rode back to the steps of the hotel, then pulled a piece of paper from his shirt pocket. Reading aloud, his voice rose to be heard over the flames.

"Therefore, be it resolved that the League for Law and Order will be disbanded. That, as law-abiding citizens, we believe the civil authorities and the courts can and will guarantee protection to life, liberty, and property. That those arrested for those crimes will receive a fair and impartial trial by a jury of their peers. And that we extend to our honored governor and adjutant general our sincere thanks for the interest they have manifested in this county. Gentlemen! Throw down your masks! You are dismissed!"

Some voices could be heard as the original torchbearers then rode back to the fire, taking off their bandanas and masks and throwing them into it. Others began following suit, and the members of the Bald Knobbers stood bare-faced before the public.

"You are dismissed!" Nat's voice rang out.

Alonzo nearly clapped. He was smiling and shaking his head at Nat's sense of drama when he realized that William and Kate were not watching Nat. Instead, he followed their gaze to their son, who was watching Nat Kinney closely from the hotel veranda, directly behind the big red-headed man. Their stiffness, and the intensity with which they watched Billy, could hardly be ignored by their son, Alonzo thought. Yet not once did Billy look in their direction, his eyes solely on the back of Nat Kinney.

What the hell was going on? Alonzo wondered, and began to speak when suddenly, gunfire erupted. The Bald Knobbers were going out the same way they had started, guns speaking to the skies and riding off in every direction.

Below the balcony, Nat Kinney rode out a few feet, then turned his horse. He mockingly bowed to Jamison, and lifted the bottle in his left hand to his mouth. Drinking the remainder of the brandy within, he rode back across Jefferson to the bonfire, and tossed the bottle onto the flames. Without another glance in the direction of the hotel, he joined his former lieutenants, and they rode out of town.

"Bravo!" Alonzo wrote. "It was truly a great performance."

He sat back, massaging his cramped hand. Looking around, he

saw his back door was still open, and he rose to close it. Then he blew out the candle, and disrobed, exhausted but happy that tomorrow, he would finish his letter to his wife, and tell her to come home.

CHAPTER 42
Late April, 1886

Eva DeLong and her little sister, Georgia Kinney, arrived home from their extended stay at their grandfather's Kansas ranch only a few hours after the Bald Knobbers were officially disbanded by their father.

It took some time for Maggie to adjust to having her daughters home. She had missed them terribly, but changing her focus from Nat--who was brooding--to the girls was difficult at first. Nat, too, wanted and needed her attention, and his inability to keep his hands off her any time he was near her began to stifle her even more.

Eva had lost a considerable amount of weight, and took long walks every morning and evening. Nat spent his days in the fields, never leaving the property. And Georgia, who went to Miranda's home the first chance she had, was terribly behind in her lessons.

It was enough to turn her hair white, Maggie thought irritably as she pulled one such hair from her right temple one morning. She was standing at the mirror in their bedroom when a knock sounded on the door.

She opened it to find Georgia in tears. Kneeling down, she grabbed her youngest daughter and pulled her close. "What is it, honey? What's wrong?"

"They're leaving..." and there were more tears as Georgia collapsed in her mother's arms.

"Who is leaving?" Maggie asked softly. "Come now, child, you can tell me." She rose, bringing Georgia with her, and stumbled into the kitchen, nearly carrying the crying child. Sitting in her rocker, it was awkward to get Georgia on her lap and comfortable, but she managed and began the soothing motion of back-and-forth. "Georgia? Who is leaving?"

"Miranda's mother is taking a position in Forsyth. They're moving away!"

"Oh, my darling..." and Maggie crooned to Georgia for some time, trying to calm her. "It won't be the end of your friendship, you know. You can still see her on occasion, and write to her!"

"But..."

"Do you know what position her mother found?"

Absolution | 421

Georgia sat up, searching her mother's face. She had been very homesick while in Kansas, both for her family and friends, and for the hills of Taney County. Already, Maggie thought as she calmly looked Georgia back in the eye, she was running barefoot and turning brown from being outside. While she was exultant from Georgia's news--it would only help her civilize her child--she hid it carefully while waiting for the answer.

"Mr. Snapp found a place for the Widow Maggie at some restaurant," Georgia replied, sobbing and hiccoughing. "He says her food is so good, she needs to run a diner, so he talked to some friend of his." She fell onto her mother's shoulder again.

Unbeknownst to Maggie, Nat had seen Georgia running back home in tears, and came quickly behind her. He was watching his wife and daughter through the window of the kitchen, and heard Georgia's words.

An irrational fury began to rise through him, seeming to come from the earth itself. Sam Snapp was causing his daughter to be hurt. Sam Snapp was becoming a threat to him once more, and now it was his daughter, whose pain was felt as his own, who was a victim.

Some voice in his mind, from his heart, told him he was wrong. The Widow Maggie certainly was a good cook, if her sandwiches were anything to judge from. But why not have her open a diner in Kirbyville, where she would have the teamsters who constantly traveled through as customers? It was a rational, reasonable idea.

He argued with himself for only moments before he decided to act. Then he left his porch, running for the barn. He now owned a building in Kirbyville that, while small, would do as a diner for the Widow. He should've thought of it earlier.

Nat Kinney forgot that he had not encouraged Georgia's friendship with Miranda, and that he himself had shot and killed Andrew Coggburn, a close friend of Miranda's mother. All he could think of was that his child was crying, and he might have a way to make her feel better. Saddling Grey Ghost, the horse sidestepped and danced before Nat gave him his head and left the farm.

৯ ৶

Riding down the slope to the Widow's home, Nat saw the neatly-planted garden. Flower and herb beds were also arranged with care, some in the shade of trees and some in what sun reached the yard. Over across a ravine, he saw the Widow and her children in the corn field. The smell of pigs reached him, and he glanced further down the hill below the house, hearing several piglets squealing. Riding further down to inspect the fenced pig pen, he felt a tremor go through his horse as they approached. A mean-looking black sow rose from her side, ignoring her litter as she tried to see through the stout fence surrounding her.

"Hey! Hey! Don't go near her!" a woman's voice called, urgent and breathless. "You fool!"

Nat had turned to see the Widow and several children running toward him around the head of the ravine, and as he clicked the reins to turn Ghost, a loud "slam!" reverberated. Even louder squeals were heard as the sow began trying to get out of her pen and attack the horse and rider.

Ghost reared, and hastily left the immediate vicinity of the pig pen, Nat agreeing with his horse's assessment of their danger. Repeated slams could be heard as they made their way back up to the dooryard of the cabin, arriving just as the Widow and the children did, red-faced and out of breath.

"You...FOOL!" yelled the Widow Maggie, panting. "Don't you know better--?"

"How in the hell was I to know you have a rabid sow down there?" Nat asked crossly.

"Not rabid..." the Widow said.

"How the hell do you feed her?" he asked her, then instantly regretted it. He looked at the house instead of at the indignant woman. An admiring look came over his face as he realized the amount of work the woman and her daughters had put into the place.

Once her breathing slowed, Widow Maggie sent the children to take a bucket of slops down to the still-enraged sow. "Don't fergit to call her name as you go, so she'll know who's close by," she told the girls. Miranda grabbed Phebe's hand, and the girls walked toward the summer kitchen, where the fetid bucket of day-old food was waiting.

"It's early to feed her, but..." the Widow pushed her hair back off her face, and finally turned to Nat Kinney, who had dismounted and was leaning on the gate post, inspecting her house like he owned the place.

"What do you want?" Her tone was unfriendly, Nat decided.

"I came to see how you were doing," Nat told her, turning to inspect her as well.

Insulted, the Widow Maggie's color rose once more. She glared at him, her hands twitching at her side.

"We been fine. What do you want?"

Nat smiled. "My daughter says you're moving. Are you selling this place?"

"Ain't your business!" The Widow stood defiantly in front of Nat, daring him to tell her otherwise.

"Are you opening a diner in Forsyth?" he asked.

"Why do you ask?" The heat left her voice, and it was cold. She could not have mimicked his wife any better, Nat thought.

Still admiring her--he knew how to handle angry women--he answered the Widow. "I have a small building in Kirbyville that is empty. It would be a good investment if you opened a diner in it. With the drivers and residents there, you would have more customers than in Forsyth."

Incredulous, the Widow eyed Nat. "You want me to open a diner in your building?"

He nodded, misunderstanding her. "I'd be happy to get it ready for you. It's close enough, you can ride home every night."

She was too stunned to reply for a few seconds, Nat saw. She opened her mouth to speak at least twice, finally managing to growl, "I already have plans."

"Yes, I hear Sam Snapp is helping you out. I'm rather surprised, frankly. One would think the man would rather marry you than help you move away," Nat spoke without thinking. He realized the dress she was wearing was the one he had paid for anonymously last year. His eyes fell to her bare feet, traveled up her legs and body.

The Widow's head jerked back as if he'd slapped her. Through clenched teeth, her words came slow and furious. "You'll find paradise in hell before I do business with you, Kinney," her cold voice finally reached through to his more rational self. "Get off my place!"

"I am so sorry, I did not mean to insult you," Nat began. Then he looked at her face, and was surprised to see she had not accepted his apology.

The squeals from below had stopped, and suddenly Miranda was back by her mother's side, carrying an axe. "Ma!" The two younger girls were slower to climb the hill, but as the Widow took the axe from Miranda's hands, Nat realized he was in some danger.

"Hey! I just wanted to make you an offer!" he said, backing off as the Widow took a step toward him, the axe held in front of her like a shield. Suddenly, her left hand slipped down the handle to join her right, and the axe was over her head.

It was all the Widow Maggie could do, not to follow through with her swing. Nat Kinney quickly jumped on his horse, which was doing its fancy sidestepping.

"GET OFF MY PLACE!" the Widow Maggie yelled.

Her voice echoed up the slope as he urged the horse back toward home. Once on the level road, he let Ghost run, wondering how he had managed so many men if he couldn't handle two women named Maggie all by himself.

It was several hours later when Nat Kinney's wife found him behind the barn, drinking from a stashed whiskey bottle and morosely contemplating the loss of companionship he had found with the Bald Knobbers.

Slight amusement won out over sheer aggravation, at least for the moment. He had not heard her approach, so he jumped when she spoke.

"Nat....why are you out here by yourself?" Maggie asked, then smiled when he started. The basket in her hands held a stoppered jug of hot coffee, for Nat had not been inside to get coffee since leaving the house this morning. Besides consoling Georgia and setting her to lessons, she had been doing laundry, and her dress sleeves were rolled above her elbows.

He squinted up at her, for the sun was at an angle behind her. "Bah," he said.

She could smell whiskey, and the fact that he had not taken a bath in days. Her lip curled in disgust as the amusement faded. "What's wrong with you?" she asked. Damn. It was just like Nat to become upset when Georgia was, too.

"Sam Snapp."

Her eyebrows rose. First, Georgia, now Nat.

"What about Sam Snapp?" she asked. How did he know--?

"I went to see the Widow Maggie today."

Absolution | 425

She pursed her lips, eyeing the lout on the ground in front of her. "About what?" She would be polite. She hadn't liked their last fight over the Widow, and Nat was drunk this time.

"I wanted to rent her the building in Kirbyville."

"To what purpose?"

"So she would not move, make Georgia cry anymore." His words were slurred, and she stepped back just a little. Ah. He *had* heard Georgia this morning.

"Nat, you cannot go around telling people what to do now. You made a promise..." Maggie began, but Nat raised his hand in a gesture that quieted her.

"I know, I know. Just thought I'd make the offer."

"And just what did you offer her?" Maggie was curious, if angry.

"That I would fix the building to suit her opening a diner in it."

"What building is this?"

"The empty one I own now in Kirbyville."

Ah. She didn't know Nat owned a building in Kirbyville. Her heart began to pound, "What else? What else? What else?" didn't she know, it said, a growing discordance traveling along her veins. Carefully, she sat the basket down, knelt down beside Nat, despite the assault on her sense of smell.

"What does Sam Snapp have to do with anything?" she asked, nonchalant. Georgia had told her; she had her innate suspicions about Andy Coggburn's death, and remembered Nat's fury the night of his meeting with the adjutant general.

Nat reached a hand over and patted her knee through the fabric of her dress. The pat became a rub, but instead of comforting him as she used to, Maggie rose and shook out her skirts.

"Nat, I asked you a question."

"Come here," he wheedled, and she took another step back.

Despite being drunk, his reflexes were good enough to grab her ankle, and she nearly fell. He was stretched out on the ground, and rolled over, looking up at her face as she regained her balance.

"Come here, I said," he told her, his voice lowering. His grip on her ankle loosened as he tried to stroke the back of her leg, but she stepped back once more.

"You bitch! I'm not done with you!" he growled at her, rolling over and getting on his hands and knees. She continued to back away until she hit the fence post of the pasture, still in the shadows behind the barn.

"Mother! I'm done with my lessons!" came Georgia's voice from the house.

"Just a minute, darling! I'll be right there!" Maggie called, hoping Georgia would not come out. Nat was beginning to rise to his feet, and she suddenly lifted a foot, kicking him and knocking him back down to the ground.

"Your daughter needs me," she told her husband. "And you, you filthy-smelling bastard, you're not man enough to take me now!"

Turning to look over her shoulder as she walked away--in case he hadn't been as drunk as she thought--Maggie's heart almost melted at the sight of her husband lying on the ground. Then she remembered his offer to the Widow and Nat's wife continued to walk away from him, wondering why she hadn't kicked him after he was down.

ᔦ ᔐ

"Mother, would you play the piano tonight?" Eva was pushing food around on her plate. It was only Eva and Georgia at the table with Maggie tonight. Nat had not come in from the barn, and Maggie was glad. She had water on the stove, heating for a bath, just in case Nat did appear, but did not want to push the issue in front of the girls.

It was a warm night, one to have the windows and doors wide open. Swallowing at the thought of similar nights now in the past, Maggie nodded. "You girls clean up."

She had only played one or two times since the girls had been home, although she dusted the piano every day. She pulled the bench out, lifted the lid, and settled herself. First, she played the scales, warming up her fingers and hands. They were sore from doing the laundry, and she was flexing and massaging them when she heard footsteps on the porch outside. Then, a knock on the door frame.

Eva's voice carried happy notes in it, and Maggie recognized the answering response from Robert Prather. Ah. She stood, preparing to go to greet the young man when she heard him speak in low tones, "Why is there a bonfire on the bald tonight?"

Maggie came from the bedroom to the entryway, and out onto the porch. It was twilight, and there was a big fire on the bald behind the

Absolution | 427

house. She could see Nat's silhouette as he stoked the fire higher.

"It has nothing to do with us, you said," Eva responded to Robert's question. "You wrote me that you were sorry, I was right. Nothing our parents do has to do with us."

Maggie bowed her head. She had just seen horsemen riding over the crest of the hill, and wondered what to do. For lack of anything better, she returned to her piano, and began to play while her daughter and a young man she liked discussed their future. For she would no longer stand in their way.

And she did not play the song Nat liked so much. Whatever he thought he was doing, up there with his men and the bonfire, she was not going to be happy with him when he decided to come home.

ৎ৽ ৵৹

Nat was gratified when Wash Middleton and Gabe Branson rode up. Then, slowly, others appeared, including John Haggard and Bill Hensley. He was sitting on the same large log he had used to stand on for speeches, and made no attempt to rise or speak until there were a dozen men in front of him.

The moon was just rising when he finally spoke, his voice clear considering the amount of whiskey he'd consumed, he thought.

"We meet by the fire."

The men around him responded with a muttered, "We ride in the dark."

"My friends." Nat stood with some difficulty and the men realized he was drunk. He had consumed Maggie's coffee earlier, and was now back to whiskey. A dangerously-awake drunk.

Somehow, Maggie's last words to him were confused with the Widow Maggie, and he knew he had to find a way to rid himself of Sam Snapp, his nemesis, his enemy, the taker of women who buried them too soon. His daughter's tear-stained face rose up before him while he heard both Maggie's voices, condemning him, betraying him.

Damn, he was drunk. He smiled at the confused men before him, and began pacing.

"My friends, there is a threat to me."

Muttering from the men.

"And to my family."

A bit louder now.

"Sam Snapp is a dangerous man."

John Haggard began to lose patience. "Aw, Cap'n, no, he's not. He's not done anything to threaten you."

Nat raised his head, looking at John, who was some distance from him. "John Haggard, come before me now." John hesitantly walked to stand in front of Nat. "You promised me there was no threat from Sam Snapp. You know him, you said. He would not be a problem, you said."

"And I meant it. He ain't been a threat."

"Ah, but I see it differently than you do." Nat pulled one of his ivory-handled pistols from his waistband, and moved so quickly, he had John collared and the gun pointed at his heart before anyone else made a move.

"I tell you, he is a threat." Nat's tone was menacing. "And you will take care of it."

With Nat's fist at his shirtfront, and the gun pointing straight at his heart, John Haggard was sweating freely. "H-h-how do…w-w-what do you mean?" he asked Nat.

"You will kill Sam Snapp tonight."

John began to shake slightly. "I cain't do thet, Cap'n. Sam's my brother-in-law, I cain't do thet."

"Well, he's about got another wife, so he won't be your brother-in-law much longer," Nat chuckled, malicious in his threat.

"Who?"

"The Widow Maggie." Nat's proclamation brought laughter to the other men, but his eyes bore into John's and the laughter died off as they saw he meant what he said.

"Cap'n, thet un ain't gonna marry again," Wash said. "She like to 'ev stabbed me last year!"

"Bah." Nat threw Haggard off, and John fell in the dust at the feet of the other men. Gabe reached down to help him up, and he dusted himself off.

"None of you listen," Nat paced once more. "I tell you, the man is a threat. Who else would have told Jamison about Coggburn? Who buries wives quicker? The answer to the question is clear. Sam Snapp."

"He's had a run of bad luck, thet's all," Gabe said loudly. "We all know men who have buried more than one wife."

Absolution | 429

"I want Sam dead." There was no mistaking the menace. "If you will not do it, John Haggard, I will ride down there tonight and do it myself."

John shook his head. "He is no threat, Cap'n, I promise."

"Your promises mean nothing, apparently. Did you not take the oath? Did you not promise to go to the aid of your brethren in need? You obviously didn't mean it."

"I did, Cap'n, but Sam is…"

"I am in need, John Haggard. And you have been chosen."

Wash Middleton eyed John, then sidled over to Nat. "Cap'n, let me do it. I'll do it for you tonight." Together, they watched John recoil.

"No! I'll do it," John was almost shouting. "Not tonight, though. I need time."

The expression on Nat's face was shocking. "Oh, it'll be tonight, Haggard, or we'll just bury you up here on this hill."

In the firelight, it was difficult to tell if anyone would side with him, John thought. Kill Sam? As far as he knew, Sam had only been off the farm to visit the store and his sister in Kirbyville. He'd occasionally taken time off from his own farm to check, and every time, he'd seen Sam at home. What possible threat was Sam to Captain Kinney?

"Alright, alright. I'll go."

Kinney's smile was vulpine in the dark, gleaming by the firelight. "Report back at once."

John walked to his horse, and swung up in the saddle. He was certain he must be home asleep, and having a nightmare. Why had he responded to the summons of the bonfire? He rode off without a word to the others.

୨ଡ଼ ଡ଼ଜ

He tied the horse some distance from the house. Carefully, he made his way down the wide trail, knowing if he walked through the woods, the dogs would alert Sam. They knew John's step, and would recognize him on the trail.

The front door was open. John sensed a disturbance in the dogs, and paused before continuing on to the back of the cabin. There were a couple of tail thumps, but they were well-trained. Sam had

430 | Vonda Wilson Sheets

told them to "stay," and they did not leave the porch. Well, good so far.

Pulling his pistol, John slipped to the wall, and crept around the corner, to the side nearest his horse.

The window was open, and he could hear the sounds of a family eating dinner. Nannie and Serelda had made a stew, and as John looked in, he could see Sam smiling at Allie, holding her in his lap with his knee propped up on the table. He was feeding her broth, and she appeared to like it, by the expression on Sam's face.

More tail thumps on the porch. Sam heard them this time, and glanced up at the window. He could not see out because of the light within. Then Tom said something to divert his attention, and he once again gave Allie a spoon of broth.

John's hands were shaking, and he nearly dropped the gun. Kill Sam? This man who was caring for his children, tending his farm, minding his own business? He pulled back out of the window's light, and his hand hit the wall.

It wasn't a loud noise, as such noises go, but it was enough. The dogs rose to their feet. They might know John, but they could smell fear. And it was coming from John Haggard in waves.

The restlessness on the porch, combined with a noise he didn't recognize, caused Sam to hand Allie to Nannie. He stood, grabbing his rifle, and went out onto the porch, instantly moving to the shadows between the door and window.

"Who's there?" he asked. He crouched low, duck-walked under the window, and made his way to the end of the porch, where he stood once more to peer into the darkness. As his eyes adjusted, he could sense no movement, nothing untoward.

John Haggard was less than six feet from his target, and raised his pistol. All he needed was for Sam to step off the porch, and he would--

Susie Haggard Snapp's voice sounded clearly in his mind. "Leave us alone," she told her brother. "He's done nothing to you." And while Sam was fondling the head of one of the dogs, trying to see into the night, his wife's spirit moved between her husband and her brother.

"Leave! Not by your hand!" she told John once more, and he nodded. Then Granny Haggard was there, a sad smile on her face, and suddenly there were more spirits, more loved ones long gone,

Absolution | 431

protecting Sam.

John listened as his brother-in-law's footsteps receded, went back into the house. The dogs moved around, lying down and adjusting themselves.

He walked away, his pace once more normal and he knew the spirits were moving with him, protecting him, too, and masking his retreat. He prayed they would remain with him, because he certainly was going to need them when he told Nat Kinney that Sam was still alive and that he, John Haggard, would not be the one to kill him.

CHAPTER 43
George Washington Middleton

To say George Washington Middleton was a follower was telling the truth. To say he missed the camaraderie of the Bald Knobbers was an understatement. To say he was beholden to Nat Kinney for giving him a chance to rise up in the ranks of the Bald Knobbers to become the captain's right-hand man--beholden wasn't a strong enough word to describe the tie that bound Wash to Nat.

He was a fearsome man to most women and children, but his own wife and children thought him a fond parent who couldn't bear to whip them. His overalls hung slack on his skeletal body, but he had plenty to eat. He wore a hat made of skunk fur in the wintertime, enjoying the looks of disgust from women who happened to see him, and embarrassment on the faces of the men he associated with. Aside from his own family, only Nat Kinney seemed to find something of value in Wash Middleton, the same something that Wash himself valued.

Wash wasn't uncivilized. He simply had never been more than a son, husband or father until the Civil War happened, and then he was a Union soldier. Like soldiers before him and after him, the bonds formed during wartime with other men were necessary when life was basic survival under heavy fire. Although he was a scout, he also fought with units on the front. This brotherhood, this feeling of fraternity, was the strongest connection he had ever made, aside from his family.

Until Nat Kinney moved to Taney County. The big red-headed man was able to discuss scouting tactics and other things that brought forth some aspect of Wash's personality which made him a potential threat to anyone he felt was unnecessary, or even dangerous.

The fact that John Haggard had been chosen, and failed, to kill Sam Snapp was a crippling blow to Wash. Why had Cap'n Kinney chosen Haggard, when Wash stood ready to do whatever he was ordered to? It was the first time he had felt slighted by Cap'n Kinney, and it rankled down his spine, making him slump even more when he thought about it.

He had jumped on his horse, ready to ride to Snapp's cabin when Haggard's voice stopped him.

Absolution | 433

"You can't kill him tonight, Cap'n," Haggard cried. "Serelda Coggburn and all his children are there."

Nat called out to Wash, "Hold!" Wash rode back to the circle of men, and listened to the discussion. It was determined, by the end of the impromptu meeting, that any death related to Andy Coggburn's would open an investigation into Nat's actions the day Andrew was killed. For Sam Snapp had been the only witness to know Andrew had not had a gun, and he had seen Wash Middleton place a pistol in Andy's dead hand.

Cap'n Kinney had put a hand on Wash's shoulder, gripping it tightly. The smell of stale sweat and whiskey, the captain's bloodshot eyes, the desperation on his face--these things triggered a response in Wash that forgave the captain's earlier slight and made his own urge to serve even stronger.

For Wash Middleton knew he was the only one, the only man, who could save Cap'n Kinney now.

The spring had been rather warm, but the second weekend in May was rainy, with a slight chill in the air.

Sam Snapp ground the last of his carefully-hoarded coffee beans, and made a pot of coffee. Impatiently waiting for it to be ready, he paced on the porch, shooing the dogs off for a while. Tom had been sent to collect eggs, using the diversionary method of throwing food scraps in the chicken yard while going in the coop and checking the nests. The rooster was crowing and scolding Tom for the intrusion, but Sam heard no yelling from his son in return.

Tom had just turned three. He aped Sam in many of his motions, and was coddled by any female within sight. The Widow Maggie had enjoyed watching Tom and Sam together; her three daughters and the four girls living in Sam's house were one collective sound similar to that of the chickens he was now listening to. An involuntary smile crossed Sam's face, thinking of one recent afternoon when the girls and the Widow had been out collecting greens and mushrooms, while he and Tom were pulling weeds in the vegetable garden. Tom had found a garden snake, and somehow managed to put it in the pocket of his breeches. The snake attempted to escape during dinner, slithering out of Tom's reach and causing general pandemonium. Sam had laughed until he cried, unable to help capture the enraged jewel-colored creature. The Widow had swept the snake out with the

434 | Vonda Wilson Sheets

broom while the girls stood on their chairs and Tom frantically tried
to prevent the snake from harm.

It had been a week since the Widow Maggie and her daughters
had left their farm, renting it to one of the McClary boys. The rent
was cheap enough, in exchange for taking care of the pigs and the
gardens, as well as making weekly deliveries to Forsyth once the
gardens began yielding their produce.

Sam had written his brother Robert over a month ago, asking if he
knew of a situation in Forsyth for the widow and her daughters. He
vouched for the widow's cooking skills, noting that her daughters
needed schooling and the Oak Grove school was simply not an
option. Within days, Robert had spoken with the new owner of the
former Everett properties, Jim Berry. Berry was very interested in
purchasing and improving the diner on the town square, Robert's
reply stated. And the Widow's reputation as a cook spoke for her
well enough, by virtue of the sandwiches she had been selling at
Kintrea's store in Kirbyville.

So her life was moving forward, and Sam was happy for her. They
had slipped into an easy friendship, neither placing any demands
on the other, in the fields and around both farms, dealing with the
children and meals and heavy work. It had been too easy, Sam
thought as he poured himself a cup of coffee. It was a little over five
months since Susie died, and he missed her constantly. He wasn't
whole, not even close, he knew. The ache was easing, though.

The Widow Maggie had been more direct in one of their
conversations. "You need to be sad for a while," she'd told him. Her
own history made her wary, and after Nat Kinney visited her place a
couple weeks ago, she felt unsafe.

So the deed was done. There would be no haste in their friendship,
no pressure for it to be more, unless both of them were comfortable
with making it more.

Sam's face brightened as he considered riding into Kirbyville
this morning. Maybe there would be a letter. He certainly needed
coffee, and a rattle of the empty sugar tin by Serelda--who loved
sugar on her oatmeal--caused him to nod. "I'm going into Kirbyville
this morning," he told her.

Tom came in and tried to hand the egg basket to Nannie, who
ignored him while she looked anxiously at her father. "Pa," she
began.

Absolution | 435

"What?" Sam leaned over to count the eggs, then asked Tom, "How many did you find?" Tom was learning his numbers.

"Theven," Tom said proudly, beaming at his father. Nannie took the basket, and began to crack the eggs for breakfast.

"There might be a letter from Miranda," Sam coaxed his worried daughter. Serelda was putting Alma in the high chair. The baby was sitting up well now. Allie still had to be propped, and depended mostly on a bottle for sustenance, but Alma was eating soft foods with the rest of the children, taking a bottle only for thirst and comfort.

Nannie stopped what she was doing and sent a direct stare at her father. "Well, you kin stay here and 'Rilda and me kin go."

"Next time," Sam said. He put his coffee mug on the table. "I think I'll go now. Don't pour out my coffee. I'll be back soon." He smiled as he put on his coat and hat. "I won't stop at Aunt Addie's, but I do need to talk to her about you and 'Rilda going to school."

The girls both smiled at the thought of school, then continued on with breakfast as Sam saddled his horse and left.

Although it was Sunday, the Kintreas would be open today. During the months of good weather, teamsters hauled products seven days a week, and John Kintrea saw little reason to close the store on Sundays. He and his wife attended church in Kirbyville, letting their young assistant open the store early in the morning, then giving him the afternoon off.

This particular Sunday, May 9, the clerk was in bed with a spring cold, and John Kintrea himself was behind the counter when Sam walked in. Business appeared to be good, and Sam eyed the rolls of fabric. He would need to arrange for summer dresses for the girls, he thought, then turned as Kintrea greeted him.

"Coffee and brown sugar, one pound of each," Sam told Kintrea after pleasantries were exchanged.

"You have mail, too, Sam," the storekeeper said, turning to the slot marked "Snapp, S." and pulling out two letters.

He handed them to Sam, who looked at the writing on the outside while Kintrea weighed and bagged his purchases. One letter was from his brother Matt. The other was written in a child's hand, and Sam knew Miranda had written for her mother. He smiled, tucking the letters into his coat pocket without opening them. The anticipation of seeing Nannie and Serelda's faces when he got home made his smile wider. More pleasantries with Kintrea as he paid for his purchase, and then he was walking to the door, ready to get home.

Glancing around while crossing the porch, he saw one of the Prather boys playing marbles, his eyes focused on the proper angle of his shot, his rump in the air. Going down the steps, the thought crossed Sam's mind that if Alonzo Prather had brought his family home, it meant that things were going to be peaceful. A fresh hope suddenly burst into his heart, causing him to whistle.

He was some feet away from the porch when a gravelly voice entered his consciousness.

"You hadn't oughta be whistling, you damned bushwhacker," it said.

Sam whirled and froze. Wash Middleton was sitting on a bench by the door of the store, his whittling knife lying next to him as he used his bandana to polish the gun in his hand. Sam had walked right past him.

"Excuse me?" Middleton called him a bushwhacker? What the hell?

"You heard me, you bushwhacker." Middleton's voice was easy while he continued to rub his gun, not looking at Sam. "You promised to keep yer mouth shut, and you didn't."

Threat. All of Sam's nerves were cold with danger. This was not happening, he told himself. Aloud, "I haven't said anything!"

"You talked to the governor's man."

Sam shook his head. "I never did!"

"You're a liar!" Middleton's voice rose slightly.

There were several people, including the Prather boy, who were scrambling to get away. Sam himself could not move, except for shaking his head.

"I never did lie!"

"You know Coggburn had a gun in his hand!" Accusation.

Sam returned the accusation, forgetting he had no weapons but truth. "Andy was unarmed!"

Wash brought his gun up, setting its sights squarely on Sam's chest. Sam dropped his package, throwing up his left arm to halt Middleton.

"Don't!"

The gun fired, and Sam pulled his bloodied left arm to his body in agony. His knees went weak, and the second shot entered his left shoulder, the force spinning him, turning his back to Middleton. He fell to his knees, and he heard his children screaming as he knelt, breathing hard to put the fire inside out.

The third shot knocked him to the ground, face in the mud. It was no small effort to turn his head, but he could no longer breathe. A pair of boots walked past his open eyes, but Sam Snapp could no longer see.

Sam Snapp was dead, Wash Middleton noted with satisfaction, ignoring the chaos around him. Unhurriedly, he almost strolled to the gazebo in the park across the road, and mounted his horse.

He had been prepared for days. Every morning, he had kissed his wife and left their home, sitting and carving and waiting for Sam Snapp to appear. He had a bedroll and supplies in his saddlebags, as he would go down to his brother's home in Boone County to wait out the fuss that would be made over Sam's death.

Wash knew Cap'n Kinney would be mighty pleased with him. He watched Doc Anderson, Sam's brother-in-law, come running to the front of Kintrea's store, then turn to stare hard at him. Other eyes were watching him, wary of Wash Middleton, Cap'n Kinney's lieutenant.

It was time to go.

CHAPTER 44
Late Spring, Summer, Fall of 1886

Sam Snapp's mortal remains were laid to rest the next day in the family cemetery. In the dreary rain, his livestock and other moveable goods were parceled out to family members. The children, with the exception of Serelda Coggburn, went home with their Aunt Addie, who had been married to Dr. Elisha Anderson for several years and had no children of her own.

Serelda, orphaned once again, went to stay with the Widow Maggie for a few days until a permanent place could be found for her. The small room allotted for the widow's use by her employer was already cramped. Serelda made herself as small as possible and sat in the room during the day while her friends Miranda and Phebe were in school. Small Celie, too young for school until the fall term, sat in a corner of the kitchen while her mother cooked and served food to hungry people in the diner, brightening the Widow Maggie's mood with her chatter and play.

On her next day off from work, the Widow Maggie left Miranda in charge of her sisters and rented a horse from the livery. There was an extra bed in the cabin she rented to the McClarys, and she felt Serelda needed to be around people all day, instead of cooped up in a basement room. The McClary son who rented the farm had a wife and new baby; Widow Maggie knocked the price of her monthly rent down for the couple to accommodate Serelda.

She took her time on the way back to Forsyth. The rain had finally cleared, and she stopped by the Van Zandt Cemetery to lay fresh-cut flowers on Andy's grave. She did the same for Sam and the graves of both his wives at Snapp Cemetery.

Clear about her own part in the men's lives, she grieved for the loss of their companionship. Both had taught her about friendship, and Sam, so recently bereft of Susie, had, by example, taught her that grief could be lessened when shared.

She looked north to the town of Forsyth. She had made a new start, was doing work she enjoyed, and would soon be able to rent a small house in Forsyth for her little family.

Someday, it might not be enough. But it was enough for now.

Wash Middleton turned himself into the sheriff a few days after Sam's death. The circuit-riding judge would not be holding court in Taney County until October, so Wash was allowed to go home, on the condition that he would not leave Taney County.

Twice in the summer, Sheriff McHaffie called a posse to chase outlaws. John Haworth served on one successful manhunt, and realized everyone else in the posse were Bald Knobbers. A few comments made got the preacher fired up, but no threat materialized when the others saw he would not join their politics.

❧ ❧

Eva DeLong and Robert Prather took their time in renewing their relationship. By the end of summer, Maggie Kinney felt certain her daughter would become engaged.

Over the years, Maggie had taught her daughters how to quilt. Small pieces of fabric were saved, and sewn into pretty designs for the quilt tops. As each top was finished, she showed them how to attach the tops to worn blankets and sheets, making pretty blankets. This summer, Georgia was sewing her piecework for a quilt top while Eva began sewing lengths of finely-woven linen into hemmed sheets and pillow cases. Feathers had always been saved; Eva's feather bed was complete, and Georgia's would be in a short time. The trunk Maggie set aside for Eva's hope chest held cast iron cookery that could be used on a stove or a grate in a fireplace. There was also a set of dishes packed away, and flatware in a wooden cabinet that had belonged to Maggie's mother.

Preparing for a wedding without a proposal was delicate work.

The relationship between Nat and Maggie was even more delicate. Nat had been in the house when Sam Snapp was killed, so she knew Nat was not involved. The posses called up by Sheriff McHaffie had been legitimate needs, but Nat had not served.

He spent his days in Forsyth or Kirbyville, always arriving home in time for dinner about 6 p.m. With the exception of touch and music, their lives continued on as always. She sent for and spent what she needed to on the house and the children; he paid the bills. He hired a crew to cut hay on the farm periodically, and she fed them lunch the days they worked. She drank a glass of wine each evening, but he never joined her. And he didn't ask her to play the piano for him.

Except for Georgia's music lessons, the lid on the piano remained closed. Like the other children, Georgia was developing technical skill, but she did not have the gift of music in her heart. She enjoyed it, but wasn't passionate about it.

Alonzo and Ada Marie were living in a large house in Kirbyville now. Robert lived in the smaller house on the farm next to the Kinneys, coming over to spend evenings with Eva under chaperonage. As the summer wore on, and no proposal was forthcoming, Maggie began to worry that maybe the young people had been through too much to want to marry anytime soon.

Nat did not seek solace in Maggie as he had in the past. They seldom spoke to each other, except in the way of worried parents, and they never touched each other, even in sleep. Paul, who was attending summer term in Forsyth, came home one weekend to find his parents strained and concerned, and not at all friendly toward each other. They were barely polite, he felt.

He returned the following weekend after summer term was over. Within days, the atmosphere in the house felt so strained, Paul worried for his mother's health. She was too pale, too thin, and too quiet.

It was election season.

Nat came home from a day in Forsyth the last Monday in August, jubilant and secretive. He waited until everyone, including Robert Prather, was seated at the kitchen table for dinner before he announced he was running for the office of state representative.

Amid the congratulations and cheers, Nat looked down the table at his wife. She was watching him closely, and he knew she did not want to move with him to Jefferson City, should he win the election. But their separation was intolerable, and he had been at a loss on how to mend things between them. He wasn't sure what had caused her to stop loving him, but he would do his best to bring that love back. He smiled at her, and watched her rub her lips together before she gave him a slight smile in return.

"One more thing," Nat told them. He rose, and went out into

Absolution | 441

the hallway which served as an entry. When he returned, he was carrying a large dress box. He walked to Maggie's end of the table, and solemnly looked down at his wife.

"There is a ball at the Masonic Lodge in a week," Maggie turned her head and looked up at him. Her eyes widened when she realized he was begging. Her chin came up. Continuing, Nat asked, "Would you do me the honor of wearing this and being the most beautiful woman there?"

She took the box, stunned delight on her face. As she lifted the lid and moved the tissue paper, she saw beautiful red silk. Pulling the garment out, she realized it was a dress, cut in a fashionable style that suited her build. A second box was brought out, in which there were gorgeous high-heeled shoes and long gloves to match.

"You'll be the envy of every woman there," Nat whispered in her ear, and she gave him a genuine smile. Careful to keep it away from her work dress--she didn't want to stain it--she felt tears in her eyes. Hastily, she took the dress and its accessories into the bedroom and composed herself while she lovingly put it in her wardrobe. It had been many, many years since Nat had surprised her in this way.

She patted her hair and took a deep breath, then turned to find Nat watching her. They stared at each other. He began to move toward her, when Robert Prather came out from the kitchen.

"Good, you're both here," he said.

Not taking his eyes off Maggie, Nat said, "What is it, Robert?"

"I've been waiting for a chance to ask the both of you, but it's hard to catch you in the same room." Maggie reluctantly broke the stare with Nat to look at Robert, who had an odd look on his face. Suddenly, she knew.

"Go ahead, Robert," she encouraged him.

"I would like permission to marry your daughter," Robert found it easier to look at Maggie than at Nat, who he was standing beside.

"Yes?" Nat's voice was purring. He had no idea what Robert had said, Maggie knew, and she didn't dare look back at him. She smiled at Robert instead.

"We'll be happy to welcome you into the family," Maggie told him as she came toward the doorway. Nat did not move, so she touched his chest lightly. "Don't you want to congratulate Robert?"

"What?" Recovering, Nat turned to the young man, stuck out his hand, and obeyed. "Congratulations!"

442 | Vonda Wilson Sheets

Robert shook Nat's hand, but hugged Maggie. "Now I've only to ask her," he told Maggie.

"You've not asked Eva?" she said, surprised.

"No, it hasn't felt right to do so, all summer long," Robert replied. "Now, it does." He turned with a soft "Excuse me," and went back into the kitchen.

Eva, Paul and Georgia had not begun to eat, waiting politely for the others to conclude their business. Robert walked to Eva, took her hand, and pulled her to her feet. He knelt in classic fashion, and said solemnly, "Eva Gertrude DeLong, will you marry me?"

Eva's eyes filled with tears as she looked down into Robert's face, unable to speak. She nodded once, twice. He stood, picking her up, and filled the air with cheers, joined by Paul and Georgia.

Nat and Maggie stood in the doorway, watching the happy young couple. Tears once again returned to Maggie's eyes as she remembered when Nat proposed to her so many years ago. Goodness, it was nearly twenty years! Her hand reached for his, but he pulled her close, and she knew he was remembering that magic evening as well.

It was much, much later, after everyone was asleep in the house and she lay curled up with Nat, skin to skin, that she realized Robert hadn't felt right about proposing to her daughter until Nat made things right with her. That would be something to consider in the days--and nights--to follow.

ᤫ ᤢ

August heat was worse than January cold.

He had never been on his own before, nor had he lived in town until he left home. The saloons held little allure for Billy Miles, and he didn't purchase much in the stores of Forsyth. The work ethic instilled in him by his parents kept him busy.

He'd cleaned out the basement and prepared the other small room for the Widow Maggie and her daughters in April. She was adapting to living in the basement when Sam was killed in early May. Once the spring session of school was over, Billy anticipated being kept awake by the widow's daughters during his daytime sleep, but he never heard them, except in the late afternoons.

There was something about the widow's eyes that reminded him

Absolution | 443

of his mother. Some strength, some determination. He only saw her in the mornings at the diner, as he picked up breakfast orders for the hotel guests. She wasn't unfriendly, but they never exchanged more than idle chitchat. The former waitress had left to marry, and the widow not only cooked the meals but learned to run the cash register.

It was a hot morning, much too hot to sleep. Cross and tired, Billy decided to get a meal at the diner, so he dressed and went up the basement stairs to the side door of the hotel which served as an employee entrance. The heat in town was incredible, and Billy thought longingly of swimming in the creek below his childhood home.

There had been little communication between himself and his parents in recent weeks. He knew they worried, especially after thinking he was losing control of himself the morning Nat Kinney disbanded the Bald Knobbers. He shook his head ruefully as he entered the diner, where fans were moving hot air let in by the open door. He knew what he was doing, he thought, as he sat down at the counter. He had no intention of spending time in jail for shooting a man in the back.

Water. Where was a glass of water?

He could hear a woman's voice from the kitchen. It was accompanied by a young girl's voice. Billy rose, walked through the pass-through, and listened.

The oldest daughter was teaching her mother to read. What was her name? Ah, Miranda. He peeped around the door jamb, and saw the two younger daughters playing dolls in the corner while listening to their sister and mother read.

Carefully, Billy walked back out the door and thought for a minute. Swan Creek still had enough water in it for a child to swim. The diner was closed in the afternoons for two hours, until it was time for folks to be wanting supper. He turned back into the doorway, this time careful to make loud footsteps.

The voices broke off, and the Widow Maggie came out, greeting him. He asked for water and breakfast, and sat down at the counter again. Miranda brought him a glass of water with precious ice in it, and Billy held it to his forehead.

"Aren't you hot?" he asked the little girl after taking a long drink, emptying his glass and holding it out to her.

444 | Vonda Wilson Sheets

"Yes, sir, I am." She took his glass back to the kitchen, returning in seconds with another glass of ice water.

It didn't take long for his meal to be served, and he ate it all. The food had gotten much better since the Widow Maggie had taken over the diner. Billy decided the smoked ham was probably the best he had ever eaten.

He paid up, and handed Miranda three pennies. "One each for you and your sisters," he told her. The Widow Maggie started to protest, but Billy smiled and shook his head.

Exhaustion hit him, and he knew he wouldn't be going swimming today. But....the Widow was turning away, preparing to pick up his dishes and wash them. "Ma'am?" he asked.

The widow hesitated, then continued toward the kitchen door. "Yes?"

"There's a swimming hole just upstream from the livery barn," Billy told her. "I was thinking about going, but--"

"Thank you, Mr. Miles. We don't swim." With that, the widow continued into the kitchen, not looking back at Billy.

"I'm not going, ma'am," he called. "I have to work tonight."

Silence.

"Thank you, Mr. Miles," the widow stuck her head back around the door jamb. She looked tired and sticky herself, but Billy didn't know if she would take the girls swimming this afternoon or not.

He decided it didn't matter, put his hat on, and returned to his basement room to sleep through the hot day.

ာ ၐ

Sam's children, except for Allie, were adjusting to life with Aunt Addie and Uncle Lish.

At three, Tom had lost his mother, stepmother, and father in less than two years. It almost seemed natural to him, the constant upheavals and moves occasioned by those deaths.

Baby Alma was cheerful and thriving. She began cutting teeth and crawling during the summer months. Uncle Lish found an iron ring meant for oxen for her to gnaw on; she began gurgling and smiling whenever she saw him.

Nannie had vivid memories of her parents and stepmother. She turned ten in August. Since the day her father left, telling her not to throw out the coffee because he would be back soon, she felt bewildered and lost. Miranda no longer lived close, and Serelda was no longer by her side. Loneliness was a new feeling for her, and now that she lived in town with her aunt, she found herself with fewer responsibilities and less work. Aunt Addie somehow understood this without being told, and borrowed some schoolbooks from the Prathers, who lived nearby. Their daughter, Mary Elizabeth, was a year younger than Nannie. As the summer's flat, dusty skies gave way to the deep blue of fall, Nannie began doing something she had not done a great deal of in recent years....she began to play with the Prather children, and other children who lived in Kirbyville.

Allie, frail since birth, and used to being carried about in a sling on her father's chest, was having problems swallowing. Aunt Addie and Nannie took turns feeding her, a long process involving stroking her throat and coaxing her with the bottle, using gentle coos. By September, her bones were showing through her pale skin. Uncle Lish, doctor that he was, knew the baby would not live. And indeed, the baby who resembled her mother so much, died before the month was over.

Even with only three children, the Anderson home was crowded. Sam's brothers and sisters made two important decisions: one, to build a new house for the Andersons in Kirbyville, with two stories and room for an office for Uncle Lish; and two, they agreed it was too soon to sell Sam's property in Taney City and west of Kirbyville. No one had time to run the farms, but Nannie still visited the small cabin in the quiet little valley and her special place in the woods nearby.

In October, Wash Middleton was indicted by the grand jury for the premeditated murder of Sam Snapp. He was arrested, jailed. The bond was a huge amount, $3,000, but it was mysteriously paid. Both the state and Wash's defense lawyers asked for a continuance until the next session of court, and again, Wash Middleton went home under the condition that he remain within the borders of Taney County.

The elections of November resulted in Tom Layton remaining

as the county clerk; Samp Barker was the deputy clerk. McHaffie was re-elected as sheriff, and W.E. Havens won the seat for state representative in his race against Nathaniel N. Kinney.

CHAPTER 45
1887

Nat Kinney seldom preached at the Oak Grove school after losing the 1886 election for state representative. There were sporadic reports of night riders still threatening citizens around the county, but Maggie knew Nat had nothing to do with the men still riding--he was home every night, unless he had to stay in Forsyth with James on business, or made trips to Springfield.

For Nat had decided he no longer wanted to be a farmer or horse breeder. His legs and hips hurt him much of the time, and he had difficulty working in the fields. In 1886, he had been in Springfield on a business trip, and was walking through a poorly-marked construction site when he fell. As time went by, the injury to his leg and hip had failed to heal, and he walked with a cane much of the time. He also decided to file a lawsuit against the city, seeking damages and compensation for lost income.

Aside from the lawsuit with the city of Springfield, Nat was also involved in a number of frivolous lawsuits in Taney County. When he first told Maggie about one or two, he claimed that the Slickers were merely hoping to annoy him.

She noticed that whenever Nat left the farm, he was met in the road not far from the house by at least two of his men, and all of them were heavily armed. She didn't know some of them, and when she mentioned it to Nat, he told her that most of the men weren't allowed in his house anymore after she'd beaten the hell out of Pat Fickle. He chuckled when he said it, but Maggie sensed there was more to the story than he was telling her. She set it aside, and as the new year began, she forgot about it.

While Robert courted Eva most diligently, he was studying law and learning business from Alonzo. He did not discuss Alonzo in the Kinney home, and he did not discuss the Kinneys while visiting his parents in Kirbyville. Nat and Alonzo met infrequently in the course of business while in Kirbyville or Forsyth. Both men were polite, and there was even some conversation that passed the time. Their friendship could not be resumed.

Robert and Eva seemed to be holding off on the wedding until they were sure their fathers would not shoot each other, Maggie reflected one snowy night in February. The long courtship had a benefit she did not foresee the night of Robert's proposal. And that was Nat himself, who appeared to be more and more hungry for her body even while Robert sat with Eva in the kitchen and held her daughter's hand.

Their separation had caused Nat to realize he was losing her, he had told her during the first delirious days and nights after their reunion. Aside from being unable to be near her and not touch her, they were swept into the social circle of political candidates, and they spent a number of nights in Forsyth. They traveled to Jefferson City for a very short visit, complete with armed escort, but Maggie was uncomfortable, and was happy to come home.

This night in February, in which thick, fat snowflakes were piling up outside, was cozy and comfortable. Maggie's hair was down, reaching past her hips. She had been wearing it so in the evenings at Nat's request--he liked to play with tendrils of it while she played music. She was running her fingers over the keys of her piano, warming her hands up, preparing to play, when a knock on the door frame caused her to look up.

It was Eva.

"Do come in, dear," Maggie scooted to her left, closer to Nat, who was sitting in his rocking chair with his legs propped on an ottoman. He was close enough to Maggie to play with her hair. She patted the bench, and Eva sat down.

"What is it, love?" Maggie asked her daughter.

Taking a deep breath, Eva turned her eyes from Maggie's face. "Robert and I have been talking, and--"

Nat chuckled. "When are you not talking?" he teased.

"Father!" Eva smiled, then resolutely continued. "We've been talking, and we've decided we don't want a big wedding in the church."

Nat's feet hit the floor with a "thump," dropping the dark tress in his hand. Maggie was stunned, but managed to put her hand out to halt his outburst. The plan had been to hold the wedding ceremony in Oak Grove church, with Nat officiating. Eva's dress had been special-ordered from New York, and would arrive in about a month. Ada Marie had ordered the cake. "But your dress--"

Eyeing her mother in a side glance, Eva kept her face toward the candle on the back of the piano. "Yes," she said. "I plan to wear the

Absolution | 449

dress, Mother. We just don't want a big wedding."

"What's wrong with the church?" Nat asked. It was a mild question, given that Maggie knew his feelings were hurt.

Eva sighed, blowing her cheeks out, and then turned to face Nat. Her mother leaned back so she could see Nat's face.

"It's not 'church,' so much as it's that church," Eva said. "There are too many sad memories there, Father."

"I see."

Nothing else was said for several seconds. Then Maggie patted her daughter's hand. "So what plans have you made, then?"

A knock on the outside door, and Georgia came out of the kitchen to admit Robert inside, Eva going to join him. She helped him brush the snow off, and took his hat and coat, hanging them on the rack near the foot of the stairs. They came into Nat and Maggie's room holding hands, smiling.

"Good evening, Mr. and Mrs. Kinney," Robert greeted Eva's parents, then seated her next to her mother. He looked from Maggie's face to Nat's, and then said, "I see Eva already told you our decision."

Maggie nodded without looking at Nat, who said, "It's a raw night to be out, Robert."

"It is." He beamed. "But I knew Eva wanted to tell you about our change in plans tonight, so I tried to get here as quickly as I could."

"Mother, Father, Captain Van Zandt has agreed to marry us," Eva continued.

Robert maintained a steady gaze at Nat, all the while holding Eva's hand. "We thought it less likely to cause any trouble if we have a simple ceremony, Mr. Kinney."

"Ye-es," Nat was rubbing his chin as if his beard itched. Then he put both hands on his knees and stood. "I think you can call me Nat, Robert," he said as he reached for his cane. "After all, you are marrying my daughter."

Robert smiled down at Eva as Maggie added, "And I am Maggie."

Nat excused himself, and walked into the hallway. He could be heard putting his coat and hat on, grunting with pain. The door opened, and he walked outside.

Looking at Maggie, Robert said, "I do apologize if he is offended, Mrs. Kinney."

"Maggie."

"Well, then, Maggie."

"I have a question, Robert," Maggie looked at her daughter's face, then up at Robert's. "Whose idea was it to ask Captain Van Zandt to do the service?"

"Mine, Mother." Eva's voice was soft as Maggie searched her eyes. "Father could not give me away if he does the ceremony."

Maggie nodded, thinking things through. "Have you set a date?" she asked.

"The night my dress arrives." Eva took her hand from Robert's, and grabbed her mother's hand, hoping she would understand. "We've waited long enough."

The expression on Eva's face looked familiar to Maggie, but she could not remember seeing it there before. Trying to gather her thoughts, she told Eva, "Don't worry about your father. I'll set it right with him."

She was rewarded with a smile from both of them, and they left the room hand-in-hand once more, to go sit in the chairs by the kitchen fireplace.

Robert left during her third song. Eva came in to say good-night afterward, while Maggie was flexing her fingers and massaging them. "Father hasn't returned?"

They heard Nat at the door just then. Once he had taken his coat into the kitchen to dry on the back of a chair, he made his way back to the bedroom, when Eva reached up and gently kissed his cheek. Pleased, Nat studied her face and nodded with a smile. The smile grew wider as Eva smiled back, and Nat said, "You look just like your mother did the night we were married." He touched the hair at Eva's temple with the side of his knuckle.

Saying good-night, Eva joined Georgia, and the girls went upstairs, closing the door at the top to conserve heat in their sleeping area.

Nat added wood to the fire, then re-crossed the room to close the door. Feeling safe and surrounded by love, Maggie's hands returned to the piano, and the first notes of "Moonlight Sonata" began.

"I haven't heard that for a long time." Nat was standing behind her, looking at her face in the mirror above the piano. Maggie smiled, but her fingers faltered when Nat bent down, his hands running down the front of her body as he leaned over to her left ear and told her, "She looked like you do when I'm making love to you." Her breath left her in almost a sob, but she continued to play his favorite song, even as he began unbuttoning her dress in back, loosening her corset, and his cold hands reached around to fondle her warm flesh. A flush came over her and through her. All thoughts of her daughter's change in wedding plans fled.

"Keep playing."

She finally finished the sonata while his hands and fingers stayed busy. Straightening, Nat brought her up with him, watching her face in the mirror as she glanced once at the reflection, then did a double-take.

Now she knew where she'd seen the expression on Eva's face. It was on her face, as Nat had said. He pushed the dress off her shoulders, exposing the straps of her flannel chemise. The loosened corset was also pushed away, and Nat's fingers then rubbed her nipples through the flannel, which added roughness of its own.

With the girls home, the days of early spring were busy and full, and they would tease each other in the ways parents have, with vicarious glances, touches and whispers. Some nights, they were too tired to do more than kiss each other good-night, and fall asleep holding hands. But there were a few nights, like this cold one, when the fire was roaring and there was time, there was no one else in the world, and they were not two passionate people, but one lovely flame.

Ada Marie Prather was happy to feed the now-aligned families of Prather and DeLong/Kinney in her house the night of March 28.

It was a Monday afternoon. Robert, Eva, and their parents stood before Captain J.R. Van Zandt, who read the marriage lines for the happy couple. Nat and Alonzo shook hands, but neither had much to say to the other during the hour everyone was eating. It wasn't long after the late-afternoon dinner before Robert picked Eva up and carried her out to Alonzo's buggy.

Robert spent two days prior to their wedding taking Eva's hope chest and other homemaking items to the house on the farm. He placed the cookery and china in the cabinets and on the hooks he had built in the kitchen, made the bed, and sat a new rocking chair before

452 | Vonda Wilson Sheets

the hearth in the front room.

Neither spoke on the short journey to the old house that Robert now called his own. Eva's hands were tucked inside a muff, her lovely hair rolled into a bun, and her lowered lashes hid the intensity with which she watched Robert's hands on the reins of the horse.

He pulled up to the front of the house, barely able to say "Whoa!" while pulling on the reins. The perfectly-executed stop presented the steps to Eva, and she knew once she climbed them, the house--and Robert--would belong to her.

Lifting her out of the buggy, Robert took her across the threshold, and she began laughing in delight, kissing him as he opened the door.

"I love you," she said softly as he shifted to allow her body to slide down his until her feet were on the floor.

"Don't go anywhere," he told her. "I'll be right back." He backed out of the door, looking at her until he turned to go back down the steps and retrieve her portmanteau and a basket of food his mother sent with them.

She stood waiting while he put the portmanteau in the bedroom and the basket of food on the kitchen table. Once more, he gazed at her…and reached for the fur stole around her shoulders.

"Aren't you going to take the horse to the barn?" Eva asked softly.

He nodded, tossing the stole and her muff to the new rocking chair.

"Don't move," Robert was halfway out the door. "Don't move."

"But I have a gown…"

Shaking his head, Robert came back to stand in the open doorway.

"No."

"But…"

He smiled. "You aren't going to need it tonight."

Her eyebrows rose, and there was a soft "Oh!" and a pretty blush spread along her cheeks.

"Don't move," he said again, and closed the door.

Eva remained in the middle of the front room. Her heart was racing, but she wasn't nervous. She had grown up on a farm, so she had some knowledge of what sex actually was. Besides, watching her mother and stepfather had taught her that bedding one's husband was something to be sought, wanted, desired. The years of waiting for this day had shown her there was nothing to fear from Robert.

The horse put away, Robert opened the door and found Eva, just where he'd left her. "Good!"

The tenderness on his face nearly took her breath away. He picked her up once more, and shouldered his way into the bedroom, where he sat her on the bed.

Kneeling before her, he picked up her right foot. He removed the shoe, and sighed as he ran a finger along her instep, to her ankle and up to her knee. Repeating the action with her left shoe, both of his hands ran up to her knees.

"Robert."

"Hmm?" He looked at her face.

Taking his hands, she stood, the train of her dress falling to the floor. Eva released Robert's hands, and went for the button of his trousers.

"I really can't wait any longer," Eva told her new husband as she unbuttoned his trousers and slid her hands along his shoulders. He shrugged his suit coat off.

That was the last coherent thought either of them had for several hours.

The new Mrs. Robert Prather was definitely Maggie Kinney's daughter.

✎ ✎

Not quite a year after Billy Miles began working overnight at the Berry Hotel, he was promoted to junior day clerk. He ran errands for guests and learned other duties, including bookkeeping.

The best part about his promotion was he now had some evenings free. Not wanting to appear eager to hang out in the saloon, he was on his way back from supper at the diner one evening when Jim Berry hailed him from the porch in front of the Berry Brothers Saloon.

Reluctantly, Billy continued past the hotel, crossing the street and receiving a hearty handshake from Berry.

"Congratulations on the promotion," Berry told him, nearly dragging him into the saloon. "The wife told me you're making her mornings easier now."

Billy smiled as he sat on a stool at the bar while his employer

454 | Vonda Wilson Sheets

walked behind the counter and poured Billy a shot of whiskey. "This one's on the house," Berry said, a broad grin on his face.

"Thank you, Mr. Berry," Billy took the glass, appreciative. He sipped the bourbon as Berry poured himself a drink as well.

"I don't often drink while I'm here," Berry nodded to Billy as he tapped his glass against the one in the young man's hand. "It's hard to please my wife, me being gone so much."

"You just got back yesterday, didn't you?" Billy made conversation.

"Yep, brought in some wine and dress goods from the St. Louis area," answered Berry. "I'm leavin' tomorrow for Kansas."

"Not much time at home, Mr. Berry," observed Billy.

"No, it's not," Berry agreed. "Gotta make money while it's easy. So…"

Billy took another sip from his glass, his eyebrows raised inquiringly.

"How would you like to work in here sometimes?"

Billy considered his reply. "Well, how often are you talking about?"

Berry shrugged. "Three, four nights a week, while I'm gone. The missus don't like the guy I hired a couple months ago. Says he's got sticky fingers. She figures if someone else is also working, he won't be able to steal so much."

"Are you gonna fire him, or just cut his time?"

"Think we'll just cut his time for now. Should be a difference in the books if he is stealing."

"Well, I don't want to take someone else's job." That was a sure way to borrow trouble he didn't want, Billy thought.

"Eh." Berry shrugged again. "He's been missing work a couple nights a week. Says he's sick. She don't like being in here by herself at night."

Billy nodded slowly, considering. Then he shrugged, and finished off his drink. "I'm willing to try it," he told Berry. "When do you want me to start?"

"Now's as good a time as any."

It was different, being on the working side of the counter. Billy knew most of the men who came in, and made tips that went into his savings account. He was saving every cent he could, to buy the

Absolution | 455

Snapp farms whenever Sam's family decided to sell.

Morning fog, summer haze, the season was hot and muggy. He discovered he enjoyed working in the saloon, listening to other men talk politics and make plans for Forsyth's progress.

The talking rose to a fever pitch when plans were announced for a September gathering of Civil War veterans. In Taney County, for the first time since the end of the war, Union and Confederate men and women would meet and mingle, enjoy activities, listen to politicians speak, and watch battle re-enactments. It promised to be a "great event," as Nat Kinney told his friends in the saloon one night.

Billy had just cleaned the table next to the group seated around Nat Kinney, in the far corner of the saloon. On this night, he was not paying a great deal of attention to conversations because his father and younger brothers were shooting a game of pool.

"Billy!" It was Nat Kinney. Billy turned, holding the tray of dirty beer mugs and tucking a white linen bar towel in his back pocket.

"Yes, sir?" Tenseness sat on the young man's shoulders, Nat noted. He found it interesting that Billy had not spoken more than a few words to his father or brothers.

"You live here in town now," Nat said. "What do you think of our plans for the reunion of our fine veterans?"

Billy smiled. "I think it'll be good for business," he said as his free hand indicated the saloon.

"Ah, yes." Nat rubbed his chin, glancing at Gabe Branson, Charles Groom, Bill Hensley, James DeLong, his son Paul, and the other men at his table. Then he looked Billy straight in the eye. "Would you like to participate in the battle re-enactment?" It seemed the entire bar was listening for Billy's answer, except for Jimmy, who was racking the balls for another game against his father. Emanuel moved abruptly to Jimmy's side.

Taking the time to think for a few seconds, Billy finally shook his head. "Mrs. Berry will likely need me to work, if the town's going to be as busy as you say." He turned to walk away, tossing a polite "Thank you for asking" over his shoulder. Jimmy lifted the triangle off the loosely-packed balls.

"Will you help clean up the town square?" Nat's voice was commanding, so Billy halted and half-turned to answer the man. The action at the pool table came to a stop as William Miles held his shot, apparently waiting for his son's answer.

456 | Vonda Wilson Sheets

"I can do that," Billy nodded.

William's shot cracked the racked balls, sending two into the far corner pockets. One was the eight ball.

"Pa!" Jimmy protested, then set about gathering the balls once more. William grimly took a sip of his beer, and walked over to the half-rail on the wall. His back was to Billy and Kinney's table.

"Mebbe you should do it right, then," was his only comment to Jimmy, as the saloon's noise level began to rise.

When the table was ready--Emanuel showing Jimmy how to pack the triangle--William took another sip of beer, then resumed his rack-breaking stance.

Nat Kinney and his cronies were paying for their drinks and leaving, and Nat stopped as William bent to eye his shot.

"Mr. Miles, will you be joining us?"

William straightened slowly, eyes on Jimmy and Emanuel at the far end of the table. He squinted a little, then pivoted on his left heel to face Nat. He shook his head. "Nope."

"But we need representatives of the Confederacy's fine soldiers," Nat cajoled. "It will be a grand event!"

William Miles smiled slightly, and reached for a chalk to use on his cue stick.

"Reckon I had enough of those kinds of 'grand events,' Mr. Kinney," he said. "Ain't gonna change the outcome."

Nat's gesture was rather grandiose as he indicated Billy, who was watching from behind the bar. "Your son seems to think it will be good for the town. He has volunteered to help."

William's smile left his face, and his head tilted toward Billy. "Got his reasons," William replied. Then he set his gaze on Nat and his friends, and snorted. "So do I." He bent once more to the pool table.

"Very well," Nat conceded. "It will be a good time."

The stick hit the cue once more. This time, three balls went into the pockets, but the eight ball remained on the table. Jimmy whooped as William tilted his head, squinting, fully aware that Nat was still watching him as he leaned to make his next play. Billy brought his father and brothers fresh beer; there were no smiles, no recognition of their relationship.

"I hope you reconsider, Mr. Miles. There is still time. It will be a reunion, you know." Nat clapped his hands on James and Paul's shoulders, and smiled broadly.

William took his time, hit his marks, and another ball went into the pocket. He continued to focus on his game, fully aware that Billy was standing between him and Nat Kinney. Father and son met gazes, one's features hardening, the other dropping any hint of emotion. Billy was the first to drop his eyes, and he made his way back through the men to the bar.

"Reckon it just ain't time," William bent once more to his game.

Nat nodded, his hands pushing James and Paul toward the door. "I understand," Nat told William.

While Nat Kinney was riding home to Maggie that night, he pondered the relationship between William Miles and his namesake. "Do you know what happened?" he asked Gabe while they were letting the horses drink.

"No, not exactly," Galba Branson answered. "Billy wanted to buy a farm, and took a job in town to make some money, from what I gathered."

"Yes, I know that. Is he attending school?"

"Not that I know of, Cap'n," Gabe thought for a moment. "But he is speaking better than he used to."

"Find out, would you?" Nat turned his horse off toward his home, where he knew Maggie would be waiting for him.

"Why?" Gabe asked.

Nat rode back to Gabe's side. "He's a smart young man, Gabe. I'm just....curious. That's all."

The men parted without another word, Gabe riding off into the darkness. Tired as he was, Nat's mind was busy. Despite the number of legal issues he was having, Nat was slowly building up prospects to buy several businesses in Forsyth. Billy Miles would bear watching, especially if the break with his family continued.

Well over a thousand people were in Forsyth during the soldiers' reunion in September. It was a festive occasion for visitors and residents alike, and seemed to indicate that whatever trouble Taney County had in the past was over. Taney County was tamed, civilized, even polite as the blue and the gray fought once more on the banks of Swan Creek, cheered on by the audience. Veterans of the Union and the Confederacy smiled, shook hands, and marched off with their families to enjoy a picnic and the chance to socialize.

Maggie Kinney wore her red silk dress to the dance on the last night. Nat, flushed with the success of his planning, danced with his wife and thought maybe it was time for them to move to Forsyth.

He didn't see the distance in her eyes, nor did he notice that she was not enjoying herself in the role of hostess. She danced with other men, smiling politely and saying the correct words as the rules of society dictated. But when she was tired, she sat by herself, sipping lemonade and wondering if she dared return to their room at the hotel.

Nat roamed the square filled with people, accepting words of congratulations and drinking toasts. He was in his element. He occasionally looked for the red of Maggie's dress, and seemed to always find her in the middle of the dancing.

The Miles and Barker families were there. So were the Moores, Haworths, Stallcups, Gideons, Hensleys....Nat spoke to everyone, it seemed. He didn't notice when Maggie finally left, just before midnight.

॰ ॰

The harvesting was easier this year in some ways. The men didn't have as many fields to thresh or pick, since Sam's farm had not been planted.

But Kate and William Miles felt the absence of Sam and Billy left little room for jocularity and fun. It was a somber group who ate supper each night at the Miles or Barker homes, and the men fell into bed, exhausted and sore. Samp Barker was working as deputy circuit clerk in Forsyth, and was only able to work the farms for a few days.

Kate and Sally were tired as well. They had been canning produce from the vegetable gardens, fruit from the various trees and vines, and keeping the men fed.

One night, it was simply too much to attempt to sleep. Kate sat in her rocker on the front porch, smoking her pipe and listening to the sounds of the night. Samp had gone down in his back, so Sally took him home to sleep in his own bed. She was alone.

The front door of the house was open to let in air. She raised her skirts to allow the slight breeze access to her bare legs and feet. She didn't turn her head when William spoke from the darkened house.

Absolution | 459

"You best come to bed."

"I'm too hot. Too tired."

"Mebbe too sad right now?" He lifted her feet and sat on the wooden box she used as a footrest, depositing her feet on his lap.

"There's that, too."

"You still think you're gonna work in the corn tomorrow?" She couldn't see his features distinctly, but heard the disapproval in his voice.

"Someone has to," she answered, unwilling to give in on that issue. "We'll be fine."

William snorted, but kept silent for a while. He began to rub her feet absently. "Damn, it's hot."

Kate sighed. "I'd give anything for things to be the way they were."

His hands stopped. Jerking his head, William put her feet down, and stood, holding out his hand. "Come on."

"I'm not ready to sleep, William." Sensing him shake his head, she brushed his hand away. "I'm not!"

"Nah, got a better idea." There was a teasing note in his voice.

"What? It's too hot for that, too," she told him as he stuck his hand back in front of her face.

"Jist come on." He would not give in, so she took his hand and stood.

He led her off the porch and toward the barn, familiarity guiding him in the dark. Dropping her hand at the barn door, William said, "Don't go anywhere." He stepped inside, and was back out within seconds. Then he took her hand once more, and led her on.

Realizing where they were going didn't take her long. Their bare feet made no sound on the path down the hill. She moved to grab his waist with both hands, walking in his trail, her pipe clenched between her teeth.

They had not done this in many years. Matter of fact--

"Yeah, bin a while." He stepped over a rock. She did, too.

Adjusting her gait to his, she giggled. "You were going to move that rock."

"Still goin' to." He chuckled in response to her giggle.

When they reached the bottom of the hill, his gait slowed over the creek gravel. As calloused as their feet were, it could still be painful to walk on.

460 | Vonda Wilson Sheets

It was lighter down here than at the house. The white gravel seemed to glow with starlight, and Kate felt some of her agitation ease as she sat on the big boulder overlooking the creek. William handed her the flask he'd brought from the barn.

"Ladies first."

She took a healthy swallow, wiped her face with her forearm, then drank again. Ah. He'd brought some of his prized stash. Smiling, she watched him undress, his dark arms and face contrasting with the whiteness of his body and upper legs.

"Did you plan this?" she asked, curious.

He took his turn with the flask, then pulled her up. "Fer a while," he admitted. "Raise your arms."

Once she was down to her chemise, they both drank some more, then waded into the water. The swimming hole wasn't too deep, but they held hands and submerged together.

The small boulder she used to sit on in the water was no longer there, gone in a flood, she supposed. They sat on the shelf-rock bottom of the creek, feeling the wet moss along their buttocks and legs, floating gently with the water's flow.

"Better?"

She smiled. "Much."

William floated a little closer to his wife. "Now, 'bout my even better idea…"

"Yes. Tell me more."

Taking her hand under the water, William began massaging it, slowly rubbing his thumb in her palm. "Whyn't I show you?" he murmured.

On the way back up the hill an hour later, William stubbed his toe on the problem rock in the path. Kate began to laugh, and once started, she couldn't stop. She sat down hard on the rock, her back to him, and once her laughter became sobs, he sat down behind her, wrapping her with his arms. The flask was empty, so he just held her until she was done.

They were both sad and grieving. Billy would return some day, they knew. But until then…

"I'm moving thet goddamned rock while you're in the corn field tomorrow."

"Mmmm." She leaned back against him, her head on his shoulder. "You keep right on saying that."

Wash Middleton's trial for the murder of Sam Snapp finally began in the October court session. Between special appointments and continuances, it was seventeen months after Sam died when Wash finally was in court.

He wasn't a friendly man, but he was a family man. Special Prosecutor James DeLong wondered why Wash Middleton did not appear to be worried when the jury handed down a sentence of forty years in the state penitentiary. Sheriff McHaffie handcuffed Wash and took him across the town square to the jail.

The next morning, the appointed judge approved a reduction in Wash's sentence to fifteen years, but it didn't matter. Someone had unlocked the jail and aided Wash Middleton with escape.

Rumors of a manhunt, a shootout in Arkansas, and another escape flew through Forsyth on angry wings.

Fayette Snapp met with his brothers Robert and Matt to form a plan. While the county and the state posted rewards for information leading to Middleton's arrest, the brothers decided to hire a detective to find him. Since Wash's first arrest, Fayette had been in favor of letting the law mete out justice for Sam's murder. It was a clear case of premeditated murder, the brothers thought. Now that Wash was on the loose, however, Fayette put a bounty of $500 for capture, and another $500 for proof of Middleton's death.

"I'll get him with money," Fayette told his brothers.

Within a month, Jim Holt was on Wash Middleton's trail.

CHAPTER 46
Holt Finds His Man

Jim Holt's instructions from the Snapp family had been quite clear. "Take your time, make sure it's the right man," Fayette Snapp said.

That proved difficult, but Jim Holt took his time.

৯ ৵

Taking a narrow dirt trail off the heavily-traveled road, he rode to his brother's barn. The sun was rising as he came out, saddlebags over his shoulder. He paused at the dooryard gate, looking south. The northern edge of the Boston Mountains could just be distinguished in the clear, lightening purple distance.

Twists and folds of rocky land filled the valleys, and the wide open ridge-tops between him and the mountains were numerous. The miles were waiting for him to travel further, but he could not.... not yet.

Noise from the house meant someone was up. He smiled, half-turned toward the back door, then glanced south again as Joe came out with the bucket to milk the cow.

Joe greeted him and went on to the barn.

When it came--and it would--trouble would be from the north. But so would his family, and he would wait for them.

That evening, shouts from outside woke him.

It was the Boone County sheriff, along with a posse. His brother stoutly denied his presence, and he grinned.

None of the lawmen dismounted, and Joe didn't step down off the stoop.

"Tell your brother to be out of Boone County tonight, Joe," the sheriff said.

"If he was here, I'd tell him, but he ain't," Joe retorted, then said loudly, "You kin search the house."

The grin fell off his face as he pursed his lips, considering. That would not do.

This sheriff was a smart one. "Nope, thet's askin' to get shot."

Absolution | 463

Indeed. He brought his gun hand down, peering through a gap in the shuttered window.

A few more shouts, and Joe stomped back inside, slamming the door. The lawmen rode away.

He came down a minute later, to find his sister-in-law and brother having a heated discussion in whispers. Martha fell silent when he walked in, but glared at Joe. The children ranged in age from eighteen down, and they, too, were silent, watching their father and uncle.

Joe rubbed his face, rolled his head, and stretched his neck, massaging the back of it. His face was tight as he picked up his fork and stirred gravy into his mashed potatoes and peas.

"You're gonna hev to go, Wash," Joe finally said, then shoved a mouthful of food in.

George Washington Middleton nodded, then took the plate of food Martha was offering him. "Think I'll go west some," he said, kneeling down by the stove to eat.

Joe chewed his food with difficulty, then took a drink of water to aid him in swallowing. "How long before they get here?"

Wash shrugged. "Few days."

Pushing his chair back, Joe stood and went to the door. "I'll get your horse ready. Finish eating.'"

Within a short time, Wash was ready to go. Martha packed him some food, and he took it from her, stuffing it in his saddlebag. She also handed him a blanket roll, a distinctly old quilt tied with stained twine.

It was full dark. He stepped outside, quickly shutting the door so he would cast no silhouette. Joe had not returned from the barn, and Wash made his way through the dooryard to the gate, opening it.

A shot ricocheted off the vine-covered pergola, and he pulled his gun from his waist, crouching low. Cries from within the house were punctuated by the posse's shouts. They had not ridden away after all, Wash reflected. He duck-walked through the gate, and made his way along the fence to the west end of the dooryard, where the woods offered cover.

Joe was raising hell in the barn, shouting at the lawmen who were holding him inside with Wash's horse.

"Damn." The word was hidden in his beard. He was going to have to leave the horse.

A couple more shots rang out. If he responded, they would know exactly where he was.

Joe was still denying his presence. "I done tole you, go search the house."

There were stealthy movements along the near side of the barn. Taking a chance, Wash ran for the trees.

"Hold!" A man's voice called. It was the sheriff.

"Don't fire at my house!" Joe Middleton was pissed.

The trees grew sporadically down the hill toward the valley of Long Creek, offering just enough cover for him to get away. He made his way around the village of Denver and crossed the big creek, soaking himself past his knees. He knew he was in Carroll County now.

There were friends in the area. Wash stayed in an old shack, out in the woods, and sent word to his brother. After a week of whittling, he began watching the road west of Denver at night. The third night, the noise of a wagon crossing the creek echoed up to him. Cautiously, he made his way down from his lookout point, his saddlebags and blanket under a pile of dead branches just off the road.

A lantern was swinging from the left side of the wagon, its light a feeble thing in this dark, misty night. There was just enough glow for him to ascertain who was driving the oxen. Wash scrabbled for his bags and blanket, walking out of the woods as his son kept the team going up the hill. He trotted to the back of the wagon, and tossed his things in. Then he leapt and hauled himself over the gate, falling into the arms of his wife and children.

They headed south, for the mountains. Joe and Martha had lived near Jasper, down in Newton County, a few years before. There, Wash figured, he'd be able to live in peace.

Wash and Tempa had moved frequently during their marriage, and that experience stood them in good stead now, living in a rented place near Parthenon.

The advantage of their isolation overlooking the Little Buffalo river was that they saw few people except on church Sundays, and it took no little time for Wash to get used to a new name. The children went to school, adapting easily to a different surname. There were occasional letters from Joe, read by one of children while Wash worked his knife, carving constantly. He could work wood into beautiful things.

Spring became full summer, and the family settled in. There was to be a big Independence Day celebration, and the children clamored to go. Since he had no good reason to refuse, Tempa packed baskets of food, and they rode in the wagon to the wide spot in the road that served as a gathering place and post office.

As early in the day as it was, people were already tossing blankets on the ground under trees, and children were playing, anticipation in the air. They walked about, looking for a good place to land, the younger children running in circles around their parents.

It was crowded and noisy, Wash noted, as Tempa threw a blanket down under a big oak. One of her church friends waved at her, and she waved back. Then she sat down, patting the blanket and smiling at Wash.

He smiled back, and sat next to her, awkwardly crossing his legs.

The younger children were soon besieged by friends, scattering like guinea fowl and every bit as noisy. The older children were more sedate. Later, there was to be dancing, and the choices of dance partners would not be made lightly.

Neighbors and friends filled the small park. Wash and the boys stood with other men, joking and talking about this and that. He was alert to being called by his newly-assumed name, and found himself on the receiving end of odd looks but twice. When the food began to be brought out and put on long tables, the chatter fell only slightly in volume.

A very necessary urge made itself known to Wash. He excused himself from the table, and crossed the park to find the privy. Except for this basic urge, Wash was as relaxed as he'd been in months.

"Wash Middleton!"

Too late, he realized he had stopped walking, half-turning to respond to his name, the one nobody here knew him by.

"You are Wash Middleton?" The man's voice was mild, and Wash turned to see the owner.

"I am. Who are you?"

"Name's Holt. You're under arrest."

The world around him shifted. He was only a few feet from the trees. He eyed the man.

"I don't know thet I am," Wash replied, raising his left hand as he shifted his right behind his back, and pulled his pistol.

The last thing Wash Middleton heard was gunfire, and it wasn't from his gun.

It took no short time for Jim Holt to collect the various rewards and bounty money that had been placed on the head of George Washington Middleton. But he persevered, and got it.

CHAPTER 47
Forsyth, 1888

Jim Berry was gone on one of his interminable sales trips in February, 1888, when his wife decided to leave Billy Miles in charge of the hotel and saloon and take her own trip.

She was gone for four days and nights. The morning after she arrived home, Billy waited in the office behind the counter to show her the books and receipts he kept. She opened the door from the room behind the office, where she lived, clad in her cloak and hat.

"Oh, good morning, Billy," she said, and waved her fur muff at him. "Don't bother about those now. I have an appointment. I should be back before lunch."

He raised an eyebrow, but nodded. She seemed entirely too cheerful to him, he decided. Still, it was none of his business. The other clerk merely shrugged into his jacket, to fetch breakfast for the hotel's few guests from the Widow Maggie's Diner.

The widow and her daughters had rented a small house on the south side of Forsyth, near the river. She recently bought the diner from the Berrys, and rechristened it. Jim Berry did not want to sell, but his wife did, so it was sold and the widow was doing very well, indeed.

While thinking about the widow, Billy was surprised to see his boss walk into the lobby, disheveled and filthy. "Where's my wife?" Berry asked, coming behind the counter and peering into the office.

"She said she had an appointment, Mr. Berry," Billy resisted the urge to shrug. He had enough money to buy both of Sam's farms from the Snapp family. Now he was saving money for seed and other things to get them up and running.

"Oh, hell," Berry was obviously agitated. "Do you know where?"

"No, sir."

Berry strode out the door, his bulky form speeding out of sight. Billy waited for the night clerk to return with breakfast.

A single gunshot went off across the square, and like everyone else in town, Billy ran to the window to see what was going on.

Jim Berry had shattered the window of George Taylor's law office with his shot. His wife came out of the office, shrieking. She

468 | Vonda Wilson Sheets

pounded Berry on the arms, forcing him to drop the gun, which was then picked up by George Taylor. Almost lazily, Taylor aimed the gun on its owner.

"I'll sue you for that," Taylor shouted.

"You lying, cheating, thieving bastard!" Mrs. Berry's high-pitched voice carried well as she continued to pound on Jim.

He ducked, moving to get away from her, shouting back curses of his own. "What the hell were you doing in Taylor's office?" as he scurried around.

"Getting a divorce!" She ran at him, and he took off once more, headed for his saloon. "You dumb son-of-a-bitch, you shouldn't leave your mail where I can find it!" It seemed Mrs. Berry had found a letter from a woman in Kansas addressed to Jim Berry. Jim slammed the saloon door shut and locked it against his wife.

The entire town was entertained by the Berrys' problems over the next few weeks, then months. Jim stayed in the saloon and store building, sleeping on the counter in the store. Mrs. Berry had not only hired George Taylor to be her lawyer--Billy came upstairs one morning to find Taylor coming out of her room. He smiled conspiratorially at Billy, then left for his office.

When Jim discovered George Taylor was living in his own hotel, with his own wife, he began keeping a shotgun and several pistols near him all the time. He tried to persuade Billy to quit the hotel, and work only for him in the store and saloon.

Living in town was suddenly complicated. Billy found a room for rent off the square, and moved out of the hotel. Carrying his winter weight suit while wearing the summer wool one, he climbed the stairs of the basement, to find Mrs. Berry waiting for him.

"Are you quitting?" she asked him, watchful.

Billy nodded, adjusting the suit over his shoulder. "Yes, ma'am." He reached into the chest pocket of his jacket, and pulled out a letter. "There's my resignation."

She glanced through it, then tore it up, dropping the pieces on the ground. Defiantly, she eyed Billy narrowly.

"I'll give you a raise." Billy shook his head, raising his hand to halt her, when she added, "It'll be enough to pay for that room of yours. I know you're saving money." Seeing him hesitate, she wheedled, "I'll even let you work for Mr. Berry as well."

Someone must have overheard Jim offering him a raise a couple nights ago, Billy realized. He eyed Mrs. Berry.

"I'll stay on the same terms I offered Mr. Berry," he said carefully.

"What terms are those?"

"I don't discuss or listen to his private matters."

She smiled, a gleam in her eyes. Then she stuck out a hand, and Billy switched his winter suit around to shake it. "Done." Craftily, she added, "Since you are not discussing my private business with Jim, I'm gonna tell you now. I want you to stay, because George is going to get me this hotel." The smile widened. "You're the best clerk I've got. I'm gonna need you."

Billy sighed. "Mrs. Berry--"

"I know, I know. You don't want to talk about it."

Billy began to walk away. "I'll work for you, but not if you force me to listen."

"Billy, don't--" She grabbed his arm. "I'm sorry. Jist don't go yet." Pointedly, he looked down at her hand on his arm, and she removed it. Then she took a deep breath. "You drive a hard bargain."

He smiled slightly. "I'm late for work, Mrs. Berry."

She sent him a dirty look, but said only, "I'll see you in the morning."

"Yes, ma'am."

That night, Billy noticed Nat Kinney watching him from his customary seat. While he continued in conversation with his friends, Nat kept glancing over at Billy behind the bar or cleaning tables.

It was quite late when he approached the young man to pay for his drinks. When Billy handed him his change, a cool "Thank you" was all he heard in Billy's voice.

"Mr. Miles," he began.

"Sir?" Billy halted washing the beer mugs.

Nat looked around, but saw no one close enough to hear them. "Congratulations on your promotion," he said in a low voice.

"Sir?" Startled, Billy looked up at Kinney's face. It was quite a sincere face, Billy thought. "What promotion?" he asked.

"George Taylor is a friend of mine," Nat said. "I understand that Mrs. Berry is attempting to seize Mr. Berry's businesses."

Billy resumed washing the mugs. "I don't discuss the Berrys, sir. Both of them have been good to me."

"But this is your business, Billy." Nat's voice was bland, but there was a cocky smile on his face when Billy snorted and looked up again.

"Nobody's said anything about a promotion," he retorted.

Nat averted his gaze, and dropped his voice even more. "I will be coming into some money from a lawsuit quite soon," he said. "I intend to use it to purchase a store…" He paused, leveled a stare directly at Billy, then continues, "and a saloon. I'm even considering a hotel."

Billy's head nodded slightly, absorbing this piece of news. He returned Nat's stare. "What's that got to do with me?" he asked.

"I'd like to hire you," Kinney's voice remained soft, inveigling Billy. "Now that my son is going to run for election, I'll need a young man to manage….things."

At that point, Jim Berry came in, yelling. "That's it. I'm filing for divorce." There was blood on his hands, and it was evident he'd been hit more than once with something hard. His nose was bleeding, and he had a black eye forming. He entered the counter's pass-through, reaching for the rag in Billy's hands. Ignoring Nat, Jim said, "She hit me with a cane, but I taught the bitch a lesson. Close it down, Billy." He took the wet rag and left the saloon, going into the store.

"Excuse me, Mr. Kinney," Billy said, and he took a key from a nail in the wall. "Alright, it's time to call it a night!" he called out to the few remaining patrons.

Nat didn't leave until he caught Billy's eye again. "Don't forget what I said, Billy," he told the young man.

Billy's face went blank as he passed Kinney en route to the door. Nat was the last to leave, and as Billy pushed the doors shut behind Kinney, locking them, he realized he was tired, and hung his head, to ease the tension in his neck and shoulders.

Berry had beat his wife after she came at him with a cane. He'd been skulking around the hotel, and she caught him. Enraged, the two of them went for each other's throats, fighting dirtier than Emanuel and Jimmy Miles had ever seen. The brothers were walking around the square in the late evening, discussing ways to persuade Billy to move back home when they heard the fight start.

Jim Berry wasn't the only one with a black eye, Billy found out when he left the saloon building a short time later. His brother Jimmy had been on the receiving end of a punch intended for Mrs. Berry, and had a nice shiner of his own.

They walked companionably for a little way.

"Pa wants you home now," Manny told him.

Billy shook his head. "Can't do it right now," he told his brothers. Then, almost as an afterthought, he added, "I just got offered a job. A good one."

Jimmy, who was gingerly touching the flesh around his now-shut eye, asked, "By who?" while Manny stopped and exclaimed, "Doing what?"

They saw Billy's smile, even in the darkness off the square. He answered both questions with one statement that made Jimmy bang his sore eye.

"Running Nat Kinney's new store."

"Ow!"

"It could be." With that, the brothers continued to the room Billy had rented at the boardinghouse.

Billy Miles moved back home in mid-August. By that time, Jim Berry had filed for bankruptcy, and what with all his charges and lawsuits, the businesses involved were shut down by the circuit judge. Nat Kinney was assigned to inventory the store.

He spent several days at home before returning to Forsyth to begin the arduous task of counting every item in the store.

Life was good, he felt.

Eva had announced her "delicate condition" some weeks before, and the prospect of a grandchild to spoil brightened Maggie's mood considerably. Georgia was doing well in her schoolwork, and she sent her youngest child to stay with Eva for a few days. James was campaigning for the office of prosecuting attorney, and he and Paul were traveling the county, speaking to small groups and meeting the electorate. It was James' first attempt to run for office. Maggie encouraged him to seek all voters, not just former Bald Knobbers who could be counted on to support the son of Nat Kinney.

It was late. Maggie doused the lantern in the kitchen, and walked out to sit on the porch, carrying a bottle of wine and enjoying the cooler air. It had been incredibly hot, and the house was stifling. It would be nice to sleep outside, and she said as much to Nat, who came up from checking the barn.

472 | Vonda Wilson Sheets

He agreed, and together, they went into the bedroom. She began to take the sheets from the feather mattress when Nat stopped her. "Let me," he said, and began to roll the mattress into an awkward bundle.

At times like this, Maggie appreciated his strength more than usual. She fanned herself, and decided to strip down, putting on a sleeveless cotton shift that only reached to her knees.

Nat shooed the dogs off the porch, and dropped the mattress on the floor. When Maggie finally joined him, he was laying on his back with his feet up on the cabin wall, looking at the stars.

"I'm going to miss being able to do this," he said as she slipped down to lay beside him.

"Mmmm. Yes, I'm sure it would be difficult to do this at the hotel," she responded, not really listening. They lay companionably together for several minutes, watching the moon's path.

He turned on his side to face her, propping himself with an elbow. It was too hot to lie close together, and the air wasn't moving at all. He liked to play a game on these hot nights, when her mind was far away. He would touch her with one small fingertip, and count to see how long it took her to notice. If she was playing the piano when he did it, she never noticed until it was time for her to close the lid.

Her mind had not been with him in some time, he thought, and moved his hand to touch the outside of her hip. For so long, they had read each other's thoughts, and he spoke with her about many things. But in the past two years or so, while he was concentrating on becoming a legitimate businessman, he had stopped discussing his daily life with her. He didn't understand her anymore, either.

A frown crossed his face. His finger twitched against her hip.

That business of leaving the dance at the veterans' reunion last fall! When he'd stormed into the room at the hotel, long after she'd left, Maggie calmly told him she was having "women's trouble." Understanding her to mean she was experiencing one of her increasingly-rare cycles, he had noted the flush on her face and the damp, cool rag she held against her head.

He was certain she wasn't experiencing a cycle tonight. But she was very far away, and she hadn't played her piano but one night this week.

"Maggie?"

"Hmmm?" Her eyes remained focused on the sky.

"I said, 'I'm going to miss doing this.' Do you not understand?"

"Understand what, Nat? You're leaving for Forsyth in the morning. Of course, you're going to miss doing this." Her eyes remained on the sky.

"No." He paused, then reached to stroke her cheek, to get her attention. Finally, she was looking at him, and she watched his mouth move by star- and moonshine. I should pour some wine, she thought, then she realized she was not listening to him, and his words jumped in front of her.

"...so when we move into town, we won't be able to do this anymore." His hand slid down the side of her neck, and he began to massage her breast.

He failed to notice that she froze. Any thought of wine or lovemaking shattered against his statement.

"What do you mean, move into town?" she asked in a strange voice he didn't recognize.

"I'm buying the Berry store and saloon building, so we'll have to live in town."

Maggie brushed Nat's hand away with no little force.

"Don't be absurd. We don't have to--"

"It's time, Maggie. You can run the store and--"

She sat up. "I'm not running a store," she told him.

"Well, I think Billy will be fine, but one of us should be there--"

Her head was shaking "no," and suddenly Maggie understood something about Nat Kinney that she'd never seen before, in nearly twenty-two years of marriage.

He not only controlled her, but he didn't know her.

She was so ill-suited to run a store of any kind....why didn't Nat see it?

He stopped talking, letting her think about his plans. He laid down once more, this time watching his hand, dark on the cotton, as it ran up and down her breast, ever so gently. Then he let it fall down to her lap, and he touched her lightly down her leg.

She did not appear to notice until he tried to reach under the gathers of her gown, then she pushed his hand away. "It's too hot," she told him, still considering his plans. Once more, he reached for her, this time for her chin, to turn her face toward him for a kiss.

A drop of sweat fell on his hand, so he let her turn away from him. She lay on her side, facing away, and said only, "I will think on this. Good night, Nat." She forgot about the wine entirely. He didn't understand, she knew. She didn't mind if he wanted the world, but her world was him, especially now that the children were nearly all grown. She accepted that she wasn't the world to him, and had come to terms with that years ago.

Nat Kinney sighed, and realized he, too, was sweating. It really was too hot. And he felt an odd vibration from his beloved wife, the woman he wanted to give the world to.

On Monday morning, August 20, 1888, Nat Kinney was eating breakfast at the Widow Maggie's diner with Galba Branson and Charles Groom when it occurred to him to send food out to the two men who accompanied him everywhere these days. He asked Miranda to take care of it, and she nodded in understanding.

None of the men who took turns standing guard over him now held a candle to Wash Middleton, he thought. Wash would have come inside with him, and it would have been Wash listening to him, as he pretended to now listen to Charles Groom and Gabe Branson.

When Bill Hensley joined them, he realized it was getting late in the morning. If he finished the store inventory today, Nat decided he would ride home. Maybe he could bring Maggie back to town later in the week. He smiled, then realized that Gabe Branson was telling him about Jim Berry's latest shenanigan.

"...so he says he's going to shoot you, and he's got Matt Snapp on the front porch of the hotel with him, just waiting for you."

Nat scoffed. "Jim's been 'waiting' for me since I started the inventory," he told the men. "What happened to his wife?"

"She's got a room over to the boardinghouse," Gabe answered.

"Ah." Nat pushed his chair back, and stood. He reached for his wallet and tossed money on the table for the food. He never asked for a bill at the diner--he liked the thought of appearing to be rich enough he didn't have to worry about money. His men appreciated the fact that he usually paid for their food and drink.

Outside, Gabe left the others, going over to the jail to check on things. Charles Groom and Bill Hensley accompanied him down the sidewalk, and the bodyguards trailed a discreet distance behind. It was easy duty, they got paid daily, and there had been no threat from anyone since Wash Middleton died.

Except for Jim Berry. Because Nat scoffed at Berry, so did the guards. No one appeared to take him seriously.

The three men continued talking as they walked into the stuffy store. Sweat began forming on their skins immediately, and Nat stripped down to his shirtsleeves, including taking his shoulder holster with its ivory-handled pistols off and setting it on the counter. The leather was sweat-stained, but Nat preferred it over keeping his pistols in his pockets or his waistband.

"Captain, why are you involved in this business?" Charles Groom was curious. Nat had never struck him as the business owner-type. The demands of a business called for daily work, and he felt Nat would much rather have some variety in his days.

"I've someone in mind to run it." Nat's answer was abrupt as he took up the pad of paper, and tried to remember where he'd left off last night. Ah...

"You're buying the store?" Bill Hensley was curious now.

"I plan to, yes." Nat strode took two steps over to a table filled with pants. He frowned. Did he need to mark the sizes down as well? The answer to that question had been eluding him for three days, but now he only had clothing and shoes to count.

Better do sizes, too.

The other two men hesitated, then Bill interrupted him.

"Who do you aim to get in here?" He walked to the crock of water on the counter, then reached for a cup.

Nat, his patience strained, was brief. "Billy Miles."

Bill choked, then coughed, but Charles beat him to the next question. "Why Billy Miles? Surely there are others--"

Irritation crossed Nat's face. "I've been watching him for some time now. He's a hard worker, and reliable. I've already spoken to him."

Bill had recovered his breath. "I thought he was buying the Snapp farms."

Nat smiled, then bent once again to counting pants. "Oh, he did. His brothers are working on them." He did not raise his head again, but asked, "Now, if you'll excuse me..." his voice trailed off.

"Oh. Certainly." Charles tilted his head toward the door, and he and Bill Hensley went out the open door. The two guards were sitting on one side of the door, and one was pulling out a deck of cards.

Glancing across the street--yes, Jim Berry was sitting there, accompanied by Matt Snapp. Both men were heavily armed.

"Are you watching them?" Bill asked.

Both guards chuckled. "They ain't gonna do anything," he said dismissively. "It's been three days, and they ain't yet."

Bill stayed to remonstrate with the men; Charles spied Gabe across from him, and went to speak with him.

Both men noted Jim Berry had a rifle next to the chair he was leaning back in. Matt Snapp, coatless, had a shoulder harness with two pistols. He was leaning forward, looking toward the east; Gabe and Charles heard him exclaim.

"Well, damn me if it ain't Billy Miles!"

Charles and Gabe looked as well.

It *was* Billy. He was tanned from working at his farm over the recent weeks, since the hotel and saloon had closed. He was wearing farmer's clothing, and Charles realized that the heavy twill pants, with a plaid shirt and work boots, suited Billy much more than the suits he'd been wearing for over two years. He was also wearing at least one gun.

"That's interesting," Gabe mused.

"It's been two years since I've seen him in anything but a suit," Charles said slowly.

"Ye-es."

Ignoring Matt and Jim, Billy dismounted and tossed his reins over the horse rail in front of the hotel. He met the eyes of Gabe and Charles, and nodded in their direction.

Charles moved forward with his hand outstretched to grasp Billy's in a firm handshake, Gabe right behind him. "I understand you are to be congratulated on your new position."

There was a slight smile on the young man's face as he shook hands with Gabe. "Maybe. The details have not been worked out yet."

Gabe was puzzled, but Charles restrained him from speaking. "I'll tell you shortly." Then, to Billy, he indicated the store. "Captain Kinney is in the store."

"Ye-es." Billy glanced in the direction of the store, then over at Jim Berry and Matt Snapp.

"Billy has been hired to run the store when it re-opens," Charles was telling Galba.

It made no sense to Gabe, but then Billy murmured, "There's a couple things that must be worked out," and began to walk toward

Absolution | 477

the store.

Jim Berry heard Charles' explanation, but looked stupefied. Matt shook his arm, and said, "Hey! He's gonna get your store!"

Both men reached for their guns, and stood. Gabe moved in their direction, as did the bodyguards across the street. Berry was fluent in his disgust with his former employee.

"I'll be goddamned if that little runt's gonna run my store," yelled Berry, and ran out into the street, Matt hot on his heels.

The bodyguards met them in the middle of the street, then Gabe joined in, remonstrating with the irate Berry. Charles began to move in their direction, when he saw Billy Miles' younger brothers walking toward the store. Then Charles Groom ran, and tried, without success, to get Gabe's attention.

Jimmy and Emanuel Miles were both carrying guns.

The store should've been dim, Billy thought, but he didn't have to wait for his vision to adjust. The window curtains were thrown aside, trying to catch any tease of a breeze.

The shaking in his legs stopped the second he walked in. It was time. He had been waiting for more than two years.

Kinney had not heard him entering, or else ignored him. He took two steps more, then spoke easily. "Hot enough for you, Mr. Kinney?"

Upon hearing Billy Miles' voice, Nat whirled in impatience. "I told you not to come in this building, didn't I? I didn't want Jim Berry to know..."

"Oh." Billy shrugged, then took a couple more paces, closer to the counter and at an angle to Nat. "I just want a drink of water."

Nat's shoulders slumped, then he shrugged, a hand gesturing toward the crock of cool water. "Help yourself." Trying to remember where he was, he bent his head to his notes. Ah, there...

Billy took a drink of water, satisfying his thirst. Then he deliberately set the cup on the counter with a thump.

Later, he would remember hearing loud voices outside.

Now, though, he could hear Nat Kinney breathing.

"Sam Snapp was a friend of mine."

The big head rose, a stunned expression on Nat's face. He stood and stared at Billy, who was standing empty-handed.

Nat lunged for his pistol holster, and Billy gave him enough time to touch it. Then he pulled his pistol and fired.

The first one shattered Nat's left forearm, and he dropped his hand, roaring at the pain. He held one of his pistols in his right hand, and brought it up to aim at Billy.

The second bullet went straight into his heart, tearing a great hole in the deputy's badge he still wore, and he fell to the floor, his gun still in his right hand.

Billy walked over and stared down at Kinney's face, waiting for the life spark to fade. It did not take long.

Footsteps on the porch, and he turned.

Jimmy and Manny were standing at the door. Behind them were Gabe Branson and Charles Groom, and the two guards.

Billy walked to the doorway. His brothers stepped aside to allow him through, forcing the older men to back away.

Stopping on the edge of the porch, he waited until a good number of people were in front of him. They had come running at the sound of gunfire. Then Billy Miles raised his hands, his pistol still smoking, and announced, "I have killed Captain Kinney in self-defense."

Before anyone could pull a weapon on him, clicks from many guns sounded throughout the square.

William and Kate Miles, Samp Barker, Robert and Fayette Snapp, Will Moore, the Haworths, and several others had been hidden around the square for hours. Now their guns were trained on people in the street, on the front porch of the store, and at the door.

"You men just hold up there," William was speaking easily, but with a tone that no soldier ever disobeyed.

James DeLong was the only person moving beneath the guns, walking with a numb expression on his face to the porch. Then Sheriff McHaffie appeared from the direction of his house, throwing a linen napkin on the ground as he ran.

"Billy, you all right?"

"Yeah, Pa, he didn't hit me."

Sardonic note. "I didn't hear his gun," William said.

Kate's eyes were on her sons, and she shouted, "Sheriff McHaffie! You see my boy safe!"

William snorted, and before Polk McHaffie could get on the porch, shouted, "You're gonna arrest my boy, Mr. McHaffie. And your prosecutor will press charges of murder on him, ain't thet right?"

McHaffie nodded.

"Thet's how things work around here, so I've seen, Sheriff. Just so's you know, Sheriff, there ain't a jury in the state thet will find my boy guilty of murder."

James DeLong's face hardened and he shook, one hand pointing to Billy. "I'm running for prosecutor, Miles!"

Snorting once more, William noticed Kate was training her sights on DeLong.

"Just so's you know, DeLong, just so's you know."

It was James DeLong and Galba Branson who rode to the Kinney farm, just north and west of Kirbyville, on the Springfield/Harrison Road. When Maggie saw them ride up together, her knees gave way, and she fell to the floor, unable to even moan.

CHAPTER 48
Aftermath of Kinney's Death

Sheriff McHaffie took Billy Miles to the Greene County Jail in the days following Nat Kinney's death. He wasn't absolutely sure he could keep Billy alive long enough to stand trial for the killing. Danger from the Bald Knobbers had lain dormant for months; Nat's focus had been on his lawsuits and the businesses he wanted. However, some members had continued to ride sporadically, led by one of Kinney's lieutenants. McHaffie worried that one of those lieutenants would step forward and claim leadership of the entire group of night riders.

Jim Berry, charged as an accessory, was taken to Springfield as well. Although Polk McHaffie didn't think the charges were frivolous, he did think there was little chance a jury would convict Berry of any plotting in Kinney's death. It was natural emotion on Berry's part, McHaffie felt, and the fact that his two prisoners did not speak to each other during the entire trip convinced the sheriff of it.

For more than two years, Billy Miles had plotted, schemed, and taken advantage of circumstances that led to Nat Kinney attempting to throw a gun on him. He had appeared to be estranged from his family; had been cut off from his lifelong friends, such as the Snapps; had lived in town and worked a job requiring a suit.

The anger at Andrew's death, the rage at Sam's death, those things sustained him through it all. He was too much his mother's son to let those emotions rule him, and too much his father's son not to use them to best advantage.

He had done so.

Now, he was at loose ends, despite sitting in a cell and waiting to be bonded out of jail. For the first time in many months, he had time to think, to explore the future, to make plans for the rest of his life.

There was a certain satisfaction in the fact he had done what he said he would do, in such spectacular fashion. Relief throbbed in his veins, and he looked forward to working his farms and maybe even finding a wife someday. Girls had been a luxury these past two years, one he was unable to afford. Now, as his life stretched before him, he realized he had nothing to do but get through the trial, and everything would be good.

He was not foolish enough to think there would be no more trouble. He did feel he had a good understanding of the men Nat Kinney had led, and didn't believe any of them would cause him a great deal of grief. At twenty-one, he felt he could handle them. As his mother had pointed out, at some point, the feuding in Taney County would have to cease. The death of the organizer, the leader, of the Bald Knobbers, would cause that cessation.

One thing which never crossed his mind was becoming a gunman, going out West and making a living by virtue of the reputation he would have after his trial. There was no honor in that.

Honor and family. Those were words to base his life on, he felt. He had proven it.

To say rage sustained Maggie Carriger DeLong Kinney after the death of her second husband would be giving too much credit to Billy Miles. A complexity of emotions, ranging from guilt, bewilderment, and camouflaged anger at Nat, to elation when her son James won his election for prosecutor in November, and the birth of Eva and Robert's son Jay in December, forced her to let the piano alone. She was afraid if she opened it, or even dusted it, she would completely fall apart. And she could not, would not, do that.

She spent a great deal of time simply dealing with Nat's lawsuits and the children. Maggie was very well-rehearsed in putting her emotions aside, no matter the reason. When one stray feeling crossed her heart or mind, she clamped down on it immediately.

The public perception of Nat Kinney as a wealthy man was proving to be untrue, as Maggie read through files and papers and instructed his lawyers on her wishes. Although she cared not a whit about her own reputation, it became important that Nat's reputation as a smart businessman remain intact.

Maggie's reputation as a snob, as a bluestocking, was no deterrent to some men. Those men were willing to overlook those obstacles as they considered the woman who kept Nat Kinney faithful throughout his marriage, for no one had ever seen Nat Kinney eye another woman lasciviously. Such a woman must be really something in the

482 | Vonda Wilson Sheets

marriage bed, these men would tell each other.

One came visiting in November, after the election. Unsuspectingly, Maggie let him in the front door of her house, and politely offered coffee. The kitchen table was full of paper, tucked in folders and with notes written in her beautiful handwriting. After fifteen minutes of the man's self-important conversation, Maggie could feel the tug of the paperwork, and began to fidget while making impersonal responses. After another fifteen minutes, the man offered help with her paperwork if he were allowed to call on her. Once she understood what he was after, it took less than a minute before he was on the road back to Forsyth, his ears burning, a red handprint on his left cheek, and coffee dripping down the front of his suit jacket.

By March, when she received a settlement check from the city of Springfield for Nat's injury, she was finished with his lawsuits and court cases. The appeals court upheld the decision of the lower court, awarding the settlement, but reducing it to fifteen hundred dollars.

Maggie spent a lot of time watching Big Bald during those first months of 1889. Paul and Georgia were living in Forsyth with James, who purchased a house off the square. While depositions were being taken by witnesses of the killing, Maggie rocked in her chair, occasionally rising to put wood on the fire, and fix herself a small meal she would have difficulty in swallowing.

She missed him.

The process of the trial for Billy Miles, the work James was doing to secure conviction on first-degree murder charges, she had no part of. And with little to occupy her time except for afternoon visits with Eva and her first grandchild, the absence of Nat's specter began to haunt her.

She had been living with this lack by retreating to the habits that withstood her before, when he'd be gone for weeks at a time while they lived in Kansas. She made mental lists of things she would discuss with him when he got home, despite the fact she was handling legal problems he'd left to her.

Grey Ghost was in the pasture below the barn one day in late March, and she wondered where Nat was. Putting on her shawl, she walked out to the barn, calling for Nat. When the horse came to her, nuzzling for attention over the fence, and Nat did not, it finally came

Absolution | 483

to her--he was gone.

Really gone.

He was not coming home. Ever.

Sinking down to sit by the fence, she looked back up the hill at the house that was so empty now. No big booming laugh, no smells of tobacco in his hair and clothes, no need for the fresh coffee she had continued to brew throughout the day since he left. No one to listen while she played the piano, encouraging her, touching her, loving her.

She was so very alone, she didn't know what to do. So she sat on the ground, hearing echoes of love and anger, and finally seeing the ghost of Nat Kinney up on the bald, building a bonfire.

There were two weeks until the trial. James had told her the defense lawyers, JJ Brown and Babe Harrington, would likely move for a change of venue. In this, he proved correct, and the trial was relocated to Greene County, and postponed for a time. After the change of venue, Billy was bonded out of jail, and began working on his Kirbyville farm.

Eva picked up her mail and brought Maggie the letter from James, telling her that Billy Miles was walking free. She paled while reading, and for once, had no desire to play with her grandson. She was choking, suffocating, while Eva looked at her strangely.

"Mother?"

"Don't mind me, darling. I must be getting a cold."

"Are you sure?"

Maggie nodded, then rose to leave the kitchen. "I think I'll just go feed the horses, and then go to bed." She leaned over, kissed her daughter on the cheek. "I'd best not be close to him, we don't want him to get sick."

She was successful in diverting Eva's attention to leaving. "No, we don't. I'll see you for dinner tomorrow?" Eva asked. "Robert's parents will be there as well."

"Best not, darling." Maggie made no excuses during the necessary time it took to send Eva on her way.

As soon as Eva was out of sight, Maggie once more grabbed her shawl and left the house. This time, she ran down the hill, crossing the stream, and up the hill to the top of Big Bald. It was the first time she'd been there since Nat died. There were still pieces of charred

484 | Vonda Wilson Sheets

wood from bonfires, but she didn't notice as she came to a halt, raising her fists and howling in fury. Then she turned and ran back down to the barn, putting a bridle on Grey Ghost and taking off for Galba Branson's home. Galba was the sheriff of Taney County now, and could be of help.

Billy Miles was free, and according to James, was likely to remain so, despite the fact the trial wasn't going to be held for a time, because of the crowded Greene County court docket. James felt the evidence was in Billy's favor, as well as the passage of time. He was going to pursue the conviction of first degree murder anyway, for love of his stepfather.

This, she thought - this she could do something about.

Billy Miles, free, while her husband lay in his grave, leaving her so alone?

Oh, no.

Not if Maggie Kinney had anything to do with it. And fifteen hundred dollars should buy her plenty of action, she thought, urging Ghost on and for the first time since he had died, feeling as if Nat was right beside her, touching her, loving her.

                                                  ৡ ৶

It was merely an obstacle that Gabe wasn't home. She tersely asked his wife, Betsy, if Gabe would call upon her at his earliest convenience. Betsy, alarmed at the color in Maggie's face and her disheveled appearance, promised Gabe would be home the next day, and would send him to Maggie immediately. To be polite, she invited Maggie to join her and the children for dinner, but she was not dismayed when Maggie declined.

Frankly, she admitted to herself, Maggie Kinney had always been aloof, somewhat intimidating. But now, she thought as the older woman rode off, astride the big horse with her hair blowing loose in the wind, her cheeks more flushed than Betsy had ever seen them, now....Maggie Kinney was terrifying.

It was late the next afternoon before Gabe rode to the Kinney farm. He knew Maggie better than most of Nat's friends, so it was natural that she turn to him for help. Betsy had blushed scarlet in

Absolution | 485

describing Maggie's visit to him, telling him about Maggie riding bareback and astride on Nat's horse.

When Polk McHaffie declared he would not seek reelection, Nat prodded Galba Branson into running for the office of sheriff. Nat's death played no small part in Galba's win, since the sentiment in the county was against the Slickers.

Gabe often visited the cemetery above Swan Creek, telling his friend about events, and imagining he could hear Nat's voice in reply. He had not spoken of this to anyone, not even his wife.

Maggie had bathed and dressed in her newest black gown, an at-home gown that accentuated the pallor in her cheeks and the intensity in her eyes. The lace played peek-a-boo with her bosom and hands, displaying her femininity to best advantage. Her hair poured down her back, restrained only by two combs at her temples.

She poured coffee, inquiring as to Gabe's health and made the usual polite noises. He had imagined some crisis, but there was none apparent as they made conversation.

When Maggie poured him a third cup of coffee, his defenses and worry allayed by her manner, she struck.

Galba Branson's eyes grew wide as Maggie, never changing from her most feminine voice and manners, told him she wanted him to find her a gunman. To kill Billy Miles.

Declining at first, by the end of his visit, he agreed to seek out such a man. Till his own death, he never understood exactly how Maggie managed to convince him to instigate a murder, and re-open the wounds of Taney County. But he agreed, loyal friend to Nat Kinney that he was, and as Maggie continued her persuasion, he believed she was right.

Nat would expect it of them.

A storm was brewing. Gabe agreed to her wishes, leaving when it became apparent he would have scarcely enough time to get home. It never occurred to Maggie to ask him to wait the storm out. It was doubtful he would have agreed to do so, being more aware of social conventions than she was, and knowing he was expected home.

As she watched the storm coming in, angry and gray and tossing her hair about her, she walked through the first floor of the house, opening the windows. The pressure from the storm bore down on her, but her eyes were calm as she gazed at her piano.

486 | Vonda Wilson Sheets

Quickly, so quickly, she threw wood on the fire in the bedroom. Then she retrieved her beeswax and the rag she used on the precious wood, allowing the wax to soften as the storm grew in intensity. Her touch was gentle as she dusted, grew more demanding as she polished.

The center of the storm was directly over her house as she opened the lid over the ivory keys, tucking it back tenderly. Without warming her hands and fingers on scales, she began to play "Moonlight Sonata" in the dark, the wind coming through the windows and lifting the tendrils of her hair in a familiar manner.

§∽ ∾§

In less than two weeks, she received word of a meeting in the sheriff's office. At night, as she had requested.

Maggie rode Grey Ghost astride into Forsyth early one afternoon, telling her scandalized children she merely wished to exercise him, and he would not allow a sidesaddle. She honestly didn't know if Ghost would accept a sidesaddle--she never tried.

Paul and Georgia went back for the afternoon school session, and James returned to his office. Alonzo Prather was the state representative for Taney County, and was seeking state money to build a new courthouse. Until it was finished, however, elected officials worked in various buildings around the square. James was using Alonzo's office for his public work. As Maggie inspected the house the children were living in, she noted the big desk in James' room was covered with law books. She drifted in, idly lifting one book up to inspect it. Inside the front cover were the words, "From the law office of Alonzo Prather."

She would sleep in Georgia's room tonight, she thought, and wandered into the small room her daughter used. Paul slept in the attic of the one-story house. Maggie lifted Georgia's hairbrush, then other items on the shelf used as a dresser. Restless. It was soon going to be time to leave.

It was twilight when she opened the unlocked jail door. Her eyes were burning under the heavy veil that hid her hair and face, draping all the way to the floor from the widow's hat on her head. No one was being held prisoner, a savvy move on Gabe's part, she thought.

Absolution | 487

She moved back into the shadows of the unlit jail, seeking to remain hidden unless--or until--she was needed.

Gabe entered a short time later. It was nearly dark, nearly time. He lit a single lantern, instead of the wall sconces, and placed it on the desk, where he perched, waiting.

Two horses were ridden up to the rail outside. Footsteps and then a knock on the door. Gabe opened it, ushering two men inside. They introduced themselves as James Hull and Ed Funk as Gabe closed the door behind them and invited them to sit in the chairs in front of his desk.

They declined.

Tersely, Galba spoke of the expectations of work he had for Funk and Hull. They were negotiating on price when Maggie lost patience.

"Oh, for God's sake, Gabe," she stepped out from the shadows, lifting the veil from her face. Gabe wasn't surprised, and the two visitors reacted by touching their guns until it was obvious she was a woman. "There is fifteen hundred dollars for you to split when you are finished. Understand this….if Billy Miles is not killed, I will not pay."

Unable to mask his irritation, Gabe opened the desk drawer and pulled out two deputy badges. "This may make things easier for you," he told the gunmen.

Both of them shook their heads. "We're used to operating on the other side of the badge," Funk said, a slight smile on his face. "We'll do it our way."

Maggie smiled back. "Does that mean you'll do it?"

Funk's smile grew wider. "Yes, ma'am, it does. Lot of money to be turning down."

Hull nodded as well, and stepped forward to shake Galba's hand. When Maggie put her hand out, he hesitated only briefly, but managed to shake hers as well. Funk did the same, and the two men left.

"Did you notice her shake was as strong as a man's?" Funk asked his partner as they forded Swan Creek to the west, riding in the direction of Walnut Shade.

Hull grunted. "Women are vicious creatures," was all he said.

488 | Vonda Wilson Sheets

After the men rode off, Gabe turned to Maggie.

"You might have had some money left if you'd let me finish," he told her.

Maggie brought the veil back over her face, and shook her skirts out. It was a woman's gesture, Gabe noted, but he'd never heard of a woman demanding vengeance in such a manner.

"I want Billy Miles dead. They seem as if they might be able to do it," Maggie walked to the door, then turned, her hand on the knob.

"I want justice as badly as you do, Mrs. Kinney," Gabe said, sitting down in his chair.

He thought he heard contempt in her voice. "I doubt it, Gabe," said Maggie. "I really doubt it."

Galba Branson reached into the open drawer of his desk, and pulled out a deputy's badge with a hole through it, tossing it on the desk. He looked up at Maggie, wishing he could see her face under the veil.

"Don't, Mrs. Kinney, don't doubt me at all."

Maggie lifted her veil, and stared straight into Gabe's face. Then she eyed the badge. "I think you should be calling me Maggie, Gabe." The veil fell down once more, her voice gentle now. "Thank you."

She left Gabe sitting in his office with the lantern light gleaming on the stained badge Nat Kinney was wearing when he died of a gunshot wound to the heart.

Jim and Manny Miles came out of the saloon after a couple of hours playing pool and drinking two beers each. The new owner was a nasty man who'd snarled when the younger Miles boys returned to play their occasional games of pool. Now, however, he was most respectful--William Miles had had a word, promising he'd beat the boys himself if they caused any trouble in the saloon. There had been no issues since then. William cautioned them about playing all night, telling them other men might want to use it as well. Mindful of Al Layton's behavior that night he killed Jim Everett, the boys limited their time and kept a close watch on the other customers.

It wasn't often William let them come into town, and they were due at Billy's farm the next day, so they took their time and enjoyed their few hours of freedom. It had just fallen night, and they were considering riding home when they saw two men on dark horses, dressed in dark clothing, dismount in front of the jail.

While it wasn't uncommon for a light to be on in the jail, the source of the light was different than usual. Jim nudged Manny. "Wonder what that's about?" he asked.

"Might be able to find out," Manny commented. "We can wait a while."

The two of them made their way to a bench in front of the closed diner, and sat down. They didn't have very long to wait. Within a half-hour, the men came out and rode west.

It was quite dark, and Manny was considering sneaking around the jail to look in the windows when the door opened and a woman's form was briefly silhouetted.

"Wonder who that is?" Jimmy spoke in low tones.

Manny shook his head. "Didn't someone say something about Nat Kinney's wife being in town this afternoon? Cain't think of anyone else thet'd be wearing black like that."

"What, in the saloon?" Jimmy considered. "Didn't hear it."

The light went out, and someone else exited the jail, obviously leaving it empty. The young men sat for a few minutes more, then rose to walk toward their horses. Neither of them heard, nor saw, Gabe Branson ride south as they mounted and left town toward home.

CHAPTER 49
July 4, 1889

John Haggard looked down the trail toward the former home of his sister. He could see two of the Miles brothers outside, working on fencing a dooryard for the house. Wondering if they'd already heard about the Widow Maggie's big black sow, he clucked his horse, descending the slope to the valley floor.

Of course the dogs heard, and began barking. His horse shied a little as the dogs approached, and John yelled, "Call them off!"

At a sharp word from one of the brothers, the dogs fell silent, escorting him across the creek branch and to the front of the cabin, where Billy and Emanuel Miles were shirtless, gleaming with sweat. Jim was standing in the doorway, also shirtless, holding a rifle aimed straight at John Haggard's heart.

"I'm not here to cause trouble, Billy," John told him, holding his hands up palm-out.

Scratching his neck, and reaching for a canteen of water, Billy tilted his head toward Jim. "Hold." The youngest Miles boy moved the rifle a scant two inches. Squinting, Billy looked up at Haggard.

"What do you want?"

John looked around, taking in the peaceful aura of the valley where Sam and Susie were so happy. "You're doing a good job."

"That's not what you came for." Emanuel spoke this time.

"No," John agreed, and shook his head. Then he nodded at the fencing rolled and waiting to be put on posts. "Heard about the Widow Maggie's sow?" he asked.

Billy shook his head. "No, but she's a mean one. Did she eat one of the McClarys?" he joked. He had seen the sow who was the original provider of fresh pork for the Widow Maggie's diner in Forsyth. Her piglets grew fast and big. Andy had done well with that one, he thought.

"She's loose."

Billy nearly shivered, and Jim and Emanuel were looking around to see if the sow had arrived. In less than five seconds, the three of them realized the dogs weren't concerned, so neither should they be. Regarding Haggard with something more than displeasure for a change, Billy said, "Thanks for the warning. How'd she get out?"

Absolution | 491

"Finally knocked a big enough hole in the shed. The Widow is gonna be unhappy with McClary when she finds out. That was one of the conditions for him to live there, making sure that razorback was secure when she had a litter." John paused. "But that ain't why I'm here."

"Of course not." Jim snorted, impatient, but Billy silenced him, "So why are you here?"

Taking a moment to look around, John finally said, "My sister was happy here." Realizing the Mileses were getting impatient, he hurriedly added, "I figure I owe him."

"Who?" Billy's tone was sharp.

"Sam."

"Ah." Billy took another drink, then rubbed his chin. "You do, at that."

"There's a man looking for you." John's words were brief.

Eyebrows raised, Jim stepped down off the porch, carrying the rifle. Again, Billy halted Jim's movements, watching John Haggard.

"We know of two men. Who's this one?" he asked.

"One of the two, I guess," John shrugged.

One of Billy's eyebrows raised. "Why just one?"

"Guess the other one got shot by his partner."

The brothers laughed. "Now, thet's funny," Emanuel said.

"He's dead." Two words brought silence. Digesting this news, Billy walked over to the porch, stirred his bandana in the bucket of water there, and began wiping his face under his hat.

"How?" Jim asked Haggard. "Did he want the reward money for himself?"

John pushed his own hat back, exposing more of his face. "No, I heard it was a bad scrape. They were chasing some robbers over on Bear Creek, got mistook for a robber."

"Wal…" Emanuel joined his brother, soaking his own bandana. "Thet's good and bad."

Jim's puzzlement continued as he asked, "How'd ye figger?"

Emanuel thought for a moment, then answered slowly, "It's good, b'cuz it means they ain't bright. Bad b'cuz whoever lived is a good shot."

Billy walked back over to his post-digging shovel and picked it up. Sinking it into the hole he'd just begun, he told John, "Thanks for the news."

John was studying his hands as if seeing bloodstains on them, and well he might, Billy thought. A little more nerve on Haggard's part, and Sam Snapp would still be living on this place. The hell in Haggard's eyes when he finally rolled his head to look at Billy showed he'd been thinking the same. Billy turned back to digging again, but Haggard's voice stopped him.

"They're s'sposed to be hunting you today," John said, suddenly weary.

Billy threw his hands wide, letting go of the post-digger. "I'm right here." Manny and Jim were just behind him.

Shaking his head, John went on. "They won't come here. They want it public."

All right. That brought Billy up short momentarily. Thinking hard, he barely remembered to ask, "Where?"

Haggard's voice held the echoes of a death knell. "Kirbyville. Today, at the picnic."

It was Jim's turn to rub behind his ear, as if he'd been bitten by a mosquito. "Why's there a picnic today?"

Emanuel laughed, then pushed at Jim. "It's the Fourth of July, dunce."

Billy was staring at John Haggard, his face white beneath the tan. His voice and hands were steady, though, when he commented, "One year since Wash Middleton was kilt, down in Arkansas."

John nodded. "Yep. Someone thought it was fittin'."

"We'll be there." Billy straightened. He had expected trouble, but not at a community gathering. It was worrisome.

"I'll put a bottle in the spring, just below the fall," Haggard told him. In so many words, he gave Billy a place to force the situation, if he could.

Billy, assessing the situation and realizing he was being forced into it, nodded. "I guess I better show up," he responded, and leaned over to pick up the post-digger once more. His gloved hands lifted it high, and after he stabbed it down again, he told Haggard, "You said your piece. Get on."

John began to speak once more, but Jim cocked the rifle he was still holding. "You heard him."

If John Haggard was seeking forgiveness, absolution, for allowing Sam Snapp to be killed, he wasn't getting it from the Miles brothers.

Absolution | 493

Not today, maybe not ever. He finally rode away.

Emanuel picked up a post, and stuck it in the hole Billy just finished. He held it while Billy traded shovels, and poured dirt into the hole. Jim was impatient.

"Well?" he asked. "What are we doing?"

Emanuel wiggled the post, and Billy began tamping the dirt down, packing the hole. Then he wiped his forearm across his face again as sweat stung his eyes.

"Is he gone?" he asked Jim, who looked up the trail.

"Yeah."

"You take Nellie, ride to Pa's. Stop in at Robert Snapp's place, let him know. Tell 'em..." and Billy held on, thinking. "Tell 'em to be down at the spring, around the falls. I'll lead 'em down soon's I can."

"Like Forsyth?" Jim asked.

Billy nodded. "I think so. Can't think of any other way out." He switched back to the post-hole digger, and paced off the length to the next post. Then he pushed it into the ground. Emanuel and Jim hadn't moved. Another thought struck him. "Emanuel, you go tell the McClarys, some of the others around here. I'll meet you all at the picnic, say..." he looked at the sun, "about four o'clock."

His brothers continued to stand there. "What?" he said, allowing some exasperation to show.

"What are you going to do?" Jim asked.

"Me? I'm gonna dig post holes. There's a wild sow on the loose."

The Kirbyville Independence Day festivities were the largest in the county. People came from all over, even Arkansas, to picnic and visit, and enjoy the fireworks. The gazebo provided shelter for musicians to play, and there were plenty of shade trees, with tables and benches scattered around the perimeter. John Kintrea provided the makings for ice cream to any who wanted to crank the mixture, and there were watermelons from the river bottoms near Moore Bend.

A blonde woman was singing in a unique, gravelly voice when Maggie Kinney arrived on the arm of her son Paul. James escorted Georgia, and the four of them joined Eva at the tables around the tree claimed by the Prather family.

If James had been the one to lift Maggie down from the wagon, he would've known instantly there was something in the air. He knew her well, and may have even inquired. But he was distracted, and had promised himself that he would dance with every pretty girl at the picnic. Aside from the Miles case, his career was going well, and he was thinking about getting married.

Paul was leaving in a few weeks for university. Maggie maneuvered to be by his side, knowing her other children would think she was storing up memories in preparation for his absence.

Georgia looked for Mary Elizabeth Prather and a few other girls she knew. As they circled the picnic area, she happened to look up and see Miranda arriving with some other young people from Forsyth. She envied Serelda Coggburn for running to hug her friend, joined by Nannie Snapp. The three girls made a pretty picture, Georgia thought, and she made no move to join them. She felt awkward, almost shy, and it was a feeling she tamped down immediately. Then Mary Elizabeth asked her a question, and her attention diverted, she did not see the brief sad expression on Miranda's face, aimed in her direction.

There was some dancing, and lots of laughter as the day wore into mid-afternoon. Billy Miles, who was sparking a girl named Emmy Johnson, arrived to find Emanuel already on the dance floor. Politely, Billy asked Emmy to dance, receiving a gracious nod from her parents. The blonde woman called a square dance, her voice carrying well over the noise of many conversations. Then a fiddle player announced a contest, and several joined him as they challenged each other to more and more intricate music.

Returning Emmy to her parents, Billy joined Emanuel at the community tables, heaped high with food. They filled plates and set off toward a table under a tree that already held several other young men.

"You notice how many are wearing guns?" Emanuel asked in a low voice as he and Billy left the ribald conversation at the young men's shady table.

"Yeah." A few more paces. "It's hard to tell some of them firecrackers from…"

"Yeah." Emanuel was as brusque as Billy as he, too, was thinking about what was coming.

They walked to the table with fruit punch and lemonade, killing

Absolution | 495

time. Without pulling a pocket watch, Emanuel and Billy knew it was nearly four o'clock.

Then a hot and dusty Jim Miles appeared, walking to the tables and filling his own plate. He was quickly joined by his brothers. He took one bite of his food before he answered their unspoken question. "They're here." Then he swallowed, shoveling another mouthful in. While he chewed this one, Jim glanced around what he could see of folks.

"I wonder why the sheriff's family ain't here," Billy leaned back against a tree, raising one foot to support himself while he pulled a wooden toothpick from his pocket.

Emanuel snorted. "I don't see Haggard lying to us."

"No-oo," Billy agreed.

Jim had eaten about a dozen forkfuls before Billy espied the sheriff, accompanying a dark-complexioned man, working his way through the dancers instead of around the floor. "Well, I'm gonna go down to the spring," he said loudly. "I need to dunk my head."

A line for the latest batch of ice cream was forming, and none but Billy's brothers took heed. "Shit!" Jim murmured, but this once, none of them could taste their mother's cuss concoction. Jim grabbed one last bite of food before tossing his plate on the table, disgusted.

"Didn't get breakfast nor lunch," he told Billy as they walked toward the trail leading down to the spring. Billy merely raised an eyebrow, but Emanuel asked, "Didn't Ma at least give you a sandwich?"

"Nope," Jim replied as they entered the woods. "Don't know why not. She seemed to be arguing with Pa."

Emanuel and Billy stopped, then resumed walking. "Thet's strange," Emanuel said. "Tain't like Ma at all."

Jim shrugged, pulling his gun and checking it as they made their way down to the spring. "Guess Pa told her off for wanting to be here."

Billy shook his head. "She's got the right, I expect," was all he said. His pace never faltered, but he wished Kate had won the argument. Then he attempted a smile, thinking of Kate's need to look after her sons. Well, he'd simply think of her shooting that rattlesnake...

And they were at the falls, some distance below where the trail crossed the creek. Jim splashed into the water, heedless of the wet except for his gun. He reached down and pulled out the bottle promised by John Haggard.

"Whoooo-eeeeeee!" he crowed, then uncapped it and took a drink, amid the shushing by his brothers. Walking out of the water, he took off his hat, handing the bottle to Emanuel. "It's 'most as good as yours," he told his brother.

Billy refused a drink of John Haggard's moonshine, instead walking into the water himself. Jim moved off to the side, out of the immediate view of the trail. Emanuel stood on the bank, the small sip he took of the moonshine rolling around in his mouth.

He spat, and commented, "It's good, but…" just as the brothers heard, "There they are!" from up on the trail.

§∾ ∾§

It had been a pleasant afternoon.

Maggie enjoyed the small group she was a part of, however unwillingly. At one point, she surprised her children, for Alonzo asked if she was going to sell her farm, and she replied that she would.

"Where are you going to live?" Eva asked.

"What are you going to do?" James wanted to know.

Maggie smiled, a bittersweet thing that suggested she had no intentions of answering those questions today.

Then she saw Gabe Branson and Ed Funk arriving.

She had been worried ever since Funk had unwitting shot his partner during a side job they had taken on while getting to know folks. Hull had no family that acknowledged him, so Gabe buried him on the ridge of his farm that overlooked the river.

But Ed Funk assured her during a late-night visit all was well, which made Maggie wonder if the shooting had been intentional.

"I wonder where Betsy is," she heard Ada Marie say to Alonzo. "There's Gabe with that man he's been showing around."

Maggie did not hear Alonzo's response. She watched the men making their way through the dancers, disappearing from her view. She clambered to her feet, Paul too slow to help her up, and shook him off when he asked her what was wrong.

Then there was gunfire, and the sound of horses running.

Absolution | 497

Billy froze for a split-second, then took off his hat and dunked his head. "That feels good," he told Emanuel during the few seconds it took Sheriff Galba Branson and Ed Funk to reach them. His back remained toward Emanuel, and he unsnapped the leather strap holding his pistol in its holster. Somehow, he had managed to keep from getting his gun wet, even as he shook the water from his head.

"Are you Billy Miles?" the voice was unfamiliar.

"I am." With that assertion, Billy turned and fired. Jim also fired from his position on the side. Emanuel fell to the ground and rolled, also firing at the sheriff and Ed Funk. A fusillade sounded. The two men fell to the ground, Funk's body nearly landing in the creek. Then William was there, with Matt and Robert Snapp, some McClarys, Moores, and others. William ran to Jim, who was yelling--oh, he was shot, Billy noted with detachment as he put his gun back in the holster.

"They're dead," someone said, examining the bodies of the two men.

"Well, of course they are," Robert Snapp answered impatiently. "Did we aim to miss?"

Horrified, Maggie watched John Haggard disappear down the trail, riding one horse and leading two more. She almost fainted, then struggled, screaming "You traitor!"

James grabbed her just as she began to run after Haggard.

"Mother! What are you doing?" he asked her in shock.

"They're going after Billy Miles!" she screamed at her son, struggling to get free.

Ada Marie and Alonzo stared at Maggie, even as she continued to resist James' hold on her body.

Slowly, Alonzo said, "How do you know that, Maggie?"

As other women's screams reached her ears, she stopped cold.

Betsy Branson wasn't here at the picnic. She was supposed to be, Maggie remembered. Everything else was a blur.

Horses were coming down the trail, and the men in the clearing at the waterfall began to scatter. However, shouts indicated that it was John Haggard, leading the horses belonging to the sons of William Miles. He rode up, breathless and anxious.

"You gotta get outta here," he told Billy. In response, Billy grabbed the reins John threw at him, and mounted his horse, as did Emanuel.

"Pa!" He was ready to go. Somehow, there were bedrolls and saddlebags on the horses, where there hadn't been earlier.

William and Matt Snapp had tied a tourniquet on Jim's thigh, Matt muttering, "He needs a doctor!" They helped the sixteen-year-old stand, and shoved him up on his horse.

"Go!" William yelled, just as shouting began again, this time coming from the picnic area above, echoing down the trail. He slapped the rump of Jim's horse, and the gelding reared, Jim barely hanging on.

The boys went, leaving their father to deal with what was coming.

As the braver men from above made their way down, first making sure there was no further gunfire, William Miles turned to John Haggard and attempted a smile. Failing, he held out his bare right hand, and John Haggard clasped it in a strong shake.

"Reckon you done good," was all William had to say. Then he shook his head, bewildered. "Did I see a bedroll and saddlebags on Jim's horse?"

John Haggard was grateful, more than he could voice. Instead, he said, "I was ready to bring the horses when your wife ran up and began tying them on. That's why it took me so long to get down here," he said, shrugging slightly to indicate some unease. "I had to help."

Stunned, one of the first faces William saw of the group that burst into the clearing was Kate's, her eyes checking him for injury as she ran to his arms. He simply looked at her, and shook his head. If forced, he would admit he was glad to see her.

There was mingling and additions to the men gathered to take up Galba Branson and Ed Funk's mortal remains, until no one was sure who was in the clearing when. Once the bodies taken back to the picnic area, someone left for the coroner.

Maggie Kinney was sitting on a bench near her family, unable to speak or move after she recognized that Branson and Funk were dead. Ada Marie sent her daughter scrambling for bed linens to wrap the bodies in, and someone else left to bring Betsy Branson to town.

Betsy arrived long before the coroner did, running and falling on her knees next to the body of her husband, their children being taken care of by women who were still there. The deep, chest-racking sobs and cries of "Why?" reached the ears and broke the hearts of everyone.

Alonzo and Ada Marie took Betsy to their home, and others began to clear the picnic grounds, deeply saddened and enraged by the killings. When the coroner, Madison Day, arrived, he didn't even ask what happened.

It was obvious. Two men were dead, one of them the sheriff of Taney County, the other a stranger only a few knew of. At the hands of the Miles boys, who were long gone. Unbeknownst to anyone now alive except for Maggie Kinney, the person truly responsible was in their midst, wringing her hands and silent.

CHAPTER 50
Absolution

Jim Miles, shot in the groin muscles, turned himself in, Billy by his side, less than three days after the Kirbyville shoot-out. Orchestrated by William Miles, Dr. Anderson visited the jail to tend Jim on a daily basis, until the brothers were bonded out.

The next grand jury session indicted the Miles brothers on the deaths of Galba Branson and Ed Funk. Those charges stacked up on top of the trial for the death of Nat Kinney, and Billy began to wonder if he'd been optimistic in planting crops on his farms.

It took a lot of work on the part of his parents, and his aunt and uncle, but the harvest was made and successful in the face of all the distractions in court.

It was nearly three months after Maggie Kinney saw destruction.

She was trying to prepare to sell the farm. Most of the time, she wandered around the property, Grey Ghost following her like a big dog. He no longer stayed in the pasture below the barn--Maggie gave him his head, allowing him the freedom to leave. It was irony of the highest form that the big stallion wouldn't leave--he stayed in the dooryard, making his way to the barn if the weather wasn't to his liking. She left the gate open for him to do as he pleased. Much like herself, he was under the control of a higher power, a force that made him do as the training of his youth bid. She saw no reason to laugh.

She didn't know what she was going to do. She had the hotel in Forsyth, the biggest part of what was left of Nat's estate. But she felt ill-suited to run it, to be at the beck and call of her customers. What else was there for an old woman?

One day in late September, just before Billy Miles was to stand trial in Greene County for killing Nat Kinney, Maggie was sitting on her porch, watching the trees change color at the foot of Big Bald. A smart little buggy rolled down the lane to the barn, and a woman stepped down from it.

Her breath caught when she realized it was the Widow Maggie.

She seemed a small woman when her daughters weren't around, Maggie Kinney thought. She continued to rock, awaiting the woman's approach and remembering that Nat had admired her. She forgot that her admiration had become jealousy in the face of Nat's respect for another woman.

"Mrs. Kinney." The widow's voice was uncultured, but respectful.

Maggie merely nodded, continuing to gaze at the trees and Big Bald.

The Widow lifted her chin. Kinney's wife wasn't going to make it easy for her. Well, she'd never asked for easy, had she?

"I came to offer you a business proposition."

Maggie rocked, but a quick glance sideways indicated interest.

"The hotel's bin closed fer some time, and my business has suffered."

No recognition.

"If you ain't interested, tell me, and I'll go talk to John Hilsabeck, see if he has something fer me. Since yer place is closed, his is always full."

The Widow stood there, waiting for a response. Nothing.

Without an invitation, she sat on the steps, her back to Maggie Kinney, and joined her in the gaze at Big Bald. For some time, the Widow admired the view, but she had to be getting back to Forsyth. The rented horse stomped its feet, shaking its head.

"Jist thought I'd ask." With that, the Widow stood and shook her skirts down. She began to walk away when the hoarse, sad voice reached her.

"Will you let me eat free?"

The Widow halted, then half-turned. "If you'll give me the breakfast and supper trade."

"Done."

As simple as that, Maggie Kinney thought while packing her china that evening. She had a direction to go in, similar to what Nat had planned all along. Maybe he'd known her better than she thought.

She made a wry face as she latched the small china trunk. It would be difficult, but she could stand the thought of living in town and running a business now. She had nothing else, and it would be intriguing, watching life pass her by.

The next morning, she rode into Kirbyville to post a letter to James. She needed help moving, she had written to her oldest son. Would he send someone from town?

Three days later, James DeLong took time off from his duties as county prosecutor, and moved his mother into the hotel she intended to clean up and run. That night, she and James walked down the sidewalk in the square of the city of Forsyth to the Widow Maggie's diner. When they walked in, Miranda took them to a booth in the back corner, with high-backed benches and a clean table.

Just before they ordered, Georgia came in and joined them, but there was none of the friendship between herself and Miranda left over from their childhood. Even though they attended school together, when it was in session, neither of the girls sought the other's company. Miranda saw Nannie Snapp and Serelda Coggburn as often as she could, writing letters when she couldn't. They were all well into their sixteenth year, but even Miranda's miraculous ability to defeat obstacles could not overcome Georgia's feelings of inadequacy and grief.

She, too, was Maggie Carriger DeLong Kinney's daughter.

Billy's trial in Springfield went much like James had expected. JJ Brown, the head lawyer on defense, died two months before Billy finally went to trial in March, 1890, for the murder of Nat Kinney. Babe Harrington and his team took JJ's notes and staged a masterful defense, but it wasn't necessary. The jury acquitted Billy on the grounds of self-defense.

Jim Berry figured out Nat Kinney's death was largely due to circumstances which played into Billy's hands by the time William Miles visited him in jail. He was effusive in his praise, to the point of embarrassing William. He left Berry sitting in his cell, no longer anxious there would be more feuding between the Bald Knobbers and Anti-Bald Knobbers. True, Berry never had been a Bald Knobber, William reflected. But one couldn't tell, sometimes.

In September, 1890, Billy once more stood before a jury on charges for the murder of Galba Branson. James DeLong made the decision to try Billy and Jim separately, and filed for a completely different trial for charges related to the death of Ed Funk. However, the jury in Christian County made it clear that once again, Billy Miles had acted in self-defense. Bitter and angry, James threw the case against Jim Miles, knowing the verdict would be the same. He dropped the charges for Ed Funk's murder, unwilling to seek vengeance in the courtroom any further.

During the months he spent waiting for the judicial system to grind justice out, Billy worked his farms and came to terms with his life. The night riders came to visit twice, but there were no threats made against the Miles family, nor were there shots fired. They were merely making their presence known.

The night he rode home after his final acquittal, Billy told his parents of his decision to move to explore the Indian Territory. For the first time in nearly five years, Billy's life was his own, and he could not stay in Taney County. Kate, who was standing behind her son and rubbing his shoulders, noted some gray hair mixed in with the various shades of blonde and brown hair that was thinning on top of his head. He was only twenty-three, she thought, and bowed her own chin. She would not stand in his way.

He left the next morning, riding down to Forsyth from Taney City, wondering at the beginning of fall in Taney County. He would miss the changing of the trees, he thought. Waiting for the Parrish ferry at Forsyth, he realized he could take some of Taney County with him, and grabbled up a handful of dirt. He reached into the stuffed saddlebags, and pulled a jar of Emanuel's moonshine out. Well, he'd rather have the dirt than the moonshine. So he filled the jar, and stuffed it back in the bag.

No doubt he'd have second thoughts about that in the days to come, he wryly told himself. Then he shrugged. Not much choice, he felt, and hailed the ferryman as the barge came up on the gravel bar to unload and reload passengers and freight.

A jarful of dirt and his mother's food in his saddlebags, Billy Miles left for the Indian Territory. He didn't know if he'd stay there, but it was time for him to move on.

৵ ৶

A little more than a year later, Maggie Kinney was preparing to go to the diner for her evening meal. She wasn't feeling well, and

Georgia would be along soon to cover for her at the desk. The only times Maggie left the hotel were for meals; otherwise, if she wasn't working, she stayed in the room behind the hotel office and desk, listening for the bell in case a guest needed her.

Much was changed for Maggie Kinney. She had aged considerably since she condemned Betsy Branson to widowhood, and her hands were knobby with arthritis. She used Nat's cane in her walks to the diner, and her once dark, thick hair had gone white and thin. Her memories of her mother were tossed back at her every time she looked in the mirror. Continuing to wear black, she was faded, she knew, and considered it earned.

The bell over the door rang, and she looked up from her newspaper at the stranger who turned to close the lobby door gently. The rain outside had darkened the felt of his hat, and dripped off the brim as he approached the desk. There was a halt in his step, then he continued on.

"I need a room for the night," the gruff voice seemed to emanate from the wet hat. Maggie didn't look too closely--the times were wild still, and if this man did not want her to see his face, she would not force the issue.

"Two dollars a night, fifty cents extra if you want a hot bath," Maggie told him. She could see a beard, brown streaked with gray, but not much else beneath the hat brim. There was a distinct aroma of horse and leather, as well as that of hard-traveled dirt roads.

"I'll take that bath tonight," the man said, handing over the money.

"Will you sign the register?" she asked, putting the money into her bank bag and laying it on the desk. He reached for the fountain pen, only pausing for a moment as he signed his name. Then he took the key Maggie was holding out to him.

"Up the stairs, second door on the right, room 203," she said. She was going to have to heat up the water, and the requested bath meant several trips up the stairs, unless Georgia arrived soon.

The man took his saddlebags and she heard his heavy boots on the stairs. Funny. The sound was different than that of most of her guests. She thought no more of it, however, since Georgia and James chose that moment to arrive.

There was a guest in the hotel who was being interviewed to take over the newspaper in town. Although James was no longer the editor, Alonzo was stuck in Jefferson City, and sent a telegraph asking him to see to the man, a Mr. Oscar Lowell. The name seemed familiar, but James did not give it a great deal of thought as he waited for the man to come down.

Maggie eyed Georgia, who eloped last year, then lost her husband to illness a few weeks ago. She seemed to be holding up well, taking over the task of heating the bathwater for the man in Room 203. After several trips with heavy buckets, she went into Maggie's room, leaving the door open so she could hear noise in the lobby. James and Maggie were still waiting for Mr. Lowell to come downstairs.

When he finally appeared, the face also appeared familiar to James, but he could not remember why. Resplendent in a new suit, the man made a moue of distaste with his mouth as he looked out the window.

"I see it's quite nasty out," Lowell said. "I shall go up for my overcoat."

Maggie donned her cloak and picked up her umbrella. "I do hope he'll be ready to leave in a minute," she told James. "I don't like to keep the Widow Maggie late." James could only nod. He was doing Alonzo a favor, that was all.

Gunfire erupted, and she dropped the umbrella in panic. Rushing to the window, Maggie pushed the curtain aside as booted feet quickly dropped down the stairs. The man who was supposed to be taking a bath in 203 was fully dressed, and held a gun in his hand. He used the tip of it to shove the curtain on the door aside, standing in the shelter of the wooden frame.

Lowell also came down the stairs, stuttering in panic.

"Is t-t-that the Bald Knobbers?" he asked, wringing his gloved hands.

James, who had been watching the masked riders through the same window Maggie was looking out, turned and said, "No. What do you know of the Bald Knobbers?"

Maggie turned the other way, to gaze at her latest guest. He had taken his hat off, his hair was long and streaked with gray, as was his beard. What skin she could see was bronzed from the outdoors, except where his hat normally protected his face.

The face. She knew that face, those eyes that landed on her, wary and watchful.

Mr. Lowell was telling James that he had lived in Forsyth some

506 | Vonda Wilson Sheets

years ago, and heard of the Bald Knobbers after he moved away.

"I really d-d-don't know a great deal, except they rode at n-night with masks, shooting up the t-town," Lowell said.

"No. That's over now," said Billy Miles, eyes still locked on Maggie Kinney's face.

She nodded slightly, so slightly. "Yes," her voice a mere echo fading into the night, falling with the rain. "It's over."

That night, Maggie was soaked in her walk back to the hotel after dinner. The next morning, Eva and Robert brought their three children to see their grandmother, the youngest a girl only four months old. Alarmed at the sight of her feverish mother, Eva asked Robert to take Maggie to their new home, where she could take care of her and the children.

Taking turns with Maggie, her daughters and sons--for Paul came home as soon as James telegraphed him--sat with her, leaving the hotel to young Miranda, whom Maggie was training.

She died of heart failure on October 11, 1891, just as Billy Miles was preparing to leave Taney County for the last time, now determined to move to Texas. He felt no need to rush, for he and Maggie had made their peace. He left as the funeral procession wound up the hill to the old cemetery.

They lay her in the ground beside Nat Kinney, whose actions had caused both of them to seek absolution, in life....and in death.

THE PEOPLE - EPILOGUE

Eva Gertrude DeLong Prather Blair Allman

Eva was born about July, 1865, in Auburn, Shawnee Co. KS.

Her father, William Henry DeLong, died Nov 1864 of injuries suffered during a Civil War battle in the Kansas City area.

Her mother was Maggie Carriger DeLong Kinney.

Eva married Robert Prather Mar 28, 1887, in Kirbyville. He was the son of Alonzo and Ada Maria McMillan Prather, born Jun 1865 in IN.

Robert died Sep 2, 1896, and is buried in Van Zandt Cemetery in Taney County. Eva and Robert had three children.

She married Joseph C. Blair Mar 25, 1897, in Taney County, and they appear in the 1900 Taney County census. Not long after the 1900 census, JC moved Eva and the family to Washington, where they owned a hotel, appearing in the 1910 Lewis County, WA, census. Son Harry Neville Blair was born Jan 6, 1901, in WA. JC died Sep 25, 1915, in Lewis County at the age of 68. Eva then married J.M. Allman, appearing with him and son Harry Neville Blair in the 1920 Lewis County, WA, census.

Eva died Feb 13, 1927, in Gray's Harbor Co. WA, and is buried under the name "Eva Allman" in Sunset Memorial Park, Hoquiam, Gray's Harbor Co. WA.

Sampson Linford "Samp" Barker

Samp was born Nov 30, 1832, in Virginia, to John S. "Slimjack" Barker and Sarah Bays.

He married Sarah "Sallie" Frazier about 1853, and they had four children: James, Rufus, Martha Catherine, and Edward.

"Samp" served in Company D, 25th Regiment of the Virginia Cavalry, and also 48th Regiment of the Virginia Infantry for the Confederacy during the War Between the States.

He died Jan 22, 1911, in Taney County, and is buried in the Barker Family Cemetery.

Sarah Frazier "Sallie" Barker

Sallie was born Mar 28, 1833 in Virginia to Henry Sr. Frazier and Sarah Livingston. After the Civil War, she and Samp moved to Taney County with her brother, Henry, and his family, and her sister, Kate Miles, and her family.

Sallie died Sep 21, 1905, in Taney County, and is buried in the family cemetery.

John Jasper "JJ" Brown

J. J. Brown was born Oct 22 1834 in TN, the son of Elias Brown and Elizabeth Alsup. His parents were in Arkansas by 1850, when Elias died.

JJ served under the command of William Fenex in a Taney County-based state militia during the Civil War.

His first wife was Mary Jane Fenex, born Dec 9, 1848. They were married in August, 1866, and she died Oct 17, 1867, and is buried in a cairn in Ragsdale/Everett Cemetery.

JJ married Nancy Caroline Tennyson, the half-sister of James "Jim" and Barton Isaac "Yell" Everett, Dec 13, 1868. Caroline was born May 28, 1852, in Arkansas.

JJ died Jan 3, 1890, and was buried in the Vaughn Cemetery in Ozark, Christian Co. MO.

Caroline died Nov. 13, 1904, in Republic, MO, and may be buried in Evergreen Cemetery in Republic.

Andrew J. "Andy" Coggburn

Andy was born about 1867 in Taney Co. MO, the oldest child of Frances Serelda Springer Hamblin and James Victor Coggburn.

Both of his parents were dead by 1880, and he is living with his half-brother, James M. Hamblin/Coggburn, in the Taney County federal census. The household next to them is that of an aunt, Frances Minerva Coggburn, and her husband, Albert Webb. The Webbs were shot and killed in 1881, and may be buried at Van Zandt Cemetery.

Andrew was killed by Nat Kinney Feb 28, 1886, near the Oak

Grove church, and was buried in an unmarked grave Van Zandt Cemetery.

John Jackson "Seck" Coggburn

Seck was born Feb 9, 1859 in Missouri to John Shell and Elizabeth Allen Coggburn. He was a first cousin to **Andrew and Serelda Coggburn**.

Among other family deaths in the early 1880s, his sister Rebecca died of miscarriage on Sep 20, 1882, and is buried next to her husband, Colonel Tapley "Kern" McNally (b about 1855 AR d May 20, 1883, Taney Co.) in Van Zandt Cemetery.

Not long after Andrew was killed, Seck moved his family to Oregon, living near his in-laws, William and Mary Margaret Brooks Boston, for a time. Seck died in 1910, and is buried in Canyon Hill Cemetery, Canyon Co. ID.

Robert S. Coggburn

Robert was a brother to Seck, was born about 1864 in Miller Co. MO.

He and his wife, Ida Belle Teener, moved frequently, but are in Snohomish Co. WA for the 1920 federal census.

Robert died Mar 30, 1930, Snohomish Co. WA.

James A. DeLong

James simply disappears from documentation after the death of his mother. He may have changed his name, or removed to California, where he had Carriger family members living.

Margaret J. Carriger DeLong "Maggie" Kinney

Maggie was born Jul 1, 1840 at Carriger's Landing in Carter Co. TN, the daughter of Christian Elliot Carriger and Angelina Rhea Allen. Elliot Carriger was college-educated, an unusual occurrence for the times.

Maggie died October 11, 1891 in her daughter Eva's home after being ill with pneumonia for a week. Her obituary stated that she had been improving, but "heart failure" was the cause of death.

She is buried by the side of her second husband, Nathaniel Napoleon Kinney in Old Forsyth Cemetery.

According to *Kansas And Kansans, Volume Three*, the Carrigers floated down the Ohio River to the Mississippi, then up to St. Louis to the Missouri River, disembarking in Independence, MO. The following spring, Elliot's brothers and father left for California on a wagon train. Although Elliot and Angie stayed behind in Missouri with their children, when Kansas Territory opened up in the mid-1850s, he moved them to Shawnee Co. KS, establishing a large ranch and a sawmill.

Maggie's first husband was William Henry DeLong, the son of Isaac and Mary Moore DeLong, b in 1832 in OH. William died as a result of injuries suffered in a battle known as Price's Raid in October. He had been captured and shot in the right shoulder, and died in the Kansas City general hospital November, 1864. His tombstone states he died November 17, but his Masonic chapter noted his death as November 19.

Nathaniel Napoleon "Nat" Kinney

Nat was born about 1845 in Doddridge Co. VA, the son of George William and Mary J. Steele Kinney.

Doddridge County was one of several which broke away from the state of Virginia during the Civil War, to form the state of West Virginia.

Nat served as a private in Company L, Sixth Regiment, of the West VA Volunteer Infantry.

After the war, he traveled west to Kansas, where he met Maggie and married her Dec 6, 1866, in Shawnee Co. KS.

Nat was involved in breaking the railroad strike in Topeka, KS, in the late 1870s.

Shortly after the 1880 census, he moved his family to Springfield, Greene Co. MO, where he joined the light infantry and worked in a saloon owned by Abel Kinney, who later claimed no relation to Nat.

A customer died during an altercation at the saloon in December, 1882, in which Nat was involved.

In January, 1883, Nat bought land and a homestead in Taney County, situated along the heavily-traveled Springfield-Harrison road.

Paul Crook Kinney

Paul was born in 1871 in Auburn, Shawnee Co. KS, the son of Maggie and Nat Kinney.

After his mother's death in 1891, he left Taney County and was living with Carriger family members in the 1895 Kansas State Census, in Shawnee Co. KS.

He married Clara between 1895 and 1905, when they appear with son Nathaniel in the KS state census, living in Douglas Co. In the 1910 federal census, the family is in Jackson Co. MO.

Between 1910 and 1920, Paul and Clara were alternately in Denver Co. CO and the Kansas City area, as their daughter Lindianola was buried in Jefferson Co. CO in 1918; by 1930, Paul and his family were settled in the Denver, CO, area.

He died in 1932, and is buried with his wife near their daughter in Crown Hill Cemetery in Jefferson Co. CO.

Serelda Ann Coggburn McClary

Serelda was born Jan 13, 1877, the youngest child of James Victor Coggburn and Frances Serelda Springer.

Her father, a deputy sheriff, died in the line of service, chasing horse thieves into Arkansas, April 30, 1879. His body was never recovered.

Frances died before 1880, and is believed to be buried in Van Zandt Cemetery.

Serelda married Clarence McClary Jan 21, 1903, in Taney County. They made their home near Kirbyville.

She was passed from relative to relative throughout her childhood, and learned accounting, where a natural gift with mathematics aided her in later years.

She died Oct 1, 1952, and is buried alongside her husband in Ozarks Memorial Park Cemetery in Taney County.

Catherine "Kate" Frazier Miles

Kate was born in 1835 in Scott Co. VA, the daughter of Henry and Sarah Livingston Frazier.

She outlived her husband by at least 15 years, appearing in the 1920 Fannin Co. TX federal census in the household of her son Jim.

She was a daughter of Henry Sr. Frazier and Sarah Livingston, and sister to Sallie Barker.

Kate appears as a widow in her son Jim's household in the 1910 Taney County federal census. In 1920, she again appears in Jim's home, this time in Fannin Co. TX. There is no record of her in the 1930 federal census, and the location of her grave is unknown at this time.

The Miles Children

Sarah J. Miles

Sarah J. Miles b ca 1859 VA md 1879 Taney County, MO, to John Frank Grant b 1854 IL. They appear in Crawford Co. AR in 1900, Grady Co. OK in 1910, and back in Crawford Co. AR in 1920.

America Melvina Miles

America Melvina Miles b Mar 16 1861 VA md Reuben David Pruitt in Taney County in 1879. They appear in the 1880 census of Taney County at the home of Robert Snapp; Reuben is listed as a laborer. In 1900, they are living next door to William and Kate Miles in Franklin Co. AR. In 1920, they appear in Lamar Co. TX. In 1930 and 1940, they lived in Nueces Co. TX. Melvina died in 1941, and Reuben died in 1946. Both are buried in Nueces Co. TX.

Elisha J. Miles

Elisha J. Miles b Oct 7 1862 VA married Anetta Jane Wood about 1885 in Taney Co. MO. They lived out their lives in the Swan and Taney City area of Taney County. Elisha died Jun 7 1928 in Taney County, and is buried in Helphrey Cemetery.

Henrietta Francis Miles

Henrietta Francis Miles b 1865 VA married to Thomas C. Appleberry about 1883, probably in Taney Co. MO. They lived in Springfield, Greene Co. MO. She is buried in an unmarked grave in the Appleberry family plot, next to her father.

John Miles

John Miles b 1874 died after the 1880 Taney County census, but before or during 1883, as there is no mention of him in any other documentation. He is likely the unknown male child buried in the Barker Family Cemetery in Taney Co.

Emanuel "Manny" Miles

Manny was born Mar 15, 1869, in Washington Co. VA, shortly before his parents, William and Kate Frazier Miles moved to Taney Co., MO.

He married Nellie Barker (b Apr 28, 1886 to Rufus and Martha Compton Barker, and the granddaughter of Sampson and Sallie Barker) April 29, 1903, in Taney County.

The couple lived in the Fall Creek valley of Taney County, near the community of Flag, and later in the small town of Branson.

Manny died Mar 27, 1953, and Nellie died May 7, 1961; both are buried in Lewallen Cemetery in Taney County.

James Robert "Jim" Miles

James (Jimmy) was born Nov 28, 1872, in Taney Co., MO.

He joined his brother Billy in Texas in the early 1890s, marrying Mary E. Alexander in Fannin Co. TX, Jun 3, 1894.

In 1910, he and his family were living in the Branson area of Taney Co., MO. In 1912, Jim got into an argument with a butcher in Branson over money the man owed him, and killed him.

Although Enos Rush's Missouri death certificate states he is buried in Randolph Co. AR, there is no burial listing for him at this time.

Jim was sentenced to ten years in the state penitentiary. However, he is listed in the 1920 Fannin Co., TX census, and was in Collingsworth Co., TX, by 1930.

He died Apr 15, 1955, in Curry Co. NM, and is buried in Memorial Gardens Cemetery, Collingsworth Co. TX.

William Marion "Billy" Miles, Jr.

Billy was born January 8, 1867 in Scott Co. VA.

While still a toddler, his family joined other relatives and moved to the Taney City (now called Taneyville) area of Taney County.

After his legal issues in Missouri were finished in 1890, he left Taney County and moved to Texas, finally settling in San Saba County.

He married Ida Mae Lawrence October 6, 1897, in Montgomery Co. TX.

He died November 29, 1950, and his lifelong occupation was farming.

William Marion Miles, Sr.

William was born about 1834 in Scott Co. VA, the son of Pascal and Susannah Halfacre Miles.

William married Catherine Frazier about 1857. He served in the Confederate Army, probably as a member of the 30th Battalion, Clarke's Virginia Sharpshooters, entering and mustering out as a private.

He moved his family to Taney County in 1869, farming near Taney City. He, Kate, and Emanuel left Taney County not long after Billy did, and lived in Franklin Co. AR during the 1900 federal census, not far from their daughter Sarah's family in Crawford Co. AR. By 1904, Kate and William were in Springfield, Greene Co. MO, when their daughter Henrietta Frances Miles Appleberry died Mar 28, and was buried in Maple Park Cemetery. William died April 16, 1905, in the small pox camp north of Springfield, and is buried in an unmarked grave next to "Ritta" in Maple Park Cemetery. (Ritta is listed in the 1880 Taney County census as William and Kate's daughter, under the surname "Miller.")

Georgia Kinney Thurmond Patterson

Georgia was born Feb 10, 1875, in Auburn, Shawnee Co. KS, the youngest child of Nat and Maggie DeLong Kinney.

She married first to Thomas Preston Thurmond on Mar 2, 1890, in Taney Co. He died Sep 14, 1891, and is buried in the Old Forsyth Cemetery.

Georgia married Robert J. Patterson Mar 25, 1897. They had three children.

Georgia died Mar 17, 1923, and is buried in the Old Branson Cemetery.

Alonzo Smith Prather

Alonzo was born Jun 25, 1840, in Indiana.

He served in the Civil War, and was instrumental in the early days of the Arkansas Industrial College, which is now the University of Arkansas at Fayetteville. Highly-educated for the times, Alonzo was also a lawyer and newspaperman, and owned several businesses.

He served four terms as a state representative for Taney County.

He married Ada Maria McMillan Oct 20, 1863, in Indiana.

Alonzo died June 3, 1910, in Taney County, and is buried in VanZandt Cemetery.

Ada Marie died Mar 2, 1940, in Kern Co. CA.

Alonzo and Ada Marie had nine children, Grace, Mary Elizabeth

(Mahnkey) Adelia, Benjamin, Robert (who married Eva Gertrude Kinney, daughter of the famous Captain Kinney of the Bald Knobbers) Frank, Richard, Joseph, and Maggie.

Made in the USA
Charleston, SC
25 November 2012